I'll Walk Alone

Mary Higgins Clark

THORNDIKE
WINDSOR
PARAGON

This Large Print edition is published by Thorndike Press, Waterville, Maine USA and by AudioGo Ltd, Bath, England.
Copyright © 2011 by Mary Higgins Clark.
The moral right of the author has been asserted.
Thorndike Press, a part of Gale, Cengage Learning.

Thorndike Press® Large Print Basic.
The text of this Large Print edition is unabridged.
Other aspects of the book may vary from the original edition.
Set in 16 pt. Plantin.

LIBRARY OF CONGRESS CATALOGING-IN-PUBLICATION DATA

Clark, Mary Higgins.
  I'll walk alone / by Mary Higgins Clark.
    p. cm. — (Thorndike Press large print basic)
  ISBN-13: 978-1-4104-3516-3 (hardcover)
  ISBN-10: 1-4104-3516-4 (hardcover)
  1. Identity theft—Fiction. 2. Women architects—Fiction. 3. Manhattan (New York, N.Y.)—Fiction. 4. Large type books. I. Title.
PS3553.L28715 2011b
813'.54—dc22   2011008089

BRITISH LIBRARY CATALOGUING-IN-PUBLICATION DATA AVAILABLE
Published in the U.S. in 2011 by arrangement with Simon & Schuster.
Published in the U.K. in 2011 by arrangement with Simon & Schuster UK Ltd.
U.K. Hardcover: 978 1 445 85760 2 (Windsor Large Print)
U.K. Softcover: 978 1 445 85761 9 (Paragon Large Print)

Printed and bound in Great Britain by the MPG Books Group
1 2 3 4 5 6 7 15 14 13 12 11

ACKNOWLEDGMENTS

I have often said, seemingly in jest, that my favorite two words are "THE END."

They *are* my favorite two words. They mean that the tale has been told, the journey completed. They mean that the people who at this time last year were not even figments of my imagination have lived the life I chose for them, or to put it better, they chose for themselves.

My editor, Michael Korda, and I have made this same journey for thirty-six years, since that first day in March 1974 when I received the unbelievable call that Simon and Schuster had bought my first book, *Where Are the Children?*, for three thousand dollars. All this time, Michael has been the Captain of my literary ship, and I cannot be more joyful and honored than to have shared our collaboration. Last year at this time he suggested, "I think a book about identity theft would make a good subject for you." Here it is.

Senior Editor Kathy Sagan has been my friend for many years. A decade ago, she was the editor of *The Mary Higgins Clark Mystery Magazine,* and for the first time has worked with me, in conjunction with Michael, on a suspense novel. Love you, Kathy, and thank you.

Thanks always to Associate Director of Copyediting Gypsy da Silva and my readers-in-progress Irene Clark, Agnes Newton, and Nadine Petry and to my retired publicist, Lisl Cade.

Once again Sgt. Steven Marron and Detective Richard Murphy, Ret., of the New York District Attorney's office have been my guides in presenting accurately the step-by-step law enforcement that occurs when a major crime is committed.

Of course, and always, love beyond measure to my spouse extraordinaire, John Conheeney and our combined family of nine children and seventeen grandchildren.

Finally, to you, my readers, thank you for all the years we've shared together. "May the road rise to meet you . . ."

In memory of
Reverend Joseph A. Kelly, S.J.
1931–2008

Always a twinkle in this Jesuit's eye
Always a smile on his handsome face
Always faith and compassion
overflowing his soul
He was the stuff of which
saints are made
When all heaven protested his absence
His Creator called him home

1

Father Aiden O'Brien was hearing confessions in the lower church of St. Francis of Assisi on West Thirty-first Street in Manhattan. The seventy-eight-year-old Franciscan friar approved of the alternate way of administering the sacrament, that of having the penitent sit in the Reconciliation Room with him, rather than kneeling on the hard wood of the confessional with a screen hiding his or her identity.

The one time he felt the new way did not work was when, sitting face-to-face, he sensed that the penitents might not be able to allow themselves to say what might have been confided in darkness.

This was happening now on this chilly, windswept afternoon in March.

In the first hour he had sat in the room, only two women had shown up, regular parishioners, both in their mideighties, whose sins, if any had ever existed, were long behind them. Today one of them had confessed that when she was eight years old she remembered telling a lie to her mother. She had eaten two cupcakes and blamed her brother for the missing one.

As Fr. Aiden was praying his rosary until he was scheduled to leave the room, the door opened and a slender woman who looked to be in her early thirties came in. Her expression tentative, she moved slowly toward the chair facing him and hesitantly sat down on it. Her auburn hair was loose on her shoulders. Her fur-collared suit was clearly expensive, as were her high-heeled leather boots. Her only jewelry was silver earrings.

His expression serene, Fr. Aiden waited. Then when the young woman did not speak, he asked encouragingly, "How can I help you?"

"I don't know how to begin." The woman's voice was low and pleasant, with no hint of a geographical accent.

"There's nothing you can tell me that I haven't already heard," Fr. Aiden said mildly.

"I . . ." The woman paused, then the words came rushing out. "I know about a murder that someone is planning to commit and I can't stop it."

Her expression horrified, she clasped her hand over her mouth and abruptly stood up. "I should never have come here," she whispered. Then, her voice trembling with emotion, she said, "Bless me, Father, for I have sinned. I confess that I am an accessory to a crime that is ongoing and to a murder that is going to happen very soon. You'll probably read about it in the headlines. I don't want to be part of it, but it's too late to stop."

She turned and in five steps had her hand on the door.

"Wait," Fr. Aiden called, trying to struggle to his feet. "Talk to me. I can help you."

But she was gone.

Was the woman psychotic? Fr. Aiden wondered. Could she possibly have meant what she said? And if so, what could he do about it?

If she was telling the truth, I can do nothing about it, he thought, as he sank back into the chair. I don't know who she is or where she lives. I can only pray that she is irrational and that this scenario is some kind of fantasy. But if she is not irrational, she is shrewd enough to know that I am bound by the seal of the confessional. At some point she may have been a practicing Catholic. The words she used, "Bless me, Father, for

I have sinned," was the way a penitent used to begin to confess.

For long minutes he sat alone. When the woman exited, the green light over the Reconciliation Room door had automatically gone on, which meant that anyone waiting outside would have been free to enter. He found himself praying fervently that the young woman might return, but she did not.

He was supposed to leave the room at six o'clock. But it was twenty minutes after six when he gave up hope that she might come back. Finally, aware of the weight of his years and the spiritual burden of his role as confessor, Fr. Aiden placed both hands on the arms of his chair and got up slowly, wincing at the sharp thrust of pain in his arthritic knees. Shaking his head, he began to walk to the door but stopped for a moment in front of the chair where the young woman had been sitting.

She wasn't crazy, he thought sadly. I can only pray that if she really has knowledge that the crime of a murder is about to be committed, she does what her conscience is telling her to do. She must prevent it.

He opened the door and saw two people lighting candles in front of the statue of St. Jude in the atrium of the church. A man was kneeling on the prie-dieu in front of the Shrine of St. Anthony, his face buried in his hands. Fr. Aiden hesitated, wondering if he should ask the visitor if he wanted to go to confession. Then he reflected that the posted hours for hearing confessions had been over for nearly half an hour. Maybe this visitor was begging for a favor or giving thanks for receiving one. The Shrine of St. Anthony was a favorite stop for many of their visitors.

Fr. Aiden walked across the atrium to the door that led to the passage to the Friary. He did not feel the intense gaze of the man who was no longer deep in prayer but had turned, pushed up his dark glasses, and was studying him intently, taking note of his rim of white hair and slow gait.

She was only in there less than a minute, the observer thought. How much did she tell that old priest? he wondered. Can I afford to take the chance that she didn't spill her guts to him? The man could hear the outer doors of the church being opened and the sound of approaching steps. Quickly he replaced his sunglasses and pulled up the collar of his trench coat. He had already copied Fr. Aiden's name from the door.

"What do I do about you, Fr. O'Brien?" he asked himself angrily, as he brushed past the dozen or so visitors entering the church.

For the moment he had no answer.

What he did not realize was that he, the observer, was being observed. Sixty-six-year-old Alvirah Meehan, the cleaning woman turned columnist and celebrity author who had won forty million dollars in the New York Lottery, was also there. She had been shopping in Herald Square and then, before going home to Central Park South, had walked down the few blocks to the church to light a candle in front of St. Anthony's Shrine and drop off an extra donation for the breadline because she had just received an unexpected royalty check for her memoir *From Pots to Plots.*

When she saw the man seemingly deep in prayer in front of the shrine, she had paid a visit to the grotto of Our Lady of Lourdes. A few minutes later, when she saw Fr. Aiden, her old friend, leave the Reconciliation Room, she had been about to run up and say a quick hello to him. Then to her astonishment, the man who had seemed so engrossed in prayer suddenly jumped up, his dark glasses raised. No mistake about it, he was watching Fr. Aiden make his way to the door of the Friary.

Alvirah dismissed any passing thought that that guy might have wanted to ask Fr. Aiden

14

to hear his confession. He wanted to get a good look at Father, she thought, as she watched the man pull his glasses back over his eyes and turn up the collar of his coat. She had taken off her glasses so he was too far away for her to see him clearly, but from the distance she judged him to be about six feet tall. His face was in the shadows but she could see he was on the thin side. Her impression, when she had passed him at the statue, was that he had no gray in his full head of black hair. He had been covering his face with his hands.

Who knows what makes people tick, Alvirah asked herself as she watched the stranger, now moving quickly, exit by the door nearest him. But I'll tell you this much, she thought. As soon as Fr. Aiden left the Reconciliation Room, whatever that guy had to say to St. Anthony, he wound it up fast.

2

It is March 22. If he is still alive, my Matthew is five years old today, Zan Moreland thought as she opened her eyes and lay still for long minutes, brushing back the tears that often dampened her face and pillow during the night. She glanced at the clock on the dresser. It was 7:15 A.M. She had slept almost eight hours. The reason, of course, was that when she went to bed, she had taken a sleeping pill, a luxury she almost never permitted herself. But the awareness of his birthday had left her almost sleepless for the last week.

Fragments of her recurring dream of searching for Matthew came back to her. This time she had been in Central Park again, searching and searching for him, calling his name, begging him to answer. His favorite game had been hide-and-seek. In the dream she was telling herself that he wasn't really missing. He was just hiding.

But he *was* missing.

If only I had canceled my appointment that day, Zan thought for the millionth time. Tiffany Shields, the babysitter, had admitted that while Matthew was sleeping she had positioned his stroller so that the sun would not be in his face and had spread a blanket on the grass and fallen asleep herself. She had not realized he wasn't in the stroller until she woke up.

An elderly witness had phoned the police after she read the headlines about the missing toddler. She reported that she and her husband had been walking their dog in the park and noticed the stroller was empty nearly half an hour before the babysitter had told the police she had looked into it. "I didn't think anything of it at the time," the witness said, sounding upset and angry. "I just thought that someone, the mother maybe, had taken the child over to the playground. It never occurred to me that young woman could possibly be watching anyone. She was out like a light."

Tiffany had also finally admitted that because Matthew was asleep when they left the apartment, she did not bother to strap him in.

Did he climb out by himself and then someone noticed he was alone and took his hand? Zan asked herself, the question dull with repetition. There are predators who hang around. *Please, God, don't let it be that.*

Matthew's picture had been in newspapers all over the country and on the Internet. I prayed that some lonely person might have taken him and then was afraid to admit it, but finally would come forward or leave him in a safe place where he'd be found, Zan thought. But after almost two years, there was not a single hint of where he might be. By now he's probably forgotten me.

She sat up slowly and twisted her long auburn hair back on her shoulders. Even though she exercised regularly, her slender body felt stiff and achy. Tension, the doctor had told her. You're living with it, 24/7. She slid her feet to the floor, stretched, and stood up, then walked over to the window and began to close it as she absorbed the early-morning view of the Statue of Liberty and New York Harbor.

It had been that view that had made her decide to sublet this apartment six months after Matthew disappeared. She'd had to get away from the building on East Eighty-sixth Street where his empty room with his little bed and toys were daily arrows piercing her heart.

That was when, realizing she had to try to have some semblance of normalcy in her life, she had thrown her energies into the small interior design business she had started when she and Ted separated. They had been together for such a short time, she didn't even know that she was pregnant when they split.

Before her marriage to Ted Carpenter, she had been the chief assistant to the famed designer Bartley Longe. Even then she'd been recognized as one of the bright new stars in the field.

A critic who knew that Bartley had left an entire project in her hands while he was on a lengthy vacation had written about her stunning ability to mix and combine fabrics and color and furnishings for a home that reflected the taste and lifestyle of the owner.

Zan closed the window and hurried to the closet. She loved a cold room for sleeping, but her long T-shirt was no protection from the drafts. She had deliberately given herself a busy schedule for today. Now she reached for the old wraparound robe that Ted had so hated and which she laughingly had told him was her security blanket. To her it had become a symbol. When she got out of bed and the room was freezing, the minute she put on the robe she was warm as toast. Cold to warm; empty to overflowing; Matthew missing; Matthew found; Matthew in her arms, home with her. Matthew had loved to snuggle inside it with her.

But no more hide-and-seek, she thought, blinking back tears, as she knotted the belt of the robe and wiggled her feet into flip-flops. If Matthew climbed out of the stroller himself, was that what he was trying to play? But an unattended child should have been noticed by other people. How long was it before someone took his hand and disappeared with him?

It had been an unseasonably hot day in June and the park had been filled with children.

Don't get into that, Zan warned herself as she walked down the hallway to the kitchen and headed straight for the coffeemaker. It had been set to go at seven o'clock, and now the pot was full. She poured a cup and reached into the refrigerator for the skim milk and the container of mixed fruit she had bought at the nearby grocery store. Then, on second thought, she ignored the fruit. Just coffee, she thought. That's all I want now. I know I should eat more than I do, but I'm not planning to start today.

As she sipped the coffee, she mentally ran through her schedule. After she stopped at the office, she was meeting the architect of a stunning new condominium high-rise on the Hudson River to discuss decorating three model apartments for him, a significant coup if she got the job. Her principal competition would be her old employer, Bartley, whom she knew bitterly resented her opening her own business instead of coming back to work for him.

You may have taught me a lot, Zan thought, but boy that nasty temper of yours wasn't anything I was going to be around again. Not to say anything about the way you came on to me. Then she closed her mind to that embarrassing day when she had had a breakdown in Bartley's office.

She carried the coffee cup to the bathroom, laid it on the vanity, and turned on the shower. The steaming water took some of the tautness out of her muscles, and after she poured shampoo on her hair, she massaged her scalp with deep pressure from her fingertips. Another trick for reducing stress, she thought sardonically. There's really only one way for me to reduce stress.

Don't go there, she warned herself again.

When she was toweling dry, she picked up the pace, briskly drying her hair, then, back in her robe, she applied the mascara and lip gloss that were her only makeup. Matthew

21

has Ted's eyes, she thought, that gorgeous shade of dark brown. I used to sing him that song, "Beautiful Brown Eyes." His hair was so light but I think it was starting to get some reddish tones in it. I wonder if he'll get the bright red I had as a kid? I hated it. I told Mom that I looked like Anne of Green Gables, stick thin and with that awful carrot hair. But on him, it would look adorable.

Her mother had pointed out that when Anne grew up, her body had filled out and her hair had darkened to a warm, rich auburn shade.

Mom used to joke and call me Green Gables Annie, Zan thought. It was another memory not to be dwelt on today.

Ted had insisted they have dinner tonight, just the two of them. "Melissa will certainly understand," he'd said when he phoned. "I want to remember our little boy with the only other person who knows how I'm feeling on his birthday. Please, Zan."

They were meeting at the Four Seasons at 7:30. The one problem with living in Battery Park City is the traffic jams to and from midtown, Zan thought. I don't want to bother coming back downtown to change, and I don't want to bother dragging a different outfit with me to the office. I'll wear

22

the black suit with the fur collar. It's dressy enough for the evening.

Fifteen minutes later she was on the street, a tall, slender young woman of thirty-two, dressed in a black fur-collared suit and high-heeled boots, wearing dark sunglasses, her designer shoulder bag in hand, her auburn hair blowing across her shoulders as she stepped down from the curb to hail a cab.

3

Over dinner, Alvirah had told Willy about the funny way that guy was looking at their friend Fr. Aiden when he was leaving the Reconciliation Room, and at breakfast she brought it up again. "I was dreaming about that guy last night, Willy," she said, "and that's not a good sign. When I dream about a person, it usually means there's going to be trouble."

Still in their bathrobes, they were sitting cozily at the round table in the dining area of their Central Park South apartment. Outside, as she had already pointed out to Willy, it was a typical March day, cold and blustery. The wind was rattling the furniture on their balcony, and they could see that across the street, Central Park was almost deserted.

Willy looked affectionately across the table at his wife of forty-five years. Often referred to as the image of the late legendary Speaker of the House Tip O'Neill, he was a big man with a full head of snow-white hair and, as Alvirah told him, the bluest eyes under the sun.

In his fond eyes, Alvirah was beautiful. He didn't notice that no matter how hard she tried, she'd always be trying to lose ten or fifteen pounds. Neither did he notice that only a week after coloring her hair, the gray roots became visible around her hairline, the hair that, thanks to Dale of London, was now a subdued russet brown. In the old days, before they won the lottery, when she colored it herself over the bathroom sink in their apartment in Queens, it had been a flaming red-orange shade.

"Honey, from what you tell me that guy had probably been getting up the courage to go to confession. And then when he saw Fr. Aiden leaving, he was trying to decide whether or not to catch up with him."

Alvirah shook her head. "There's more to it than that." She reached for the teapot and poured herself a second cup and her expression changed. "You know that today is little Matthew's birthday. He'd be five years old."

"Or *is* five years old," Willy corrected her. "Alvirah, I have intuition, too. I say that little guy is alive somewhere."

"We talk about Matthew as if we know

him," Alvirah sighed as she added a sugar substitute to her cup.

"I feel as though we do know him," Willy said, soberly.

They were silent for a minute, both remembering how nearly two years ago, after Alvirah's column about the missing child in the *New York Globe* had been posted on the Internet, Alexandra Moreland had phoned her. "Mrs. Meehan," she had said, "I can't tell you how much Ted and I appreciate what you wrote. If Matthew was taken by someone who desperately wanted a child, you conveyed in that article how desperately we want him back. The suggestions you made about how someone could leave him in a safe place and avoid being recognized on security cameras might just make a difference."

Alvirah had agonized for her. "Willy, that poor girl is an only child, and she lost both her parents when their car crashed on their way to pick her up at the Rome airport. Then she splits with her husband before she realizes she is pregnant, and now her little boy disappears. I just know she must be at the point where she doesn't want to get up in the morning. I told her that if she ever wanted to have someone to talk to, she should just call me, but I know she won't."

But then shortly thereafter Alvirah read on Page Six of the *Post* that the tragedy-haunted Zan Moreland had gone back to work full-time at her interior design firm, Moreland Interiors, on East Fifty-eighth Street. Alvirah immediately informed Willy that their apartment needed to be redone.

"I don't think it looks so bad," Willy had observed.

"It's not bad, Willy, but we did buy it furnished six years ago, and to tell you the truth, having everything white, curtains, rugs, furniture, has made me feel sometimes as though I'm living in a marshmallow. It's a sin to waste money, but I think in this case it's the right thing to do."

The result was not only their transformed apartment, but also a close friendship with Alexandra "Zan" Moreland. Now Zan called them her surrogate family and they saw her frequently.

"Did you ask Zan to have dinner with us tonight?" Willy asked now. "I mean, this has got to be a horrible day for her."

"I did ask," Alvirah replied, "and at first she said yes. Then she phoned back. Her ex-husband wants to be with her, and she didn't think she could refuse. They're meeting at the Four Seasons tonight."

"I could see where the two of them might

be some comfort for each other on Matthew's birthday."

"On the other hand, that's a pretty public place, and Zan is too hard on herself about letting her emotions show. When she talks about Matthew, I wish she'd let herself cry once in a while, but she never does, not even with us."

"I'll bet there are many nights when she cries herself to sleep," Willy said, "and I agree it won't do her any good to be with her ex tonight. She told us that she's sure Carpenter has never forgiven her for allowing Matthew to go out with such a young babysitter. I hope he won't bring that up again on Matthew's birthday."

"He is — or was — Matthew's father," Alvirah said, then more to herself than to Willy added, "From everything I've ever read, in a case like this, even if they're not present, one parent takes the blame for the situation, be it a careless babysitter, or being away when he or she had wanted to stay home that day. Willy, there's always blame, more than enough to go around when a child is missing, and I just pray God that Ted Carpenter doesn't have a couple of drinks and start in on Zan tonight."

"Don't borrow trouble, honey," Willy cautioned.

"I know what you mean." Alvirah debated then reached for the other half of her toasted bagel. "But, Willy, you know it's true that when in my bones I feel trouble coming, it always does come. And I know, I just know, that impossible as it seems, Zan is going to be hit real hard with something more."

4

Edward "Ted" Carpenter nodded to the receptionist without speaking as he strode through the outer room of his thirtieth-floor suite on West Forty-sixth Street. The walls of the room were filled with pictures of his current and former celebrity clients covering the past fifteen years. All were inscribed to him. Usually he made a left turn into the large room where his ten publicity assistants worked. But this morning he headed directly for his private office.

He had warned his secretary, Rita Moran, not to bring up the subject of his son's birthday to him and not to bring any newspapers to work. But when he approached her desk, Rita was so absorbed in reading a news story on the Internet that she did not even see him when he stood over her at the computer. She had an image of Matthew pulled up on her screen. When she finally heard Ted, she looked up. Her face turned crimson as he leaned over her, grabbed the mouse, and turned off the computer. In quick strides, he went into his office and took off his coat. But before he hung it up, he went to his desk and stared at the framed picture of his son. It had been taken on Matthew's third birthday. Even then he looked like me, Ted thought. With that high forehead and dark brown eyes, there was no mistaking that he was my son. When he grows up, he'll probably look just like me, he thought as he angrily turned the frame face down. Then he went to the closet and hung up his coat. Because he was meeting Zan at the Four Seasons, he had chosen to wear a dark blue suit instead of his preferred sport jacket and slacks.

At dinner last night, his most important client, the rock star Melissa Knight, had been visibly upset when he told her he could not escort her to some affair this evening. "You're having a date with your ex," she had said, her tone apprehensive and angry.

He could not afford to antagonize Melissa. Her first three albums had all hit over a million sales and, thanks to her, other celebrities were signing up with his public relations firm. Unfortunately, somewhere along the way, Melissa had fallen, or thought she had fallen, in love with him.

31

"You know my plans, princess," he had said, trying to keep his tone mild. And then added with the bitterness he could not conceal, "and you certainly should understand why I'm meeting the mother of my son on his fifth birthday."

Melissa had been instantly remorseful. "I'm sorry, Ted. I'm truly sorry. Of course I know why you're meeting her. It's just . . ."

The memory of that exchange was grating. Melissa's suspicion that he was still in love with Zan was always there, a constant jealousy that caused her to explode regularly. And it was getting worse.

Zan and I separated because she said our marriage was just an emotional reaction to her parents' sudden death, he thought. She didn't even realize she was pregnant when we broke up. That was well over five years ago. What has Melissa got to be upset about? I can't afford to let her get angry at me. If she were to walk out, it would be the end of this place. She'd take all her friends with her, which would mean the most lucrative ones we have. If only I hadn't bought this damn building. What was I thinking?

A subdued Rita was carrying in the morning mail. "Melissa's accountant is a dream," she said with a tentative smile. "The monthly check and all the expenses came in this morning right on time. Don't we wish all our clients were like that?"

"We sure do," Ted said heartily, knowing that Rita had been upset by his curtness when he arrived.

"And her accountant wrote a note telling you to expect a call from Jaime-boy. He just fired his PR firm and Melissa recommended you. That would be another terrific client for us to have."

Ted felt genuine warmth now as he looked at Rita's troubled face. Rita had been with him every day for the last fifteen years, ever since as a cocky twenty-three-year-old he had opened his PR firm. She had been at Matthew's christening and at his first three birthday parties. In her late forties, childless and married to a quiet schoolteacher, she loved the excitement of their famous clients and had been enraptured when he brought Matthew here to the office.

"Rita," Ted said. "Of course you're remembering that it's Matthew's birthday, and I know you've been praying for him to come home. Now start praying that a year from now we'll be celebrating his next birthday with him."

"Oh, Ted, I will," Rita said fervently, "I will."

When she went back outside, Ted stared

for a few minutes at the closed door, then with a sigh reached for the phone. He was sure Melissa's maid would pick it up and take a message. Melissa and he had attended a red carpet movie premiere the night before and Melissa often slept in. But she answered on the first ring.

"Ted."

The fact that his name and phone number had come up on her caller ID still caught him off guard. Not that kind of service when I was growing up in Wisconsin, he thought, but it probably wasn't happening in New York then, either. He forced a cheerful note into his voice as he greeted her, "Good morning, Melissa, the queen of hearts."

"Ted, I thought you'd be too busy planning for your date tonight to even think of calling me today." As usual her tone was petulant.

Ted resisted the temptation to slam down the phone. Instead, in the even tone that he used when his most valuable client was being both impossible and insensitive, he said, "Dinner with my ex won't last more than two hours. That means I'll be leaving the Four Seasons around 9:30. Could you make room in your calendar for me around 9:45?"

Two minutes later, sure that he was back in Melissa's good graces, he hung up and put his head in his hands. Oh, God, he thought, why do I have to put up with her?

5

Zan unlocked the door of her small office in the Design Center, the magazines under her arm. She had promised herself that she would avoid any references to Matthew that might be in the media. But as she passed the newsstand she had not been able to keep from buying two weekly celebrity magazines, the two most likely outlets for any follow-up stories. Last year on Matthew's birthday both of them had extensive write-ups about his kidnapping.

Only last week someone had snapped her picture when she was walking to a restaurant near her home in Battery Park City. She was bitterly aware that it would probably be used in some sensational article rehashing Matthew's abduction.

In a reflex gesture, Zan turned on the lights and took in the familiar trappings of her office, with several bolts of cloth stacked against the stark white walls, carpet samples scattered on the floor, and shelves filled with heavy books containing swatches of fabrics.

When she and Ted separated, she had started her venture as an interior designer on her own in this small office and, as satisfied clients sent her referrals, had elected to keep it that way. The antique desk with the three Edwardian chairs surrounding it was wide enough for her to sketch suggested designs for homes and rooms and lay out possible color combinations for a client's approval.

It was here in this room that she could sometimes not think about Matthew for hours and thus force the heavy unsettled pain of losing him to retreat into her subconscious. She knew that wouldn't be the case today.

The rest of the suite consisted of a back office barely large enough to hold a computer desk, files, a table for her inevitable coffeepot, and a small refrigerator. The clothes closet was opposite the lavatory. Josh Green, her assistant, had observed with ironic accuracy that the dimensions of closet and lavatory were exactly the same.

She had resisted Josh's suggestions that they lease the suite next door when it became available. She wanted to keep her overhead to a minimum. That way she would be able to hire yet another private detective agency that specialized in finding lost children to look for Matthew. She had gone through what was left of the money that she had received from her parents' modest life insurance in the first year that Matthew had been missing, spending it wildly on private investigators and psychic quacks, none of whom had turned up a shred of evidence that might lead to finding him.

She hung up her coat. The fur trimming on the collar was one more reminder that she was going to meet Ted tonight for dinner. Why does he bother? she asked herself impatiently. He blames me for letting Tiffany Shields take Matthew out to the park. But he loved Matthew passionately and no amount of blame that he could throw at her could possibly match the blame and guilt she carried herself.

To get it out of the way, she opened the celebrity magazines and scanned them quickly. As she had suspected, one of them was carrying the picture of Matthew that had been released to the media when he vanished. The caption read, "Is Matthew Carpenter still alive and celebrating his fifth birthday?"

The article ended with the quote Ted had

made the day Matthew disappeared, a caution to parents about leaving their children with a young babysitter. Zan ripped out the page, crumpled it, and threw both magazines in the wastebasket. Then wondering why she had subjected herself to looking for this kind of article, she hurried to the big desk and settled in a chair.

For the hundredth time in the past few weeks she unrolled the drawings she was going to submit to Kevin Wilson, architect and part owner of the thirty-four-story apartment building that overlooked the new walkway bordering the Hudson River on the lower west side. If she did get the job of furnishing three model apartments, it would not only be a major breakthrough for her, it would be her first successful toe-to-toe with Bartley Longe.

It still was incomprehensible to her that the employer who had so valued her while she was his assistant had so utterly turned on her. When she first began to work for him nine years ago, right after she graduated from FIT, the Fashion Institute of Technology, she had eagerly embraced the demanding schedule and put up with his volatile temper because she knew she was learning a lot from him. Divorced, then in his early forties, Bartley was very much a man about town. He had always been extremely difficult, but it was when he turned his attention to her and she made it clear that she was not interested in an involvement that he had begun to make her life miserable with his biting sarcasm and endless criticism.

I kept putting off going to see Mom and Dad who were living in Rome, Zan thought. Bartley would get furious if I said I needed a couple of weeks off. I delayed that trip for six months. Then when I finally told him I was going, whether he liked it or not, it was too late.

She had been in the airport in Rome when the car her father was driving to meet her had crashed into a tree, killing him and her mother instantly. An autopsy showed that her father had suffered a heart attack at the wheel.

Don't think about them today, she warned herself. Concentrate on the model rooms. Bartley will be submitting his plans. I know the way he thinks. I'll beat him at his own game.

Bartley would have undoubtedly created designs for both a traditional and an ultra-modern décor and one that combined elements of both. She made herself concentrate to see if there were any better way she could find to improve the sketches and color samples she would be offering.

As though it mattered. As though anything mattered except Matthew.

She heard a key turn in the door. Josh was there. Her assistant was also a graduate of FIT. Twenty-five years old, smart, looking more like a college kid than a gifted interior designer, Josh had become something of a younger brother to her. It almost helped that he had not been with her when Matthew disappeared. Somehow she and Josh just clicked.

But today the expression on his face made Zan realize that the concern she was seeing was different. Josh began without a greeting, "Zan, I stayed here last night catching up on the monthly statements. I didn't want to call you because you said you were going to take a sleeping pill. But, Zan, why did you buy a one-way ticket to Buenos Aires for next Wednesday?"

6

The little boy heard the sound of a car coming down the driveway even before Glory heard it. In an instant, he slid off the chair at the breakfast table and ran down the hall into the big closet where he knew he must stay "like a little mouse" until Glory came back for him.

He didn't mind. Glory had told him it was a game to keep him safe. There was a light on the floor of the closet, and a rubber raft just big enough for him to lie down and go to sleep on if he was tired. It had pillows and a blanket. When he was there, Glory told him, he could pretend he was a pirate and sailing on the ocean. Or, he could read one of his books. There were lots of books in the closet. The one thing he must *never do,* however, was to make a single sound. He always knew when Glory was going to go out and leave him alone because she would make him go to the bathroom even if he didn't have to go, then she would leave a bottle in the closet for him to pee in. And she would leave a sandwich and cookies and water, and a Pepsi.

It had been that way in the other houses, too. Glory always made a place for him to hide, then put some of his toys and trucks and puzzles and books and crayons and pencils in it. Glory told him that even though he never played with other children he was going to be smarter than all of them. "You read better than most seven-year-olds, Matty," she told him. "You're really smart. And it's because of me that you're so smart. You're really *lucky.*"

In the beginning, the boy didn't feel lucky at all. He would dream of being wrapped up in a warm, fuzzy robe with Mommy. After a while he couldn't exactly remember her face, but he still remembered how he felt when she hugged him. Then he would start to cry. But after a while the dream stopped coming. Then Glory bought soap and he washed his hands just before he went to bed, and the dream came back because the way the soap made his hands smell was the way Mommy smelled. He remembered her name again and even the feeling of being wrapped with her inside her robe. In the morning he took the soap back to his room and put it under his pillow. When Glory kept asking him why he did it, he told her, and she said it was okay.

Once he wanted to play a game and hide from Glory, but he didn't do that anymore. Glory raced up and down the stairs calling his name. She was *really* mad when she finally looked behind the couch and found him. She shook her fist in his face and said not to ever, ever, ever do that again. Her expression was so angry that he was really scared.

The only time he saw other people was when they were driving in the car, and that was always at night. They didn't stay long in any place and wherever they stayed, there weren't other houses around them. Sometimes Glory would take him out in the back of the house and play a game with him and take his picture. But then they would move to another house, and Glory would make a new secret room for him again.

Sometimes he would wake up after Glory had locked him in his room at night and hear her talking to someone. He wondered who it was. He could never hear the other voice. He knew it couldn't be Mommy because if she was in the house, she would definitely come upstairs to see him. Whenever he was sure someone was in the house, he would hold the soap in his hand and pretend it was Mommy.

This time the door of the closet opened almost right away. Glory was laughing. "The owner of this place sent over the guy from the security system to make sure it works. Isn't that a riot, Matty?"

After Josh told Zan about the airline charge to her credit card, he suggested they check all the other cards in her purse.

Bergdorf Goodman had new purchases of expensive clothing charged to her account, clothing that was in her size, but that she knew nothing about.

"On this day of all days," Josh muttered as he notified the store to cancel the card. Then he'd added, "Zan, do you think you can handle this appointment alone? Maybe I should go with you?"

Zan promised she would be okay, and promptly at eleven o'clock she was standing at the door of the office of Kevin Wilson, the architect of the stunning new apartment building overlooking the Hudson River. The door was partially open. She could see that the office was a makeshift space on the main floor of the new building, the kind an architect would keep for convenience to observe the progress of an ongoing project.

Wilson's back was to her, his head bent over the papers on the table behind the desk. Were they Bartley Longe's drawings? Zan wondered. She knew his appointment had been earlier than hers. She knocked on the door and Wilson, without turning around, called out for her to come in.

Before she reached his desk, Wilson swiveled around in the chair, stood, and pushed his glasses up on his head. Zan realized that he was younger than she expected, certainly not more than midthirties. With his tall, lanky frame, he looked more like a basketball player than an award-winning architect. His firm jaw and keen blue eyes were the most prominent features in his ruggedly handsome face.

He extended his hand. "Alexandra Moreland, glad to meet you and thank you for accepting our invitation to submit design plans for our model apartments."

Zan tried to smile as she took his hand. In the almost two years since Matthew disappeared, she had usually managed to compartmentalize herself, to force Matthew from her mind when she was in a business situation. But today the combination of Matthew's birthday and the shock of knowing that someone was piling up bills on her credit card and charge accounts was suddenly breaking down the wall of reserve she had built so carefully.

She knew her hand was ice cold and was glad that Kevin Wilson didn't seem to notice it, but she could not trust herself to speak. First she had to let the lump that was crowding her throat begin to dissolve, otherwise she knew that silent tears would begin to run down her face. She could only hope that Wilson would mistake her silence for shyness.

Apparently he did. "Why don't we take a look and see what you've come up with?" he suggested, gently.

Zan swallowed hard, then managed to speak in an even tone. "If you don't mind, let's go up to the apartments and I can explain to you how I've chosen to put things together."

"Sure," he said. In a long stride, Wilson was around the desk and had taken the heavy leather folder from her. They walked down the corridor to the second bank of elevators. The lobby was in the final stages of construction, with overhead wires dangling and narrow strips of carpet scattered on the dusty floors.

Wilson kept up a running conversation, surely, Zan felt, to help her get over what he must have thought was her nervousness. "This is going to be one of the most energy-efficient buildings in New York," he said. "We've got solar energy and we've maximized the window sizes throughout to give all the apartments the constant feeling of sun and light. I grew up in an apartment house where my bedroom faced the brick wall of the building next door. Day and night it was so dark I could hardly see my hand in front of my face. In fact I put a sign on the door when I was ten years old, 'The Cave.' My mother made me take it down before my father came home. She said it would make him feel bad that we didn't have a better place to live."

And I grew up living all over the world, Zan thought. So many people think that's wonderful. Mother and Dad loved the diplomatic life, but I wanted permanence. I wanted neighbors who would still be there in twenty years. I wanted to live in a house that was ours. I didn't want to have to go to boarding school when I was thirteen. I wanted to be with them, and even sometimes resented them for being on the move so much.

They were stepping into the elevator. Wilson pushed a button on the panel and the elevator door closed. Zan searched for something to say. "I guess you may have heard that since your secretary phoned and invited me to submit design plans for the model apartments, I've been in and out of here any number of times."

"I heard that."

"I wanted to see the rooms at different times of day, so that I could get a feel for them, and of how it would be for different kinds of people to walk in and say, 'I'm home.' "

They started in the one-bedroom, one-and-a-half-bath apartment. "My guess is that the people looking at this one fall into two categories," Zan began. "The apartments are expensive enough so that you're not getting any kids just out of college, unless Daddy is paying the bills. I think you'll probably have a lot of young professionals looking at this model. And unless it's a romance situation, most of them won't want roommates."

Wilson smiled. "And the other category?"

"Older people who want a pied-à-terre, and even if they could afford it don't want a guest room because they don't want overnight guests."

It was getting easier for her. She was on safe territory. "This is what I've come up with." There was a long counter separating

50

the kitchen from the dining area. "Why don't I lay out my sketches and swatches here?" she suggested as she took the portfolio from him.

She was with Kevin Wilson for nearly two hours as she explained her alternate approaches for each of the three model apartments. When they were back in his office, he laid her plans on the table behind his desk and said, "You've put an awful lot of work into this, Zan."

After the first time he had called her Alexandra, she had said, "Let's keep it simple. Everybody calls me Zan, I guess because when I was starting to talk, Alexandra was too big a mouthful for me."

"I want to get the job," she said. "I'm excited about the layouts I showed you and it was worth the time and effort to give them my best shot. I know you invited Bartley Longe to submit his plans, and of course he's a superb designer. It's that simple. The competition is stiff and you may not like anything that either of us has planned."

"You're a lot more charitable about him than he is about you," Wilson observed dryly.

Zan was sorry to hear the note of bitterness in her throat when she answered, "I'm afraid there's no love lost between Bartley

51

and me, but on the other hand I'm sure you're not treating this assignment as a popularity contest." And I know I'll come in at least a third cheaper than Bartley, she thought, as she left Wilson at the imposing entrance to the skyscraper. That will be my ace in the hole. I won't make much money if I get this job, but the recognition will be worth it.

In the cab going back to the office, she realized that the tears she had been able to hold back were streaming down her cheeks now. She grabbed her sunglasses out of her shoulder bag and put them on. When the cab stopped on East Fifty-eighth Street, as usual she gave a generous tip because she believed that anyone who had to make a living driving every day in New York traffic deserved one.

The cabbie, an elderly black man with a Jamaican accent, thanked her warmly, then added, "Miss, I couldn't help notice you were crying. You're feeling real bad today. But maybe tomorrow everything will look a lot brighter. You'll see."

If only that were true, Zan thought, as she whispered, "Thank you," gave a final dab to her eyes, and stepped out of the cab. But everything *won't* look brighter tomorrow.

And maybe it never will.

8

Fr. Aiden O'Brien had spent a sleepless night worrying about the young woman who, under the seal of the confessional, had told him that she was taking part in an ongoing crime and would be unable to prevent a murder. He could only hope that the very fact that her conscience had driven her to begin to unburden herself to him would also force her to prevent the grave sin of allowing another human being's life to be taken.

He prayed for the woman at morning Mass, then with a heavy heart went about his duties. He especially enjoyed helping with the meals or the clothing distribution that the church had been carrying on for the needy for eighty years. Lately the number of people they fed and clothed had been rising. Fr. Aiden assisted at the breakfast shift, watching with satisfaction as hungry people's faces brightened when they began to eat cereal and scrambled eggs and sip steaming hot coffee.

Then, in the midafternoon, Fr. Aiden's own spirits were cheered considerably when he received a call from his old friend Alvirah Meehan, inviting him to dinner that evening. "I've got the five o'clock Mass in the upper church," he told Alvirah, "but I'll be there about 6:30."

It was something to look forward to, even though he knew that nothing could remove the burden the young woman had laid on his shoulders.

At 6:25 he got out of the uptown bus and crossed Central Park South to the building where Alvirah and Willy Meehan had lived ever since the forty-million-dollar lottery windfall. The doorman got on the speaker to announce him, and when the elevator stopped at the sixteenth floor, Alvirah was waiting to greet him. The delicious aroma of roasting chicken floated into the hall and Fr. Aiden gratefully followed Alvirah to its source. Willy was waiting to take his coat and prepare his favorite drink, bourbon on the rocks.

They had not been sitting too long before Fr. Aiden realized that Alvirah was not her usual cheery self. There was a concerned look in her expression and he got the feeling she was trying to bring something up. Finally he decided to put it on the table. "Alvirah, you're worried about something. Anything I can do to help?"

Alvirah sighed. "Oh, Aiden, you can read a person like a book. Well, you know I've told you about Zan Moreland, whose little boy disappeared in Central Park."

"Yes. I was in Rome at that time," he said. "No trace of the child ever?"

"Nothing. Absolutely nothing. Zan's parents died in a car accident and she spent every cent of their insurance money hiring private detectives, but there simply hasn't been a trace of the little guy. He'd be five today. I'd asked Zan to come to dinner, but she's meeting her ex-husband, and that's a mistake, too. He blames her for allowing a young babysitter to take Matthew out."

"I'd like to meet her," Fr. Aiden said. "I sometimes wonder which is worse, to bury a child or to have a child disappear."

"Alvirah, ask Fr. Aiden about that guy you saw in church last evening," Willy urged.

"That was something else, Aiden. I stopped in at St. Francis yesterday —"

"Probably to slip a donation into St. Anthony's box," Aiden interrupted with a smile.

"Actually, yes. But there was a guy there

and his face was in his hands, and you know sometimes you get the feeling you don't want to crowd next to someone?"

Fr. Aiden nodded. "I understand, and that was very thoughtful of you."

"Maybe it wasn't such a good idea," Willy disagreed. "Tell Aiden what you saw, honey."

"Well, anyhow, I walked across the back to the last pew, where I could watch for this fellow when he left. Unfortunately, I didn't get a good look at him, but then you came out of the Reconciliation Room and started across the atrium to the Friary. I was going to see if I could catch up with you, but then Mr. Devout, whoever he is, jumped up, lifted his dark glasses, and Aiden, let me tell you, he didn't take his eyes off you for one minute until you were out of sight."

"Perhaps he wanted to go to confession and couldn't work up his courage," Fr. Aiden suggested. "Unfortunately, that happens, too. People want to unburden themselves, but then can't bring themselves to admit to what they've been doing."

"No. It's more than that. It just has me worried," Alvirah said firmly. "I mean it does happen sometimes that some crazy person decides he's mad at a priest. If there's anyone you know who's mad at you, keep an eye out for him."

The wrinkles on Fr. Aiden's forehead deepened as a thought occurred to him. "Alvirah, you say that this person was kneeling at the Shrine of St. Anthony for a few minutes before I left the Reconciliation Room?"

"Yes." Alvirah put down the glass of wine in her hand and leaned forward. "You suspect someone, don't you, Aiden?"

"No," Fr. Aiden protested unconvincingly. That young woman, he thought. She said she was powerless to prevent someone from being murdered. Was she followed into church or did someone accompany her? She had rushed into the Reconciliation Room. Maybe she came in on an impulse and then obviously regretted it?

"Aiden, do you have security cameras at the church?" Alvirah asked.

"Yes, at all the doors that lead into the church."

"Well, couldn't you check them and see who might have come in between 5:30 and 6:30? I mean there weren't many people there."

"Yes, I could do that," Fr. Aiden agreed.

"Would you mind if I took a look at them tomorrow morning?" Alvirah asked. "I mean I couldn't see that guy's face, but I did get

57

an impression of him. On the tall side, an all-weather coat, like a Burberry. He did have a lot of black hair."

A tape will also show that young woman coming into church, Fr. Aiden thought. Not that I have any hope of learning who she is, but it would be interesting to get a sense of whether she was being followed. The burden of concern that he had been carrying all day deepened.

"Of course, Alvirah, I'll meet you in the church at nine A.M." If someone followed the young woman and was afraid of what she might have told him, would that young woman's own life be in danger now?

It did not occur to the gentle friar to ask himself if his own life might be at risk because somebody feared the information that the troubled young woman had confided to him.

9

Promptly at 7:30 P.M., Zan was at the desk of the Four Seasons Restaurant. She had only to scan the Grill Room to see that Ted was already there, as she had expected he would be. Seven years ago, when they began to date, he had told her that always being early for an appointment was good business. "If it's a client situation, I'm sending a message that I value their time. If it's someone looking for something from me, that person is already nervous and it puts them at a disadvantage. Even if they're on time, they feel as if they're late."

"What would someone want from you?" she had asked him.

"Oh, the manager of a would-be actor or singer who wants me to handle his client. That kind of thing."

"Ms. Moreland, nice to see you again. Mr. Carpenter is waiting." The maître d' led her across the room to the table for two that

Ted always booked.

Ted was on his feet when she reached the table. He leaned over to kiss her cheek. "Zan." His voice was husky. When they sat down, his shoulder brushed against hers. "How bad a day have you been having?" he asked.

She had decided not to say a word about the charges on her credit cards. She knew that if Ted learned about them he would want to help, and she did not want to initiate anything that would keep them in contact, except of course if it involved Matthew. "Pretty bad," she said quietly.

Ted's hand closed over hers. "I will not give up hope that someday the phone will ring and it will be good news."

"I make myself believe that, but then I think that by now Matthew has probably forgotten me. He was only three years and three months old when he disappeared. I've lost nearly two years of his life." She stopped. "I mean we've lost nearly two years," she added carefully.

She saw the flash of anger in Ted's eyes and was sure she knew what he was thinking. The babysitter. He would never forgive her for the careless babysitter she had hired because she had an appointment with a client. When would it come up? After he had

60

had a couple of drinks?

There was a bottle of her favorite red wine by the table. At Ted's nod, the waiter began to pour it. When Ted picked up his glass, he said, "To our little boy."

"Don't," Zan whispered. "Ted, I can't talk about him. I simply can't. We both know what we are feeling today."

Ted took a long sip from his glass without answering. As Zan studied him, she thought for the second time that day that Matthew would grow up to look like him, with those wide-spaced brown eyes and even features. By any standards, Ted was a handsome man. Then she forced herself to realize that just as badly as she did not want to talk about Matthew, Ted needed to share some memories of him. But why here? she asked herself bitterly. I'd have cooked dinner for him at my apartment.

No, I wouldn't, she corrected herself. But we could have gone to some small, out-of-the-way place, where you don't get the feeling that the other diners may be people-watching. How many of them in this room might have seen the articles in those maga-zines today?

She knew she had to allow Ted to talk about Matthew. "This morning I was think-ing how when he grows up, he's going to look just like you," she said tentatively.

"I agree. I remember one day, only a few months before he disappeared, I picked him up from you and took him for lunch. He wanted to walk and I had his hand going down Fifth Avenue. He was so darn cute that people were looking at him and smiling. I ran into one of my old clients and he joked, 'You'll never be able to deny that child.' "

"I don't think you'd ever have denied him." Zan tried to smile.

As if he realized what an effort she was making, Ted changed the subject. "How's the design business going? I read somewhere that you were bidding to decorate those model apartments in the Kevin Wilson building."

It was safe ground. "I honestly think it went well." Because she thought Ted was genuinely interested and because she absolutely had to steer the conversation away from Matthew, Zan described the designs she had suggested and said she felt she had a good shot at getting the job. "Of course, Bartley Longe is in there pitching, and from a chance remark Kevin Wilson made, I guess he's been badmouthing me again."

"Zan, that man is dangerous. I've always felt that about him. He was jealous of *me* when we started going out together. It isn't just that he's a business rival now. He didn't want to let you out of his sight then, and I would bet anything he's still crazy about you."

"Ted, he's twenty years older than I am. He's been divorced and has had numerous affairs. He's got a nasty temper. If he has any feelings about me, it has to do with the fact that I didn't feel flattered by his attention when he decided to try to hit on me. The great regret of my life is that I kept allowing him to bully me when something in my very soul was telling me to fly to Rome and visit Mom and Dad."

She remembered it all: Arriving at Da Vinci Airport. Looking for their faces when she came through security. The letdown. Then the worry. Then collecting her bags and waiting uncertainly in the terminal. Then the call on her international cell phone. The Italian authorities telling her about the accident that had killed them.

The hustle and bustle of Rome at the airport in the early morning. Zan could see herself, standing with the phone frozen at her ear, her mouth shaped into a silent scream. "And then I called you," she told Ted.

"I'm glad you did. When I got to Rome

you were absolutely out of it."

I was out of it for months, Zan thought. Ted took me in like some kind of stray. That's how good he is. There were plenty of women who would have loved to marry him. "And you married me to take care of me, and I rewarded you by allowing an inexperienced babysitter to lose your son." Zan could not believe she had said those words.

"Zan, I know I said that the day Matthew disappeared. Can't you ever understand that I was distraught?"

Around and around we go and where we stop nobody knows, she thought. "Ted, no matter what you say I still blame myself. Maybe none of those private detective agencies I hired did us any good . . ."

"They were a waste of money, Zan. The FBI has the case open and so does the NYPD. You fell for every charlatan who claimed they could find Matthew. Even that weird psychic who had us riding down Alligator Alley in Florida."

"I don't think anything that might help us find Matthew is ever a waste of money. I don't care if I have to consult every private agency in the phone book. Maybe I'll eventually find the one person who can follow Matthew's trail. You asked me about this model apartment job. If I get it, it will open a lot of doors. I'll be making more money, and every cent I make over my living expenses will be spent trying to find Matthew. Somebody must have seen something. I still believe that."

She knew she was trembling. The maître d' was standing near them. She realized her voice had been raised and he was discreetly trying to pretend that he had not overheard her.

"Ready for the specials?" he asked now.

"Yes, we are," Ted said heartily. Then he whispered, "For God's sake, Zan, try to keep it down. Why do you keep torturing yourself?" A surprised look came over his face and she turned.

Josh was hurrying across the room. His face ashen, he stopped at their table. "Zan, I was just leaving the office when some reporters with cameras from *Tell-All Weekly* came in looking for you. I said I didn't know where you were. Then they told me some guy from England who was in the park the day Matthew disappeared just had some photos he took that day enlarged for his parents' wedding anniversary. The reporter told me this guy realized that in the background of a couple of those enlarged photos you can see a woman lifting a child out of a stroller that was parked beside a woman asleep on a blanket . . ."

"Oh, dear God," Ted cried. "How much can they tell from them?"

"When they blew them up even more, other background details were clear. The boy's face isn't visible, but he's wearing a matching blue plaid shirt and shorts."

Zan and Ted stared at Josh. Through lips almost too dry to form words, Zan said, "That's what Matthew was wearing. Did that man bring the photos to the police?"

"No. He sold them to that rag *Tell-All*. Zan, this is crazy, but they swear that you're the woman who's picking up the child. They say there's no mistaking that it's you."

As the sophisticated diners in the Four Seasons Grill Room turned their heads to find the source of the sudden outburst, Ted grabbed Zan by the shoulders and pulled her to her feet. "Damn you! Damn you, you self-pitying lunatic," he shouted. "Where is my son? What did you *do* to him?"

10

Penny Smith Hammel, like many heavyset women, moved with natural grace. When she had been young, despite her weight she had been one of the most popular girls in high school, with her pleasant features, infectious humor, and ability to make even the most awkward partner on the dance floor feel as if he were Fred Astaire.

A week after high school graduation she had married Bernie Hammel, who immediately started work as a long-distance truck driver. Content with where they grew up, Bernie and Penny had raised their three children in rural Middletown, New York, a little more than an hour drive from Manhattan and eons away in lifestyle.

Now fifty-nine years old, the children and grandchildren scattered from Chicago to California and with Bernie on the road so much, Penny had kept happily busy by being available as a babysitter. She loved all her charges, giving them the affection that she would have showered on her grandchildren if they had lived nearby.

The only real excitement in her life had occurred four years ago, when she and Bernie, together with Bernie's ten fellow drivers, had won five million dollars in the lottery. They were one of the larger groups ever to win, and after taxes it netted them each about three hundred thousand dollars, which Bernie and Penny immediately put into a college fund for their grandchildren.

Part of the excitement was that they accepted an invitation to go into Manhattan and meet Alvirah and Willy Meehan and attend a meeting of their Lottery Winners' Support Group. The Meehans had started the group to help people learn not to squander their winnings on crazy investments or by playing Santa Claus to newly discovered relatives.

Penny and Alvirah had immediately realized they were kindred souls and kept in touch regularly.

Penny's best friend since childhood, Rebecca Schwartz, was a real estate agent who kept Penny informed about houses being bought or sold in her local neighborhood. On March 22, she and Penny had lunch in their favorite diner and Rebecca filled Penny in on the fact that the farmhouse on the dead-end road near her had finally been rented. The new tenant had moved in on March 1.

"Her name is Gloria Evans," Rebecca confided. "About thirty. Really attractive. Natural blonde. You know I can always tell when it's being helped along. Great shape, not like you and me. She just wanted a three-month rental, but I told her that Sy Owens wouldn't dream of renting it for less than a year. She didn't bat an eye, just said she was willing to pay for the year in advance because she's finishing a book and needs to be by herself without interruptions."

"Not a bad deal for Sy Owens," Penny commented. "Then I guess he rented it furnished?"

Rebecca laughed. "Oh sure. What else would he do with all that tacky stuff? He wants to sell that place as is, lock, stock, and barrel. You'd think it was Buckingham Palace!"

As was her custom with any new neighbors, the next day Penny drove over to welcome Gloria Evans with a plate of her homemade blueberry muffins. When she knocked on the door, even though there was a car in the breezeway, it was a few minutes before the door was cautiously opened.

Penny had one foot poised to step inside, but Gloria Evans kept the door partially closed and Penny could tell right away that this woman wasn't the least bit happy at the interruption. Penny was immediately apologetic. "Oh, Miss Evans, I *know* you're writing a book, and I'd have called if I had your cell phone number. I just want to welcome you to town with some of my famous blueberry muffins, but please don't think I'm one of those people who will be pestering you with phone calls or drop-in visits —"

"That's nice of you. I did come here to be completely isolated," Evans snapped, as with obvious reluctance she took the plate of muffins from Penny's extended hand.

Refusing to be affronted, Penny continued. "Don't worry about the plate. It's a throwaway. I wrote my phone number for you on a Post-it I stuck on the bottom, just in case you should ever have an emergency."

"That's very kind, but unnecessary," Evans replied stiffly. She had been forced to open the door wider to accept the plate, and looking past her Penny spotted a toy truck on the floor.

"Oh, I didn't know you had a child," Penny exclaimed. "I'm a good babysitter if you ever need one. I have references from half the people in town."

"I don't have a child!" Evans snapped. Then following Penny's glance she turned and saw the toy truck. "My sister helped me get settled. That belongs to her son."

"Well, if she ever visits and you two want to go off for lunch, you have my phone number," Penny said amiably. The last three words were addressed to the door that had closed in her face. For the moment she stood uncertainly, then wishing she had the courage to ring the bell again and grab her blueberry muffins out of the woman's hand, she turned and hurried back to her car.

"I hope Gloria Evans isn't writing a book on manners," she sniffed as, thoroughly humiliated, she backed up her car, turned it around, and sped away.

11

Alvirah and Willy heard the breaking news that Zan Moreland might have been responsible for the disappearance of her son on the eleven o'clock news that night. They had been preparing for bed after their dinner with Fr. Aiden. Shocked, Alvirah called Zan and left a message when she did not answer her cell phone.

In the morning, Alvirah met Fr. Aiden in the Friary adjoining St. Francis of Assisi Church. Together with Neil the handyman, they went to the office to view the playback of the tapes from the security cameras starting at 5:30 P.M. on Monday evening. For the first twenty minutes there was nothing unusual in the frames of people entering or leaving the chapel. As she waited, Alvirah, her voice filled with concern, told Fr. Aiden that the media was reporting that Zan might be involved in Matthew's disappearance.

"Aiden," Alvirah said, insistently, "they

might just as well be saying that Willy and I stole Matthew from his stroller. It's so absolutely ridiculous that you wonder how anyone would swallow it. If they have some kind of pictures, I can only say that that guy in England doctored them to make money from that magazine." Then she leaned forward and gasped. "Neil, can you stop the video? That's Zan. She must have paid a visit here on Monday evening. I know how upset she had to have been because Matthew was turning five yesterday."

Fr. Aiden O'Brien had also recognized the expensively dressed young woman in the dark glasses with the long hair. It was the woman who had come into the Reconciliation Room and told him that she was involved in an ongoing crime and that there was a murder about to be committed. He tried to keep his voice calm as he asked Alvirah, "Are you sure that is your friend Zan?"

"Aiden, of course I'm sure. Look at that suit. Zan bought it last year after it was reduced. She's so careful about money. She went through every cent her mother and father had left her, spending it on private detectives to help find Matthew. Now she's saving so that she can get someone new to start hunting for him."

Before Aiden could reply, Alvirah urged

Neil to start running the tape again. "I'm dying to see if I can pick up the guy who was eyeing you, Aiden."

Aiden phrased his words carefully. "Do you think he might have been accompanying or following your friend, Alvirah?"

Alvirah seemed not to have heard the question. "Oh, look," she exclaimed, "there he is coming in, the guy I'm looking for." Then she shook her head. "Oh, you can't see his face, and his collar is up. He's got those dark glasses on. All you can see is that mop of hair."

For the next half hour, she reviewed the rest of the tapes. They could easily distinguish the agitated figure of the woman Alvirah identified as Zan leaving the church. She was still wearing her dark glasses, but her head was bent and her shoulders shaking. Holding a handkerchief to her mouth as if she were trying to stifle sobs, she had rushed out of the church and out of the sight of the camera.

"She didn't stay five minutes," Alvirah said sadly. "She's so darn afraid of breaking down. She told me that after her parents were killed in that accident, she simply couldn't stop crying. She was afraid to go out in public. She said that if that happened again because of Matthew, she wouldn't be able to work and she needed to work to keep herself from going insane."

"Insane." Fr. Aiden whispered the word so softly that neither Alvirah nor Neil could possibly have heard it. "I am an accessory to a crime that is ongoing and to a murder that is going to happen very soon. I don't want to be part of it, but it's too late to stop." In the last two days that frantic statement was embedded in his mind.

"There's that guy again, leaving. But you can't tell anything about him." Alvirah signaled to Neil to turn off the tape. "You see how upset Zan appears Monday night? Can you imagine how she feels right now with the news story about her kidnapping Matthew?"

That was the other thing the young woman told him, Fr. Aiden thought: *You'll read about it in the headlines.* Had the murder she claimed she could not prevent already *been* committed? Had she already killed her own child, or probably even worse, was the poor thing still alive and about to die?

12

After Ted's explosive accusation, Josh grabbed Zan's hand and pulled her through the tables of shocked diners at the Four Seasons, rushed her down the stairs, through the lobby, and onto the street. "God, they must have followed me," he muttered as paparazzi lunged forward and cameras began flashing.

A cab had stopped in the street in front of the entrance. Josh, his arm now around Zan, sprinted to it and the instant the previous occupant had both feet on the ground, pushed her into it. "Just move," he snapped to the driver.

The driver nodded and started the cab, catching the light at Fifty-second Street and Third Avenue. "Make a right on Second Avenue," Josh told him.

"Is she a movie star or a rock singer?" the cabbie asked, then shrugged when he did not get an answer.

Josh still had his arm around Zan. Now he removed it. "You okay?" he asked her.

"I don't know," Zan whispered. "Josh, what does it mean? Are they crazy? How could they possibly have a photo of me taking Matthew out of his stroller? For God's sake, I have proof that I was at the Aldrich town house. Nina Aldrich had invited me over there to discuss doing the interior for her."

"Zan, take it easy," Josh said, trying to sound calm even as he visualized what it was going to look like when Ted's outburst hit the news. "You can prove where you were that day. Now what do you want to do? I'm afraid if you go home, the paparazzi may be waiting for you there."

"I have to go home," she said, her voice becoming stronger. "You can drop me off, but if there are any photographers, have the cab wait and walk with me until I can get inside. Josh, what's going on? I feel as if I'm living in a nightmare and I can't find my way out of it."

You *are* living in a nightmare, Josh thought.

They were silent the rest of the way to Battery Park City. When the cab pulled up to Zan's apartment building, as Josh had anticipated the cameras were waiting for

77

them. Ducking their heads, they ignored the cries to "Look this way, Zan," or "Over here, Zan," until they were safely inside the lobby.

"Josh, the cab is waiting. You go ahead home," Zan told him as they stood at the elevator.

"Are you sure?"

"I'm sure."

"Zan . . ." Josh bit off what he was about to say. He was going to warn her that the police would undoubtedly want to question her again and that before she spoke to them, she had better get a lawyer.

Instead, he squeezed her hand and waited until she was safely inside the elevator before he left. Outside, the paparazzi, seeing him alone and sensing that there would be no more photo opportunities, were beginning to disperse. They'll be back, Josh thought, as he got back in the cab. If there's anything at all we can be sure of, it's that they'll be back, damn them.

13

After his outburst in the Four Seasons, Ted Carpenter had gone down to the men's room. When he had jumped up and grabbed Zan, the glass of red wine he'd been holding had spilled all over his shirt and tie. Grabbing a towel, he'd futilely dabbed at the spots then looked in the mirror.

I look as if I'm bleeding to death, he thought, momentarily distracted from the stunning revelation that a tourist's camera had caught Zan taking Matthew from Central Park.

He felt the vibration of his cell phone in his jacket pocket. He knew it would be Melissa.

It was.

He waited until he was sure she had finished leaving a message, then listened to his voice mail. "I know you can't talk now, but meet me at Lola's by 9:30." There had been nothing of Melissa's normally sexy voice in her message. Ted knew it was clearly an order. "It'll be just the two of us. Then we'll go down to the Club around 11:30," Melissa continued. Then her voice turned petulant: "Don't kiss your ex good night."

I can't be seen out partying when it's just been reported that my ex-wife has kidnapped and probably hidden my child, he thought, aghast. When I call Melissa back and tell her what has happened, she'll surely understand that.

The photos.

She probably hasn't heard about them yet.

Why am I worried about Melissa? he asked himself. The question I should be screaming is: Are those photos fakes?

I know how photos can be manipulated. How many times have we eliminated unimportant people from our publicity shots? If you can take them out, you can put them in, too. It's common practice to put a star's face on a better-shaped body. Is this claim that Zan took Matthew just trick photo editing? How much did that tourist get for selling them to that *Tell-All* rag?

A man entering the restroom looked at Ted sympathetically. Ted exited quickly, not wanting to engage in conversation. If those photos turn out to be phonies, I'll look despicable for attacking Zan the way I did, he thought in near despair. I'm supposed to be a master of public relations when it comes to crisis management.

He had to talk to Melissa. He would meet her. He had time to go home, change his shirt, and meet her at Lola's. If the media was waiting outside, he would tell them that, on reflection, he abjectly begged Matthew's mother's pardon that he had been so quick to believe she had abducted their son.

Bracing himself, he walked out the lobby door where, as he had expected, camera crews were waiting for him. A microphone was stuck in his face. "Please," he said, "I want to make a statement but can't if you won't give me room."

As the shouted questions diminished, he took the microphone from the hand of one reporter. His voice firm, he said, "First, I must apologize to Matthew's mother, my former wife, Alexandra Moreland, for my unspeakable behavior this evening. Both of us are desperate to find our little boy. When I heard that there were photographs in existence showing that Matthew's mother had taken him, I quite literally lost it. A moment of reflection would have made me realize that those photos have got to be fake, or doctored, whatever name you want to give it."

Ted paused, then added, "I am so sure that the photos are a hoax that I am going now to meet my client, the talented and beautiful Melissa Knight, for dinner at Lola's Café. As you can see, in my unfortunate response to hearing about those pictures, I spilled wine on my shirt. I am going home to change, then to Lola's."

Ted could not conceal a tremor in his voice. "My son, Matthew, is five years old today. Neither his mother nor I believe that he is dead. Someone, perhaps a lonely woman who desperately wanted a child and seized the opportunity to steal him, is with him at this moment. If that person is watching us, please tell Matthew how much Mommy and Daddy love him and long to see him again."

The reporters kept a respectful silence as Ted walked to the curb where Larry Post, his high school friend and long-time driver, was holding the car door of the backseat open for him.

14

After Josh left her, Zan went upstairs, double-locked the door of the apartment, and stripped off her clothes, wrapping herself in her warm old bathrobe as she had done when she woke up in the morning. The message light was blinking on the telephone. She walked over and turned off the ringer. For the rest of the night, she sat in the bedroom chair with one single light shining on Matthew's picture. Her eyes searched each feature of his face longingly.

The spike of hair that by now had probably developed into a cowlick. The hint of red in that mop of sandy hair. Was he now an out-and-out redhead?

He had always been a friendly child, sunny and welcoming to strangers, not like some children who are naturally shy at age three. Dad was an extrovert, Zan thought. So was Mother. What happened to me?

So many of those months after they died

are a blur. Now they are saying that *I* took Matthew out of his stroller that day.

"Did I?" she whispered aloud.

The shock of the question, the enormity that she could actually voice it, stunned her. She forced herself to ask the logical next question. "But if I took him, what did I do with him?"

She had no answer.

I would never have hurt him, she told herself. I never laid a finger on him. Even when I had given him a "time out" if he was behaving badly, my heart would melt for him, sitting in his little chair, looking so miserable.

Is Ted right? Do I wallow in self-pity and want other people to pity me? Does he mean that I'm one of those crazy mothers who harm their children because they need to be pitied and comforted?

She had thought she was beyond it, that sense of numbness, the feeling that she was withdrawing into herself from the pain. In the airport in Rome that day, when she had called Ted only minutes after she learned of her parents' death, she had felt her legs crumble under her. But even though she could not reach out to the people who had gathered around her, who had lifted her onto a stretcher, who had rushed her to the hospital in an ambulance, she had been aware of every word they said. It was just that she couldn't open her eyes, or make her lips form words, or lift her hand. It was as if she had been in a sealed room and could not find her way back to tell them that she was still with them.

Zan knew that was happening to her again. She leaned back in the soft armchair and closed her eyes.

A merciful emptiness engulfed her as she whispered his name: "Matthew . . . Matthew . . . Matthew . . ."

15

How much had Gloria told that old priest? It was the question that haunted him day and night. She was beginning to crack, and now at this crucial time, when it all was coming to a head, when everything he had planned during these two years was about to happen, she had rushed into that room.

He had been born a Catholic, and knew that if what Gloria said was under the seal of the confessional, the priest would have to keep his mouth shut. But he wasn't sure if Gloria was a Catholic, and if she wasn't, and just had gone in for a little heart-to-heart chat, maybe the old priest would consider it okay to say that Zan had a looka-like, someone who was impersonating her.

If that happened the cops would keep digging, and it would soon be all over. . . .

The old priest. That neighborhood around West Thirty-first Street wasn't any great shakes, he thought. And stray bullets were hitting people all over the city these days. Why not one more?

He would have to take care of it himself. He couldn't take the chance of having one more person alive who could tie him to the disappearance of Matthew Carpenter. The best thing would be to go back into the church, and try to get a line on when that priest was hearing confessions. There must be a schedule.

But that might take time. Maybe if I call, he thought, and ask when Fr. O'Brien is scheduled to hear confession next, whoever answers won't think it unusual. I'm sure some people want to talk to the same guy about their problems every time they go. Besides I can't sit around like this and wait for him to go to the cops.

The decision made, he placed the call and was told that Fr. O'Brien was scheduled for the next two weeks, Monday through Friday from four to six P.M.

It's about time for me to go to confession, he thought.

Before he paid Gloria to mind the child, he'd known that she was a consummate makeup artist. She told him that she sometimes made up herself and her friends to look like celebrities, and that they'd fooled everyone. She said they all had a good laugh when according to Page Six of the *Post* the celebrities they were mimicking were sighted having a quiet dinner at an out-of-the-way spot and graciously signing autographs.

"You wouldn't believe how often we don't get a check," she had giggled.

I always wear the wig she gave me when we meet in town, he thought. With that wig and the raincoat and dark glasses, even my best friends wouldn't know me.

He laughed aloud. As a kid, he'd always enjoyed being in plays. His favorite was when he had played Thomas à Becket in *Murder in the Cathedral*.

16

After speaking to the reporters outside the Four Seasons, Ted Carpenter turned on his iPhone on his way downtown and found the photos of the person who seemed unmistakably to be Zan taking Matthew from the stroller. Shocked, he stopped at his duplex condo in the newly gentrified Meatpacking District of lower Manhattan. There he had agonized briefly about whether or not to meet Melissa at Lola's Café. What will it look like for me to be there when these photos are showing my ex-wife stealing my child?

He phoned the Central Park Precinct and was put through to a detective who told him that it would be at least twenty-four hours before they could verify that the pictures were not doctored. At least if I'm questioned by the paparazzi, I can tell them that, he thought, as he changed his shirt and rushed back to the car.

The paparazzi on the sidewalk outside the popular café were kept back behind velvet ropes. One of the bouncers had held the door of his car open and he had ducked out toward the entrance. But then he stopped, unable to ignore the shouted question, "Have you seen those photos yet, Ted?"

"Yes, I have and I have been in touch with the police. I believe they are a cruel hoax," he snapped.

Inside the café he braced himself, knowing he was a half hour late meeting Melissa. He fully expected to find her in a filthy mood, but she was sitting at a large table with five old friends from the band she had once been in as the lead singer. She was clearly enjoying their adulation. Ted knew all of them and was grateful for their presence. If Melissa had been waiting alone, there would have been hell to pay.

Her greeting to him, "Hey, you're getting more coverage than I am," was met with hoots of laughter from her tablemates.

Ted leaned over Melissa and kissed her on her lips.

"What'll you have, Mr. Carpenter?" The waiter was at the table. There were already two bottles of their most expensive Champagne chilling in a bucket beside him. I don't want that damn Champagne, Ted thought as he sat down next to her. I always get a headache from it. "A gin martini," he said. Only one, he promised himself. But I need it. What in the hell does it look like for me to be here when there may be a break in the search for my son?

He was careful to drape his arm lovingly around Melissa and keep his eyes fixed on her for the benefit of the stringers who were paid to contribute items to the columnists. He knew that tomorrow Melissa would want to read something like "Top recording artist Melissa Knight has bounced back from her well-publicized breakup with rock singer Leif Ericson and is now madly in love with public relations dynamo Ted Carpenter. They were canoodling at Lola's last night."

I remember hearing about the time Eddie Fisher, then married to Elizabeth Taylor, sent a telegram from Italy signed "The Princess and her love slave," Ted thought. That's the kind of rot I'm supposed to provide for Melissa. She's kidding herself into thinking that she's in love with me.

But I need her. I need her nice fat check every month. If only I hadn't bought the building when our lease was up. It's been draining me dry. Melissa will move on from me fast enough, he thought, as he gulped rather than sipped the gin martini. The trick is to make sure that when she decides to drop me, she doesn't go to another PR firm and take her buddies with her.

"The same, Mr. Carpenter?" the waiter asked when he came by.

"Why not?" Ted snapped.

At midnight Melissa decided to leave for the Club. Another four a.m. morning once they get settled there. Ted knew he had to escape. There was only one way he could do it.

"Melissa, I feel lousy," he said, speaking under the din of the noisy café. "I think I may be getting a bug or flu or something. I can't expose you to it any longer. You've got a full schedule and you can't afford to get sick."

Keeping his fingers crossed, he saw the appraising look she gave him. Odd how her genuinely exquisite features could suddenly become distorted and lose all semblance of beauty when she was upset or angry. Her depth-of-the-ocean dark blue eyes narrowed and she twisted her long blond hair into a single curl that she pulled forward over her shoulder.

She's twenty-six years old and as totally self-centered as any personality I've ever dealt with in this business, Ted thought. I wish I could tell her to go to hell.

"You're not hooking up with your ex, are you?" she demanded.

"My ex-wife is the last woman I want to see right now. You ought to know by now that I'm crazy about you." Taking a chance, Ted deliberately let a note of irritation creep into his expression and tone of voice. He could afford to do that only occasionally but he knew, when he did, it sent the message to her that it would be insane to imagine he could look at another woman.

Melissa shrugged and turned to the others at the table. "Teddy's chickening out," she laughed. "Everyone who's going with me to the Club, let's split."

They all got up.

"You have your car?" Ted asked.

"No. I walked. For God sake, of course I have my car." She tapped him on the cheek, a playful slap for the benefit of the onlookers.

Ted signaled to the waiter to put the bill on his house account as usual and the group left the café together. Melissa held his hand and stopped to smile for the paparazzi. Ted walked her to her limo, wrapped her in his arms, and kissed her a long, deep kiss. A little more fodder for the gossip mills, he thought. That should keep her happy.

Her former bandmates piled into the limo with her. As his own car was brought up to the curb, a reporter stepped forward, holding something in his hand. "Mr. Carpenter, have you seen the photos the English tourist took that day your son was kidnapped?"

"Yes, I have."

The reporter held up an enlarged version of them. "Would you care to comment?"

Ted stared at them, then taking them, he moved closer to the brightly lit window as if to get a better look. Then he said, "As I said before, I believe these pictures will turn out to be a cruel hoax."

"Isn't that your ex-wife, Zan Moreland, picking up your child from the stroller?" the reporter demanded.

Ted was aware of the cameras surrounding him now. He shook his head. Larry Post was holding open the door of his car. He rushed to get into it.

When he got home, too shocked to feel anything, he undressed and took a sleeping pill. His night filled with tortured dreams, he awoke aching and nauseous, feeling as though the fictitious flu bug had become a reality. Or was it those damn gin martinis? he asked himself.

At nine o'clock the next morning, Ted called

his office and spoke to Rita. Cutting off her shocked reaction to the photos, he told her to call Detective Collins, who had been in charge of the investigation the day Matthew disappeared, and make an appointment for him to see Collins tomorrow. "I'm going to stay home at least until mid-afternoon," he told Rita. "I may have a fever, but I've got to get in by then. I need to look at the proofs of that photo shoot that Melissa did for *Celeb Magazine* before I can okay them. Tell anyone in the media who calls that I will have no statement until the police have investigated the authenticity of those pictures."

At three o'clock, ghastly pale, he finally arrived at the office. Without asking, Rita made a cup of tea for him. "You should have stayed home, Ted," she said matter-of-factly. "I promise I'm not going to say another word about it, but there is one fact that you should keep in mind. Zan adored Matthew. She would never hurt him."

"Notice you use the word 'adored,'" Ted snapped. "That's past tense in my book. Now where are the *Celeb* proofs of Melissa?"

"They're gorgeous," Rita said reassuringly, as she took them from an envelope she had laid on his desk.

Ted stared at them. "To you they're gorgeous. To me they're gorgeous. But I can tell you right now that Melissa is going to hate them. There are shadows under her eyes, and her mouth looks too thin. And don't forget I was the one who told her she ought to accept posing for that cover story. Good God, can it get any worse?"

Rita looked at her boss of fifteen years with compassion. Ted Carpenter was thirty-eight years old but he looked years younger than his actual age. With his thick hair, brown eyes, firm mouth, and lean frame, she always believed that he was better looking and had a lot more charisma than many of the clients he represented. But right now he looks as if someone attacked him with a machete.

And to think of all the pity I've wasted on Zan these two years, Rita thought. If she'd done something to that darling little boy, I honestly think I could shoot her myself!

17

Zan blinked, opened her eyes, and closed them again. What happened, she asked herself. She wondered why she was sitting in the chair, why even though she was wearing the bathrobe, she felt so chilled, why her whole body ached.

Her hands were numb. She rubbed them together, trying to get feeling back into her fingers. Her feet were asleep. She moved them in a circular motion, almost unaware of what she was doing.

She opened her eyes again. Matthew's picture was directly in her vision. She could tell that the bulb in the lamp next to it was still on, even though dim, cloud-filled light was filtering through the partially drawn shade.

Why didn't I go to bed last night? she asked herself as she tried to get past the dull throbbing in her head.

Then she remembered.

They think I took Matthew from the stroller. But that's impossible. That's crazy. Why would I do that? What would I have done with him?

"What would I have done with you?" she moaned, as she stared at Matthew's picture. "Can anyone seriously believe I could harm you, my own child?"

Zan sprang to her feet, then in quick strides crossed the room to grab Matthew's picture and hug it against her body. "Why do they think that?" The question was now a whisper. "How could those pictures be of me? I was with Nina Aldrich. I spent that afternoon in the new town house she bought. I can prove it. Of course I can prove it.

"I know I didn't take Matthew out of his stroller," she said aloud, trying to control the quavering tone of her voice. "I can prove it. But I can't let what happened to me last night happen again. I can't have those blanks in my memory, the way I did after Mom and Dad died. If there is a photo of a woman picking up Matthew from the stroller, it would be the first real break in trying to trace him. I've got to think like that. I can't let myself retreat again. Please, God, don't let me be overwhelmed again. Let me hang on to the hope that there may be something in those photos that will give some clue, some lead, to finding Matthew . . .

It was only six o'clock. Instead of showering, Zan turned on the taps in the Jacuzzi, knowing that the swirling hot water would help relieve the aching of her body. What should I do? she asked herself again. I'm sure that Detective Collins must have those photos by now. After all, he was the lead investigator on the case.

She thought of the way the media had been outside the Four Seasons waiting for her last night, how they had been here outside the apartment when Josh took her home. Would they try to follow her around today? Or would they be at the office waiting for her?

She turned off the taps of the Jacuzzi, tested the water, then realized it was too hot. The phone, she thought. She remembered that she had turned off the ringer when she got into the apartment last night. She walked into the bedroom and over to the night table. The message light was blinking. There had been nine phone calls.

The first eight were from reporters asking to interview her. Determined not to allow them to upset her, Zan carefully deleted the calls one by one. The final one was from

Alvirah Meehan. Gratefully, Zan listened to it, savoring Alvirah's reassurance that that guy who claimed he had a picture of Zan picking up Matthew in the park must be some con artist. "It's a shame you have to go through nonsense like this, Zan," Alvirah's outraged voice boomed. "Of course it will be exposed as a sham, but it's still terrible on you emotionally. Willy and I know that. Please call us and come over and have dinner tomorrow. We love you."

Zan listened to the message twice. Then, when the computerized voice instructed, "Push three to save, push one to delete," she pushed the save button. It's too early to call Alvirah, she thought, but I'll get back to her when I'm in the office. It would be good to be with her and Willy tonight. Maybe by then, if Detective Collins can see me this afternoon, all this will be cleared up. And maybe, oh, please, God, if that man from England was snapping photos when someone was taking Matthew from the stroller, Detective Collins will have something to go on.

Somewhat comforted at the thought, Zan reset the coffeepot from the seven-o'clock setting so that it would begin to brew at once. She got into the Jacuzzi and felt the healing warmth of the water begin to deflate the tension in her body. Coffee cup in hand, she dressed in slacks, a turtleneck sweater, and low-heeled boots.

When she was dressed, it was still only a few minutes before seven, but she realized it might be early enough to leave the apartment without running into reporters. That possibility made her twist her hair into a bun and drape a scarf securely around it. Then she dug into a dresser drawer and found an old pair of sunglasses with a wide, round frame that was a totally different shape from the kind she usually wore.

Finally she grabbed a faux-fur vest from the closet, picked up her shoulder bag, and took the elevator down to the basement. From there she made her way through the rows of parked cars in the garage and exited onto the street at the back of the building. With swift steps she hurried toward the West Side Highway, encountering only the early-morning dog walkers and joggers. When she was sure she was not being followed she hailed a cab and started to give the office address on East Fifty-eighth Street, then changed her mind. Instead she directed the cabbie to drop her on East Fifty-seventh Street. If there's any sign of the media I can go in through the delivery entrance, she thought.

It was only when she was able to sit back, knowing that at least for the length of the trip uptown she could be sure that no one would shout questions at her or aim a camera in her direction, that she was able to focus on the other problem, the fact that someone was charging clothes and an airline ticket to her name. Will that affect my credit rating? she worried. Of course it will. If I get the job with Kevin Wilson, I'll be ordering very expensive fabrics and furniture.

Why is all this happening to me?

Zan found herself pushing back against the almost physical feeling of being caught in a riptide, of a fierce current dragging her underwater. She gasped for air, as the sense of not being able to breathe overwhelmed her.

Panic attacks.

Don't let them come back, she pleaded to herself. She shut her eyes and forced herself to inhale deep, measured breaths. By the time the cab pulled to the corner at Fifty-seventh Street and Third Avenue, she had managed to regain some measure of calm. Even so, her fingers were trembling as she handed the cabbie the folded bills.

It had begun to drizzle. Cold, wet drops brushed her cheeks. The vest was a mistake, she thought, I should have worn a raincoat.

Ahead of her a woman was hurrying a little boy who looked to be about four years old toward a waiting car. Zan rushed to pass them so that she could look into the child's face. But of course it wasn't Matthew.

When she turned the corner there didn't seem to be any sign of the media waiting for her. She pushed the revolving door and went into the lobby. The newsstand was to the left. "The *Post* and the *News* please, Sam," she told the elderly clerk.

There was nothing of his usual friendly smile in Sam's demeanor when he handed the folded copies to her.

She did not permit herself to look at them until she was safely in her office. Then she laid them on her desk and unfolded them. The front page of the *Post* was a picture of her bending over the stroller. The front page of the *News* was a picture of her carrying Matthew away.

Disbelieving, her eyes darted from one to the other. But it *isn't* me, she protested. It *can't* be me. Someone who *looks* like me took Matthew. . . . It made no sense.

Josh wasn't due in until later. Zan tried to focus, but by noon she gave up. Zan grabbed the phone. I've got to call Alvirah back. I know she has the *Post* and the *Times* delivered every morning.

103

Alvirah answered on the second ring. When she heard Zan's voice, she said, "Zan, I saw the papers. You could have knocked me over with a feather. Why would someone who looks like you take Matthew?"

What does Alvirah mean by that question? Zan asked herself. Was she asking what reason someone would have for making herself look like me and taking Matthew, or does she mean that she thinks I took him?

"Alvirah," she said, choosing her words carefully, "someone is doing this to me. I don't know who, but I have my suspicions. But even if Bartley Longe would go to this length to harm me, there is one thing I'm sure of: He would never hurt Matthew. Alvirah, thank *God* for those pictures. Thank God for them. I'm going to get Matthew back. Those pictures are going to be my proof that someone is impersonating me, that someone hates me enough to steal my child and now is stealing my identity . . ."

For a moment there was silence, then Alvirah said, "Zan, I know a good private detective firm. If you don't have the money to pay for it, I do. If these pictures have been doctored, we'll find out who paid to have it done. Wait a minute. Let me correct myself. If you say these pictures are phonies, I absolutely believe you, but I think that whoever has done this has overplayed his hand. I guess you lit a candle to St. Anthony the other night when you stopped into St. Francis of Assisi."

"When I stopped in . . . where?" Zan was afraid to ask the question.

"Late Monday afternoon at 5:30, quarter of six. I had dropped in to the church to make a donation I promised to St. Anthony and I noticed that some guy was eyeing my friend Fr. Aiden, and I didn't like it. That's why I checked the security camera tapes this morning to see if he was anyone Fr. Aiden might know. With all the crazies in New York, forewarned is forearmed. I didn't see you then, but you are on the tape. You came into the church and left just a few minutes later. I figured you were saying a prayer for Matthew."

Monday afternoon at 5:30 or quarter of six. I decided to walk home, Zan thought. I went straight home. I did go west on Thirty-first or Thirty-second Street, but by then I knew I was tired and took a cab the rest of the way.

But I didn't stop in the St. Francis chapel. I *know* I didn't.

Or did I?

She realized that Alvirah was still speaking and was asking about dinner.

"I'll be there," Zan promised, "at 6:30." She replaced the phone on the cradle and put her head in her hands. Am I having blackouts again? she asked herself. Am I going crazy? Did I kidnap my own son? And if I took him, what did I do with him?

If I can forget what happened less than forty-eight hours ago, what else have I blacked out? she asked herself in despair.

18

In the days when he had worked as an undercover cop it had been easy for Detective Billy Collins to pass as a down-and-out drifter. Thin to the point of boniness, with a sharp-angled face, sparse graying hair, and mournful eyes, he was easily accepted by drug dealers as a likely customer to purchase a fix.

Now that he was assigned to the Central Park Precinct, and arriving for work in a business suit, shirt, and tie, together with his mild, self-effacing manner, people tended to dismiss him on first acquaintance as an ordinary, run-of-the-mill guy, who probably wasn't too bright.

That judgment was shared by many suspected felons who were deceived by Billy's routine questions and seeming acceptance of their version about a criminal event. For most of them, that turned out to be a serious mistake. Billy's forty-two-year-old steel-trap mind retained information that had seemed trivial and unimportant at the time it was given, but when circumstances changed, he could retrieve that data from his memory bank in a heartbeat.

Billy's private life was simple. Despite his funereal appearance, he had a keen sense of humor, was a good storyteller, and was devoted to his wife, Eileen, whom he'd started dating when they were in high school. He said she was the only person alive who considered him handsome, and that was the reason he had fallen permanently in love with her. His two sons, who fortunately for them resembled their very attractive mother, were both students at Fordham University.

Billy had been the first detective to arrive on the scene when the 911 call came that a three-year-old was missing in Central Park nearly two years ago. He had rushed there with a sinking heart. For him the worst part of his job was to respond to a crime involving a dead or missing child.

That hot summer day in June it had been Tiffany Shields, the babysitter, who sobbed hysterically that she had fallen asleep next to the stroller and when she woke up Matthew was gone. While every inch of the park was being searched and nearby visitors questioned, the divorced parents had arrived separately. Ted Carpenter, the father, had been on the verge of attacking Shields, who admitted that she had fallen asleep; Zan Moreland, the mother, had been eerily calm, a reaction that Billy had attributed to shock. Even as the hours had passed without a trace of Matthew, and not one single witness who might have observed him being taken had come forward, the mother had remained impassive in demeanor.

In the nearly two years since that day, Billy Collins had kept Matthew's file on the top of his desk. He had scrupulously followed up on both parents' explanation of where they had been when their child disappeared, and both their statements were backed up by other witnesses. He asked them about any enemies who might have hated them enough to kidnap their child. Zan Moreland had hesitantly confided that there was one person she did consider an enemy. He was Bartley Longe, a prominent interior designer, who scoffed at the idea that in any way he would kidnap the child of a former employee.

"That statement from Zan Moreland validates everything I have ever said about her," Longe had told Billy, his tone furious and disgusted. "First she practically accused me of causing her parents' deaths, because if they hadn't been on their way to pick her up at the airport, her father might have had his heart attack at home and wouldn't have been in the accident. Then she told me that it was because she was working for me that she didn't see her parents more often. Now she's telling you that I kidnapped her child! Detective, do yourself a favor. Don't waste your time looking anywhere else. Whatever happened to that poor child was because his deranged mother made it happen."

Billy Collins had listened, but then trusted his own instincts. From what he had learned, Bartley Longe's anger at Zan Moreland was triggered by the fact that she had become his business competitor. But Billy had quickly decided that neither Longe nor Moreland had anything to do with the little boy's disappearance. In his heart and soul he firmly believed that Zan was a victim, a deeply wounded victim who would have moved heaven and earth to get her child back.

That was why when he received a call on Tuesday evening about a breaking development in the Matthew Carpenter case, Billy had been tempted to jump in his car and drive from his home in Forest Hills, Queens, to the precinct.

His boss told him to stay put. "For all we know those photos that were sold to that gossip magazine may have been doctored. If they're on the level, you need to have a clear mind to start reworking the case."

On Wednesday morning, Billy woke at seven A.M. Twenty minutes later, showered, shaved, and dressed, he was on his way into the city. By the time he arrived there, the photos that were published in *Tell-All Weekly* and online were on his desk.

There were six in all; the original three the English tourist had taken, plus the three he had blown up for the family album. They were the ones whose background seemed to indicate that Zan Moreland had kidnapped her own son.

Billy whistled softly, his only physical response to the fact that he was both shocked and chagrined. I really did believe that sob-sister, he thought, as he studied the three photos that showed Zan bending over the stroller, then picking up the sleeping child, and finally walking down the path away from the camera. There's no mistake, Billy thought as he went from one photo to the next. The long, straight auburn hair, the slender frame, the fashionable sunglasses . . .

He opened the file that was always on the corner of his desk. From it he extracted pictures that had been quietly taken of Zan by the police photographer when she rushed to the crime scene. The short flowered dress and the high-heeled sandals she was wearing when she arrived in the park that day were identical to the clothing worn by the kidnapper.

Billy normally patted himself on the back that he was an excellent judge of human nature. His sharp sense of disappointment in his own bad judgment was immediately vanquished by his overriding concern about what Zan Moreland might have done with her own son.

Zan's alibi about her whereabouts that day had seemed straightforward. Clearly he had missed something. I'm starting with the babysitter, Billy thought grimly. I'll pick apart Zan Moreland's account of every minute of that day and find out how she's gotten away with lying. Then by God, I'm going to make her tell me what she did with that little kid.

19

Tiffany Shields was still living at home, completing her second year at Hunter College. The day that Matthew Carpenter disappeared had been a turning point in her life. It wasn't only that she had been in charge of Matthew and had fallen asleep, it was that whenever the case came up in the media, she was branded as the careless babysitter who had not only not bothered to strap him into the stroller, but who had stretched out on a blanket and, as one reporter wrote, "passed out."

Almost every article referred to the hysterical call she had made to 911. The tape of it was played on some of the TV coverage. In the past two years when a child was missing anywhere, Tiffany had been forced to read or hear that it was or wasn't a Tiffany Shields-sleeping-babysitter kind of situation. Whenever she read or heard those media reports, Tiffany's anger at the unfairness of it grew into a block of solid fury.

The day was still vivid in her mind. She woke with what felt like the beginnings of a cold. She canceled plans to meet some of her girlfriends to celebrate their impending graduation from Cathedral High School. Her mother had gone to work at Bloomingdale's where she was a sales clerk. Her father was the superintendent of the apartment building where they lived on East Eighty-sixth Street. At noon, the phone rang in their apartment. If only I hadn't answered it, Tiffany thought over and over again in the next twenty-one months. I almost didn't. I figured it was some tenant calling to complain about some damn leaking faucet.

But she did answer it.

It was Zan Moreland. "Tiffany, can you possibly help me?" she had pleaded. "Matthew's new nanny was supposed to start this morning and just phoned that she can't be here until tomorrow. I've got a terribly important appointment. It's with a potential client, and she's not the kind of person who would care about my babysitting problems. Would you be an angel and take Matthew out to the park for a couple of hours? I just fed him and it's his naptime. I promise you he'll probably sleep the whole time."

I used to mind Matthew once in a while

when the nanny had an evening off and I loved that little guy, Tiffany thought. But that day I told Zan that I thought I was getting sick, but she was so insistent that I finally gave in. And ruined my life in the process.

But on Wednesday morning, as she glanced at the morning paper over a glass of orange juice, Tiffany had two reactions. Explosive anger that Zan Moreland had manipulated her, and unbelievable relief that she would no longer be the victim of Matthew's disappearance. I told the cops that I had taken some antihistamines and felt kind of groggy and that I didn't really want to babysit, she thought. But if they come back to talk to me again, I'm going to rub it into them that Zan Moreland *knew* I was feeling tired. When I picked up Matthew, she offered me a Pepsi. She said it would make me feel better, that the sugar in it was beneficial when a cold was coming on.

Looking back, Tiffany thought, I wonder if Zan may have put something in that soda to make me really sleepy? And Matthew never even stirred while he was in the stroller. That's why I didn't bother him to put the strap on . . . He was out like a light.

Tiffany reread every word of the story and

studied the photos carefully. That's the dress Zan was wearing, she thought, but the shoes aren't the same. By mistake, Zan had bought two pairs that were alike and had another pair that was almost the same. All of them were high-heeled beige step-in sandals. The only difference between the two styles was that one crossover strap was narrower than the other. She gave me one of the identical pairs with the narrower strap. We were both wearing them that morning. I still have them.

I'm not going to tell that to anyone. If the cops knew they may want my sandals and by God I *earned* them!

Three hours later, when she checked the messages on her cell phone after her history class, Tiffany saw that one of them was from that Detective Collins who had questioned her over and over again when Matthew disappeared. He wanted to talk with her again.

Tiffany's narrow mouth hardened into a slit. Her normally pert features suddenly lost their attractive, youthful expression. She pressed the button to return Billy Collins's call.

I want to talk to you, too, Detective Collins, she thought.

And this time I'll be the one to make *you* squirm!

20

Glory was putting that gooey stuff on his hair again. Matthew hated it. It made his scalp feel burned and some of it almost got in his eye. Glory rubbed hard to catch it, but the washcloth went in his eye and it hurt. But he knew that if he said he didn't want her to put the stuff in his hair, she would only say, "I'm sorry, Matty. I don't want to do it, but I have to."

Today he didn't say one single word. He knew Glory was really mad at him. This morning, when the doorbell rang, he had run into the closet and closed the door. He didn't mind this closet at all because it was bigger than some of the other ones, and it had a light big enough that he could see everything. But then he remembered he had left his favorite truck in the hall. It was his favorite because it was bright red and had three speeds, so when he played with it in the hall he could make it go very fast or

117

really slow.

He had opened the closet door and ran to get it. Just then, he saw that Glory was closing the door and saying good-bye to some lady. After Glory locked the door she turned around and saw him. She looked so mad he was scared that she would hit him. "Next time I'll stick you in the closet and never let you out," she had said in a mean, low voice. He'd been so scared that he ran back into the closet and started to cry so hard that he couldn't get his breath.

Even after a while, when Glory said it was all right to come out, that it wasn't really his fault, that he was just a little kid, and that she was sorry she had yelled at him, he still couldn't stop crying. He was saying, "Mommy, Mommy," over and over, and he wanted to stop but he couldn't.

Then, later, when he was watching one of his DVDs, he heard Glory talking to someone. He tiptoed to the door of his room, opened it, and listened. Glory was on the phone. He couldn't hear what she was saying but her voice sounded really mad. Then he heard her shout, "I'm sorry, I'm sorry," and he could tell she was really scared.

Now he sat with the towel around his shoulders and the stuff dripping on his forehead and waited until Glory told him to get over to the sink, that it was time to rinse out his hair.

Finally she said, "Okay, I guess you're about ready." When he leaned over the sink, she said, "It's really too bad. If you ever get the chance, you'll be a cute redhead."

21

With intense satisfaction, Bartley Longe sauntered down the corridor to his office at 400 Park Avenue with the morning newspapers under his arm. Fifty-two years old, with silver threads in his light brown hair, ice blue eyes, and an imperious manner, he was the kind of man who could intimidate a headwaiter or a subordinate with a single chilling glance. On the flip side of his personality, he was a charming and welcome guest among his many clients, both the current celebrities and the quietly wealthy.

His staff always nervously anticipated his 9:30 A.M. arrival. What kind of mood would Bartley be in? A furtive peek at him answered that question. If his expression was pleasant and he graced them with a hearty "Good morning," they relaxed at least for the present. If he was frowning and tight-lipped, they knew something had displeased him and that somebody was in for a nasty dressing-down.

By now, every one of the eight full-time employees had read or heard the stunning news that Zan Moreland, who had once worked for Bartley, was a person of interest in the disappearance of her own son. They all remembered the day she had burst into the office after her parents died in that accident and screamed at Bartley: "I hadn't seen my mother and father in nearly two years and now I'll never see them again. You made it impossible for me to leave because you said I was too valuable on this project or that project. You're a nasty, self-centered bully. You're more than that. You're a stinking devil. And if you don't believe it, ask any of these people who work for you. I'm going to open my own firm and you know what, Bartley? I'm going to rub your nose in my success."

She had broken into racking sobs and Elaine Ryan, Bartley's longtime secretary, had put an arm around her and taken her home.

Now Bartley opened the door of his office, the smirk on his face a clear signal to both Elaine and the receptionist, Phyllis Garrigan, that all was well for his employees, at least for the present. "I guess unless you're deaf, dumb, and blind, you know about Zan Moreland?" Bartley asked the women.

"I don't believe a word of it," Elaine Ryan said flatly. Sixty-two years old, her dark brown hair stylishly shaped, her hazel eyes the best feature in her narrow face, she was the single employee in the office with enough courage to occasionally challenge Bartley. As she often told her husband, the only thing that kept her working for Bartley was the good pay and the fact that at any time she could afford to walk out if he got too nasty. Her husband, a retired state trooper, was now head of security at a discount department store. Anytime Elaine came home fuming at something Bartley had said or done, he silenced her with one word, "Quit."

"It doesn't matter what you believe, Elaine. The proof is in the photos. You don't think that magazine would have bought them if there was any doubt about what they show, do you?" The smirk was leaving Bartley's face. "It is clear now that Zan picked up her own little boy and walked out of the park with him. It's up to the police to find out what she did with him after that. But if you want my theory, I'll give it to you."

Bartley Longe pointed his finger at Elaine

for emphasis. "When she worked here, how often did you hear Zan whine that she wished she had grown up in one home in the suburbs instead of moving from place to place because of her father's job?" he demanded. "My theory is that all the sympathy she got after her parents' death was over and she needed a new tragedy in her life."

"That's absolutely crazy," Elaine said, heatedly. "Zan may have mentioned that she would have preferred not to have moved around all the time, but she said it in a general way when we were talking about our backgrounds. It certainly doesn't mean she said it all the time to gain sympathy. And she was crazy about Matthew. What you're insinuating is disgusting, Mr. Longe."

Elaine realized that Bartley Longe's cheeks were becoming flushed. Thou shall not contradict the boss, she thought. But how could he possibly suggest that Zan might have kidnapped Matthew to get sympathy?

"I forget how partial you were to my former assistant," Bartley Longe snapped. "But I will bet you that, as we speak, Zan Moreland is hunting for a lawyer, and I can assure you that she's going to need a good one."

22

Kevin Wilson admitted to himself that it was almost impossible to concentrate on the drawings on his desk. He was looking at the landscaper's sketches for the plantings in the lobby of 701 Carlton Place, as the new apartment complex would be called.

The name had been agreed upon only after a heated discussion with the directors of Jarrell International, the multibillion-dollar company that was financing the building. Several members of the board of directors had suggestions of names they thought would be more appropriate. Most of them were in the romantic or would-be historical vein, Windsor Arms, Camelot Towers, Le Versailles, Stonehenge, even New Amsterdam Court.

Kevin had listened with increasing impatience. Finally it had been his turn. "What is considered to be the most exclusive address in New York?" he had asked.

Seven of the eight board members named the same address on Park Avenue.

"Exactly," Kevin had told them. "My point is that we've got a very expensive building to fill. As we speak, there are many very expensive residential buildings in Manhattan under construction. I don't have to remind you that this is a tough economy, or that it's our job to make our pitch to potential buyers a very special one. Our location is spectacular. Our views of the Hudson River and of the city are spectacular. But I want us to be able to tell our prospective buyers that when the name 701 Carlton Place is mentioned, everyone hearing that address will know that the person giving it is lucky enough to be living in a privileged location."

I guess I carried the day, he thought as he turned his chair from the table to the desk, shaking his head. Dear God, if Pop were around what would he think if he heard that spiel? His grandfather had been the superintendent of the building next door to where he and his parents had lived. The name, Lancelot Towers, had been carved in stone over the six-story walk-up with its dreary railroad flats, creaking dumbwaiters, and ancient plumbing, on Webster Avenue in the Bronx.

Pop would have thought I was crazy, Kevin acknowledged, and so would Dad, if he were still alive. Mom is used to my salesmanship pitch by now. After Dad died, when I finally got her to move to East Fifty-seventh Street, she said I could sell a dead horse to a mounted policeman. Now she loves Manhattan. I swear she falls asleep at night humming "New York, New York."

All these random thoughts are going nowhere, he acknowledged silently, as he leaned back in his chair. From down the hall he could hear the relentless sound of hammering and the shrill, ear-piercing whine of machines beginning to polish the marble floors.

To Kevin, the din of construction was more beautiful than hearing a symphony in Lincoln Center. From the time I was a kid, I told Dad I'd rather go to a construction site than to the zoo, he thought. Even then, I knew I wanted to design buildings.

The landscaper's sketches weren't right, he decided. He'll have to start all over, or I'll get someone else. I don't want the entrance to look like a conservatory, Kevin thought. This guy just doesn't get it.

The model apartments. Last night he had studied both Longe's and Moreland's submissions for hours. They were both mighty impressive. He could understand why Bartley Longe was considered one of the foremost interior designers in the country. If he got the job, the apartments would be spectacular.

But Zan Moreland's sketches were marvelously attractive, too. He could see how she had studied under Longe, but then broken off from his ideas to pursue her own. There was more warmth, more of a sense of this-is-my-home in the deft way she put small touches in her layouts. And she was 30 percent cheaper in her prices.

He admitted to himself that he had not been able to get her out of his mind. She was a beautiful woman, there was no doubt about that. Slender, even a shade too thin, those enormous hazel eyes dominating her face . . . Odd that she was so shy, almost to the point of diffidence, until she got into explaining her vision for the model apartments. Then it was as if a light turned on and her face and voice became animated.

When she left yesterday, I watched her walk out to the curb and hail a cab, Kevin thought. It had gotten so windy that I wondered if that suit she was wearing was warm enough for her, even though it had a fur collar. I had the feeling that a strong gust of wind would have knocked her to the ground.

There was a tap on the door of his office. Before he could respond, his secretary, Louise Kirk, was in the office and walking to his desk. "Let me guess. It's exactly nine o'clock," he said.

Louise, a forty-five-year-old pear-shaped dynamo, with a head of fluffy blond hair, was the wife of one of the construction chiefs. "Of course it is," she replied briskly.

Kevin was sorry he had given Louise that opening. Now he hoped she wouldn't repeat her oft-told comparison of herself to Eleanor Roosevelt. As Louise, a history buff, explained it, Eleanor was always exactly on time, "Even to the moment when she descended the stairs in the White House to arrive precisely when the ceremony at FDR's casket in the East Room was about to begin."

But today Louise clearly had other things on her mind. "Did you have a chance to read the papers?" she asked.

"No. The breakfast meeting started at seven o'clock," Kevin reminded her.

"Well, then take a look at this." Gleeful at being able to be the bearer of startling news, Louise laid the morning papers, the *New York Post* and the *Daily News,* on his desk.

Both of them had a picture of Zan Moreland on the front page. Their headlines were similar, and sensational. Both alleged that Zan Moreland had kidnapped her own child.

Kevin stared at the photos in disbelief of what he was seeing. "Did you know her child was missing?" he asked Louise.

"No, I didn't connect her name with it," Louise said. "Don't forget, I was in the main office yesterday. Of course, I knew the child's name, Matthew Carpenter. The papers were full of the story when he disappeared, but as I remember they always referred to the mother as Alexandra. I didn't put two and two together. What are you going to do about it, Kevin? She's bound to be arrested. Should I return her sketches to her office?"

"I would say that we have no choice," Kevin said quietly, then added, "The funny thing is I'd just about decided to give her the job."

23

On Wednesday morning, after celebrating the seven-o'clock Mass, Fr. Aiden watched CNN news as he sipped a cup of coffee in the kitchen of the Friary. Deeply disturbed, he shook his head as the breaking news unfolded that Alexandra Moreland had kidnapped her own child. He watched as the camera showed the same young woman who had come into the Reconciliation Room Monday leave the Four Seasons Restaurant last night. She tried to hide her face when she was rushing into a cab past the reporters and photographers, but there was no mistaking her.

Then he saw the photos that seemed to be the unmistakable proof that she had abducted little Matthew.

"I am involved in an ongoing crime and I am unable to prevent a murder that is about to be committed," she had said.

Was the ongoing crime the fact that Alexandra Moreland had taken her own son and lied to the authorities about his disappearance?

Fr. Aiden watched as the news anchorman spoke to June Langren, a nearby diner in the Four Seasons, about the shocking outburst by Ted Carpenter. "I honestly thought he was going to attack her," Langren said, breathlessly. "My boyfriend jumped up to restrain him if necessary."

In the fifty years he had been hearing confessions, Fr. Aiden thought he had heard virtually the full range of iniquities that the human spirit is capable of committing. Many years ago he had listened to the wrenching sobs of a young woman, little more than a girl herself, who had given birth to a child, and in fear of her parents had left it to die in a garbage bag in the Dumpster.

The saving mercy was that the child had not died, that a passerby had heard the cries of the wailing infant and saved it, he reflected.

This was different.

"A murder is about to be committed."

She did not say, "I am going to commit a murder," Fr. Aiden thought. She spoke of herself as an accomplice. Maybe now that those pictures have proven that she stole the child, whoever she is involved with will be frightened off. I can only pray that that will be the case.

Later that morning after he had reviewed the security tapes with Alvirah and she had gone home, Fr. Aiden opened his calendar. He had several dinner appointments in the next week with generous sponsors of the friars' ongoing food and clothing charity who had become close personal friends. He wanted to verify the time he was meeting the Andersons this evening.

His memory was accurate: 6:30, at the New York Athletic Club on Central Park South. Right down the street from Alvirah and Willy, he thought. That's perfect. I just realized I left my scarf in their apartment last night. I guess Alvirah didn't notice it or she would have mentioned it when she was here. After dinner, I'll give them a call and if they're home, I'll run over and get it. His sister, Veronica, had knitted that scarf for him, and if she noticed that he wasn't wearing it on a cold day, he'd be in big trouble.

As he was leaving the Friary after lunch, Neil was coming out of the chapel, a dustcloth and can of furniture polish in his hands. "Father, did you see that the woman, I mean the one your friend recognized on our security tape, is the one who stole her own kid?"

"Yes, I did," Fr. Aiden said abruptly, making it very clear to Neil that he did not wish to hear anything more about it.

Neil had been about to make the comment that when he had seen the tape it had jostled something in his mind. He'd been walking home to his apartment on Eighth Avenue Monday night around the time that Moreland woman had been caught on the security tape, but just as he got to the corner, a young woman who was walking ahead of him had darted out in traffic and hailed a cab. She damn near got hit by a car, he thought. I got a good look at her.

That was why he had gone back and run the security tape again, stopping it where Alvirah Meehan had recognized her friend. You'd swear the woman getting in the cab was the one who's on the tape, he thought. But unless she can change clothes in the middle of the street, it can't be the same person.

Neil shrugged. That was what he'd been about to tell Fr. Aiden, but it was clear Fr. Aiden didn't want to hear it. None of my business anyhow, Neil decided. In his forty-one years, thanks to his drinking problem, Neil had run the gamut of jobs. The one he'd liked best was being a cop, but that had only lasted a few years. No matter how much you pleaded that you'd go on the wagon, getting drunk three times when you were on duty meant getting tossed out on your ear.

I had the makings of a good cop, Neil thought reflectively, as he headed for the utility closet. All the guys joked about me that I could see a mug shot once and pick the guy out of Times Square a year later. Wish I'd lasted in the department. Maybe by now I'd be the police commissioner!

But he hadn't gone to AA then. Instead, after drifting from job to job, he'd ended up on the streets, begging for handouts and sleeping in shelters. Three years ago when he'd come here for food, one of the friars had sent him to the Inn at Graymoor where they had a rehab program for men like him, and there he'd finally kicked the booze.

Now, he liked working here. He liked staying sober. He liked the friends he'd made at the AA meetings. The friars called him their majordomo, a fancy way of saying handyman, but still, it had a certain dignity.

If Fr. Aiden did not want to talk about the Moreland woman, that's the way it is, Neil decided. Mum's the word. He probably wouldn't care anyhow that I saw someone

who looked just like her.
   Why should he?

24

The elderly man who timidly entered the offices of Bartley Longe was clearly not a potential customer. His thinning white hair was straggly on his skull, his worn Dallas Cowboys jacket in need of replacing, his jeans hanging loose on his body, his feet clad in old sneakers. He made his way slowly to the reception desk. At the first sight of him, Phyllis, the receptionist, took him to be a messenger. Then she dismissed that possibility. The frailness of the man's body and the sallow complexion of his wrinkled face suggested that he was, or had been, seriously ill.

She was glad that the boss was huddled in a meeting with Elaine, his secretary, and two fabric designers, and that his door was closed. Bartley Longe would have thought that whatever this man wanted, he didn't belong in the rarefied atmosphere of these surroundings. Even after six years, kind-hearted Phyllis cringed at the way Bartley treated any person with a shabby appearance. Like her pal Elaine, Phyllis stayed at the job for the pretty decent salary, and the fact that Bartley was out of the office often enough to give them all a break.

She smiled at the obviously nervous visitor. "How can I help you?"

"My name is Toby Grissom. I'm sorry to bother you. It's just that I haven't heard from my daughter in six months and I can't sleep at night because I'm so worried that maybe she's in some kind of trouble. She used to work here about two years ago. I thought someone in your office, maybe, might have heard from her."

"She worked *here?*" Phyllis asked, as she mentally reviewed the list of employees who might have quit or been fired around two years ago. "What is her name?"

"Brittany La Monte. At least that's her stage name. She came to New York twelve years ago. Like all kids she wanted to be an actress, and she did get a little part off-Broadway now and then."

"I'm sorry, Mr. Grissom, but I've been here six years, and I can absolutely tell you that no one named Brittany La Monte was working in this office two years ago."

As though afraid of being dismissed out

of hand, Grissom explained, "Well, not exactly worked for you *here.* What I mean is that she made her living as a makeup artist. Sometimes when there were cocktail parties to show off those model apartments Mr. Longe decorated, he asked Brittany to do the makeup for the models. Then he invited her to be one of the models. She's a real pretty girl."

"Oh, that could be why I never met her," Phyllis said. "What I can do is ask Mr. Longe's secretary about her. She's at all those model-apartment parties, and she has a phenomenal memory. But she's tied up in a meeting now and I know she won't be free for a couple of hours. Can you come back later?"

Make it after three, Phyllis reminded herself. King Tut said he was going to his place in Litchfield tonight, and he's leaving after lunch. "Mr. Grissom, anytime after three would work," she said sweetly.

"Thank you, ma'am. You're very kind. You see, my daughter always wrote to me regularly. She did say she was going on a trip two years ago, and sent me twenty-five thousand dollars to make sure I had something in the bank. Her mother passed away a long time ago and my little girl and I have been real pals. She said she wouldn't be in touch too often. Every once in a while I would get a letter from her. The postmark would be New York, so I know she's been back here. But like I say, it's been six months and no letter, and I've just got to see her. The last time she was in Dallas was almost four years ago now."

"Mr. Grissom, if we have an address for her, I promise we'll have it for you this afternoon," Phyllis said. Even as she spoke she knew that there probably wasn't any financial record of payment to Brittany La Monte. Bartley always paid people like her off the books so that he could get away cheaper than paying union wages.

"You see, I just got a pretty bad report from my doctor," Grissom explained, as he turned to go. "That's why I'm here. I don't have long and I don't want to die before I see Glory again and be sure she's okay."

"Glory? I thought you said her name was Brittany."

Toby Grissom smiled reminiscently. "Her real name is Margaret Grissom, after her mother. Like I said, her stage name is Brittany La Monte. But when she was born, I took one look at her and said, 'Little girl, you're so gorgeous your mama may call you Margaret, but my name for you is Glory.'"

25

At 12:15, a few minutes after they had spoken, Alvirah called Zan back. "Zan, I've been thinking," she said. "There's no question but that the police are going to want to talk to you. But before they do, you need to have a lawyer."

"A lawyer! Alvirah, why?"

"Zan, because the woman in those pictures looks just like you. The police are going to be knocking at your door. I don't want you answering questions without a lawyer beside you."

Zan felt the numbness that had pervaded her mind and body begin to change into a deadly calm. "Alvirah, you really aren't sure whether I'm the woman in those pictures, are you?" Then she added, "You don't have to answer that. I understand what you are saying. Do you know a lawyer you would recommend?"

"Yes, I do. Charley Shore is a top-drawer

criminal defense attorney. I did a column on him for my newspaper, and we became good friends."

Criminal defense lawyer, Zan thought, bitterly. Of course. If I *did* take Matthew, I committed a crime.

Did I take Matthew?

Where would I have taken him? Who would I have given him to?

Nobody. It can't have happened that way. I don't care if I forgot that I stopped in at St. Francis's the other night. I was so desperately unhappy with Matthew's birthday coming up that maybe I did go in and light a candle for him. I've done that before. But I know that I never could have taken him out of that stroller and put him out of my life.

"Zan, are you still there?"

"Yes, Alvirah. Can you give me that lawyer's number?"

"Sure. But don't call him for ten minutes. I'll get in touch with him first. After I speak to him, he'll want to help you. I'll see you tonight."

Slowly Zan put the phone back on the cradle. A lawyer will cost money, she thought, money I could use to hire someone new to search for Matthew.

Kevin Wilson.

The thought of the architect's name made her sit bolt upright. Of course he would see those photos and think that she had kidnapped Matthew. Of course he would expect her to be arrested. He'll give the job to Bartley, Zan thought. I've spent so much time on it. I can't lose it. I'll need the money more than ever. I've *got* to talk to him!

She wrote a note for Josh and hurried out of the office, going down in the service elevator, and leaving the building by the service entrance. I don't even know if Wilson will be there, she thought, as she hailed a cab. But if I have to sit outside his office all afternoon, I'll do it.

I've got to ask him to give me a chance to clear myself.

It took nearly forty minutes in even heavier than usual traffic for Zan to reach the newly named 701 Carlton Place. The cab fare with tip was twenty-two dollars. It's a good thing I have a credit card, she thought, as she looked in her wallet and realized she had only fifteen dollars in the billfold section.

It had been her cardinal rule to use the credit card as sparingly as possible. Whenever she could, she walked to her appointments. Funny how you concentrate on something like cab fare, she thought, as she entered the apartment building. It's like when Dad and Mother died. At the funeral Mass I kept thinking that there was a spot on the jacket I was wearing. I kept asking myself why I hadn't noticed it. I had another black jacket that I could have worn.

Is it that I'm taking refuge in trivia again? she asked herself, as she pushed the revolving door and walked into the deafening sound of the machines polishing marble in the lobby.

Kevin Wilson obviously only wants working space, she thought, as she walked down the equipment-laden corridor to the room he was using as an office. She knew that when everything was in place that area would serve as a delivery drop for tenants' packages.

The door of his temporary office was partially open. She knocked, and without waiting for a response went in. There was a woman with blond hair standing at the table behind Wilson's desk. From the astonished expression on her face when she turned around and saw her, Zan knew she had read the morning papers.

Even so, she introduced herself. "I'm Alexandra Moreland. I met with Mr. Wilson yesterday. Is he here?"

"I'm his secretary, Louise Kirk. He's in the building, but . . ."

Trying not to cringe as she saw the agitation that was exuding from the other woman, Zan interrupted her. "It's a beautiful building, and from what I saw of it yesterday the people who move in here will be very, very happy. I certainly hope to be part of it."

I don't know how I can sound so calm, she thought. And then immediately she had the answer. Because I must get this job. Zan waited silently, her eyes fixed on the other woman's face.

"Ms. Moreland," Kirk began, hesitantly. "There really isn't any point in your waiting to see Kevin — I mean Mr. Wilson. Earlier this morning, he asked me to pack your proposal and return it to you. In fact, it's right there if you want to take it now, or else I'll have it delivered to you, of course."

Zan did not look at the package on the table. "Where is Mr. Wilson?"

"Ms. Moreland, he really doesn't . . . ."

He's in one of the model apartments, Zan thought. I know he is. She turned, walked around the desk and picked up the package of her fabrics and sketches. "Thank you," she said.

In the lobby she headed straight for the elevators.

Wilson was not in the first apartment or

in the second. She found him in the third, the largest unit. Sketches and fabric samples were laid out on the kitchen counter. Zan knew they had to be Bartley Longe's designs for this apartment.

She walked over to stand next to Wilson and set her package down. Without greeting him, she began, "I'm going to tell you right now," she said, "if you go with Bartley, the effect will be ravishing and damn hard to live with." She picked up a sketch. "Beautiful," she said. "But take a look at that love seat. It's too low. People will avoid it like the plague. Look at those wall hangings. Simply gorgeous, and so-oo-oo formal. But this is a very large apartment. Maybe somebody who has kids will be interested in it, but this design isn't going to inspire them. And no matter how much money you have, when you come home you want a home, not a museum. I offered you three different apartments that will make people feel comfortable."

She realized that for emphasis she had grabbed his arm. "I'm sorry for barging in," she said, "but I had to talk to you."

"You have, so are you finished?" Kevin Wilson asked quietly.

"Yes, I am. You've probably heard that photographs have surfaced that appear to show me kidnapping the child I've been hungering to find for almost two years. We'll know soon enough if I can prove that no matter how much the woman in those photos looks like me, it's not me. Just answer one question. If the photos that I'm talking about didn't exist, would you have given the job to Bartley Longe or me?"

Kevin Wilson studied Zan for a long minute before answering. "I was inclined to give it to you."

"Well, then, I ask you, I beg you, don't make a decision yet. I am going to be able to prove that whoever the woman in those photos is, it isn't me. I'm going to see the client who is the reason I hired the baby-sitter to take Matthew to the park that day, and ask her to come with me to the police and prove that I could not have been in the park at that time. Kevin, if you go with Bartley simply because you prefer his designs, that's one thing. But if you would have given me the job because you like my designs better, I implore you to let me clear my name. I implore you to wait before announcing a decision."

She looked up into Wilson's face. "I need this job. That doesn't mean I'd expect you to give it to me out of pity, because that would be ridiculous. But every cent I can save is being squirreled away so that I can hire another agency to try to find my Matthew. And something else that you should think of. I bet I'm thirty percent cheaper than Bartley. That ought to count for something."

Suddenly all the energy and fire was gone from her. She pointed to the package with her samples and sketches on the counter. "Would you consider looking at them again?" she asked.

"Yes."

"Thank you," Zan said, and without looking at Kevin Wilson again left the apartment. As she passed the floor-to-ceiling window at the elevator bank, she could see that the earlier drizzle had turned into a hard, driving rainstorm. She stopped for a moment to look out. A helicopter was hovering over the West Side Heliport preparing to land. She watched as the wind tossed it from one side to another. Finally, it settled down safely on the tarmac. It made it, she thought.

Dear God, please let me make it through this storm, too.

26

Billy Collins's partner was Detective Jennifer Dean, a handsome African-American woman his own age whom he had met at the Police Academy, where they had become fast friends. After a stint in the Narcotics Division, Jennifer had been promoted to detective and transferred to the Central Park Precinct. There, to their mutual satisfaction, she had been assigned to be his partner.

Together, they met with Tiffany Shields at Hunter College during her lunch break. By that time Tiffany had convinced herself that Zan Moreland had deliberately drugged both her and Matthew. "Zan insisted I have that Pepsi that day," she told them, her mouth tightened into a narrow line. "I felt lousy. I didn't want to babysit. She gave me a pill. I thought it was Tylenol for colds, but I think now it was the kind that makes you sleepy. And let me tell you something else.

Matthew was out like a light. I bet anything she drugged him, too, so that when she grabbed him out of the stroller, he wouldn't wake up."

"Tiffany, you didn't tell me that you thought Zan Moreland drugged you the day Matthew disappeared. You never hinted that you thought that," Billy said quietly. His tone did not reflect the fact that to him what the girl was saying made sense. If Moreland had been looking for a way to kidnap her own child, Tiffany may have given her a priceless opportunity. That day was unseasonably warm, the kind that made anyone sleepy, never mind someone who was drowsy from having a cold and then possibly drugged.

"There's something more I've been thinking about," Tiffany went on, her voice sullen. "Zan put an extra blanket at the foot of the stroller just in case I wanted to sit on the grass. She said that it was so warm that every bench in the park would probably be filled. I thought she was being nice, but now I think she was just hoping that I'd fall asleep right away."

The detectives looked at each other. Was Moreland possibly that manipulative? they both wondered. "Tiffany, you never suggested the day Matthew disappeared — or

any time after that when we spoke to you —
that you had been drugged," Jennifer Dean
reminded her calmly.

"I was hysterical. I was so scared. All those
people and cameras around and then Zan
and Mr. Carpenter coming, and I knew they
were blaming me."

Because of the heat, the park had been
unusually crowded that day, Billy thought.
If Moreland had waited her chance, then
casually walked past the stroller and picked
up Matthew, no one would have thought it
unusual. Even if Matthew had awakened,
he wouldn't have cried. We attributed
Moreland's calm to shock. When Ted Carpenter arrived on the scene, he did what
most fathers in his position would have
done. He tore into the babysitter for falling
asleep.

"I've got a class," Tiffany said, as she
stood up. "I can't be late for it."

"We don't want you to be late for it,
Tiffany," Billy agreed, as he and Jennifer
rose from the hallway bench where they had
been sitting.

"Detective Collins, those photos prove
that Zan Moreland took Matthew and set
me up to be the fall guy. You don't have a
clue how miserable these two years have
been for me. Try listening to my 911 call to

you. You can still find it on the Internet."

"Tiffany, we can understand how you feel." Jennifer Dean's tone was soothing.

"No, you can't. No one can. But do you think Matthew might still be alive?"

"We have no reason to think that he is not alive," Billy hedged.

"Well, if he's not, I just hope that that lying, lousy mother of his spends the rest of her rotten life in a jail cell. Just promise me that I get a front seat at her trial. I've earned it."

Tiffany spat out the words.

27

He had put the plan in motion. Step by step he was now bringing it to a head. He knew it was time. Gloria was getting too restless. Also, he had made a terrible mistake when he told her that it would be necessary to kill Zan and make it look like a suicide. Gloria had only gotten into it for the money he promised her. She didn't understand that it would not be enough simply to make Alexandra Moreland dangle in the wind to public ridicule.

He would not be happy until Zan was dead.

Last night when he called Gloria, he told her that he was planning to have her come back to the church with him soon, but he didn't tell her why. She started to object, and he shouted her down. He didn't tell her that he planned to get rid of the old priest and that she had to be caught looking like Zan on the security cameras.

Zan's suicide would be believable.

The plan was that on the same day, Gloria would abandon Matthew in a public place where he would be noticed. He could see the headlines already: MISSING CHILD FOUND HOURS AFTER MOTHER'S SUICIDE.

He could savor the story that would follow. "Alexandra 'Zan' Moreland was found dead in her apartment in Battery Park City, an apparent suicide. The troubled interior designer, suspected of kidnapping her own child . . ."

Those photos that the tourist has taken. Why had they come to light now? The timing couldn't be worse. On the other hand, they could be a magnificent, unexpected gift.

He had pored over them himself, studied them, enlarged them on his computer. Gloria looked just like Zan. If the cops believed they were authentic, Zan's denials about making all the purchases to her credit cards would only be one more proof that she was crazy, that she had staged the kidnapping herself.

By now they were undoubtedly wondering if she might have done away with her own child.

But if the cops, or anyone else, could find one single discrepancy in those photos, they wouldn't believe that any of the rest was true. The whole thing would fall apart.

Would they interview the babysitter again?

Of course they would.

Would they interview Nina Aldrich, the potential client Zan claimed to have been with when her son disappeared?

Of course they would.

But Nina Aldrich had had a good reason to be vague about that time frame two years ago and that reason still existed. She wouldn't want to be pinned down now, he thought.

The greatest threats to him were Gloria herself, and the photos that tourist had taken.

He never phoned Gloria during the day. There was always the chance that the boy might be within earshot and no matter how much he warned her, Gloria had a bad habit of calling him by name when they talked.

He looked at the clock. It was almost five. He couldn't wait any longer. He had to talk to Gloria. He had bought two prepaid cell phones, one for her and one for himself. He locked the door of his office and tapped in her number.

She answered on the first ring. From the angry tone of her voice he could tell that the call was going to be trouble.

"I've been seeing the story plastered all over the Internet," she said. "They keep showing those pictures."

"Was the boy nearby when you were on the computer?"

"Of course he was. When he saw his picture, he loved it," Gloria snapped.

"Don't try your lamebrained sarcasm on me. Where is he?"

"He's in bed already. He didn't feel well. He threw up twice."

"Is he getting sick? I can't have him going to a doctor."

"Not that kind of sick. I put that coloring stuff in his hair again this afternoon and he hates it. This crazy life is getting to him. It's getting to me, too. You said one year tops, and it's been nearly two years."

"It's going to be over very soon. I can promise you that. Those pictures of you in the park will bring it to a head. But you've got to rack your brain. Look at them on the Internet again. See if there's *anything* that the cops might notice that would make them suspect that the woman there isn't Zan."

"You paid me to follow her around, to study her photos, to learn how to walk and talk like her. I'm a damn good actress and that's what I want to be doing, not babysitting that little kid and keeping him from his mother. God Almighty, he keeps a bar of soap under his pillow because it's the kind she used and the scent reminds him of her."

He had not missed the moment of hesitation in Gloria's voice and then her answer, first defensive, then trying to steer the conversation to the subject of the child.

"Gloria, concentrate," he warned firmly. "Is there *anything* about the way you dressed, or jewelry that you wore, that would make the police take seriously Zan's claim that she was not the woman in that picture?"

Enraged when she did not answer, he asked, "And something else, exactly *what* did you tell that priest?"

"If you keep bugging me about that, I'll go crazy. So here's the way it was. I told him that I am a participant in an ongoing crime, that a murder is going to be committed, and that I can't stop it."

"You told him that?" The caller's voice was deadly calm.

"I told him that, damn you. But I told him under the seal of the confessional. If you don't know what that seal means, look it up. And I'm giving you fair warning. One week more and I'm out of here. And you better have two hundred thousand dollars in cash for me. Because if you don't, I'll go to the cops and tell them you forced me to keep the kid because otherwise you would have had him killed. I'll trade everything I know about you for immunity from prosecution. You want to know something? I'll be a hero! I'll get a book contract for a million dollars. I've got it all figured out."

Before he had time to answer, the woman, known to Matthew and her father as Glory, had pressed the END button on her cell phone.

Despite his frequent and frantic efforts to reach her again, she did not answer his calls.

28

After she left Kevin Wilson, Zan went directly back to the office, once again using the delivery entrance to get into her building.

Josh was waiting for her. She had left the note saying that she was going to try to meet with Wilson. When she saw the expression of deep concern on the face of her young assistant, she attributed it to his fear they might have lost the job of decorating the model apartments, and said reassuringly, "Josh, I think we might get a break with Wilson. He'll hold off making a decision until I can clear myself."

Josh's expression did not change. "Zan, exactly how can you clear yourself?" he asked, his voice trembling with emotion. He pointed to the front page of the two newspapers that were lying on the desk.

"Josh, I'm not in those pictures," Zan said. "That woman looks like me, but she isn't me." The protest came from lips that were suddenly dry. Josh has been my dear friend as well as my assistant, she thought. Last night he came rushing to get me out of the Four Seasons and past all those reporters. *But he hadn't seen the pictures yet.*

"Zan, a lawyer named Charles Shore called you," Josh told her. "He said that Alvirah had recommended him. I'll dial him back for you. You need to be protected right away."

"Protected from whom?" Zan demanded. "The police? Ted?"

"You need to be protected from yourself," Josh shot back, as tears glistened in his eyes. "Zan, when I first came to work for you after Matthew disappeared, you told me about those blackouts you had after your parents died." He came around the desk and put his hands protectively on her shoulders. "Zan, I love you. You're a brilliant interior designer. You're the big sister I never had. But you need help. You've got to prepare a defense before the cops start questioning you."

Zan pushed his hands away and stepped back. "Josh, you mean well, but you've got to understand. I can prove I was with Nina Aldrich when Matthew was taken from the stroller. I'm going to see her right now.

Tiffany took Matthew to the park at about 12:30. By two when she woke up, he was gone. I can prove I was meeting with Nina Aldrich during that time. I tell you, I can prove it! Something crazy is going on, but I am *not* the woman in those photos."

Josh did not look convinced. "Zan, I'm calling that lawyer for you right now. My uncle is a cop. I talked to him this morning. He said it's obvious you're a suspect now in Matthew's disappearance, and he'd be surprised if you're not brought in for questioning before the end of the day."

Nina Aldrich is my only hope, Zan thought. "Call that lawyer," she said. "Tell me his name again."

"Charles Shore." Josh reached for the phone.

As Josh was dialing, Zan steadied herself by putting both palms on the desk. The panic was building up. She felt herself wanting to retreat to escape it. Not now, she prayed. Please God, not now. Give me the strength to hang on. Then from a distance, she heard Josh shout her name, but she no longer had the strength to answer him.

It all became a blur. She thought she felt people pressing around her, people shouting at her, the wail of an ambulance. She heard herself sobbing, calling for Matthew.

Then she felt a prick in her arm. It was real.

When she finally woke, she was in the emergency room of a hospital. Josh and a man with iron gray hair and steel-rimmed glasses were sitting beside her in the curtained-off cubicle. "I'm Charley Shore," the older man said. "I'm Alvirah's friend, and your lawyer if you'll have me."

Zan struggled to focus on him. "Josh called you," she said slowly.

"Yes. Don't try to talk now. We'll have plenty of time tomorrow. As a precaution, the doctor would like you to stay here overnight."

"No. No. I have to go home. I have to talk to Nina Aldrich." Zan tried to pull herself up.

"Zan, it's nearly six o'clock." Shore's voice was soothing. "We'll talk to Mrs. Aldrich tomorrow. It would be better if you stayed here, I promise you."

"It would be so much better if you stayed, Zan," Josh told her soothingly.

"No. No. I'll be all right." Zan felt her head clearing. She had to get out of here. "I'm going home," she said. "But first, I promised Alvirah I would have dinner with her and Willy tonight. I want to go there now." Alvirah will help me, she thought. She'll help me prove that I am not the woman in those photos.

Things were coming back to her. "I fainted, didn't I?" she asked. "And then I was in an ambulance?"

"That's right." Josh covered her hand with his.

"Wait a minute. Am I wrong, or were people crowding around me? Were reporters there when they took me out to the ambulance?"

"Yes, Zan," Josh admitted.

"I had another blackout." Zan pulled herself up, then realized a hospital gown was hanging loosely from her shoulders. She folded her arms, hugging herself. "I'll be okay. If you two will just wait outside, I'll get dressed."

"Of course." Charles Shore and Josh rose quickly but were stopped by her sudden, anxious question.

"What is Ted saying about all this? Obviously, he's seen the photos himself by now."

"Zan, get dressed," Shore told her. "We'll talk on the way to Alvirah and Willy's place."

As they left the emergency room, Zan realized, in a moment of absolute clarity, that neither Josh nor Charley Shore had responded to her insistence that Nina Aldrich would verify the fact that she had been with her when Matthew disappeared.

29

On Wednesday afternoon, Penny Hammel phoned her friend Rebecca Schwartz and invited her to come over for dinner. "I cooked a nice pot roast for Bernie because the poor guy's been on the road for two weeks and it's his favorite meal," she explained. "He was supposed to be home by four o'clock but wouldn't you know it, his darn truck started having problems in Pennsylvania. He's got to stay in King of Prussia overnight while they figure out what's wrong. Anyhow, I pulled out all the stops for the dinner and I'm not going to eat it alone."

"I'll be there with bells on," Rebecca assured her. "I don't have anything in the house for dinner, as it happens. I was going to get takeout from Sun Yuan, but honest to God, I do that so often I feel as if I'll turn into a fortune cookie."

At 6:15 the two friends were sipping

Manhattans in Penny's combined kitchen-family room. The mouthwatering aromas emanating from the stove combined with the warmth of the fireplace filled both women with the sense of well-being.

"Oh, have I got a story to tell you about the new tenant in Sy's farmhouse," Penny began.

Rebecca's expression changed. "Penny, that woman made it clear that she was holing up there to finish her book. You didn't go over, did you?"

Even as she asked the question, Rebecca knew the answer. She should have guessed that Penny would want to get a look at the new tenant.

"I had no intention of paying a visit," Penny said defensively. "I brought over six of my blueberry muffins just to be neighborly, but that woman was downright rude. I mean I started by saying that I didn't want to interrupt her but thought she might enjoy the muffins, and I'd put my phone number on a Post-it on the bottom of the plate. If I were the one moving into a strange neighborhood, I'd like to know that there was someone to call if an emergency came up."

"That was real nice of you," Rebecca conceded. "You're the kind of friend everyone should have. But I wouldn't go there again. She's a loner, that one."

Penny laughed. "For two cents I would have asked her for my muffins back. And anyhow, when you think about it, she has a sister she can call if she needs help."

Rebecca drained the last of her Manhattan. "A sister? How do you know she has a sister?"

"Oh, I saw a toy truck on the floor in the hall behind her and I told her that I'm a good babysitter. She told me that the truck belonged to her sister's kid. Her sister helped her move in and had left it."

"That's funny," Rebecca said slowly. "When I gave her the key, she said she had a meeting with her editor and would be arriving late at night. I drove by early the next morning and saw her car in the breezeway. There wasn't another car there. So I guess her sister and her kid came later."

"Maybe there *is* no sister and she likes to play with toy trucks herself," Penny laughed. "I can tell you, with a nasty attitude like hers, I bet she doesn't have many friends."

She got up, reached for the cocktail shaker, and split the last of the Manhattans between them. "Dinner's about ready to be put on the table. Why don't we sit down and get started? But I do want to catch the 6:30 news. I'd love to know if they arrested that crazy woman who kidnapped her own child. I can't believe that she's still running around loose."

"Neither can I," Rebecca agreed.

As they had expected, the photos taken in Central Park allegedly showing Alexandra Moreland lifting her son Matthew out of the stroller were the lead story on the evening news. "I wonder what she did with him, poor kid?" Penny sighed as she swallowed a succulent bite of pot roast.

"Moreland wouldn't be the first mother to kill her own child," Rebecca said soberly. "Do you think she was nuts enough to do that?"

Penny did not answer. Something about those photos was bothering her. What *is* it? she asked herself. But then the segment about the missing child ended and she clicked the television off with a shrug. "Who needs three minutes of sales pitches about sex pills and nose sprays?" she asked Rebecca. "Then you hear all the problems that stuff can give you, like heart attacks and ulcers and strokes, and you wonder who would be dopey enough to buy them."

For the rest of the meal the two good friends gossiped about their mutual friends in town, and whatever it was about the photographs that had disturbed Penny retreated into her subconscious.

30

The meeting Bartley Longe had been conducting in his office when Toby Grissom stopped in to inquire about his missing daughter lasted all morning. Then, contrary to his usual pattern, instead of going out, Bartley ordered a lunch delivered from a nearby restaurant.

As was their habit, his secretary, Elaine, and the receptionist, Phyllis, shared their diet-conscious salads in the kitchenette down the hall from the reception room. A weary-looking Elaine confided that Bartley was in as terrible a mood as she'd ever seen him and that was saying a lot. He had bitten off poor Scott's head when Scott suggested not putting valances in the smaller bedrooms of the Rushmore job, and he tore Bonnie apart over the fabric designs she chose for him to approve. Both of them were almost in tears. "He's treating them the way he treated Zan," she said.

"Scott and Bonnie are not going to last any longer than all the other assistants he's had since Zan," Phyllis said vehemently. "But I've been looking at those photos in the newspapers. He's right about one thing. There's no question but that Zan stole her own child. I only hope she left him with someone she can trust."

"I blame Bartley for causing her to have a breakdown," Elaine said sadly. "And you know what's crazy? In the midst of all that was going on with Scott and Bonnie, he kept the television on the whole morning. It was on mute, so there was no sound, but he kept an eye on it and the minute those photos of Zan taking Matthew were shown, he was all attention."

"Is that what has him all fired up today?" Phyllis asked. "I thought he would be thrilled to see that Zan was lying about Matthew."

"You wouldn't believe how much he hates Zan, and how he loves to see her twisting in the wind. And actually it was when Scott suggested that those photos might have been staged that Bartley lost it. Don't forget Zan just bid against him for that job with Kevin Wilson. If Zan could somehow prove those photos are phonies and she gets that job, it will be a horrible blow for Bartley.

There's no question about that. There are at least four younger designers besides Zan who have been cutting into his business."

Phyllis glanced at her watch. "I'd better get back to the desk. I swear he begrudges me breaking for lunch, even though if anyone rings the doorbell, I can buzz it open in about ten seconds. But first, do you remember someone named Brittany La Monte?"

Elaine sipped the last of her diet soda. "Brittany La Monte? Oh sure I do. She started out doing makeup for the models or would-be actresses that Bartley hired to serve cocktails and hors d'oeuvres when he was showing off those model apartments a couple of years ago. Just between us, I think Bartley took a big shine to Brittany. He told her he thought she was prettier than the girls she was making up and gave her a job passing out Champagne. I always thought he was seeing her on the side. We haven't done one of those apartments in at least a year, and he's never brought her to any of his other events. I guess he dumped her the way he dumps all of them."

"Brittany's father, Toby Grissom, was in this morning looking for her," Phyllis explained. "The poor old guy's worried. The last postcard he got from her was six months ago, from Manhattan. He's sure she's in trouble. I told him I'd talk to you because you would remember her if she worked on any of those jobs. He's coming back after three. I figured Bartley would be on his way to Litchfield by then. What can I tell Grissom?"

"Only that she did some freelance work for us a few years ago and that we have no idea where she might be working or living now," Elaine said. "That's the truth."

"But if you think Bartley might have had a thing going with Brittany, could you ask him if he's been in touch with her? The father said that he's had some bad news about his health, and I can tell he's desperate to see her."

"I'll ask Bartley," Elaine agreed nervously. "But if there was any romance going on between them, he won't like to have her name brought up. He's still steaming about that model who sued him for sexual harassment. He settled big on that one and might be afraid that this will develop into that kind of problem. Was there a postmark on the card Brittany sent her father?"

"Yes, New York. That's why he's here. But Mr. Grissom did say that just about two years ago, Brittany told him that she had some kind of job and wouldn't be in touch

171

with him often."

"Oh, brother," Elaine sighed. "I wonder if Bartley got her pregnant? What time did you say Brittany's father is coming in?"

"Anytime after three o'clock."

"Then let's just hope that Bartley takes off for Litchfield, and I can talk to the father quietly."

But at three o'clock when Toby Grissom timidly rang the bell and Phyllis released the lock, Bartley Longe was still incommunicado in his office. Grissom's sneakers were squishing and Phyllis looked with horror as they deposited muddy soil on the Aubusson carpet.

"Oh, Mr. Grissom," she said, "I wonder if you'd mind wiping your feet on that mat." She tried to soften the request by adding, "The weather certainly is miserable today, isn't it?"

Like an obedient child, Grissom walked back to the mat and rubbed the soles of his sneakers on it. Seemingly oblivious to the stain on the carpet, he said, "I've spent the day chasing down the girls my daughter lived with while she was in New York. I want to see Bartley Longe now."

"Mr. Longe is tied up in a meeting," Phyllis said, "but his secretary, Elaine Ryan, will be happy to speak to you."

"I didn't ask to speak to Longe's secretary. I'll sit in this fancy waiting room no matter how long it takes until I see that Bartley Longe fellow," Grissom said, his manner unquestionably determined.

Phyllis could see the weariness in his eyes. His jacket and jeans looked soaked through to the skin. I don't know what else is wrong with him, but he's lucky if he doesn't catch pneumonia, she thought. She picked up the phone. "Mr. Grissom is here," she told Elaine. "I explained Mr. Longe is in a meeting, but Mr. Grissom plans to wait until he's free."

Elaine caught the cautionary note in the receptionist's voice. Brittany La Monte's father was going to wait Bartley out. "I'll see what I can do," she told Phyllis. She replaced the phone in the cradle, and deliberated. I have to tell our fearless leader about this guy, she thought. I've got to warn him. The light on the phone panel showed that Bartley had made an outside call himself. When the light went out, she got up and knocked on Bartley's door. Without waiting for a response she went into his private office.

The television was still on, muted. Bartley's lunch tray was pushed to one side of his massive desk. The norm would have been for Bartley to call for someone to take out the tray when he had finished eating. Now he looked at Elaine, his expression both surprised and angry. "I wasn't aware I sent for you."

It had been a long day. "Nobody sends for me, including you, Mr. Longe," Elaine said, crisply. Fire me if you don't like that, she thought. I'm sick of the sight of you. She did not wait for Longe to react before continuing. "There is a man out here who insists on seeing you. I gather he'll wait in the reception room until the cows come home, so unless you want to sneak out the back door, you'd better meet with him. His name is Toby Grissom and he's Brittany La Monte's father. I'm sure you'll remember her name. She freelanced for you about two years ago when we were showing the Waverly apartments."

Bartley Longe leaned back in his chair, a puzzled expression on his face, as if trying to remember Brittany La Monte. He knows perfectly well who I'm talking about, Elaine thought, as she noticed the way he clasped his hands tightly together.

"Of course I remember that young woman," he said. "She was trying to be an actress and I even introduced her to some people who might have helped her. But as I

174

recall, the last time we had one of those situations where we used the models, she wasn't available."

Neither Elaine nor Bartley Longe had heard Toby Grissom come through Elaine's office and stand at the partially opened door. "Don't give me that stuff, Mr. Longe," Grissom said, his voice rising in fury. "You gave Brittany a line about making her a star. You had her up to your fancy place in Litchfield plenty of weekends. Where is she now? What did you do to my little girl? I want the truth and unless I get it, I'm going straight to the cops."

31

It was 7:30 P.M. by the time Zan, against all medical advice, was in a cab on her way to Alvirah and Willy's apartment with Charley Shore. She had insisted Josh go home after flatly refusing his offer to sleep on the couch of her apartment. If there's anything I need now, she thought, it's to be alone later on and gather my wits about me.

"Shouldn't you be on your way home, too?" she asked Shore as the cab inched its way along York Avenue.

Charley Shore decided not to tell Zan that he and his wife had theatre tickets for a play they both wanted to see and that he had phoned his wife to tell her to leave his ticket at the box office, that he'd be there when he could make it. Once again he thanked heaven for the fact that Lynn was always understanding when a situation like this came up. "I don't think I'll be terribly late," he had told her. "Zan Moreland is in no condition to have a long discussion with me tonight."

That opinion was more than reinforced by the deadly paleness of Zan's complexion and the way she was shivering inside the fake-fur vest she was wearing. I'm glad she's going to be with Alvirah and Willy, Charley thought. She trusts them. Maybe she'll even tell them where her son is.

When Alvirah had called him earlier this afternoon about Alexandra Moreland, she had been direct with him. "Charley, this is someone you've got to help. I thought a tree had fallen on me when I saw those photographs. I don't see how they can be fake. But there's nothing fake about the way she's been suffering and trying to find Matthew. If she took him, she doesn't remember it. Don't people go into zombielike states when they've had breakdowns?"

"Yes, it's not frequent, but sometimes they do," he told her.

Now in the cab, Charley wondered if Alvirah had not diagnosed Moreland's condition with deadly accuracy. When he got to the hospital earlier, she had still been out of it, but was mumbling her son's name over and over again. "I want Matthew . . . I want Matthew . . ."

The words had torn his heart. When he

was ten years old, his two-year-old sister had died and he could still vividly remember that terrible day at the grave, and his mother's plaintive wail. "I want my baby. I want my baby."

He looked at Zan. The cab was dark, but from the headlights of other cars and the brightly lit signs on stores along the way, he could clearly see her face. I am going to help you, he vowed. I've been in the business forty years and I'm going to give you the best defense that I possibly can. You're not faking this memory loss. I'll bet my life on it.

He had expected to go up with her to the Meehans' apartment and stay for a while, but as the cab approached Central Park South, he changed his mind. Alexandra Moreland obviously trusted Alvirah and Willy. She'd be better off alone with them this evening. Certainly it was no time to start to question her about details.

The cab stopped in the semicircular driveway, and he told the cabbie to wait for him. Despite Zan's insistence that he didn't need to get out, he escorted her up in the elevator. The doorman had announced them and Alvirah was waiting in the hall when they got off on the sixteenth floor. Without a word, she wrapped her arms around Zan and looked at Charley. "You go ahead, Charley," she directed. "What Zan needs is to relax now."

"I couldn't agree more and I know you'll take good care of her," Charley said with a smile, as he stepped back into the elevator and pushed the button for the lobby. The cab got him to the theatre in time for the curtain, but even though the show was lighthearted and amusing, and he had been looking forward to it, he still could not settle down and enjoy it.

How do I defend a woman who may not be capable of contributing to her own defense? he asked himself. And how long will it be before they decide to slap handcuffs on her?

He had an ominous feeling that when that happened, it would push her over the edge.

A blanket wrapped around her, a pillow behind her head, sipping hot tea with honey and cloves, all had the effect of making Zan feel as though she was coming out of a kind of dark alley. At least those were the best words she could use to explain to Alvirah and Willy about why she had collapsed. "When I saw those photos, I thought I was dreaming. I mean, I can prove I was with Nina Aldrich when Matthew was in the park. But why would anyone go to the trouble of looking exactly like me? I mean, isn't that crazy?"

Not waiting for a response, she said, "You know what I was running through my head . . . that song from *A Little Night Music . . .* 'Send in the Clowns.' I love that song and it seemed so appropriate. This is a farce. It's a circus. It has to be. But I know it will be all right when I talk to Nina Aldrich. I was going to do that today and then I fainted."

"Zan, it's no wonder you fainted with all this going on. You may remember that Josh was on the phone with Charley Shore and Charley dropped everything to be with you. That's the kind of lawyer and friend he is. Josh told me about last night at the Four Seasons with Ted. The way I figure it, you never did get to have dinner last night, and how much did you eat today?" Alvirah asked.

"Well, not much. Just coffee this morning, and I hadn't had lunch by the time I got back to the office. And then I fainted." Zan sipped the last of the tea. "Alvirah, Willy, you both believe that those photos show me taking Matthew. I heard it in your voice this afternoon, Alvirah. Then when Josh told me right away that I needed a lawyer, I could see that he believes they're real, too."

Willy looked at Alvirah. Of course she thinks they're the real McCoy, he thought. I do, too. But that doesn't mean this poor gal isn't positive they're not her. What's Alvirah going to say now?

Alvirah's response was hearty but evasive. "Zan, if you say those pictures are not of you, then I would guess Charley's first job will be to get a copy of the negatives or whatever they do with those cell phone cameras if that's what the man used, and get an expert to prove that they're phony. Then my bet is that the time frame when you saw that woman about decorating her new town house would vindicate you. Didn't you say Nina Aldrich was her name?"

"Yes."

"Charley's the kind of lawyer who will make sure that every second you spent with Nina Aldrich is accounted for."

"Then why didn't Josh or Charley respond when I told them that my meeting with Aldrich would prove I couldn't have been in the park?" Zan asked.

Alvirah stood up. "Zan, from what I gather, you didn't have any real conversation with Josh before you fainted. Buh-lieve me, we're not going to leave a stone unturned until we get at the truth and find

181

Matthew," she promised. "But the first thing you've got to remember is that you are going to be bombarded from all sides and you can't go through all this unless you're strong. And I mean physically strong. Dinner's simple. When you promised to come I put on my thinking cap and remembered that you love chili. So that's what it is, chili, a salad, and hot Italian bread."

Zan tried to smile. "Sounds good to me."

And it *was* good, she decided, as the warmth of the comfort food and a glass of red wine made her feel that she was getting her balance back.

She had told Alvirah and Willy about the possibility of decorating the model apartments for the architect Kevin Wilson at his ultra chic building, 701 Carlton Place. "It's between me and Bartley Longe," she explained. "I realized that when Wilson read the morning papers, he'd probably believe that I had staged that kidnapping. I went straight to his office and asked him to give me a chance to prove that I couldn't have taken Matthew that day."

Alvirah knew she had only a small sense of how much Zan had worked on her designs for those apartments. "Did he give you that chance?"

Zan shrugged. "We'll see. He let me leave

my sketches and fabrics, so I guess I'm still in the running."

They all passed on dessert, deciding to have just cappuccino. Knowing that Zan would be getting ready to leave, Willy got up from the table, went into the bedroom, and quietly picked up the phone and ordered a car to take her to Battery Park City then bring him back. Just in case they're hanging around her building, there's no way I'm letting that girl face a battery of reporters and photographers alone, he decided. I'm going to escort her home and get her upstairs.

"Fifteen minutes, Mr. Meehan," the car dispatcher assured him.

Willy had just gotten back to the table when the phone rang. It was Fr. Aiden. "I'm crossing the street from the club," he announced. "If it's still all right, I'd like to pick up my scarf."

"Oh, that's perfect," Alvirah assured him. "There is someone here I've been hoping you'd arrive in time to meet."

Zan was finishing the last of her coffee. As Alvirah replaced the phone, Zan said, "Alvirah, I honestly don't want to meet anyone. Please, let me get away before whoever that is arrives."

"Zan, this isn't just anyone," Alvirah

pleaded. "I didn't say anything but I was really hoping that you'd still be here when Fr. Aiden dropped by. He's an old friend and he left his scarf here last night, and because he had dinner practically across the street, he's stopping by to pick it up. I don't want to interfere with your plans, but I'd love it if you got to know him. He's a wonderful priest at St. Francis, and I think he could be a real comfort to you."

"Alvirah, I'm not feeling very religious these days," Zan said, "so I'd like to just slip away fast."

"Zan, I called a car. I'm riding home with you. That's that," Willy said.

The phone rang. It was the doorman to announce Fr. O'Brien. Alvirah rushed to open the door and a moment later the elevator stopped at their floor.

A smiling Fr. O'Brien was hugged by Alvirah, shook hands with Willy, and then turned to be introduced to the young woman who was their guest.

The smile vanished from his face.

Holy Mother of God, he thought, she's the woman who's involved in a crime.

She's the one who claims she can't prevent a murder.

32

On the short drive over from Hunter College to the Aldrich town house on East Sixty-ninth Street, Detectives Billy Collins and Jennifer Dean admitted to each other that never for one minute had either of them suspected that Zan Moreland had abducted her own child.

They reconstructed the day Matthew Carpenter disappeared. "All I was thinking was that we were looking for a predator who sized up the situation and acted on it," Billy said somberly. "The park was crowded, the babysitter asleep on the grass, the little boy asleep in the stroller. I saw it as a perfect set-up for a pervert on the lookout for a child."

"Tiffany was absolutely hysterical," Jennifer said, reflectively. "She was screaming, 'How can I face Zan, how can I face her?' But why didn't we dig further? The thought that Tiffany may have been drugged never crossed my mind, either."

"It should have crossed our minds. It was a hot day, but not many teenagers, even with the onset of a cold, would pass out midday in a deep sleep on the grass," Billy said. "Oh, here we are." He pulled to a stop in front of the handsome residence, double-parked, and slapped his ID on the wind-shield. "Let's keep reconstructing our first impressions for a couple of minutes," he suggested.

"Alexandra Moreland had a hard-luck story that would make a sphinx take pity on her," Jennifer Dean said. "Parents killed on the way to the airport for a long-delayed reunion, marriage when she was an emo-tional wreck, a single mother struggling to start a business, and then her little guy gets abducted." Her voice was becoming more disgusted with every word.

Billy tapped his fingers on the steering wheel as he tried to recall every detail of the events that had taken place nearly two years ago. "We spoke to the Aldrich woman that night. She backed up Moreland's story right away. They had an appointment. Moreland was with her going over sketches and fabrics in the new town house Aldrich just bought when I called Moreland to tell her her son was missing." Billy stopped, then added

186

angrily, "And we didn't ask any more questions."

"Let's face it," Jennifer said as she fished in her pocket for her handkerchief. "We had it all figured out. Working mother. Irresponsible babysitter. Predator snatching the opportunity to grab a child."

"When I got home, Eileen had been watching television," Billy recalled. "She told me she cried when she saw the expression on Moreland's face. She said that she thought it was going to be like Etan Patz, that little boy who disappeared all those years ago and was never found."

Looking out at the blustery wind and the persistent rain, Jennifer raised the collar of her coat. "All of us were willing to believe the sob story. But if those photos are legit, they prove that Moreland couldn't have been with Nina Aldrich that whole time," she said. "And if Aldrich can swear they were together, then the photos are probably fakes."

"They're not going to be fakes," Billy said grimly, "so Aldrich wasn't on the level when I spoke with her. But why would she have lied?" Without waiting for an answer, he said, "Okay, let's go in."

With that they dashed from the car to the door of the town house and rang the bell. "I imagine Aldrich paid a minimum of fifteen million bucks for this little nest," Billy muttered.

They could hear the chimes inside, but before they had stopped ringing, the door was opened by a Latina woman in a black uniform. She appeared to be in her early sixties. Her dark hair, streaked with gray, was drawn back into a neat bun. Her face was lined and there was a weary expression in her heavily lidded eyes.

Billy gave her their cards.

"I am Maria Garcia, Mrs. Aldrich's housekeeper. She is expecting you, Detective Collins and Detective Dean. May I take your coats?"

Garcia hung the coats in the closet and invited them to follow her. As they walked down the hall, Billy glanced into the formal living room and slowed his pace to get a longer look at the painting over the mantel. He was a frequent visitor to museums and said to himself, I bet that's a genuine Matisse.

The housekeeper led them into a large room that seemed to serve a double purpose. Butter-soft dark brown leather sofas were grouped around a recessed flat-screen television. Floor-to-ceiling mahogany bookcases covered three walls. All the books on the shelves were aligned in perfect symmetry. No casual reading in here, Billy thought. The walls were dark beige and the carpet a geometric brown and tan pattern.

Not my taste at all, Billy decided. Probably cost a fortune, but a little dab of color would go a long way in here.

Nina Aldrich kept them waiting close to half an hour. They knew she was sixty-three years old. When she swept into the room with her impeccable carriage, flowing silver hair, flawless complexion, patrician features, black caftan, silver jewelry, and frosty expression, she gave the impression of a monarch greeting an intrusive visitor.

Billy Collins was not impressed. As he stood up, for a split second he remembered what his uncle, a chauffeur for a family in Locust Valley, Long Island, had told him. "There are a lot of smart people in this town, Billy, who have plenty of money they made on their own. I know, because that's the kind of people I work for. But they're not the same as the really rich, who have been that way for generations. Those people live in a world of their own. They don't think like the rest of us."

It was clear to Billy, as it had been the first time he met her, that Nina Aldrich fit into that category. And she wants to put us on the defensive, he thought. Okay, lady, let's talk. He opened the conversation. "Good afternoon, Mrs. Aldrich. It's very accommodating of you to see us on short notice, because it's obvious you're having a very busy afternoon."

From the narrowing of her lips, he could see that she had gotten his point. Without being invited, he and Jennifer Dean both sat down again. After a moment's hesitation, Nina Aldrich took a seat behind the narrow antique desk opposite them.

"I've seen the morning papers and the Internet," she began, her voice cold and contemptuous. "I can't believe the way that young woman could have been so flagrant as to kidnap her own child. When I think of the sympathy I felt for her and the caring note I wrote to her, I am simply outraged."

Jennifer Dean opened the questioning. "Mrs. Aldrich, when we spoke to you hours after Matthew Carpenter disappeared, you verified that you had an appointment with Alexandra Moreland, and that she was with you when I first phoned her to tell her that her child was missing."

"Yes, that was about three o'clock in the afternoon."

"What was her reaction to our call?"

"Looking back, after having seen those

photos, I can tell you that she's quite a marvelous actress As I told you at our previous meeting, after speaking to you, Ms. Moreland went white as a sheet and jumped up. I wanted to call a cab, but she ran out of the house and raced to the park on foot. She left all her books with her fabric and paint samples and pictures of antique furniture and lamps and carpets and so forth scattered here."

"I see. The babysitter took Matthew to the park between 12:30 and 12:40. From my notes I see that your appointment with Ms. Moreland was at one P.M.," Jennifer continued.

"That's right. She called me on her cell phone to say that she'd be just a few minutes late because of the babysitter problem."

"You were here."

"No. I was in my former apartment on Beekman Place."

Billy Collins was careful to keep his expression from showing his excitement. "Mrs. Aldrich, I don't think you told me that the first time we spoke. You said that you met Ms. Moreland here."

"That's the way it turned out. I told her I didn't mind her being a little late, but then when an hour passed, I called her back. By then she was sitting in this house."

"Mrs. Aldrich, you are now telling me that when Alexandra Moreland spoke to you after two o'clock that you still hadn't seen her?" Billy persisted.

"That's exactly what I'm saying. Let me explain. Zan Moreland had a key to this house. She had been letting herself in while she was preparing to submit her suggestions for the décor. She just assumed we were meeting here. So actually it was closer to an hour and a half before we got together. When we finally did talk, she apologized for the confusion and offered to come to Beekman Place, but I was meeting friends at the Carlyle for cocktails at five so I told her I would come meet her up here. Frankly, by then I was getting pretty irritated with her."

"Mrs. Aldrich, do you keep a written record of your appointments?" Dean asked.

"Of course I do. I keep them in one of those daily planners."

"Would you happen to have kept yours from two years ago, and is it on hand?"

"Yes. It would be upstairs." With an impatient sigh, Nina Aldrich got up, walked to the door of the room, and called the housekeeper. Glancing at her watch, a gesture Billy Collins was sure was intended for them, she directed Garcia to go to her desk, open the top drawer, and get the appointment book for the year before last.

While Nina Aldrich and the detectives waited, she said, "I do hope we're not going to be involved in this situation beyond this meeting. My husband despises this sort of sensationalism, and he was not happy when the papers made so much of the fact that Moreland's meeting was with me that day."

Billy did not deem it wise to tell her that if this came to trial, she would end up being a star witness. Instead he said quietly, "I'm sorry about the inconvenience."

Maria Garcia returned, a small red leather book in her hand. She had already opened it to June 10.

"Thank you, Maria. Wait right here." Nina Aldrich glanced at the page and handed the book to Billy. Next to the one P.M. slot was Alexandra Moreland's name. "This doesn't say where you were planning to meet her," Billy observed. "If you were discussing decorating this house, why would you meet her at the other residence?"

"Ms. Moreland had taken extensive pictures of all the rooms here. We had no furniture other than a card table and a couple of chairs in the entire house. Why would I not make my choices in comfort? But since, as I said, I was planning to meet friends at the Carlyle for cocktails at five, I told Ms. Moreland to wait for me instead of coming down to Beekman Place."

"I see. Then you weren't here long before we called her?" Jennifer asked.

"Little more than a half hour."

"When you arrived here, how would you describe Ms. Moreland's demeanor?"

"Flurried. Apologetic. Anxious."

"I see. And how big is this house, Mrs. Aldrich?"

"It's five stories high and forty feet wide, which as you can see makes it one of the larger town houses in the area. The top floor is now an enclosed garden. We have eleven rooms." There was no mistaking the pleasure Nina Aldrich displayed in disclosing the dimensions of her town house.

"What about the basement?" Billy asked.

"It has a second kitchen, a wine cellar, and a very large finished room, which my husband's grandchildren enjoy when they are visiting. Also a storage area."

"You say there were only a few chairs and a card table here the day Matthew disappeared and you met Ms. Moreland here?"

"Yes. The architectural renovation had been done by the previous owners. Because of sudden financial problems, the house went on the market and we bought it. For the most part we were very satisfied with the architect's work and wanted no part of long delays by starting any further renovations. The interior decorating had not begun and that was when Alexandra Moreland was recommended to me."

"I see." Billy looked at Jennifer and they both got up to go. "You say Ms. Moreland had a key to the house. Did she ever come back after Matthew disappeared?"

"I never saw her. I know that she did come back at some point for her briefcase, samples, and so forth. Frankly, I don't remember if she ever did return the key, but of course we had all the locks changed when we moved in."

"You did not have Ms. Moreland do the interior design work for you?"

"I thought it was quite obvious that she would be in no emotional condition to take on such a project, and I wouldn't have expected it of her. And obviously I couldn't take a chance that she wouldn't have some kind of breakdown and leave me in a mess."

"May I ask who decorated this house?"

"Bartley Longe. Perhaps you've heard of him. He's quite brilliant."

"I guess what I'm asking is, when did he come on the job?" Billy's mind was racing. This house had been empty the day Matthew disappeared. Zan Moreland had access to it. Was it possible that she brought her child here and perhaps had hidden him in one of the rooms or in the basement? No one would have dreamt of looking for him here. She could have come back in the middle of the night and, alive or dead, taken him somewhere else.

"Oh, Bartley took over quite soon," Nina Aldrich said. "Don't forget, I hadn't given the job to Moreland at that point. I was only considering hiring her. And now, Detective Collins, if you don't mind —"

Billy interrupted her. "We're on our way, Mrs. Aldrich."

"Maria will see you out."

The housekeeper escorted them down the hall and retrieved their coats from the closet. Although her face remained impassive, inwardly she was churning with anger. You bet Bartley Longe took right over from that nice young woman, she thought. Mrs. High-and-Mighty began having a fling with him after she let that nice young Moreland woman do all those design plans. She won't admit it now, but she was going to turn down Moreland's designs even before the child disappeared.

Jennifer began to button her coat. "Thank you, Ms. Garcia," she said.

"Detective Collins," Maria began, then

stopped. She had been about to say that she was in the room when Mrs Aldrich absolutely told Alexandra Moreland to meet her here, not at Beekman Place. But who would take my word against hers? Maria Garcia asked herself. Besides, what difference does it make? I saw those photos in the paper. There's no question. Whatever her reason, Ms. Moreland stole her own child.

"Did you want to tell me anything, Ms. Garcia?" Billy asked.

"Oh, no, no. I just wanted to wish you both a nice day."

33

He had tried Gloria again and again that evening, but the phone just rang. Was she playing a game with him? He finally reached her at midnight and was quick to notice that at some point her defiant bravado had collapsed. Her voice sounded tired and listless when she answered. "What do you want?"

He was careful to keep his tone moderated and warm. "Gloria, I know how tough this has been for you." He was about to add that it had been tough for him, too, but clamped his teeth over that sentence. It would have given her an opening and, worse than that, a golden opportunity to rekindle her sense of being entrapped.

"Gloria," he continued, "I've been thinking. I'm not going to give you two hundred thousand as we agreed. I'm going to triple it. I'm going to give you six hundred thousand dollars in cash by the end of next week."

He was delighted to hear her astonished gasp. Was she stupid enough to really fall for it? "You only have one more thing to do," he continued, "and that is to show up in the Franciscan church one more time about quarter of five. I'll let you know what evening."

"Aren't you afraid I'll go to confession again?"

If she were in this room, I'd kill her right now, he thought. Instead he laughed. "I looked it up. You're right about the seal of the confessional."

"Aren't you torturing Matthew's mother enough? Why do you have to kill her?"

Not for the same reason I'm going to kill you, he thought. You know too much. I'd never be sure that so-called conscience of yours wouldn't start bubbling to the surface. As for Zan, I won't be happy until they are planning her funeral.

"Gloria, I'm not going to kill her," he said. "That was just angry talk."

"I don't believe you. I know how much you hate her." The edge of anger and even panic was creeping back into Gloria's voice.

"Gloria, how did we start this conversation? Let me remind you. I'm going to give you six hundred thousand dollars in cash, in genuine U.S. dollars, that you'll be able

199

to put in a safe-deposit box and live on while you give yourself a chance to do the only thing you really want to do and that is to walk across the stage in a Broadway play or on a movie set. You're a beautiful woman. Unlike most of the look-alike Barbie dolls in Hollywood, you're also a chameleon. You can look and walk and talk like someone else. You remind me of Helen Mirren in *The Queen.* You've got that level of talent. I'm asking you for a week. At the most ten days. I'll want you to go to that church, and I'll let you know what to wear. The minute you leave, it's all over. We'll meet someplace nearby and I'll give you five thousand dollars right away. That's as much cash as you should carry in case your bags are opened in an airport."

"Then what?"

"You go back to Middletown. You wait until about nine or ten o'clock that night, then drop Matthew off in a department store or mall. After that, you're on a plane to California, or Texas, or wherever you like, to start your new life. I know you're worried about your father. You can tell him you were on a mission for the CIA."

"Not more than ten days." Now her voice was tentative, almost convinced. Then she added, "But how will I get the rest of the cash?"

You'll never have that problem, he thought. "I'll have the money packaged and mailed to you anywhere you want."

"But how can I trust that the package will arrive or that, if it does, that it won't be stuffed with old newspapers?"

You can't trust me, he thought. Reaching for the straight-up double scotch that he had promised himself he wouldn't touch until after he spoke to her, he said, "Gloria, if that ever happened, and it won't, you can go back to plan B. Get a lawyer, tell him your story, get him to arrange a book deal, and then go to the cops. In the meantime, Matthew has been found, nice and healthy, and the only thing he knows is that Glory took care of him."

"I read him a lot of books. He's smarter than a lot of kids his age."

I'm sure you were a real Mother Teresa, he thought. "Gloria, this will be over soon and you'll be rich."

"All right. I'm sorry I got so upset before. It's just that this woman who lives near here showed up with some stupid muffins this morning. I know she was just sniffing around to see what kind of person I am."

"You didn't tell me about her earlier," he

said quietly. "Did she see Matthew?"

"No, but she saw his toy truck and told me she was such a great babysitter if I ever needed one. I told her my sister had helped me move in and that it was her little boy's truck."

"That sounds all right to me."

"The real estate agent is this woman's big friend. I had told the real estate agent that I was coming in by myself at night. She's another nosy one. I know she drove by early the morning after I got here."

He felt himself begin to perspire. *For want of a horse the rider is lost . . .* Incongruous that he should remember that old saying right now. His mind explored the possible scenarios. The nosy blueberry muffin lady checking with her real estate friend. He didn't want to think about that.

Time was running out.

It was hard to keep the reassuring note in his voice. "Gloria, you're borrowing trouble. Just start counting down the days."

"You bet I will. And not just for my sake. This little kid doesn't want to stay hidden anymore. He wants to go look for his mother."

34

Kevin Wilson arrived at his mother's apartment at seven P.M., just as the evening news on Channel 2 was ending. He had rung the bell twice, then let himself in with his own key. It was an arrangement that was long in place. "That way if I'm on the phone or still dressing, I don't have to run to the door," was the way his mother put it.

But when he walked in, diminutive, white-haired, seventy-one-year-old Catherine "Cate" Kelly Wilson was neither in her bedroom nor on the phone. She was glued to the television set and did not even look up as he entered the living room.

The three-room apartment he had bought for her was on Fifty-seventh Street, near First Avenue, a location which offered a crosstown bus stop on the corner, a movie theatre within walking distance, and, most important to her, St. John the Evangelist Church only one block away.

The unwillingness with which his mother had vacated the old neighborhood three years ago when it had become financially possible for him to buy her this new apartment still amused Kevin. Now, she loved it.

He went over to her chair and kissed her forehead.

"Hello, dear. Sit down a minute," she said, switching the channels without looking up at him. "*Headline News* is coming on now and there's something I want to see."

Kevin was hungry and had been looking forward to going immediately to Neary's Pub. It was not only a favorite dining spot, but also had the advantage of being directly across the street.

He settled down on the couch and looked around. The couch and the matching chair where his mother was sitting had been part of her original furniture, and no amount of persuasion had induced her to part with them when she moved. Instead Kevin had both pieces reupholstered for her as well as having her bridal bedroom set refinished. As she pointed out, "That's ribbon mahogany, Kevin, and I'm not giving it up." He'd also repaired her dining room furniture, which was "too good to throw out." She did allow him to replace the threadbare, machine-made Oriental carpet with one in a similar design. He did not tell her how much the new one cost.

The result was a cozy apartment filled with pictures of his father and grandparents, various cousins, and lifelong friends. Whenever he walked into it, no matter how busy his day, it lifted his spirits. It felt like a home. It *was* a home.

That was just what Zan Moreland had pitched to him in her plea to withhold judgment on his decision between her and Bartley Longe until she could prove her innocence in the alleged kidnapping of her own child. People want to feel as though they're living in a home, not a museum, she had told him.

Kevin realized that he had spent a good part of the day wondering why he hadn't simply returned Moreland's sketches and fabric samples to her with a brief note saying he had decided that Bartley Longe was the right person for the project.

What was keeping him from doing it? God knows he'd taken enough flak from his secretary, Louise, about how astonished she was that he would waste his time on a lying kidnapper. "I can tell you, Kevin, it took my breath away when that woman had the nerve to come here, and then ignore what I told her, that she could take her stuff, or I'd mail it to her. What did she do? Go running up to find you, and try to hold on to her chance of getting the job. Mark my words, she'll be on Rikers Island in handcuffs before this is over."

Not bothering to hide his annoyance, he had told Louise dryly, "If she's arrested, I believe she'll be out on bail." Finally he had told Louise flat out to drop the subject altogether, which of course had brought on a wounded, reproachful attitude from her that she made doubly clear by calling him "Mr. Wilson" for the rest of the day.

"Kevin, watch! They're showing those pictures of that Moreland woman picking up her child out of the stroller. The nerve of her, lying to the cops. Can you imagine how the father must be feeling all this time?"

Kevin sprang up and rushed across the room. There was a picture of Alexandra Moreland taking a little boy out of a stroller, and then one of her carrying him down the path. They stayed on the screen as the commentator continued, "She is seen here when she rushed back to Central Park after learning from police that her son was missing."

Kevin studied the image. Zan Moreland looked in shock. The suffering in her eyes was unmistakable. That same look had been there this afternoon, he thought, when she begged him to give her the chance to prove her innocence.

Begged? That was too strong a word. And she had given him an out by saying that if he preferred Bartley Longe's designs, she would understand.

She looks so wounded, he thought. He listened intently as the news announcer said, "Yesterday was Matthew Carpenter's fifth birthday and now the speculation is about whether his mother gave him to someone to keep for her — or if he is no longer alive."

In this past month or two Zan had been going back and forth to the apartments any number of times and putting hours upon hours of work into creating the designs for them, Kevin thought. I realize now that when I met her at Carlton Place yesterday, I could sense her suffering even though she seemed so calm. Why would she be in so much pain if she knew her child was safe? Is it possible she killed him?

No, it was not possible, he thought. I'd stake my soul on that. She's not a killer.

Kevin realized that his mother had stood up. "It's hard not to believe that kind of solid evidence," Catherine Wilson said. "But the look on Zan Moreland's face when she found out her child was missing! Of course, you're too young to remember, but when the Fitzpatrick baby fell out the window of our apartment building and was killed, that's the expression I saw in Joan Fitzpatrick's eyes, so much pain that you bled for her. That Moreland woman must be some actress."

"*If* she's acting." Kevin was surprised to hear himself defending her.

Startled, his mother looked at him. "What do you mean, if? You saw those pictures, didn't you?"

"Yes, I did, and I don't know what I mean. Come on, Mom, let's eat. I'm starved."

It was later, at their usual table in Neary's, that Kevin told his mother over coffee that he had been considering hiring Alexandra Moreland to decorate three model apartments.

"Well, of course this ends that," Catherine Wilson said decisively. "But tell me, what's she like?"

Her face would haunt you, Kevin thought. Those expressive eyes, that sensitive mouth. "She's about five eight, I would say. She's very slender and graceful. She moves like a dancer. Yesterday her hair was loose on her shoulders, the way you see it in the pictures. Today, she had tied it back in a bun or chignon or whatever you call it." He realized he was describing Zan to himself as much as to his mother.

"My God, you sound as though you have a crush on her," his mother exclaimed.

Kevin thought for a long moment. That's crazy, he decided, but there is something about Zan. He remembered the feeling of having her shoulder brush his when she was pointing out some of the aspects in Bartley Longe's sketches that she felt would put off a prospective buyer. By then she had seen those photos from Central Park and she knew what she was up against.

"She asked me to give her time to prove that those photos are fakes," he said. "I don't have to make a decision between her and Bartley Longe yet. And I'm not going to. I'm sticking to my guns and giving her the chance she asked for."

"Kevin, you've always been for the underdog," his mother said. "But this may be carrying it too far. You're thirty-seven years old and I was beginning to worry that I would be stuck with an Irish bachelor on my hands. But, for God's sake, don't get involved with someone in a hopeless situation."

Just then their longtime friend Jimmy Neary stopped at their table to say hello. He'd caught Catherine's last words. "I couldn't agree more with your Mom, Kevin," he said. "And if you're ready to settle down, I've got a list a mile long of young ladies who already have their eye on you. Do yourself a favor. Steer clear of trouble."

35

As he had promised, Willy took Zan home in a hired car. He offered to drop Fr. Aiden along the way, but he did not accept the ride. "No, you go along. I'll visit with Alvirah for a little while," he said.

When Fr. Aiden said good-bye to Zan, he looked directly into her eyes and said, "I will pray for you." Then he reached out and took her hands in his.

"Pray that my little boy is safe," Zan answered. "Don't bother to pray for me, Father. God has forgotten that I exist."

Fr. Aiden did not try to reply. Instead he stepped aside to let her pass into the hallway. "I'll just stay five minutes, Alvirah," he promised after the door closed behind Zan and Willy. "I could see that the young woman wanted no part of my company, and I didn't want to wish it on her even for a short ride in the car."

"Oh, Aiden," Alvirah sighed. "I'd give

anything if I could believe that Zan didn't take Matthew out of his stroller that day, but she did. There's no question about it."

"Do you think the child is alive?" Fr. Aiden asked.

"I could no more conceive of her hurting Matthew than I could imagine running a knife through Willy."

"I think you told me that you only came to know Ms. Moreland after her son disappeared," Fr. Aiden said. *Be careful,* he warned himself. There is no way you can possibly let Alvirah think that you've met Alexandra Moreland before.

"Yes. We became friendly because I wrote a column about her, and she phoned to thank me for it. Oh, Aiden, I believe that Zan must have been in some sort of catatonic state, or maybe even has a split personality. The point is, I don't know anyone she has ever mentioned who might be raising Matthew for her."

"There are no other family members?"

"She was an only child. So was her mother, and her father had one brother who died when he was still a teenager."

"How about a close friend?"

"I'm sure she has friends, but I don't care how good a friend you are, who would be party to a kidnapping? But, Father, suppose she just abandoned Matthew somewhere and doesn't know where? The one thing I would swear is that in her mind, her child is missing."

In her mind, her child is missing. Fr. Aiden was still pondering that thought when, a few minutes later, the doorman hailed a cab for him downstairs.

I am an accessory to an ongoing crime and to a murder that is about to be committed.

Does that young woman indeed have a split mind — or what is the new term for it, a dissociative identity disorder? And if so, was it Alvirah's friend, the real personality, trying to break through when she rushed into the Reconciliation Room?

The cab the doorman hailed was waiting. Grunting from the pain in his arthritic knees as he climbed into the backseat, Fr. Aiden thought, I am bound by the seal of the confessional. There is no way I can hint as to what I know. She asked me to pray for her child. But oh, dear Lord, if a murder is in the offing, I beg you to intercede and stop it.

What the elderly friar could not even begin to imagine was that there were now three murders being planned. And that *he* was first on the list.

36

Josh was already in the office when Zan arrived at eight A.M. Thursday morning. From the expression on his face, she knew immediately that something else had happened. By now too numb to feel anything except cold acceptance, she merely asked, "What is it?"

"Zan, you told me that Kevin Wilson agreed to hold off on deciding between you and Bartley over those model apartments."

"Yes. But I know with those pictures in this morning's papers of me being carried out to the ambulance yesterday, it's all over for that job. I'll be surprised if everything I left with him isn't back here before noon."

"Zan," Josh said passionately, "that's probably true, but it's not what I'm talking about. Zan, how could you have ordered all the fabrics and furniture and wall hangings for those apartments before you got the okay on the job?"

"You've got to be joking," Zan said flatly.

"Zan, I wish I were. You put the order in for the fabrics and the wall hangings and the custom furniture and the fixtures. My God, you've ordered *everything*. We've got delivery notices on the fabrics. Forget the money! Where are we going to *put* all that stuff?"

"They never would have begun delivering without being paid," she said. This, at least, I can prove is a mistake, Zan thought frantically.

"Zan, I called Wallington Fabrics. They have a letter from you requesting deferment of the usual ten percent down because time is of the essence, and saying you'll be able to pay in full as soon as the contract with Kevin Wilson comes in. You claim he's already signed it, and the check will be arriving very soon."

Josh grabbed a paper from his desk. "I asked them to fax me a copy of the letter. Here it is. On our stationery and that's your signature."

"I didn't sign that letter," Zan said. "I swear on my life that I didn't sign that letter, and I didn't order anything for those model apartments. Absolutely all I ever took from any of our suppliers were the upholstery fabric, drapery and wall hanging

215

samples, and pictures of the furniture and Persian carpets and window treatments that I would use if we got the job."

"Zan," Josh began, then shook his head. "Look, I love you like you're my own sister. We've got to call Charley Shore right now. When I phoned Wallington Fabrics, I thought someone had made a mistake. Now they're going to start worrying about getting paid. And you *did* send minimal deposits to hold the carpets and some of the antiques. You must have written the checks from your personal account."

"I didn't sign that letter," Zan said, her voice now quiet. "I didn't write any checks from my personal account. And I am not crazy." She saw the look of combined disbelief and concern on the face of her associate. "Josh, I accept your resignation. If this is going to turn out to be a scandal with our suppliers suing us, I don't want you caught in it. They might accuse you of being in some kind of rip-off scheme along with me. So why don't you get your stuff together and take off?"

As he stared at her, she added, sarcastically, "Admit it. You think I kidnapped my own son and that I've lost my mind. Who knows, maybe I'm dangerous? Maybe I'll clobber you over the head when your back is turned."

"Zan," Josh snapped. "I'm not leaving you, and I'm going to find a way to help you."

The phone rang, a sharp, ominous sound. Josh picked up the receiver, listened, then said, "She's not here yet. I'll give her the message."

Zan watched as Josh scribbled a phone number. When he hung up, he said, "Zan, that was Detective Billy Collins. He wants you to come to the Central Park Precinct with your lawyer today, as soon as possible. I'm going to call Charley Shore right now. It's early but he told me he always gets to his office by 7:30."

Yesterday I fainted, Zan thought. I can't, I won't, do that again.

During the night, after Willy dropped her off, she lay in bed in quiet, absolute despair, a single light shining on Matthew's picture again. For some reason, the look of compassion in the eyes of the priest who was Alvirah's friend kept coming back to her. I was rude to him, she thought, but I could feel that he wanted to help me. He said he'd pray for me, but I told him to pray for Matthew instead. When he took my hands, it felt as though he were blessing me. Maybe what he was doing was helping me to face the truth?

All night long, except for brief periods when she dozed off, Zan had kept her vigil, looking at Matthew's picture. As dawn was breaking she said quietly, "Little guy, I don't believe that you're still alive. I've always sworn that I would know if you were dead, but I've been fooling myself. You are dead, and it's over for me, too. I don't know what's happening, but I can't fight anymore. I guess in my soul, all these many months, I've really believed that you were grabbed by a predator who abused and then killed you. I wouldn't have thought I would come to this, but there is a bottle of sleeping pills in this drawer that will bring us back together. It's time to take them."

A sense of relief and exhaustion had come over her, and she finally closed her eyes. With Fr. Aiden's face before her, she had prayed for forgiveness and understanding before she reached for the pills.

It was then that she heard Matthew's voice calling out to her. "Mommy, Mommy." She had leapt up from the bed screaming, "Matthew! Matthew!" In that moment, against all rational belief, she knew with absolute certainty that her little boy was still alive.

Matthew is alive, she thought fiercely, as she heard Josh talking to Charley Shore.

When he replaced the receiver, Josh said, "Detective Collins wants to question you this morning. Mr. Shore will pick you up at 10:30."

Zan nodded. "You said that I must have paid any deposits on the furnishings for the model apartments out of my savings account. Pull my bank account up for me on the computer."

"I don't have the password for your account."

"You'll have it now. It's 'Matthew.' I have a little over twenty-seven thousand dollars in it."

Josh sat down in front of the computer and began to send his fingers flying across the keyboard.

Zan saw the expression on his face, troubled, but not surprised. "What is my balance?" she asked.

"Two hundred thirty-three dollars and eleven cents."

"Then there is a computer hacker at work," she said flatly.

Josh ignored that. "Zan, what are we going to do about all the orders you placed?" he asked.

"You mean, what are we going to do about all the orders I *didn't* place," Zan said. "Look, Josh, I'm not afraid to go to the police station and talk with Detective Collins. I believe there is an answer to all this. Somebody hates me enough to try and destroy me, and his name is Bartley Longe. I told Detective Collins and his partner about him when Matthew disappeared. They didn't take me seriously. I know they didn't. But if Bartley hates me enough to try to destroy my reputation and my business, I think he may hate me enough to kidnap my son and maybe turn him over to a friend who wanted a child."

"Zan, don't repeat that to the cops. They'll turn that kind of talk against you in a heartbeat," Josh implored.

The intercom phone rang. Josh picked up the receiver. It was the service manager of the building. "Shipment arriving for you. It's a large load and pretty heavy."

Ten minutes later twenty long rolls of fabric were delivered to the office. Zan and Josh had to push the desk to one side and pile the chairs in the back room in order to make room for it. When the delivery men left, Josh opened the statement that was attached to one of the rolls and read it aloud. "One hundred yards of discontinued fabric at one hundred and twenty-five dollars a yard. Special arrangement nonrefundable purchase agreement. Full payment due within ten days. Total including tax, thirteen thousand eight hundred and seventy-four dollars."

He looked at Zan. "We have forty thousand dollars in the bank and sixteen thousand in accounts receivable. You've been concentrating so much on the model apartments, you haven't done anything on at least four of the smaller jobs we have lined up. The rent is due next week and so is the payment on the start-up loan you got to open this place, to say nothing of the usual overhead and our salaries."

The phone rang again. This time Josh made no effort to answer, and Zan hurried to pick it up. It was Ted. His voice bitter and angry, he snarled, "Zan, I'm on my way to meet Detective Collins. I have rights as Matthew's father, rights that you have willfully taken from me. I am going to insist that they arrest you immediately, and I'll move heaven and earth to make you tell me what you have done with my son."

37

Toby Grissom pushed open the door of the 13th Precinct in Manhattan and, ignoring the comings and goings in the busy reception area, approached the sergeant behind the desk.

"I'm Toby Grissom," he began timidly, but there was nothing timid in his voice when he added, "My daughter is missing and I think some big shot interior decorator may be the reason for it."

The sergeant looked at him. "How old is your daughter?"

"Thirty last month."

The sergeant did not show the relief he felt. He'd been afraid that it might be another case of a young teenage runaway who sometimes gets picked up by a pimp and ends up a hooker or disappearing for good. "Mr. Grissom, if you'll just take a seat, I'll ask one of our detectives to take down the information."

There were a couple of benches in the area near the desk. Toby, his wool cap in hand, a manila envelope under his arm, sat on one of them and watched with detached curiosity as uniformed cops went in and out of the building, sometimes accompanying people in handcuffs.

Fifteen minutes later, a large-framed man in his midthirties with thinning blond hair and a quiet manner approached Toby. "Mr. Grissom, I'm Detective Wally Johnson. Sorry to keep you waiting. If you'll follow me to my desk, we can talk."

Obediently Toby stood up. "I'm used to waiting," he said. "Seems to me I've been waiting for one thing or another most of my life."

"I think we all have times when we feel like that," Wally Johnson agreed. "It's this way."

The detective's desk was one of many in a large, cluttered room. Most of the desks were empty, but the files strewn on them suggested that each of the missing occupants was actively working cases.

"We got lucky," Johnson said as, arriving at his desk, he pulled up a chair beside it. "I not only got promoted to being next to the window with the view, such as it is, but it's one of the quieter spots in the whole precinct."

Toby did not know where he got his courage to speak up. "Detective Johnson, I don't really care if you like where you sit. I'm here because my daughter is missing, and I think either something has happened to her, or she's mixed up in some kind of trouble that she has to get out of."

"Can you explain what you mean by that, Mr. Grissom?"

By now, after visiting Bartley Longe's office and speaking with the two young women Glory had been living with when she disappeared, Toby felt as though he could not go through the full story again. But that's crazy, he told himself. If I don't come across to this detective as a guy to believe, he'll just blow me off.

"My daughter's legal name is Margaret Grissom," he began. "I always called her Glory because she was such a glorious, beautiful baby, if you know what I mean. She left Texas when she was eighteen to come to New York. She wanted to be an actress. She won best actress in the senior play at her high school."

Oh God, Johnson thought, how many of those kids who were best actress in the school play come running to New York? Talk about the "field of dreams." It was an effort to keep his mind on what Grissom was telling him, about his daughter taking the name of Brittany La Monte, and what a good person she was. She was so pretty she was offered jobs in porno films but wouldn't touch them, how she got started doing makeup because that way she could make enough money to support herself and even send nice little gifts to him on his birthday and Christmas. And —

It was time for Johnson to interrupt. "You say she came to New York twelve years ago. How many times have you seen her since then?"

"Five times. Like clockwork. Glory always spent Christmas with me every other year. Except almost two years ago this coming June, she phoned and said she wouldn't be coming next Christmas. She said she was working on a new job that was real hush-hush, but that she'd be getting paid a lot of money for it. When I asked if she was talking about some guy keeping her, she said, 'No, Daddy, no, I promise you.' "

And he believes that, Wally Johnson thought sympathetically.

"She said that she had an advance payment for the job and was giving almost all of it to me. *Twenty-five thousand dollars.* Can you imagine? It was to be sure I wouldn't need anything, because she had to be out of touch. I thought maybe she was working for the CIA or something."

Or more likely, Margaret-Glory-Brittany found herself a billionaire, Detective Johnson thought.

"The last I heard from her was a postcard from New York six months ago saying that the job was taking longer than she expected and that she was worried about me and missed me," Grissom continued. "That's why I finally came to New York. I got some real bad news from my doctor, and besides that I have a feeling now that maybe somebody is holding Glory somewhere. I went to see the girls she shared an apartment with and they told me that this big shot designer was snowing her about how he'd introduce her to theatre people and make her a star. He made her go up to his house in Connecticut on weekends so she could meet important people."

"Who was this designer, Mr. Grissom?"

"Bartley Longe. He has fancy offices on Park Avenue."

"Did you speak to him?"

"He gave me the same line he gave Glory. He told me that he hired her as a kind of model when he was showing off places he'd decorated and he'd introduced her to a lot of theatre big shots. But they all told him that Glory didn't have what it takes, and finally he couldn't pester people about her anymore. And according to him, that was that."

And it probably was, Wally Johnson thought. The usual thing. The guy promises her the moon, has a little fling, gets tired of her, and tells her not to bother showing up at his place next weekend.

"Mr. Grissom, I'm going to follow up on this, but I warn you that I'm afraid that we're not going to get very far. I'm more interested in the job your daughter was so mysterious about. Is there anything more specific you know about it?"

"Not a thing," Toby Grissom said.

As he asked the question, Wally Johnson felt like a phony. I'd be better off telling this poor old guy that his daughter is a hooker who got involved with some guy, and it's worth her while to stay under the radar, he thought.

Nevertheless, he asked the usual perfunctory questions. Height. Weight. Color of eyes. Color of hair.

"All this is on Glory's publicity shots," Toby Grissom said. "Maybe you'd like one." He reached into the envelope he was carrying and brought out a half dozen eight-by-ten photographs. "You know, they want the girls to look kind of sweet and innocent in one picture, and kind of sexy in another, and if they have short hair like Glory, they try them with different wigs or extensions or whatever you call that stuff."

Wally Johnson rifled through the photos. "She *is* very pretty," he said sincerely.

"Yeah, I know. I mean, I always liked her better with long hair, but she said that it's easier to have good wigs 'cause you can be anybody you want."

"Mr. Grissom, why don't you leave me the photograph with the montage showing her in her different poses. That will be more useful to us."

"Of course." Toby Grissom stood up. "I'm going back to Texas. I need my chemo treatments. They won't save my life, I guess, but maybe they will keep me alive long enough to see my Glory." He started to walk away, then came back to Johnson's desk. "You will talk to that Bartley Longe?"

"Yes, I will. And if anything develops we'll be in touch with you, I promise."

Wally Johnson tucked Margaret-Glory-Brittany's glossy photo montage under the clock on the corner of his desk. His gut instinct was that the young woman was alive and well and probably involved in something dirty, if not illegal.

I'll give that Longe guy a call, Johnson thought, then I'll put Glory's picture where it belongs, in the dead letter file.

38

At nine A.M. Thursday, Ted Carpenter arrived at the Central Park Precinct. Haggard and worn from the events and the emotional seesaw of the past day and a half, his tone was brusque when he said he had an appointment with Detective Billy Collins. "And I believe he said something about his partner would be with him," Ted added before the desk sergeant could respond.

"Detectives Collins and Dean are expecting you," the sergeant said, ignoring the hostility in Carpenter's voice. "I'll let them know that you're here."

Less than five minutes later, Ted was sitting at a conference table in a small office, facing Billy Collins and Jennifer Dean.

Billy thanked him for coming in. "I hope you're feeling better, Mr. Carpenter. I know that when your secretary phoned yesterday to make an appointment, she said you were ill."

"I was and I am," Ted replied. "And it's not just physical. Knowing what I've gone through for almost two years, to see those photos and realize that my ex, Matthew's mother, has been guilty of abducting my son, just about drove me over the edge."

An unmistakable note of anger crept into his voice. "I have wasted my time blaming that babysitter who fell asleep when she was supposed to be minding my son. Now I have begun to wonder if she wasn't in collusion with my ex-wife. I know Zan regularly gave Tiffany clothes she no longer wore."

Billy Collins and Jennifer Dean were trained not to show surprise at anything that was said to them, but each knew the other's thoughts. Was this an angle they had not considered? And if there was any truth to it, what made Tiffany Shields turn on Zan to the point of suggesting that both she and Matthew had been deliberately drugged that day?

Billy chose not to follow up on Ted Carpenter's reasoning that Shields was involved. "Mr. Carpenter, you and Ms. Moreland were married for how long?"

"Six months. What has that got to do with it?"

"Her mental health is what we're getting at. At the time of Matthew's disappearance,

231

she told us that after her parents' death, you flew to Rome and saw her through the funeral, the packing of their personal items, the usual details following a demise. She made it clear that she was very grateful to you."

"Grateful! That's one way of putting it. She didn't want me out of the room. She had hysterical crying fits and fainting spells. She blamed herself for not having visited her parents sooner. She blamed Bartley Longe for not letting her take a vacation. She blamed the traffic in Rome for causing her father's heart attack."

"But with that kind of emotional baggage, you still chose to marry her?" Jennifer Dean asked quietly.

"Zan and I had been dating, somewhat casually, but we were definitely becoming interested in each other. I guess I was half in love with her then. She is a beautiful woman, as I'm sure you've observed, and very intelligent. She is a gifted interior designer, thanks, I might add, to the fact that Bartley Longe took her on after she graduated from FIT and gave her the chance to be his right-hand apprentice."

"Then you don't feel that Ms. Moreland was fair when she blamed Bartley Longe for making it impossible to visit her parents earlier?"

"No, I don't. She knew perfectly well that much as he might rant and rave if she took a few weeks off, he never would have fired her. She was far too valuable to him."

"You say you were dating and half in love with Ms. Moreland during that time. Did you express your feelings about her job with Longe at that time?"

"Of course I did. The fact is, Longe had given her the chance of a lifetime for a young designer. He had taken on a high-profile job to decorate the TriBeCa penthouse of Toki Swan, the rock star, but because he was up to his elbows doing a Palm Beach mansion, he virtually turned the job over to Zan. She was thrilled. You couldn't have dragged her onto a plane at that point."

"Did Ms. Moreland show any signs of overwork, or of approaching a breakdown, before she flew to Rome?"

"From what I understand, after she finished that job Longe wanted her to stay a few weeks longer and help him finish the Palm Beach place. That's when the big quarrel took place and she quit. As I just told you, that so-called firing was a joke."

"After her parents' death, couldn't you have helped her without marrying her?" Jennifer Dean asked.

"That's like asking a bystander watching someone trapped in a burning car, why didn't you dial 911 instead of taking immediate action? Zan needed to feel as if she had a home and a family. I gave that to her."

"But she left you very quickly."

Ted bristled. "I didn't come in here to have a consultation about my brief marriage to the woman who abducted my son. Zan felt that she had taken advantage of me, and decided to move out. It was only after she was gone that she realized she was pregnant."

"What was your reaction?"

"I was pleased. By then I realized there was nothing between us, and I told her I would give her generous support so that she could always live comfortably and raise our child. She told me she intended to open her own interior design business. I understood that, but after my son was born, I did insist on meeting the nanny she planned to hire so I could judge for myself if that person was competent."

"Did you do that?"

"Yes. And the nanny, Gretchen Voorhees, was a blessing. Frankly, I would say that she was more of a mother to Matthew than Zan. Zan was consumed with her need to beat out Bartley Longe for jobs. I can tell you the amount of time she spent working to get that job with Nina Aldrich was unconscionable."

"How do you know that?"

"Gretchen told me that on the last day she worked for Zan. I was picking Matthew up for the afternoon. Gretchen was flying back to Holland because she was getting married."

"Had Ms. Moreland hired a new nanny, and if so, did you meet her?"

"I met her once. Her references were good. She seemed perfectly pleasant. However, she was obviously not reliable. She didn't show up the first day for work, and Zan grabbed Tiffany Shields to take my son to Central Park so she could fall asleep on the grass, if indeed she *did* fall asleep."

Ted Carpenter's face turned a deep crimson red. He swallowed, unable to go on. Then, his hands clenched into fists, his voice raised, he said, "I'll tell you what happened that day. Zan realized that Matthew was going to be in her way. Maybe she had realized it for a long time before that. Gretchen told me of the many times she had to work on her day off because Zan was too busy to stay home with her child. Zan was, and is, all about becoming a famous interior designer. That's it! She's well on her way to it. That baloney about spending every cent she can scrimp to have private detectives search for Matthew is strictly PR. If anyone should know, it's me. I'm in the business. Take a look at that article *People* magazine did on her last year on the first anniversary of Matthew's disappearance. She's showing them her modest three-room apartment, whining about how she walks rather than take cabs so that every cent she makes is saved to try to find Matthew and so on . . . Then notice how she always talks about what a great interior designer she is."

"You are saying that you believe your ex-wife got rid of your child because he had become a liability?"

"That's *exactly* what I'm saying. She's a born martyr. How many people have lost their parents in an accident and even though they're grieving, have gone on with their lives? If she had asked me to take full custody of Matthew, I would have done it in a heartbeat."

"Did you *request* full custody?"

"That would have been like asking the earth to stop revolving around the sun. How would that have looked in the newspapers?"

Ted stood up. "I have nothing more to say to you except this. I assume that by now you have checked out those photos that were taken in Central Park. Unless they are doctored — and you have given me no indication that you think that is the case — then I want to know why Alexandra Moreland has not been arrested. You have proof positive that she stole my son. Clearly she lied to you every step of the way. I'm sure there is a law about withholding a child from the other parent who has visitation rights. But the charge you really should be pursuing now is that Matthew was abducted and murdered by his own mother. What are you waiting for?"

As he pushed back his chair and stood up, Ted Carpenter, tears running down his cheeks, again demanded, "What are you waiting for?"

39

It was not just the pain in his arthritic knees, which he ruefully referred to as his nocturnal visitor, that kept Fr. Aiden awake for a good part of Wednesday night. It was the woman who had confessed to being part of an ongoing crime and an impending murder, the woman whose name he now knew: Alexandra Moreland.

The incredible irony of meeting her at Alvirah and Willy's apartment! Between two and four in the morning, Fr. Aiden relived every second of those few moments they had been together. It was apparent to anyone that Zan, as Alvirah had called her, was suffering. The expression in her eyes was like that of a soul in hell, if such a comparison could be imagined. She had said, "God has forgotten that I exist."

She truly believes that, Fr. Aiden thought. But she did ask me to pray for her child. If only I could help her! When she confessed, she was clear about what she was doing, and about what was being planned. No mistake about it, and no mistake that it was her.

Alvirah, who knew Zan well, had recognized her face on the security camera in the church and said that she was absolutely the person in those Central Park pictures. If I could only broach the subject that if Zan has a split personality, they might try to have a doctor give her some medication to release what is hidden in her mind, Fr. Aiden thought. But I cannot reveal anything, even if it would help her. . . .

He would pray that in another way, some way, somehow, the truth would come out to save her child, if it was not already too late. After a while his eyes began to close. Just before dawn, he woke again. Zan's face filled his mind. But there was something else. Something he had dreamed. And it troubled him. There was a seed of doubt in him, and he didn't know where it was coming from.

Once again he whispered a prayer for her and her little boy, then mercifully fell back asleep until his alarm woke him in time to be ready to celebrate the eight o'clock Mass in the lower church.

■ ■ ■ ■

At almost half past ten, while Fr. Aiden was going through the mail on his desk, a call was put through to him. It was Alexandra Moreland. "Father," she said, "I'll have to make this quick. My attorney is going to be here in a minute to go with me to the police station. The detectives on Matthew's case want to talk to me. For all I know, I'm going to be arrested. I apologize for being so rude to you last night, and thank you for praying for Matthew. And I want you to know this: I was as close as you can get to swallowing a bottle of sleeping pills early this morning, and something about the kind way you looked at me and then took my hands in yours stopped me. Anyhow, I won't think of that again. I had to say thank you and please keep praying for Matthew, but if you don't mind, say a word for me as well."

Then there was a click in his ear. Stunned, Fr. Aiden sat quietly at his desk. That's what I've been trying to remember, the feel of her hands when I held them, he thought.

But what is it?

What could it possibly be?

40

After the cozy dinner she had shared with her friend Rebecca, and the fact that they both had enjoyed several glasses of wine, Penny had slept soundly through the night and even allowed herself the luxury of bringing her morning cup of coffee back to bed. Propped up on pillows, she had watched the news on television. Once again the Central Park photos of Zan Moreland taking her child out of the stroller and the others of her being carried to the ambulance were briefly shown.

"Unless those photos are proven to be doctored, in my opinion, the arrest of Alexandra Moreland is imminent," the network's legal expert explained on the *Today* show.

"Should have happened yesterday!" Penny barked to the television screen. "What are they waiting for, a sign from heaven?" Shaking her head, she got out of bed a second time, put on a warm robe, and carried the coffee cup to the kitchen, where she began to prepare her usual generous breakfast.

Bernie phoned as she was running the last scrap of toast over the plate to catch the remnants of the yolk of her fried egg. His voice sounded disgruntled as he told her that it would be another couple of hours before the truck was fixed, so he wouldn't get home till midafternoon. "Hope you and Rebecca didn't eat all the pot roast," he told her.

"More than plenty for you," Penny assured him before saying good-bye. Men, she thought, shaking her head indulgently. He's upset because he's stuck in a gas station in King of Prussia, and he's trying to find a reason to get mad so he can have a fight with me and get it off his chest. I should have told him that Rebecca and I ate the whole thing and tonight we're having frozen pizza.

As she loaded the dishwasher, Penny saw that the mailman was delivering to their box at the end of the driveway. After his van disappeared, she tightened the belt on her robe and hurried outside. Spring may have just arrived, but boy you'd never know it, she thought, as she opened the box, closed her hand on the small pile of letters, and at an even quicker pace made her way back to the warmth of the house.

The first few envelopes were solicitations from various charities. The next contained a fingernail-sized sample of a new facial cream. The last envelope brought an unconscious smile to Penny's face. It was from Alvirah Meehan. Quickly she ripped it open. It was a notice that the semiannual meeting of the Lottery Winners' Support Group was being held the following week in Alvirah and Willy's apartment.

Alvirah had written a personal note on the notice. "Dear Penny, hope you and Bernie can make it. Always so good to be with you."

We can make it, Penny thought happily, as she mentally reviewed Bernie's schedule. I'd love to get her opinion on that Moreland woman now. I know Alvirah's been friendly with her.

The sense of pleasant anticipation wore off as Penny went upstairs, showered, and dressed. Something was gnawing at her and it had to do with that snippy Gloria Evans, who was renting the Owens farmhouse. It wasn't just the fact that Gloria Evans had been so rude when I gave her the blueberry muffins, and it wasn't just the toy truck on the floor, Penny decided. That woman was supposed to be finishing a book, but even writers who want privacy don't practically slam the door in a person's face, do they?

Penny was by nature thrifty. That was why another thing that Rebecca had told her about Gloria Evans — that Evans didn't bat an eye about paying for a year's lease when she only planned to stay for three months — seemed strange.

There's something going on with that lady, she decided. She wasn't just being rude. She was downright nervous when she answered the door. I wonder if she's doing something illegal, like selling drugs out of there? No one would know if someone came late at night and turned onto that dead-end road. Sy's is the only house on it.

I'd love to keep an eye on the place, she thought. The trouble is, if Gloria Evans happens to be at the window she'll see me driving past, then turning around and coming back. If she is up to anything, I'd be tipping her off.

As Penny, her lips pursed, applied bright red lipstick, her only tribute to glamour, she began to laugh, smearing the lipstick on her cheek. "Oh, for heaven's sake," she said aloud. "I know what's bugging me about that Evans bird. She reminds me of the Moreland woman. Isn't that a riot? Wait till I tell Alvirah that I was trying to hatch a mystery. She'll get a real laugh out of that!"

41

Charley Shore could not conceal his look of astonishment when Josh opened the door of Moreland Interiors and he saw the rolls of carpet stacked against the walls and covering the floor of half the office.

"It's a misunderstanding with one of our suppliers," Josh began to explain.

"No, it isn't," Zan corrected him. "Mr. Shore, or Charley, since we've agreed we're on a first-name basis, somebody is ordering materials on a contract that we don't have yet and has hacked into my bank account."

She really is out of it, Shore thought, but was careful not to show any reaction except concern. "When did you find out about this, Josh?"

"The first indication was the other day, when someone bought a first-class one-way ticket to South America in Zan's name for next week and charged it to our business account," Josh said, his tone carefully matter-of-fact. "Then there are bills for expensive clothes charged to Zan's store accounts. Now we're hearing from our suppliers about carpets and fabrics and wall hangings that we didn't order."

"Josh is trying to convey to you that he thinks I'm delusional and doesn't believe that there's a computer hacker at work," Zan said, calmly, "but there is, and that shouldn't be too hard to prove."

"How did the orders to the suppliers get placed?" Charley Shore asked.

"By phone, and — ," Josh began.

"Give Charley the letter, Josh," Zan interrupted.

Josh handed it to the attorney, who read it carefully. "This is your stationery," Charley Shore asked.

"Yes," Zan said.

"Is this your signature, Zan?"

"It looks like mine, but I didn't sign that letter. In fact, I'd like to take it to the police station with us. I believe that someone is impersonating me and trying to ruin my life and my business, and I think that person has taken my son."

Charles Robert Shore was an experienced criminal lawyer with an impressive list of verdicts that favored his clients to the point that he was a thorn in the side of many prosecutors. But now for a split second he regretted that his friendship with Alvirah Meehan had put him in the position of defending her clearly psychotic friend.

Choosing his words carefully, he asked, "Zan, have you reported this identity theft crime to the police?"

Josh answered for her. "No, we haven't. Too much has been going on in the past few days. You can understand that."

"I would agree," Charley said, quietly. "Zan, I don't want this problem to come into the conversation with Detectives Collins and Dean today. Can you promise me that you won't bring it up?"

"Why wouldn't I bring it up?" Zan demanded. "Can't you see? This is part of an ongoing scheme, and when we get to the bottom of it, we will know where Matthew is being kept."

"Zan, trust me. We must thoroughly discuss this before we decide if and when we tell the detectives." Charley Shore looked at his watch. "Zan, we'd better get going. I have a car waiting downstairs."

"The delivery entrance is my usual mode of entrance and exit," Zan told him. "There's always someone from the media hanging out around the front door."

Charley Shore studied his new client.

There was something different about her. When he delivered her to Alvirah last night, she'd been fragile in every way, pale, shivering, and broken in spirit.

Today, there was a resolute firmness in her. She was wearing light makeup that enhanced her beautiful hazel eyes and long lashes. The auburn hair that she had worn in a tight bun yesterday was flowing on her shoulders. Yesterday she had been wearing jeans and a fake-fur jacket. Today, her slender, fine-boned body was fashionably dressed in a dark gray pantsuit with a multicolored scarf draped around her neck.

Charley's wife, Lynn, dressed well. If he ever needed confirmation of that fact, he received it from the American Express bill he got every month. He considered her mild extravagance a small price to pay for the many times he missed a dinner party or was late for an event at Lincoln Center because he was preparing for an important trial. But if he had to choose, he much preferred the image of Zan Moreland as a victim than the one the media would see if they took pictures of her today.

There was absolutely nothing he could do about it. He reached for his cell phone and directed his driver to meet them at the back of the building.

The day was still unseasonably cold, but the sun was shining and the drifting white clouds held no hint of rain. Charley glanced up, hoping that the brightness of the day might be a good omen, but he had serious doubts that would be the case.

When they were in the car, choosing his words carefully, he said, "Zan, this is terribly important. You have got to follow my lead on anything I tell you to do. If Collins or Dean asks you a question and I tell you not to answer, that's the way it has to be. I understand that there will be times when you're burning to try to put them straight, but you must *not* do that."

Digging her nails into her palms, Zan tried not to show how frightened she was. She liked Charley Shore. He had been so kind, so fatherly at her bedside in the hospital yesterday, then in the cab when he escorted her to Alvirah's apartment. She also knew that he didn't doubt for one minute that she was the woman in the Central Park photos. And even though he tried not to show it, it was obvious he believed the letter to Wallington Fabrics with her signature was on the level as well.

One of her favorite books as a child had been *Alice in Wonderland*. Now the words "Off with her head, off with her head," ran through her mind. But Charley does want to help me, and the least I can do is trust his advice. I don't have any choice.

"Mommy . . . Mommy . . ." I heard Matthew's voice this morning, she reminded herself. I must keep holding on to the certainty that he is alive and that I will find him. It's the only way I can possibly keep going.

The cab was pulling up to the Central Park Precinct. There were people with television cameras and microphones at the entrance.

"Oh, hell," Charley Shore muttered. "Somebody tipped them off that you're expected here."

Zan bit her lip. "I'll be all right."

"Zan, remember, do *not* answer their questions. If they shove a mike in your face, ignore it."

The cab stopped and Zan followed Shore out of it. The reporters rushed to intercept them. Zan tried to close her eyes to the shouted questions, "Will you be making a statement, Ms. Moreland?" "Where is Matthew, Ms. Moreland?" "What did you do with him, Zan?" "Do you think he is still alive?"

As Charley Shore, his arm around her back, tried to propel her forward, she broke

251

away from him and turned around to the cameras. "My son is alive," she said, her voice steadily rising. "I believe I know who hates me enough to go to the level of kidnapping him. I tried to tell that to the police two years ago and they didn't listen, but I am going to make them listen now."

She turned and looked straight into Charley Shore's eyes. "Sorry," she said, "but it's about time somebody starts to listen to me and look for the truth."

42

Kevin Wilson's present home was a furnished sublet in TriBeCa, the area below Greenwich Village that at one time had been the location of grimy factories and printing presses. It was a roomy loft with an open area that included a kitchen with a well-equipped bar, a living room, and a library. The furniture was starkly modern, but the den beyond it was equipped with a roomy leather sofa and matching chairs with hassocks. His bedroom was comparatively small, but that was because the owner had moved the wall to accommodate a fully equipped gym. An oversized corner room served as his office. The large windows in every room guaranteed sunshine from dawn till dark.

Kevin was happy to sublease the loft and recently had put in a bid to buy it. He already was making plans for the architectural changes he would make, like leaving the exercise room only big enough to hold a few pieces of equipment, enlarging the master bedroom and bath, and turning the corner room into two other bedrooms with a shared larger bath.

As for the furnishings, he already was marking which ones he would keep and which would end up at Goodwill. His mother told him he was getting the nesting instinct. "You're the last one of your good friends to be single," she regularly reminded him. "It's about time you got over the casual dates and found a nice girl and settled down." Lately she had begun to expand on that. "By now all my friends are bragging about their grandchildren," she complained.

After having dinner with his mother, Kevin had gone straight home to bed. He slept soundly and in the morning awoke at his usual six A.M. Cereal, juice, and coffee with a quick glance at the front page of the *Wall Street Journal* and the *Post* was followed by an hour on the gym equipment. He watched the morning news, catching a segment of the *Today* show with some legal expert giving his opinion that the arrest of Alexandra Moreland was imminent.

My God, Kevin thought, is that really possible? He felt again the electrical reaction that he had experienced when their shoulders brushed. If those pictures in Central Park aren't doctored, then there is something wrong with her, he regretfully acknowledged.

As he showered and dressed, he could not get Zan's face out of his mind. Her eyes, so beautiful and expressive, had been so sad. It didn't take a Rhodes scholar to see the pain in them. Louise had made the initial call to Moreland Interiors inviting Zan to bid on the job for decorating the apartments. Oddly enough, in all the times she had come and gone, he had not run into her until the other day when she delivered her sketches and samples. She had brought them in herself. Bartley Longe, on the other hand, had been accompanied by his assistant walking behind him carrying his designs.

That's another reason I don't like that guy, Kevin thought. Longe's attitude was galling. "I look forward to working with you, Kevin," as though it were a done deal.

It was ten minutes of eight, and he was ready to go. Because he was planning to be at 701 Carlton Place all day, he had dressed casually in a sport shirt, sweater, and khakis. He took a quick glance in the mirror. It was about time to get a haircut, and he wanted to be sure that his hair was brushed down sufficiently.

When I was a kid, I had such curly hair that Mom used to say that I should have been a girl. Zan Moreland has long, straight hair, the dark auburn of a Japanese maple. I didn't know I was a *poet,* he thought, as he reached for a jacket and left the apartment.

If Louise Kirk did not come in at the stroke of nine, Kevin had to endure her usual indignant outburst about her belief that one day, all the traffic in New York will just stop dead. Today, though, she arrived fifteen minutes early.

Kevin had told her he surfed the channels during his workout.

"Kevin, did you by any chance catch the *Today* show when they were talking about Zan Moreland?" she asked eagerly.

I guess we're friends again, he thought. I'm back to being on a first-name basis with her.

"Yes, I did," he said.

Louise did not seem to notice his abrupt answer. "Everybody can see that unless those pictures were doctored, which I'd give ten years of my life to say that they're not, the poor girl is deranged."

"Louise, the 'poor girl,' as you describe Alexandra Moreland, is an extremely gifted interior designer and a very attractive human being. Could we withhold judgment and drop the subject?"

Kevin almost never played employer/employee with anyone in his office or on a job, but this time he did not try to hide his genuine anger.

When he was a child, at his mother's insistence, he had taken piano lessons. It had become painfully obvious to all three — his mother, his teacher, and himself — that he had absolutely no talent as a musician, but that had not diminished his pleasure in playing. There was one song that he had learned to play very well, "The Minstrel Boy."

Now a fragment of the words echoed through his head. *"Tho' all the world betrays thee . . . One sword, at least, thy rights shall guard . . . One faithful harp shall praise thee!"* Who did Zan Moreland have to praise or defend her? Kevin wondered.

Louise Kirk got the message. "Of course, Mr. Wilson," she answered, her voice subdued.

"Louise, will you knock off the 'Mr. Wilson' stuff? We're going to take a tour through this whole building. Bring your notebook. I've been seeing some sloppy work, and I have a number of people who are going to hear about it today."

At ten o'clock, as Kevin, trailed by Louise, was pointing out uneven grouting in three of the shower stalls in apartments on the thirtieth floor, his business cell phone rang. Not wanting to be interrupted, he gave the phone to Louise to answer.

She listened, then said, "I'm sorry, Mr. Wilson is not available but I'll give him your message." She disconnected and handed him back the phone. "That was Bartley Longe," she said. "He wants to invite you to have lunch with him today, or if that doesn't work, to have dinner this evening or tomorrow night. What shall I tell him?"

"Tell him to forget it for now." Longe's probably gloating that he has the job, he thought, and then reluctantly concluded that maybe he did. The model apartments needed to be finished. The consortium that owned the building was already grumbling about the cost overruns and the inevitable delays in construction. They wanted the apartments decorated so that the sales department could take over. Certainly if Zan Moreland was arrested, she wouldn't have any time to oversee the day-to-day progress. A decorator had to be on top of the job when any interior work was done.

At quarter of eleven, when he and Louise

were finally back in his office, one of the workmen came in to see him. "Which apartment do you want us to stack the fabrics and all that other stuff in, sir?"

"What do you mean, where do I want to put what stuff?" Kevin asked.

The workman, a leathery-faced man in his sixties, seemed bewildered by the question.

"I mean all the stuff that decorator ordered for the model apartments. It's starting to arrive."

Louise answered for Kevin. "Tell whoever is delivering anything for those model apartments to take it right back to where it came from. Not one single order has been authorized by Mr. Wilson."

Kevin did not believe what he heard himself saying. "Put any deliveries in the largest apartment." He looked squarely at Louise. "We'll sort this out," he said, "but if we don't accept whatever is coming, we'll be part of the sensational stories about Zan Moreland. Those suppliers will go screaming to the media. I don't want potential buyers to see this building in that kind of light."

Not daring to show what she was thinking, Louise Kirk nodded. You're attracted to that young lady, Kevin Wilson, she thought. *Fools rush in . . .*

43

Matthew had begun to be really scared of Glory. It had started yesterday when she yelled at him for forgetting his truck and leaving it where that lady saw it. He had run back into the closet and then she locked him in and then after a while she said she was sorry, but he couldn't stop crying. He wanted Mommy.

He kept trying to think about Mommy's face but it was like seeing shadows. But he could remember her wrapping him inside her bathrobe, and he could even remember when her long hair would tickle his nose and he would brush it away. If she was with him now, he wouldn't brush it away. He'd hold it so tight that he'd never let go even if it hurt her.

Later on, after Glory had put that smelly stuff in his hair, she gave him one of the muffins the lady brought. But afterward he felt sick and threw up. It wasn't the muffin.

He knew that. It was because some days when Mommy didn't go to work, she used to bake muffins with him. It was like the soap that he kept under his pillow. The muffins made him think of Mommy.

After that Glory had tried to be nice. She read a story to him, but even though she told him he was really smart and read grown-up words better than any kid his age, he hadn't felt any better. Then Glory told him to make up a story. He did make up one — that a little boy had lost his mother and knew he had to go out and find her. Glory didn't like that. He could tell that she was tired of taking care of him. He was tired, too, and went to sleep early.

After he had been asleep for a long time, he woke up when he heard a phone ring. Even though his door was only opened a little, he could hear some of what Glory was saying. He heard her talking about keeping this kid from his mother. Was he the kid she was talking about? Was it her fault he wasn't with Mommy? She had told him that Mommy wanted him to hide because bad people were going to steal him.

Was she lying to him?

44

When he left the police station at ten A.M., Ted Carpenter pushed through the assembled media, his eyes resolutely fixed on his waiting car. But when he reached it, he stopped and spoke into the microphone that had been thrust in front of him. "For nearly two years, despite her emotionally unstable personality, I have tried to believe that my ex-wife, Alexandra Moreland, was in no way responsible for my son's disappearance. Those pictures are absolute proof that I was wrong. I can only hope that she will now be forced to tell the truth and that by the grace of God Matthew is still alive."

As questions began to be thrown at him, he shook his head. "Please, no more." Tears glistening in his eyes, he got into the car and buried his face in his hands.

His driver, Larry Post, pulled away, then when they were clear of the police station, asked, "Will you be going home, Ted?"

"Yes, I will." I can't face going into the office, he thought. I can't face talking to people. I can't face trying to persuade Jaime-boy, that no talent, egocentric, crude jackass whose so-called reality show is making him millions, that he should sign up with me. What in the hell was I doing even going to dinner with that blood-sucker Melissa and her hangers-on the night of Matthew's birthday? My ex-wife is going to be grilled by the cops, and maybe she'll say or do something that will break this wide open.

Larry glanced in the rearview mirror and took in the haggard, strained expression on Ted's face. "Ted," he said, "I know it's none of my business, but you look as though you're getting sick. Maybe you should see a doctor."

"There's no medicine available to solve my problems," Ted said wearily. He leaned his head back and closed his eyes. His meeting with the detectives replayed itself, moment by moment, in his mind. The expression on both their faces had been inscrutable.

What's the matter with them? he asked himself. Why haven't they arrested Zan? Is there something wrong with those photos? And if so, why wouldn't they tell me? *I'm* the father. I have every right to know. Zan had always insisted that Bartley Longe hated her enough and was jealous enough of her success to do anything to hurt her. But did those cops honestly believe that a high-class interior designer would go to the extent of kidnapping and maybe even killing a child just to get back at a former employee? His head pounded at the notion.

Larry Post knew what was going through Ted Carpenter's mind. Ted was worried sick. It's really a crime that he ever met that Moreland woman who dumped him after he was so good to her and then didn't even want him when she started to get better, he thought, even though she was pregnant with his kid.

Larry's weathered skin and balding hair made him seem older than his thirty-eight years. His tightly muscled body was the result of rigorous daily exercise. That had started when he was twenty and serving a fifteen-year sentence for killing a drug dealer who had been trying to cheat him. When he got out he couldn't find a job anywhere in Milwaukee and phoned Ted, his closest friend in high school, begging for help. Ted had told him to come to New York. Now Ted called him his right-hand man. Larry cooked for him when Ted wanted a night home, chauffeured him everywhere, and did general maintenance in the building Ted had so foolishly bought three years ago.

Ted's cell phone rang. As he had expected, it was Melissa. When he answered, she said, "I didn't like the fact that you claim you were too sick to go to the Club with me the other night. I notice that you were able to be at the police station bright and early today."

Enraged, Ted waited a long moment, then forced a reasonable tone into his voice. "Melissa, sweetheart, I told you that the police needed to talk with me. I put them off yesterday and anyhow I didn't want you to catch any kind of bug I may be carrying. I still feel absolutely lousy and much as I want to meet Jaime-boy, I'm not up to it today. I've got to just get home and sit by the phone. My ex is meeting with the detectives in less than an hour. With any luck they'll arrest her and maybe get her to talk. I'm sure you can understand how I'm feeling right now."

"Forget Jaime-boy. He made up with his publicist. But don't worry. He'll break up with him again before the week is over. Listen, I've figured out a great way to get publicity. Call the media and tell them to be in your office for a three o'clock news release. I'll be with you, and I'll announce that I'm offering a five-million-dollar reward for anyone who finds your kid alive."

"Melissa, are you totally crazy?" Ted's raised voice made Larry Post look quickly into the rearview mirror.

"Don't you *dare* talk to me like that. I'm trying to *help* you." Melissa made no attempt to hide her fury at Ted's response. "Think about it. Suppose that Bartley Longe, that miserable snob who I hate — you know the remarks he made about my last album, when he told the paparazzi why he hadn't invited me to that big party he threw. . . . Anyhow, you told me your ex keeps saying Longe took your kid. Maybe he did."

"Melissa, think this through. You're on record as saying, not once but many times, that you believe that Matthew was molested and killed by a predator the same day he was abducted. Why would anyone believe you would change your mind now? That kind of offer will only look like a cheap publicity stunt and will hurt your career. They'll compare it with O. J. Simpson putting up a reward to find the person who killed his wife and her friend. Added to that, it will open the door to hundreds of people calling in claiming they saw a child who looks like Matthew. I put up a million-dollar reward myself when Matthew disappeared, and the police ended up wasting valuable time tracking down the bunch of lunatics who called."

"Look," Melissa insisted, "they've got those pictures of your ex taking the kid. Suppose she doesn't break down? Suppose the kid is alive somewhere and someone is minding him? Don't you think that person would jump at the chance to get five million bucks?"

"That same person would have a long time to wait in prison before being able to spend that money."

"That's not true. Look at that mob guy who killed a zillion people and didn't even go to jail because he helped the cops convict his buddies. Maybe there's more than one person in on it. Maybe one of them will confess and help the cops find your son. Then that person gets a good deal from the DA and a lot of money from me. Listen, Ted, I *like my* idea. Your kid is going to be in the headlines when your ex is arrested and for a long time after until she goes to trial. My sister's husband, no great shakes of a guy, is a public defender. God help the poor slobs he defends, but he does know law. You know how much money I make. If I had to pay the five million, I can afford it, and just the offer makes me look like a saint. Angelina Jolie and Oprah get all that publicity doing good for kids. Why not me? So be at your office at three o'clock and have a statement for us to give them."

Without any good-bye, Melissa's phone went dead.

Ted leaned his head back against the seat and closed his eyes. *Think,* he told himself. *Think.* Get control of yourself. Consider the consequences if she goes ahead with this. If I could only afford to quit right now. If I could only afford to kiss her good-bye. If only I didn't have to put up with her moods and tantrums and outbursts and have to cover her backside when she makes a fool of herself . . .

He touched the REDIAL button on his cell phone. As he expected, Melissa did not answer. "Leave a message" was the response he heard. At the signal he took a deep breath. "Baby," he began, his tone wheedling, "you know how much I love you and how every minute of my life is dedicated to building you up to be the number one star that you deserve to be. But I also want the public to know the sweet and generous side of you. I can't begin to thank you for this breathtaking offer, but as your lover, your best friend, your publicist, I want you to think about making this offer in a different way."

A beep told him that his allotted time to leave a message was up. Gritting his teeth, Ted pressed REDIAL again. "Sweetheart, I have an idea that will have a long-lasting effect. We'll call a press conference tomorrow or whenever you want to arrange the meeting. At it, you announce that you are donating five million dollars immediately to the Foundation for Missing Children. Every parent of a missing child will love you and that way you won't have to respond to the sleazes who will try to turn your generosity into something it isn't. Think about it, darling. And call me."

Ted Carpenter turned off his cell phone and managed to wait until he reached home before he went into the bathroom and became violently sick to his stomach. Minutes later, chilled and shaking, he went into the bedroom and picked up the phone.

Rita Moran answered, her voice motherly and concerned. "Ted, I saw you on the breaking news on the Internet. You look terrible. How are you doing now?"

"Just as bad as I look. I'm going to bed. No calls at all unless . . ."

Rita finished the sentence for him. "Unless the witch dials from her broom."

"She won't for a while. Some common-sense advice I gave her may be filtering into her brain as we speak."

"How about your appointment with that Jaime-boy nut?"

"It's been canceled, or maybe just postponed." He knew that Rita understood the financial ramifications of losing that potential client.

"Maybe it's just been postponed."

Ted caught the false hardiness in her tone. She was the only one of his employees who knew the degree to which the purchase of the building had been a big drain and a horrible mistake. "Who knows?" he asked. "I'll talk to you later. Zan is being questioned by the detectives right now. If Collins or Dean happens to call, tell them they can reach me here."

Stripping off his clothes to his underwear, he got into bed and pulled the covers around him until only the top of his head was showing.

For the next four hours, he dozed intermittently.

Then at three o'clock, his phone rang again.

It was Detective Collins.

45

Zan remembered keenly the kindness with which Detectives Billy Collins and Jennifer Dean had treated her when Matthew disappeared. That day, after Ted's outburst about leaving Matthew with a young babysitter, they had even said to her, "At times like these, some people have to handle tragedy by blaming it on someone. Try to understand that."

She knew they had then interviewed Nina Aldrich, who had verified their appointment that day. When Tiffany Shields had finally calmed down, she had told the detectives that the new nanny had not shown up, and that Zan had called her at the last minute and begged her to watch Matthew because she had an important client she could not risk losing.

Zan had told them that the only person who she felt honestly hated her was Bartley Longe, but even then she had realized that they were dismissing him as a possibility.

They had tried to suggest that Ted's outburst about hiring an inexperienced babysitter might suggest some underlying hostility, a scenario Zan had dismissed. She had told them that Ted had approved both Matthew's first nanny and the new one she had hired just before Matthew disappeared.

The photos. Of course they had to be doctored! With her newfound strength in the sure knowledge that she had heard Matthew's voice early that morning, Zan, with Charley Shore guiding her arm, followed Detectives Collins and Dean into the room where they would be questioning her.

They all took seats, Charley Shore next to her, Billy Collins and Jennifer Dean across from them. In the weeks immediately following Matthew's disappearance, Zan realized she had originally seen the detectives only in a blur. This time she studied them carefully. They were both in their early forties. Billy Collins had the kind of face that blended into the crowd. He had no distinguishing features. His eyes were narrowly set, his ears a little too large for his long, thin face. His eyebrows shaggy. His manner low-key. He looked slightly rumpled, as though he hadn't taken the time to straighten his tie. When they were settled in the seats, Billy solicitously asked if they would like to have coffee or water.

On the other hand, Jennifer Dean, his attractive African-American partner, immediately made Zan feel uncomfortable today. There was a crisp, no-nonsense air about her now. Zan remembered the warmth of her touch when Zan almost fainted shortly after she arrived in Central Park that day. Jennifer had been the one who rushed forward and grabbed her before she fell. Today she was wearing a dark green suit with a white turtleneck sweater. Her only jewelry was a wide gold wedding band and small gold earrings. Streaks of gray were untouched in her midnight black hair. Unsmiling, she looked appraisingly into Zan's face as though she were seeing her for the first time.

Zan had shaken her head at the offer of coffee, but the unexpected change in Dean's attitude startled her. "Maybe I will have that coffee," she said.

"Sure thing," Collins said. "Anything in it?"

"Nothing, thanks," Zan said.

"I'll be back in a minute."

It was a long minute. Detective Dean made no attempt to start a conversation.

In a casual gesture, Charley Shore gently

placed his arm over the back of Zan's chair, a reassuring move that signaled to her he was there to protect her.

But protect her from what?

Billy Collins was back with a paper cup filled with coffee that was little more than tepid. "Starbucks it's not," he commented.

Zan nodded her thanks as Collins took his seat and handed her the enlarged photographs of a woman taking the sleeping Matthew from his stroller in Central Park. "Ms. Moreland, is that you in these pictures?"

"No, it isn't," Zan said firmly. "It may look like me, but it isn't me."

"Ms. Moreland, is this your picture?" He held up another one.

Zan glanced at it. "Yes, that must have been taken right after I got to Central Park after you called me and said that Matthew was missing."

"Can you see any difference in the women in these pictures?"

"Yes. The woman taking Matthew out of the stroller is an imposter. The one of me arriving in the park after he was kidnapped is genuine. You certainly must know that by now. I was with a client, Nina Aldrich. I know you checked that out immediately."

"You did not tell us that instead of meeting Mrs. Aldrich at her Beekman Place home where she waited for you for well over an hour, you were in her town house on East Sixty-ninth Street alone for all that time," Jennifer Dean said, her tone accusing.

"I was there because she told me to meet her there. I was not surprised she was late. Nina Aldrich was chronically late for our appointments whether they were in the town house she was decorating or the apartment where she still lived."

"The town house is minutes from the spot in Central Park from which Matthew disappeared, isn't it, Ms. Moreland?" Billy Collins asked.

"I would guess it's about a fifteen-minute walk. When I got the call from you, I ran all the way."

"Ms. Moreland, Mrs. Aldrich is very sure that she told you to meet her on Beekman Place," Detective Dean said.

"That's not true. She told me to meet her at the town house," Zan said heatedly.

"Ms. Moreland, we're not trying to attack you," Collins said, his voice soothing. "You say Mrs. Aldrich was chronically late for appointments."

"Yes, she was."

"Do you know if she has a cell phone?" Collins asked.

"She has a cell phone, of course she does," Zan answered.

"Do you have the number of her cell phone?" As he spoke, Billy Collins took a sip of his own coffee and made a face. "Even worse than usual," he commented amiably.

Zan realized she was still holding the cup in her hand and took another sip of it. What had Collins just asked her? Of course. He asked me if I had Nina Aldrich's cell phone number. "Her number is in my phone," she said.

"How long since you've spoken to Mrs. Aldrich?" Dean asked, her voice steely.

"Almost two years. She wrote me a note about Matthew and said she knew that it would be far too much responsibility for me to take on such a major project as decorating her large home, meaning, of course, she was afraid to take a chance on me concentrating on the job."

"Who got the job of decorating her town house?" Collins asked.

"Bartley Longe."

"Isn't he the person you claim might be responsible for kidnapping Matthew?"

"He is the only person I know who thoroughly hates me and is jealous of me."

"Where are we going with these questions?" Charley Shore asked as he applied

276

slight pressure to Zan's shoulder.

"We're simply asking if Ms. Moreland was frequently in touch with Mrs. Aldrich at the time she was bidding for the job of decorating her town house."

"Of course I was," Zan broke in.

Again she felt the light pressure of Charley's hand on her shoulder.

"Were you friendly with Mrs. Aldrich?" Dean asked.

"In a client-relationship kind of way, I guess you'd call it. She liked my vision for how I saw the town house should be decorated to best show off, or rather emphasize, some of the architectural features that exist in those wonderful late nineteenth-century homes."

"How many rooms are in that town house?" Jennifer Dean asked.

I can't imagine why they're so interested in the layout of that place, Zan thought as she mentally retraced the rooms in the Aldrich home. "It's very large," she said. "Forty feet wide, which I assure you is unusual. There are five stories. The top floor is an enclosed roof garden. There are eleven rooms as well as the wine cellar, and a second kitchen and storage room in the basement."

"I see. So you went there to meet Nina

Aldrich. Were you surprised she didn't show up?" Collins asked.

"Surprised? No, not really. She was always late. The one time she wasn't and I was five minutes late, she let me know how important her time was and that she wasn't in the habit of being kept waiting."

"Didn't the fact that the babysitter minding Matthew had a cold and didn't feel well make you anxious enough to pick up your cell phone and call her?" Dean asked.

"No." Zan felt as though she were in a morass where everything she said made her sound as though she were lying. "Nina Aldrich would have resented my reminding her that she was late."

"How often did she keep you waiting as long as an hour or more?" Dean asked.

"That was by far the longest."

"Wouldn't it have been reasonable to phone and ask if you had been mistaken about the time and place of your meeting?"

"I knew the time and place she had told me. You don't remind the Nina Aldriches of this world that they may have made a mistake."

"So you stood or sat there for an hour or more before she finally called you?"

"I was going over my sketches and the pictures of antique furniture and chandeliers and sconces that I was planning to show her. In a few cases, I was choosing between several selections as my top recommendations. The time went quickly."

"I understand there was almost no furniture in the town house," Collins commented.

"A card table and two folding chairs," Zan answered.

"So you sat at the card table for more than an hour going over your sketches?"

"No. I went up to the master bedroom on the third floor. I wanted to check once more and see how the patterns I had chosen worked in the strong sunlight. Remember the day was unusually warm and sunny."

"Would you have heard Mrs. Aldrich if she had come in while you were on the third floor?" Jennifer Dean asked.

"She would have seen my portfolio and sketches as soon as she walked through the door," Zan said.

"You had your own key to the town house, Ms. Moreland?"

"Of course. I was submitting plans to decorate the entire house from top to bottom. I went back and forth regularly for weeks."

"You got to know the house pretty well, then, didn't you?"

"I would think that's obvious," Zan snapped.

"Including the basement with its second kitchen, wine cellar, and storage room. Were you planning to decorate the storage room?"

"That space was large and dark and virtually inaccessible. It was really a kind of sub-cellar reached by a door at the back of the wine cellar. There were plenty of other storage areas in closets throughout the house. I suggested painting the room, putting in good lighting, and building shelves to accommodate items like skis for Mrs. Aldrich's step-grandchildren."

"It would have made a pretty good hiding place if someone wanted to hide something — or someone — wouldn't it?" Jennifer Dean asked.

"Don't answer that question, Zan," Charley Shore ordered.

Billy Collins did not look disturbed. "Ms. Moreland, when did you give Mrs. Aldrich her key back?"

"It was about two weeks after Matthew disappeared. That was when she wrote the note saying that she thought the stress of Matthew's disappearance would be too much for me to handle the job."

"In those two weeks, did you still think you had the job?"

"Yes, I did."

"Could you have handled it, given the fact that your son was missing?"

"Yes, I could have handled it. In fact, concentrating on it was the only way I thought I could preserve my sanity."

"Then you went back and forth often to that empty house after your son disappeared?"

"Yes."

"Did you go there to visit Matthew?"

Zan jumped up from the chair. "Are you crazy?" she demanded. "Are you trying to tell me that you think I kidnapped my own child and hid him in that storage room?"

"Zan, sit down," Charley Shore said firmly.

"Ms. Moreland, as you have said several times, that is a large town house. Why would you suggest that we think you hid Matthew in the storage room?"

"Because you *are* suggesting it," Zan cried. "You are insinuating that I stole my own child, brought him back to that house, and hid him there. Why are you wasting your time? Why aren't you finding out who doctored those photos to make them look as though I'm taking Matthew from the stroller? Don't you understand that's the key to finding my son?"

Detective Dean shot back at her, "Ms. Moreland, our tech people have gone over the photographs very carefully. They are not 'doctored,' as you put it. These photos have not been altered."

Try as she would, Zan could not hold back the sobs that racked her shoulders. "Then someone is impersonating me. Why is this happening?" she cried. "Why don't you listen to me? Bartley Longe hates me. From the minute I opened my own firm, I took business from him. And he's a womanizer. He used to come on to me when I worked for him. He's the worst kind of sleaze. He can't stand to be rejected. That was another reason to hate me."

Neither Collins nor Dean showed any emotion. Then when Zan, her tearstained face buried in her hands, managed to stifle her anguished reaction to the relentless questions, Jennifer Dean said, "Ms. Moreland, this is a new twist on your story. You never once referred to Bartley Longe as having come on to you sexually."

"I didn't because I didn't think it was that important at the time. It was only a part of the pattern."

"Zan, how often did you suffer fainting spells and memory lapses after your parents died?" Collins asked. Now his voice was concerned and kindly.

Zan tried to brush away tears, realizing that he, at least, was not openly antagonistic to her. "Everything was a blur for those six months," she said. "Then I started to be able to think clearly and realized I had been so unfair to Ted. He was putting up with my crying spells and my spending days in bed and he was giving up evenings to be with me when he should have been out at clients' events and openings, and endless awards events. When you run a public relations firm, you just can't neglect that."

"Did you tell him you were leaving as soon as you decided?"

"I knew he would be too worried about me and try to talk me out of it. I looked around and found a small apartment. My mother and father had insurance policies, no fortune, fifty thousand dollars in all, but it gave me a safety net to get started. And I took out a small loan."

"What was your husband's reaction when you finally told him you were leaving and wanted a divorce?"

"He had to go to California for the premiere of Marisa Young's new movie. He was planning to get a nurse to stay with me. That was when I told him that I was eternally grateful to him, but I couldn't be a burden to him any longer, that our marriage was a total act of kindness on his part, but now I knew I could go it alone and give him his life back. I told him I had decided to move out. He was kind enough to get me settled."

At least they're not accusing me when they ask me about Ted, she thought.

"At what point did you realize you were pregnant with Matthew?"

"I didn't have a period for several months after my parents died. The doctor told me that wasn't unusual in cases of extreme stress. Then my periods were irregular. So it was a few months after I left Ted before I realized that I was expecting Matthew."

"What was your reaction to finding out you were pregnant?" Dean asked.

"Shocked, then very happy."

"Even though you had taken out a bank loan to start your own business?" Collins asked.

"I knew it would be hard, but that didn't bother me. Of course I told Ted, but I told him that he should not feel any financial responsibility."

"Why not? He was the father, wasn't he?"

"Of course he was," Zan said heatedly.

"And he has a very successful public relations firm," Dean pointed out. "Weren't you as much as telling him that you wanted no part of him having anything to do with your child?"

"*Our* child," Zan said. "Ted insisted that until I got my business going that he would pay for the nanny I would need to hire, and that if I didn't need his financial help, he would put the money he would normally pay for support into a trust fund for Matthew."

"You paint a rosy picture, Ms. Moreland," Jennifer Dean observed sarcastically. "Wasn't it a fact that Matthew's father was concerned over the amount of time you left Matthew with the nanny? In fact, didn't he indicate that he was willing to take over full custody of Matthew when you became more and more involved in your business?"

"That's a lie," Zan shouted. "Matthew was my life. In the beginning I only had a part-time secretary and unless I had a client in the office or was outside on appointments, Gretchen, the nanny, would bring Matthew to the office on her way to and from the park. Look at my appointment books from the time he was born till he disappeared. I was home almost every night with him. I didn't want to be out. I loved him so much."

"You *loved* him so much," Dean snapped. "Then you do think he is dead."

"He is not dead. He called out to me this morning."

The detectives could not conceal their astonishment. "He called out to you this morning?" Billy Collins demanded.

"I mean, early this morning, I heard his voice."

"Zan, we're leaving now," Charley Shore said, himself clearly rattled. "This inquisition is over."

"No. I'm going to explain. Fr. Aiden was so kind when I met him last night. I know that even Alvirah and Willy don't believe that I'm not the one in those photos in Central Park. But Fr. Aiden gave me a sense of peace that stayed with me all night. Then just as I was waking up this morning, I heard Matthew's voice as clearly as though he were in the room and I knew he was still alive."

This time, when Zan stood up, she pushed back the chair so quickly that it toppled over. "He is alive," she shouted. "Why are you torturing me? Why aren't you searching for my little boy? Why won't you believe me that those photos are not of me? You think I'm crazy. You're the ones who are blind and stupid." Her voice now hysterical, she screamed, " 'There are none so blind as those who will not see.' In case you don't know, that's a quote from Jeremiah in the Bible. Two years ago, when the pair of you wouldn't listen to me about Bartley Longe, I looked it up."

Zan turned to Charley Shore. "Am I under arrest?" she demanded. "If not, let's get the hell out of here now."

46

Alvirah had called Zan's office and learned from Josh that Charley Shore had taken Zan to the police station for questioning. And then Josh told her about the one-way ticket to Buenos Aires and the orders Zan had placed with their suppliers.

With a heavy heart, Alvirah filled Willy in on that conversation when he returned from his morning walk in Central Park. "Oh, Willy, I feel so helpless," she sighed. "There's no mistake about those pictures. Now Zan has bought herself a one-way ticket to Buenos Aires and is ordering stuff for a job she doesn't even have."

"Maybe she thinks they're closing in on her, and is planning to run away," Willy suggested. "Listen, Alvirah, if she *did* take Matthew out of the stroller, maybe he's in South America with a friend. Didn't Zan tell you that she speaks a couple of languages, including Spanish?"

"Yes. She moved around with her parents a lot when she was growing up. But oh, Willy, that's as much as saying that Zan is a schemer. I don't think that's true. I think the problem is that she has lapses of memory, or is a split personality. I've read a lot about people like that. One personality simply has no idea of what the other one is doing. Remember that book *The Three Faces of Eve?* That woman was three different people and one didn't know about the other. Maybe Zan, in another persona, took Matthew from the stroller. Maybe she did give him to a friend who took him to South America and in that persona is planning to join him."

"This split personality stuff sounds like hocus-pocus to me, honey," Willy said. "I'd do anything for Zan, but I honestly think she's mentally ill. I just hope that when she was irrational, she didn't do anything to that little kid."

While Willy was out on his morning walk, Alvirah had been cleaning the apartment. Even though they had put most of the lottery money they'd won in triple-A bonds and solid stocks so that they had a nice dividend income, she had never been able to bring herself to hire a cleaning woman. Or at least, when she did try one at Willy's urging, she had immediately realized that she was three times as fast and ten times as thorough as the person they hired to come in once a week.

Now their three-room apartment over-looking Central Park South was sparkling, and the sun that had finally broken through was cheerfully reflected in the shiny surface of the glass-topped coffee table and the mirror on the back wall that reflected the park. Vacuuming and dusting and mopping up the kitchen had helped calm Alvirah, and while she was working she had put on her "thinking cap," as she called the imaginary head covering that helped her find solutions to problems.

It was almost eleven. She turned on the television to the news station just in time to see Zan get out of a car and Charley Shore try to rush her past the media. When Zan stopped and began to speak into the micro-phone, she could see the dismay on Char-ley's face. "Oh, Willy," Alvirah sighed. "Anyone listening to Zan now would be sure that she knows exactly where Matthew is. She sounds so positive that he's alive."

Willy had settled in his club chair with the morning papers, but looked up at the sound of Zan's voice. "She sounds so posi-tive because she knows where that kid is, honey," he said emphatically. "I have to say that judging from her performance when Charley brought her here last night, she's one hell of an actress."

"How was she when you took her home in the car?"

Willy ran his fingers through his thick mane of white hair and frowned in concentration. "Just the way she was here, like a wounded doe. She said we've become her best friends and she doesn't know what she'd do without us."

"Then if she's hidden Matthew somewhere, she doesn't know it herself," Alvirah said positively as she pushed the remote to turn off the television. "I'd be interested to know what impression Fr. Aiden had of Zan. When he said he'd pray for her, I heard what she said to him, to pray for Matthew but that God had forgotten she existed. That almost broke my heart. I just wanted to put my arms around her and hug her."

"Alvirah, I think that dollars to donuts, Zan is going to be arrested," Willy said. "You might as well be prepared for that."

"Oh, Willy, that would be awful. Would they let her out on bail?"

"I don't know. They sure won't like the fact that she bought a one-way ticket to South America. That could be reason enough to keep her locked up."

The telephone rang. It was Penny Hammel calling to say that she and Bernie would be thrilled to join the Lottery Winners' Support Group meeting on Tuesday afternoon.

With her worry about Zan, Alvirah had wished that she had waited to call a Support Group meeting, but the sound of Penny's cheerful voice lifted her spirits. She knew that she and Penny were kindred spirits in a lot of ways. They both wore size fourteen. They both had a good sense of humor. They both had preserved their lottery windfall. They both were happily married. Of course, Penny had three children and six grandchildren and Alvirah had never been blessed with a child. However, she considered herself a surrogate mother to Willy's nephew, Brian, and surrogate grandmother to Brian's kids. Besides that, she had never wasted time wishing her life away for something she could do nothing to change.

"Solved any crimes lately, Alvirah?" Penny asked.

"Not a one," Alvirah admitted.

"Have you been watching television and seeing that Zan Moreland kidnapped her own kid? I've been glued to the set."

Alvirah did not intend to get into a discussion with the loquacious Penny about Zan Moreland, nor admit she knew her well. "It's a pretty sad case," she said, carefully.

"I'd say so," Penny agreed. "But I've got a funny story to tell you when I see you next week. I thought I was on my way to uncovering a drug deal or something sinister like that, and then I realized that I was getting excited about nothing. Oh well, I guess I'll never write a book about solving crimes like you did. Did I ever tell you that I thought the title *From Pots to Plots* was downright inspired?"

Every time I see you, you tell me that, Alvirah thought indulgently, but said, "I'm pretty happy about the title myself. I think it's catchy."

"Anyhow, maybe you'll get a laugh when you hear about the crime that didn't happen. My best friend in town is Rebecca Schwartz. She's a real estate agent."

Alvirah knew it was impossible to cut off Penny without seeming abrupt. Carrying the phone, she walked across the living room to the club chair where Willy was now attempting to solve the daily puzzle and tapped him on the shoulder.

When he looked up, she mouthed the name "Penny Hammel."

Willy nodded, went to the front door of

the apartment, and stepped out into the hall.

"Anyhow, Rebecca rented a house near me to a young woman and I'll tell you why I thought there was something strange about her."

Willy rang the bell, keeping his finger on it long enough that Penny would be sure to hear it.

"Oh, Penny, I hate to interrupt but the doorbell is ringing and Willy isn't in the apartment. I can't wait to see you next Tuesday. Bye, dear."

"I hate to lie," Alvirah said to Willy. "But I'm too worried about Zan to listen to one of Penny's long stories, and it wasn't a lie to say you weren't in the apartment. You were outside in the hall."

"Alvirah," Willy smiled, "I've said it once and I'll say it again. You'd have made a great lawyer."

47

At eleven A.M. Toby Grissom checked out
of the Cheap and Cozy Motel where he had
spent the night on the Lower East Side and
started to walk to Forty-second Street
where he could get a bus to LaGuardia
Airport. His plane wasn't until five o'clock,
but he had to be out of his room and
anyhow he didn't want to stay in it any
longer.

The weather was cold, but the day was
clear and bright and it was the kind of day
on which Toby used to enjoy taking long
walks. Of course, it had been different since
he started getting the chemo treatments.
They really knocked the stuffing out of him
and now he wondered if there was any point
in taking them any longer if all they could
do was to keep him out of pain.

Maybe the doctor could just give me some
pills or something so I wouldn't have to be
so tired, he thought, as he trudged up

Avenue B. He glanced down at his canvas bag to reassure himself that he hadn't forgotten it. He had put the manila file with the pictures of Glory in it. They were the most recent ones she had sent him before she disappeared.

He always carried the postcard Glory had sent him six months ago folded in his wallet. It made him feel near to her, but ever since he came to New York, his sense that she was in trouble had gotten steadily worse.

That Bartley Longe guy was bad news. You could tell that in a minute. Sure, he wore clothes that any dope could tell were expensive, and he was good looking but in that narrow-nose, thin-lip kind of way. When he looked at you, it was like you were dirt under his feet.

Bartley Longe had work done on his face, Toby thought. Even a run-of-the-mill guy like me would know that. His hair is too long. Not like those rock stars with those wild mops that make them look like a bunch of bums, but still too long. Bet it cost him four hundred dollars to get a haircut. Like the kind of money those politicians pay to barbers.

Toby thought about Longe's hands. You'd never guess he ever did an honest day's work in his life.

Toby realized he was gasping for breath. He was walking close to the curb. Slowly, he worked his way through the stream of oncoming pedestrians, until he reached the nearest building and, leaning on it, dropped his bag and took out his inhaler.

After he used it, he took deep breaths to force more air into his lungs. Then he waited for a few minutes until he felt ready to resume walking. While he waited, he observed the passersby. All kinds of people in New York, he decided. More than half of them were talking on cell phones, even the ones who were pushing strollers. Yak. Yak. Yak. What the devil did they have to say to each other? A group of young women, maybe in their twenties, passed him. They were talking and laughing and Toby eyed them sadly. They were dressed nice. They all were wearing boots that went anywhere from their ankles to past their knees. How did they ever wear those crazy high heels? he asked himself. Some of them had short hair, others had hair down past their shoulders. But they all looked as if they'd just stepped out of the shower. They were so clean they glistened.

They all probably had pretty good jobs in stores or offices, he thought.

Toby resumed his walk. I can understand

now why Glory wanted to come to New York. I just wish she'd decided to get a job at an office, instead of trying to be an actress. I think that's what got her into trouble.

I know she's in trouble and it's the fault of that Longe guy.

Toby thought about how his sneakers had made a stain on the carpet in Longe's reception area. Hope they can't get it out, he thought as he dodged a homeless woman pushing a cart laden with clothes and old newspapers.

Longe's private office looks phony, too, Toby mused. Real formal. You'd think you were in Buckingham Palace, but not a paper on the desk. Where does he do all that fancy planning of those houses he decorates?

Deep in thought, Toby almost stepped from the curb after the light turned red. He had to jump back to avoid being sideswiped by a sightseeing bus. I better watch where I'm going, he told himself. I didn't come to New York to get splattered by a bus.

His thoughts immediately turned back to Bartley Longe. I wasn't born yesterday. I know why Longe snowed Glory into going up to his country home. That's the way he talked about his house in Connecticut. "His country home." Glory was a sweet, innocent girl when she came to New York. Longe didn't bring Glory up to Connecticut to play tiddlywinks. He took advantage of her.

If only Glory had married Rudy Schell right out of high school. He was crazy about her. Rudy went to work when he was eighteen and has a big plumbing business now. Big home, too. He only got married last year. When I'd run into him, he always asked about Glory. I could tell he still really liked her.

Toby realized he was not that far from the 13th Precinct, where he'd met Detective Johnson yesterday. A thought struck him. That guy never asked to see Glory's postcard. She printed what she wrote on it, and I thought it was because the card was small and her handwriting was kind of big with all those loops. But suppose she never sent the card herself? Suppose someone figured that I'd be getting nervous about her and decided to put me off looking for her? Maybe that person knows that I'm on my way out.

I'm going to see that Detective Johnson again and sit at his desk that he says is such a privilege to have, Toby decided, and I'm going to ask him to check this postcard for fingerprints. Then I'm going to tell him that I want him to see Mr. Bartley Longe right now if he hasn't already. Does Detective Johnson think he's kidding me? All he's probably planning to do is to call up Longe and apologize for the inconvenience and then tell him that this old bird came in and he has to follow through. Then he'll ask him if he knew Glory, and what was the nature of their relationship. Longe will give him the same kind of bull he gave me about trying to help Glory's career and that he doesn't hear from her anymore. And Detective Johnson, sitting at his window desk, which doesn't have a view, will apologize for bothering Mr. Longe and that will be that.

If I miss the flight, I miss the flight, Toby thought as he turned down the block heading to the 13th Precinct. But I can't go home until that detective checks the fingerprints on that postcard and until he goes face-to-face with that creep Longe and pins him down about when he last saw Glory.

48

"Ms. Moreland, you are not under arrest, at least not at the present," Billy Collins told Zan as she started for the door. "But I would suggest you wait."

Zan looked at Charley Shore and he nodded. As she sat back down, to give herself time, Zan asked for a glass of water. While she waited for Collins to get it, she tried to steel herself against making another outburst. Charley had immediately put his arm over the back of her chair again and for a brief moment pressed his hand on her shoulder. But this time she did not find the gesture reassuring.

Why wasn't he objecting to their insinuations? she asked herself. No, they're not insinuations. They're accusations. What good is it to have a lawyer if he won't defend me against these people?

She turned her chair a little to the left to avoid having to look directly at Detective

Dean, then realized that Dean was looking down into a notebook that she had taken from her pocket.

Billy Collins returned with the glass of water and took his seat across the table from Zan. "Ms. Moreland —"

Zan interrupted him. "I would like to speak with my lawyer privately," she said.

Collins and Dean stood up immediately. "We'll get a cup of coffee," Collins told her. "Why don't we come back in fifteen minutes?"

The second the door closed, Zan yanked her chair to face Charley Shore directly. "Why are you letting them attack me with those accusations?" she demanded. "Why aren't you taking my part? You're just sitting there and patting my shoulder and letting them suggest that I kidnapped my child and brought him back to that town house and locked him in the storage room."

"Zan, I understand how you feel," Charley Shore said. "I have to do it this way. I need to know everything they'll be using to try to build a case against you. If they don't ask those questions, we won't be able to start building a defense."

"Do you think they're going to arrest me?"

"Zan, I'm sorry to tell you that I believe they will get a warrant for your arrest.

Maybe not today but definitely within the next few days. My concern is what charges they may bring against you. Obstruction of justice. Perjury. Depriving your ex of his parental rights. I don't know whether they'd go so far as to charge you with kidnapping since you're the mother, but they may. You just told them that Matthew spoke to you today."

"They knew what I meant."

"You *think* that they know what you meant. They may be deciding that you were on the phone with Matthew." Looking at Zan's stunned expression, Charley added, "Zan, we have to anticipate the worst-case scenario. And I need you to trust me."

They passed the next ten minutes in silence. When the detectives returned to the room, Collins asked, "Do you want more time?"

"No, we don't," Charley Shore answered.

"Then let's talk about Tiffany Shields, Ms. Moreland. How often did she babysit for Matthew?"

It was an unexpected question, but easy to answer. "Not that often, just sometimes. Her father is the superintendent of the apartment building where I lived when Matthew was born and until six months after he disappeared. His original nanny, Gretchen, was off on weekends, which was fine with me, because I liked to take care of Matthew myself. But after he was past the infant stage, if I did go out for the evening after he was in bed, Tiffany stayed with him."

"Did you like Tiffany?" Detective Dean asked.

"Of course I did. I thought she was a very intelligent, sweet girl and it was clear she loved Matthew. Sometimes on a weekend if I was taking him to the park, she'd come along to keep me company."

"Was your friendship so close that you gave her presents?" Collins asked.

"I wouldn't call them presents. Tiffany is pretty much my size, and sometimes when I was going through my closet and realized I had a jacket or scarf or blouse that I hadn't worn in a while and that I thought she'd like to have, I'd offer it to her."

"Did you consider her to be a careful babysitter?"

"I never would have left my child with her if I didn't think so. That is, of course, until that terrible day when she fell asleep in the park."

"You knew Tiffany had a cold, wasn't feeling well, and did not want to babysit that day," Detective Dean snapped. "Wasn't there anyone else you could have called to help you out?"

"No one who lives close enough to drop everything and rush over. Besides that, almost all of my friends are in the same business I'm in. They're working. You have to realize I was frantic. You just don't call someone like Nina Aldrich and break an appointment at the last minute. I had put untold hours into my sketches and designs for the town house and it wouldn't have been unlike her to dismiss me if I had made that call. I only wish to God I *had* made it."

Zan knew that even though she was trying to follow Charley Shore's instructions that he wanted to know where the detectives were going with their questions, it was impossible to conceal the nervous tremor in her voice. Why were they asking her all these questions about Tiffany Shields?

"So Tiffany reluctantly said she would help you out, and came to your apartment?" Detective Dean said, her tone level and without emotion.

"Yes."

"Where was Matthew?"

"He was asleep in the stroller. Because the weather was so warm overnight I had left his window open, and he woke up that morning at five o'clock from the racket the sanitation trucks were making. He usually sleeps until seven, but he didn't go back to sleep that morning and we got up and had breakfast very early. That was why I gave him an early lunch, and because Tiffany was coming to get him, I laid him down in the stroller and he was out like a light."

"What time would you say it was when you put him in the stroller?" Collins asked.

"I would say about noon. Right after I fed him."

"And what time did Tiffany come to your apartment?"

"Around 12:30."

"He was asleep when Tiffany came to get him, and he was still asleep when he was lifted out of the stroller approximately an hour and a half later." Now there was no mistaking the sneer in Jennifer Dean's voice. "But you didn't bother to strap him in, did you?"

"I had planned to fasten the strap when Tiffany came."

"But you didn't do it."

"I had covered Matthew with a light cotton blanket. I asked Tiffany to make sure the strap was fastened before we left the apartment."

"You were in too much of a rush to make sure your only child was secure in the stroller?"

306

Zan knew she was about to start screaming in frustration at the detective. *She's twisting everything I'm telling her,* she thought. But then she again felt the firm pressure of Charley Shore's hand on her shoulder and knew he was warning her. She looked straight into Dean's impassive face. "When Tiffany came up, it was obvious she didn't feel well. I told her that I had put an extra blanket at the foot of the stroller so that if she couldn't find a bench in a quiet place where Matthew could nap, she could spread it on the grass and sit on it."

"Didn't you also offer her a Pepsi?" Detective Collins asked.

"Yes, Tiffany said she was thirsty."

"What else was in the Pepsi?" Dean snapped.

"Nothing. What are you getting at?" Zan demanded.

"Did you give Tiffany Shields anything else? She believes you put something in that soda to make her pass out once she sat down on the grass in Central Park. And you gave her a sedative instead of a cold pill."

"You've got to be out of your minds," Zan shouted.

"No, we're not," Detective Dean said scornfully. "You portray yourself as being so kind, Ms. Moreland. Isn't it a fact that this child was getting in the way of your precious career? I've got kids. They're in high school now, but I remember the nightmare it was if they woke up too early and were cranky for the day. Your career was all that mattered to you, wasn't it? This unexpected little treasure from heaven was getting to be a pain in the butt, and you knew you had the ideal situation to take care of it."

Detective Dean stood up and pointed her finger at Zan. "You deliberately went to Nina Aldrich's town house when she was expecting you at her home on Beekman Place. You went to the town house with all your sketches and fabrics and left them there. Then you walked to the park knowing that it wouldn't be long before Tiffany passed out. You saw your chance and you got it. You grabbed your child and took him back to that nice big, empty town house and hid him in that storage space behind the wine cellar. The question is, what did you do to him, Ms. Moreland? What did you do to him?"

"I object!" Charley Shore shouted and pulled Zan up from her chair. "We're out of here now," he said. "Are you two through with us?"

Billy Collins smiled indulgently. "Yes, counselor. But we do want the names and addresses of the two people you mentioned, Alvirah and the priest. And let me offer a suggestion. Maybe if Ms. Moreland hears her son's voice again real soon, she can tell him — and whoever is hiding him — that it's time for him to come home."

49

The real estate business in Middletown, as in most of the country, had been miserable for months. Rebecca Schwartz's thoughts were glum as she sat in her office and stared out at the street. The windows were filled with taped pictures of houses for sale. A number of the pictures had the word SOLD slashed across the front, but some of them were of houses that had been sold five years ago.

Rebecca was a master at describing available housing. The smallest, dingiest Cape Cod was depicted in the flyers she tacked up around town, as "cozy, intimate, and utterly charming."

Once she got prospective buyers to take a look at that kind of house, she painted a verbal picture of how special it would be when a talented homemaker brought out its latent beauty.

But even with her spectacular ability to

bring out the hidden virtues of a house that needed a lot of work, Rebecca was experiencing tough sledding. Now, as she anticipated another fruitless day, she reminded herself that she was a lot better off than most of the people in this country. Unlike other fifty-nine-year-olds who were having a lean time, she could afford to keep going until the economy improved. An only child, her parents deceased, she had inherited from them the split level that had been her home all her life and the income from the two rental properties they owned on Main Street.

It isn't just about the money, she thought. I like to sell houses. I like to see people's excitement the day they move in. Even if the house needs a lot of work, it's a new chapter in their lives. I always bring over a present for the new owners on moving day. A bottle of wine, and cheese and crackers, unless I know they're teetotalers. In that case I bring a box of Lipton tea bags and a crumb cake.

Her part-time secretary, Janie, wasn't due in until twelve. The other agent, Millie Wright, who worked with her on a commission-only basis, had had to give up and take a job in the A&P. As soon as the market picked up, she had promised Rebecca that she'd be back.

So lost was Rebecca in her thoughts that she jumped when the phone rang. "Schwartz Real Estate, Rebecca speaking," she said, keeping her fingers crossed that this was a potential buyer, not just someone else wanting to sell their house.

"Rebecca, this is Bill Reese."

Bill Reese, Rebecca thought, and then felt a surge of hope. Bill Reese had come back twice last year to look at the Owens farm, then decided against buying it.

"Bill, it's good to hear from you," she said.

"Did that Owens place ever sell?" Reese asked.

"No, not yet." Rebecca switched immediately into real estate jargon. "We have several people very interested in it, and one of them seems to be ready to make an offer."

Reese laughed. "Come on, Rebecca. You don't have to try to snow me. On your honor as a girl scout, how many potential buyers are ready to be reined in at this minute?"

Rebecca pictured Bill Reese as she laughed with him. He was a smart, pleasant, heavyset guy in his late thirties with a couple of young kids. An accountant, he lived and worked in Manhattan, but he had been raised on a farm and last year had told her that he missed that kind of life "I like to grow things," he'd said. "And I'd like my kids on weekends to be able to have the fun of being around horses, the way I did."

"There aren't any offers on Sy's farm," she admitted, "but I'm telling you this right now, and this isn't the usual sales pitch: that is a beautiful piece of property, and when you get rid of all those heavy shades and tired furniture and do some painting and update the kitchen, you'll have a lovely, roomy house that you'll be proud to own. This bad market isn't going to last forever, and somebody is going to come along sooner or later and realize that twenty acres of prime property with a basically sound house is a good investment."

"Rebecca, I tend to agree with you. And Theresa and the kids fell in love with it. Do you think Sy will budge on the price?"

"Do you think an alligator will start singing love songs?"

"All right. I get you," Bill Reese laughed. "Look, we'll take a ride up on Sunday and if it's what we all think we remember, we'll go into contract."

"We have a tenant there now," Rebecca said, "it's a year's lease and she paid it all in advance, but that doesn't matter. In the contract, it clearly says that with one day's notice, we can show the place to a potential buyer, and if the place is sold, the tenant has to be out within thirty days. Of course, her money will be refunded on a per diem basis. But it won't be a problem. Even though this woman has a year's lease, she told me she only planned to stay for three months."

"That's fine," Reese said. "If we decide to buy it, I want to take over by the first of May so I can do some planting. How's this Sunday around one o'clock in your office?"

"It's a date," Rebecca said happily. But when she hung up, some of the exhilaration faded. She did not relish the thought of phoning Gloria Evans to tell her she may have to move. On the other hand, Rebecca reassured herself, the contract was clear and Gloria Evans would have thirty days' notice to get out. I can show her some other places, Rebecca thought, and I'm sure I can find one that will rent on a month-to-month basis. She said she only needed three months to finish her book. This way I can point out that she'll be refunded for the whole time she doesn't use Sy's place.

Gloria Evans answered on the first ring. Her voice sounded annoyed when she said, "Hello."

I've got good news and bad news, Rebecca thought, as she drew in her breath and began to explain the new development.

"*This* Sunday? You want people marching through here this Sunday?" Gloria Evans demanded.

Rebecca caught the unmistakable anxiety in her voice. "Ms. Evans, I can show you at least half a dozen very nice houses that are more up to-date, and you can save a lot of money by going on a month-to-month basis."

"What time are those people coming on Sunday?" Gloria Evans asked.

"Sometime after one o'clock."

"I see. When I was willing to pay a year's lease for only the three months I plan to use this house, you could have pointed out that you might have people trooping in and out of here."

"Ms. Evans, it was clearly there in the lease you signed."

"I asked about that. You told me that I didn't have to worry about anyone coming near it for the three months I planned to be here. You said the market would be dead until at least early June."

"I honestly thought that. But Sy Owens would not have allowed you to rent the house without that provision in the lease."

315

Rebecca realized she was talking to herself. Gloria Evans had clicked off. Too bad about her, she thought as she picked up the phone to give Sy the good news that she might have a sale on the house.

His reaction was exactly what she had expected. "You made it clear that I'm not budging five cents off the price, didn't you, Rebecca?" he asked.

"Of course that's what I told him," she replied, silently adding, you old skinflint.

50

Detective Wally Johnson looked at the tattered postcard Toby Grissom had handed him. "Why do you think your daughter didn't write this card?" he asked.

"I don't say she didn't write it. Like I told you, I've started to think that because it was printed, maybe she didn't, maybe somebody did something to her and then tried to make it look like she's still alive. Now, Glory has big, fancy handwriting, with lots of loops, if you know what I mean, and that's why it didn't occur to me till now that maybe she hadn't sent this card at all."

"You said you received this six months ago," Johnson said.

"Yeah. That's right. And you never asked, but I thought maybe you should check it for fingerprints."

"How many people have handled this card, Mr. Grissom?"

"Handled it? I don't know. I showed it to

some of my friends in Texas, and I showed it to the girls Glory used to room with here in New York."

"Mr. Grissom, of course we'll check it for fingerprints, but I can tell you right now that whether your daughter sent it or somebody else did, we'll never be able to get prints off it. Think about it. You've shown it around to your friends and to Glory's roommates. Before that a number of postal clerks and your mailman handled it. Too many people have touched that card."

Toby spotted Glory's photo montage on the corner of Johnson's desk. He pointed to it. "Something happened to my girl," he said. "I know it." Then in a voice tinged with sarcasm, he asked, "Have you called that Bartley Longe, that guy who was taking her up to his country house, yet?"

"I had some other pressing assignments last night. Mr. Grissom, I assure you it is my top priority to talk with him."

"Don't assure me anything, Detective Johnson," Toby told him. "I'm going nowhere until you pick up that phone and make an appointment with Bartley Longe. If I have to miss my plane, that's okay with me. Because I intend to sit here until you've seen that guy. If you want to arrest me, that's okay, too. You just got to get it straight. I won't leave this police station until you're on your way to see Longe, and don't go there with your hat in your hand apologizing for the visit, saying her father is a pest. Go there hard-nosed and get some of the names of the other theatre people who that jerk claims he introduced Glory to, and find out from them if they ever met her."

This poor guy, Wally Johnson thought. I don't have the guts to break his heart and tell him that his daughter is probably a high-priced hooker by now who's with some fat-cat boyfriend. Instead, Johnson picked up the phone and asked information for the phone number of Bartley Longe. When the receptionist answered, he introduced himself. "Is Mr. Longe there?" he asked. "It's very important that I speak with him immediately."

"I'm not sure if he's still in his office," the receptionist began.

If she's not sure if he's in his office, that means that he *is* in his office, Johnson thought. He waited and a moment later the receptionist was back on the phone.

"I'm afraid he's already left, but I'll be happy to take a message," she said, soothingly.

"I'm afraid I'm not planning to leave a

message," Johnson answered firmly. "You and I both know that Bartley Longe is there. I can be there in twenty minutes. It is absolutely essential that I see him now. Brittany La Monte's father is sitting at my desk and he needs some answers about her disappearance."

"If you'll just hold . . ." After a brief pause the receptionist said, "If you can come right over, Mr. Longe will wait for you."

"That will be fine." Johnson hung up the phone then looked compassionately at Toby Grissom, taking in the exhaustion in the elderly man's eyes and the deep creases in his face. "Mr. Grissom, I could be gone as long as a few hours. Why don't you go out and get something to eat, then come back here? What time did you say your plane was?"

"Five o'clock."

"It's just a little after twelve now. I could get one of our guys to run you out to La-Guardia after I report back to you. I'm going to speak to Longe, and then, as you suggest, get a list of the people he claims met her at his home. But you staying in New York doesn't make sense at all. You told me that you're supposed to be having chemo treatments. You shouldn't skip them. You know you shouldn't."

Toby suddenly felt as though all the starch were going out of him. The long walk in the cold had taken its toll even though he had enjoyed it. And he was hungry. "I guess you're right," he said. "There's got to be a McDonald's near here." With a humorless smile, he added, "Maybe I'll treat myself to a Big Mac."

"That's a good idea," Wally Johnson agreed, as he got up and reached for the photo of Glory that he had kept on his desk.

"You don't need to bring that," Grissom said angrily. "That guy knows just what Glory looks like. Trust me, he does."

Wally Johnson nodded. "You're right. But I'll take it with me when I talk to the people who met Glory at Bartley Longe's home."

51

"I'm leaving for an hour or so," Kevin Wilson told Louise Kirk, and did not respond to the obvious curiosity in her expression by explaining where he was going. He knew that after his sharp response to her remarks about Zan Moreland she would not have the nerve to question him. He also knew that later, if he gave her a receipt for a luncheon, she would look it over carefully to see if he had marked a client's name on it or if he had charged it on his personal card.

There had been two more deliveries this morning. One contained rolls of wall coverings, the other boxes of table lamps.

Louise did manage to get in one more question. "Do you want any other deliveries from Zan Moreland's order to be put in the largest apartment? I mean, I could see that some of them were meant for the middle one."

"Keep it all together," Kevin said as he reached for his windbreaker.

Louise hesitated, then said, "Kevin, I know I'm overstepping myself, but I'll bet the ranch that you're on your way to Zan Moreland's office. As your friend, I beg you, don't let yourself get caught up in anything to do with that girl. I mean, she's very attractive, anyone with two eyes can see that, but I think she's mentally ill. When she went into the police station this morning, she told the reporters that her son was alive. If she knows that, she knows where he is, and she's been putting on a big act for nearly two years. On the Internet, they have links to some of the video that the media posted that day after the child was reported missing in Central Park. They show her in the park by the empty stroller. You can tell she's the same woman as in the photos that tourist took."

Louise paused for breath.

"Anything else?" Kevin asked evenly.

Louise shrugged. "I know you're mad at me, and I don't blame you. But as your friend as well as your secretary, I hate to see you get hurt. And any kind of involvement with her will hurt you professionally as well as personally."

"Louise, I'm not getting involved. I'll tell

you where I'm going. It's to Alexandra Moreland's office. I spoke to her assistant, who sounds like a nice guy. I'd like to settle all this with as little fanfare as possible. Quite frankly, I don't like Bartley Longe. You heard him when he called. He's like the cat who ate the canary, just assuming that I wouldn't dream of having anything to do with Zan Moreland now."

Kevin's hand was on the door, but then he turned and added, "I've studied and compared both of their proposals, and I like hers much more. As Zan pointed out, Bartley Longe doesn't provide a homelike quality to his designs. He's too damn grandiose. That doesn't mean I'll hire Moreland, by the way. But it does mean that I might accept her proposal, use her materials, make some sort of financial deal with her for all the work she's done, and get someone else to execute it. Does that make sense to you?"

Louise Kirk could not resist a parting shot. "It makes sense, but is it sensible?"

Josh had braced himself for the meeting with Kevin Wilson. He had his story straight. He and Zan believed that a hacker had gotten into their computer, and they were having it checked. As soon as they could validate that a hacker had made the orders, they could insist that the vendors who had delivered any goods pick them up immediately.

That will only buy us a little time, he thought. There's no hacker. Zan ordered that stuff from her laptop. Who else would know exactly what to order?

She must have written that letter on her laptop, too.

The phone rang. It was the desk saying that Mr. Kevin Wilson was there and was it all right to send him up?

Kevin did not know what to expect, but he was not prepared to find Moreland Interiors to be headquartered in a relatively small office that was packed with rolls of carpet piled almost to the ceiling and covering half the floor space. He noticed that the furniture had obviously been pushed as far as possible toward the opposite wall to make room for all of it. Nor did he expect Josh Green to be so young. Not more than his midtwenties, Kevin thought, as he extended his hand to Josh and introduced himself.

Recognizing the supplier's name stamped on the heavy paper covering the carpet, he asked, "Is all that stuff intended for my model apartments as well?"

"Mr. Wilson," Josh began.

"No need for formalities. It's Kevin."

"All right, Kevin. This is what happened. A hacker must have gotten into our computer and placed those orders. That's the only explanation I can offer."

"Do you know that we've had three deliveries so far this morning to 701 Carlton Place?" Kevin asked. Then, seeing the stunned expression on the young man's face, he said, "I gather you *didn't* know that?"

"No, I didn't."

"Josh, I know Zan went into the police station with her lawyer this morning. Do you expect her back soon?"

"I don't know," Josh said, making no effort to hide the concern in his voice.

"How long have you been working with her?" Kevin asked.

"Almost two years."

"I chose her to submit a plan for my model apartments based on the fact that I was a guest in a home in Darien, Connecticut, and in an apartment on Fifth Avenue, two separate jobs that she had just finished decorating six months ago."

"That would be the Campion home and the Lyons apartment."

"Did you actively work on those jobs?" Kevin asked.

Where is this going? Josh asked himself. "Yes, I did. Of course, Zan is the designer and I'm her assistant. Since we were doing both jobs at the same time, we alternated covering the day-by-day activity of each project."

"I see." I like this guy, Kevin thought. He's a straight shooter. Whatever Zan Moreland's problems, she designed exactly what's right for those apartments. I don't want to deal with Bartley Longe and I don't like his designs as much. And I can't start inviting other designers to submit plans. The board is already screaming about the delays in having the model apartments completed.

The door opened behind him. He turned to see Zan Moreland come into the office, with some older man who he guessed would be her lawyer. Zan was biting her lip trying to hold back the sobs that were racking her shoulders. Her eyes were swollen from crying and tears were streaming down her cheeks.

Kevin knew he had no business there. He looked at Josh. "I'll call Starr Carpeting," he said, "and tell them to pick up all this stuff and deliver it to Carlton Place. If any more deliveries like this come in, don't accept them. Send them to Carlton Place as well as all the invoices. I'll be in touch."

Zan had turned her back to him. He knew she was embarrassed for him to see her weeping. He left without speaking to her, but as he waited for the elevator he knew that, more than anything, he wanted to go back and put his arms around Zan.

Sense and sensible, he thought wryly, as the elevator door opened and he stepped into it. Wait till I tell Louise what I've done.

52

Melissa had listened with mounting fury to Ted's message suggesting that instead of putting up a five-million-dollar reward for information leading to Matthew's return, she make it a five-million-dollar donation to the Foundation for Missing Children.

"Can he be serious?" she asked Bettina, her personal assistant.

Bettina, a savvy, sleek forty-year-old with a cap of gleaming black hair, had come to New York from Vermont at age twenty, hoping for a career as a rock singer. It hadn't taken her long to realize that her reasonably good voice would go nowhere in the music world and instead she had become the personal assistant to a gossip columnist. Melissa had noticed Bettina's efficiency and offered her more money to work for her. Bettina promptly dumped the columnist who, as she aged, had come to count on her.

Now Bettina's emotions ranged between sharing Ted's loathing of Melissa and loving the excitement of being part of a major celebrity's life. And when Melissa was in a good mood, she would grab an extra one of the expensive gift bags that were meant only for the stars at a concert or awards show for Bettina, while she was getting one for herself.

The minute Bettina walked into Melissa's apartment at nine o'clock that morning, she had known it would be a long day. Melissa had immediately sprung on her the notion of offering the reward for Matthew's safe return. "You notice I say 'safe return,' " Melissa said. "Almost everybody believes that little kid is dead, so I'll get some nice publicity and it won't cost me a nickel."

Ted's negative response had infuriated Melissa. Then, when he left the suggestion that she donate the money to a foundation instead, she was livid. "He wants me to give five million dollars to a foundation. Is he crazy?" she asked Bettina.

Bettina liked Ted. She knew how hard he worked promoting Melissa. "I don't think he's crazy," she said, soothingly. "It certainly would make you seem very, very generous, which of course you would be, but you'd need to write the check in front of the cameras."

"Which I don't intend to do," Melissa snapped, pushing back the blond hair that hung almost to her waist.

"Melissa, I'm here to do anything you want. You know that," Bettina said. "But Ted is right. Ever since you and he became an item, you let everyone know that you think his son was abducted and killed by a child molester. To offer a reward for information leading to his safe return now would be begging for nasty comments on the late-night shows and the Internet."

"Bettina, I intend to make that offer. Call a press conference for one o'clock tomorrow. I know exactly how I'll word it. I'll say that while I have always felt that Matthew is not alive, that uncertainty is destroying Matthew's father, my fiancé, Ted Carpenter. This offer may make someone come forward, maybe someone whose relative or friend is raising Matthew as her own child."

"And if someone does come forward, you're prepared to write him or her a check for five million dollars, Melissa?" Bettina asked.

"Don't be silly. First of all, that poor kid is probably dead. Second, if someone really knew where he is and hasn't come forward all this time, that person is considered an

331

accomplice of some kind and therefore cannot profit from the crime. Got it? Everybody thinks I'm some kind of airhead, but we'll get hundreds of tips from all over the world, and every one of them will be mentioning Melissa Knight's promised reward."

They were in the living room of Melissa's penthouse apartment on Central Park West. Before answering Melissa, Bettina walked over to the window and looked down at the park. It all began there, she thought. One sunny afternoon in June nearly two years ago. But Melissa is right. That little boy is probably dead. She'll get her free publicity and it won't cost her a dime.

53

"Well, we rattled Moreland's cage," Billy Collins observed with satisfaction as he and Jennifer Dean munched on hot pastrami sandwiches and coffee at their favorite delicatessen on Columbus Avenue.

Detective Dean finished the last bite of the first half of her sandwich before she answered. "What scares me is that this case is almost too perfect. Do you believe that Moreland meant she had heard her son's voice in a kind of dream, or do you think she was actually talking to him on the phone?"

"Whether she was on the phone or dreaming, she said that boy is alive and I believe he's alive," Billy Collins said positively. "The question is where is he, and will whoever is holding him panic with all the publicity about the case now? I'm getting another cup of coffee. Want one?"

"No, I've had enough caffeine today. Why

don't I try Alvirah Meehan again and see if she's back yet? Her husband said that she should be finished at the hairdresser by now."

Alvirah answered the phone herself. "Come over, if you want, but I don't know how I can help you," she said cautiously. "My husband and I have been good friends of Zan ever since she decorated our apartment about a year and a half ago. That was after her son disappeared. She's a wonderful young woman and we love her."

"Why don't we just come anyhow? You're practically around the corner," Jennifer Dean said, as Billy returned with his second cup of coffee.

Ten minutes later they were parking in the semicircular driveway at 211 Central Park South. It was wide enough so that other vehicles could pass, and when Tony the doorman saw Billy put his police department ID face up inside the windshield, he made no objection to leaving the car there. "Mrs. Meehan said you should go right up when you get here," he told them. "It's apartment 16B."

"You do realize that some of our guys know Alvirah Meehan?" Jennifer asked Billy as they rode up in the elevator. "She's the cleaning woman who won big in the lottery and became an amateur sleuth, and has even written a memoir about it."

"Just what we don't need is an amateur sleuth involved with the case," Billy commented as the elevator stopped at the sixteenth floor. But after two minutes of being in Alvirah and Willy's home, like everyone else who had ever met them, he felt as if they'd been friends forever.

Willy Meehan reminded Billy of the pictures of his grandfather, a big man with snow white hair who had worked all his life as a cop. Alvirah, her hair freshly set, was wearing slacks and a cardigan sweater. Billy knew her clothes had not come out of a bargain basement, but still Alvirah's outfit reminded him of the housekeeper for the people down the block who had some money.

He was surprised when Jennifer accepted the coffee Alvirah offered. It was not something they usually did, but he suspected that it would not be wise to make an enemy of Alvirah, who had already established on the phone that she was Zan Moreland's good friend. And probably her defender, he thought.

I was right about that one, Billy said to himself a few minutes later as Alvirah emphasized the heartbreak she believed that

Zan had been suffering since her son disappeared. "I've known all kinds," Alvirah said emphatically, "and there are some things you can't fake. The suffering I've seen in that girl's eyes has made me want to cry."

"Did she talk about Matthew very often?" Jennifer Dean asked, softly.

"Let's put it this way, we never brought it up. I'm a contributing columnist for the *New York Globe* and at the time Matthew disappeared, I wrote a column begging whoever took him to understand the agony his parents were going through. I suggested that that person bring Matthew to a mall, and point out a security guard. Then tell the boy to close his eyes, count up to ten, then go up to the guard and tell him his name and the guard would find Mommy for him."

"Matthew was only a little past three when he disappeared," Billy objected. "Not every child that age can count up to ten."

"I had read in the paper that his mother had said that hide-and-seek was the favorite game they played together. In fact, one of the times that Zan did talk about Matthew, she said that when she got the call that he was missing, she was praying that he had woken up and gotten out of the stroller himself and maybe thought he was playing hide-and-seek with Tiffany." Alvirah paused, then added, "She told me that Matthew could count up to fifty. He was obviously a very bright child."

"Did you see the photos of Zan Moreland taking Matthew out of the stroller on television or in the papers today, Mrs. Meehan?" Jennifer Dean asked.

"I saw the photos of a woman who looked like Zan taking the child out of the stroller," Alvirah said carefully.

"Do you think that was Zan Moreland in those pictures, Mrs. Meehan?" Billy Collins asked.

"I wish you'd call me Alvirah. Everyone else does."

She's stalling for time, Collins thought.

"Let me put it this way," Alvirah began. "It certainly looks as though the woman in those pictures is Zan. I don't know nearly enough about technology because it's going so fast these days. Maybe those pictures were altered. I do know that Zan Moreland is torn in two with missing her son. She was here last night and she was a basket case she was so upset. I know she has friends both here and abroad who invited her to visit them over the holidays. She stayed home by herself. She couldn't bear to go out."

"Do you know what other countries her

friends live in?" Jennifer Dean asked, quickly.

"Well, they're from the countries where her parents lived," Alvirah said. "I know one of them is Argentina. Another one is in France."

"And remember her parents were living in Italy when they were killed in that accident," Willy chimed in.

Billy Collins knew that there was nothing more they could learn from Alvirah or Willy. They believe those pictures are of Zan Moreland, he thought as he got up to go, but they won't admit it.

"Detective Collins," Alvirah said, "before you leave, you must understand that if those photos really are Zan taking Matthew out of the stroller, she doesn't know that she did it. I would swear to that."

"Are you suggesting that she may be a split personality?" Collins asked.

"I'm not sure what I'm suggesting," Alvirah said. "But I do know that Zan is not acting. In her mind she has lost her child. I know she's spent money on private detectives and on psychics to try to find him. If she was playing a game, she wouldn't have had to go that far, but she isn't playing a game."

"One more question, Mrs. Meehan — uh,

Alvirah. Zan Moreland mentioned a priest, Fr. Aiden O'Brien. By any chance do you know him?"

"Oh, yes, he's a dear friend. He's a Franciscan friar at St. Francis of Assisi Church on Thirty-first Street. Zan happened to meet him here last night. She was just about ready to leave when he came in. He told her that he'd pray for her and I think that gave her some comfort."

"She had never met him before that?"

"I don't think so. Although I *do* know she stopped into St. Francis just before I was there on Monday evening to light a candle. Fr. O'Brien was hearing confessions that evening in the lower church."

"Did Zan Moreland go to confession?" Billy asked.

"Oh, I don't know, and of course I didn't ask. But you might be interested to hear that I had my eye on some guy who I thought was acting funny. I mean he was kneeling in front of the Shrine of St. Anthony with his hands in his face. But the minute Fr. Aiden stepped out of the Reconciliation Room, he jumped up and didn't take his eyes off Aiden until he was out of sight in the Friary."

"Was Ms. Moreland still in church when this happened?"

"No," Alvirah said, positively. "I only know she was there because yesterday morning I went back and asked to have a look at the tape on the security cameras. I wanted to see if I could spot that guy just in case he ever caused any trouble. I couldn't pick him out in the crowd, but on the camera I did see Zan coming in. That would be about fifteen minutes before I got there. The security tapes showed that she only stayed a few minutes. The guy I was trying to get a look at left just before I did, but there was no way to pick him clearly out of the crowd that was coming into the church."

"Did you think that was unusual for Ms. Moreland to pay a visit there?"

"No. The next day was Matthew's birthday. I thought she might have wanted to light a candle to St. Anthony for him. He's the saint people pray to when they're missing something."

"I see. Thank you both very much for your time," Billy Collins said as he and Jennifer Dean got up to leave.

"Well, that didn't get us very far," Dean commented as they went down in the elevator.

"Maybe, maybe not. What we did find out is that Zan Moreland has friends in a number of countries. I want to see if she's

340

made any trips to any one of those countries since her son disappeared. We'll get a subpoena and check her credit cards and bank accounts. And tomorrow we'll go down and pay a visit to Fr. O'Brien at St. Francis of Assisi. Wouldn't it be interesting if Zan Moreland went to confession to that priest? And if she did, I wonder what she had to say to him."

"Billy, you're *Catholic*," Jennifer Dean protested. "I'm not, but I know that no priest will ever discuss what was said in the confessional."

"No, he won't, but when we question Zan Moreland again, maybe if we work her hard enough, she'll break down and share her dirty little secrets with us."

54

Matthew had never seen Glory cry, not even once. She had sounded real mad when she was talking on the phone, but after she slammed it down, she started to cry. Just like that. Then she looked at him and said, "Matty, we can't hide like this any longer."

He thought that meant that they'd be moving to a new place to live, and he wasn't sure if he was glad or sorry. The room he slept in was big enough so that he could put all his trucks on the floor and move them one after the other just like he would see big trucks on the road at night when he and Glory moved to a new house.

And there was a bunk bed and a table and chairs in that room that had been there when they moved in. Glory had told him that some other kids must have lived there because the table and chairs were just right for a kid his size to sit down and draw pictures.

Matthew loved to draw. Sometimes he would think about Mommy and draw a lady's face on the paper. He never could get it to look just like her, but he always remembered her long hair and how it felt when it tickled his cheek, so he would always give the lady in his pictures long hair.

Sometimes he would take the bar of soap that smelled like Mommy from under the pillow and have it next to his hand on the table before he opened his box of crayons.

Maybe the next place they moved wouldn't be as nice. He didn't mind being locked in the big closet in this house when Glory left him alone. She always left the light on, and it was big enough for his trucks, and she always saved some new books for him to read until she got back.

Now Glory looked mad again. She said, "I wouldn't put it past that old bag to make some excuse to come barging in here before Sunday. I've gotta remember to keep the bolt on the front door."

Matthew didn't know what to say. Glory wiped her face with the back of her hand. "Well, we just move up the schedule. I'll let him know that tonight." She walked over to the window. She always kept the shades down all the way and if she looked out, she did it by pushing the shade to one side.

She made a funny sound as if she couldn't get her breath, then said, "That damn muffin jerk is driving by again. What's she looking for?" Then she added, "You got her started, Matty. Go upstairs and stay in your room and make sure none of your trucks are ever downstairs again."

Matthew went up to his room, sat down at the table, reached for his crayons, and began to cry.

55

Bartley Longe sat behind closed doors in his Park Avenue office, trying to talk himself into indignation at the rudeness of the detective who had, in effect, ordered him to put off any appointments he might have until they met.

But he could not conceal, even from himself, that he was frightened. Brittany's father had kept his threat to go to the police. He couldn't have them digging into his background again. That sexual harassment suit the receptionist had filed against him eight years ago hadn't looked good in the newspapers.

The fact that he had been forced to settle for a lot of money had hurt him, financially and professionally. The receptionist had alleged that he'd become outraged when she rejected his advances and had slammed her against the wall, and that she had been in fear of her life. "His face had darkened with anger," she had said to the cops. "He can't stand rejection. I thought he would kill me."

How was that going to sit with this cop when he does some digging into my background? Longe asked himself. Should I bring it up right away so that I seem straightforward? Brittany's been missing nearly two years. The only way they'll believe that I didn't do something to her is if she turns up in Texas and visits her Daddy very, very soon.

Something else. Why hadn't Kevin Wilson taken his call this morning? Surely he, or someone in his office, had seen Zan going into the station house with her lawyer. Surely Wilson had to be figuring that she'd probably be arrested, and if she was, how much time would she be able to put into his model apartments?

I *need* that job, Bartley Longe admitted. It's a showcase for whoever gets it. Sure, I get enough business from the celebrities, but an awful lot of them drive a hard bargain. They say they'll get a magazine to do a photo layout of their new homes, and that it would be free advertising for me. I don't need that kind of free advertising.

I lost some of my big-money/old-money customers after that lousy publicity. If I'm involved in another scandal, I'll lose more of them.

Why doesn't Wilson call me back? In his letter when he asked me to bid for the job, he said it was of the utmost importance that I submit my plans as soon as possible because they were already behind schedule. But now, not a word from him.

The intercom on his telephone buzzed. "Mr. Longe, are you planning to go out after your meeting with Detective Johnson, or do you want me to send for something after he leaves?" Elaine asked.

"I don't know," Longe snapped. "I'll decide after I see him."

"Of course. Oh, Phyllis is calling. That means he must be here now."

"Send him in."

Nervously, Bartley Longe opened the top drawer in his desk and looked at the mirror he kept there. The small job that had been done on his face last year had been terrific, he comforted himself. It wasn't obvious, but it got rid of the suggestion of a jowl that had begun to form below his chin. Having the touch of silver in his hair was exactly the right way to go as well. He had worked carefully on his distinguished exterior. He tugged at the sleeves of his Paul Stuart shirt so that the monogrammed cuff links were in place.

Then as Elaine Ryan tapped on the door and opened it with Detective Wally Johnson in tow, Bartley Longe stood up and, with a courtly smile, welcomed his unwelcome guest.

56

The minute Wally Johnson entered Longe's office, he took an instant dislike to the man. Longe's condescending smile reeked of superiority and disdain. His opening statement was that he was delaying a meeting with a very important client and hoped that whatever questions Detective Johnson had for him would not take more than fifteen minutes to complete.

"I hope not, either," Johnson answered, "so let's get right to the purpose of my visit. Margaret Grissom, whose stage name is Brittany La Monte, is missing. Her father is sure that something has happened to her or that she is in trouble. Her last known job was working for you as a hostess in your model apartments, and it is also known that she was having an intimate relationship with you and spent many weekends at your home in Litchfield."

"She spent some weekends at my home in

Litchfield because I was doing her a favor, introducing her to theatre people," Longe contradicted. "As I told her father yesterday, none of them thought Brittany had that certain something, that almost indescribable spark that would make her a star. They all predicted that at best she would be doing low-budget commercials or independent films where she would not need a SAG or Equity card. In her ten or eleven years in New York, she had never managed to achieve either."

"On that basis, you stopped inviting her to Litchfield?" Johnson asked.

"Brittany was beginning to see the big picture. At that point, she tried to turn our casual relationship into wedding bells. I have been married once to an aspiring actress and it cost me plenty. I have no intention of making that same mistake twice."

"You told her that. How did she accept it?" Johnson asked.

"She made some very uncomplimentary remarks to me and stormed out."

"Of your Litchfield home?"

"Yes. I might add that she took my Mercedes convertible with her. I would have filed charges, but I did receive a phone call from her telling me that she had parked it in the garage in my apartment building."

Johnson watched as Bartley Longe's face darkened with anger. "Exactly when was that, Mr. Longe?" he asked.

"Early June, so that would make it nearly two years ago?"

"Can you give me a more definite date?"

"It was the first weekend in June and she left late Sunday morning."

"I see. Where is your apartment, Mr. Longe?"

"It is at 10 Central Park West."

"Were you living there two years ago?"

"It has been my New York residence for eight years."

"I see. And after that Sunday in early June nearly two years ago, have you ever seen or heard from Ms. La Monte again?"

"No, I have not. Nor did I care to either hear from or see her."

Wally Johnson let a long minute pass before he spoke again. This guy is scared to death, he thought. He's lying and he knows that I'm not going to stop looking for Brittany. Johnson also knew that he wouldn't get more from Longe today.

"Mr. Longe, I'd like to have a list of the guests who would also have been at your home on the weekends that Brittany La Monte was there."

351

"Of course. You must understand that I entertain frequently in Litchfield. Being a good host to the wealthy and to celebrities opens the door to many of them becoming very good clients. It is quite possible I will miss some names," Longe said.

"I can understand that, but I would suggest you dig deep into your memory and give me a list by tomorrow morning at the latest. You have my card with my e-mail on it," Johnson said as he rose to leave.

Longe stayed behind his desk, not even rising from his chair. Johnson deliberately walked over to the desk and reached out his hand, giving the designer no choice but to accept it.

As the detective suspected, Bartley Longe's finely manicured hand was wringing wet.

On the way back to the precinct, Wally Johnson decided to make a detour and drive to the garage at 10 Central Park West. He got out of the car there and showed his badge to the attendant who was approaching him, a handsome young African-American. "No parking today," he said. "I just want to ask a few questions." He glanced at the nameplate the young man was wearing. "How long have you worked here, Danny?"

"Eight years, sir, since the doors opened," Danny answered proudly.

Johnson was surprised. "I didn't take you for more than your early twenties."

"Thanks. A lot of people say that." With a smile, Danny added, "It's a mixed blessing. I'm thirty-one, sir."

"Then of course you know Mr. Bartley Longe?"

Johnson was not surprised to see the change in Danny's formerly pleasant expression as he confirmed that he knew Mr. Longe.

"Did you ever know a young woman who was a friend of his, Brittany La Monte?" Johnson asked.

"Mr. Longe has many young women who are his friends," Danny answered, hesitantly. "Different ones come in with him all the time."

"Danny, I have a feeling you remember Brittany La Monte."

"Yes, sir. I haven't seen her in a while, but that's not surprising."

"Why is that?" Johnson asked.

"Well, sir, the last time she came here, she was in Mr. Longe's convertible. I could tell she was mad as hell." Danny's lips twitched. "She had Mr. Longe's toupees and wigs with her. She had cut patches of hair out of all six of them. While we stood there, she Scotch-taped them over the wheel and the dashboard and the hood so no one could miss them. There was hair all over the front seat. Then she said, 'See you guys,' and marched off."

"What happened then?"

"The next day, Mr. Longe came in boiling mad. The manager had put his wigs and toupees in a bag for him. Mr. Longe had a baseball cap on and we guessed that Miss La Monte had rounded up his whole collection. Between us, sir, Mr. Longe isn't very well liked in this garage, so we all got a good laugh out of it."

"I'll bet you did," Wally Johnson agreed. "He looks like the kind who stiffs you at Christmas."

"Forget Christmas, sir. He never heard of it. But his tip when he picks up his car is one dollar, if you're lucky." Danny's expression became concerned. "I shouldn't have said that, sir. I hope you won't repeat it to Mr. Longe. I could lose my job."

"Danny, you don't have to worry about that. You've been an immense help to me." Wally Johnson began to get back in his car.

Danny held the door for him. "Is Miss La Monte okay, sir?" he asked anxiously. "She was always really nice to us when she came in with Mr. Longe."

"I hope she is okay, Danny. Thanks a lot."

Toby Grissom was sitting at Johnson's desk when he got back to the precinct.

"Did you have that Big Mac, Mr. Grissom?" Johnson asked.

"Yes, I did. What did you find out from that big phony about Glory?"

"I found out that your daughter and Mr. Longe had a blowup and she drove his convertible to his apartment here in the city and left it parked there. He claims that he never saw her again. The young man in the garage confirmed that she never came after that, at least not to the garage."

"What does that tell you?" Grissom asked.

"It tells me that they broke up for good. As I mentioned to you before, I'm going to get a list of as many of the other weekend guests as we can locate and see if any of them has heard from Brittany, or, as you call her, Glory. I'm also going to visit her roommates and find out exactly when she left that apartment. I promise you, Mr. Grissom, that I am going to follow this through to the end. And now, please, let me get you a ride to the airport and promise me that you'll be in your doctor's office tomorrow morning. As soon as you're on your way, I'm going to call your daughter's roommates and make an appointment to see them."

Leaning on the sides of the chair for support, Toby Grissom stood up. "I've got a feeling I'll never see my girl again before I die. I'm going to trust you to keep your promise to me, Detective. I'll see the doctor tomorrow."

They shook hands. With an attempt at a smile, Toby Grissom said, "All right. Let's find my police escort to the airport. If I ask real nice, do you think he'll turn the sirens on for me?"

57

On Thursday afternoon, after her breakdown in her office, Zan let Josh take her home. Emotionally exhausted, she went straight to bed, allowing herself a rare sleeping pill. On Friday morning, feeling heavy and drugged, she stayed in bed, arriving at the office at noon.

"I thought I could handle it, Josh," she said, as they sat at the desk and ate the turkey sandwiches he had ordered from the local delicatessen. Josh had brewed coffee in the coffeemaker, making it extra strong, as she had requested. She reached for her cup and sipped from it, savoring the flavor. "It's a lot better than what Detective Collins served at the station house," she said wryly.

Then, seeing how concerned Josh was, she said, "Look, I know I fell apart yesterday, but I'll be all right. I've got to be. Charley warned me not to talk to the media, and now I'm sure they're twisting what I said about Matthew being alive just the way those detectives did when they questioned me. Maybe next time I'll listen to him."

"Zan, I feel so useless. I just wish I could help you," Josh said, trying to keep the emotion out of his voice. But there were still some questions he needed to ask, too. "Zan, do you think we should report the airplane ticket to Buenos Aires that was charged to your credit card? And the clothes at Bergdorf's and all the stuff that was ordered as if we got the job for the Carlton Place apartments?"

"And the fact that my bank account has been virtually cleaned out?" Zan asked. Then she added, "Because you don't believe that I didn't order any of it, or have any part in those transactions, do you? I *know* that. And I know Alvirah and Willy and Charley Shore all believe that I'm mentally ill, and that's putting it kindly."

She did not give Josh a chance to answer. "You see, Josh, I don't blame you a bit. I don't blame Ted for what he's saying about me, I don't even blame Tiffany who, I just learned from the detectives, thinks that I sedated her so that she would fall into a drugged sleep on a blanket in Central Park, and I could take my own child to that damn town house and leave him tied up and gagged in the storeroom — unless, of course, I'd already murdered him."

"Zan, I love you. Alvirah and Willy love you. And Charley Shore wants to protect you," Josh said, feebly.

"The saddest part is that I know all that is true. You, Alvirah, and Willy love me. Charley Shore wants to protect me. But none of you believe that someone who *looks* like me has taken my child, and that person, or whoever hired her, is trying to destroy my business as well.

"To answer your question, I don't think we should give these detectives any more so-called evidence that I'm a mental case to help them when they continue their inquisition."

Josh looked as if he wished he could deny what she had told him, but Zan could see that he was honest enough not to try. Instead she waited until she had finished her coffee, silently handed him the cup to refill, and then waited until he came back before she spoke. "I was obviously in no state to talk to Kevin Wilson when I got back here yesterday, but I heard what he said to you. Do you think he really means it, that he'll take on the obligation of paying our suppliers?"

"Yes, I do," Josh answered, relieved to get

onto a safer subject.

"That's more than decent of him," Zan said. "I can't imagine what the media would have made of it, if he'd said in public that he had never okayed any of the designs I had submitted. In all, the orders amount to tens of thousands of dollars. He wanted top-of-the-line and we gave him top-of-the-line."

"Kevin said he liked our — I mean *your* — plans better than Bartley Longe's," Josh told her.

"*Our* plans," Zan emphasized. "Josh, you're gifted. You know that. You're like me nine years ago when I started working for Bartley Longe. You had a lot of input when I was discussing those model apartments with you."

She picked up the second half of her sandwich, then put it down. "Josh, you know what I think is going to happen? I may be arrested for kidnapping Matthew. I believe in my heart he is alive, but if I am wrong I can assure you that the state of New York won't have to prosecute me for his murder to put me in prison. Because if Matthew is dead, my life will be a prison anyway."

58

On Friday morning, the first thing to hit Ted as he walked into the office was bad news. Rita Moran was waiting for him, her expression tight with anger and frustration. "Ted, Melissa is calling in the media to her apartment to announce she is offering five million dollars for Matthew's safe return. Her assistant phoned to tip us off. She didn't want you to be blindsided. Bettina *did* say Melissa is making it clear she believes Matthew is dead, but said that the uncertainty is killing you."

Sarcastically Rita added, "She did it for you, Ted."

"Good God," Ted shouted. "I told her, I begged her, I implored her . . ."

"I know," Rita said. "But, Ted, keep something in mind. You can't afford to lose Melissa Knight as a client. We just got a new estimate for repairing the plumbing in this building, and let me tell you, it's a horror. Melissa and the friends she's already brought in are keeping your head above water and if Jaime-boy does come through, we've got breathing space. I suggest you discount this white elephant of a building until you find a buyer, take the business loss, and concentrate on getting more clients like Melissa. Only be sure you don't get that lady mad at you. You can't afford it."

"I know I can't. Thanks, Rita."

"I'm sorry, Ted, I know how much you have on your shoulders. But remember, we still have some terrific singers and actors and bands, who, when their big break comes, won't forget how much you've done for their careers. So I suggest you call the witch when she's finished offering her five million dollars and tell her how grateful you are and how much you love her."

59

On Friday Penny Hammel drove past the Owens farmhouse slowly enough that she noticed the movement of the shade in the front window. That woman must have been right there and heard my van rattling down this bumpy road, she thought. What's Gloria Evans got to hide in there? Why is every shade pulled down to the sill?

Sure that she was still being watched, Penny deliberately made a U-turn instead of going as far as the dead end. In case the mystery woman has any doubts, let her know that I've got my eye on her, she thought. What's she doing in there anyhow? It's a gorgeous day, wouldn't you think she'd want to be able to see it? And she claims she's writing a book! I bet most writers don't sit at the computer in the dark when the sun could be pouring in the window!

Penny had made the detour impulsively

while she was on her way into town. She wanted to pick up a few groceries and she also wanted to get out of Bernie's way. He was in one of his Mr. Fixit moods, puttering around in his workshop in the basement. The only problem was that every time he finished a job like replacing the handle of a pot or gluing together the broken lid of the sugar bowl, he would yell for her to come down and see what a great job he'd done.

I guess being alone in the truck so much of the time, he likes to have someone hear the sound of his voice, Penny mused as she turned onto Middletown Avenue. She hadn't intended to drop in on Rebecca, but when she found a parking spot it was practically in front of Schwartz Real Estate and she could see her sitting at the desk.

Why not? she decided as with quick steps she walked across the sidewalk and turned the handle on the door of the agency. "*Bonjour,* Madame Schwartz," she boomed in her best imitation of a French accent. "I am here to buy that beeg, ugly McMansion on Turtle Avenue that has been on the market for two years. I wish to tear it down because it is an eyesore. I am carrying four million Euros in the trunk of my limousine. Do we have what you Americans call a deal?"

Rebecca laughed. "Very funny, but let me

tell you something that is nothing short of a miracle. I have a buyer for Sy's place."

"What about the tenant?" Penny demanded.

"She has to be out within thirty days."

Penny realized that she felt a twinge of disappointment and that she actually had been having fun building up a mystery surrounding Gloria Evans. "Have you told Evans that?" she asked.

"I did, and she is one unhappy lady. She hung up the phone on me. I told her I could show her at least five or six places that would be much more attractive and that she could use on a month-to-month basis so that she isn't stuck with a year's lease."

"And she hung up on you anyway?" Penny dropped into the chair nearest to Rebecca's desk.

"Yes. She was really upset."

"Rebecca, I just drove past Sy's place. Have you been inside since she moved in?"

"No. Remember, I told you that I drove by early the morning after she was supposed to arrive and saw her car in the carport, but I haven't been inside."

"Well, maybe you should make an excuse to go in. Maybe you can knock on her door and apologize to her about the inconvenience of the sudden sale and tell her you're sorry she's so upset. If she doesn't have the courtesy to invite you to come in, I'd say that it's proof positive something is going on."

Warmed up to the subject, Penny searched her mind for possible reasons to spur Rebecca into taking action. "That would be a perfect place for distributing drugs," she theorized. "Quiet country road. Dead-end street. No neighbors. Think about it. And if the cops ever raided her, who knows what might happen to your sale? Suppose she's already running from the police?"

Knowing that she had absolutely no basis in fact to support what she was suggesting, Penny said, "You know what I think I'll do. I won't wait until Tuesday. I'll call Alvirah Meehan later on today and tell her everything about Ms. Gloria Evans and ask her for her advice. I mean, suppose Evans is running from the police and there's a reward for finding her? Wouldn't that be just too much?"

60

Fr. Aiden O'Brien began his Friday at seven
A.M. serving the breadline outside the
church. Today, as usual, there had been
more than three hundred people waiting
patiently for breakfast. Some of them, he
knew, had been on line for at least an hour.
One of the volunteers whispered to him,
"Notice that we're seeing a lot of new faces,
Father?"

The answer was that yes, he had noticed.
Some of those people attended the senior
citizen activities that were now his principal
assignment. He had heard from many of
them that it was getting to be a choice
between food and the medicines they absolutely needed.

Those concerns were with him always, but
today, as he woke up, he had prayed for Zan
Moreland and for her child. Was little Matthew still alive, and if so, where had his
mother been keeping him? He had seen the

suffering in Zan Moreland's eyes when he took her hands in his. Was it possible, as Alvirah seemed to believe, that Zan was a split personality and didn't know what was happening in her other persona?

If that were true, was it the other persona who had come to confession and admitted to being part of an ongoing crime and unable to prevent a murder?

The problem was that no matter which one came to confession, he was bound by the seal never to reveal what he had been told.

He remembered how chilled Zan Moreland's elegant hands had felt when he closed his own over them.

Her hands. What was it that was nagging him about those hands? There was something, and it was important, but try as he might he simply could not remember it.

After lunch in the Friary, Fr. Aiden was barely back in his office when he received a call from Detective Billy Collins, requesting to pay him a visit. "My partner and I would like to ask you a few questions, Father. Would it be possible for us to come down immediately? We could be there in twenty minutes at the most."

"Yes, of course. May I ask what this is about?"

"It concerns Alexandra Moreland. We're on our way, Father."

Exactly twenty minutes later Billy Collins and Jennifer Dean were in his office. After the introductions, sitting at his desk facing them, Fr. Aiden waited for one of them to open the conversation.

It was Billy Collins who spoke first. "Father, Alexandra Moreland paid a visit to this church on Monday evening, did she not?" he asked.

Fr. Aiden chose his words carefully. "Alvirah Meehan identified her on our security tape as having been here on Monday evening."

"Did Ms. Moreland go to confession, Father?"

"Detective Collins, your name suggests that you are Irish, which means there is a good chance that you are Catholic or, at least, were raised as one."

"I was raised as one and I still am one," Billy said. "Not that I make it to Mass every Sunday, but pretty regularly."

"That's good to hear." Fr. Aiden smiled. "But then, as you must know, I cannot discuss anything about the confessional — not only what may have been said within it, but also who was or wasn't there."

"I see. But you did meet Zan Moreland at Alvirah Meehan's home the other evening," Jennifer Dean asked quietly.

"Yes, I did. Very briefly."

"Anything she said to you then wouldn't be under the seal of the confessional, would it, Father?" Dean persisted.

"It wouldn't necessarily be. She asked me to pray for her son."

"She didn't happen to mention that she just had cleaned out her bank account and bought a one-way ticket to Buenos Aires for next Wednesday, did she?" Billy Collins asked.

Fr. Aiden tried not to show how startled he was. "No, she did not. I repeat, we spoke for less than fifteen seconds."

"And it was the first time you were face-to-face with her?" Jennifer Dean shot the question at him.

"Please don't try to trick me, Detective Dean," Fr. Aiden replied sternly.

"We're not trying to trick you, Father," Billy Collins said. "But you might also be interested to know that after several hours of questioning, Ms. Moreland didn't share with us the fact that she's planning to leave the country. We just found it out ourselves. Well, Father, if you don't mind we'll take a look at those security tapes that show Ms.

Moreland coming into the church and leaving it."

"Of course. I'll have Neil, our man for all seasons, show them to you." Fr. Aiden reached for the phone. "Oh, I forgot. Neil isn't here today. I'll ask Paul from our bookstore to help you out."

While they waited, Billy Collins asked, "Father, Alvirah Meehan was worried because she thought somebody was observing you too carefully the other night. Are you aware of anyone who might be antagonistic to you?"

"No one, absolutely no one," Fr. Aiden replied emphatically.

After Paul escorted the detectives to show them the tapes, Fr. Aiden put his head in his hands. She must be guilty, he thought. She was planning to escape.

But what is it about Zan Moreland's hands that I can't remember?

Two hours later, Fr. Aiden was at his desk when Zan called him again. Still holding out hope that he might be able to prevent the murder she had told him would happen, he said, "I was hoping to hear from you, Zan. Do you want to come in and talk with me? Maybe there is some way I can really help you?" Fr. Aiden said.

"No, I don't think so, Father. My lawyer just called. I'm going to be arrested. I have to go with him to the police precinct at five o'clock today. So maybe, if you don't mind, pray for me, too."

"Zan, I *have* been praying for you," Fr. Aiden said fervently. "If you . . ." He did not get to finish the sentence. Zan was no longer on the phone.

He was scheduled to be in one of the Reconciliation Rooms at four o'clock. I'll wait till after I'm finished there, then call Alvirah after six, he thought. By then she may know whether or not Zan is going to be released on bail.

At that moment Fr. Aiden O'Brien had no inkling that someone would be coming into the Reconciliation Room, and that his purpose would be not to confess to a crime but to commit one.

61

At 4:15 on Friday afternoon, Zan called Kevin Wilson. "I don't know how to begin to thank you for taking responsibility for everything that was ordered for the apartments," she said, her voice calm, "but I can't let that happen. I'm about to be arrested. My lawyer thinks I'll be given bail, but whether or not I am, I won't be of much use to you as an interior designer."

"You're going to be arrested, Zan?" Kevin could not keep the shock out of his voice even though Louise had warned him that she was surprised the arrest had not already happened.

"Yes. I'm to be at the police precinct at five o'clock. The way it was explained to me is that I'll be processed after that."

Kevin could hear the effort Zan was making to keep her voice from breaking. "Zan, this doesn't change the fact that —" he began.

She interrupted him. "Josh will call the suppliers and explain that everything must go back, and that I'll try to work out some sort of settlement with them," she told him.

"Zan, please don't think that my decision to accept the deliveries was some random act of kindness. I like your designs and I don't like Bartley Longe's. That's the beginning and the end of it. Before you came in, Josh told me that you and he worked on two jobs concurrently, and that while you were at one, he was at the other. Isn't that true?"

"Yes. It is. Josh is truly gifted."

"All right, then. On the business level, I am hiring Moreland Interiors to take over the decorating of my model apartments. Whether or not you receive bail, my decision is firm. And, of course, I need a separate bill for your usual fees over and above the actual cost of the furnishings."

"I don't know what to say," Zan protested. "Kevin, you've got to be aware of the kind of publicity my case is generating and it is bound to get worse. Are you sure that you want people to know that a woman accused of kidnapping and maybe murdering her own child works for you?"

"Zan, I know how bad it looks, but I believe in your innocence, and that there is another explanation for everything that has happened to you."

"There is, and please God, it will be found." Zan attempted to laugh. "I want you to know that you have the distinction of being the first person to express any belief at all in my innocence."

"I'm glad if I'm the first, but I'm sure I won't be the last," Kevin said firmly. "Zan, you've been on my mind constantly. How are you able to handle all this? When I saw you, you were so upset that I was heartsick for you."

"How am I now?" Zan asked. "I've been questioning myself about that, and I think I have the answer. Years ago, when my parents were stationed in Greece, we flew to Israel and visited the Holy Land. Have you ever been there, Kevin?"

"No, I haven't. I've always wanted to go. For a long time I didn't have the money. Now I don't have the time."

"What do you know about the Dead Sea?"

"Not much other than that it's in Israel."

"Then to explain how I feel, I swam in it when we were there. It's a salt lake that is twelve hundred and ninety-three feet below sea level. That means it's the lowest point on earth. It's so thick with salt that you're warned not to get the water in your eyes

375

because if you do, they'll be terribly burned."

"Zan, how does that relate to you now?"

Zan's voice broke as she said, "I feel as if I'm at the bottom of the Dead Sea with my eyes wide open. Does that answer your question, Kevin?"

"Yes, it does. Oh, God, Zan, I'm sorry."

"I really believe you are. Kevin, my lawyer just came in. Time to go get fingerprinted and booked. Thanks again."

Kevin replaced the phone on the cradle, then turned away so that Louise Kirk, who was opening the door of his office, would not see the tears in his eyes.

62

Friday afternoon he called Glory. When she answered, as he had expected, her voice was sullen and angry. "It's about time I heard from you," she snapped. "Because your one-week-or-ten-day plan just isn't going to pan out. I probably have to get out of here within thirty days, and Sunday afternoon the real estate broker is going to come trooping in here with the guy who's buying the house. And if you think you're going to dump me in another godforsaken hole like this, you're wrong. By Sunday morning, you'd better have the money in my hands or I go to the police and claim that five-million-dollar reward."

"Gloria, we can wind this up by Sunday. But if you think you can make a deal to collect that reward, you're dumber than I thought. Remember Son of Sam? If not, look him up. He killed a couple of people and shot three or four others. He was writing a book about his crime spree and they passed a law saying that no criminal can profit from his crime. Lady, whether you know it or not, you're up to your neck in this one. You kidnapped Matthew Carpenter and you've been holding him captive for two years. You get caught, you go to prison. Got it?"

"Maybe they make exceptions," Gloria said defiantly. "But this little kid is bright. If you think that once they find him, he won't tell them that Mommy didn't take him that day, you are wrong. I'm pretty sure he remembers. When he woke up in the car, I was still wearing the wig. He started shrieking when I took it off. He remembers *that.* And once, when I thought the door was locked, I tried on the wig after I washed it. My back was to him. He opened the door and came in before I could get it off. He asked me, 'Why do you try to look like my Mommy?' Suppose he tells them that Glory took him out of the stroller? Won't that be great for me?"

"You haven't let him see any of the tapes they've been showing on television, have you?" he asked, as the appalling truth washed over him. If Matthew tells the police he knew his mother had not taken him, every plan I have made would collapse.

"You do ask stupid questions, don't you? Of *course* I haven't," she said.

"I think you're crazy, Brittany. That happened almost two years ago. He's too little to remember."

"Just don't count on him being a dumb bunny when they find him. And don't call me Brittany. I thought we agreed on that."

"All right, all right. Look, we're going to change our plan. Forget about making yourself up to look like Zan and going back to that church. I'll take care of that myself. Pack your car with everything you own. We'll meet tomorrow night instead at LaGuardia Airport. I'll have the money for you, and a plane ticket home to Texas."

"What about Matthew?"

"Do what you've always done, only this time it will have to be a little longer. Put him to bed in the closet, leave the light on, and give him enough cereal or sandwiches and soda to last him. You say those people are coming in on Sunday to go through the house?"

"Yes. But suppose they don't come? We can't leave that little boy locked in the closet."

"Of course not. Tell that real estate agent that you're leaving Sunday morning and that you'll notify her where to send your refund. You can be sure that by noon on Sunday she'll be checking out that house, whether or not she has the new buyer with her. And then she'll find Matthew."

"Six hundred thousand dollars, five thousand in cash, the rest wired to my father's bank account in Texas. Get out your pen. I'll give you the account number now."

His hand was perspiring so much that he couldn't keep the pen from slipping, but he managed to jot down the numbers she was snapping at him.

It was the one possibility that he had never considered — that Matthew would remember it was not his mother who had kidnapped him that day.

If that happened, Zan's story would be believed. All his carefully laid plans would be useless. Even if he killed her, as he had planned to do, they would still start looking to see who else might have planned this hoax and kidnapping.

And somehow they would get to the truth. The same vigilance with which they were hounding Zan would be turned from her in other directions.

He was sorry. He was truly sorry, but Matthew could *not* be found in that closet. He had to be gone when the real estate agent arrived on Sunday afternoon.

I never intended to kill him, he thought regretfully. I never thought that it would have to end like this. He shrugged. And now it was time to go to church.

"Bless me, Father, for I have sinned," he thought grimly.

63

This time, Zan did not respond to the media when she and Charley Shore arrived at the Central Park Precinct. Instead, ducking her head, she ran from the car to the front door with Charley's arm under her elbow. They were escorted to the now familiar interrogation room, where Detectives Billy Collins and Jennifer Dean were waiting for them.

Without greeting her, Collins said, "I hope you didn't forget to bring your passport, Ms. Moreland."

Charley Shore answered for her. "We have the passport."

"Good, because the judge will want it," Billy said. "Ms. Moreland, why didn't you share with us that you were planning to fly to Buenos Aires next Wednesday?"

"Because I wasn't," Zan said calmly. "And before you ask, neither did I clean out my bank account. I'm sure you've checked that by now."

"What you are saying is that the same imposter who stole your child also bought you a one-way ticket to Argentina and helped herself to your bank account?"

"That is *exactly* what I am saying," Zan said. "And in case you don't know it yet, that same person ordered clothes at the stores where I have an account, and also ordered all the supplies I would have needed for the interior design job I bid on."

The frown on Charley Shore's face reminded her that he had told her to answer questions, but not to volunteer any information. She turned to him. "Charley, I know what you're thinking, but I don't have anything to hide. Maybe if these detectives look into all those activities, they'll discover that even just one of them couldn't have been done by me. And maybe then it is possible they will look at each other and one of them will say, 'Well, maybe she was telling the truth.' "

Zan looked back at the detectives. "Clap if you believe in miracles," she said. "I am here to be arrested. Can we possibly begin the process?"

They stood up. "We do that downtown at the courthouse," Billy Collins told her. "We'll drive you there."

It doesn't take long to be an accused felon, she thought an hour later, after the arrest warrant was issued, a number was assigned to it, and she had been fingerprinted and had her mug shot taken.

From there she was taken into a courtroom to stand in front of a stern-faced judge. "Ms. Moreland, you are being charged here with kidnapping, obstruction of justice, and interference with parental custody," he told her. "If you can make bail, you cannot leave the country without the permission of the court. Do you have your passport with you?"

"Yes, Your Honor," Charley Shore answered for her.

"Surrender it to the court clerk. Bail is set at two hundred fifty thousand dollars." The judge stood up and walked out of the courtroom.

Zan turned to Charley, panic-stricken. "Charley, I can't raise that much money. You know I can't."

"Alvirah and I spoke about this possibility. She's putting up the deed to her apartment for security with a bondsman and will lend you the bondsman's fee. As soon as I call Willy, he'll be on his way here with it. When the bail is straightened out, you'll be free to go."

"Free to go," Zan whispered, looking down at the black smudges she had not been able to scrub from her fingers, "free to go."

"This way, ma'am." A court officer took her arm.

"Zan, you have to wait in a holding cell until Willy puts up the bail. As soon as I talk to him, I'll come back and wait with you," Charley told her. "You've got to understand this is all routine stuff."

Her feet leaden, Zan allowed herself to be walked through a nearby door. It opened onto a narrow passage. At the end of it was an empty cell with an open toilet and a bench. At the slight prodding of the uniformed officer, she stepped inside the cell and heard the key turn in the lock behind her.

No Exit, she thought wildly, remembering the Sartre play by that name. I played the role of the adulteress in it in college. *No exit. No exit.* She turned and looked at the bars, then tentatively put her hands on them. My God, how can it have come to this? she thought. *Why? Why?*

She stood there unmoving for nearly half an hour, then Charley Shore returned. "I spoke to the bail bondsman, Zan," he said. "Willy should be here in a few minutes. He has to sign a few papers, turn over the deed, pay the fee, and you'll be out of here. I know how it must feel for you, but this is the moment your lawyer, meaning me, knows what we're up against and starts to fight."

"An insanity defense? Isn't that what you're thinking, Charley? I'll bet it is. In the office before you got there, Josh and I had the television in the back room on. The CNN anchor was interviewing a doctor who specialized in multiple personalities. In his brilliant opinion, I may be a very likely candidate for that kind of defense. Then he cited a case where the defense pleaded that the core person did not know what the personality who committed crimes was doing.

"You know what the judge said to that defense argument, Charley?" Zan shrieked. He said, *I don't care how many personalities that woman has. They all have to obey the law!"*

Charley Shore looked into Zan's blazing eyes and knew there was no way he could either reassure or comfort her.

He decided not to insult her by attempting to do either.

64

Gloria Evans, born Margaret Grissom, called "Glory" by her adoring father, stage name Brittany La Monte, was not sure if she could believe that it really would be over within forty-eight hours. A thousand times in these nearly two years she had whispered, "If only," to herself during sleepless nights when she had begun to realize the enormity of her crime.

Suppose it doesn't work out? she thought. Suppose they do track me down? I'll go to prison for the rest of my life. What's six hundred thousand dollars? It will only last me a couple of years by the time I get set up, buy new clothes, have new pictures made, take some more acting lessons, and try to get a publicist and an agent. He said he could introduce me to people in Hollywood, but what good were all the people he introduced me to in New York? *Zip.*

And Matty. He was such a nice little kid. I

knew I'd mess myself up if I got too tight with him, Glory thought, but how can you *not* like the kid?

I love the boy, she thought, as she packed the clothes that were the same as the ones Zan Moreland wore. By God, I'm good, she thought with a tight-lipped grin. I pay attention to detail. Moreland is a little taller than I am. I had an extra lift put on the heels on those sandals just in case anyone got a picture of me when I took the kid.

Warming to her self-congratulatory stream of thought as she packed her suitcases, Glory remembered how she had worked on that wig to get her hair just right, the color and the blunt cut. Glory padded the shoulders of that dress because Moreland was more broad shouldered than she was. I bet right now the cops are doing all that digital stuff and they'll come back saying that no way was the woman in the picture not Moreland. My makeup was perfect, too.

She looked around the bedroom with its bleak white walls, tired oak furniture, and rag of a carpet. "And what the hell did it all get me?" she asked aloud. Two years of jack-assing from one hidden house to another. Two years of leaving Matty locked up in the closet while I went to the store or once in a while to a movie. Or to New York, to make it look like Moreland had been some place or other.

That guy could break into Fort Knox, she thought as she remembered how one day he had met her at Penn Station and thrust the fake credit card into her hand. He had cut out ads of clothes on sale. "This is what I want you to buy," he said. "She already has duplicates of them."

Other times he had mailed her a box of clothes that were identical to some that Moreland had bought. "In case I really want to rub it in," he said.

Glory had been wearing one of those suits, the black one with the fur trimming, and all her makeup when she drove into Manhattan on Monday. He'd told her to buy clothes at Bergdorf's and charge them to Moreland's account. She didn't know exactly what else he planned for her to do, but when she met him, she could tell he was upset. "Just get back to Middletown," he had told her.

That was late Monday afternoon. I got mad, Glory thought. I told him to go to hell and that I'd walk to the parking lot. I should have taken off my wig and tied my scarf around my neck so I didn't look like her, but I didn't. Then when I passed the church, it was crazy, but I stopped in. I don't know

389

what made me go to confession, or start to anyhow. My God, was I losing it? And I ought to have known that he'd be following me. How else would he have known I was there?

"Glory, can I come in?"

She looked up. Matthew was standing at the door. Focusing on him, Glory could see that he had lost weight. Well, he hadn't been eating much lately, she thought. "Sure. Come in, Matty."

"Are we going to move again?"

"I have very good news for you. Mommy is coming to get you in a couple of days."

"She is?" he said excitedly.

"You bet she is. That's why I won't be minding you at all anymore. And the bad people who were trying to steal you are all gone. Isn't that wonderful?"

"I miss Mommy," Matthew whispered.

"I know you do. And believe it or not, I'm going to miss you, too."

"Maybe you'll come and visit us some-time?"

"Well, we'll see." Looking into Matthew's intelligent, seeking gaze, Glory suddenly thought, In two years if he sees me on television or in a movie, he'll say, "That's Glory, the lady who minded me."

Oh my God, she thought, that's the way

he's thinking, too. He knows he can't let Matty be found. Could he possibly . . ?

Yes, he could. She already knew that.

I can't let it happen, Glory thought. I've got to call and try to get that reward. But right now, I'll do what he said. In the morning, I'll call the real estate woman and tell her I'm leaving Sunday morning. Then I'll meet him in New York tomorrow night, like we planned, but before that I'll go to the cops and make a deal with them. They can tape me so that they'll have absolute proof that I'm on the level.

"Glory, can I go downstairs and get a soda?" Matthew asked.

"Sure, honey, but I'll go down with you and get you something to eat."

"I'm not hungry, Glory, and I don't believe you that I'll see Mommy soon. You always tell me that."

Matthew went downstairs for a soda, brought it back up, lay on his bed, and reached for the bar of soap. But then he pushed it away. Glory tells lies, he thought. She's always telling me that I'll be seeing Mommy soon. Mommy doesn't want to come for me.

65

Fr. Aiden made his way from the Friary to the lower church at ten minutes of four on Friday. He walked slowly. He had been sitting at his desk for hours and the arthritis in his back and knees always pained him when he'd been in one position for too long.

Today, as always, there were people queuing up at the two Reconciliation Rooms in the entrance area where confessions would be heard. He could see that someone was paying a visit to the Lady of Lourdes grotto and someone else was at the kneeling bench before St. Jude. A few people were sitting on the bench against the outside wall. Resting their feet, he wondered, or waiting to work up courage to go to confession? It shouldn't take courage, he thought. It only requires faith.

As he passed the recessed Shrine of St. Anthony, he noticed a man in a trench coat with a thick head of dark hair kneeling there. The thought crossed his mind that maybe this was the man who Alvirah claimed was taking an odd kind of interest in him the other night. Fr. Aiden dismissed that thought. If it is, maybe the fellow simply was working his way up to unburdening himself, he thought. I hope so.

At five of four, he put his name on the outside of the Reconciliation Room, went in, and settled in his chair. His personal prayer before he began to receive the penitents was always the same, that he would meet the needs of those who came for healing.

At four o'clock, he pressed the button so that the green light would go on, and the first person on the line would know it was permissible to enter.

It was an unusually busy afternoon even for the Lenten season, and nearly two hours later, Fr. Aiden decided that since there were only a few others waiting, he would not leave until he had heard all their confessions.

Then, at five minutes of six, the man with the unruly hair came in.

The collar of his trench coat was up around his neck. He was wearing oversized dark glasses. His thick mop of dark hair covered his ears and forehead. His hands were in his pocket.

Fr. Aiden felt an instant sense of fear. This man was not a penitent, he was sure of that. But then the man sat down and, his voice husky, said, "Bless me, Father, for I have sinned." Then he paused.

Fr. Aiden waited.

"I'm not sure you'll want to forgive me, Father, because the crimes I am going to commit are quite a bit more serious than the crimes I have been committing. You see, I am going to kill two women and a child. You know one of them, Zan Moreland. And beyond that I can't take a chance on *you*, Father. I don't know what you have heard, or what you suspect."

Fr. Aiden tried to rise, but before he could the man drew a gun out of his pocket and held it against the Friar's robe. "I don't think they'll hear this," he said. "Not with a silencer, and anyway they're all too busy praying."

Fr. Aiden felt a fierce, sharp pain in his chest, and then as everything went black, he felt the man's hands guiding him back into his chair.

Hands. Zan Moreland. That was what he had been trying to remember. Zan had long, beautiful hands.

The woman in confession who he had

thought was Zan had smaller hands and
short fingers . . .

Then the image passed out of his mind,
leaving him in silent darkness.

66

When they were finally able to leave the courthouse, Willy stepped out through a sea of cameras, ran out into the street, and hailed a cab.

Biting her lip to keep it from trembling, and holding Charley Shore's hand, Zan raced to get in the taxi. But she could not escape the flashing bulbs and the microphones that were thrust in front of her. "Any statement for us now, Zan?" a reporter called.

Stopping in her tracks, she screamed, "I am not the woman in those photos, I am not, I am not."

At the curb Willy was holding the cab door open. Charley helped her into it. "The big guy will take care of you now," Charley said quietly.

For minutes after the cab pulled away, neither Zan nor Willy said anything. Then when they were almost at Central Park, she turned to Willy. "I simply don't know how to thank you," she began. "My apartment is a sublet. My bank account is nonexistent. There's no way I could have made that bail. I'd be in the Tombs tonight in an orange jumpsuit if it weren't for you and Alvirah."

"There was no way you were going to be in the Tombs tonight, Zan," Willy said. "Not on my watch."

When they reached the apartment, Alvirah was waiting with glasses on the coffee table. She said, "Charley called me, Willy. He said Zan needs something stronger than red wine. What will it be, Zan?"

"I guess a scotch." Zan tried to smile as she untied her scarf and slipped off her outer jacket, but it was a forlorn effort. "Or maybe two or three," she added.

As she reached to take the jacket from her, Alvirah wrapped her arms around Zan. "When Charley called to say you were on your way, he asked me to remind you that this is only the first move in a long process and that he is going to fight every step of the way for you."

Zan knew what she had to say, but she was not sure how to put it. Stalling for time, she sat on the couch and looked around the room. "I'm so glad that you went ahead with these matching club chairs, Alvirah.

Remember we debated about having one of them be a wing chair?"

"You told me all along that I should get the matching club chairs," Alvirah said. "When Willy and I were married we, and everyone we knew, bought a couch, a wing chair, and a club chair. And the end tables matched the cocktail table. And the lamps matched, too. Let's face it. There weren't too many interior decorators running around Jackson Heights, Queens, at the time."

As she spoke, Alvirah was studying Zan, taking in the deep shadows under her eyes, the alabaster white of her skin, the fact that although she was naturally slender, she now seemed actually frail.

Zan picked up the drink Willy had prepared for her, shook it slightly to rattle the ice cubes against the side of the glass, and began, "This is terribly hard for me to say because it seems so ungrateful."

She looked up at their concerned faces. "I can read your minds," Zan said quietly. "You think I'm going to come clean and tell you that yes, I did kidnap and maybe even kill my child, the flesh of my flesh.

"That's not what I'm going to say. I am going to tell you that I am not bipolar. I am not neurotic. I am not a split personality. I know what it looks like, and I don't blame you for believing any or all of that."

Her voice rising with passion, she said, "Someone else took Matthew. Someone who cares enough to look exactly like me is the woman in those photos in Central Park. I just read about a woman who spent a year in prison because two of her ex-fiancé's friends claimed she had held them up at gunpoint. Finally one of them broke down and admitted he was lying."

Zan stared into Alvirah's eyes, beseeching her understanding. "Alvirah, on Matthew's life, I swear before God, I am innocent. You're a good detective. I've read your book. You've solved some pretty important crimes. Now I am going to ask you to rethink this awful mess. Say to yourself, 'Zan is innocent. Everything she has told me is true. How do I go about proving her innocence instead of just pitying her?' Is that possible?"

Alvirah and Willy looked at each other, knowing they could read each other's minds. Ever since they had seen those pictures of Zan — or the woman who strikingly resembled her — they had passed judgment on her. *Guilty.*

I never even considered that she isn't the woman in the pictures, Alvirah thought.

Maybe there *is* another explanation for all this. "Zan," she began slowly, "I am ashamed, and you are right. I am a pretty good detective, and I've been too quick to judge you. You *are* presumed innocent, which is the foundation of justice, something which I, like many people, have forgotten in your case. Where do I look for answers?"

"I swear Bartley Longe is behind this," Zan said promptly. "I rejected his advances — never smart if you worked for him. I quit and opened my own firm. I've taken some of his clients. Today I learned the job of doing the model apartments at Carlton Place is mine."

She saw the surprised expression that came into both their eyes. "Can you believe that Kevin Wilson, the architect, hired me even though he knew I might be going to jail? Of course, now that I'm out on bail, I can work with Josh, but Kevin hired us knowing that Josh might have had to handle the job himself."

"Zan, I know how much that assignment means to you," Alvirah said. "And you won it over Bartley Longe!"

"Yes, but if he hates me now, can you imagine how much more he'll hate me when he hears this?"

Alvirah had a frightening thought that Zan may have missed something. If she was right and some woman was skillfully impersonating her, and if Bartley Longe had hired a woman to dress up like Zan and kidnap Matthew, what might happen now? And what might Longe do to Matthew given this new insult of Zan getting a prestigious job that he wanted himself? If Longe is guilty and if Matthew is still alive, will Longe be driven even further in his need to harm Zan?

Before Alvirah could speak, Zan said, "I've been trying to sort everything out myself. For some reason Nina Aldrich told those detectives that I was to meet her at her apartment on Beekman Place. That simply isn't true. Maybe the housekeeper was within earshot when Nina told me to meet her at the town house on Sixty-ninth Street that day."

"All right, Zan, that may be a good lead. I'll try to get to the housekeeper. I'm good at making friends with someone like that. Don't forget I was a cleaning woman for years." Alvirah hurried to get the pad and pen on the shelf under the kitchen phone.

When she returned, Zan said, "And, please talk to Tiffany Shields, the babysitter. She asked for a Pepsi and when I went to get it she followed me into the kitchen. She took it out of the refrigerator and opened it herself. I never touched it. She asked me if I had any cold pills. I gave her a Tylenol for colds. I've never had the Tylenol with a sedative in my home. Now she's decided that's what I gave her."

The phone rang. "It always rings when we're about to have dinner," Willy grunted, as he went to pick it up.

An instant later his expression changed. "Oh my God! What hospital? We'll go right over. Thanks, Father."

Willy replaced the receiver, then turned to Alvirah and Zan who were staring at him.

"Who, Willy?" Alvirah asked, her hand over her heart.

"Fr. Aiden. Some guy with a lot of heavy black hair shot him in the Reconciliation Room. He's in NYU Hospital, Alvirah. He's in intensive care. His condition is critical. He may not last through the night."

67

Alvirah, Willy, and Zan had stayed at the hospital outside the intensive care unit until three in the morning. Two other Franciscan friars were there, keeping watch with them. They had all been allowed to stand at Fr. O'Brien's bedside for a moment.

His chest was swathed in bandages. A breathing tube covered most of his face. Intravenous fluid was dripping into his arm. But the doctor now was cautiously optimistic. Miraculously, all three bullets had missed his heart. While his condition was extremely critical, his vital signs were improving. "I'm not sure if he can hear you, but talk to him briefly," the doctor said.

Alvirah whispered, "Fr. Aiden, we love you."

Willy said, "Come on, Padre. You've got to get better."

Zan covered Fr. Aiden's hand with hers. "It's Zan, Father. With all that's going on, I know it is your prayers that have given me hope. Now I'm praying for you."

When they left the hospital, Alvirah and Willy took Zan home in a cab. Alvirah waited in it while Willy saw her to the door of her apartment. When he returned, he grunted, "It's too cold for the vultures. Not a camera in sight."

They slept until nine o'clock the next morning. On awakening Alvirah grabbed the phone and called the hospital. "Fr. Aiden is holding his own," she reported. "Oh, Willy, I knew when I saw that guy in the church Monday night that he was trouble. If only we could have gotten a good look at him on the security camera, we might have been able to identify him."

"Well, the police are sure going over that security camera with a fine-tooth comb now to see if they got a better view of him last night," Willy assured her.

Over breakfast, they looked at the front page of the tabloids. Both the *Post* and the *News* had a picture of Zan, leaving the courthouse with Charley Shore. Her denial, I AM NOT THE WOMAN IN THOSE PHOTOS, was the headline of the *News*. "NOT ME," SCREAMS ZAN, read the *Post* headline. The *Post* photographer had gotten a close-up that revealed the agonized expression that accompanied her words.

Alvirah cut the *Post* front page and folded it. "Willy, it's Saturday, so maybe that babysitter is home. Anyhow, Zan gave me her address and phone number. But instead of calling, I'm just going to go there. Zan said that Tiffany Shields took the Pepsi from the refrigerator herself. That means there's no way Zan could have tampered with it. And as for the cold pill, Zan says she never bought the kind that has a sedative. You heard her. That young woman fell asleep when she was minding Matthew and now is trying to throw the blame for doing that on Zan."

"Why would the girl have made up a story like that?" Willy asked.

"Who knows? Probably to justify herself for falling asleep on the job."

An hour later, Alvirah was ringing the superintendent's bell at Zan's former apartment building. A young woman in a bathrobe answered the door.

"You must be Tiffany Shields," Alvirah guessed, plastering her warmest smile on her face.

"So? What do you want?" was the hostile reply.

Alvirah had her card in her hand. "I'm Alvirah Meehan and I'm a columnist for the *New York Globe*. I'd love to interview you for a story I'm writing about Alexandra Moreland." That's not a lie, Alvirah told herself. I am going to write a column about Zan.

"You want to write about the stupid babysitter who everybody blamed for falling asleep while all this time it was his mother who was the kidnapper," Tiffany snapped.

"No. I want to write about a teenage girl who was sick and only agreed to babysit because the child's mother had to see a client and the new nanny hadn't showed up."

"Tiffany, who's there?"

Looking past Tiffany into the foyer, Alvirah could see a broad-shouldered, balding man approaching them. She was about to introduce herself when Tiffany said, "Dad, this lady wants to interview me for an article she's writing."

"My daughter has taken enough of a pounding from you people," Tiffany's father said. "Just go home, lady."

"I don't intend to pound anyone," Alvirah said. "Tiffany, listen to me. Zan Moreland has told me how much Matthew loved you, and that you and she were real friends. She told me that she knew you were sick and she blamed herself for insisting that you mind Matthew that day. That's the story I want to tell."

Alvirah kept her fingers crossed as the father and daughter looked at each other. Then the father said, "I think you should talk to this lady, Tiffany."

As Tiffany opened the door wide to allow Alvirah to enter, her father escorted Alvirah into the living room and introduced himself. "I'm Marty Shields. I'll leave you two. I've got to get upstairs to check out someone's lock." Then he looked down at the card. "Hey, wait a minute. Aren't you the lady who won the lottery and wrote a book about solving crimes?"

"Yes. I am," Alvirah acknowledged.

"Tiffany, your mother loved that book. She went to a bookstore and you signed it for her, Mrs. Meehan. She said she had a nice talk with you about it. She's at work now. She's a sales woman in Bloomingdale's. I can tell you right now she'll be real sorry she missed you. Okay, I'm on my way."

What a piece of luck that his wife liked my book, Alvirah thought happily, as she took a straight chair near the couch where Tiffany was curling up. Tiffany is just a kid, she decided, and I can understand what kind of stress she's been under all this time. I've heard her phone call played on the news and so have millions of other people.

"Tiffany," she began, "my husband and I have been good friends with Zan almost since the time Matthew disappeared. I have to stress that I never once heard her blame you for what happened that day. I never ask her about Matthew because I know how hard it is for her to talk about him. What was he like?"

"He was adorable," Tiffany said promptly. "And so smart. That isn't surprising. Zan read to him every night, and on weekends she would take him everywhere. He loved to go to the zoo and he could name all the animals. He could count to twenty and never miss a number. Of course, Zan is a real artist. Her sketches of rooms and furniture and window treatments that she does for her job are wonderful. Even at three you could tell that Matthew had a real talent for drawing. He had big brown eyes that could look so solemn when he was thinking. And his hair was starting to turn red."

"And you and Zan were real friends?"

Tiffany's expression became wary. "Yes, I guess so."

"Over a year ago, I remember she told me

that you two were good friends, and that you always admired her clothes. Didn't she sometimes give you a scarf or gloves or a pocketbook that she didn't need?"

"She was nice to me."

Alvirah opened her purse and took out the folded front page of the *Post*. "Zan was arrested last night and is charged with kidnapping. Just take a look at her face. Can you see how much she's suffering?"

Tiffany glanced down at the picture, then quickly looked away from it.

"Tiffany, the detectives told Zan that you think she may have drugged you."

"She may have. That's why I was so sleepy. There may have been something in that Pepsi and then that cold pill. I bet it was a sedative."

"Yes, that's what I understand that you told the detectives, but Tiffany, Zan remembers it clearly. You asked for a soda because you were thirsty. You followed her into the kitchen and she opened the refrigerator door for you. You took the can out and you opened it yourself. She never touched it. Isn't that true?"

"I don't remember it that way." Tiffany's tone of voice was now defensive.

"And you asked Zan if she had any cold medicine. She gave you a Tylenol, but she

409

never kept nighttime Tylenol in the house. At your request she gave you the one that is a cold medication. Now, I grant you that those antihistamines can make you a little drowsy, but you asked for medication. Zan didn't offer it."

"I don't remember." Tiffany was sitting up straight now.

She remembers, Alvirah thought, and Zan is right. Tiffany's trying to rewrite history to make herself look good. "Tiffany, I wish you'd look at that picture again. Zan is suffering from these accusations. She swears she is not the woman in that picture taking Matthew. She doesn't know where he is, and the only thing that's keeping her going is the hope that he'll be found alive. She will be put on trial and you'll be a witness. I just hope that you think carefully when you're under oath, and if Zan's account of that morning is accurate that you will tell the truth. Now, I'm on my way. I promise that when I write this story, I will stress that Zan has always blamed herself, not you, for Matthew's disappearance."

Tiffany did not get up with her.

"I left you my card, Tiffany. It has my cell phone on it. If there's anything else that you think of, call me."

At the door she was stopped. "Mrs. Meehan," Tiffany called. "It may not mean anything, but —" She got up. "I have some sandals to show you. Zan gave them to me. When I saw those pictures of Matthew being taken out of the stroller, I noticed one thing. Wait a minute."

She went down the hall and came back a moment later with a shoebox in one hand and a newspaper in the other. She opened the shoebox. "These sandals are exactly the same as a pair Zan has. She gave them to me. When I thanked her, she said that she had bought a second pair the same color by mistake, and not only that, she had another pair exactly the same except that it had wider straps. She said it was practically like having three pairs of the same shoes."

Not knowing what to expect and not daring to hope that it would be significant, Alvirah waited.

Tiffany pointed to the newspaper she was holding and said, "You see the shoes Zan, or the woman who looks like her, is wearing when she's bending over the stroller?"

"Yes. What about them?"

"See how the strap is wider than it is on this pair?" She took a sandal from the shoebox and held it up.

"Yes. It is different, not much, but Tiffany, what about it?"

"I noticed and I can swear that Zan was wearing the ones with the narrow straps the day Matthew disappeared. She and I left this building together. She rushed into a taxi and I pushed the stroller to the park."

Tiffany's face became troubled. "I didn't tell that to the cops. I've been so mad about the way people think of me that I know I was blaming Zan. But last night when I began to think about it, it didn't make sense. I mean, why would Zan have come back home that day and changed into her sandals with the wide strap?"

Her eyes searched into Alvirah's pleadingly.

"Does that make sense to you, Mrs. Meehan?"

68

On Saturday morning, Detective Wally Johnson pushed the intercom button under the name ANTON/KOLBER 3B in the foyer of the brownstone shared by Angela Anton and Vita Kolber. They were the young women who had been Brittany La Monte's roommates before she disappeared.

When they did not answer the messages he left them on Thursday evening, he'd been prepared to go directly to their apartment the next morning and take a chance on catching them at home. But then Vita Kolber called him back at eight A.M. on Friday asking if he could meet with them on Saturday morning instead. They both had early-morning rehearsal calls and the rehearsals were expected to last through the day.

It was a reasonable request and Wally spent Friday following up on the other names Bartley Longe's secretary phoned in to him. "These are regular theatre people who would have met Brittany when she was in Mr. Longe's country home," she explained.

Two of the names were film producers who were both out of the country. The third was a casting director who had to search her brain to remember Brittany La Monte. "Bartley always has a bevy of blondes around him," she explained. "It's hard to tell them apart. If I can't place this girl Brittany, it says to me she didn't grab my attention."

Now as soon as he announced himself a musical voice said, "Come right up." At the sound of a buzzer he pushed the inner door open and climbed to the third floor.

The door of 3B was opened by a tall, slender young woman with long blond hair that cascaded down past her shoulders. "I'm Vita," she told him. "Please come in."

The small living room had clearly been furnished from make-dos and family cast-offs, but was cheerful and coordinated with bright pillows on the vintage couch, colorful blinds on the long, narrow windows, and playbill posters of Broadway hits on the whitewashed walls.

When, at Vita's invitation, he sat in one of the armless upholstered chairs, Angela An-

414

ton came in from the kitchen carrying two cups of cappuccino. "One for you, one for me," she announced as she laid them on the round metal coffee table. "Vita's a tea drinker but doesn't want a cup now."

Angela Anton was not more than five feet tall, with medium brown hair cut into bangs, and hazel eyes that Wally immediately noticed were more green than brown. There was something in the graceful way she moved that made him suspect she was a dancer, an observation that was absolutely on target.

Both young women settled on the couch and looked at him expectantly. Wally took a sip of the coffee and complimented Anton on it. "I usually have my second cup at my desk," he said, "but, this is much better. As I said in my message, I need to talk to you both about Brittany La Monte."

"Is Brittany in trouble?" Vita asked, anxiously, then didn't give him a chance to answer. "What I mean is that she's been gone almost two years and when she left she was so mysterious about it. She took Angela and me out to dinner and said it was on her. She was all excited. She said that she had gotten an offer of a job that would pay really well, but would take a while, and after that, she was going to

California because hanging around New York trying to get in a Broadway show hadn't worked for her."

"Brittany's father is concerned about her, as you know," Johnson said. "He told me he came here to see you."

Angela was the one who answered. "Vita only spoke to him for a couple of minutes. She had a casting call. I had time so I listened to Mr. Grissom's life story, then I had to tell him that we just haven't heard from her."

"He told me that he showed you the postcard Brittany sent him six months ago. It was from New York. Do you think it was genuine?" Johnson asked.

The two young women looked at each other. "I don't know," Angela said slowly. "Brittany's handwriting had curlicues and loops. I can see why she would have printed on a small card. But I just don't know why she wouldn't have called one of us if she was back in Manhattan. We were pretty tight with each other."

"How long did you actually share an apartment together?" Wally asked as he put the coffee cup back on the table.

"It was four years for me," Angela said.

"Three years," Vita responded.

"What do you know about Bartley

Longe?"

Wally Johnson was surprised to hear both young women laugh. "Oh, my God," Vita said. "Did you know what Brittany did with that guy's wigs and toupees?"

"I heard about it," Johnson said. "What was that situation? Was Brittany involved with him, or was she in love with him?"

Angela took a sip of her coffee, and Wally wasn't sure if she was considering the question or finding a way to be loyal to Brittany. Finally she said, "I think Brittany underestimated that guy. She was having a fling with him, but she did it for one reason only and that was to meet people at his Litchfield house who might do her some good as an actress. I can't tell you how much she wanted to be famous. It drove her. She made fun of Bartley Longe. She put us in stitches imitating him."

Wally Johnson thought of what Longe had told him, that Brittany wanted to turn their affair into marriage. "Did she want to marry him?" he asked.

Both young women began to laugh. "Oh, good God," Vita said. "Brittany would no more have married him than . . ." She paused. "I swear, I can't come up with a comparison."

"Then what happened that caused her to

destroy his hairpieces?" Johnson asked.

"She saw that most of the people he had up to that house in Litchfield were potential clients, not theatre people. She decided he was wasting her time. Or maybe by then this mysterious other job had come up. Bartley Longe had given Brittany some jewelry. I guess he could tell that she was sick of going up there, and he swiped it from her jewelry box. That's what really ticked her off. They had a big fight. He wouldn't give it back. So when he was in the shower, she collected all his wigs and toupees and drove his convertible back to New York. She told us she cut up all the 'rugs,' as she called them, and scattered them all over the convertible so that no one in the garage could miss seeing them."

"Did she ever hear from Longe after that?"

"He left her a message," Vita said, the smile gone from her face. She played it for us. "He wasn't ranting the way he would be if she was late getting to Litchfield. He said. 'You will regret this, Brittany. *If* you live to regret it.' "

"He threatened her that directly?" Wally Johnson asked, his interest aroused.

"Yes. Angela and I were frightened for her. Brittany just laughed. She said he was a big bag of wind. But I made a copy of the voice

418

mail. As I said, I was frightened for her. It was only a few days later that she packed her stuff and left."

Wally Johnson considered what he had heard. "Do you still have that copy of Longe's voice mail?"

"Oh, sure," Vita said. "I was worried that Brittany just laughed it off, but when she left town I figured Bartley Longe would eventually cool down."

"I'd like to have that tape if it's handy," Johnson told her. When Vita went to get it he spoke to Angela. "You're in show business, too, I guess."

"Oh, yes. I'm a dancer. Right now I'm rehearsing for a show that's going to open in two months." Before he asked, she said, "And just so you know, Vita is a really good singer. There's a revival of *Show Boat* opening off-Broadway and she's in the chorus."

Wally Johnson took in the Broadway playbill posters on the walls. "Was Brittany a singer or dancer?" he asked.

"She could get by in both areas, but basically she was a dramatic actress."

Johnson could tell by the hesitancy in Angela Anton's voice that she was not going to be lyrical about the theatrical talents of Brittany La Monte. "Angela," he began, "Toby Grissom is a dying man and is

419

agonized by his worry that his daughter may be in some kind of trouble. How good an actress was Brittany?"

Angela Anton looked reflectively at the framed playbill over the chair where Johnson was sitting. "Brittany was okay," she said. "Would she have made it to become a star? I don't think so. I remember one night about four years ago, when I got home, she was sitting here crying because once again an agent had turned her down. You see, Detective Johnson, she was a fabulous makeup artist. I mean *fabulous!* She could change the way someone looked in a heart-beat. Sometimes, when the three of us didn't have jobs, she'd make us all up to look like celebrities. She had a collection of wigs that would knock you over. We'd get dressed up and go somewhere and everyone would think we were the celebrities we were imitating. I told Brittany that she could be the leading makeup artist to celebrities and that would be her path to success. She didn't want to hear it."

Vita Kolber had come back into the living room. "Sorry," she said. "It wasn't in the drawer where I thought I had put it. Would you like me to play it for you, Detective Johnson?"

"Please."

Vita pushed the button of her tape machine. The voice of Bartley Longe, powerful in its fury, threatening and frightening in its message, reverberated through the room. *"You will regret this, Brittany. If you live to regret it."*

Wally Johnson asked to have it played again. It sent chills down his spine. "I'll have to take that tape with me now," he said.

69

Penny Hammel knew she should not take the chance of driving past the Owens farmhouse and being spotted by Gloria Evans. But as she told Bernie, she also knew that something was going on in that house and it was probably a drug deal. "And maybe there's a reward," she said. "You know you can be an anonymous caller, I mean they won't blab all over the news that you're the one who blew the whistle."

There were times when Bernie didn't mind being on the road so much, and one of those times was when Penny got it into her head that something mysterious was going on around her. "Honey, remember the time you thought that stray poodle you found was the missing champion that ran away in the airport? When you checked it out, he was a foot higher and twelve pounds heavier than the other one."

"I know. But he was a nice dog, and

then I advertised and his owner came for him."

"Your thank-you was a bottle of the cheapest wine that guy could find in the liquor store," Bernie reminded her.

"So what? The dog was so happy to be found." Philosophically, Penny had shrugged off the incident. It was Saturday morning. Over breakfast they had seen the news clip of Alexandra Moreland leaving the station house last night still screaming denials that she had kidnapped her child. Penny had thoroughly reasserted her opinion of what should be done to that heartless mother.

Bernie was about to leave for an overnighter that would bring him back on Monday evening. Penny had reminded him several times that he absolutely could not miss the Lottery Winners' reunion in Alvirah and Willy's apartment on Tuesday evening.

He zipped up his jacket and pulled on his wool cap. It was then that he noticed that Penny was wearing her tracksuit and thick boots. "Are you going for a walk?" he asked. "It's pretty cold out."

"Oh, I don't know," Penny said dismissively. "I'm considering going into town and stopping by to say hello to Rebecca."

"You're not going to walk into town, are you?"

"No, but I may do a little shopping or something."

"Uh-huh. Well, just don't overdo it." Bernie planted a kiss on Penny's cheek. "I'll call you tomorrow, honey."

"Drive carefully. If you get sleepy, be sure to pull over. Remember I love you and I don't want to be a merry widow."

It was their traditional parting when Bernie went on the road.

Penny gave him plenty of time to get out of town, then around ten o'clock went into the closet to get her heavy jacket, snow hat, and gloves. She had already put the binoculars on the sideboard behind a lamp where Bernie wouldn't see them. I'll park the car on the street that borders the end of Sy's property, she thought, then I'll sneak up and hang out in the woods for a while. It might be silly, but who knows? That Evans woman is up to something. I can feel it in my bones.

Twenty minutes later she was standing behind an evergreen tree with heavy branches. From there she had a good view of the house. She waited for nearly an hour and then, her hands and feet cold, decided to leave. It was at that moment that the side door of the farmhouse opened and she saw Gloria Evans come out carrying two suitcases.

She's leaving now, Penny thought. What's her big hurry? Rebecca said that she has thirty days to get out if the house sells. On the other hand, Rebecca told her that she was bringing the buyers in tomorrow for a look around the house. That's probably what Missy Evans is worried about. Dollars to donuts, I'm right. What's she got to hide in there?

Gloria Evans had put the suitcases in the trunk of her car and returned to the house. When she came out again, she was dragging an oversized trash bag that seemed to be heavy. That, too, she started to put in the trunk. As Penny watched, a paper fell out of the top of the bag and blew back into the yard. Evans looked after it, but did not chase it. Then she went back into the house and for the next half hour did not come out.

Too cold to wait any longer, Penny went back to her car. It was nearly noon and she drove straight into town. Rebecca had left a note on the door: "Back soon."

Disappointed, Penny started to drive home but then, on an impulse, returned to her observation spot behind Sy's farmhouse. This time to her chagrin, the Evans car was gone. Oh, boy, that means nobody's in there, she thought and, holding her breath, walked up to the back of the house. The shades were drawn to the sill except for one of them that was raised about six inches. She peered in and could see into the kitchen with its heavy old furniture and linoleum floor. Can't tell much from here, she thought. I wonder if she's gone for good?

Making her way to the wooded area again, she saw that the sheet of paper that had blown away was caught on a shrub. Pleased, she ran to get it.

It was coloring paper and a childish hand had obviously sketched it. It had the outline of a woman's face with long hair, a face that in some way resembled Evans. Under the sketch was a single word, "Mommy."

So she *has* a kid, Penny thought, and she doesn't want anyone to know it. I bet she's hiding it from the father. That would be just her style. I wonder if she cut her hair recently. No surprise that she didn't want me to see the toy truck. I know what I'll do. I'll call Alvirah and tell her — maybe she can trace Ms. Gloria Evans. Maybe if she's been hiding a kid from his father, there'll be a reward. Wouldn't that really be a surprise for Bernie?

With a satisfied smile, Penny went back to

the car, the drawing securely held between her gloved fingers. She laid it on the passenger seat, looked down at it, and frowned. Something was sticking in her mind, it felt like a sore tooth that was starting to throb again.

Darned if I know what, she thought as she started the car and drove away.

70

On Saturday morning, the normally intense satisfaction he would have felt at seeing the pictures of Zan splattered all over the tabloids was missing. He had endured a miserable night of restless dreams involving him trying to outrun the hordes of people who were relentlessly chasing him.

Shooting the priest had unnerved him. He had tried to hold the gun against the old man's robe, but at the last minute the priest had pulled to one side. According to the news report, he was in critical condition.

Critical condition, but not dead.

What was he going to do now? He had told Gloria to meet him at LaGuardia tonight, but thinking about it, that was a lousy idea. She was worried about being caught. She was suspicious that he would not deliver on the money. I know her mind, he thought. I still wouldn't put it past her to try to get some of that reward money. I wouldn't be surprised if she was dumb enough to think she could make a deal with the cops and let them put a wire on her before we meet. If she gives them my name now, it's all over.

But if she thinks it through, and is greedy enough to hang on, waiting to get her hands on my money and not go to jail, she may opt for that, he thought.

I can't take a chance of someone spotting me in broad daylight around that farmhouse. But I've got to get up there before she leaves to meet me at LaGuardia. I'll take everything personal in the house that belonged to her and Matthew with me. Then when the real estate agent finds them dead, nothing will be around to suggest that Gloria was impersonating Zan.

He had planned to kill Zan and make it look like a suicide. In a way this was better. She would never get over losing Matthew for good.

When he thought about it, that was infinitely more satisfactory than putting a bullet through her heart. How much fun it had been all these years, even before Matthew was born, being able to observe almost every moment of Zan's life at home whenever he wanted to tune in. In these last two years, he had loved being able to watch her lying in bed, hear her sobbing in her sleep, then waking up in the morning, and, not knowing he was watching, reach over and touch Matthew's picture.

It was eleven o'clock. He dialed Gloria. But she did not answer her cell phone. Maybe she was already on the way into New York, and on her way to the cops?

The thought terrified him. What could he do? Where could he run?

Nowhere.

At 11:30 and then at 12:30, he called her again. By then his hands were shaking. But this time she answered. "Where are you?" he demanded.

"Where do you think I am? I'm stuck here in this damn farmhouse."

"Were you out?"

"I went to the store. Matty just isn't eating anything. I got some hot dogs for his lunch. What time do you want me to meet you?"

"Eleven o'clock tonight."

"Why that late?"

"Because there's no need to do it earlier. And by then, Matthew will be sound asleep, so you won't have to lock him up alone for too long. I'll have all the money. It might raise too many questions to wire it. You can take your chances on carrying it through airport security or sending it parcel post to your father, but this way you'll know you have it, Brittany . . ."

"Don't call me that! You shot that priest, didn't you?"

"Gloria, I need to remind you of something. If you still have any thoughts of going to the police and making a deal, it won't work. I'll tell them that it was you who begged me to kill that good old man because you were stupid enough to blab to him in confession. They'll believe me. You'll never go scott free. This way you still have a chance of doing what you want to do, to have a career. Even if you cut a deal, you won't get away with less than twenty years. Believe me, there isn't much of a market for either actresses or makeup artists in prison."

"You'd better have that money with you."

He could tell that if she had had any intention of going to the cops, she was wavering. "I'm looking at it right now."

"Six hundred thousand dollars?" she asked. "All of it."

"I'll wait tonight while you count it."

"What about Matthew saying I took him from the stroller?"

"I've been thinking about what you said. He was just three years old. There's nothing to worry about. They'll think he's mixed up about whether his mother or someone else, meaning you, took him that day. You know they arrested Zan last night? The cops don't believe a word that she's saying."

"I guess you're right. I just want this to be over."

You're making it easy for me, he thought. "Don't leave around any of the stuff you wore when you looked like Zan," he said.

"Stop worrying. Every bit of it is packed. Did you get my airline ticket?"

"Yes. I'm sending you by way of Atlanta. It's better if you don't have a direct flight. I'm just being careful. Use your own ID when you fly from Atlanta to Texas. You're booked on the 10:30 Continental tomorrow morning from LaGuardia to Atlanta. That way if you want to send the money to your father, parcel post, which I think is a good idea, you'll have time to do it. I'll meet you in the parking lot of the Holiday Inn on the Grand Central Parkway. I made a reservation for you there."

"I guess you're right. And like you say, if I meet you at eleven o'clock, I only have to put Matty in the closet at 9:30."

"Exactly." Then, making his voice sound tender, he added, "You know, Gloria, you are a superb actress. These times you've been out, you've not only looked like Zan but you moved like her, too. I could see that in the photos that tourist took. It's uncanny. I'm telling you, those cops are convinced it's Zan in them."

"Yeah. Thanks." She clicked off.

I wasted a night's sleep, he thought. She won't go to the cops. Once again he picked up a newspaper with Zan's face on it. "I can't wait to see your expression tomorrow when that real estate woman and her buyer find Brittany and Matthew, and you get the sad tidings," he said aloud.

And like that he figured out the solution that was at his fingertips. It would take money, but that kind of money he could willingly spare.

He just didn't have the heart to kill the child himself.

71

It was late morning when he got to his desk
after seeing Brittany La Monte's roommates. Wally Johnson leaned back in his
chair. Totally ignoring the phones and
conversations going on in the big room, he
studied Brittany's photo montage. There is
a slight resemblance to the Moreland
woman, he thought. Angela Anton had said
that La Monte was a consummate makeup
artist. He held the montage against the front
page of the *Post* showing Alexandra Moreland coming out of the courthouse. The
headline read: ZAN SCREAMS, "I AM NOT
THE WOMAN IN THOSE PHOTOS."

Was there even the faintest chance that
she was right?

Wally closed his eyes. On the other hand,
was Brittany La Monte still alive, or had
Bartley Longe managed to carry out his
threat to her? She had not been seen in
nearly two years, and the postcard could

well have been a phony.

The tape of that phone call was enough to bring Longe in for questioning. But suppose . . . Wally Johnson did not finish the thought. Instead, he reached for his cell phone and called Billy Collins. "Wally Johnson, Billy, you at your desk?"

"On the way in. I had to stop at the dentist. Be there in twenty minutes," Billy answered.

"I'll take a run up. I want to show you something."

"Sure," Billy said, mildly curious.

The night before, Billy had gone directly from Zan Moreland's arraignment to a play at Fordham University on the Rose Hill Campus in the Bronx. His son, a senior, had one of the leading roles in it. Billy and Eileen had heard about the shooting of Fr. Aiden O'Brien in the car on their way home to Forest Hills.

"I'm sorry we won't get this case, but it happened in another precinct," he had told Eileen heatedly the night before. "To shoot a seventy-eight-year-old priest when he's in the process of offering you forgiveness has to be the worst form of lowlife. I just spoke to Fr. O'Brien earlier today, something about the Moreland case. The crazy thing is that Fr. O'Brien was warned about that guy. Alvirah Meehan, the friend of Zan Moreland I told you about, had seen someone watching that priest Monday evening. She even went to view the church security camera tape, but couldn't get a decent look at him."

All Friday night, Billy had kept waking up, feeling as if he had, in some way, personally failed Fr. O'Brien. But we *did* look at the tape, he thought. The glimpse we got of that guy with a lot of dark hair was useless. He could have been anybody.

The first thing he did in the morning was to phone the hospital, where a police guard had been placed outside the intensive care unit. "He's holding his own, Billy," was the reassuring answer to his inquiry.

At the precinct, Jennifer Dean was waiting at his desk with David Feldman, one of the detectives assigned to investigate the shooting of Fr. O'Brien.

Although Jennifer Dean was outwardly calm, Billy knew her well enough to sense that she was tense. "Wait till you hear what Dave has to tell us, Billy," she began. "It's pretty explosive."

Feldman didn't waste time on preliminaries. "Billy, as soon as the medics got the priest on the way to the hospital, we looked at the security cameras." The crinkles around David Feldman's eyes were proof that the detective was by nature a man who frequently smiled, but now his expression was grave. "We had a description from some of the people who were in the atrium after they heard three popping sounds. They saw a six- or six-foot-one man with a bushy head of black hair, trench coat, upturned collar, and dark glasses run out of the Reconciliation Room. It was easy to pick him out on the camera, entering and leaving the church. I think that mop of hair is a wig. No way that we could get a decent look at his face."

"Anyone see which way he headed?" Billy snapped.

"A woman came forward who saw a man running toward Eighth Avenue. He may or may not have been our guy."

"Okay." Billy knew David Feldman had more to say but would do it his way, meticulously covering the step-by-step of the investigation.

"This morning the church handyman, Neil Hunt, came back. He had been to an AA meeting last night and went straight home and to bed after it. He didn't hear about the shooting until this morning. But get this." Feldman pulled his chair closer to Billy's desk and leaned forward. "Hunt used to be a cop. He got thrown off the force after being sent to the farm twice to dry out. Drinking on duty. The third time he was told to turn in his shield."

"Billy, wait till you hear the rest of it," Jennifer said, a note of barely concealed astonishment in her voice. "Remember that Alvirah Meehan told us that she had been in church Monday evening, and didn't like the way that man sprang up from supposedly praying when Fr. O'Brien came out of the Reconciliation Room? It bothered her enough that she went back and looked at those security tapes."

Feldman darted an annoyed glance at Dean for interrupting him. "We took a look at those tapes from Monday night, Billy," he said. "It's the same guy who was on the cameras last night going into the atrium of the lower church and leaving it a few minutes later, the one who shot the priest. You couldn't miss him. Mop of black hair, big dark glasses, same trench coat. The priest had no idea who he was.

"But, Billy, get this. We believe that Zan Moreland was in the church Monday night, too. She came and left before Alvirah, but the man in the black hair may have followed her in. He didn't leave until he saw what Fr. Aiden looked like."

"Was Moreland dropping in to say a prayer, or do you think she's connected to the guy who shot the priest?" Billy snapped. "Or did she go to confession and maybe that guy got worried?"

"I think it's a possibility," Feldman answered. "Billy, there's something else going on. As I said, the handyman who showed us the security tapes, Neil Hunt, used to be a cop."

"He wasn't the one who showed us the security tape yesterday," Jennifer Dean interrupted again.

"He claims he has a photographic memory," Feldman continued. "He bragged that I should look up his record in the department on that. He swears that Monday night, right after the Moreland woman left the church, he was walking home and a block away, a woman who looked just like her stepped in front of him and got in a cab. He said he'd have thought it was the same person, except the one who got in the cab had slacks and a jacket on. The one in church was dressed up."

Billy Collins and Jennifer Dean looked at each other for a long minute, each thinking the same thing. Was it possible that Alexandra Moreland was telling the truth, that there really *was* someone who looked ex-

439

actly like her out there? Or was this ex-cop-trying to capture a moment of self-importance by making up a story that no one might be able to prove or disprove?

"I wonder if our former brother in New York's Finest has read the morning papers and figures this is a good way to get some-one to pay him for an interview?" Billy sug-gested, even as his gut told him that wouldn't be the case. "Dave, let's get Neil Hunt in here and see if he sticks to his story."

Billy's cell phone began to ring. Deep in thought, he picked it up and barked his name. It was Alvirah Meehan. He did not miss the triumphant note in her voice. "I wonder if I can come right over and see you," she said. "I have something of great interest to tell you."

"I'll be right here, Mrs. Meehan, and I'll be glad to see you." He looked up.

Wally Johnson was making his way swiftly through the uneven rows of desks to come to him.

72

Kevin Wilson spent more than an hour in the exercise room of his apartment late Saturday morning. During that time he switched the remote from channel to channel, trying to see every possible news clip showing Zan leaving the courthouse. Her agonized protest, "I am not the woman in those photos," cut through him like a knife.

Frowning, he watched as a psychiatrist compared the photos of Zan in Central Park after Matthew disappeared and the ones of her taking Matthew from the stroller and carrying him away. "There is no way that woman is not the mother kidnapping her own child," the psychiatrist was saying. "Look at these photos. Who else would be able to find and change into the exact same dress in the space of a few hours?"

Kevin knew he had to see Zan today. She had told him she lived in Battery Park City, only fifteen minutes away. She had given him her cell phone number. Keeping his fingers crossed, he dialed it.

It rang five times, then her voice came on. "Hi, this is Zan Moreland. Please leave a number and I'll get back to you."

"Zan, this is Kevin. I hate to do this to you, but I'd really like to get together with you today. We're getting the workmen started Monday on the apartments and there are a few things I need to go over with you." Then he added, hastily, "No problems, just choices."

He showered, then dressed in his favorite kind of clothes: jeans, a sport shirt, and a sweater. He wasn't hungry, but he had some cereal and coffee. He sat at the small table that overlooked the Hudson while he read in the paper about the charges that had been placed against Zan. Kidnapping, interfering with parental custody, lying to the police.

She was ordered to surrender her passport and could not leave the country.

Kevin tried to imagine what it would be like to stand in front of a judge and have charges like that hurled at him. He had been a juror in a manslaughter trial once and had watched the frightened defendant, a twenty-year-old kid who'd been high on drugs when he rammed a car, killing two people,

442

sentenced to twenty years in prison.

His story was that someone had slipped something into his soda. Kevin still wondered if that was possible, but the kid had a history of being arrested for pot.

I am not the woman in those photos. Why against all the odds do I believe her? Kevin asked himself. I know, I absolutely *know,* that she is telling the truth.

His cell phone rang. It was his mother. "Kev, did you see the newspaper about the Moreland arrest?"

You know I did, Mom, he thought.

"Kevin, are you going to hire that woman after all this?"

"Mom, I know it sounds crazy but I believe that Zan is a victim, not a kidnapper. Sometimes you just know something about someone else and that's the way I feel."

He waited, then Cate Wilson said, "Kevin, you've always had the biggest heart of anyone I know. But sometimes people aren't deserving of it. Just think about that. Goodbye, dear."

She had disconnected.

Kevin debated, then pushed Zan's number again. He hung up when her voice started to direct him to leave a message. *I'll get back to you.*

It was nearly 1:30. You're not going to get back to me, he thought.

He got up, put a few dishes in the dishwasher, and decided to go for a walk. A walk that will take me to Battery Park City, he thought. I'm going to Zan's apartment and knock on her door. If nothing else, I would guess that this job is more important to her than ever — her legal bills have to be piling up already.

He was reaching in the closet for his leather jacket when the phone rang again. It better not be Louise crowing about Zan's arrest, he thought. If she is, I'll fire her.

His "Hello" was close to a bark.

It was Zan. "Kevin, I'm sorry. I left my cell phone in my coat last night and the ringer was off. Do you want me to meet you at Carlton Place?"

"No, I've had enough of being on the job for a week. I'm just about to go out for a walk. You're fifteen minutes away. May I come to your apartment and we can talk there?"

There was a moment of hesitancy, then Zan said, "Yes, of course, if that works better for you. I'll be here."

73

Come on, Matty, eat your hot dog," Gloria coaxed. "I made a special trip to the store to get it for you today."

Matthew tried to take a bite, then put it down. "I can't, Glory." He thought she'd be mad, but she just looked sad and said, "It's a good thing this is the end, Matty. Neither one of us is going to last, the way we're living."

"Glory, why did you pack up my stuff? Are we moving to a new house?"

Her smile was bitter. "No, Matty, I told you, but you don't believe me. You're going home."

He shook his head in disbelief. "Where are *you* going?"

"Well, for a while I'm going home to visit my daddy. I haven't seen him in the whole time you haven't seen Mommy. After that, well, I guess I'll try to get my career on track. Okay, I'm not going to make you eat that hot dog. How about some ice cream?"

Matthew didn't want to tell Glory that nothing tasted good anymore. She had packed away almost all his toys and cars and coloring books and crayons. She had even taken the picture he was drawing of Mommy, the one he had put back in the box because he didn't want to finish it. He didn't want to throw it away, though. And she had packed the bar of soap that smelled like Mommy.

Every single day he kept trying to remember what it was like to be with Mommy. Her long hair that sometimes tickled his nose. Her robe and how it felt when she wrapped him inside with her. All the animals in the zoo. Sometimes he said their names over and over when he was in bed. Elephant. Gorilla. Lion. Monkey. Tiger. Zebra. Like A, B, C, D. Mommy had told him that it was fun to put letters and words together. E is for elephant. He knew he was forgetting some of them and he didn't want to. Glory sometimes gave him DVDs with animals in them, but it wasn't the same as seeing them with Mommy at the zoo.

After lunch, Glory said, "Matty, why don't you watch one of the movies on your DVD. I have to finish packing. Close the door of your room."

Matthew knew that Glory probably wanted to watch television. She did that every day, but never let him see it. His television only worked on the DVD setting, and he had a lot of movies. But he didn't want to watch one now.

Instead when he went up to his room, he laid down and pulled the blanket up over him. He forgot and his hand crept under the pillow for the soap that smelled like Mommy, but it wasn't there. Matthew was so sleepy, he closed his eyes and hardly noticed that he was crying.

Margaret/Glory/Brittany finished the hot dog that Matthew had barely touched and sat reflectively at the kitchen table. She looked around. "Crummy house, crummy kitchen, crummy life," she said aloud. Her anger at herself for having gotten into this situation in the first place had been mingled with a sense of sadness. It had come over her during the night and she knew it had to do with her father.

Something was wrong with Daddy. She knew it in her bones. Her hand reached for her cell phone, but then she pulled it back. I'll be with him by tomorrow night, she thought, I'll surprise him.

She said it aloud. "I'll surprise him."

The words sounded hollow and even fool-
ish to her ears.

74

Alvirah was reveling in her story as she sat at Billy Collins's desk, and word for word she described her meeting with Tiffany Shields to him and his fellow detective Jennifer Dean. The shoebox with the sandals Tiffany had given her was on the desk. She had taken one of the sandals out. What she didn't know was that she had placed it on top of Brittany La Monte's photo, which Collins had hastily turned over, facedown.

"I don't blame Tiffany," she said. "She's had one hard time of it being lambasted by the media and all the do-gooders. When she thought Zan had kidnapped Matthew, you can understand why she'd feel furious and betrayed. But when I explained to her that Zan had never blamed her, and reminded her that she would be under oath in a trial, she soon changed her tune."

"Let me get this straight," Billy said. "Ms. Moreland bought two pairs of identical shoes and had a third pair that was very similar, except for the strap."

"You've got it," Alvirah said heartily. "We talked about it, and Tiffany remembered a little more. Zan told her that she had ordered them online and by mistake got two pairs in the same color. Then when she realized that the sandals looked so close to a pair she already owned, Tiffany said, Zan just gave her one of the new pairs."

"Tiffany's memory seems to move around a bit," Jennifer Dean suggested. "Why is she so positive that Zan Moreland was wearing the sandals with the thinner strap that day?"

"She remembered because Zan happened to be wearing the same ones that Tiffany was, the pair with the thin strap. She said she had noticed it that day, but she wasn't in the mood for joking and Zan was nervous and in a hurry."

Alvirah looked at the two detectives. "I came straight here after I talked to Tiffany. I didn't happen to have with me those pictures showing Zan wearing one pair of sandals when she supposedly kidnapped Matthew and a different pair when she came back to the park after he was gone. But *you* do. So go look at them. And tell your experts to study them. And then wonder why any woman about to kidnap her child would bother to go home and change her shoes."

Billy and Jennifer Dean looked at each other, once again knowing what the other was thinking. If what Alvirah Meehan was telling them was true, the case against Zan Moreland was unraveling. They had both been startled by the resemblance of Brittany La Monte to Zan Moreland, once Wally Johnson pointed it out, and by the fact that La Monte was a makeup artist who had disappeared in exactly the time frame when Matthew Carpenter had been kidnapped, and who had worked for Bartley Longe, the rival Zan Moreland insisted was responsible for Matthew's disappearance.

In this high-profile case it was necessary to move very carefully. Billy did not want to admit that he was shaken — more shaken than he had ever been in any investigation he had ever worked.

We spoke to Longe, Billy thought. We dismissed him as a suspect. But now? With all this going on? Was the ex-cop Neil Hunt on target when he said he saw someone who looked like Zan Moreland getting into a cab near that church? He even remembered the hack number so we could check cab records for Monday night at that time. That was next on Billy's list.

Was Tiffany Shields a reliable witness? Probably not. The kid had changed her version of the morning she began to baby-sit Matthew Carpenter to suit her imagination.

But what if she was right about the shoes?

Alvirah was getting up to go. "Mr. Collins, last night after her terrible experience of being arrested and placed in a holding cell, Zan Moreland, Matthew Carpenter's mother, begged me to start out with the premise that I believed in her innocence. The minute I decided to do that, I sought out Tiffany and reminded her that she'd be under oath in a trial and she told me what I believe is the truth."

Alvirah took a deep breath. "I think you're a decent man who wants to protect the innocent and punish the guilty. Why don't you do what Zan begged you to do, too? Assume that she is innocent. Really investigate the man she believes to be responsible for Matthew's disappearance, Bartley Longe, and start digging. You see, even though she's been arrested, she still got the big job instead of Longe — of decorating some fancy new apartments. If Longe did figure out how to kidnap Matthew, and if Matthew is still alive, this might be enough to make him try to get back at Zan again and with the only weapon he may have. Her son."

Billy Collins stood up and extended his hand to Alvirah. "Mrs. Meehan, you are quite right. Our job is to protect the innocent. That is all that I am free to tell you right now. I'm very grateful that you encouraged Tiffany Shields to tell you what is perhaps a more accurate account of what happened when she met Ms. Moreland at her apartment the day Matthew disappeared."

As he watched Alvirah make her way to the exit, his instinct was telling him that she was the one on the right track and that time was running out.

As soon as she was out of sight, he yanked open the drawer and pulled out the photos of Zan Moreland that had been in newspapers all over the world these past few days, the original ones of her at the park after the kidnapping and the ones that just surfaced from the British tourist. He laid them on the desk and reached for a magnifying glass. He studied them and handed the glass to Jennifer.

"Billy, Alvirah's right. She's not wearing the same shoes," Jennifer whispered.

Billy turned over the photo montage of Brittany La Monte and aligned it with the other pictures. "What could a good makeup artist do to change a similarity to a look-alike?" he asked Dean.

It was a rhetorical question.

75

When Zan opened the door for Kevin at 1:45, he looked at her for a long minute, then, feeling as if it were the most natural thing in the world for him to do, he put his arms around her. For long seconds they stood still, her hands at her side, her eyes searching his.

Kevin said firmly, "Zan, I don't know how good your lawyer is, but what you need is a private detective agency to turn this situation around."

"Then you *do* believe that I'm not a wacko?" Zan's tone was tentative.

"Zan, this is me. I trust you. Trust me."

"I'm sorry, Kevin. My God, you're the first person to say you believe me. But it goes on. The Mad Hatter's tea party goes on. Look around you."

Kevin looked around the warm and tastefully decorated living room with its eggshell walls, roomy pale green sofa, striped chairs, and deep green and cream geometric carpet. Both the couch and the chairs had open boxes on them from Bergdorf's.

"These just arrived this morning," Zan said. "They're charged to my account. I didn't buy them, Kevin, I didn't buy them. I spoke to a salesclerk in Bergdorf's I know pretty well. She said she didn't handle the sale Monday afternoon, but she recognized me and was a little hurt that I hadn't asked for her. She said that I bought the same suit a few weeks ago. Why would I do that? The one I have is in the closet. Alvirah thought she saw me on the security camera in the church on Monday evening wearing a black suit with a fur collar. I didn't wear that suit Monday evening. I wore it the next day, when I met you." Zan threw up her hands in a gesture of despair. "Where does it end? How can I stop it? Why? Why?"

Kevin covered her hands with his. "Zan, hang on. Come on. Sit over here." He guided her to the couch. "Have you ever noticed anyone following you?"

"No, but Kevin, I feel as if I'm living in a fishbowl. I've been arrested. Someone is impersonating me. The media is hounding me. I feel as if someone is walking in my footsteps, shadowing me, imitating me. *That person has my child!*"

"Zan, let's go back. I saw the photos of the woman you swear is not you in the paper, taking your son out of the stroller."

"She was wearing the same dress that I have, the same everything."

"That's my point, Zan. When did you wear that dress on the street where you could be seen?"

"I went out on the street with Tiffany. Matthew was asleep in his stroller. I grabbed a cab to Sixty-ninth Street to go to the Aldrich town house."

"That means even if someone saw you, and wanted to look like you, in the space of an hour or so, she would have had to find a dress that was exactly like yours."

"Don't you see? One of the columnists brought that up in the newspaper. They said it would be impossible for anyone to do that."

"Unless someone saw you while you were getting dressed, and already had a dress identical to the one you chose to wear?"

"There was absolutely no one in the apartment except Matthew while I was getting dressed."

"And this identical clothing continues to this day." Kevin Wilson stood up. "Zan, do you mind if I look around the apartment?"

"No, take your time, but what for?"

"Just humor me."

Kevin Wilson walked into the bedroom. The bed was made and piled with pillows. A picture of a smiling child was on the night table. The room was orderly, with a single dresser, a small writing desk, a slipper chair. The valance of the large picture window matched the blue and white pattern on the bed.

But even though Kevin's subconscious was aware of the pretty bedroom, his eyes were darting around the room. He was thinking of the time three years ago when a client had bought a condo after a bitter divorce between the sellers. When the workmen started to pull out the wiring, they had discovered a spy camera in the bedroom.

Was it possible that Zan might have been under scrutiny when she chose the dress she was wearing the day Matthew disappeared? And was it possible that she was still under scrutiny from an unknown observer?

With that in mind, he went back to the living room. "Zan, have you got a stepladder?" he asked. "I need to take a look around this place."

"Yes, I have one."

Kevin followed her to the hall closet, then reached past her and took the ladder from her hands. She followed him into the bedroom as he stood on it and slowly, carefully, began to examine and run his finger over the crown molding on the bedroom walls.

Directly opposite her bed, and over the dresser, he found what he was looking for, the tiny eye of a camera.

76

The *Post* and the *Times* were delivered to the Aldrich town house every morning. Maria Garcia put them in the pocket on the side of the breakfast tray for Nina Aldrich, who enjoyed breakfast in bed. But before Maria brought up the tray, she looked at the headline with Zan Moreland's cry, "I AM NOT THE WOMAN IN THOSE PHOTOS," splattered across the front page.

Mrs. Aldrich lied to the police, Maria thought, and I know why. Mr. Aldrich was away and Bartley Longe dropped in on her. And *stayed.* And stayed a long time. She knew she was keeping that young woman waiting and she didn't care. And then she lied bald-faced to those detectives. It was easier than to try to make an excuse for keeping Ms. Moreland waiting so long.

She brought up the tray and Nina Aldrich, propped up on pillows, grabbed the *Post* and saw the front page. "Oh, they did arrest her?" she said. "Walter will be furious if I'm dragged in to testify. But I'll simply repeat what I told the detectives, and that will be that."

Maria Garcia left the bedroom without answering. But by noon, she could stand it no longer. She had the card Detective Collins had given her and, being careful to see that Mrs. Aldrich was not on her way down in the elevator, dialed his number.

In the precinct, Billy Collins was waiting for Bartley Longe who, in a rage, had accepted Detective David Feldman's invitation to come in to the Central Park Precinct. Billy picked up the phone. He heard a tremulous voice say, "Detective Collins, I'm Maria Garcia. I'm afraid to call you because I don't have my green card yet."

Maria Garcia, the Aldrich housekeeper, Billy thought. What now? His voice soothing and reassuring, he said, "Mrs. Garcia, I didn't hear you tell me that. Is there something else that you want to say?"

"Yes." Maria took a long breath, then nervously burst out, "Detective Collins, I swear on my mother's grave that Ms. Moreland was told by Mrs. Aldrich to meet her here at the town house that day almost two years ago. I heard her and I know why she's lying about it. Bartley Longe, the designer, had stopped in to see Mrs. Aldrich on Beekman Place. They were having an affair. She let poor Ms. Moreland do all the work to get the job and gave it to him instead when he started flattering her. But that day, she was leaving to meet Ms. Moreland here on Sixty-ninth Street when Mr. Longe arrived. She knew perfectly well that Ms. Moreland was waiting for her, and that she'd sit there waiting until Mrs. Aldrich decided to show up."

Billy was about to respond when Maria Garcia gasped, "Mrs. Aldrich is on the way down. I have to go."

There was a click in his ear, and Billy Collins was processing this new chink in the evidence in the case against Alexandra Moreland when, accompanied by his lawyer, a furious Bartley Longe arrived at the precinct.

77

At quarter of one on Saturday afternoon, Melissa phoned Ted. "Have you seen the papers?" she asked. "They're all talking about how generous I am to offer that wonderful reward for your son."

Ted had managed to beg off from seeing her again on Friday night on the basis of his ongoing flu-like symptoms. At Rita's loyal insistence, he had called Melissa after her announcement to the media and groveled his gratitude to her.

Now, clenching his teeth, his voice robotic, he said, "Beautiful lady, I predict that a year from now, you'll be the number one star on this planet, maybe in the universe."

"You're sweet." Melissa laughed. "I think so, too. Oh, good news. Jaime-boy had a fight with his publicist again. Isn't that a riot? The big all-is-forgiven scene lasted only twenty-four hours. He wants to meet you."

Ted was standing in the living room of his

handsomely furnished duplex apartment in the Meatpacking district, the apartment where he had lived for eight years. It had been his crowning achievement when he had been established enough to buy and furnish it. Bartley Longe and Zan Moreland, his assistant, had done the interior decorating. That was how he had met Zan.

That was running through his head as he reminded himself that he could not afford to offend Melissa. "When does Jaime-boy want to meet me?" he asked.

"Monday, I guess."

"That would be *great.*" Ted's reaction was genuinely enthusiastic. He was not up to meeting Jaime-boy today. And Melissa was flying to London to attend a celebrity birthday party. He knew that, concerned as she was with catching a flu bug, she still did not want to go unescorted to the party.

He felt an almost uncontrollable desire to laugh. Wouldn't it be perfect if someone did somehow find Matthew, and Melissa had to shell out five million dollars?

"Ted, if you start feeling better, hop a plane to London, or else I'll find someone else at the party. British guys are soooooooooooo attractive."

"Don't you dare." His slightly stern voice, his "Daddy knows best," was a good sign-off. Finally he was able to get off the phone. He opened the door of the terrace and went outside. The cold air snapped at him. He looked down.

Sometimes I wonder if it wouldn't be good to jump and be done with it, he thought.

78

When Willy got back from his daily walk in Central Park, he realized that he was hungry. The problem was that he and Alvirah often liked to have lunch out on Saturdays, then drop in on a museum or go to a movie.

He tried to call her cell phone, but she didn't answer. *I should think that whatever that Tiffany Shields kid has to say, it would be said by now,* he thought, *but maybe Alvirah stopped to do a little shopping.*

I won't spoil my appetite, he decided when she still hadn't returned. But fifteen minutes later, he was wavering. And then the phone rang.

"Willy, you just won't begin to guess what I'm going to tell you," Alvirah began. "I'm so excited, I can hardly stand it. But listen, I just left Detective Collins and Detective Dean at the Central Park Precinct. Let's meet at the Russian Tea Room for lunch."

"I'm on my way," Willy promised. He

knew that if he began to ask Alvirah questions, she would spill the beans immediately about what was exciting her and he'd rather hear it over the lunch table.

"See you there," Alvirah confirmed.

Willy replaced the receiver and headed for the closet in the foyer. He pulled out his jacket and gloves. As he was opening the front door of their apartment, the phone rang. He waited in case it was Alvirah calling back. Instead, when he did not pick up, he heard the beginning of a message. "Alvirah, this is Penny Hammel. I tried you on your cell phone but you're not answering. You won't believe what I'm going to tell you, Alvirah," she began. "I swear I think I'm right. This morning —"

Willy let the door close behind him on Penny's message. Later, Penny, he thought as he rang for the elevator.

The message he did not wait to hear was Penny telling Alvirah that she was willing to bet that Matthew Carpenter was the child Gloria Evans was hiding in the farmhouse.

"What should I do?" Penny asked the answering machine. "Call the cops now? But I guess it would be better to hear from you because I have absolutely no proof. Alvirah, *call me!*"

79

Kevin, what does this mean?" Zan asked. "You're telling me that my bedroom has had a camera recording every minute I'm here?"

"Yes." Kevin Wilson did not waste time thinking about the terrible sense of invasion that Zan would be feeling when the full awareness of all that this discovery involved sank in on her. "Zan, somebody installed this or had it installed. Somebody probably bugged your other apartment as well. That's why it was possible for your look-alike to dress in exactly the same clothes."

From staring into the camera, he turned to look at her. Zan's face was ghastly white. She was shaking her head in protest. "My God, my God. Ted sent that guy he knew from his hometown in Wisconsin, Larry Post," she cried. "He's Ted's driver, cook, and handyman. He does everything for him. He installed the lighting fixtures and set up the television here and in the other apart-

ment and my computer system in my office
Maybe that is how my accounts were hacked
into. And all this time I've been blaming
Bartley Longe.

"Ted has done this to me!" she shrieked,
her voice rising with every word. "It's Ted.
But what has he done to my son?"

80

Shortly after two o'clock Larry Post reached Middletown. The job that Ted had laid out for him was not easy. *I'm supposed to make it look like Brittany shot the boy and then killed herself. That's easier said than done.*

Larry had not been surprised that Ted had changed his mind about driving up there and finishing them off himself. Ted was worried sick that Brittany would go to the police, and he now realized that the boy might be able to convince the cops that Zan had not taken him from the park. If that happened, Ted knew the police would eventually come to him.

Larry could understand why Ted couldn't bring himself to kill his own son, but why was it at this point even necessary? *I'm no bleeding heart, but I can't say that I ever thought that working for Ted would ever end up like this,* Larry thought. *But he did point out to me that if the cops keep dig-*

ging and find those cameras in Zan's apart ment, she'll know that I was the one who installed all the lighting and set up her computer.

When Zan decided to leave Ted and take that apartment on East Eighty-sixth Street, and then again when she moved to Battery Park City after Matthew disappeared, big-hearted Ted was the one who had helped her get settled both times. He sent a plumber to check all the pipes and me to install new lighting fixtures. And the cameras. The day she moved from Eighty-sixth Street I got rid of the original cameras. I had already installed the second cameras in her new apartment.

For the first three years it was enough for Ted to just spy on her anytime he wanted. But then she was getting successful in her business and she and Matthew were such a team that he couldn't stand it. And that was just the time when he met Brittany at a party and hatched this whole crazy plan.

Ted is right. If we don't act now, the cops will be knocking on my door before too long. I'm not going back to prison. I'd rather be dead. And he's going to give me the money he's already put in Matthew's trust fund. Let's face it. Ted needs me and I need him.

Ted had said that Brittany had become too much of a loose cannon and was now a big threat to both of us. He said that she's nutty enough to think that she might be able to make a deal with the police and still get the five-million-bucks reward that witch Melissa has put up in her big publicity stunt.

Larry laughed out loud. If that kid ever got home safely, Melissa would have a coronary. But that's not going to happen. He and Ted had figured out how he would get this done.

Brittany will recognize the truck when I pull up the driveway, he thought. Hopefully she won't panic when she sees me because she knows that I've been in on everything all along. When I'm near the house I'll phone her and say that I've got two big boxes full of cash, six hundred thousand dollars. I'll say that Ted wanted me to show her that he wouldn't double-cross her about the money and give her time to send it to Texas. In case she gets suspicious and is scared to open the door, I'll be carrying one of the boxes and she can look through the window and see the hundred-dollar bills on the top layer of the box. She won't be able to tell that the rest of the box is stuffed with newspapers.

When she lets me in, I'll do what I have

to do. If she doesn't let me in, I'll blow the lock off the door. If that happens, it won't look like a murder-suicide, but there's nothing I can do about it. The main thing is that neither one of them will ever be able to talk.

81

Billy Collins was unimpressed by Bartley Longe's show of bravado. "Mr. Longe," he said, "I'm glad you have your lawyer with you. Because before we exchange a meaningful word, I am telling you that you are a person of interest in the disappearance of the woman known as Brittany La Monte. Her roommates kept a tape of your threat to her."

Billy had no intention of telling Longe that he had just come under suspicion of hiring Brittany La Monte to impersonate Zan Moreland and to kidnap her child. *That* possibility he was hugging to his vest.

"I never saw Brittany La Monte after she left my home in early June almost two years ago," Longe snapped. "That so-called threat was made because she had vandalized my property."

Wally Johnson and Jennifer Dean were sitting with them. "Your wigs and toupees, Mr.

Longe?" Johnson asked. "By any chance have you replaced them with a set that includes one with a thick mop of black hair?"

"Absolutely not," Longe snapped. "Let's get this straight. I never saw Brittany after that day. Give me a lie detector test. I'll pass it with my eyes closed." He turned to Wally Johnson. "Have you followed up on any of those names my secretary gave you?"

"Two are out of the country," Wally Johnson shot back. "Perhaps you knew they're not easily reachable."

"I don't keep track of my many friends who are successful producers." Longe turned to his lawyer. "I would like to insist on having a lie detector test immediately. I will not be hounded by these detectives any longer."

Jennifer Dean had not said anything. Sometimes they worked an interrogation that way. Billy asking the questions, she listening to the answers. Billy Collins felt that his partner was sometimes better than a lie detector test for spotting the liars.

But not always, he reminded himself. If Zan Moreland is right about being impersonated, we both sure missed it.

And if she was, it didn't answer the question, Where is Matthew Carpenter? Is he still alive?

His telephone rang. It was Kevin Wilson.

Billy picked up his phone and listened, his face impassive. "Thank you, Mr. Wilson. We'll get right on it."

He turned to Bartley Longe. "You can leave at any time, Mr. Longe," he said. "We will not press any charges against you for the threatening phone call. Good-bye."

Billy jumped from his chair and headed out of the room. Trying not to show their surprise, Jennifer Dean and Wally Johnson followed him. "We've got to get to Ted Carpenter's apartment," Billy told them tersely. "My guess is that if he happens to be looking into his computer, he'll know that it's all over."

82

She couldn't wait any longer. She had to hear her father's voice. She had to tell him that she was coming home. But first . . . Glory tiptoed upstairs to make sure that Matthew's door was closed.

She had expected that he'd be watching one of the movies, but he was asleep on the bed, under a blanket. He looks so pale, she thought, as she bent over him. He's been crying again. The realization of what she had done to him swept over her as, careful not to awaken him, she tiptoed out of the room, closing the door behind her.

Standing in the kitchen, she picked up the last of the unregistered cell phones that he had given her and dialed her father's home in Texas. The call was answered by a stranger.

"Uh, is Mr. Grissom there?" Panicked, Glory knew that she was going to hear bad news.

"Is this a family member?"

"It's his daughter." Glory's voice became high-pitched and breathless. "Is he sick?"

"I'm sorry. I'm with the EMT service. He called 911 and we got here immediately but it was too late to save him. He had a massive heart attack. Are you Glory?"

"Yes. Yes."

"Well, ma'am, I hope what I am going to say is some comfort to you. Your father's final words were, 'Tell my Glory that I love her.' "

She pushed the button to disconnect the call. I have to go home now, she thought wildly. I have to put my arms around him one last time. What was the reservation that had been made for her? Yes, 10:30 tomorrow morning at LaGuardia, Continental Airlines to Atlanta. I'll change the reservation. I'll go straight home. I have to see him. I have to tell Daddy, I'm sorry. I'm sorry.

She opened her laptop. Half out of her mind with grief and regret, her fingers moved automatically to the Continental Airlines Web site. For a few minutes her fingers raced over the keys. Then she stopped. I should have known, she thought. I should have known.

There was no reservation in the name of Gloria Evans to Atlanta at 10:30 A.M.

478

There was no Continental Airlines plane leaving at that time to Atlanta.

Margaret/Glory/Brittany closed the computer. He'll be here soon. He won't have the money. I'll never escape him. He'll hunt me down with the same hatred he has hunted Zan Moreland. Her sin was not to want him and mine is that I am a threat to him.

He would be here soon. She knew it. She was standing at the window facing the road. A white truck was slowly passing the house. She gasped. Larry Post had been waiting in a white truck when she left Central Park with Matthew. If he was coming here now, it was to make sure she never had the chance to give Ted up to the cops.

It was too late to get Matthew and go to the car. Her eyes wild, she knew what might work. Rushing upstairs, she picked up Matthew, who was still asleep on the bed. The same way he was when I took him out of the stroller, she thought. She carried him downstairs and put him on the inflated mat in the closet.

"Are you going now?" Matthew asked drowsily.

"Very soon, Matty." She knew she didn't have to warn him not to make a sound until she came back for him. I taught him well, poor kid, she thought.

The sound of the bell ringing resonated through the house.

She locked the door of the closet and dropped the key behind the server in the dining room on her way to the door.

A smiling Larry Post was looking in the kitchen window. "Brittany, I've got a present for you from Ted," he called out.

83

"That was a good lunch," Willy said complacently as he sipped the last of his cappuccino.

"Yes, it was. And, oh, Willy, I just know that Detective Collins is looking at all this in a different way. I mean, it's going to be as plain as the nose on your face that no woman about to kidnap her own child would bother to change her shoes for an almost identical pair. But what scares me is that whoever is behind this might start to panic if he finds out that the detectives are starting to believe Zan.

"And the question is whether after all this, even if Zan can prove her innocence, there's a limit on how much longer she can keep herself going if Matthew isn't found."

Willy agreed, his expression now weighted with concern. Then, as he reached for his wallet, he said, "Honey, just as I was leaving the apartment to meet you, Penny Hammel called. I didn't pick up."

"Oh, Willy, I feel kind of mean. I had my cell phone turned off when I was meeting Detective Collins, but when I called you I saw there was a message from Penny and frankly I didn't want to be bothered listening to it. I was too excited thinking about the fact that maybe the tide was turning for Zan."

She looked around. "I know it's not polite to use your cell phone in the restaurant, but I won't be talking, just listening." Alvirah turned away from the table, trying to give the impression she was reaching down for her pocketbook. She opened her phone and pressed the number to receive her messages. Then as she listened her face went pale.

"Willy," she said, her voice shaking. "I think Penny may have found Matthew! Oh, sweet Lord, it makes sense. But the woman who looks like Zan is packing to leave, oh, Willy . . ."

Not waiting to complete the sentence, Alvirah sat up straight and dialed Billy Collins's cell phone number.

A number she now knew by heart.

84

Would it work? Ever since he had sent Larry to Middletown over an hour ago, Ted Carpenter had agonized over what he had set in motion. He knew he had no choice. If Brittany went to the cops, he'd spend the rest of his life in prison. Even that wouldn't be as bad as watching the joyful reunion of Zan and Matthew.

My son, he thought. She didn't want me. I gave her a child and she claims she didn't know she was expecting him when she dumped me.

Thank you very much for your kindness and good-bye, he said to himself, playing her role. You never expected to have a child, so you don't have to pay for him. That wouldn't be fair. But how nice of you to check out the apartment I moved into and then the one that I rented after Matthew disappeared. How kind to see that the plumbing and the heating and the light fixtures work.

Of course it wouldn't be fair, Ted raged, because you really didn't want to share him. He was *yours*. You told me to start a trust fund for him but that really wasn't expected of me. Well, lady, that trust fund is going to pay for speeding your little precious into eternity today.

I wonder if she's home now? I didn't bother to watch her last night. I was too tired and worried, but now Larry is on his way to Middletown. With any luck, things will work out.

Ted turned on his computer and entered the code that would get him into Zan's apartment. Then, horror-struck, he watched as, directly facing the camera, Zan shrieked his name.

85

Cold and stiff, Penny Hammel was waiting in the woods behind Sy's old farmhouse. After studying the childish drawing and being sure that she was right, that Gloria Evans resembled Zan Moreland, she had driven down the road and called Alvirah and left a message. Then she came back and saw that the Evans car was back, so she drove around the road again and took up her vigil.

She couldn't let Evans get in that car and drive away. If I'm right that she had Matthew Carpenter in Sy's house, I can't let her disappear again, Penny thought as she stamped her feet and flexed her fingers to keep them from freezing. If she tries to leave, I'll follow her to see where she goes.

She wondered if she should try calling Alvirah again. But she was sure that the minute she got the message Alvirah would call back. I called her at home and on her cell phone, Penny reasoned. But after a while she thought, Maybe I should try once more.

She took her phone out of her pocket and opened it. Her fingers were inside her mittens. Impatiently, she pulled off a mitten but before she could go to her list of numbers, her phone rang.

As she had hoped, it was Alvirah. "Penny, where are you?"

"I'm watching that farmhouse I told you about. I don't want that lady to get away and she was packing this morning. Alvirah, I'm sure she has a child in there. And she looks like Zan Moreland."

"Penny, be careful. I called the detectives who are on this case. They're calling the Middletown police. They'll be there in a few minutes. But you —"

"Alvirah," Penny interrupted. "There's a white truck stopping in front of the house. It's parking in the driveway. The driver is getting out. He's carrying a big box. Why would she want any big box if she's planning to leave? What would she want to put in it?"

86

Billy Collins, Jennifer Dean, and Wally Johnson were being driven in a squad car to Ted Carpenter's apartment. Billy had briefed the other two on Kevin Wilson's call. "We never looked at the father," he berated himself. "Carpenter never made a single false move. Never. Outraged at the babysitter falling asleep. Outraged at Moreland for hiring a young babysitter. Then publicly apologizing to Moreland. Then outraged after the pictures in the paper. He was playing us all along."

Billy's cell phone rang. It was Alvirah relaying Penny Hammel's message. Billy turned to Jennifer Dean. "Get the Middletown police to the Owens farmhouse on Linden Road pronto," he snapped. "Tell them to proceed with caution. We have a tip that Matthew Carpenter may be hidden there."

Ted Carpenter's apartment was downtown. "Turn on the siren," Billy directed the officer who was driving. "That guy has got to be feeling cornered."

But even as he said it, he had a feeling it would be too late.

When they arrived, the crowd milling around the building told him that what he had feared might have happened. Even before he got out of the squad car, he knew that the body that had just plummeted through the canopy and was lying on the sidewalk was that of Ted Carpenter.

87

Help me, Brittany prayed. I don't deserve it, but help me. With a smile she waved to Larry Post, as she walked over to the living room window. She still had her cell phone in her pocket. He was opening the cover of a large box. She could see rows of hundreds lined up in it, each packet with a printed tape around it.

I'll open the door, she thought. Maybe I can stall him. I don't have the security system on. If he tries to open or break a window, he could do it in a minute. He thinks I'd never call the police for help. I don't have a chance. But maybe . . .

"Hi, Larry," she called. "I know what you've got. I'll open the door for you."

As she turned her back to him, she took out the phone and dialed 911. When an operator answered, she whispered, "Home invasion. I know the man. He's dangerous." Knowing that the local police were familiar with the location of the farmhouse, she cried, "The Owens farmhouse. Hurry. Please hurry."

88

I'm going in there, Penny decided. If that guy gets Evans and the child into that truck, no telling what will happen. I'll bring in the drawing and say that I found it when I was walking and thought it had to belong here. The cops may be on the way, but those 911 calls can get mixed up.

She hurried from her observation post in the woods. She ran across the field and stumbled over a heavy rock. Some instinct made her bend down and hoist it up. Maybe I'll need this, was the thought that ran through her head. She rushed up to the house and looked in the kitchen window. The Evans woman was standing there. The man Penny had seen carrying the box from the truck was a few feet away from her, holding a gun.

"You're too late, Larry," Brittany was saying. "I dropped Matthew in a mall an hour ago. I'm surprised you haven't heard about it if you had your car radio on. It's a big story, but I guess it won't make Ted too happy."

"You're lying, Brittany."

"Why would I lie, Larry? Isn't that the plan? That Matthew would be in a place where he's surely found, and I go home with the money and we're all happy — happy that we're finished with it?

"I know Ted is worried about leaving me out there as a potential problem, but you can reassure him that I won't be one. I want a life again. If I turn him in, I'll go to prison, too. And now you've brought the money. All of it, I guess. All six hundred thousand dollars. The trouble is that I can't celebrate because my father just died."

"Brittany, where is Matthew? Give me the key to the closet where you hide him. Ted told me about it."

Brittany saw the look of desperation in Larry Post's eyes. He'd find the closet easily enough. It was right at the end of the hall and he would find a way to open it even without a key. How could she stop him before help came?

"I'm sorry, Brittany." Larry was pointing the gun at her heart. His eyes were devoid of emotion.

■ ■ ■ ■

Penny had not been able to hear what was being said, but she could see that the man in the kitchen with Evans was about to shoot her. There was only one thing she could do. She pulled back her hand and with her ample strength sent the rock she was holding crashing through the window.

Startled at the slivers of glass that cascaded around him, Larry Post fired the gun but the shot sailed over Brittany's head.

Realizing her one chance, Brittany threw herself on Larry, causing him to lose his balance, stumble, and fall. He opened his hand to protect himself from smashing against the stove and dropped the gun.

Brittany swooped down and picked it up as police cars raced up on the lawn. Holding it on Larry Post, she said, "Don't move! I don't care if I use it on you and I know how to do it. My daddy and I used to go hunting together in Texas."

Without taking her eyes off him, she backed up and opened the kitchen door for Penny. "The blueberry lady," she said. "Welcome. Matthew Carpenter is in the closet down the hall," she said. "The key is behind the server in the dining room."

Larry Post scrambled to his feet and began to run. He threw open the front door and ran into a sea of blue uniforms. Other policemen pounded past them into the house. Margaret Grissom/Glory/Brittany La Monte had slumped into a chair at the kitchen table. The gun she was holding was dangling from her hand.

"Drop the gun! Drop the gun!" a cop shouted.

She laid it on the table. "I only wish I had the courage to use it on myself," Brittany said.

Penny found the key and rushed to the closet, then paused. Slowly she opened it. The little boy, who had obviously heard the shot, was huddled in the corner, his expression terrified. The light was on. She had seen enough of his pictures in the paper to be sure it was Matthew.

As a broad smile came over her face and tears filled her eyes, Penny bent down, picked him up, and held him close to her. "Matthew, it's time you went home. Mommy has been looking for you."

89

Detectives Billy Collins, Jennifer Dean, and
Wally Johnson were standing in the lobby of
the late Ted Carpenter's trendy apartment
building. The detectives from the local
precinct had cordoned off the area around
Carpenter's body and were waiting for the
arrival of the crime scene unit and the medical examiner's van.

Their expressions grim, they were desperate to hear the outcome of Billy's urgent
call to the Middletown police to respond to
the possibility that Matthew Carpenter was
being held in the Owens farmhouse.

Was Alvirah Meehan's friend in Middletown correct? Was it possible that a woman
who strongly resembled Zan Moreland was
hiding Matthew Carpenter all this time?
And following Kevin Wilson's phone call
about the camera in Zan's apartment, where
was Larry Post now? They had just run his
name through the computer at headquar-

ters, and discovered that he had served time for manslaughter. It's a sure bet that he's got some part in this whole scenario about Matthew and not just the bugging of Moreland's apartment, Billy thought.

Billy's cell phone rang. Holding their breath, Jennifer Dean and Wally Johnson watched as a broad smile came over Billy's face. "They've got the kid," he said, "and he's okay."

Jennifer Dean and Wally Johnson answered in unison. "Thank God," they said, "thank God."

Jennifer, her voice low, said, "Billy, we were *all* wrong about Zan Moreland. Don't beat yourself up. Everything pointed to her."

Billy nodded. "I know it did. And I'm very happy to be wrong. Now let's call Matthew's mother. The Middletown police are on their way to our precinct with him."

Fr. Aiden O'Brien heard the breaking news from the police officer who was guarding him at the hospital. His condition now upgraded to "critical but stable," he whispered a prayer of thanksgiving. The sacred seal of the confessional that had cloaked his sure and certain knowledge that Zan Moreland herself was a victim would no longer haunt him. Her innocence had been proven in another way. And her child was coming home.

90

Zan and Kevin raced to the Central Park Precinct to find Alvirah and Willy already there. Billy Collins, Jennifer Dean, and Wally Johnson were waiting for them. Billy had told Zan on the phone that the Middletown Police assured him that while Matthew was very pale and thin, he looked okay. He'd explained to her that while ordinarily the police would want to have Matthew checked out by a doctor right away, that could be done later today or tomorrow. Billy had told them to get him home.

"Zan," he cautioned her, "from what they know so far, Matthew has never forgotten you. Penny Hammel, the woman we can thank for finding him, showed the police a drawing that they think Matthew made. She found it in the backyard of that farmhouse. I hear it looks a lot like you and it has the word 'Mommy' printed on the bottom. But it would be a good idea if you brought a toy or a pillow or something that he loved. It might comfort him after what he's been through."

From the moment she entered the precinct, other than fiercely thanking and hugging Alvirah and Willy, Zan had not said another word. Kevin Wilson, his arm protectively around her, was carrying a large shopping bag. When they heard the sound of sirens approaching the entrance to the precinct, Zan reached into the bag and pulled out a blue bathrobe. "He'll remember this," she said. "He loved to cuddle with me inside of it."

Billy Collins's phone rang. He listened and smiled. "Come into this private room," he said gently to Zan. "They're bringing him in downstairs now. I'll go get him."

Less than a minute later, the door opened and little Matthew Carpenter stood bewildered and looked around. Zan, with the robe draped over her arm, ran to him and dropped to her knees. Trembling, she folded him into the robe.

Tentatively, Matthew reached for the lock of hair that was falling over her face and held it against his cheek. "Mommy," he whispered, "Mommy, I missed you."

EPILOGUE

One year later

Zan, Alvirah, Willy, Penny, Bernie, Fr. Aiden, Josh, Kevin Wilson, and his mother, Cate, watched with hearts overflowing as six-year-old Matthew, now restored to being a fiery redhead, blew out the candles of his birthday cake.

"I got them all," he announced proudly. "With only one breath."

Zan ruffled his hair. "Good for you. Do you want to open your presents before I cut the cake?"

"Yes," the boy answered decisively.

He's made a remarkable recovery, Alvirah thought. Zan had brought him regularly to a child therapist and he had blossomed from the timid child whom Zan had wrapped in her bathrobe when Penny brought him home to an outgoing, happy little boy who would occasionally still cling to Zan saying, "Mommy, please don't leave me." Most of the time he was an enthusiastic first-grader who couldn't wait to go to school and be with his friends.

Zan knew that as Matthew got older and began to ask questions, she would have to deal with his inevitable anger and sadness about what his father had done and how he had died. It will be one step at a time, she and Kevin had agreed. And they would handle it together.

The party was being held in Zan's apartment in Battery Park City, but she and Matthew wouldn't be there much longer. She and Kevin had chosen their wedding day to be just four days from now, on the anniversary of Matthew's return home. Fr. Aiden would be presiding at the ceremony. After the wedding, they would be moving into Kevin's apartment. His mother, Cate, who had already become Matthew's trusted babysitter, relished her soon-to-be role as grandmother.

Alvirah thought of the tabloids she had read this morning over breakfast. On page three they were rehashing the story of Matthew's kidnapping, the impersonation of Zan, the suicide of Ted Carpenter and the sentencing of Larry Post and Margaret Grissom/Glory/Brittany La Monte. Post had received life in prison and La Monte got twenty years.

As Matthew began to open his packages, Alvirah turned to Penny. "If it weren't for you, this wouldn't be happening."

Penny smiled. "Thank my blueberry muffins and the truck I saw in the foyer that day and then the drawing that I found stuck in the bush behind Sy's farmhouse. As Bernie had to admit, sometimes being nosy can pay off. The most important thing, the only thing, is that Matthew is safe. The reward money from Melissa Knight is a bonus."

She means it, Alvirah thought indulgently. Penny really means it. Melissa Knight had used every trick in the book to weasel out of paying the reward, but in the end she had written the check.

Now Alvirah watched as Matthew, suddenly serious, finished opening his presents and put his arms around Zan. He brushed a lock of her hair against his cheek.

Then he said contentedly, "Mommy, I just had to make sure you're still here." Matthew smiled. "Now, Mommy, can we please cut the cake?"

ABOUT THE AUTHOR

Mary Higgins Clark, #1 *New York Times* bestselling author, has written thirty suspense novels; three collections of short stories; a historical novel, *Mount Vernon Love Story*; a children's book, *Ghost Ship*, illustrated by Wendell Minor; and a memoir, *Kitchen Privileges*. She is the coauthor with Carol Higgins Clark of five suspense novels. Her books are international bestsellers, with over one-hundred million copies in print in the U.S. alone. Visit her online at www.maryhigginsclark.com.

Managing in
Developing Countries

Managing in Developing Countries

Strategic Analysis and Operating Techniques

JAMES E. AUSTIN

THE FREE PRESS
A Division of Macmillan, Inc.
NEW YORK

Collier Macmillan Publishers
LONDON

THE FREE PRESS
A Division of Simon & Schuster
1230 Avenue of the Americas
New York, NY 10020

THE FREE PRESS and colophon are trademarks
of Simon & Schuster Inc.

Manufactured in the United States of America

10 9 8 7 6 5 4 3 2 1

Library of Congress Cataloging-In-Publication Data

Austin, James E.
        Managing in developing countries : strategic analysis and
Operating techniques / James E. Austin.
        p.   cm.
Includes bibliographical references.
ISBN : 0-7432-3629-7
1. International business enterprises—Developing countries—
Management.   2. Business and politics—Developing countries.
3. Industry and state—Developing countries.   I. Title.
HD62.4.A88   1990   89-23784
658'.049—dc20   CIP

For information regarding special discounts for bulk purchases, please contact Simon &
Schuster Special Sales at 1-800-456-6798 or business@simonandschuster.com

To Cathy

*Whose concern for others first led me
to the developing world and whose
sense of humanity remains an inspiration*

Contents

PART 1

Analyzing the
Business Environment

PART 2

Managing the Functional Areas

Appendixes

Preface

This book has evolved out of my research, teaching, and work in developing countries over the past twenty-five years. A critical step in that intellectual journey was taken twelve years ago when I began to develop the Management in Developing Countries course for the Harvard Business School MBA program. The impetus for that effort came from a recommendation by the faculty in the school's General Management Area that it was essential that our students, as future business leaders, gain an understanding of management in the Third World. It involved extensive research on management problems in developing countries and the preparation of many case studies of Third World business situations. The testing grounds were classroom discussions with the MBAs and with managers in Harvard's executive education programs, and in seminars in many developing countries. Through this iterative process over the years the book's analytical framework and concepts emerged, as well as an identification of the most critical issues facing managers in developing countries.

The writing of this book was not a race toward publication. Each draft was exposed to the intellectual scrutiny of my academic colleagues and the pragmatic probing of business managers. Although those rewriting cycles were often painful, the richness of the reviewers' insights more than rewarded the perseverance. The generosity with which they gave of their time was a great source of encouragement. I gained much from my Harvard Business School colleagues. Hugo Uyterhoeven's vision and support gave birth to the undertaking. Lou Wells faithfully plowed through my many drafts, responding with amazing rapidity and his customary thoroughness. Ben Gomes-Casseres and Ravi Ramamurti, whose nearby offices were easily invaded by my manuscripts, provided valuable, frank appraisals and concrete suggestions. Bob Stobaugh's observations guided me toward greater substantiation. Dennis Encarnation helped bring lucidity to the analysis of business–government relations and to the presentation of economic cost-benefit analysis. David Yoffie's collaboration extended my conceptualization of political forecasting. Tom Piper and David Meerschwam shared their expertise in international finance. Therese Flaherty and Alice Amsden deepened my analysis of production and technology issues. Kash Rangan provided insights on marketing. George Lodge sharpened my appreciation for a holistic approach. Willis Emmons helped conceptualize and substantiate several key areas. Marc Lindenberg of Harvard's Kennedy School of Government shared his wisdom and experience in political analysis. This effort also greatly benefited from the dedicated and skilled work of several research assistants who have contributed to the project over the years: Roberto Artavia, Lohki Banerji, Brizio Biondi-Morra, Madeleine Costanzas, Jill Dalby, Jonathan Fox, Seok Ki Kim, Tomás Kohn, Walter Kruger, Constantinos Markides, Dale Murphy, Frankie Roman, and Alvin Wint. It was a privilege and a pleasure to have them as collaborators.

Jerry Meier of Stanford's Graduate School of Business, Stephen Kobrin of the Wharton School, Thomas Brewer of Georgetown University, Taieb Hafsi of the École des Hautes Études Commerciales, Henry Lane of the University of Western Ontario, John Ickis of the Instituto Centroamericano de Administración de Empresas, George Kastner of the Instituto de Educación Superior de Administración, Malcolm Harper of the Cranfield School of Management, H. E. Beaton of The Polytechnic of Central London, and Eduardo Roberto of the Asian Institute of Management provided helpful observations and encouragement. The faculty of the Lahore Business School also contributed many constructive comments on the manuscript. Fifty more professors from the United States and abroad kindly responded to my request for their judgments about the utility and focus of the book.

Dozens of managers shared their experiences and insights on handling the special demands of business in developing countries. Many managers from multinationals and Third World companies who were participating in Harvard's executive education programs met with me in small discussion groups and provided invaluable feedback on the manuscript. Additionally, Ken Hoadley and R. A. Barakat of Arthur D. Little (ADL); Martin Webber of Louis Berger, Inc.; Kevin X. Murphy of J. E. Austin Associates; and Fred Epprecht of F. E. Zuellig (Bangkok) Ltd. offered many useful suggestions based on their years of experience in developing countries. My understanding of the complexities of Third World business environments has also been deepened by my interaction over several years with Jonathan Coles of MAVESA in Venezuela and Pedro Pick of ADL. Many officials from developing country governments and individuals from several international development agencies have helped me comprehend more clearly the public policy perspective and governments' views of business. In addition to benefiting through the years from the thoughtful analyses of hundreds of graduate students in my courses, I also received suggestions from several who carefully read drafts of the manuscript and indicated how it could be adjusted to meet their needs.

This research effort would not have been possible without the truly exceptional intellectual, financial, and administrative support of the Harvard Business School. I particularly appreciate Dean John McArthur's unswerving support of my endeavors. My colleagues who have ably guided the Division of Research during the life of this project—Ray Corey, Jay Lorsch, Tom McCraw, and Mike Yoshino—have given wise counsel and continual encouragement. Keith Larson's superb editorial skills have strengthened the book and instructed the author. Lynn Lazar's administrative abilities preserved order where chaos could easily have reigned. The artistic skills of George Nichols transformed my mental images into lucid graphics.

The final stages of revising the manuscript were aided by David Oot's and Jean Baker's generous offer of the use of their Nairobi home. The solitude, comfort, computer, and stimulation of being in Kenya were the right combination for creative writing. Bob Wallace, Senior Editor and Vice President of the Free Press, provided invaluable support, unfailingly high quality standards, and impeccable professionalism in guiding the manuscript expeditiously into print.

Clearly, I am indebted to many. They taught me, helped me, encouraged me. I hope the quality and utility of this book will meet their expectations and justify their assistance. The challenges of management in developing countries are complex and demanding, and businesses have a vital role to play in the development process of the Third World. It is my hope that this book will help managers meet those critical challenges.

1

The Management Challenge

WHAT IS DIFFERENT ABOUT MANAGING IN DEVELOPING COUNTRIES?

The fundamental difference is the distinctive nature of the business environment, which varies considerably from that of the more developed nations. This carries significant managerial implications. A few examples will illustrate.

When Cummins Engine Company set up one of its first overseas operations to manufacture diesel engines in India, it encountered a host of new problems: government controls, production difficulties, financial restrictions, and market disruptions.[1] The government required that Cummins incorporate as a joint venture with a local partner. Manufacturing problems arose because of difficulties in transferring technology, difficulties in training employees in new techniques, and the local partner's different perceptions of and attitudes toward quality. Further complicating production was the inadequacy of the industrial infrastructure: Local parts suppliers were technically unable to meet Cummins's quality standards, yet the government required Cummins to use local inputs anyway. The required types of steel were not locally available and had to be imported. Import financing was restricted by the scarcity of foreign exchange in the country and cumbersome bureaucratic procedures to obtain import licenses from the government. This caused long delays that further disrupted production schedules. Initial sales projections were based on the expected demand for diesel engines that would result from the government's emphasis on heavy industry in its national development strategy. But demand collapsed when the government shifted priorities and resources away from industry and toward agricultural production. The government also tightened credit to counter rising inflationary pressures, which reduced the financial resources needed by the buyers of engines

1

(several of which were state-owned enterprises). Finally, Cummins was faced with intensified competition from lower-priced Japanese imports after receiving assurances from the government that such imports would be prohibited. For Cummins, the Indian startup clearly was not going to be a case of doing business as usual. This was a very different environment.

The macroeconomic environment also poses special problems. In Mexico a local family-owned company had operated a very successful electrical appliance distribution business for many years.[2] But in the 1980s its success and even its survival were threatened when double-digit inflation broke out. Its traditional policies for pricing, consumer credit, supplier payables, and bank financing began causing losses and decapitalization. The changing macroeconomic environment in Mexico also battered foreign companies, such as the successful Pepsico subsidiary, Sabritas.[3] The government unexpectedly devalued the peso, which, in dollar terms, wiped out the company's peso profits. Furthermore, the acute balance-of-payments problem led the government to require Sabritas and other firms to begin exporting as a condition for continuing to import their production equipment and inputs.

In many developing countries the macroeconomic situation and business environment are significantly affected by loans and economic aid provided by developed country governments and such multilateral agencies as the International Monetary Fund (IMF) and the World Bank. Egypt, for example, received in 1989 about $2.8 billion in aid from the United States, an amount equal to Egypt's budget deficit.[4] Such aid often comes with requirements for policy changes, e.g., fiscal austerity or devaluations. Such actions can dramatically affect the operations of firms as well as disrupt political conditions. IMF agreements that led to reductions in government subsidies and food price increases triggered bread riots in Egypt in 1977. Many Egyptian officials feared a repeat, if cuts were too severe in 1989 and 1990. Thus, dependence on external aid complicates the political economy of less developed countries (LDCs). At the same time, the additional capital resources often create business opportunities related to the development projects they fund.

A tumultuous political environment often confronts companies. The management of Standard Fruit, the Castle & Cooke subsidiary in Nicaragua, found itself in 1978 in the middle of an armed insurrection, with pressures coming from both the existing government and the revolutionaries. Standard later had to develop strategies for dealing both with the new revolutionary government, which had different conceptions of private property and the societal role of business, and with workers, whose expectations about sharing the control and benefits of companies were dramatically changed by the revolution.

Socioeconomic conditions in the Third World can create distinct marketing environments. Nestlé and other manufacturers of infant formula came under intense attack for their use in developing countries of their developed country marketing practices that stimulated the consumption of infant formula. Unsanitary living conditions, lack of potable water, and low levels of education and incomes of poor consumers of the infant formula greatly increased the chance of product misuse and possible injury. Pervasive poverty requires of managers a heightened social sensitivity and responsibility.

Cultural diversity in the Third World also dictates the need for distinct strategies. In some Islamic countries, for example, the charging of interest is prohibited by religious norms, so different approaches to financial transactions are called for. In some countries sharp differences in social class and language among groups and areas within a single country demand drastic adjustments in, for example, marketing messages and personnel management.

Distinctive business environments derive directly from differences in development levels and processes between the LDCs and the more developed nations. Those differences significantly affect all functional areas of management as well as overall strategies.

Many of the firms mentioned so far were able to deal effectively with the problems they encountered and to reap corresponding financial rewards; others were not and suffered the economic consequences. A distinguishing feature of more successful companies in developing countries is their superior ability to understand and interact with their business environment. A key to formulating effective business strategies in LDCs is the capacity to analyze and comprehend thoroughly the firm's external environment. Management's challenge is to devise a systematic approach to environmental analysis that enables effective managerial response. The purpose of this book is to present such an approach. It will set forth an analytical framework for environmental analysis and techniques for applying that framework to issues of strategic importance to a firm's viability and success. The book is both conceptual and applied. The goal is to enhance managers' capacity to deal with the distinctive challenges of management in developing countries.

WHOM IS THIS BOOK FOR?

This book is primarily for current and future managers involved in or interested in doing business in or with developing countries. It is particularly oriented toward individuals from more developed nations who wish to learn more about the LDC business environment; my teaching experiences at Harvard Business School and in various Third World nations, however, indicate that managers from developing countries will also find the framework and techniques relevant and useful. Readers of this book will differ considerably in their knowledge and experience of developing countries. The more experienced will find some portions of the book to be familiar terrain; the value-added for them is in the analytical framework and techniques. For the less experienced, in addition to the value of the analytical approach, the book tries to provide a basic understanding of the business environment in developing countries. Lastly, although government officials and public policy analysts are not the direct target audience of this book, my teaching experiences suggest that they too will find the book relevant to their tasks involving interaction with businesses.

I have also prepared with Tomás Kohn a companion volume, *Strategic Management in Developing Countries* (The Free Press, 1990) that contains over thirty case studies of companies operating in developing countries. That book will be particularly suited for classroom discussions but would also give practitioners more detailed views of business situations to which the analytical framework and techniques in this book can be applied.

HOW IS THE BOOK ORGANIZED?

We shall now present the "map" of how this book will provide an understanding of the complex and diverse LDC business environment. This introductory chapter provides an overview by discussing the importance of the developing countries to the global business economy and by describing the diversity among Third World nations. The remainder of the book is divided in two parts. Part I, "Analyzing the Business Environment," provides an analytical approach for examining and understanding the distinctive nature of the LDC business environment. Part II, "Managing the Functional Areas," focuses on how to deal with critical issues in each of the core functional areas of management.

Part I (chapters 2 through 5) presents the components of what I have labeled the Environmental Analysis Framework (EAF). Chapter 2 provides an overview of the EAF. Chapter 3 discusses the first component of the framework, the four kinds of environmental factors by which the salient characteristics of a developing country can be systematically identified and the distinctive nature of its business environment understood. Those readers experienced in developing countries will find much of this chapter's information familiar, but its organization may provide additional insights; others will find in it a useful organizing framework and information base for building an understanding of the LDC context. Chapters 4 and 5 discuss two other components of the EAF. Government's strategies and policies are a fundamental force shaping the business environment, so Chapter 4 presents the analytical approach for understanding this phenomenon. A firm's immediate competitive environment is its industry, and Chapter 5 provides a way of viewing the distinctive nature of industry structure and competitive dynamics in developing countries.

Part II (Chapters 6 through 10) discusses special management issues that arise in the functional areas of business–government relations, finance, production, marketing, and organization. Management control issues are dealt with as a dimension of each of the other functional areas rather than in a separate chapter. The chapters are selective rather than exhaustive; they focus on those issues considered to be of particular strategic importance to successful management in LDCs. Part II extends and applies the EAF through analytical techniques and guidelines for dealing with these key management issues. Given the strategic importance of government's actions to company success, I consider managing the business–government relationship to be as fundamental as the traditional functional areas; Chapter 6 examines key aspects of this relationship. Chapter 7 discusses three problematic and challenging finance issues facing LDC managers: how to manage in a high-inflation environment, how to handle foreign exchange risks, and how to deal with capital scarcity. Chapter 8 focuses on the production issues of technology management as it relates to technology transfer, choice, adaptation, and supplier development. Chapter 9 examines adjustments in the marketing mix required in the LDC environment. Chapter 10 is concerned with organizational strategy in three areas: the choice of a foreign firm's mode of entry into a developing country, issues surrounding joint ventures, and the effect of culture on organizational structure and processes.

Chapter 11 concludes the book by briefly discussing trends affecting the future business environment in developing countries and delineating some management capabilities deemed critical to success in that future environment.

HOW IMPORTANT ARE DEVELOPING COUNTRIES TO THE INTERNATIONAL ECONOMIC AND BUSINESS SYSTEM?

A basic management reality in today's economic world is that businesses operate in a highly interdependent global economy, and the 142 developing countries[5] are very significant actors in the international business arena. They are buyers, suppliers, competitors, and capital users. It is important for managers to recognize the magnitude and significance of these roles. The economic importance of the Third World is great and becoming even greater.

As Buyers

The bulk of the world's consumers live in the developing countries. About 77% of the world's 1990 population resided in the Third World: 4.1 billion out of the 5.3 billion total.[6] The LDC population is expanding at an annual rate of almost 2%, while that of the more developed countries is growing at around 0.5%. Population-driven demand growth is primarily a Third World phenomenon.

These populations, of course, contain most of the world's lower-income consumers. Consequently, their effective demand and their share of the world's economic pie is disproportionately lower. The LDCs produce

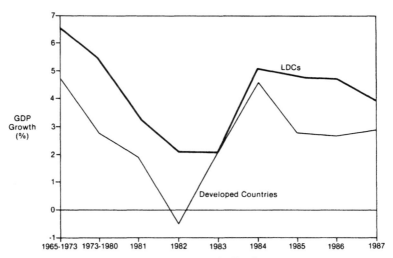

Figure 1.1 Growth Rates of Gross Domestic Product

SOURCE: *World Development Report 1986, 1987,* and *1988* (New York: Oxford University Press for World Bank, 1986, 1987, 1988).

about 20% of the output of the world's market economies.[7] Nonetheless, since 1960 these economies have been growing at a faster rate than those of more developed nations. As can be seen from Figure 1.1, Third World economic growth rates in real terms have been consistently higher and are projected to continue so in the future, despite declines in the 1980s. Thus, Third World demand is driven by rising incomes as well as population growth. It is likely that their aggregate share in the global market will grow in importance. The higher population growth rates in developing countries, however, hold down growth in per capita GNP and therefore the ability to close the income gap between developing and developed countries.

Table 1.1 reveals differences in GDP growth rates among Asia, Africa, and Latin America and the Caribbean. Asia, particularly East Asia, has been the high-growth region, and Africa one of low growth. Latin America experienced high growth during the 1970s, fell off during the early 1980s, and then began to recover. Table 1.2 shows the growth rates of economic categories of LDCs. During the 1980s the low-income countries have been growing faster than the middle-income nations, and the exporters of manufactured goods have fared better than the oil exporters. The highly indebted nations have also grown relatively more slowly.

The developing countries satisfy a significant portion of their domestic demand through purchases in the international market. In 1987 they accounted for 25% of the world's imports.[8] Their main imports in order of importance are machinery, manufactured goods, fuels, foods, chemicals, and other raw materials. The more developed nations supplied nearly 60% of these total imports; between 1978 and 1984 sales to the Third World amounted to 40–45% of the total exports of the United

Table 1.1 Growth Rates of Gross Domestic Product by Region

Regions	1965–73	1973–80	1980–85	1986	1987	1988*
East Asia	7.9	6.5	7.8	7.3	8.6	9.4
South Asia	3.8	4.4	5.4	4.6	3.1	7.6
Africa	6.1	3.2	−0.5	3.2	−1.3	3.1
Europe, Middle East & North Africa*	7.6	4.3	2.3	3.1	1.9	2.6
Latin Amer. & Carib.	6.4	5.2	0.2	3.5	1.7	1.5

* Figures for 1988 are preliminary; figures for Middle East exclude Iran and Iraq after 1980.

SOURCES: *World Development Report 1989*, p. 147; *1986*, pp. 24, 155; *1982*, p. 8.

Table 1.2 Growth of Real GDP by Country Category

Country Categories	1965 -73	1973 -80	1981	1982	1983	1984	1985	1986	1987	1988*
High-income economies	4.7	2.8	1.9	-0.5	2.2	4.6	2.8	2.7	2.9	3.7
All LDCs	6.5	5.4	3.4	2.1	2.1	5.1	4.8	4.7	3.9	5.0
Low-income	5.5	4.6	4.8	5.6	7.7	8.9	9.1	6.4	5.3	8.6
Middle-income	7.0	5.7	2.8	0.8	0.0	3.6	2.8	3.9	3.2	2.6
Oil exporters	6.9	6.0	4.1	0.4	-1.9	2.3	2.2	0.3	0.8	n.a.
Manufactures exporters	7.4	6.0	3.3	4.2	4.9	7.8	7.8	7.2	5.3	n.a.
Highly indebted	6.9	5.4	0.9	-0.5	-3.2	2.0	3.1	3.5	1.7	1.5

* Preliminary; n.a.: not available

SOURCES: *World Development Report 1987*, p. 172, Table A.3; *1988*, p. 189, Table A.4; *1989*, p. 147, Table A.4.

States, Japan, Germany, and Britain (excluding intra-EEC sales).[9] Developed nations supplied 91% of the LDCs' machinery imports, 88% of the chemicals, 77% of other manufactured goods, and 57% of the raw materials.[10] For some product categories and companies LDCs are critical markets. For example, for papermaking machinery the developing countries will constitute 41% of the world market demand for the 1986–96 period.[11] Forty percent of the Caterpillar Tractor Company's worldwide sales in 1981 were to developing countries, and the trend was strongly upward.[12]

As Suppliers

The developing countries are also important suppliers in the international marketplace. By the mid-1980s they accounted for 28% of the world's exports, with 70% of their sales going to the more developed nations and 30% to other LDCs. The industrial countries, in turn, depended upon the Third World for about 22% of their total international purchases in 1987.[13] For certain products the developed nations' dependence on the developing countries as suppliers is even greater. For example, in 1986 the United States depended on the Third World for 87% of its fuel imports, 57% of its food imports, and 39% of its raw material imports.[14] The developing countries have also become important suppliers of manufactured goods; manufactures rose from 38% of LDC exports in 1965 to 60% by 1980.[15] Figure 1.2 shows the dramatic increase in manufactured exports from developing countries into the U.S. market; they have risen fivefold between 1978 and 1987. The Third World is increasing not only the absolute value of its exports to the United States but also its share of total U.S. manufactured imports (nearly 30%). In their trade with other developing countries, LDCs tend to export their more capital-intensive goods to countries that are less developed and less abundantly endowed with capital than themselves; their exports to the developed countries tend to be more labor-intensive.[16]

Pushing the trend of more manufactured exports from LDCs has been the strategic decision of many major companies from the developed countries to move their production of components or entire products offshore. For example, Nike started out by importing running shoes from Japan; it also had a small U.S. production operation. As labor costs and the value of the yen rose, Nike shifted to Korea and Taiwan; in search of cheaper sources, it added the Philippines and Thailand. Finally, it set up production contracts and operations in the People's Republic of China, which Nike's chairman saw as the world's last great

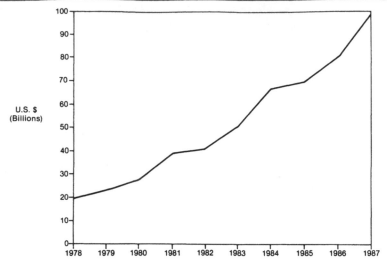

Figure 1.2 Imports of Manufactured Goods by the United States
SOURCE: Derived from *Foreign Trade Highlights* (Washington, D.C.: U.S. Department of Commerce, Office of Trade and Investment Analysis, 1987), p. A–19.

supply of cheap labor.[17] In 1988 AT&T began investing $40 million in production facilities in Thailand to produce up to 5 million phones annually, mainly for the U.S. market. This new facility would allow the company to shift its existing production of cord phones from Singapore to Thailand, so that the Singapore facilities could concentrate on the more sophisticated cordless phones.[18] Almost all U.S. semiconductor companies have shifted assembly operations to the developing countries, making Malaysia the world's largest semiconductor exporter. More than half the workforce in Malaysia's electronics industry is employed by U.S. multinationals.[19] IBM made a major investment in Mexico to manufacture microcomputers, mainly for export to the United States; other computer firms have also established export-oriented production operations in the developing countries. All U.S. television manufacturers have moved offshore. By 1978 Taiwan had become the world's largest producer of black-and-white TV sets, then was surpassed in 1981 by South Korea, which by the mid-1980s had also become the third largest producer of color TV sets.[20] In the Caribbean a large assembly industry, particularly for apparel, has emerged. Fabric is imported from the U.S., often into duty-free export zones, and re-exported to the U.S. Such exports from the Dominican Republic, Haiti, and Jamaica expanded at a 20% annual rate throughout the 1980's.[21] European and Japanese multinational firms have also increased their sourcing and exporting from LDCs. Third World countries are an integral part of global sourcing systems.

As Competitors

As the industries of developed nations mature, particularly more labor-intensive ones, their costs relative to those in the Third World tend to rise and their technologies become more internationally accessible. Developing nations, with their lower labor costs, increasingly gain comparative economic advantage in these industries and foster them as part of their industrialization. By the 1980s, for example, Brazil's manufacturing output exceeded Britain's.[22] In 1986 Taiwan exported $36 billion of manufactures and generated a trade surplus exceeded only by Japan and West Germany.[23]

The developing countries have become fierce competitors in various manufactured products, capturing market shares from producers based in the developed nations. In the aggregate, developing countries have increased their share of manufactured imports by developed countries from about 11% in 1960 to about 25% by the mid-1980s. Early inroads were made in apparel and textiles: By 1984 almost half of the world's clothing exports came from developing countries.[24] Of the world's top thousand companies ranked by sales, seventy-three were from the Third World.[25] The Munjal company in India is the world's largest manufacturer of bicycles, producing seventeen per minute; it forecasts exports of 1 million bikes per year.[26] More recently, electronics has been the growth area, with the Third World's share of global exports reaching 12% by 1980 and rising. This is not just the offshore operations of multinational corporations already mentioned. Indigenous companies such as Korea's Samsung and Gold Star or Taiwan's Sampo and Tatung are significant forces in the international consumer electronics markets.[27] By 1988 Samsung Electronics had captured 20% of the U.S. microwave market and 13% of the VCR market.[28] The competitive presence of LDC companies is being felt in other sectors as well. For example, Brazil's EMBRAER, the government's aeronautic enterprise, has successfully exported its turboprop airplanes to the United States, to Europe, and to other LDCs. Korea's Hyundai penetrated the Canadian auto market in 1983 with its fast-selling, low-priced Pony model; the $3,300 price tag generated about $8 million in sales the first year and $80 million the second. Hyundai then repeated its success in the U.S. market with its Excel model.[29] Faced with the growing competitiveness of LDC companies, many multinational corporations are creating joint ventures and other strategic alliances with them; for example, General Motors joined with Korea's Daewoo to produce subcompacts.

Becoming international class competitors has required heavy capital outlays by the developing countries. The inherent scarcity of domestic capital has required that they tap foreign capital sources.

As Capital Users

As can be seen from Figure 1.3 and Table 1.3, the developing countries receive external capital from three main sources: private creditors (mainly the international banks), foreign direct investment (mainly multinational corporations), and official governmental assistance (foreign governments and multilateral agencies).

Total net capital flows to the LDCs more than doubled in real terms between 1970 and 1981, reaching $136 billion. They declined during the 1980s, particularly because of the drop in commercial bank lending and the decline in the value of the dollar. Important shifts among the capital sources occurred during the 1970–86 period. In 1970 private lending supplied 16% of the capital, foreign direct investment (FDI) 18%, and government assistance 61%. By 1981 private lending had

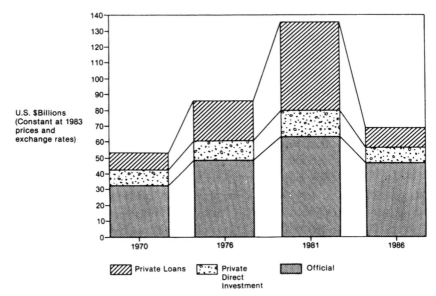

Figure 1.3 Capital Flows to Developing Countries
SOURCE: OECD, *Development Cooperation, 1987 Report*, December 1987.

Table 1.3 Total Resource Flows to Developing Countries (*$U.S. billions at 1983 prices and exchange rates*)

	1970	1973	1976	1979	1981	1982	1983	1984	1985	1986
Governmental Assistance										
Official development										
assistance	22.2	23.9	29.5	32.9	36.3	33.7	33.4	35.6	37.5	36.2
(%)	(42)	(37)	(34)	(37)	(27)	(35)	(34)	(40)	(45)	(52)
Official non-conces-										
sional flows	10.3	9.2	19.2	18.8	26.9	21.9	16.9	19.4	15.0	10.5
(%)	(19)	(14)	(22)	(21)	(20)	(23)	(17)	(22)	(18)	(15)
% subtotal										
government	(61)	(51)	(56)	(58)	(47)	(58)	(51)	(62)	(63)	(67)
Private Flows:										
Direct										
investment	9.7	8.9	12.0	13.8	16.7	11.8	9.3	11.7	7.6	9.7
(%)	(18)	(14)	(14)	(16)	(12)	(12)	(10)	(13)	(9)	(14)
Bank										
lending	7.9	18.3	21.6	20.2	50.7	25.9	34.1	17.8	13.6	4.1
(%)	(15)	(29)	(25)	(23)	(37)	(27)	(35)	(20)	(16)	(6)
Bond										
lending	.8	1.1	1.8	.7	1.4	.5	1.2	.6	3.9	2.9
(%)	(2)	(2)	(2)	(1)	(1)	(1)	(1)	(1)	(5)	(4)
Grants	2.3	2.6	1.9	2.0	3.7	2.3	2.8	3.7	5.6	5.7
(%)	(4)	(4)	(2)	(2)	(3)	(2)	(3)	(4)	(7)	(8)
% subtotal										
private	(39)	(49)	(43)	(42)	(53)	(42)	(49)	(38)	(37)	(32)
Total resource flows	53.2	63.9	86.0	88.4	135.7	96.1	97.7	88.8	83.1	69.1

SOURCE: Joseph C. Wheeler, *Development Co-operation, 1987 Report* (Paris: OECD, December 1987).

risen to 38%, FDI dropped to 12%, and governmental flows fell to 47%. By 1986, however, the private lenders' share had plummeted to 10%, while direct investments provided 14%, and governmental assistance reached a high of 67%. We shall now examine the bank lending, foreign direct investment, and official assistance flows.

Bank Lending. The principal change in the mix of annual capital flows during the 1970s was the dramatic increase in bank lending. In 1970 it constituted 15% of total flows to the developing countries and 39% of the private flows; by 1981 it had increased to 37% of total flows and 70% of private flows. By 1988 nearly 60% of the developing countries' long-term debt was owed to private creditors. The Third World's total external liabilities passed the $1 trillion mark by 1985 (see Table 1.4). With this huge debt overhang, private bank lending to the LDCs declined dramatically to only 6% of total flows by 1986.

What fueled the extraordinary expansion of international lending during the 1970s and early 1980s was the pressure on banks to recycle petrodollar deposits, along with the existence of attractive interest-rate spreads and the LDCs' insatiable demand for capital. A further incentive to borrow was the fact that real interest rates were negative—that is, the London

Table 1.4 External Liabilities of Developing Countries ($US billions)

	1982	1983	1984	1985	1986	1987	1988a	1989a
Long-term debt:								
Official sources	203	226	238	305	364	437	450	460
Private sources	359	419	449	489	530	559	570	540
Total long-term debt	562	645	687	794	894	996	1020	1000
Short-term debt (b)	169	140	132	131	119	133	140	135
Use of IMF credit	21	31	33	38	40	40	40	40
Other developing								
countries (c)	86	86	81	89	99	111	120	125
Total debt	838	902	933	1052	1152	1280	1320	1300
% Growth:								
Liabilities		7.6	3.4	11.3	9.5	11.1	3.1	−1.5

ª Preliminary estimates.
ᵇ Data reflect the known rescheduling of some $48 billion of short-term debt to banks into long-term debt in 1983–87. This category is overwhelmingly from private sources.
ᶜ Estimated data for Cyprus, Greece, Hungary, Israel, Malta, Poland, Portugal, Romania, Turkey, and Yugoslavia; excludes high-income oil exporting countries.

SOURCE: Derived from *World Debt Tables: External Debt of Developing Countries, 1988–89* (Washington, D.C.: World Bank, 1989), vol. I, p. x.

InterBank Offered Rate (LIBOR) was less than the annual percentage change in export unit values of the borrowing LDCs; for 1973–77 the real rates were −14% and for 1978–80 −5.3%.[30] Additionally, governments in developed countries often promoted such private lending to help stimulate their exports to the developing countries.[31] The enticements for LDC governments and businesses to borrow were attractive, and too many developing countries overborrowed. By 1987 Latin America's external debt was more than twice as large as its domestic bank liabilities.[32]

Initially these LDC loans were a major source of profit growth for the international banks. However, many observers contend that the banks failed to analyze adequately the LDC environments and overlent. The banks and countries were exposed to the harsh effects of market changes. LDC commodity prices plummeted in 1980–81, real interest rates soared to 18% in 1981–82 (and the dollar rose) and to 13% in 1983–85, and LDC exports fell as recession in the industrial nations reduced demand.[33] The drop in foreign exchange earnings left the LDCs unable to service their dollar-denominated, variable-interest foreign loans. The resultant international debt crisis saddled banks with serious default risks and led to extensive debt reschedulings. Between 1975 and 1980 there were about five reschedulings per year; by 1984 the number soared to 30. These reschedulings caused the export credit agencies in the developed nations (such as the Eximbank in the United States or the ECGD in the United Kingdom) to pay out large claims on insured supplier credits and guaranteed bank credits.[34] LDC loans as a percentage of total bank assets in 1985 were 14% for Bank of America, 13% for Citicorp, and 9% for Chase Manhattan, and many times greater than their equity capital. By 1987 Citibank and other international banks began a process of writing off some of these loans. Even the World Bank increased its bad debt reserve levels in 1988 for the first time in its history.

As Table 1.5 reveals, the financial burden of the debts on the Third World economies has increased significantly. Outstanding debts rose from 28% of GNP in 1980 to 50% in 1987. The debt-servicing burden for public and private foreign loans increased in 1987 to 6.2% of GNP; 26% of export earnings were needed on the average to meet the debt-servicing obligations, and interest payments alone amounted to 12% of exports. For some countries the debt-servicing burden was much higher. The need to find foreign exchange to service the debts will influence significantly the shape of government policies and, therefore, the business environment in the upcoming years.

In 1987 ten developing countries accounted for almost half the Third World's trillion-dollar debt, with Brazil and Mexico's combined $194

Table 1.5 Developing Country Debt Indicators

	1980	1981	1982	1983	1984	1985	1986	1987
Tot. ext. debt as % of GNP	27.8	30.6	43.8	39.6	40.8	45.6	48.3	49.7
Tot. debt service as % of GNP	4.3	5.0	5.5	5.4	5.7	6.2	6.2	6.2
Tot. debt service as % of exports of goods & services	19.0	22.0	25.3	24.0	24.0	26.9	28.6	26.4
Total interest as % of exports of goods and services	9.5	12.1	14.4	13.8	13.7	14.5	14.2	11.7
Private debt as % of total debt	12.9	14.2	13.6	13.7	12.9	10.7	8.9	7.7

SOURCE: World Bank, *World Debt Tables 1987–88*, pp. 2, 5; *1988–89*, p. 5; World Bank Debtor Reporting System database.

billion constituting 18% of the total.[35] The first column in Table 1.6 lists the top ten debtor nations in 1987. The bigger countries tend to have bigger debts. The plight of some of the smaller countries is revealed when the top ten debtor list is constructed in terms of external liabilities per capita, as shown in the second column. Still another perspective is gained when the ranking is made using the ratio of GNP per capita to liabilities per capita, which relates the burden of the debt to the country's resources available to service it (see third column). According to this measure, the ten countries least able to pay their debts include eight African nations whose low per capita incomes greatly weaken their debt-

Table 1.6 Developing Country Debt Rankings, 1987

Largest Debt Outstanding	Biggest Debt Per Capita	Lowest Ratio of GNP Per Capita to Debt Per Capita
Brazil	Israel	Zambia
Mexico	Panama	Nicaragua
Argentina	Oman	Mauritania
Indonesia	Nicaragua	Jamaica
India	Venezuela	Yemen PDR
Poland	Gabon	Zaire
Turkey	Jamaica	Côte d'Ivoire
Egypt	Argentina	Liberia
Venezuela	Hungary	Somalia
China	Singapore	Morocco

SOURCE: Derived from *World Development Report 1989*, pp. 164–65, 204–5.

carrying capacity. This circumstance was the main reason why the Western developed nations at their 1988 Economic Summit recommended that adjustments be made by creditor nations to alleviate the poorest African nations' debt burden.

Servicing these foreign debts has become an increasingly severe drain on the developing countries' capital and foreign exchange resources. Since 1984 debt-service payments from the Third World on their long-term debt have exceeded new loan disbursements coming into developing countries. Long-term lending has been declining since 1982. In effect, through their repayments developing countries have become net capital suppliers to the developed nations. Most of the largest debtors, except for Korea and India, are in this position. However, about 62% of the developing countries are still receiving more long-term funds than their debt-service outflows, and thus continue to be net capital users.[36]

Developing countries will remain important actors in the international credit system, for both new borrowings and repayments. The debt-servicing burden will heighten the priority that governments place on foreign-exchange generation and saving, and this will place special demands in this direction on companies.

Foreign Direct Investment. Governments sometimes prefer direct equity investments by foreign corporations over loans, because, in addition to capital, they bring technologies and, sometimes, access to international marketing networks. Furthermore, if the project fails, the government does not have any loan to pay back. Although there is considerable diversity in foreign investment strategies, there does appear to be an evolutionary pattern related to a product's life cycle that holds for many firms.[37] Production begins in the developed country and is marketed there. Next, exports to developed and developing countries are added to increase volume and achieve economies of scale. As the product advances in its life cycle, foreign manufacturing operations are set up in developed and then developing countries to serve the local markets previously handled by exports. Often this move has been prompted by governments erecting tariff walls to keep out imports and to stimulate local production in the protected markets. (This, for example, was part of the motivation that led Cummins Engine to set up its production facilities in India.) After operations have stabilized, exports are added to the domestic sales, with the target market often the foreign investor's home market. While this cycle is occurring, the parent firm is often developing new products, which then start the cycle again. More recently, firms are becoming more flexible and devising strategies and production systems that are more global. These involve developing and developed countries in an integrated network that tries to use various countries' comparative advantages to achieve global economies of scale or to make preemptive moves to achieve competitive advantage. This can in effect short-circuit the traditional life-cycle pattern and create a more complex set of strategic considerations and foreign direct investment configurations.

Foreign direct investment rose throughout the 1970s, although its share of total capital flows dropped to about 9% by 1980, as bank lending surged. However, as the international banks retrenched in the face of the international debt crisis, FDI's relative importance increased, with its share rising to 14% in 1986. In absolute real terms the FDI levels peaked in 1981, hit a low in 1985, and began to recuperate in 1986. The global recession in the 1980s cut LDC subsidiaries' profits and retained earnings, a key source of FDI. Developing country governments have been increasing their efforts to attract foreign investors. More than twenty African countries and several Caribbean nations have liberalized the foreign investment codes; the Andean Pact nations loosened their restrictions on FDI; several Asian developing countries have opened up new sectors to foreign investors (e.g., 80% of Korea's industrial sector is now open); new fiscal incentives have been offered by China, Ghana, Guinea, India, Madagascar, Thailand, and Yugoslavia; still others have reduced restrictions on capital repatriation.[38]

Prospects of good profits and favorable returns attract the foreign investor to the Third World. Latin America and the Caribbean captured two-thirds of the FDI to LDCs in 1965–69, but their share fell to about one-half in the 1980–83 period; Asia and the Middle East's share rose from 17% to 41%; Africa dropped from 17% to 11%.[39] FDI has been heavily concentrated in a small number of countries having large domestic markets or providing material resources or serving as export platforms; more than half the FDI during the 1973–84 period went to Brazil, Mexico, Indonesia, Malaysia, and Singapore.[40] About 80% of the Japanese trading companies' foreign manufacturing investments are in developing countries, with over 50% in Asian nations.[41] The annual outflow of profits of foreign direct investment in developing countries averaged $22 billion during 1980–83.[42] During this same period the reported rate of return on United States FDI in developing countries averaged 18.3%, as against 11.3% on direct investments in other developed countries.[43] Return on equity in foreign joint ventures in Korea, for example, was about 20% in 1978.[44]

Of the five hundred largest U.S. companies, 55% reported having

Table 1.7 U.S. Companies Investing in Developing Countries by Sector, 1986

	Share* of Top 500	Share* of Top 2000
Petroleum, gas, and fossil fuels	28.0%	24.5%
Machinery, electric, and manufactured goods	22.2	33.5
Transportation equipment and communication	12.8	8.7
Agriculture and food processing	10.6	6.4
Services	10.3	12.5
Metal industries	6.6	6.6
Paper and paper products	6.6	5.0
Construction	2.9	2.8

* Number of firms investing in each sector as a percentage of the total firms in the top five hundred and top two thousand investing in LDCs.

SOURCE: Calculated from Compustat Business Segment Database using data through 1986.

assets in developing countries in 1985; of the top two thousand, 27% had investments in the Third World. As Table 1.7 shows, these investments[45] were principally (over 50%) in the energy sector and in the machinery, electrical, and other manufactured goods industries. These were followed by transportation equipment and communication, services, and agriculture and food processing (about 33%). Metal industries, paper and related products, and construction constituted about 17% of the investment areas.

Smaller firms also invest abroad. Half of the 1,949 U.S. firms with foreign investments in 1982 had fewer than two thousand employees.[46] Firms with less than five hundred employees established 17% of their overseas affiliates in LDCs and companies with 501–2,000 employees set up 24% there. Larger firms chose LDCs for about 36% of their foreign operations.

Expansion of direct foreign investment in the Third World is expected in the future. Multinational corporations will remain important economic actors in developing countries, and developing countries will remain an important business environment for the MNCs. For local LDC firms the increased MNC presence is double-edged: It can mean the threat of increased competition or the opportunity for productive partnerships.

Governmental Assistance. Governments and multilateral agencies, such as the IMF and the World Bank, are important sources of short- and long-term loans for the Third World. Historically there has been a *de facto* segmentation of country recipients in terms of the sources of capital flows. Higher-income, more industrialized developing countries tend to be served more by private lenders and foreign investors, while lower-income countries rely more on official sources for their external capital flows. However, recently some of the highly indebted industrial developing countries have also had to rely increasingly on official sources. As the poorer countries develop, it is likely that they will increasingly attract private capital.

As of 1986, official sources provided two-thirds of the net flows to the Third World, an all-time high. Public-sector entities have partially filled in the capital flow void caused by the reduced lending of the international banks. In 1986 31% of the net flows were in the form of government-to-government bilateral aid from the developed countries. OPEC bilateral aid accounted for another 4%, down from its high of 10% in 1975. Aid and nonconcessional lending from multilateral agencies such as the World Bank accounted for 21%.[47] Even on the aid side, however, funds have been declining in real terms, falling from $63 billion in 1981 to $47 billion in 1986. (Part of this decline reflects the fact that official assistance is reported in dollar terms, and the value of the dollar fell during this period.)

It is clear from the foregoing sections that the developing countries play a significant role in the global economy as buyers, suppliers, competitors, and capital users. Understanding their business environments is critical for international business managers. That understanding requires an appreciation for the diversity among LDCs.

HOW DIVERSE ARE DEVELOPING COUNTRIES?

Any manager who has traveled to several developing countries will quickly point out that they differ considerably one from another. Although in this book we use the terms developing countries, Third World, and less developed countries interchangeably to refer to this large category of 142 nations, no two are alike. A basic premise of this book is that the distinctive business environments in developing countries are due to the different levels and processes of development, not just between the developing and developed but also among the developing countries themselves. These business environments are inherently unstable because countries continue to develop; rapid or significant change is the constant.

LDC diversity can be revealed by differences in levels of development. The literature on economic development is filled with debates about what development is and how to measure it. Several development indicators commonly used by international development organizations are discussed below. Our objective is not to find the "correct" one; we shall instead point out how each indicator can give the manager a different perspective on how the business environment is likely to vary among LDCs with different developmental characteristics. We shall also point out some of the limitations of these indicators.

Gross National Product per Capita

This is the most common development indicator, with countries grouped by income ranges. Appendix A ranks countries by per capita GNP. The categories used by the World Bank[48] are shown in Table 1.8. The GNP per capita indicator reveals a country's output and national income in relation to its population, thereby partially showing the level of effective demand.

One of this indicator's weaknesses is that as an average it does not reveal income distribution or real standards of living. For example, in 1983 the United Arab Emirates (UAE) had the highest per capita income in the world at $22,870, far above Switzerland, the highest industrialized nation at $16,290. Yet few would claim that the UAE or other Persian Gulf states are developed nations. Although they have made important gains, on the average only 50% of their populations are literate, and they have infant mortality rates averaging over 70 per thousand live births (versus 99% literacy and infant mortality rate under 10 in industrial economies). Furthermore, with the decline in oil prices the UAE's 1986 per capita GNP had fallen to $14,680, behind Switzerland, the United States, and Norway.[49] Another limitation of the GNP per capita figures is that they do not reveal living costs; these are often lower in LDCs, thereby allowing higher living standards in terms of goods and services acquirable than the absolute levels of GNP might imply, that is, the purchasing power of the same income levels can differ between countries.

Table 1.8 GNP per Capita in 1987*

Low-income economies	under US$480
Middle-income economies	$480–$6,000
Lower middle-income	$480–$1,940
Upper middle-income	$2,020–$6,000
Oil exporters†	average $1,520
High-income economies	above $6,000

* Figures are reported in constant dollar terms.
† This is a category based on criteria other than GNP per capita.

For example, in 1987 Japan's average income was $23,022 and in the United States it was $18,163; however, in purchasing power terms the Japanese income was 19% less than the American's, reflecting the considerably higher costs of food and housing in Japan.[50]

Total GNP

The absolute magnitude of a country's economy is indicative of aggregate demand and market size. There are ten giant LDC economies, which in total constituted 50% of the Third World's combined 1987 gross domestic products (see Table 1.9). These larger economies tend to create more diverse and complex business environments. The magnitude of their markets permits production economies of scale. The smaller economies are often more vulnerable to economic disruption and cannot support large production volume for the domestic market, although they can serve as high-volume export bases.

Table 1.9 LDCs with Largest Gross Domestic Products 1987

Country	GDP in Millions of US $
Brazil	299,230
China	293,380
India	220,830
Mexico	141,940
Korea	121,310
Taiwan	95,384
South Africa	74,260
Argentina	71,530
Saudi Arabia	71,470
Indonesia	69,670

SOURCES: *World Development Report 1989*, pp. 168–9; *Taiwan Statistical Data Book 1988* (Taipei: Council for Economic Planning and Development, 1988), pp. 99, 112.

Degree of Industrialization

Generally, as a country develops, its industrial sector contributes a growing percentage to the nation's gross domestic product. The industrial sector includes mining, manufacturing, construction, and energy. This measure can be useful to companies as an indicator of a country's current level of industrial infrastructure and technology. The phrase "industrialized nations" is often used to refer to the developed nations of North America, Europe, Scandinavia, Oceania, Japan and Russia. Some of the upper-middle-income countries with higher levels of industrial and technological development and of human resources and infrastructure are referred to as the Newly Industrializing Countries (NICs). Among these, the "Four Dragons"—South Korea, Hong Kong, Taiwan, and Singapore—have drawn special attention for their exceptionally high annual growth rates and success in exporting manufactured goods. Appendixes A and B rank developing countries by percentage contribution of industry to GDP.

This indicator can be misleading because it does not reveal the scope, quality, or technological sophistication of the industrialization. Oil countries tend to have a high industrial percentage contribution to GDP, but their infrastructure in many instances is related mainly to the oil sector. In 1987 in the People's Republic of China, industry constituted 49% of GDP and in South Korea it was 43%, yet the level and breadth of industrial sophistication in Korea clearly exceeded that of mainland China.[51] To assess the development level, one should look at the industry share in conjunction with the other sectors' shares. As industry's share rises, agriculture's declines and services' increases. At the higher levels of industrial development the supporting services in the financial, telecommunications, commercial, and professional areas expand even more rapidly, thereby decreasing industry's share. In the industrial countries the sectoral proportions in 1987 were 37% for industry, 60% for services, and 4% for agriculture; the corresponding figures for low-income countries (excluding India and China) were 27% for industry, 40% for services, and 33% for agriculture.[52]

Thus, as countries develop, companies can expect infrastructure and business opportunities to rise in the industrial and service sectors while the agricultural sector will decline in relative importance. Within these sectors important shifts also occur. In industry generally, manufacturing rises and mining falls. Agricultural products experience greater degrees of processing. For example, in low-income Bangladesh agriculture accounts for 53% of GDP and food processing industries 4%, while in the upper-middle-income country of Argentina agriculture's share was 11% and the agroindustries' share was 32%.[53]

GNP Growth Rates

Another measure is how fast the country is moving along the economic development spectrum, rather than where it lies on it. This can be ascertained by measuring growth rates of either GNP or GNP per capita.

The growth rate indicates one aspect of demand behavior and possible market dynamics. The business environment in a high-growth versus a low-growth market can be quite different. The causes of these growth rates can vary significantly even among the countries in the fast or slow groups. Understanding the business environment requires a probing of the underlying factors shaping these diverse growth patterns.

Table 1.10 lists the six fastest and six slowest growth countries in terms of average annual GDP growth rates for the 1965–80 and 1980–86 periods. Appendixes A and B rank the LDCs by growth rates.

Table 1.10 Fastest and Slowest Growing Developing Economies (*GDP growth rates*)

Fastest Six			
1965–80		1980–87	
Oman	15.2%	Botswana	13.0%
Botswana	14.2%	Oman	12.7%
Saudi Arabia	11.3%	China	10.4%
Singapore	10.1%	Korea	8.6%
Taiwan	9.8%	Taiwan	7.4%
Korea	9.5%	Cameroon	7.0%
Slowest Six			
1965–80		1980–87	
Lebanon	−1.2%	Mozambique	−2.6%
Chad	0.1%	Bolivia	−2.1%
Niger	0.3%	Niger	−1.9%
Uganda	0.8%	Nigeria	−1.7%
Kuwait	1.3%	Liberia	−1.3%
Zaire	1.3%	Philippines	−0.5%

SOURCES: *World Development Report 1989*, pp. 166–67; *Taiwan Statistical Data Book 1988*, p. 112.

Physical Quality of Life Indicator (PQLI)

The PQLI measures development in noneconomic terms. This is a composite index based on a country's literacy rate, infant mortality rate, and life expectancy. In 1981 the average PQLI for developing countries was 61; it was 96 for developed nations.[54] The PQLI rank of a country can diverge considerably from its rank based on economic indicators. For example, Sri Lanka, with a 1981 per capita income one-seventh of Brazil's, had a PQLI of 85 compared to Brazil's 74. The PQLI is useful

in suggesting the quality of human resources u̅   nter.
Appendixes A and B provide a PQLI ranking of ⸲   ries.

Income Distribution

Countries can also be characterized by the degree o   s or
inequality of its income distribution. One indicator of ir   ation
is the Gini coefficient, which measures the percenta   going
to each income bracket. In a "perfectly equitable" distribution each
1% of the population would earn 1% of the available income, and the
Gini coefficient would be zero. In a completely inequitable economy
the top percentile of the population would earn all the income, and the
Gini coefficient would be one. For example, in 1970 the Gini coefficient
for Ecuador was .63 and for South Korea .35, indicating a more equal
distribution of income in South Korea.[55] This coefficient can indicate
economic narrowness or concentration in the consumer market. It may
also reveal some pressure for political change. Appendix C lists the
Gini coefficients for several countries.

Other Diversity Indicators

One can also characterize countries according to types of *political*
systems, such as military governments, single-party regimes, and multi-
party democracies. The stability of the regime could also be used as an
indicator. Another dimension is *culture*. The cultural richness of developing countries is extraordinary. Culture is *sui generis* and thus difficult
to use as a categorizing parameter. Nonetheless, certain shared belief
systems, sometimes stemming from a common religion, can be used to
group countries. For example, Islamic countries have certain beliefs
and practices that influence business customs in a distinctive way. Certain
Asian nations have shared cultural roots that create special attitudes
toward group loyalty and individualism, which in turn affect business
organization and behavior. The social, political, and economic structures
of many African nations are influenced by tribal systems and customs.
Demographically one can categorize nations according to size, for example, the "megapopulation" countries of China, India, Brazil, Indonesia,
and Nigeria, which account for about 45% of the world's population,
or the thirty-two "minipopulation" LDCs with less than a million inhabitants. Countries can also be categorized according to population growth
rates or degree of urbanization. These demographic variables create very
different market environments. *Geographical* location is also used to

categorize countries and can capture cultural and climatological similarities, for example sub-Saharan Africa. However, considerable economic diversity exists even within regional groupings; for example, the Côte d'Ivoire (Ivory Coast) had a 1987 per capita GNP of $740 and Gabon $2,700, as contrasted to an average of $330 for the rest of the sub-Saharan region.[56]

The foregoing indicators reveal the significant diversity among developing countries. Our analytical framework will help to identify the variables that create that diversity. But along with their diversity, the developing countries share many similarities. To highlight these salient general characteristics that give rise to a distinctive context for doing business, we shall make generalizations throughout the book about developing countries in the aggregate and their "business environment." Generalization is integral to conceptualization and the distillation of critical variables. It allows us to create a more usable managerial framework. However, when we make these generalizations, the reader is urged to remember the diversity and exceptions that surround them and to adjust for that reality.

CONCLUSION

As we move toward and into the twenty-first century, developing countries will become even more important in the global economy. Improvement in the well-being of four-fifths of the world's population rests on the ability of the Third World to develop. And that development will depend, to a significant extent, on the capacity of managers in developing countries to operate the productive apparatus in an efficient, effective, and equitable manner. This book aims to contribute to that management challenge.

Analyzing the Business Environment

2

Environmental Analysis Framework

The key to effective management in developing countries is the capacity to analyze, understand, and manage the external forces enveloping the firm. The manager confronts two basic questions: *what* to analyze in the environment and *how* to assess its relevance to the firm's strategy. The LDCs' distinctive environment engulfs the firm with a complex multitude of pressures, demands, and opportunities. The risk of being overwhelmed is real. A manager must analyze systematically these environmental forces, decipher their managerial implications, and translate them into strategic decisions. Working within an analytical framework does not guarantee optimal decisions, but it provides a structure for the decision process and the answering of key managerial questions. The purpose of this brief introductory chapter is to provide a *conceptual* overview of our Environmental Analysis Framework (EAF). The subsequent three chapters will elaborate the components of the framework.

OVERVIEW: MULTIPLE FACTORS AND MULTILEVELS

The fundamental task in environmental analysis is to identify and understand the channels through which external forces impact the firm. We must take a broad view of the forces shaping the environment, systematically recognizing the connections and interdependencies. Thus, our first conceptual step is to sort external forces into four categories of environmental factors: economic, political, cultural, and demographic.

There are, of course, alternative ways to categorize. These four, however, have the advantages of being comprehensive and readily integrated with analytical perspectives and techniques derived from the underlying social-science disciplines of economics, political science, sociology and anthropology, and demography. The second step is to envision the business environment as having four levels: the international level encompassing various kinds of interaction among countries, the national level as shaped by a government's strategy and policies, the industry level involving firms' immediate competitive environment, and the company level comprising the individual enterprise's strategy and operations. These environmental levels are thus envisioned as moving from the most macro or

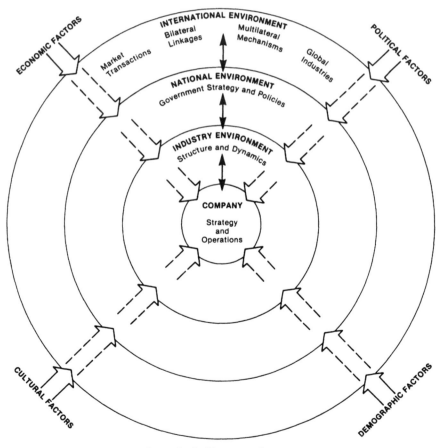

Figure 2.1 Environmental Analysis Framework

distant from the firm to the most micro at the internal level of the firm itself. Each of these four levels—international, national, industry, and company—is shaped by the overall environmental factors: economic, political, cultural, and demographic. Also, actions on each level can affect the other three levels; they are interactive.

Figure 2.1 presents a summary view of the EAF. It is a simplified conceptual map; the complexity lies in reading the map. That task involves analyzing the components and understanding their links, which we shall now describe in more detail.

ENVIRONMENTAL FACTORS

One of the big stumbling blocks facing managers attempting to carry out environmental analysis is figuring out how to sort out the external phenomena. There are so many and they seem so complex that confusion can immobilize action. A first key step is to use analytical categories that enable one to untangle and make more manageable the external complexity.

The four categories of environmental factors—economic, political, cultural, and demographic—can be divided into subcategories to facilitate systematic scrutiny. This increases one's ability to decide what managerial actions might be taken to deal with the actual or potential impact of a specific environmental factor. The economic factors consist of natural resources, labor, capital, infrastructure, and technology. The political factors include stability, ideology, institutions, and geopolitical links. The cultural factors encompass social structure and dynamics, perspectives on human nature, time and space orientation, religion, gender roles, and language. The demographic factors involve population growth, age structure, urbanization, migration, and health status.

The specification of individual factors should be accompanied by recognition of their interrelationships. A manager needs to know each of the strands and how they are woven together to create the larger environmental fabric. These factors and their interaction shape the nature of the business environment at international, national, industry, and firm levels and thus provide a common analytical lens through which to view each level.

Chapter 3 shows in detail how the four categories and their subsets can identify the salient characteristics of the business environment of a developing country. Figure 2.2 presents a summary view of these interactive factors.

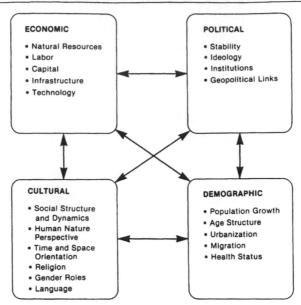

Figure 2.2 Environmental Factors

ENVIRONMENTAL LEVELS

The International Level

Since developing countries are an integral part of the international economy, the EAF must incorporate this international dimension of the business environment. Because our emphasis in this book is on the distinctive nature of the LDC business environment, and because we wish to stress the interdependent nature of the LDCs' and global economies, our approach is to integrate the international aspects into our examination of the national business environment, rather than treat it separately. We will delineate here the key aspects of the international environment, which are then used as integral parts of our analyses of government strategies (Chapter 4), industry analysis (Chapter 5), and the functional areas (Part II). The focus is on how the international environment shapes the national business environment and on the implications of the distinctive LDC environment for firms in LDCs operating in the international economy.

Countries are linked together through the cross-border flows of resources that take place through four main types of interactions. The first type is the normal market transactions in the international arena that bring about the flow of goods and services among nations. As was pointed out in Chapter 1, the LDCs operate in the international economy as buyers, suppliers, competitors, and capital users. The dynamics of that marketplace can produce important reverberations. For example, international prices of major imports or exports can significantly affect national economies, government actions, and the domestic business environment in which a firm is operating.

The second type of international interaction is the special bilateral linkages between the country in which the firm is operating and other individual countries. Such country-to-country relationships can affect the nature of market transactions as well as lead to nonmarket flows that can have a large impact on the country's business environment. These relationships can be viewed through the lens of the EAF's four environmental categories, for example: economic links—the majority of Mexico's foreign trade is with the United States, which makes Mexico's economy highly dependent on the health of the U.S. economy; political links—Poland's ties to the Soviet Union, which lead to aid flows and influence over domestic policies; cultural links—Pakistan's ties to Saudi Arabia through the shared Islamic religion, which lead to flows of workers and funds; demographic links—large numbers of males from Lesotho migrate to neighboring South Africa to work in the mines, which affects the structure of the labor supply and economies in both countries (and in the early 1980s Nigeria expelled its migrant labor force, causing a million Ghanaian workers to flood back into Ghana's already large pool of unemployed).[1] These international interdependencies frequently lead to special bilateral agreements between two countries' governments whereby economic aid, preferential market access, or other forms of assistance are granted.

The third vehicle for international interaction involves the multilateral mechanisms or formal agreements, created jointly by various countries to govern the international system as a whole or subsets of it. Examples are the General Agreement on Tariffs and Trade (GATT), the International Coffee Agreement and the Multi-Fiber Agreement for specific commodities, the IMF and the World Bank for international finances, the World Court for international law, and the United Nations for global political relations.

The fourth vehicle that links the LDCs with the international economy is global industries. In these industries, production systems and markets are spread across countries and are interdependent. Actions in one country have a direct impact on the operations of firms in that industry in other countries. The structure and competitive behavior in that global industry is shaped in part by the forces in the specific environments in each of the participating countries. In effect, through their participation in a global industry and interaction with each other, individual firms share portions of each other's country and industry environments.

An international manager in a global industry may need to utilize the EAF to examine the business environment in a country in which a competitor is operating, even though the firm itself does not do business in that country. What happens in that industry in one country may carry competitive implications for a company in another country even without immediately changing the business environment in the second country. For example, a government in one country may decide to provide export subsidies to its companies in that global industry; suddenly the company in that same industry in another country may be placed at a competitive

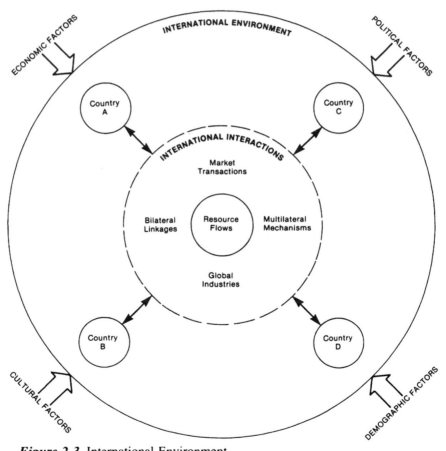

Figure 2.3 International Environment

disadvantage, even though its national environment is unchanged. The challenge to the newly disadvantaged company is then to change its environment or operations in order to overcome the competitive disadvantage.

Figure 2.3 depicts the international environment in terms of the four types of international transactions discussed above. Figure 2.4 shows the international links created by global industries in terms of overlapping environments.

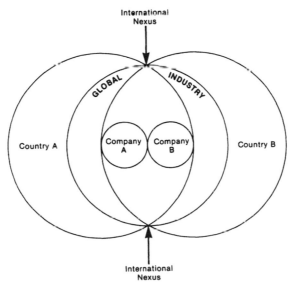

Figure 2.4 International Links of National Environments Through Global Industries

The National Level

The government is a primary shaper of the business environment, so at the national level the government's strategy becomes a critical focal point of analysis for the manager. Methodologically, one can view the nation-state as similar to a corporation: It has goals, a development strategy, policies, and policy instruments to implement that strategy. As indicated previously, a national strategy and its elements are shaped by both international and national economic, political, cultural, and demographic factors. Thus, any analysis of national strategy must consider the causal links with those factors in order to understand why the government is taking or might take certain actions.

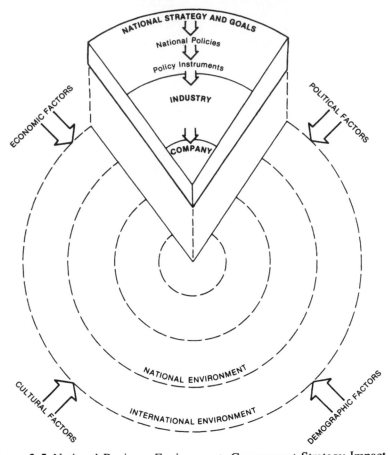

Figure 2.5 National Business Environment: Government Strategy Impact

Chapter 4 analyzes the causes, content, and impact of national strategies. We interpret the environment at the macro national level to determine the managerial implications at the micro firm level. This process will enable managers to understand national strategies and the policies, the instruments used to implement them, and their potential impact on the industry and company. Figure 2.5 highlights this government strategy component of the EAF.

Industry Level

At the industry level a manager must understand the proximate competitive environment facing the firm. This component of our framework

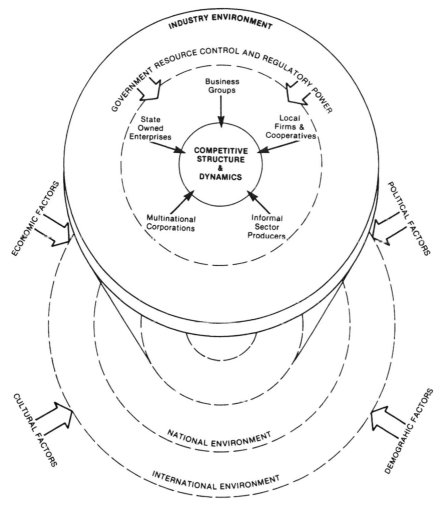

Figure 2.6 Industry-Level Analysis

focuses on industry structure and competitive dynamics, which are shaped by the LDCs' special environmental factors.

In developing countries, the government is a "mega-force" in shaping the competitive environment. Its control over resources and its regulatory powers can fundamentally determine the structure of industries, the nature of competition, and relative competitive advantage among firms.

The second focus is on institutional analysis. The LDC environment gives rise to five types of competitors with different competitive strengths and weaknesses: state-owned enterprises (SOEs), which are often very large economic entities; business groups, which are powerful, family-based, multibusiness conglomerates; local non-business-group firms and cooperatives, which can be important in single industries; multinational corporations, which have strong international links; and informal sector producers, which are the multitude of small-scale firms operating in the service and light-industry sectors. Chapter 5 delineates the distinctive dimensions of the competitive environment in developing countries. Figure 2.6 depicts the focus of the industry-level analysis component of the EAF.

The Company Level

The fourth level of the environment is the firm itself. Like the international level, the company level is an integral part of the analyses of the national and industry levels. The EAF is continually focused on the impact of the environment on the firm. Part II emphasizes the company-level focus by examining functional area issues.

CONCLUSION

The environmental system is interactive and dynamic. The actions of individual firms shape the industry-level environment, which in turn can affect government strategies and policies, which can affect the international environment, and vice versa. Similarly, as actors within the environment, international institutions, governments, industries, and firms can affect and alter the economic, political, cultural, and demographic factors. Strategic management involves both adjusting to the business environment and altering it. The next three chapters examine the analytical components of the Environmental Analysis Framework: examining the environmental factors, interpreting national strategies, and understanding industry structure and dynamics.

3

The Environmental Factors

Although countries are highly diverse, the four major interrelated categories of factors—economic, political, cultural, and demographic—can be used to analyze developing countries individually or in the aggregate. The precise nature of these factors will vary by country, but they are common to all. By examining a country's situation in each of the four general categories and their specific subcategories indicated below, a manager can systematically focus on and interpret the most managerially relevant characteristics of the environment. Table 3.1 lists the principal factors to be examined in each of the four categories.

The environmental factors listed in the table shape the business context. They constitute the variables the manager should monitor in environmental scanning. Their managerial significance can be systematically examined at each of the four levels of the business environment indicated in the EAF (international, national, industry, and company). The factors influence events in the international arena, shape national governments' development strategies and policies, affect the structure and competitive dynamics of the company's industry, and directly impinge on specific activities of the company.

The following sections examine in further detail each of the four major sets of environmental factors.[1] Each factor will be described in comparison to the situation in more developed countries. This comparative perspective will (1) reveal more clearly the distinctive nature of LDC business environments, and (2) highlight possible directions of change in the environments as these countries develop. To sharpen the contrast we shall make generalizations about the LDC environment. The reader should keep in mind, however, the previously mentioned diversity among the developing nations. After describing each environmental subfactor, we shall indicate some of its managerial implications. The purpose in this chapter is only to *illustrate* how environmental factors can influence the business context. Subsequent chapters give more detailed analyses of the factors' impact and managerial significance; these cross-references are noted in the text. This component of our analytical framework helps managers determine which variables to scan, what links to examine, and how to interpret them given their specific circumstances.

Table 3.1 Environmental Factors

Economic	Cultural
Natural resources—	Social structure & dynamics
importance and availability	Human nature
Labor—skilled & unskilled	Time & space
Capital—domestic & foreign	Religion
Infrastructure—physical & informational	Gender roles
Technology—levels & structure	Language

Political	Demographic
Instability	Population growth
Ideology	Age structure
Institutions	Urbanization
International links	Migration
	Health status

ECONOMIC FACTORS

This first major category[2] focuses on the differences in economic characteristics between the more and less developed countries, and the relevance of these characteristics to managers.

It is useful from a managerial perspective to divide the economic category into subcategories. For convenience, we start with the standard economic trilogy of land (natural resources), labor, and capital but add two other subcategories particularly relevant for LDCs: infrastructure and technology. These subcategories are summarized in Table 3.2 and discussed below. This summary provides a general view of the characteristics in countries at different points on the economic development spectrum. As mentioned, there are exceptions to the summarized generalizations. Furthermore, the indicated differences across low-, middle-, and high-income countries do not mean that these conditions will automatically hold for another country moving up the income scale. Nonetheless, they do provide a view of how the business environment can vary across different types of developing countries and the direction in which it might change as the countries develop.

Table 3.2 Summary of Economic Factors

Factors	Development Level (GDP per capita)		
	Low	Middle	High*
Natural Resources			
Importance to economy	high	--->	lower
Availability	under-developed	--->	developed
Labor			
Skilled human capital	scarce	--->	abundant
Unskilled labor: % workforce			
in agriculture	72%	44%	6%
Capital			
Domestic Capital			
Income levels	$280	$1,810	$14,430
Savings rates: % of GDP 1987	15%	25%	21%
Income skewedness	medium	high	low
Financial institutions	weak	--->	strong
Inflation: average 1973–83	14%	29%	8%
Capital flight	outflow	--->	inflow
Foreign Exchange			
Trade deficits	medium	high	low
Commodity export line	narrow	--->	broad
Exchange-rate volatility	low	high	low
Foreign debt service:			
as % of exports	21%	21%	2%
Concessional foreign aid	recipient	<---	donor
Infrastructure			
Physical infrastructure	weak	--->	strong
Information availability	low	--->	high
Technology			
Technological levels	low	--->	high
Industry structures	dualistic	--->	unitary
Technology flows	recipient	--->	supplier

* High-income oil exporters are excluded.

Natural Resources

The first economic subcategory is natural-resource endowment, including land and mineral resources. Different natural-resource endowments do not necessarily determine levels of development, but they do contribute to the diversity of LDCs and their development processes. We shall discuss two characteristics: the importance of natural resources in the national economy, and their availability.

Importance of Natural Resources to the Economy. Most LDC economies are still agriculture-based, although many countries are rapidly industrializing. Table 3.3 compares the contribution of agriculture to GDP for four development levels. (Tables and figures in the chapter are placed near each subsection's "Managerial Implications.") Note that this contribution may be greater than indicated because, first, it is difficult to measure subsistence farming, and second, significant portions of the industrial and commercial sectors involve food processing and marketing. Many are also heavily dependent on mineral resources.

The contribution of natural resources to the national economy is a general indicator of the level of economic development. LDC economies tend to rely more heavily on natural resources. This can change as alternative industries are developed or world demand changes. The dynamics of the national economy are significantly shaped by the degree of dependence on narrow commodity lines. For example, over half of Botswana's GDP and about 70% of its exports in 1986 came from minerals, mainly diamonds.[3] Between 1974 and 1986 oil and gas accounted for 77% of Indonesia's exports, and coffee ranged between 26% and 69% of Colombia's exports.[4] Many Colombians say, "As coffee goes, so goes Colombia."

Table 3.3 Contribution of Agriculture to GDP

Income Groupings	1965	1987
Low-income economies	43%	31%
Lower-middle-income economies	21%	22%*
Upper-middle-income economies	19%	10%*
High-income economies	5%	3%*

* Figures for 1986.

SOURCES: *World Development Report 1989* (New York: Oxford University Press for World Bank, 1989), pp. 168–69, and *1988*, pp. 226–27.

Managerial Implications. The more central natural resources are to an economy, the more a manager should monitor that sector, even if the company is not directly involved in it. As the dominant economic sector, it will be a magnet for government resources, and its performance will have profound effects on the national economy and government policies, and therefore other firms. For example, in Ghana agriculture produced about half of GDP, and so when a 1983 drought caused farm production to fall 7.2%, GDP fell 4.6%.[5] A revenue drop in key export sectors due to a fall in international prices could trigger a national recession, which could tighten credit and depress demand, thereby affecting a firm's finances and marketing; a revenue rise in the key sector could increase disposable income and stimulate demand throughout the economy, perhaps sparking inflation. Scrutinizing the central sector may reveal specific business opportunities in ancillary industries. As the country develops, one can expect new businesses to arise that will provide additional value-added through further processing of the primary commodity. Being aware of these dynamics and how one's company can aid government goals can contribute to a more desirable business-government relationship (see Chapter 6). If a government is trying to diversify its economy, it may provide incentives for such new businesses. The Colombian government, for example, provided significant fiscal and credit incentives to entrepreneurs developing the cut-flower industry for the export market. This assistance was important in helping Colombian producers become a dominant competitive force in the U.S. market.

Availability of Natural Resources. Much of the world's proven reserves for basic and strategic minerals lie in developing countries: They hold over 50% of twenty-six different minerals, including gold, tin, aluminum, copper, nickel, and cobalt (Table 3.4). Other types of reserves include agricultural land, timber, fuels and other energy sources, and natural tourist attractions (wildlife, unspoiled mountains, and so on). The quantity of a resource is often related to the absolute geographical size of the country, as larger nations frequently are more richly and broadly endowed with natural resources. Thus, the size of the country can be a determining variable. Development of LDC resource reserves generally lags behind that of developed countries.

One should consider not only the quantity of the resource but also its quality. The productivity of land, for example, will be determined by climatological conditions such as rainfall and temperature patterns and topographical conditions such as mountainous terrain. Although Saudi Arabia has a relatively large land mass, most of it is not arable except at a very high cost. The importance of a country's endowment of natural resources should be assessed in terms of the economic feasibility of their development as well as the technical feasibility.

Managerial Implications. Natural resources have made LDCs key in-

Table 3.4 LDCs' Share of Proven World Mineral Reserves

Rhodium	99%	Gold	71%	Silver	45%
Platinum	99%	Cobalt	70%	Iron	44%
Palladium	98%	Titanium	65%	Scandium	43%
Chromium	98%	Manganese	62%	Fluorine	42%
Tin	90%	Bismuth	56%	Cadmium	40%
Tantalum	88%	Zirconium	55%	Zinc	40%
Aluminum	85%	Copper	53%	Sulfur	39%
Gallium	85%	Arsenic	53%	Rubidium	38%
Iodine	84%	Tellurium	52%	Barium	35%
Niobium	83%	Selenium	51%	Lead	34%
Antimony	79%	Boron	50%	Vanadium	23%
Beryllium	77%	Germanium	50%	Molybdenum	23%
Nickel	73%	Thorium	47%	Mercury	14%
Tungsten	72%				

SOURCE: Derived from U.S. Department of Interior data, 1977.

ternational suppliers of strategic commodities. Historically the abundant capital and technical knowledge needed to develop and market these mineral resources led developing nations to rely on multinational companies (MNCs). Over time the LDC governments have tended to assume control and ownership of these operations, viewing them as part of the national patrimony and critical to their sovereignty. Large projects to tap resource reserves continue to be mounted in Third World countries, for example a billion-dollar coal extraction and processing operation in Colombia, a multibillion-dollar hydroelectric project in Brazil, and Occidental's coal and ARCO's natural gas projects in China.[6] The economic and technological requirements for such operations often still exceed local capabilities, especially if the resources are located in more remote areas requiring significant infrastructure investments. Business opportunities lie in finding politically acceptable modes of collaboration, such as joint ventures, licensing, management contracts, or marketing agreements. (See Chapter 10 for a discussion of these alternative organizational forms.)

Labor

Generally, skilled labor is scarce and unskilled abundant. Education and training levels in most developing countries are low by Western standards. Literacy rates are commonly under 50% (see Table 3.5), although some developing nations have achieved nearly universal literacy.

Table 3.5 Education Levels

	% in Higher Education[a]	Literacy Rate (%)
Low-income economies	5[b]	37[c]
Middle-income economies	14	64
Industrial market economies	39	97

[a] Number enrolled in higher education in 1984 as percentage of population aged 20–24.

[b] Excluding India with 9% and China with 2%.

[c] Excluding China; including China raises the average to 51%.

SOURCES: Higher education data from *World Development Report 1988*, pp. 280–81. Literacy data from John Sewell *et al.* (eds.), *U.S. Foreign Policy and the Third World*, (New Brunswick, N.J.: TransAction Books, in cooperation with the Overseas Development Council, 1985) pp. 214–15.

Less than one in five students continues past primary school in the lowest-income economies. Only 2% continue past secondary school, as against 37% in the industrial economies. The small minority who do are typically the urban upper-class elite, who may seek better career opportunities overseas. While skilled labor is scarce in developing countries, highly educated persons may not find appropriate job opportunities. Foreign education or local university programs do not always provide training in the skills that a developing country most needs; imbalances are common between the type and quantity of skills available and those demanded by companies.

The obverse of scarce skilled labor is abundant unskilled workers. Extremely high unemployment and underemployment are common in developing countries. In Latin America, for example, open urban unemployment in 1984 was 19% in Chile, 14% in Venezuela and Uruguay, and 13% in Colombia and Bolivia.[7] When underemployment is combined with unemployment, the rates often approach 50% of the labor force. Seasonal underemployment is particularly high in rural areas and in countries dependent on agriculture as a major source of national product. This rural unemployment contributes to rural–urban migration. The large pool of urban labor is tied in to dualistic industry structures (described below) in the form of large "informal sectors" (see Chapter 5). Population growth and the resulting young age structure of LDCs swell the number of unemployed. With scarce financial resources, fewer families are able to afford the education needed to gain marketable skills. Some developing countries (particularly in the Middle East) are labor short; often they solve this problem by importing laborers from other LDCs.

Managerial Implications. The lack of skilled labor creates obvious production and organizational problems. Technological choices can be limited by labor's skill level, hampering the use of sophisticated equipment. Training becomes a critical task during startup in order to remove production bottlenecks. Cummins Engine, for example, had to carry out considerable training as part of its startup in India. Once trained, workers will also have more opportunities elsewhere, given the general scarcity of skilled workers. Consequently, considerable attention must be paid to maintaining high motivation and morale to reduce desertion. Training must be seen as an ongoing function, not only to remove the skill bottleneck but also to improve worker morale. Governments and unions will generally view this form of human resource development favorably, thereby facilitating negotiations.

Despite problems of skill scarcity, the abundance of even unskilled human resources creates one of the biggest comparative advantages of developing countries: low-cost labor. Abundant labor makes labor-intensive activities viable, creates a steady labor supply, and gives firms leverage in bargaining with unions. However, the political importance of employment often leads to legislation protecting workers against layoffs and to overstaffing of public institutions. To use more labor-intensive methods, firms may have to adapt production technologies and techniques. (Chapter 8 analyzes the issues of technology choice and adaptation.)

Domestic Capital

In most developing countries private and public domestic capital is very scarce. Among the factors affecting the availability of domestic capital are low incomes and savings, skewed income distribution, weak financial institutions, high inflation, and high capital flight.

Low Incomes and Savings Rates. Only fourteen of the 142 developing countries had a gross domestic product in 1986 over $50 billion,[8] while most of the nineteen industrialized market economies' GDPs were over $100 billion. LDCs' small economic bases are insufficient to meet their high national needs. On a per capita basis, the income difference is even more striking: In 1987 the average GNP per capita was $280 in the low-income economies and $14,430 for industrial market economies. More than half the world's population lived in countries with a GNP per capita of less than $450 a year, while three-fourths of all LDCs had an average GNP per capita of less than $2,500 per year.[9] This poverty is compounded by skewed income distributions, in which a small elite and an urban middle class earn a large proportion of total disposable income. Masses of low-income individuals struggle to survive on less than a dollar a day.

Savings rates in most low-income countries were about 15% of GDP in 1987 (with salient exceptions being China at 38% and India at 22%); lower-middle-income countries averaged 21%, upper-middle-income countries 27%, and industrial market economies 21%.[10] In simple terms, there is a tradeoff between spending now for higher living standards, and saving and investing for future growth. When average income is very low, an increase in voluntary saving through a cut in current consumption is much more difficult. A low savings rate implies lower capital formation and fewer investment funds, with relatively high current expenditures.

Managerial Implications. At the consumer level, low incomes mean low effective demand; purchasing power is severely constrained. The mass market will tend to be mainly for basic items such as food and clothing. At lower income levels the largest percentage of the budget will go to food purchases; as incomes rise, food expenditures will grow in absolute terms but take up a smaller share of the total family expenditures. Low cash incomes and savings also mean that the capacity to make outlays for consumer durables is hindered. This implies that consumer and supplier credit must play a significant role in marketing programs (see Chapter 9). The extremity and pervasiveness of poverty in LDCs places a special social responsibility on business as a vehicle for creating economic progress that will help alleviate this deprivation.

At the national level, capital scarcity may lead to severe limits on the availability of bank credit or equity capital. This can constrain a firm's ability to invest in capital-intensive production or pursue new business opportunities. Within an industry, those companies able to gain preferential access to scarce domestic capital or to tap external resources will gain competitive advantage.

Income Distribution. Sharply demarcated economic classes are particularly prevalent in LDCs because of the pattern of income distribution, which is less equal in most developing countries than in most developed countries. For example, in the LDCs the top 10% of the population receive around 36% of the countries' income and much more in such nations as Brazil at 51% and Zambia, Kenya, and Mauritius at 46%, whereas in no developed country did the top 10% receive over 30%.[11] Perhaps surprisingly, distribution is better in a few lowest-income countries than in the industrialized West. Sri Lanka, for example, has a more equitable income pattern than the United States. Some analyses indicate that inequality tends to be worst in middle-income countries with rapidly growing economies.[12] The Gini coefficients discussed in Chapter 1 and the country rankings in Appendix C provide further data on income distribution patterns.

Managerial Implications. Skewed income distribution tends to create very distinct market segments, with the low end concerned mainly with subsistence goods and the affluent end having purchasing patterns similar to those of wealthier consumers in more developed countries. This creates a demand for many Western products and may even facilitate the implementation of global marketing strategies (see Chapter 9). Where income disparities are less, possibilities for mass marketing broaden. Large or worsening economic disparities can generate social discontent and political instability. For example, the severe economic hardships endured by Mexico's masses during the 1980s contributed in the 1988 presidential elections to a split in and almost the defeat of the Institutional Revolutionary Party, which had controlled the government for most of this century.

Weak Financial Institutions. Particularly in the poorer developing countries, financial institutions are weak. The scarcity of trained personnel and the narrowness of the markets hinder institutional development. The relative size of the financial system can be roughly indicated by the ratio of money supply to GDP; for developing countries this is usually less than 0.5, while for developed economies it ranges upward toward 1.0.[13] Formal capital markets such as stock exchanges are either nonexistent or quite limited in scope. Government tends to be heavily involved in the financial system either as a regulator or as a direct operator. Often the national banking system is largely state-owned. This frequently means that the financial institutions are heavily bureaucratized and politicized. Weaknesses in financial institutions reduce their ability to attract and mobilize savings, thereby accentuating capital scarcity. The population, especially in rural areas, will often place their savings in traditional nonmonetary assets, such as livestock or jewelry. Where the formal institutions are underdeveloped, informal financing mechanisms and capital markets operate.

Managerial Implications. The task of capital mobilization is much more difficult (see Chapter 7). There are fewer financing options and long-term capital is particularly scarce. Transaction costs in time and resources tend to be higher. The cost of capital, too, is generally higher because of its scarcity. On the other hand, the lack of institutionalization may create greater flexibility in structuring financing arrangements. There may also be business opportunities in providing some of the financial services lacking in the environment. Foreign firms may be able to create advantage through access to external capital sources. Local business groups often deal with the weak financial system by creating their own financial institutions (see Chapter 5).

High Inflation. In the decade 1975–85, the average inflation rate in LDCs was more than double that of developed countries. Several countries hit triple figures: In Argentina, for example, for the first half of the 1980s inflation averaged 343% per year, reaching 684% in 1984. Inflation tended to hit hardest in countries experiencing rapid growth rates, such as the upper-middle-income and Latin American countries, and generally was relatively low in the poorest developing countries. During the 1980–86 period the upper-middle-income countries' average annual inflation rate was 46%, the lower-middle-income countries' 38%, and low-income economies' 18%.[14] In Bolivia, however, the poorest country in South America, inflation skyrocketed in the 1980s to a five-figure level (11,-749%) before the government abandoned the old currency and started over.[15] Developed countries experienced an average inflation rate of 7% during the same period.

Managerial Implications. To managers used to dealing with single-digit inflation, such hyperinflation can be crippling. The firm's financial and marketing functions are hit particularly hard; planning becomes difficult. Setting prices is complicated by the need to ensure coverage of the rising replacement costs of the goods sold. Credit management on both receivables and payables becomes critical. Interest costs soar. The risk of capital erosion is great. Historical accounting methods are rendered useless for current decision-making. Companies can, however, operate successfully under inflationary conditions if they take the proper steps. (Chapter 7 deals in detail with the task of inflation management.)

High Capital Flight. The last contributor to domestic capital scarcity is capital flight, which occurs when keeping money at home is riskier or yields lower returns than abroad. It contributed significantly to balance-of-payments pressures on several countries in the early 1980s, particularly in Latin America (see Table 3.6). Capital fleeing Venezuela, for example, was one-third greater than all the capital coming into the country, thereby causing a serious deterioration in the nation's capital position. Capital flight is typically associated with high and variable inflation, low real interest rates, disadvantageous tax rates, an overvalued exchange rate, and political and/or economic instability.

Table 3.6 Capital Flight and Inflows: 1979–82

	Capital Flight ($billions)	Capital Inflows ($billions)	Flight as % of Inflows
Venezuela	22.0	16.1	136.6%
Argentina	19.2	29.5	65.1%
Mexico	26.5	55.4	47.8%
Uruguay	0.6	2.2	27.3%
Portugal	1.8	8.6	20.9%
Brazil	3.5	43.9	8.0%
Turkey	0.4	7.9	5.1%
Korea	0.9	18.7	4.8%

SOURCE: *World Development Report 1985*, p. 64.

Managerial Implications. Capital flight intensifies the scarcity of capital and signals (and often precipitates) devaluation. This outflow of capital should be monitored also because it indicates other underlying problems and usually triggers government actions. The more pronounced the flight, often, the more restrictive government's foreign-exchange controls become. A tightening of credit in general may also occur. (Chapter 4 shows how a manager can trace through the effects on the firm of such government policies.)

Foreign Exchange

Foreign exchange is a critical form of capital in developing countries because its availability determines their external purchasing power. There are three aspects of foreign exchange that merit scrutiny: scarcity, variability, and valuation. Compared with industrial economies, developing countries are even poorer in foreign exchange than in domestic capital. In 1987 the average foreign-exchange reserves per capita in low-income countries was only $17. The average for middle-income countries was $128 per capita, while in industrial economies it was $1,148.[16] Similar comparisons hold for exports per capita, another indicator of foreign-exchange availability.

Scarcity. An underlying cause of the foreign-exchange shortage is that LDCs' import needs exceed their export earning capacity. As a result, they face chronic balance-of-trade deficits, which are particularly significant when seen as a percentage of Gross National Product (see Table 3.7). Most LDC trade balances were seriously affected by the

Table 3.7 Balance of Trade, 1987

Income Groupings	Exports/ Capita	Imports/ Capita	Balance/ Capita	Trade Balance as % of GNP
Low-income	$ 34	$ 41	−$ 7	−2.5%
Low-middle-income	$ 237	$ 240	−$ 3	−0.3%
Upper-middle-income	$ 522	$ 448	+$ 14	+1.6%
Oil exporters	$ 291	$ 266	+$ 25	+1.7%
High-income	$2,476	$2,583	−$107	−0.7%

SOURCE: *World Development Report 1989*, pp. 164–65, 190–91.

oil price increases of the 1970s. Recessions and trade protectionism in the industrialized countries further eroded LDC trade balances.

To offset trade deficits, developing countries have relied on capital inflows in the form of foreign loans, foreign direct investment, or official public assistance. As was noted in Chapter 1, foreign borrowing has dropped off, and servicing the huge outstanding debt has converted this traditional source into a net drain on foreign-exchange resources, thereby accentuating the scarcity.

Managerial Implications. In the face of foreign-exchange scarcity, management must economize this resource. Government restrictions on imports become tighter, as Cummins Engine found out in its Indian venture. Consequently, the firm may have to alter dramatically its procurement patterns toward domestic sources; significant shifts in production technology may also be necessary. Foreign-exchange controls by the government will add administrative burdens and, for multinational firms, restrict profit and capital repatriation. Those firms able to earn foreign exchange will be in a favorable bargaining position with the government.

Variability. LDC supplies of foreign exchange are not only scarce but also highly variable. This is due basically to the narrowness and nature of their exports. As was mentioned in the previous section on natural resources, LDC economies are often based on one or two primary agricultural or mineral exports. Dependency on a few commodity exports often leads to boom-and-bust cycles in the national economy, corresponding to rising and falling world prices for that commodity.[17] In Guinea, for example, 95% of export earnings comes from bauxite. When the prices of bauxite jumped 48% in 1974, foreign-exchange reserves increased correspondingly. Figure 3.1 shows the export price variability of non-oil primary commodities. Foreign capital flows (loans, direct investment, and official assistance) are less erratic sources of foreign exchange

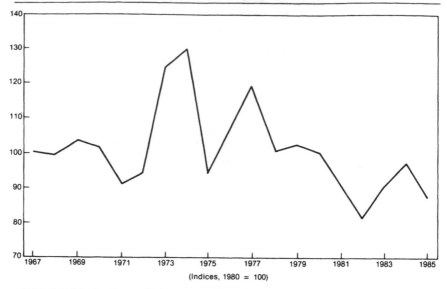

(Indices, 1980 = 100)

Index of market prices for non-oil primary commodities deflated by the export unit value index of the manufactures of industrial countries.

Figure 3.1 International Price Variability of Non-oil Primary Commodities
SOURCE: Based on *Staff Studies for the World Economic Outlook,* (Washington, D.C.: IMF, July 1986), p. 158.

but are by no means stable (as demonstrated in Chapter 1, Figure 1.3). Private flows are destabilized by political or economic disturbances, and official flows are subject to variation due to donor politics.

Managerial Implications. The main managerial significance of this variability is that uncertainty is increased and planning becomes more complex. Monitoring the prices of a country's major commodities will provide a basis for projecting foreign-exchange supply shifts and for planning the requisite operational adjustments (discussed further in Chapter 7).

Vaulation. The final aspect of foreign exchange is the rate at which the local currency exchanges for other currencies. Foreign-exchange rates in most developing countries are set by the government rather than fixed by the forces of supply and demand in a free market. The government can alter the exchange rates suddenly and significantly, for it controls the price and the allocation of the scarce foreign exchange. There is usually a parallel, unofficial "black market" for the currency, in which supply-and-demand forces yield a rate different from the official rate. Sometimes the government sets multiple rates that apply to different types of transactions. For example, essential imports might be favored with a lower exchange rate (say 4 pesos for 1 dollar), while foreign exchange to import luxury goods could be purchased only from the central bank at 15 pesos to the dollar.

Managerial Implications. The level of the exchange rate can dramatically affect companies' cost structure and competitiveness. The lower the rate, the cheaper are imports. A company would benefit from lowered costs of any inputs it imports; it would be hurt if it were competing against imports. Similarly, if it exports, lower rates would put it at more of a competitive disadvantage because its prices would be higher. For example, if the company prices its product at 4 pesos, the foreign buyer will have to pay a dollar, given the 4:1 exchange rate. If the exchange rate were 8:1, then the 4-peso sales price would equate to 50 cents. Thus, a devaluation of the currency from 4:1 to 8:1 would greatly increase the competitiveness of the export. Pricing and inventory management of imported inputs become more complicated. Exchange-rate changes can also have drastic financial effects due to currency exchange losses. For example, if a multinational subsidiary had profits of 100 million pesos, that would have been the equivalent of $25 million at the 4:1 exchange rate; the devaluation to 8:1 would cut dollar profits in half. Foreign-exchange exposure constitutes a major financial risk that requires careful management. (Chapter 7 deals in more detail with the management of the foreign-exchange risk.)

Infrastructure

Deficient Physical Infrastructure. A poor infrastructure may be the most visible distinguishing characteristic of developing countries. (We divide infrastructure into two types: physical and informational; the two are related in some areas, such as telecommunications.) Modern facilities are often lacking for transportation, postal, telecommunications, electrical, water waste disposal, and other utilities. Port capacity is often inadequate, services inefficient, and charges high. Air cargo service is often hampered by the low frequency of flights. Truck transport suffers from poorly maintained or unpaved roads, which increase maintenance costs and shorten the life of the equipment. Railroads are generally government-run and often inefficient and unreliable. Transportation networks in former colonies, for example, were often designed to facilitate the extraction and export of resources to the neglect of inland links domestically or with neighboring countries. Telecommunications facilities are typically hampered by a shortage of foreign exchange for capital investments, despite their demonstrated ability to make substantial profits. The staffing

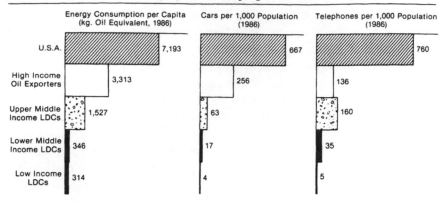

Figure 3.2 Energy, Transportation, and Telecommunication Infrastructure
Indicators by Level of Development

sources: *UN African Statistical Yearbook*, vols. 1–4 (New York: UN Economic Commission for Africa, 1985); *UN Statistical Yearbook for Asia and the Pacific 1986–87* (Bangkok: UN Economic and Social Commission for Asia and the Pacific, 1988); *Statistical Abstract of Latin America 1987* (Los Angeles: UCLA Latin American Center, 1987); *Statistical Abstract of the U.S.: Comparative International Statistics* (Washington, D.C.: U.S. Department of Commerce, Bureau of Census, 1988).

of postal operations is often based more on political patronage than on competency, thereby limiting their efficiency.[18]

Figure 3.2 reveals the dramatic differences in energy, transportation, and telecommunication infrastructure among countries at different levels of economic development. For example, whereas the United States consumes 7,193 kilograms of oil per capita and has 667 cars and 760 telephones per 1,000 people, the low-income LDCs consume 314 kilograms per capita and have four cars and five telephones per thousand. Whereas New Zealand averages 1 kilometer of paved road for every 5 square kilometers, Sudan has 1 kilometer per 5,500 square kilometers. Asia and Africa lag behind in infrastructure development, for example averaging around four telephones per 1,000 people in contrast to Latin America's forty phones or the Middle East's hundred. There is considerable variation within regions: Hong Kong and Singapore, for example, average more than 325 telephones per 1,000; Argentina produced 1,667 kilograms of energy per inhabitant and Haiti only 56.[19]

Managerial Implications. A company feels the lack of infrastructure most directly in its choice of production operations, but also in marketing, finance, and business–government relations. To the extent that the firm must take on the burden of providing or improving its own infrastructure (e.g., building access roads, maintaining generators), its investment requirements are increased. Problems in energy supply lead to production disruptions and higher maintenance and technology costs. Cummins Engine found the available energy supply insufficient for the needs of the equipment it had installed in its Indian factory. In addition, a poor transportation infrastructure limits access to markets and raw materials. Telecommunication limitations complicate purchasing, sales, and control functions and add to transaction costs. Zaire's telephone system, for example, is so deteriorated that businesses have resorted to the widespread use of walkie-talkies.[20]

For industries in the business of building infrastructure, such as construction engineering and equipment firms or telecommunications manufacturers, LDCs are growth markets. Construction expenditures in LDCs were projected to grow two to three times faster than in developed countries.[21] Frequently infrastructure projects are financed by foreign-aid loans; bilateral assistance often specifies that the developing country must give preference to the donor country's suppliers. For other industries, it may be possible to translate the necessity to build infrastructure into a bargaining chip with the government. (Chapter 6 discusses the task of managing the business–government relationship.) If a company is able to develop its own infrastructure adequately, it may use it as an entry barrier against competitors or to gain favor with the local government. For example, mining firms working in rural areas have used their private road networks to limit competitors' access and have lent their communications facilities to local government agencies.

Inadequate Information. A striking difference between developed countries and LDCs is the difficulty of obtaining reliable information in the latter. While difficult to quantify, information availability generally increases with magnitude of GDP. Poor countries lack adequate information-gathering and -disseminating infrastructure. Good information on domestic and foreign supply and demand, prices, availability of technology, financing, and government regulations is often unavailable. Such domestic information sources as trade journals, newspapers, and radio are restricted by lack of skilled research personnel, tiny markets, and inadequate budgets. In rural areas of even large, advanced developing countries like Brazil, accurate information is difficult to obtain.

Managerial Implications. Imperfect information leads to market inefficiencies and increased transaction costs. Decisions must often be made with a smaller and less reliable data base. Word-of-mouth information and personal communication networks become more important in companies' management information systems. To the extent that a manager can overcome the information vacuum, the problem can be converted into a competitive advantage. The costs of information collection may be greater, but the value of the data gained will be higher in an imperfect information market.

Technology

Three aspects of technology in developing countries stand out: technological level is low, technological development is concentrated, and technological sources are foreign. There are a multitude of causes for the low levels, including three factors previously discussed: capital scarcity, skill deficiencies, and infrastructure inadequacies. Domestic R&D capabilities tend to be quite limited, and so technologies are acquired mainly from abroad. Sometimes governments restrict technology transfer. For example, one East African country imposed high tariffs on the import of personal computers out of fear that they would displace labor.

To the extent that modern technology is employed, it tends to be concentrated in larger enterprises and certain segments of the economy. A dualistic structure emerges: modern, advanced sectors next to small-scale, low-technology, informal sectors. For example, large, highly technified agricultural plantations and subsistence farms using rudimentary tools, or capital-intensive, mass-production manufacturing plants and small, labor-intensive production shops.

Managerial Implications. A major task facing managers is achieving an appropriate fit between the technology and the LDC environment. Technology transfer often requires adaptation. Foreign technology generally has been developed for the industrialized nation's environment, which has a different factor endowment and different factor costs. For example, labor-saving technologies may not be so economically advantageous in a low-cost, surplus labor environment. The manager must thus adjust the technology to fit the environment or adjust the environment to fit the technology, or both. Appropriate sourcing and adaptation of technologies can be a major source of competitive advantage. (Chapter 8 addresses technology management issues.) The dualistic structure raises issues of how modern-sector firms will interact with informal-sector producers. (Chapter 5 describes the characteristics of the informal-sector producers and their economic roles.)

POLITICAL FACTORS

The second constellation of environmental factors focuses on four political variables: instability, ideology, institutions, and international links. Table 3.8 suggests how three of these political characteristics might vary in countries at different levels of economic development. It is important to note that political development and economic growth do not necessarily march forward in a synchronized manner. Variability among countries is large, so the indications in the table should be viewed only as suggestive.

Table 3.8 Summary of Political Factors

Factors	Development Level (GDP per capita)		
	Low	Middle	High
Instability	high	medium	low
Institutions	weak	--->	strong
International links	dependent	--->	more autonomy

Instability

The political history of many developing countries after World War II is marked by conflict and frequent military coups d'état. That has been particularly true of the newly independent nations. In sub-Saharan Africa forty-three new nations were born between 1956 and 1983, and many of these and the other newly independent African nations experienced great political turmoil: no fewer than fifty governments in twenty-eight African countries had been overthrown by 1983.[22] Even the older nations of Latin America have been fraught with instability, with Bolivia being the extreme: Since 1825 the average duration of a government has been two years, with 85% of the changes resulting from coups d'état, presidential assassinations or resignations, or new coalitions; nine times there were at least three different governments in the same year.[23]

Instability is typically accompanied by authoritarian governments that lack democratic responsibilities and pressures. There are many factors contributing to instability. One is social mobilization, which may lead to increased political participation. If the desire to participate is stifled, or if political institutions are not capable of channeling it within the system, it may boil over and cause political turmoil.[24]

It should be pointed out, however, that not all developing countries have been unstable. Some, such as Mexico and Costa Rica in Latin America or the Côte d'Ivoire (Ivory Coast) and Kenya in Africa, have been stable for decades. India has had reasonable stability since independence.

Managerial Implications. The managerial consequences of political instability are manifold; indeed, they are frequently cited as the main reason Western businesses are reluctant to enter Third World markets. Instability increases uncertainty, adds to indirect costs, causes planning problems, and leads to centralization of authority and bureaucratic bottlenecks. Radical changes in political systems can also cause domestic or foreign economic disruption. The result can be nationalization of industries, sudden restrictions on repatriation of capital, and threats to life and property. These threats can come from the right or the left in the political spectrum and from within the existing government or military or from external forces. Polarization of issues and actors is common, with resulting policy discontinuities, political stalemates, and scapegoating. Other problems include disruption to supply and distribution channels, increased security risks for personnel, and damage to infrastructure.

However, firms can and do cope with political instability, which is not necessarily equal to political risk in jeopardizing the viability of an enterprise. There are many different forms and dimensions of instability that pose different issues for different firms. One type of instability is change in regime, but to understand its implications one should further examine the ideological direction of the change, the degree of differences between the changing parties, the irregularity of the change, and the legality of the change. Regime instability does not necessarily lead to widespread changes in economic policies.[25] From a managerial perspective, political risk should be viewed as company-specific rather than country-specific. All companies in the same country are not equally exposed to or affected by political instability. The challenge is to understand the sources and kinds of the instability, how they affect the firm, and how they can best be handled (see Chapters 4 and 6).

Ideology

A government's ideological predilection toward the role of the state and the role of the private sector and property rights influences the type of political system chosen, e.g., socialism, capitalism, or a hybrid. In general, LDC governments tend to see the role of the state as being heavily involved in the economy. The perception is that such involvement will accelerate development. Perhaps even more important, economic involvement gives the government and the reigning political group more power and control over society. Some observers of political development assert that the most potent sentiment among all groups in a developing society is nationalism.[26] Newer developing countries may be more sensitive to this issue than older nations because of their colonial experience, recent independence, political and economic dependency, poverty, and instability. Nationalism and the type of political system developed can dramatically shape the dynamics of the political process and the business environment.

Ideology can be usefully viewed more broadly than just as a set of political beliefs. Lodge defines ideology as "a set of beliefs and assumptions about values that the nation holds to justify and make legitimate the actions and purpose of its institutions." He asserts further that "a nation is successful when its ideology is coherent and adaptable, enabling it to define and attain its goals, and when there is the least distance between the prevailing ideology and the actual practice of the country's institutions."[27] For example, strong ideological coherence is asserted to have contributed to Korea's and Taiwan's development success, while low coherence has held back Mexico.[28] A country's ideology is shaped by multiple forces, including social attitudes, which will be discussed in our subsequent analysis of cultural factors.

Managerial Implications. Ideologies may severely limit the scope or organization of a business and require distinct relationships with the government, because it is the prevailing set of beliefs and assumptions that ultimately constitutes managers' source of authority. Nationalistic sentiments may put foreign companies at a competitive disadvantage. Governments may place discriminatory regulations on foreigners; local businesses may have preferential access to government decision-makers, credit, and markets. Understanding a national ideology and how it is shifting will enable a manager to understand better the nature of institutional change and to manage relations with the government more effectively.

Institutions

Political institutions such as parties, bureaucracies, and other political organizations are often weak and unstable in LDCs. Institutional weakness contributes to political instability by failing to provide a continuous channel for political participation. Continuity of government policies is also hindered by frequent changes in ruling groups or individual government officials. In some instances these political groups strive to gain and consolidate their power through coercive means. Bureaucracies are often technically weak and inefficient. They frequently are overstaffed, under-qualified, and underpaid. Government institutions may also face conflicting political demands and may have inadequate authority to carry out their assigned responsibilities.

Other LDC political actors, or their roles, can be quite different from those in the more developed countries and can complicate the political scene. Universities and students are often very active in politics (typically from a socialist perspective, although more recently in Middle Eastern countries from an Islamic *sharia* perspective), even bringing down governments. The military is often highly political, either directly via military leaders in the government or indirectly as a final arbitrator of political power. Labor unions are also frequently politicized, with strikes organized more for political than for economic reasons. Peasant or agrarian organizations and cooperatives may be very active politically; they frequently provide the basis for rural uprisings. Aristocratic classes are a more dominant (or at least visible) force in LDCs, whether landowning classes in traditional societies or urban elites in more modernized ones. Businesses often organize themselves into industry associations, which serve as political vehicles. In LDCs major ethnic groups may divide a country's politics down ethnic lines, and religious issues or actors may dominate domestic politics. A final category of actors, discussed more fully later, is foreign entities. Because of the limited power of LDCs, their colonial history, and the political and economic interests of industrial countries, the latter may have a significant impact on the politics of some developing countries.

Managerial Implications. The managerial impact of weak institutions includes: inefficient, slow, and costly government services; extreme centralization and arbitrariness in governmental decision-making; pressures to bribe to elicit approvals or other actions from the bureaucracy; and increased disorder and uncertainty. High government turnover means discontinuities in government contacts, relations, and policies. In administrative terms these all result in higher transaction costs.

To manage its critical relationship with the government effectively, a business must understand who the key political actors are, what the basis and extent of their power is, and what their interests are. In addition, nongovernment political actors may adopt politically motivated, noneconomic, or "nonprofessional" agendas that must be understood. They may create disruptions, negatively affect workforce discipline, decrease managerial control over the business, and create higher costs. These hazards can be managed better with proper analysis and strategic response. The diversity of political actors provides more bargaining range for skillful negotiators, allowing a variety of coalitions to be formed and a wide range of issues to be put on the bargaining table. (Chapter 6 discusses in detail the management of the business–government relationship, including some of the managerially perplexing ethical issues related to corruption.)

International Links

The interdependence of the world's political and economic systems has been the focus of many volumes.[29] Here we focus on several political aspects of the international environment worthy of particular attention by business managers. The farthest-reaching aspect is superpower politics and strategic links in the international system. U.S.–Soviet relations still dominate the international political arena and can significantly affect the environments of specific developing countries caught in the tug-of-war.[30] Colonial ties, for example in French-speaking West Africa, also continue to have an impact in terms of economic flows, organizational ties, technical standards, and business practices.

Theories concerning dependency and imperialism assert that the current international system causes core industrial countries to create economic dependencies in peripheral developing countries.[31] Valid or not, perceived dependencies affect LDC attitudes toward foreign enterprises. A wide variety of economic links affect developing countries, including multilateral and bilateral capital flows and trade agreements. The form, substance, and continuity of these arrangements are significantly shaped by the nature of the international political links. Religious and cultural links (for example, the role of Islam in uniting the Middle East or drawing Africa to it) also can be a determining factor in the dynamics of international political relations.

Managerial Implications. Government policies and/or economic priorities are affected by political relations with foreign entities. These international links may open up opportunities (e.g., due to preferential trading arrangements) or they may create constraints (e.g., due to exclusive political alliances). For multinational enterprises, the relations between the home government and the host government become especially important. One study of technology exports from Egypt confirmed the importance of political and cultural ties in determining market destination and access; 80% of Egypt's technology exports went to Arab countries.[32] Political disputes between neighboring countries can lead to armed conflicts that inflict great havoc on the economy, so managers should closely examine the historical and prospective relations among adjacent countries.

CULTURAL FACTORS

The third category useful in examining the business environment is culture. Culture is the set of shared values, attitudes, and behaviors that characterize and guide a group of people. We shall examine the following cultural dimensions: social structure and dynamics, which concern the nature of relationships and interactions in a society; human nature, which deals with a people's perception of the basic goodness and changeability of humans; time and space orientation, which involves attitudes toward temporal behavior and physical relationships; religion, which is a source of values and institutional power; gender roles, which influence the division of tasks in society; and language, which embodies cultural traits in the communication process.

Table 3.9 summarizes how some of these cultural factors may vary between less and more economically developed countries, but culture, even less than political factors, does not evolve in a common way as countries move forward on the economic front. The correlation is tenuous at best, so the summary should be viewed as an oversimplification of very complex phenomena and diverse situations. It is offered in the spirit of speculation rather than definition. For managers the relationship between development levels and cultural attributes is not as important as scrutinizing each of the cultural variables to understand their managerial significance in their particular business setting. In approaching that task, managers should remember that even within countries there can be significant cultural diversity, and, furthermore, what holds as a cultural norm for a large group of people will not necessarily hold for a specific individual.

Table 3.9 Summary of Cultural Factors

	Development Level (GDP per capita)		
Factors	*Low*	*Middle*	*High*
Social structures	more rigid	--->	less rigid
Religious influence	stronger	--->	weaker
Gender roles	very distinct	--->	less distinct
Language	high diversity	--->	low diversity

Social Structure and Dynamics

Culture shapes the ways in which societies organize themselves and interact. Managers can usefully examine social structure and dynamics along three dimensions: attitude toward others, structure of relationships, and decision-making styles. Attitudes toward others can be viewed as ranging from individualism to collectivism, with the first placing high value on independence and self-reliance and the second emphasizing one's responsibility and obligations to one's social group, be that one's extended family, organization, ethnic group, or nation. The structure of relationships can be characterized as ranging from hierarchical to egalitarian, with the former using vertical structures with authority concentrated at the top while the latter has more horizontal structures and authority is more equally diffused. Decision-making styles can be viewed as ranging from autocratic to participative, with decisions being taken unilaterally or jointly on a consultative basis.

A study by Hofstede of 88,000 employees of one multinational firm in sixty-seven countries indicated that developing countries tend to be more receptive to hierarchical, authoritarian, and paternalistic relationships within groups, with loyalty to the group being of high concern. Collectivism rather than individualism is often the prevailing norm.[33] While it is true that industrialized countries also have demarcated class structures, they are usually less distinct and more permeable than in LDCs. Groups are structured along family, ethnic, racial, religious, tribal, geographic, and economic lines. Sometimes these social structures restrict the social and economic mobility of individuals or groups. Kinship networks are a pervasive and powerful component of LDC business environments. Family ties are often the central force in the creation and operation of ''business groups,'' which are a dominant form of business organization and major competitive force in developing countries (and are described more fully in Chapter 5). Kinship networks are also information conduits that cut across formal institutional lines, such as businesses and government organizations.

Managerial Implications. The cultural bases of a group's social structure and dynamics will significantly shape organizational design and decision-making processes. A company's human resource management strategy has to be tailored around these underlying values, behavioral norms, and social groupings. Cross-cultural communications between expatriates and nationals or between headquarters and subsidiaries also require sensitivity to cultural differences. (Organizational implications of cultural factors are analyzed in Chapter 10.) These values also shape society's view of the legitimacy of managerial authority and of business's social role, which is part of the country's ideology (discussed in the preceding section on political factors). Businesses' strategies for relating to government and other institutions will be affected by prevailing or changing ideologies.

Social structures also affect industry structure and a firm's marketing activities. Sharply demarcated social structures make markets narrower. They may lead to control over marketing and distribution channels by one ethnic or other social group, which can limit access (see Chapter 9). If the division becomes serious enough to be part of the political agenda, the government may impose regulations. For example, the government of Malaysia responded to domestic political pressures by imposing quotas limiting the hiring of ethnic Chinese minorities, who tend to exercise great influence in Southeast Asian economies.

A company can make opportunities from these divisions by creating market niches or product differentiation. The same social networks that limit access can also ease access to markets if properly approached and cultivated. Cultural norms regarding the nature and forms of interaction will shape the strategies and tactics for building alliances. Kinship relations affect the structure of business and the way firms operate. These networks, often structured as powerful business groups, can create competitive advantage through member loyalty and superior access to information. They may cause competitive disadvantage where decisions are made based on social rather than economic rationale.

Human Nature

Societies have varying perceptions of the basic nature of humans. Two aspects of these perceptions are particularly relevant for managers: the degree of inherent goodness of human beings and the changeability of their nature.[34] Societies can view humans as being mainly good or evil or neutral or mixed. These perceptions are often rooted in religious values. As for changeability, those societies believing that human nature is largely unchangeable tend to be more fatalistic and rigid. Those on the other end tend to see people as holding power over their environment and able to change it, others, and themselves.

Managerial Implications. Beliefs about the degree of goodness in humans will influence management control systems. A belief that humans are basically good and trustworthy will lead to looser controls; a view that they cannot be trusted will call forth tighter controls and supervision. Where trust is low, delegation of authority tends to be low and decision-making more autocratic; relations tend to be more adversarial and less collegial. If human nature is believed to be changeable, a firm is more likely to stress training and personnel development. Employee mistakes are more likely to be seen as learning opportunities than as reason for punishment.

Time and Space

Different cultures can have very distinct orientations toward time and space. For example, the U.S. culture is very time-conscious, whereas many LDC cultures consider time to be an abundant resource and are much less concerned about such time-related behavior as punctuality. Time perspectives can be past-, present-, or future-oriented. Attitudes toward traditions and change can vary significantly. Space can also be seen quite differently as being private or public. Cultural norms for physical proximity vary greatly.

Managerial Implications. Attitudes toward time affect scheduling activities and planning orientations (see Chapter 10). Attitudes toward space can influence office layouts and one's behavior in personal interactions. Standing close to a business associate might be deemed socially appropriate in one culture and offensive in another.

Religion

Religion exerts a significant influence in developing countries, whether it is Catholicism in Latin America, Islam in the Middle East and Africa, Islam, Buddhism, and Hinduism in Asia, or others less dominant. Religious beliefs shape individual attitudes and actions and, therefore, influence some of the values regarding human nature and social structures and dynamics. Religious institutions can also be important political actors. In some developing countries the *de facto* separation of church and state is blurred, and some (for example, the Islamic nations of Saudi Arabia and Iran) have even established religious states.

Managerial Implications. Religious norms can affect work patterns (e.g., religious holidays, Islam's month of daytime fasting, Ramadan), product preferences (e.g., cigarettes named after Hindu gods in India, no liquor in Saudi Arabia, prohibition of interest charges in Islamic banks), or interreligious tension and conflict among employees. Religion-based consumer preferences create demand for specific types of products or services, for example, specially prepared foods or travel services for pilgrims to Mecca.

Religions and other societal institutions shape morality, and moral standards vary across cultures. A foreign manager may bring to a developing country ethical precepts that conflict with local customs. (Chapter 6 examines some of the ethical issues related to "corruption.")

Gender Roles

Only recently have LDC planners begun to recognize that failure to understand women's actual and potential economic contributions entails a high socioeconomic cost to society. Women are on the whole less educated than men (Table 3.10). In urban areas they are also less active economically, but in rural areas women often provide most of the agricultural labor. Women also have more limited access to productive resources. Law and custom may prevent them from owning land and pledgeable assets, getting formal credit, or having the freedom from household tasks to pursue other productive activities. Physical mobility may be limited, as in Saudi Arabia, where women are prohibited from driving. Gender division of labor tends to be more clearly demarcated socially in the developing countries.

Managerial Implications. These constraints on women affect a firm's human resource management. It is important to identify the patterns of gender-based division of labor in a country and the nature of the environmental forces creating such patterns.[35] If women's activities are severely restricted, as in some Middle Eastern countries, the firm suffers a loss of a potential labor force. Managers may have to make special arrangements to deal with the various needs and constraints faced by female employees. Given the general pattern that places women in charge of child care and other household tasks, companies may have to provide such services as day care to enable women to work. Mobility restrictions due to social norms may require special transportation services and gender-segregated workplaces.

The roles of women are changing in many countries, with females entering the modern workplace in increasing numbers. During 1970–80 female participation in the industrial labor force in developing countries grew 56%, and in 1980 women constituted about 28% of the employment in multinationals in the Third World.[36] Most of the workers in multinational semiconductor and electronics subsidiaries in developing countries are women. Because traditional gender roles in many LDCs have excluded women from managerial positions, there is often a large untapped pool of management talent. Tapping that can bring great value to a firm, although the potential disruption of traditional roles, relationships, and

Table 3.10 Educational Status of Women*

Country	Adult Literacy: Females as % of Males 1985	Enrollment Ratio: Females as % of Males 1983–86	
		Primary school	Secondary school
Yemen AR	11.1	19.6	17.6
Afganistan	20.5	50.0	45.5
Oman	25.5 (1982)	92.5	48.8
Chad	27.5	38.2	18.2
Burkina Faso	28.6	57.1	42.9
Nepal	30.8	56.9	37.3
Somalia	33.3	56.3	52.2
Saudi Arabia	34.3 (1982)	73.0	64.7
Guinea-Bissau	37.0	49.3	44.4
Mozambique	40.0	84.9	44.4
Yemen DR	42.4	36.5	42.3
Sudan	42.4 (1986)	86.0	68.4
Guinea	42.5	45.5	33.3
Benin	43.2	50.0	41.4
Niger	47.4	54.1	33.3
Pakistan	47.5	50.0	38.1
Mali	47.8	58.6	40.0
Liberia	48.9	61.0	39.4 (1980)
Morocco	48.9	65.8	65.8
Egypt	50.8	80.9	71.2
India	50.9	71.0	53.3
Bangladesh	51.2	71.4	38.5
Senegal	51.4	69.2	50.0
Togo	52.8	61.9	30.3
Rwanda	54.1	96.8	66.7
C.African Rep.	54.7	53.2 (1982)	33.3 (1982)
Sierra Leone	55.3	70.6 (1982)	47.8 (1982)
Zaire	57.0	75.6	40.7
Côte d'Ivoire	58.5	70.7	44.4
Malawi	59.6	87.2	33.3

* Countries listed in order of increasing ratio of female to male literacy among adults, up to 60%. While there is great country variation, women's and men's educational status tends to improve with higher per capita national income.

SOURCE: UNICEF, *The State of the World's Children 1988* (New York: Oxford University Press, 1989), pp. 76–77.

remuneration practices may cause tension and require special attention. Effective personnel management requires sensitivity to the gender-specific needs of this workforce.

Language

Language is a cultural medium; all communication is culturally rooted. Developing countries tend to have greater internal cultural diversity and, consequently, greater linguistic diversity. Almost 60% of the developing countries are linguistically heterogeneous; only 26% of the developed countries are.[37] India, for example, has fourteen major languages and 3,000 different dialects.[38] In Africa there are 750 tribal languages, of which fifty are spoken by more than a million people.[39] Communication is broader than just the spoken word; the silent aspects of language, such as the style of expression (e.g., openness vs. closedness, aggressive vs. passive), the use of context (formality, special settings, or protocol), and nonverbal signaling (body language) are all culturally shaped.

Managerial Implications. Linguistic diversity carries implications for marketing promotion and advertising strategies (see Chapter 9) as well as organizational communications among employees with different languages, between headquarters and subsidiaries, and between partners in joint ventures. Cross-cultural communications, if neglected, can cause serious misunderstandings and business problems (see Chapter 10).

DEMOGRAPHIC FACTORS

The most fundamental structural difference between the more and less developed countries is the demographic context; their population profiles and dynamics stand in stark contrast. Thus, the final environmental category is demographic factors, which include population growth rates, age structure, urbanization, migration, and health status. Table 3.11 summarizes how these demographic factors vary in countries across the development spectrum.[40]

Population Growth Rates

The populations of developing countries are growing at much higher rates than those of the industrialized nations.[41] Whereas the populations in Europe and North America never grew faster than 1.5% annually, the growth rates in the developing countries rose to about 2.5%. This fact makes the demographic experience and structure of the two groups

Table 3.11 Summary of Demographic Factors

Factors	Development Level (GDP per capita)		
	Low	Middle	High
Annual pop. growth rates (1980–87)	2.8%	2.2%	0.6%
Age structure	young	--->	older
Urbanization (% of total 1987 pop.)	30%	31%	77%
Migration	low	high	high
Life expectancy (1987)	54	65	76

SOURCE: *World Development Report 1989*, pp. 164–65, 214–15, 224–25.

of countries fundamentally different. Because of the compounding phenomena (i.e., a higher rate applied each year to an ever increasing population base), small differences in annual growth rates lead to large absolute increases in population. For example, a 1% difference in annual rates over a hundred-year period would cause the population to increase 2.7 times.

In the decade of the 1960s, the average birth rate in the developing countries remained high (at around 39 per 1,000) while health improvements caused the death rate to drop (from 25 to 13 per 1,000), thereby causing a significant increase in the population growth rate. The corresponding average birth and death rates for the developed countries were 20 births per 1,000 in 1960 dropping to 17 in 1970, with 9 deaths per 1,000 throughout. Thus, for the 1960–70 decade, developing country populations were growing 2.4% annually while the industrialized nations were expanding at only 1.1%. Even though the rates in both developed and developing countries were declining by the 1970s, the differences in these rates and the larger absolute population base of the Third World meant that the increase in the world's population was (and continues to be) largely concentrated in the LDCs, as depicted in Figure 3.3. In 1990 59% of the population resided in Asia, but Africa's population is growing most rapidly (3.2%).[42]

Managerial Implications. Population growth expands markets, so from a demographic perspective the LDCs are key growth markets for many products. However, effective demand does not necessarily increase concurrently with population growth. Per capita incomes rise less rapidly than overall economic growth due to the population increase. Consequently, basic consumption goods tend to have stronger growth than luxury goods. Growing populations may cut into future economic growth by channeling scarce resources into consumption rather than productive

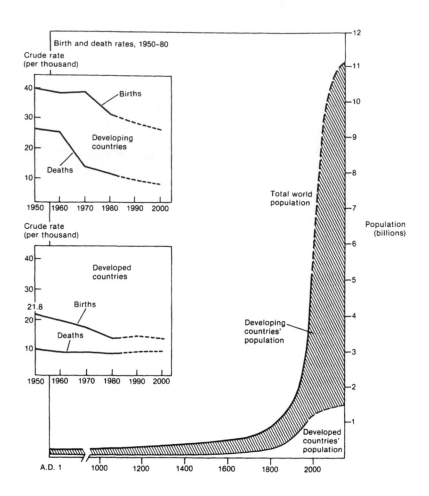

Figure 3.3 World Population Pattern
SOURCE: Adapted from *Population Change and Economic Development* (New York: Oxford University Press for World Bank, 1985), p. 3.

investment. Rapidly growing populations may also heighten labor unrest and affect the domestic political stability of a country as well as its relations with foreign countries through migration.

Age Structure

Because of declines in infant mortality and continued high fertility rates, the age structure of developing countries is dominated by the young. In developing countries in 1990, 36% of the population was

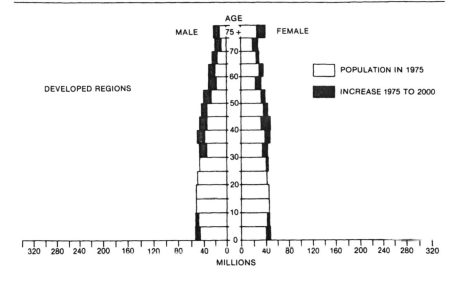

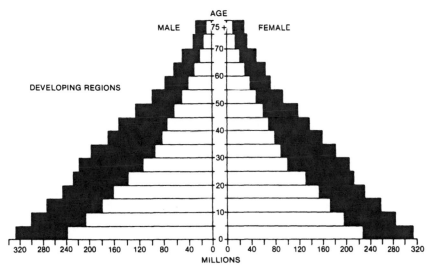

Figure 3.4 Age Structures for Developed and Developing Countries
SOURCE: Based on James E. Harf and B. Thomas Trout, *The Politics of Global Resources: Energy, Environment, Population, and Food* (Durham, N.C.: Duke University Press, 1986), p. 101.

under fifteen years of age with this share rising to 40% for the lower-middle-income countries, as against only 21% in industrialized countries.[43] This age structure is both the result of the growth rates discussed above and the source of continued momentum for that growth. Figure 3.4 shows the contrasting age structures, with the developed countries' older population structure creating a largely rectangular distribution profile, while the LDCs' distribution is pyramidal because of the preponderance of the younger ages. The broad base of the pyramid means that larger numbers of females will be entering the reproductive stage, so that even if the average number of children born per mother were reduced, the total numbers of newborns would still increase significantly. Thus, even though developing countries will eventually also go through an age-structure transition, their youth-dominated profile will remain for several decades.

Managerial Implications. Within the firm, production and marketing are affected most directly. Much of the surplus labor that exists consists of inexperienced and immature workers. One drawback of a young age structure is that a high percentage of the population is not of working age: In 1990, only 59% of the population in developing countries was of working age, versus over 67% in industrial market economies. The result is that income earners have to support larger numbers of non-wage-earners in their households, thereby lowering per capita income and consumer expenditures.

On the positive side, a young work force may be highly trainable and flexible. With fewer preconceptions about work habits and roles, young workers may identify more easily with the workplace. A young age structure allows for product development and market niches for particular products (such as baby products, educational materials, athletic equipment, certain fashions, cosmetics, and other consumer goods). As the Western world's age pyramid gets older, companies whose product demand is demographically driven have turned to the rapidly growing younger markets in the Third World. (Chapter 9 discusses in more detail the marketing implications of LDC demographics as well as demographic analysis techniques.)

Urbanization

Perhaps the most visible structural change occurring in the LDCs is the growth of the urban centers. Urban populations in developing countries are growing at twice the rate of their rural populations. This is due to natural increases as well as migration from the countryside. Excluding China (which remains overwhelmingly rural), 24% of the developing country populations were urban in 1987. Regional patterns are distinct: Latin America is the most urbanized region, with 70% of its population in cities; Asia and Africa are still generally very rural, with only 25%

urban dwellers in South Asia, 37% in East Asia, and 27% in sub-Saharan Africa.[44]

Most LDC governments do not have the financial, institutional, or human resources to provide adequate public services for this rapid urbanization. The common result is unplanned growth, sprawling slums, traffic congestion, poor sanitation, power and water shortages, and other urban ills.

Managerial Implications. Large metropolitan areas are concentrated consumer markets, easily accessible to marketing and distribution efforts. In developing countries characterized by cultural and language diversity, urban areas tend to be melting pots, homogenizing consumer demands, thereby facilitating advertising. The rapid expansion of the metropolis, however, complicates distribution and transportation logistics. Government concessions may be available to firms willing to locate outside of major urban areas. Rural populations remain large in most LDCs and constitute important markets.

Migration

Although the number of migrants is usually less than 2% of a country's total population, they may be a large share of LDCs' available skilled workers and a noticeable proportion of the workforce in the recipient country. In the mid-1970s 8% of the workforce in Belgium, France, and Germany were temporary migrants; the total number of temporary workers abroad in 1980 was 13 million to 15 million.[45] In 1980 85% of the United Arab Emirates workforce and 70% of Kuwait's consisted of temporary immigrants, while for the Middle East as a whole the 1975 figure was 40%.[46] Workers abroad constitute a loss of skills for the country but also a source of foreign-exchange earnings through their remittances.

Internal rural-urban migration does not necessarily lead to political instability. Recent urban immigrants tend to be conservative and not overly amenable to political action. Political scientists have cited four reasons for this tendency. (1) By "voluntarily" moving to the city, rural migrants have presumably improved their utility. (2) The village orientation of recent migrants may make dissident political organization and cooperation difficult. People with rural habits and values tend to support political passivity and exhibit an unwillingness to challenge traditional authority. (3) The immediate concern of the urban poor is food, housing, and jobs. In the short run at least, these are best obtained through the system, not against it. (4) Urbanization increases the power of governments in urban centers, thereby increasing the means to repress dissident political activity. Thus, urbanization may contribute to political stability, at least in the short run.[47] In the longer run, however, urban dwellers tend to become more politically active.

Managerial Implications. Internal rural-to-urban migration leads to a constant inflow of consumers whose tastes and purchasing patterns will change as they adjust to urban life. As employees the migrants might require special orientation to a different type of work environment. They may also need assistance from the firm in housing and other social services. On the political side, although migrants are not necessarily a destabilizing force, the broadening of the urban population does facilitate political organizing.

One managerial problem created by external migration is "brain drain," the emigration of managers and skilled workers. In fact, sometimes workers migrate after they have been trained by the company. Training increases mobility. Lack of opportunities for advancement in large foreign or family-run firms may also prompt professional managers to leave those firms and even the country. Changes in immigration policies or demand in the key labor-absorbing countries should be monitored, because shifts could cause a sudden increase or decrease in the domestic labor supply.

Health Status

Developing countries are plagued by short life expectancy and high sickness rates, despite impressive gains in the last few decades. Poor sanitation and nutrition, insufficient health education, and inadequate medical facilities are the main causes. Among the twenty-two low-income African countries the average life expectancy at birth is only forty-eight years. For middle-income countries the figure is sixty-three, and in industrial market economies it exceeds seventy-six.[48] In forty-four LDCs less than 50% of the population have access to potable drinking water, and in twenty-two countries less than 50% have access to health services.[49] Infant mortality rates in seventy-one LDCs exceeded 60 deaths per 1,000 births as against 10 or less in developed nations.

Managerial Implications. High morbidity rates undercut the firm from within. They lead to lower worker productivity as a result of sick leave and poor on-the-job performance. Short life expectancy, in crude economic terms, means inefficient use of human capital, high staff turnover, and increased training costs. Health needs also represent markets for medical and pharmaceutical goods and services. It may be possible for a firm to build employee loyalty through health benefits. Finally, to the extent company health programs are effective, labor productivity can be boosted, aiding the company's competitive advantage.

CONCLUSION

In this chapter we have seen that developing countries as a group present a distinctive business environment. This environment requires analyses and managerial responses different from those of developed country environments in order to deal with problems and take advantage of opportunities.

This first component in our Environmental Analysis Framework helps the manager understand the distinctiveness and untangle the complexity of the LDC business environment by dissecting it into economic, political, cultural, and demographic factors. The economic factors concern basic productive resources and include natural resources (importance and availability), labor (skilled and unskilled), capital (domestic and foreign exchange), infrastructure (physical and informational), and technology (levels and structure). The political factors examined are instability, ideology, institutions, and international links. The cultural factors examine the sets of shared values, attitudes, and behavior by analyzing social structure and dynamics (relationships and interactions), perceptions of human nature (goodness and changeability), attitudes toward time and space, religion as a source of values and as a sociopolitical institution, and language as a culturally imbedded communication process. The demographic factors are population growth, age structure, urbanization, migration, and health status.

By using these categories, managers are able to identify and analyze more systematically the environmental phenomena. Separating the phenomena into individual factors facilitates analysis and sharpens the scanning. However, managers must also recognize and examine interrelationships among the factors. Those factors are also often in a state of flux, so they need to be monitored periodically. Environmental analysis must be dynamic rather than static. The EAF categories provide a common set of variables through which to assess changes in the business environment. The task is to trace through the effects of the environmental factors on each of the four levels of the business environment (international, national, industry, and firm) in order to understand their managerial relevance. This chapter has given examples of managerial implications. To analyze the national business environment more thoroughly, we now turn to the second component of the EAF, which is government strategies.

4

Interpreting National Strategies

Every LDC government has a national development strategy. The clarity and explicitness of these strategies will vary among countries, with some being clearly set forth in national development plans and others being simply the *de facto* results of government actions. In either case, unwritten strategic agendas of competing political forces may also be present. Although each country's strategy will have characteristics peculiar to its specific circumstances, there are general types of strategies that developing countries employ. Governments shape the business environment through national strategies. It is essential, therefore, that managers be able to interpret and predict national strategies so as to ascertain their implications for company strategies and operations. The process of doing this constitutes the second component of our Environmental Analysis Framework.

The managerial questions being addressed are: What is the strategy that the government is following and why? Is that strategy likely to change and how? How is the strategy being implemented, and how is it likely to affect my industry and firm? To answer these questions the manager can analyze the environment at the national level by (1) studying how the environmental factors condition the government's strategy; (2) defining the strategy's goals and orientation; (3) examining the strategy's (a) public policies, which in effect constitute the substantive content of the strategy, and the (b) policy instruments and institutions, which are the mechanisms and agents chosen to implement the policies; and then (4) assessing their impact on the industry and the company.

Figure 4.1 illustrates how these elements are linked together in what we term the "Public-Policy Impact Chain." The economic, political,

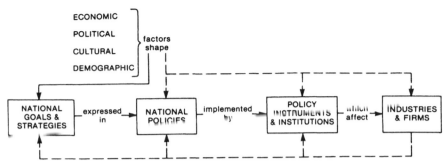

Figure 4.1 Public-Policy Impact Chain

cultural, and demographic environmental factors shape the government's strategy and influence the other elements in the chain. The national strategy contains goals and sets forth the country's major development focus. We shall describe common categories for identifying goals and strategies. National strategies are expressed in terms of a set of public policies, and we specify the types of policies commonly used by LDC governments. Policies are implemented by a variety of instruments and institutions, and we examine their characteristics. At the end of the chain comes the impact on the industry and the firm. We shall show how managers can trace the effects of different policies on the industry and on the firm's functional areas. It should also be noted that the elements in the chain are interactive and there are feedback effects. For example, the firms or industry groups will interact with both policy implementers and policy-makers, and that interaction can influence both the form and the substance of national strategies, policies, and implementation mechanisms.

In developing countries understanding government policies is often complicated by the rapidity with which policies change. There is a higher uncertainty quotient. This makes even more important the ability to monitor and interpret public policies in a systematic and efficient manner. This component of the EAF aims to strengthen that analytical capacity.

ENVIRONMENTAL FACTORS
AND NATIONAL STRATEGIES

Understanding what the government is seeking and why is a prerequisite to interpreting and predicting the dynamics of the public-policy process and to achieving effective business-government relations. Like business strategies, national strategies are shaped by the environmental forces surrounding them: Economic, political, cultural, and demographic factors influence public policy-makers' strategic decisions. These national and international environmental factors create constraints and opportunities from which policy-makers must weave the national strategy. Thus, the manager needs to identify and understand the links between environmental factors and the government's strategic choices.

The preceding chapter described each of the environmental factors and illustrated how they shape the business environment at the international, national, industry, and company levels. In this section we shall focus on the national level and provide some brief additional illustrations, using country examples of how these factors specifically affect government strategies. In later sections we analyze the other elements in the Public-Policy Impact Chain: the nature of national strategies, their implementation, and their impact on industries and firms.

Economic Factors

Mineral deposits or land endowments have often been key determinants of national strategies. For example, the development strategies of Venezuela and Saudia Arabia without oil or Chile or Zaire without copper would be very different. Similarly, a country blessed with a large land area, such as Argentina, faces very different agricultural strategy options from a land-constrained country like El Salvador. The agricultural development options for India with its fertile Punjab region are far different from those for the drought-ridden, desert-encroached countries of sub-Saharan Africa.

Land resources interplay with human resources in shaping national strategies. A large country like China with a population over 1 billion has an agricultural structure and dynamic different from that of Brazil, with a similar land base but a population of only 138 million. Analogously, the development needs and strategies of populous oil-producing nations such as Nigeria or Iran are much different from those of their less populous counterparts in the Middle East.

Large supplies of labor can create a comparative advantage in more labor-intensive industries, but this relative competitive advantage can shift as the country develops and wage rates rise. For example, South Korea's and Singapore's initial advantage due to lower wages later eroded, which led to their being increasingly displaced from more labor-intensive products by such LDCs as Thailand and Malaysia. In response to their own rising labor costs and resultant shifts in comparative advantage,

Korea and Singapore adjusted their strategies toward higher technology and knowledge-intensive industries. They were able to do this because of their long-standing efforts to increase the educational and skill levels of their populace.

Countries have chosen distinct paths for mobilizing the capital resources needed for their development. For example, Brazil made heavy use of foreign borrowing and foreign direct investment (FDI). However, India and China, despite their great need for capital, for political reasons related to their national goal of independence, traditionally used relatively little external private financing (although this strategy began to shift in the 1980s).

Obtaining technology has become a strategic issue in national planning and can, for example, lead to the formulation of a strongly pro-FDI policy. As technological levels of countries rise, governments' concerns tend to move beyond access to control. The appropriateness and cost of new technology are scrutinized. Mexico, for example, set forth specific legislation and screening mechanisms for foreign technology. Another goal that can emerge is reducing national dependence on foreign technology by developing internal capacity for technological development. This has been one of the reasons for the Brazilian government's efforts to restrict the access of foreign computer companies to the Brazilian market. At the heart of Korea's national strategy for the 1990s is the goal of gaining technological equivalency with the West by the turn of the century.

Political Factors

Political ideology can decisively shape national strategies. For example, Tanzania's socialist and communitarian ideology lead to a national strategy relying heavily on state-owned enterprises and market control, which was quite distinct from that of neighboring Kenya, where a more market-oriented ideology prevailed. The degree of consensus surrounding an ideology will influence political stability and thus the longevity of a national strategy. In Mexico, for example, the PRI party has won every presidential election in this century, but its near loss in the 1988 elections may have been due in part to its old ideology's no longer fitting new economic and social realities. Consequently, adjustments in national strategy are likely to emerge. The strength of political institutions both to control and to meet the needs of society affect the behavior of governments. For example, in both the Côte d'Ivoire (Ivory Coast) and Kenya there are single ruling parties; the Côte d'Ivoire has had the same president and Kenya has had only two presidents since their independence in the early 1960s. The single-party systems may have reduced some of the divisiveness flowing from tribalism. The breadth and control of the governments' institutional networks give them a multitude of response options ranging from co-optation to suppression. In contrast, young regimes coming to power through military coups are more fragile and tend to use control mechanisms that are more openly coercive. Their national strategies are dominated by the goal of political survival.

By assessing the political context and decision-making processes, the manager is better able to predict the likelihood and direction of shifts in public policy. However, political dynamics are also driven by specific, often unpredictable, international or national events. When these occur, one must assess their ramifications for the government's policy course. For example, the Falkland Islands War between Argentina and England triggered major political changes resulting in the ouster of Argentina's military regime and a return to a democratic government. The assassination of the opposition leaders Benigno Aquino in the Philippines and Pedro Joaquin Chamorro in Nicaragua ignited processes of political mobilization that created new coalitions that ultimately caused the overthrow of the Marcos and Somoza regimes and led to the ascension to power of new regimes, which made major shifts in national strategy. Although the specifics of these events are not foreseeable, the possibility and implications of these kinds of disruption are often discernible by careful monitoring and assessment of national and international political factors.

Cultural Factors

Cultural factors can shape national strategies in many ways. For example, religious values and institutions in Islamic nations explicitly determine government actions and legal structures. Cultural and ethnic differences can also be sources of external and internal conflicts, which can have a major impact on national strategies, as shown by the Iran–Iraq war, the Arab–Israeli conflict, and the violence between Hindus and Sikhs in India or the Tamils and Sinhalese in Sri Lanka. Cultural ideology can determine the form of governments. For instance, the South Korean government's strong role, hierarchical orientation, and bureaucratic authoritarianism have their roots in Confucian and communitarian values adapted under the colonial influences of China and Japan.[1] Emerging individualism in Korea, which had its seeds in Christianity that flourished after liberation, has increasingly affected Korea's political structures, processes, and programs.

Demographic Factors

Rapidly growing populations increase pressures on existing resources of all kinds, including public services. National consumption needs increase, thereby reducing resources available for investment. A country like Kenya, with an annual population growth rate of 4.0%, is faced with quite different pressures from those facing Sierra Leone, with a 2.6% rate, or Cuba, with a 0.9% rate.[2]

High population growth increases the labor supply. A country long on people confronts its government with tremendous pressures for employment generation and, therefore, a possible preference for labor-intensive technologies. A huge labor pool may also create relatively lower wage rates, thereby encouraging governments in such countries as Sri Lanka, Haiti, China, and Malaysia to adopt strategies to attract FDI in labor-intensive industries. However, employment opportunities do not automatically materialize, and the resultant large pools of unemployed can become politically destabilizing. Employment generation thus becomes a high priority in government strategies. Urbanization can intensify political pressures, because urban populations are more highly politicized and their demands carry greater force. More than one LDC government has fallen or has had to retreat when it tried to reduce food or transportation subsidies to urban populations.

HISTORICAL PERSPECTIVE

It is clear that environmental factors influence country strategies, but it is also important to realize that the results of past strategies create the context for future ones. History helps shape the future. For example, when Miguel de la Madrid became president of Mexico in late 1982, his administration faced huge budget and balance-of-payments deficits, rampant inflation, stagnating production, and an extremely large foreign-debt-servicing burden. These conditions were mostly the result of previous administrations' policies and falling prices for Mexico's oil exports, and they greatly reduced the amount of freedom the new government had in formulating its strategy. The resultant strategy, not surprisingly, was one of severe fiscal austerity, credit tightening, import restrictions, currency devaluation, export promotion, and IMF assistance. That strategy was also influenced by other economic, political, demographic, and cultural factors prevailing for many years in Mexico.

Where a country has been significantly influences where it will go. The manager needs to examine the evolution of environmental factors in the past, not just take a snapshot of their current state. Interpreting national strategies requires a historical perspective. The previous chapter specified variables and indicators for examining each environmental factor. One can also use these and other measures to assess the performance of a government's strategy, because that performance shapes subsequent strategy, as the Mexican example reveals. Examples of economic, social, and political performance indicators are shown in Table 4.1.

Table 4.1 National Strategy Performance Indicators

Economic Performance

Economic growth: compound growth rate in real GNP, growth rates of specific sectors

Price stability: annual inflation rates

Savings & investment: national savings and investment as a percentage of GNP

Balance of payments: trade balance, current account balance, changes in reserves

Employment: unemployment levels

Social Performance

Consumption: compound growth rate in real GNP per capita, national consumption as a percentage of GNP, protein and calorie intake per capita

Health: infant and child mortality rates, life expectancy, specific disease incidence rates

Education: literacy level, school completion levels and rates

Housing: average inhabitants per house

Income distribution: Gini coefficients

Political Performance

Stability: number and nature of regime or ministerial changes

Popular Support: incidence of civil or opposition disturbances

Openness: restrictions on basic freedoms

DEFINING NATIONAL STRATEGIES

National strategies emerge from the interplay of the above economic, political, demographic, and cultural factors. Understanding and monitoring those factors can help the manager ascertain the rationale behind, and possible changes in, national strategy. To understand a national strategy, one needs to identify its goals and focus.

The Nature of National Goals

The goals of development strategies can often be found in the govern ment's planning documents and the president's and ministers' speeches. Multiyear development plans are commonly used in developing countries, although the rigor and formality of planning processes vary. For example, formal central planning is basic to India's strategy formulation; its five-year plans set forth explicit goals and economic targets. Korea's economic growth since the early 1960s has also been guided by a series of five-year economic plans. In other countries, goals are often less clear and may even be internally inconsistent, possibly reflecting compromises negotiated by competing political forces. Some development plans are simply exercises, funded by external donors, and with little connection to the real political decison-making processes. Because goals and their relative priorities change in response to shifting environmental factors, they need to be monitored. The manager should also be alert to the existence of unwritten goals. These may involve particular objectives of the governing political forces and should be identified through political analysis.

Although each country will formulate goals to fit its specific circumstances, they tend to fall into the following categories:

- Growth: Increasing economic growth implies greater investment and requires a longer time horizon.
- Consumption: Raising the standard of living implies increased consumption, which in the short run may conflict with the growth objective, since resources invested are not available for consumption.
- Equity: Improving economic equity may mean increasing access to economic opportunities or the direct receipt of economic resources via income-redistribution measures.
- Employment: Generating jobs is a way to achieve other goals but is such a pressing need in so many countries that it becomes a main goal. Some ideologies consider having gainful employment a social goal and basic right rather than an economic means.
- Sovereignty: Preserving national sovereignty encompasses national security goals and resource control.

- Political survival: This is usually the operative goal of each ruling political group and will often dominate other goals in the short run.

In addition to these general goals, a strategy will have sector-specific goals, such as in agriculture, industry, mining, education, housing, or health. These are especially important for companies operating in those sectors. The manager should not only identify these goals but also try to assess their relative importance to the government. This might be indicated by the share of the government's national budget allocated for each one. A goal's permanency is another indicator of importance: The longer a goal has been present in national strategies, the more difficult it is to remove it, for it becomes part of the national ideology. For example, in 1951 Costa Rica abolished its army and chose to stress education over defense, with the theme "more teachers than soldiers." Today it has the most literate population in Central America and no standing army. Even faced with armed conflict in neighboring countries in the late 1980s and intense international pressure to mount a military force, Costa Rican governments have not abandoned the national goal of no army. This has continued to make scarce resources available for more economically and socially productive uses.

Development Strategy Categories

Although different governments may share the same general goals, they often choose different strategies to attain them. Every country's strategy is unique in its particulars because it responds to a distinct environment. Nonetheless, among developing countries, common categories of development strategies have emerged. In general, the strategies can be categorized as being inward- or outward-oriented, that is, focused on domestic or international markets through import substitution or export promotion. Central to almost all countries' strategies has been the development of an industrial base. Thus, within the inward- and outward-oriented strategies, two main approaches to industrialization have dominated Third World planning: Import Substitution Industrialization (ISI) and Export Promotion Industrialization (EPI). The two carry very different implications for the business environment and for strategies of individual firms.

ISI creates protected domestic markets, removing or reducing competition from imports. In fact, a major reason for direct foreign investments has been to retain markets formerly served by the company through exports, which would be excluded under ISI restrictions. Japan's Matsushita corporation, for example, set up its first overseas manufacturing facility in Thailand in 1961 not as part of a global strategy but rather to comply with the Thai government's strategy and requirements for local production to replace imports.[3] An ISI strategy aims to protect and nurture the country's "infant industries" during their developmental stage. One of this strategy's drawbacks is that the protected environment may foster inefficiency and noncompetitive behavior. Furthermore, the level of production needed to serve the domestic market may be too small to achieve significant economies of scale, thereby leading to higher-cost products.

EPI, in contrast, focuses on the export market, which implies achieving international competitiveness. It aims to use the stimulus of large external markets and the discipline of world competition to create an efficient industrial base. Under this strategy, "infant industries" nurtured under ISI are expected to graduate from protection and enter the unprotected international arena. This is seldom an easy transition for businesses used to the lower competitive pressures in a protected domestic market. Greater exposure to external competition may cause significant economic dislocation and political stress.

Latin American countries have used mainly ISI strategies, whereas East Asian countries have shifted to EPI. The development success of the "Four Dragons" (Korea, Taiwan, Singapore, and Hong Kong) in using the export-led growth model has attracted the attention of many countries, although there is some debate about the replicability of their experience.[4] From 1960 to the mid 1970s Korea's and Taiwan's exports grew at better than 20% annually, fueling GDP growth rates of about 9%.[5] It should also be noted that the development strategy of each of these four has distinct features and levels of complexity that are obscured by lumping them together under the EPI label. For example, Korea's strategy has promoted large-scale firms while Taiwan's has relied on relatively smaller companies: The average export value per footwear manufacturer in 1985 was $23 million in Korea and $2 million in Taiwan; Korea had 5,300 export traders in 1984 exporting an average of $5.2 million of industrial goods while Taiwan had 20,597 traders exporting an average of $1.4 million.[6] Hong Kong and Singapore are city-state entrepôts whose heavy involvement in shipping, commercial services, and banking stand in contrast to South Korea and Taiwan.[7]

Other NICs, such as Mexico and Brazil, have also begun to shift from ISI to EPI. In fact, Brazil achieved very strong export growth between 1968 and 1973 (16.5% annually).[8] However, such shifts are often resisted by local producers who do not wish to abandon their protected positions; they have a vested interest in preserving the old strategy and will exercise political pressure to retain it. One Argentine trade expert pointed to the interplay between managerial attitudes and public policies:

> You have to have an exporting mentality. You have to seek opportunities and design your shoes for foreign markets. You must have an exchange rate that makes it possible to export profitably, not a historically over-valued currency that protects inefficiency and unproductive concentrations of people in the cities. Argentina despised its export industries and taxed them very heavily, yet lived off them very well until markets closed and prices fell.[9]

Countries that have clung to their inward orientation rather than allow internal adjustments to external shocks, such as the oil price or debt increase, generally have ended up with overvalued currencies, rising trade deficits, and even greater borrowing needs.[10]

Given the adverse balance-of-payments situations of many LDCs, export promotion will probably continue to be emphasized. To some extent, governments can and do employ both strategies simultaneously, promoting exports while selectively restricting imports. However, there is a basic tension between the two industrialization strategies: how open a country's economy will be. That decision can greatly affect a company's competitive environment, production configuration, and market orientation. Countries that have achieved a consensus among government, business, and labor to pursue an EPI strategy have a comparative advantage over nations in which pressure groups are still clinging to ISI. As Chalmers Johnson notes, this "helps explain why 18 million Taiwanese export about the same amount as 138 million Brazilians and about four times as much as 80 million Mexicans, even though Mexico is located next door to the world's largest market and Taiwan is 6,000 miles away."[11]

Under either ISI or EPI, the manager should ascertain the type of industrial development sought by the government. For example, India's early industrialization strategy emphasized the development of heavy industry and capital goods; Taiwan's stressed light industry and consumer goods. Those choices opened windows of opportunity for some multinationals and local firms in one country but closed them in the other. The government may also have strong preferences for a type of industrial technology (e.g., labor-intensive versus capital-intensive), which could have significant production, financial, and organizational implications.

In addition to general ISI and EPI strategies, there are other types of national strategies managers should examine. In a country with a major natural resource like oil, copper, or timber, the manager will want to monitor the government's intentions and actions in that sector, because the reverberations for the rest of the economy are likely to be great. Such countries generally employ a resource-based industrialization (RBI) strategy, in which the economic linkages and surplus generated from the processing and export of the main resource fuels the development of other economic sectors.[12] In 1980, for example, the Mexican government decided to deploy its oil revenues to launch a new agricultural strategy aimed at achieving national self-sufficiency in basic foods.[13] That strategic move had important managerial implications for MNCs and national firms operating in the agribusiness sector.

Some countries have chosen to emphasize agriculture rather than industry as their engine for development. While other African nations were neglecting agriculture, the Ivory Coast stressed it. As a result it became the world's largest cocoa exporter, Africa's largest coffee exporter, and its third-largest cotton grower. It has set similar targets for rubber and aims to triple rice and corn production so as to cut down its food imports. This strategy catapulted the Ivory Coast's per capita income past most other African countries. Much of the nation's economic surplus generated by agriculture was plowed into telecommunications and transport infrastructure, thereby facilitating development in other sectors as well.[14] Kenya targeted horticultural products to broaden its exports from its traditional base of coffee and tea. Between 1970 and 1986 the value of horticultural exports grew a hundredfold, and Kenya became the fourth-largest exporter of cut flowers, its effort led by the world's largest carnation farm.[15] Given agriculture's relatively large share of most developing countries' GDP, managers should particularly scrutinize national agricultural strategy, because performance in that sector will often carry significant repercussions for the health of the economy as a whole. Failures there can disrupt the government's strategy in the industrial or other sectors.

PUBLIC POLICIES AND POLICY INSTRUMENTS

The next two links in the Public-Policy Impact Chain are the policies emanating from the national strategy and the mechanisms used to implement those policies.

Categorizing the Policies

The substance of national strategies is revealed by a corresponding set of policies, which can be grouped into the following categories: monetary (money supply, interest rates, credit), fiscal (public expenditures, taxation, borrowing), incomes (wage and price regulations), trade (foreign exchange rates and regulations, import and export controls), foreign investment (capital flow regulations, ownership requirements, incentives), and sectoral policies (industry, agriculture, natural resources, commerce, social, defense). The first five policy groups constitute the constellation of macropolicies that can have economywide and sector-specific effects. The sixth group, sectoral policies, reflects the peculiar circumstances of each sector and therefore carries additional measures beyond general macropolicies.

Using these policy categories facilitates the manager's task of separating the national strategy into its component parts, each of which can have quite different effects on the firm. Although the policies are analytically segregated, it is essential that the manager understand their linkages. Changes in one often carry ramifications for the others.

Understanding Policy Instruments and Institutions

The policy categories enable the manager to examine systematically the substance of national strategies and to make an initial assessment of their managerial implications. To determine their precise relevance to the firm, however, one must analyze the specific instruments and institutions the government uses to implement the policies. These mechanisms and agents, in effect, transform public policies into business issues.

A policy's impact and how a company should deal with it depend on the specific characteristics of the instruments and institutions selected to implement it; the same policy with different instruments can have quite distinct effects. Furthermore, the way in which the instrument is administered can significantly determine its impact on the firm. Policy instruments are of three types: (1) legal mechanisms such as laws specifying corporate income tax rates; (2) administrative mechanisms such as import licenses; and (3) direct market operations such as government purchases or the provision of credit. Table 4.2 provides examples of these three types of policy instruments in each of the above six policy categories. Laws tend to apply generally across firms. They are also rigid and difficult to get changed. Administrative mechanisms can be much more company-specific, and the bureaucrats implementing them

Table 4.2 Policy Areas and Instruments

Policy Instru-ments	Policy Areas					
	Monetary	*Fiscal*	*Trade*	*For. Inv.*	*Incomes*	*Sectoral*
Legal	Banking reserve levels	Tax rates Subsidies	Govt. import control	Ownership laws	Labor laws	Land tenure laws
Admini-strative	Loan guaran-tees	Public service fees Tax collection	Import quotas and tariffs Exchange rates and controls	Profit repatria-tion	Price controls Wage controls	Industrial licensing or Resource concessions Domestic content
	Credit regs.		Export controls	Invest. approval		Technology licensing
Direct market opera-tions	Loans Money creation	Govt. purchases Govt. sales	Govt. imports Govt. exports	Joint ventures	Govt. wages	Govt. research Sectoral SOEs

have greater discretion in determining how they should be applied. Ways of obtaining adjustments in administrative mechanisms tend to be more numerous and flexible than for laws. Market mechanisms are often the most company-specific, because they can involve direct transactions with individual firms.

The type of institution used to administer the mechanisms is also relevant to the manager. Legal mechanisms are often implemented by commissions, regulatory boards, or simply official decrees that set forth "rules"; the burden is on the company to comply, and only noncompliance elicits governmental action. Administrative mechanisms generally entail interaction of the firm with the government bureaucracy in obtaining authorizations and proving compliance. Direct market operations are often carried out by state-owned enterprises (SOEs) that produce goods or services for sale in the marketplace and thereby become competitors, customers, or suppliers of the firm (as will be discussed in the next chapter). Organizational structures, capacities, and motivations will vary across these different types of implementing institutions, and so will the ways in which a firm should interact with them. (Chapter 6 discusses approaches to business–government interactions.)

Mapping the Impact

To assess the managerial relevance of policies and their instruments, one must identify which aspects of a firm's operation will be affected by each policy and its instruments. This moves us to the end link in the Public-Policy Impact Chain. Although the specific nature of the impact will depend on the particulars of the policy and firm, the functional areas affected within a firm can be traced through at a general level. Table 4.3 presents the functions affected by various policy instruments in the six policy areas. The type of instrument (legal, administrative, or operational) is also indicated.

From the table we can see, for example, that in the area of monetary policy interest rates and credit extension would affect mainly the financial operations of the company. In fiscal policy, investment credits would bring financial benefits and possibly influence capital investments and technology choices in production. In the incomes policy area, price controls would affect marketing, and wage controls would have financial effects and perhaps carry organizational implications relating to personnel

Table 4.3 Policy Impact Points

Policy		Company Impact Points[b]			
Category	Instrument	Fin.	Mktg.	Prod.	Org.
Monetary	interest rates (A)[a]	x			
	loans (O)	x			
Fiscal	tax rates (L)	x			
	investment credits (L)	x		x	
	govt. sales (O)			x	
	govt. purchases (O)		x		
Incomes	price controls (A)		x		
	wage controls (A)	x			x
Trade	tariffs (A)	x	x		
	import quotas (A)		x	x	
	export incentives (L)	x	x		
	exchange rates (A)	x	x		
Foreign	ownership requirements (L)	x			x
investment	repatriation limits (L)	x			
	personnel regulations (A)				x
Sectoral	technology licensing (A)	x		x	x
	production licensing (A)			x	x
	SOE operations (O)	x	x	x	x

[a] Types of policy instruments: L = Legal; A = Administrative; O = Direct Market Operations
[b] Management control aspects of each of the four functional areas could also be affected.

remuneration and motivation. In trade policy, import quotas might affect marketing (if the imports were competing goods) or production (if they were supply inputs). The exchange rates will affect the cost of imports and exports. In the foreign investment area legislation requiring local equity participation would have significant effects on organizational design and processes and on financial structure; regulations might also limit the number of expatriates who could hold positions or require training of locals for top management positions. Specific sectoral policies, for example for industry, might involve particular licensing regulations concerning capacity levels, domestic content requirements that could affect production operations, or SOEs used by the government to carry out policies in that sector. These government companies might impinge on all aspects of the firm's business, depending on whether they were suppliers, buyers, or competitors.

With the above analysis, we can locate a policy's likely functional area of impact. Functional area managers can thereby concentrate on specific government policies so as to prepare contingency and action plans. Top management can focus on the interaction of the policies and their overall impact on the firm and its strategy. To gain this perspective, management can also examine how the government's policies and instruments (1) affect the firm's access to inputs, markets, and even profits, and (2) influence input costs, output prices, and profit levels. Examples of how the instrument types listed above can affect firms' resource access and levels are given below.

Access to Inputs, Markets, and Profits. Government regulations that affect access may apply to all industry participants or only to certain types of firms. The forms this type of regulation can take in LDCs are listed below.

- *Concessions.* Before a firm can engage in mining operations or drill for oil, for example, it must often first obtain a concession from the government. Concessions may also be required in certain situations in which exclusive marketing rights are to be granted, perhaps in a specific region.
- *Licenses.* In many LDCs, firms must obtain industrial licenses before they can build or expand capacity. If a firm wishes to purchase the plant, equipment, technologies, or even raw materials from abroad, import licenses may be required.
- *Permits.* Permits for construction or other activities may be required at the state or local level.

- *Allocations.* The government often allocates credit and foreign exchange through state-owned and private banks based on priorities it sets in its planning process.

- *Quotas.* Quotas are frequently set as to the percentage of domestic content of material inputs required in production. They thereby indirectly limit access to imported raw materials. In workforce composition, quotas may be set for the number of managers/workers who are expatriates or members of ethnic, religious, or other groups.

- *Preferred-supplier clauses.* The government may require that SOEs, agencies, and other governmental bodies procure supplies, when possible, from specific types of firms, e.g., SOEs, small-scale enterprises, or other domestic private companies. These regulations clearly limit access to buyer markets for certain types of firms in some industries.

- *Nontariff barriers.* A foreign-based firm may find its access to an LDC market limited partly or completely by quantitative restrictions on the import of its product or through other barriers such as stringent quality standards or lengthy inspection procedures. From the perspective of a local firm, these nontariff barriers may limit access to both capital goods and needed raw materials.

- *Repatriation restrictions.* The parent companies of LDC subsidiaries may find their access to the local firm's profits severely limited by restrictions on levels of dividend payments, management and technical fees, and interest and principal payments on parent company loans.

Input Costs, Output Prices, and Profit Levels. As a complement to regulations of access, most LDC governments have a wide array of policies that affect cost, price, and profit levels. These policies and their policy instruments will sometimes apply to all firms in all industries and at other times only to certain participants or subsectors. The major categories of cost, price, and profit-level regulation are discussed below.

- *Royalties or fees.* To the extent that concessions, licenses, and permits are necessary "inputs" for a firm, their cost will be important. Since these items are obtained exclusively from the government, their prices will be set through regulations stipulating royalties or fees to be paid to the government or other expenditures or actions to be taken by the company.

- *Interest rates.* The cost of bank credit in LDCs is often fixed by governmental interest-rate regulation. For those firms with access to bank credit, real interest rates may be quite low relative to the cost of unregulated nonbank credit. In Brazil in 1982–83, for example, the government provided preshipment financing for manufactured exports at the fixed rate of 40% when inflation was over 100%, thereby creating negative real interest rates for the exporters (see section below on subsidies).[16]

- *Foreign-exchange rates.* Most LDC governments regulate their foreign-exchange rate by tying its value to that of a major currency (often the US$) for unspecified periods of time rather than letting it float freely. Since inflation in LDCs is generally higher than in developed countries, a fixed exchange rate ordinarily leads to an increasingly overvalued currency, until the government imposes a devaluation. The overvaluation causes imports into the LDC to become artificially cheap and exports expensive; therefore both input costs and output prices may be affected. In addition, the value of a subsidiary's profits and assets to its parent MNC in the home-country currency will be affected. An overvalued currency often occurs under ISI strategies with their extensive foreign-exchange restrictions; export-oriented strategies tend to have more realistic exchange rates and fewer restrictions. It should be noted that many LDC governments employ a multitiered system of exchange rates under which certain categories of imported capital goods or basic necessities deemed essential to the country might be given a more favorable exchange rate than luxury items. For example, in 1984 the Guatemalan government instituted a multiple exchange rate system that gave oil imports a more favorable rate.[17]

- *Wage rates and employee benefits.* Many LDCs have some form of minimum-wage legislation. Government regulations may also mandate minimum levels of employee pension and health benefits and in some cases even housing or other benefits. Finally, many LDCs have regulations affecting the timing of employee terminations and levels of severance pay.

- *Tariffs.* Tariffs increase input costs for the importing local producer or the price of importing competing goods and therefore the market price. Most LDCs employ a wide variety of tariff levels rather than a single rate. The manager should determine the "effective protection" from a tariff on final imported goods because it can differ from the nominal tariff rate due to the effect of tariffs on the imported inputs for locally produced competing goods. For example, assume that an imported good faces a tariff of 60%. The locally produced good competing against that import has to import 50% of its production inputs, and these incur a 30% tariff. The resultant effective protection of the local product against the import is 90%, based on the following calculation:

$$\text{Effective Rate of Protection} = \frac{\begin{bmatrix} \text{Tariff on} \\ \text{imported} \\ \text{good (60\%)} \end{bmatrix} - \begin{bmatrix} \text{Share of} & & \text{Tariff on} \\ \text{inputs} & \times & \text{imported} \\ \text{imported (50\%)} & & \text{inputs (30\%)} \end{bmatrix}}{1 - \text{Share of inputs imported (50\%)}}$$

- *Price controls.* LDC governments often regulate the prices of a wide variety of goods and services, typically in basic consumer goods and industrial inputs. Most firms find at least some of their input costs to be determined by the government; some find their output prices to be set as well. In the case of MNC subsidiaries that source from their parent company, the government may use controls on the transfer prices of these goods to restrict the use of overinvoicing as a way of circumventing profit repatriation regulations.

- *Production specifications and other requirements.* The cost of operations can be raised indirectly through government regulations that affect the type of production process used (e.g., environmental and safety regulations) as well as the end product (e.g., technical and quality standards). The government may also require the firm to incur additional costs through contributions to regional or local development projects (e.g., construction of roads, schools, sewage systems).

- *Subsidies and tax incentives.* Government subsidies in LDCs can have several functions: (1) to keep a producer's output prices low (e.g., fuel and power subsidies); (2) to improve the profitability of firms that perform some socially desirable function during which they incur additional costs (e.g., SOEs or private firms locating in remote areas); and (3) to promote certain kinds of exports. Various tax incentives may also be available. Investment-tax credits reduce capital costs and raise after-tax profits of certain firms; tariff rebates may be available to exporters who import raw materials. Corporate taxes may be reduced or eliminated for a specified period of time for firms that locate in an especially underdeveloped region or engage in a particular type of activity (exporting, for example). Once given, subsidies are politically difficult to remove. For example, when the Guatemalan government attempted to remove the previously cited example of the preferential exchange rate for oil imports, there was such a protest from oil users that the government had to reinstitute the subsidized rate.[18]

- *Taxes and surcharges.* In addition to a general corporate tax, certain firms or industries may face additional taxes. Subsidiaries of MNCs must often pay taxes on management fees, technical fees, and dividends remitted abroad. In certain years, the government may impose special levies or surcharges to support specific development activities or simply to help reduce budget deficits.

In addition to assessing the impact of policies on the firm, the manager can also ascertain their effect on competitors and therefore the implications for the firm's competitive position and future strategy. Public policies in LDCs often do not apply equally to all firms in an industry, but even when they do, it is wrong to assume that the policies are not critical in shaping competitive dynamics. Policies may be uniform, but because companies never are, different effects are quite likely. For example, import restrictions accompanied by elaborate bureaucratic licensing procedures will probably affect small firms and big ones differently, for the latter have more resources and administrative capacity to cope with bureaucratic red tape. In effect, small firms will face new administrative barriers to entry. Again, a firm that develops local suppliers rather than uses imported inputs will be better off than a competitor that relies on imports and then finds this supply cut off. Furthermore, the way individual companies choose to respond to policies may be quite different. Public policies create strategic opportunities for competitively differentiating moves. Finally, some policies or instruments target specific firms or categories of firms; an example is dividend or capital repatriation restrictions for multinationals. The next chapter will examine further the specific links of government policies to industry structure and dynamics.

Import Substitution Industrialization Example

As an illustration of the mapping methodology, we shall take the generic ISI strategy and delineate some of its possible policies and instruments and their points of impact on the companies in a sector. Public-policy impact, like political risk, is country- and company-specific. But although its exact effects depend on the particular environment and national strategy and the specific characteristics of each firm, this abbreviated general example will illustrate the analytical process. The last section of the chapter will provide an example of a specific country and company. In this general ISI model, we shall examine the trade, monetary, fiscal, and industry-sector policy groups.

Trade Policy. This is the main policy area for the ISI strategy. Possible policy instruments include tariffs, import quotas and licenses, and foreign-exchange regulations. These instruments erect walls around the local market and protect domestic producers from international competition. Their impact can be mapped by identifying the functional areas of the firm that are affected. The initial impact is on marketing. For MNCs exporting to the country, for example, the measures will threaten the existence of the export market or at least reduce the competitiveness of the exported product. For the firm operating within the country, the instruments become an asset enhancing its competitive position by raising barriers to entry from outside firms. Specific effects will depend on the particular type of instrument and how it is administered. Tariffs will increase the price of imports and hence the price ceiling at which local products can be sold. If consumers care more about the quality of the product than its price, however, branded imports might still fare well despite tariff walls. Quantitative import controls such as quotas provide stronger protection because they shut out or limit import competition regardless of price differences and consumer preferences.

Import controls could have a significant effect also on production and finance if they cover items used in local production. Tariffs would increase production costs and thus affect working capital requirements. Quotas could create absolute shortages; these could lead to underuse of capacity or require the use of local inputs, which might not be available in adequate quantities or at acceptable quality or cost.

Foreign-exchange controls could take many forms. One might be multiple rates giving preference to certain types of imports; the effects would be similar to those of tariffs. Another might be foreign-exchange quotas that varied by type of product; their impact would be similar to that of product quotas. Managers must scrutinize how quotas are administered; this involves examining the bureaucratic machinery. Bureaucratic procedures and politics can greatly influence the results of each firm's requests; the actual impact then becomes a function of how well the firm works with the bureaucracy. In addition, the processing time required to authorize foreign-exchange or product-import requests can cause long and unpredictable delays, thereby creating problems in production scheduling and inventory management.

Monetary Policy. The general tightness of money would be of general concern to the company, but the ISI strategy might be accompanied by specific priority credit lines and preferential interest rates for import-substituting industries. The main point of impact of these instruments would be the financial area of a company's operations. Companies in these product lines would have growth opportunities and capital-cost advantages; other companies might find their credit lines shrunk and the demands on their equity bases greater.

Fiscal Policy. ISI fiscal policy instruments might include tax exemptions or investment credits and special government purchases from the new local producers. Tax exemptions could affect the financial area by increasing profits and cash flow, and hence capital resources. Investment credits will also influence the financial area and choice of technology. They could, for example, create an incentive to select more capital-intensive production technologies. To promote the local industry, the government might make preferential purchases from import-substituting companies, thereby affecting marketing and, through that, production volume levels and product characteristics. If the procurement program gave preference to companies owned wholly or partly by locals, it might be a partial inducement to multinationals to alter their organizational structure by bringing in a local partner.

Industrial Sector Policy. The ISI strategy might also include more specific policy instruments aimed at shaping the development of the industrial sector: e.g., local content requirements, capacity licensing, technology specification, and location incentives. Local content requirements would affect production and carry implications for procurement activities, product quality, and cost. Organizationally, they might also lead to backward vertical integration. Capacity licensing impinges on production but might also have financial implications. For example, fear of future restrictions on capacity might push a company to make greater capacity investments initially to avoid having to obtain permission later (or to create an administrative barrier to the entry of potential competitors). The technology specifications would affect production and possibly organization. If the specifications were oriented toward more labor-intensive technologies, the production configuration and the organization to operate it could be significantly affected. Industrial policy may include some regional development objectives for locating plants in designated areas. These incentives carry obvious financial implications, but the location decision might also affect production operations.

Table 4.4 presents a summarized and simplified "map" of the impact of ISI policy.

Table 4.4 ISI Policy Impact Points

Policy		Impact Points			
Category	*Instrument*	*Fin.*	*Mktg.*	*Prod.*	*Organ.*
Trade	Tariffs	x	x		
	Quotas		x	x	
	Multiple exchange rates	x	x		
	Foreign exchange quotas			x	
Monetary	Credit lines & limits	x			
	Special interest rates	x			
Fiscal	Tax exemptions	x			
	Investment credits	x		x	
	Government purchases		x	x	x
Industry	Capacity licensing	x		x	
	Local content requirements		x	x	x
	Technology specification			x	x
	Plant location incentives	x		x	x

Export Promotion Industrialization Example

Most of the aforementioned fiscal and monetary policy instruments used to implement an ISI strategy are also applicable to a strategy of export promotion industrialization. Both strategies seek to accelerate industrialization and growth. They differ mainly in trade policy and in how monetary and fiscal policies are linked to trade.

Trade Policy. To stimulate exports, governments sometimes use export subsidies, although the more visible forms of subsidy are generally prohibited under international trade regulations (GATT). Exemptions from import duties on production inputs or capital equipment for goods to be exported are sometimes used. Import-entitlement quotas may be authorized based on export earnings. Tariff protection against competing imports or restriction on the number of competitors may be given to increase the firms' domestic volume so as to achieve economies of scale that will enhance their competitiveness in the export markets. Such protection may be only temporary. Some empirical studies suggest that for some industries "export success may depend on having a concentrated domestic market structure." Japan's export-oriented development strategy often employed this approach. Similarly, the Korean government's favoring the *Chaebol* was driven in part to attain scale economies needed to achieve export competitiveness. Korea's exports between 1961–75 grew at the rate of 30% per year.[19]

Sometimes the government would develop infrastructure to facilitate export operations, e.g., the Kenyan government built wholesale markets and grading stations to improve quality control for its horticultural exports. Many governments have set up special export processing zones that have industrial site infrastructure, where firms can import inputs duty-free and process them for reexport. For example, since 1970 Mauritius established various zones that attracted over more than four hundred processing operations (mainly textiles); by 1986 they were producing 53% of the country's exports.[20]

Governments can also enter into bilateral trade agreements with other countries that obtain market access for exporters. Some governments sponsor market studies or promotion for their export products.

Governments also generally exercise considerable control over foreign-exchange earnings by requiring that they be converted to the local currency through the central bank within a specific period. The exchange-rate policy can be managed to enhance the exporters' competitiveness by periodic devaluations to create an undervalued currency or at least avoid an overvalued currency. Favorable exchange rates for such imports or for export earnings may also provide financial incentives.

Monetary Policy. Under EPI strategies, governments frequently provide assistance and incentives through their credit policies. They give special credit lines for export working capital, infrastructure investments, or input imports. Interest rates are sometimes subsidized. Accounts receivables from export sales can often be discounted at the central bank. One survey of sixty-five LDCs found that more than half had export refinance programs.[21] Korea used subsidized credit as a primary mechanism for directing private investment into priority sectors; it then applied the criterion of export volume as the performance measure in determining which firms would receive the credit. Amsden argues that this enabled the state to "discipline" the private firms to become internationally competitive and that other developing country governments have been less able to mobilize their private sectors in this way.[22]

Fiscal Policy. In the fiscal area, governments may use tax exemptions or rebates based on export earnings. Tax holdings on corporate profits are often given to attract investors into the export processing zones mentioned above. Governments may also give investment tax credits or allow accelerated depreciation on equipment used to produce exports. SOEs might sell raw materials to exporting firms at subsidized rates, or SOEs themselves might export at a loss, with the government covering losses through subsidies.

Foreign Investment Policy. Some governments have targeted MNCs as key vehicles for exporting, given their connections and greater access to export markets. Special incentives to induce this behavior include profit remission privileges or income tax exemptions. Several countries have set up special free trade zones in which foreign investors (and sometimes local firms) can import duty-free production inputs and manufacture goods for reexport. Such operations are generally exempt from most taxes and exchange controls. Requirements for local equity participation are sometimes waived for firms engaged mainly in exporting opera-

Table 4.5 EPI Policy Impact Points

Policy		Impact Points			
Category	*Instrument*	*Fin.*	*Mktg.*	*Prod.*	*Org.*
Trade	Export subsidies	x	x		
	Import tariff exemptions	x		x	
	Import entitlements		x	x	
	Tariff protection		x		
	Trade agreements		x		
	Infrastructure		x	x	
	Market research & promotion		x		
	Foreign exchange allocation	x		x	
	Exchange rates	x	x		
Monetary	Priority credit lines	x			
	Preferential interest rates	x			
Fiscal	Tax exemptions	x			
	Investment credits	x		x	
	Accelerated depreciation	x		x	
	Subsidized inputs	x	x		
	SOE subsidized exports		x		
Foreign	Special export zones	x			x
investment	Profit repatriation	x			
	Tax exemptions	x			
	Ownership stipulations				x

tions. Such government incentives have been found to be influential in firms' investment location decisions.[23]

Table 4.5 presents a summary of an EPI strategy's possible points of impact on a firm.

COUNTRY AND COMPANY EXAMPLF· CUMMINS ENGINE IN INDIA

To provide a more specific illustration of the national strategy analysis component of the EAF, we return to Cummins Engine's investment in India,[24] which is the first company example mentioned in Chapter 1. Cummins was one of the world's largest manufacturers of diesel engines for the transportation, construction, mining, and energy industries. By the early 1960s it had six plants in the United States and had also set up factories in England, Scotland, and Australia. Cummins had been exporting diesel engines to India for several years and in 1962 set up a manufacturing operation there. We shall examine India's national strategy to illustrate how it affected Cummins Engine's strategy and operations.

India's Strategies

Since gaining its independence from Great Britain, India's strategies have been expressed in a series of five-year development plans. The First Plan (1951–56) aimed to solve the immediate shortages and dislocations arising from independence and the partition of India and Pakistan. The government succeeded in increasing agricultural production 22% and industrial output 30%, and in strengthening the social and economic infrastructure. The First Plan was largely a collection of individual projects, and it got the country moving. The Second Plan (1956–61) was based on a more systematic development model and planning process. It was in effect when Cummins weighed its decision to invest in India.

Goals and Strategy. Using the Public-Policy Impact Chain, we first examine the main goals, which appeared to be: (1) high economic growth—needed to sustain India's huge and fast-growing population; (2) independence—as a newly sovereign state, nationalism was strong and foreign influence was to be minimized; (3) political survival—as a fledgling democracy in a huge, ethnically diverse country, the government and the ruling Congress Party wanted to consolidate control. To achieve those three goals, the government's strategy focused on industrialization as the vehicle for growth, on import substitution as a means of reducing its external reliance, and on heavy government involvement in the economy to ensure control. The goals and strategy were set forth through a central planning process that established physical capacity and output objectives and investment targets for the whole economy and specific sectors.

Policies, Instruments, and Their Potential Impact. Moving to the next links in the Public-Policy Impact Chain, we shall examine the types of policies emanating from the strategy, the instruments used to implement those policies, and the potential points of impact on Cummins Engine's strategy and operations.

Industrial Policy. Emphasis was placed on heavy industry that was to produce capital goods; these were seen as essential to achieving maximum economic growth and reducing external reliance. Government leaders were impressed by the relatively rapid and significant industrialization achieved by Russia through such a strategy. India's huge iron ore deposits and coal reserves were seen as supporting such an emphasis. Furthermore, the scarcity of foreign exchange was viewed as impeding a strategy of importing capital equipment. Industrial output expanded 41% during the Second Plan, thanks mainly to the growth of heavy industry. Further expansion through the development of original equipment manufacturers of trucks, tractors, and construction and industrial equipment was set for the Third Plan (1961–66). The government established a production target of 100,000 diesel engines, with 5% to 10% in the higher horsepower range of the Cummins product line. The government's industrial policy created a market opportunity for Cummins.

Several instruments were used to implement this industrial policy. First, the government established various SOEs to mount the heavy industries. The prevailing political ideology held that the state should control the strategic core industries. The implication for Cummins was that many of its clients would be government entities rather than private companies. Learning to do business with the government would be imperative, and government policies toward the SOEs would be critical. The second instrument was industrial licensing. All firms in the industries stressed in the plans had to register with the government; no new firms could be set up or capacities expanded without a license. This meant that Cummins's production flexibility would be constrained and that negotiating approval of the initial capacity level would be of strategic importance.

Trade Policy. An ISI strategy meant that imports would be reduced or eliminated. The strategic implication of this for Cummins was that it would ultimately be unable to continue exporting to India. Continued access to the market would require a direct investment in India. The potential advantage was that the company would then be able to operate in a market protected from import competition.

Import controls were used not only to stimulate local industrialization but also as a mechanism for rationing foreign exchange, which had become progressively more scarce. By 1962, the year of Cummins Engine's investment, India's official gold and foreign-exchange reserves had plummeted to their lowest level since independence because of a mounting trade deficit. This implied constraints on Cummins Engine's ability to obtain imported inputs for its production operations. Import controls were administered by an extensive bureaucratic network involving multiple agencies and multiple approval levels. This meant long processing times and complicated procurement scheduling. Among the required approvals was a certification of "indigenous nonavailability," which suggested a strong preference for local suppliers and thus possible impact on Cummins Engine's purchasing and production operations.

Foreign Investment Policy. The government permitted foreign investment but generally did not allow wholly owned subsidiaries. This reflected its concern about foreign control and the perceived costliness of foreign-exchange outflows due to remittances. The impact of this on Cummins would be on the organizational form, as a joint venture would be a requirement. A further concern, given foreign-exchange scarcity, would be controls over dividend remissions. Foreign firms were also required to offset any foreign exchange used up in importing by earning foreign exchange through exports. This raised the issue of whether locally produced Cummins engines could be internationally competitive.

Monetary Policy. The government exercised close control over credit markets through its own banks as well as the regulation of private banks. The money supply had been expanding at about 6% annually during the Second Plan, and the inflation rate was around 3%. Credit availability could affect the demand prospects for Cummins.

Fiscal Policy. The government had been deficit-spending at an increasing rate in the First and Second Plan periods. The deficits were covered mainly by local borrowing but also increasingly from abroad. Foreign aid was an important source of funds. This situation signaled possible inflationary pressures and perhaps constraints on continued expansion of government spending. For Cummins this would dampen demand, especially since many of its clients were SOEs. However, a growing percentage of funds was being channeled into heavy industries, which received 24% of the public investment in the Second Plan, up from a

3% share in the First Plan. Agriculture's share had dropped from 15% to 6%. On the one hand, this confirmed the expanding market base for diesel engines. On the other, the reduced emphasis on agriculture might place the whole economy at risk, since 70% of the workforce and 52% of the national income came from this sector.

Strategy Implementation and Actual Impact. The preceding analysis of India's national strategy, policies, and policy instruments reveals several potential points of impact on Cummins Engine's strategy and operations as it set up its investment in India. We shall now move the clock forward and examine the actual extent and nature of those impacts as Cummins started up its manufacturing facilities.

The first impact was on the organizational form. Cummins was required to establish a joint venture. It formed Kirloskar Cummins Ltd. (KCL) with Kirloskar Oil Engines Limited (KOEL), which produced mainly engines in the under-50-horsepower range and was part of a leading Indian business group. The corporation obtained an industrial license to build a plant with an annual capacity of 2,500 engines in the 220-h.p. and 330-h.p. categories. It encountered serious problems in production and marketing.

The problems started with a nine-month delay in the construction of the factory. A border conflict with China led the government to declare a national emergency in 1962, which resulted in a scarcity of construction materials and equipment. This illustrates the importance of identifying vulnerability points in national strategies. International political factors are one such point to which India was exposed. International conflicts will almost always subjugate other economic goals and plans to the priority needs of security.

The original production plan called for the manufacture of 250 engines the first year, 1,000 the second, and 1,500 the third. In actuality, by the second year after construction only eleven engines had been sold, and those were basically shipped in from the United States and assembled in India. Import controls had important direct and indirect effects on this production shortfall. Directly, the processing of import licenses caused delays of up to fourteen months, causing scheduling disruptions and shortages of inputs ordered by KCL. The authorities also refused some import requests on the grounds that there were local producers of the goods to be imported. For example, the government denied permission to import oil filters, even though KCL had already tested locally produced filters and found their quality unacceptable.

The indirect effects of import controls stemmed from the constraints they placed on local suppliers, most of whom were small and inexperienced with the requirements of larger, more sophisticated engines. Many were unable to meet Cummins's quality standards, in part because they did not have the foreign exchange or import licenses for needed raw materials or equipment. Their limited administrative ability and resources hindered their capacity to maneuver their way through the bureaucratic maze. The rejection rate of parts purchased from outsiders was triple that which Cummins experienced in the United States. The high product quality upon which Cummins based its international reputation was in jeopardy. Although the government had required KCL to reach a domestic content level of 90% by 1965, it reached only 20% by then, and the government was pressuring for compliance.

Projected sales had also failed to materialize. Several government policies and actions dampened demand. The inflation rate began increasing, in part because of the government's fiscal policy of deficit spending. To clamp down on inflation, the government tightened credit and constrained spending by many of its SOEs. Furthermore, agricultural shortfalls caused food imports to rise from 12% of imports to 27% between 1962 and 1967. This not only exacerbated the foreign-exchange shortage but also led the government to allocate greater investment resources to agriculture than to industry. As a result, sales to original equipment manufacturers failed to materialize. Two American manufacturers of earth-moving equipment postponed their plans to set up manufacturing facilities in India. Indian Railways cut its production of locomotive shunters in half. Even replacement sales dropped off. This points out the critical impact that fiscal and monetary policies and policies in other key sectors can have on market demand and a firm's sales projections.

Further dampening sales was the competition from imported engines. Although the government had promised to prohibit imports once KCL built its factory, the actual administration of that import regulation allowed imports to continue. Japanese imports cost much less than KCL's engines because of the low production volume and high costs of this initial phase. Lower-cost imports were particularly appealing to the SOEs and the government, given the tighteness of investment budgets.

By 1965 KCL's cumulative losses were approaching one million dollars, market demand had evaporated, factory capacity was underused, production costs were exorbitant, quality was substandard, and differences had arisen between Cummins and KOEL as to the future strategy of the joint venture. To a great extent both the company's opportunity and its predicament were due to the government's strategy. The government's policies and the ways they were implemented significantly affected the firm's production, marketing, organization, and finance, as well as its core strategic decision of entering India. Our scrutiny of Cummins's situation from the vantage point of the Public-Policy Impact Chain revealed how one can project these effects and identify both risks and opportunities emanating from the government's strategy.

In 1965 Cummins was at a critical juncture with its Indian venture. Should it cut its losses and leave India? Its local partner had offered to buy Cummins out at a 50% to 70% discount. Should it stay and try to make strategic and operational adjustments? The decision would rest, in part, on interpreting changes in the business environment caused by the government's strategy and actions. Did the government's increased emphasis on agriculture imply an abandonment of its industrialization strategy, or was this just a temporary shift to meet the imperative of confronting a food shortage? Did the larger allocation of resources to agriculture create new market opportunities? The increasing demand for small 4–16-horsepower engines had surpassed the capacity of KOEL's production facility. Should Cummins make an additional $400,000 investment to pursue this opportunity? In the Third Plan the government had begun to shift toward an export-promotion strategy to overcome its balance-of-payments problem. Export credits and subsidies were available, and a devaluation of the overvalued rupee seemed likely. Would shifting the strategy toward exports, therefore, be desirable and feasible for KCL? Given the quality problems, should Cummins risk its reputation in the international market with engines made in India?

It is clear that the strategic decisions facing Cummins Engine hinged significantly on the government's strategy and policies and the company's interpretation of and ability to deal with them. Cummins did decide to stay in India. In later chapters we shall further examine the company's efforts to deal with the challenges it encountered as a result of the government's actions and other problems arising from environmental factors.

CONCLUSION

The foregoing discussion demonstrates how critically important it is for managers to understand national strategies. The methodology presented here as the second component in the EAF enables a manager to approach this task systematically by tracing through the four links in

the Public-Policy Impact Chain. The focal points of the analysis and
the key questions addressed can be summarized as follows:

1. *National Strategy*. What is it? Why? How will it change? The
country's development strategy can be identified by delineating its objectives and high-priority areas. The rationale behind it and future directions
can be understood by examining the links between the economic, political,
cultural, and demographic factors and the strategy; they constitute the
underlying shaping forces and should be examined with a historical perspective.

2. *National Policies*. What is the substance of the strategy? This can
be answered by identifying the policies emanating from the strategy.
Using standard policy categories (monetary, fiscal, incomes, trade, foreign
investment, sectoral) enables the manager to organize and monitor policy
changes.

3. *Policy Instruments*. How are the policies being implemented? To
deal with the policies most effectively, the manager should examine
the exact form (legal, administrative, or market intervention) of the instruments and the nature of the institutions being used to carry out the
policies.

4. *Industry and Firms*. How will the industry and company be affected?
This is the critical final link. Disaggregating national strategies into increasingly specific subsets of policies and policy instruments facilitates
the task of identifying which of the functional areas in a firm is affected,
as well as the impact on its access to and levels of key resources.

Thus, the Public-Policy Impact Chain provides a conceptual map
through which general managers can interpret the strategic management
implications of changes in government policies. They can trace through
the links so as to identify the likely impact points, and thus be in a
better position to deal with a possible problem or capitalize on a new
opportunity. Top management as well as functional area managers who
understand these links will be better equipped to foresee and handle
the managerial ramifications of public policy decisions. Those managers
and companies who are less able to monitor and understand these linkages
will be relegated to reactive, *ad hoc* responses, which could put them
at a competitive disadvantage relative to those who have the capacity
for systematic public policy analysis.

5

Understanding Industry Structure and Competitive Dynamics

The immediate competitive environment for a firm is its industry, and so the third component of our Environmental Analysis Framework aims to help us understand the distinctive nature of industry structure and competitive dynamics in developing countries. An LDC's economic, political, cultural, and demographic characteristics tend to give a special shape to the competitive environment at the industry level. This shape can best be understood by focusing on who the distinctive actors are and how they behave competitively. First, there is (1) government, which is a primary rather than a residual shaper of the competitive environment. Additionally, there are five key categories of industry actors: (2) state-owned enterprises (SOEs), which have become significant producers and competitors; (3) business groups, in which significant economic power is concentrated; (4) local non-business-group firms and cooperatives, which can also be competitively significant; (5) informal-sector producers, which are small-scale enterprises that play a pervasive role in LDC economies; and (6) multinational corporations, which have increasingly operated in the Third World, often deploying global strategies.

This third component of the EAF examines the business environment at the industry level through the lens of institutional analysis. The chapter will analyze each of the six categories of industry actors to identify their salient features and competitive characteristics. When formulating competitive strategy, a manager should keep each of the six institutional categories on the analytical screen. Every industry situation will differ in its details, but this chapter will provide an institutional knowledge base and a framework for examining each type of industry actor.

THE COMPETITIVE STRATEGY MODEL

It is necessary at this point to indicate how this component of the EAF relates to existing methodologies for industry and competitive analysis. The most recent useful framework has been developed by Michael Porter.[1] The Porter "Five Forces" model is largely based on developed-country markets, industries, and experience. It needs to be modified to maximize its utility to managers in developing countries. Fusing the EAF and Five Forces frameworks accomplishes this.

The Five Forces framework delineates five competitor categories with five corresponding competitive forces:

Competitor Categories	Competitive Forces
Actual competitors	Intensity of rivalry
Potential competitors	Barriers to entry
Potential substitutes	Substitution pressures
Suppliers	Supplier bargaining power
Buyers	Buyer bargaining power

The core concept underlying this framework is "extended rivalry." At the center are the actual competitors, and the intensity of their rivalry constitutes the competitive force among them. Surrounding the existing competitors are threats of entry from potential competitors and from substitute products. Lastly, interaction with buyers and suppliers is viewed as a competitive dynamic in the form of bargaining power relationships.

The Five Forces framework contains generic elements that can apply to all industry analysis. We assume that most students of modern management are familiar with the specific analytical techniques elaborated in Porter's methodology and will not repeat them here. The two modifications of the framework needed to optimize its use in analyzing LDC environments are both additions. First, it is necessary to elevate another element, government actions, to the status of a "mega-force." In the developing countries, government's influence over industry structure and dynamics is so pervasive and powerful that it constitutes a sixth competitive force joining Porter's five. Government is the gatekeeper determining who has access to key resources; it is the controller determining many prices and costs. Its actions do not affect all actors or other competitive forces in an industry uniformly. By themselves, its actions can create competitive advantage, or, more important, companies within an industry can create competitive advantage by the nature of their response to government actions. In effect, government resource control and regulatory powers modulate the five types of competitive forces and relationships in the Porter framework. The EAF provides an analytical tool for systematically identifying how government actions shape the competitive environment.

The second modification involved in fusing the EAF and Five Forces frameworks is to add the roles of the environmental factors in shaping industry structure and competitive dynamics. These economic, political, cultural, and demographic factors affect each of the competitive forces and relationships: intensity of rivalry, buyer and supplier bargaining power, and threats of entry and substitution. A graphic depiction of the fused frameworks is shown in Figure 5.1.

In the application of the fused framework, the emphasis is on institu-

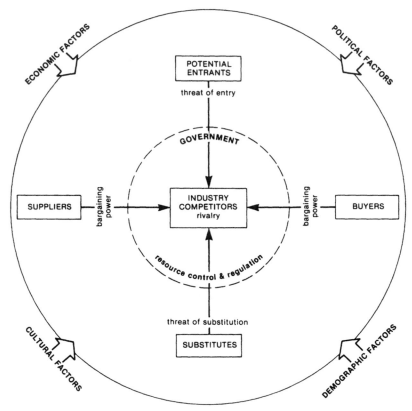

Figure 5.1 Industry Analysis Framework for Developing Countries

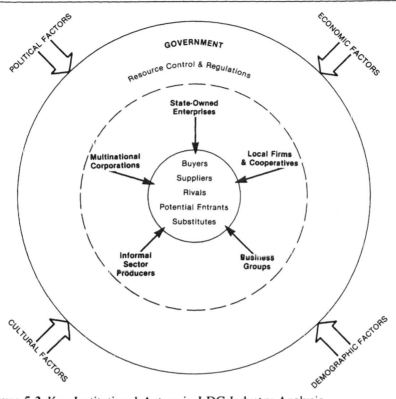

Figure 5.2 Key Institutional Actors in LDC Industry Analysis

tional analysis and the distinctive characteristics of the LDC industry actors. The environmental factors shape the form and behavior of the six categories of industry actors in developing countries: government, SOEs, business groups, local non-business-group firms and cooperatives, the informal sector, and MNCs. Each of these types of enterprise might be found performing any of the generic industry roles: rival, buyer, supplier, potential entrant, or substitute. Figure 5.2 depicts this institutional dimension. The following sections analyze the competitive characteristics of these actors.

GOVERNMENT AS SHAPER
OF THE COMPETITIVE ENVIRONMENT

One of the salient features of developing countries is the relatively greater role that governments play in the economy. Their actions often subsitute for and change the dynamics of the market forces in an industry.

Consequently, the competitive environment can be drastically altered. Government actions in LDCs can and do affect all the industry actors and competitive forces already mentioned, and the effects can differ among industry participants. Chapter 4 showed how government policies and policy instruments could have an impact on various functional areas of a firm's operations and shape the competitive environment by controlling access to resources and affecting prices and costs. We shall now give examples of how government actions (the "mega-force") can affect the other Five Forces.

Intensity of Rivalry

Because the government is the gatekeeper to many critical resources such as foreign exchange, credit, and import licenses, one of the key forms of competition within an industry is for administrative preference from the government. In effect, managing business–government relations becomes a critical competitive tool (see Chapter 6). Different firms have varying advantages in accessing government officials. Larger firms are better able to support the staff needed to wind through bureaucratic mazes. Local firms might have more personal, political, or ethnic connections with key government decision-makers than foreign firms. In many countries firms need a license from the government to expand their production capacity (as we saw in the last chapter's example of India). Companies will sometimes seek licenses for increases significantly exceeding current demand so as to ensure future expansion and avoid the costs and uncertainty of seeking frequent smaller increases. Such regulation-induced lumpy investment creates overcapacity and could lead to overproduction and price-cutting. The government's discriminatory resource allocation could result in dominance for one or a few firms, which could reduce rivalry; or it could create a more equally balanced or even an overpopulated competitive structure, which could then intensify competition.

The government can create competitive advantage for certain types of firms, such as subsidized credit to small-scale enterprises or SOEs. For example, in 1983–85 the share of bank lending going to SOEs was 56% in Guyana, 43% in Mexico, 25% in Nepal, and 18% in Brazil; the Philippines directed credit to agriculture through forty-nine programs and to industry through twelve, each with varying eligibility and financing terms depending on the type and location of the firms.[2] Governments can reduce or remove certain areas of competitive rivalry, e.g., the effect of price controls on price competition. Government often restricts foreign firms' ability to repatriate capital; this can create a form of exit barrier that, in turn, might intensify rivalry as the MNCs fight to make the best of their locked-in positions. Lastly, governments frequently have sectoral policies that significantly influence the growth rates of particular industries. Expansive policies and high growth will tend to reduce rivalry, for firms do not have to fight each other for market share to grow; restrictive policies would have the reverse effects.

Barriers to Entry

Governments affect competitive dynamics by influencing the entry of potential competitors. In many instances, government authorization is a prerequisite to entering an industry. Governments regulate how many and what kind of firms can compete, for example:

- In the Philippines the government authorized the construction of flour mills by local investors, and it created a protected market by restricting imports. The companies at first were very profitable, but as soon as the government removed the import barrier, the local companies were faced with severe competition and pushed to the brink of bankruptcy.[3]

- In Mexico, John Deere mounted a tractor manufacturing facility with the understanding that the government would license only two manufacturers and would prohibit imports. But the government later allowed in two additional MNC producers. This fundamentally altered the production economics of the factory, which had been built for a volume equal to half the market, and it now faced a possible reduction to a 25% share. Imports were also allowed to continue.[4]

- The government of Brazil instituted in 1977 a "market reserve policy" for minicomputers, whereby four national firms were selected from sixteen applicants (including seven multinationals) to be the nation's exclusive producers.[5] These firms were given access to imported inputs, and foreign imports were prohibited. This cracked the dominance of the computer industry by the multinationals and fundamentally changed the competitive dynamics of the industry.

Most LDC governments exclude foreign companies from certain industries and reserve some for SOEs.

Potential Substitutes

Substitutes increase as a competitive force in an industry as their price and function approach those of the dominant existing product. Government strategies and policies can significantly affect relative prices and, therefore, substitutability. Brazil's actions in the energy area illustrate this phenomenon. In reaction to oil price shocks in the 1970s, the government adopted the goal of self-sufficiency in energy supplies. Oil was its chief energy import, so besides increasing its domestic oil exploration, it simultaneously started a program to produce "gasohol" from its local production of sugar. The government provided investment capital to processors and support prices to farmers. It issued regulations so that cars would be equipped to use this substitute fuel and gas stations would sell it. Plummeting prices for sugar in world markets and rising prices for oil made gasohol an attractive alternative. The government's financial and regulatory inputs, however, were essential to making the substitution. By the late 1980s, falling oil prices and rising sugar prices meant that the cost of retaining this energy substitute had risen significantly, but so too had the barriers to exit.

Supplier and Buyer Bargaining Power

Governments can influence access to supplies and thus also the relative degree of bargaining power between buyers and suppliers. The most common policy instrument affecting supply access is import controls. These could be direct (quotas or tariffs) or indirect (foreign-exchange allocations for imports). The more restrictive the import controls, the greater bargaining power local suppliers have, because the purchasers' supplier alternatives are reduced. Domestic-content requirements have similar effects: The government obligates purchasers to buy locally. Government price controls on production supplies increase the *de facto* power of whatever side (supplier or purchaser) is favored by the government's price. The government's enforcement power stands behind the price, so small and relatively economically weak farmers, for example, would be able to extract a favorable price from a large, economically powerful processor. Wage controls also change the bargaining dynamics between labor suppliers and users. Through its control over entry into an industry and resources allocated to actors in an industry, a government can influence the industry's structure. If buyers become more concentrated than sellers, their bargaining power will increase, and vice versa. Government regulations prohibiting backward or forward integration can influence bargaining power. In one South American country, for example, foreign firms are prohibited from engaging in consumer distribution. Consequently, wholesalers have more bargaining power vis-à-vis foreign producers because they do not face the threat of forward vertical integration. Multinationals in Mexico cannot own farm land, so agroindustries cannot so easily threaten suppliers with backward vertical integration.

=

From the foregoing, it is clear that government is a primary actor in the industry environment, and its actions constitute a "mega-force" shaping industry structure and competitive dynamics. Government actions directly and indirectly affect the intensity of rivalry, barriers to entry, substitution pressures, and supplier and buyer bargaining power. As a business executive in one Latin American country put it, "A manager cannot increase prices, sell a product, export it, import anything, or raise salaries without government involvement."[6] In many instances businesses are operating under what is almost a government-issued franchise. Even when controls are less tight, LDC governments' influence on the business environment is pervasive.

To deepen our understanding of the distinctive nature of the LDC competitive environment, we shall now examine the characteristics of the five other major types of economic actors operating in LDC marketplaces, beginning with government-owned companies.

STATE-OWNED ENTERPRISES

The government is a competitive force not only through its regulatory powers but also through its ownership of SOEs, which directly produce goods and services in the marketplace. These SOEs (sometimes called public enterprises or parastatals) occupy an important place in many industries as competitors, suppliers, or buyers (e.g., several key clients of Cummins's Indian venture were SOEs). Their characteristics and competitive behavior are often quite distinct from that of their private-enterprise counterparts. This section discusses SOEs' economic importance, the government rationale for using them, and their competitive characteristics.

Economic Importance

While SOEs have had a long history in developing countries, the two decades 1960–80 witnessed a rapid expansion in their numbers and activities. For example, the numbers of SOEs rose in Mexico from 180 to more than 1,000, in Brazil from 150 to 600, in Tanzania from 50 to

400.[7] SOEs have broadened their presence from the traditional areas of public utilities, transportation (railroads and airlines), sumptuary products such as liquor and tobacco, and basic necessities such as salt and matches into other productive and commercial activities.[8] They are significant actors in high-technology industries in some LDCs, for example, telecommunications, energy, computers and electronics, and aircraft manufacture.[9] Within LDC economies, SOEs have emerged as dominant enterprises in the 1970s and 80s: In Brazil the ten largest companies were SOEs, as were the seven largest manufacturing firms in India and the five largest companies in Mexico.[10] SOEs rank among the largest companies in the world: Of the five hundred largest industrial corporations outside the United States in 1987, 44 were from LDCs, and 20 of them were SOEs.[11] Some developing country SOEs are global or regional leaders. More than half the world's steel production (excluding centrally planned economies) comes from SOEs.[12] South Korea's state steel company is one of the world's largest and lowest-cost producers. Ethiopian Airlines leads the African market, tripling its freight volume and almost doubling passenger volume and revenues over the 1977–87 decade, and generating profits throughout the 1980s.[13] Its outstanding maintenance facilities and personnel have made its service operations a major contributor to profits; its high quality and lower costs led Zambia to switch its overhaul contract from Aer Lingus to Ethiopian Airlines, joining Ethiopia's other African airline customers as well as Greece's Olympic Airways, Air India, and Lufthansa.[14]

In most developing countries, SOEs account for 7%–15% of the GDP[15] and 15%–30% of gross fixed capital formation.[16] The presence and economic significance of SOEs are much larger in some sectors of the economy than the average contribution would suggest. For example, the utilities sector, "a natural monopoly," is almost always dominated by public enterprises: 84% in India, 72% in South Korea, and 100% in Bangladesh.[17] Natural resources is another SOE-dominated sector: 70% of the world's petroleum is controlled by SOEs. Similarly, 70% of the productive capacity for ammonia in developing countries is in the hands of SOEs.[18] Although there is considerable diversity among LDCs, the average share of SOEs of the manufacturing sector is estimated to be around 15%.[19] In Ethiopia it was about 90%, Somalia 80%, Zambia 50%, and Cameroon 40%.[20] Although public enterprises have only a minimal presence in agricultural production, they are often quite prominent in agricultural input supplies or output marketing, thereby making them important actors in the larger agribusiness system.[21] Because of their importance in major sectors, SOEs are often main conduits for government investment funds: In 1984 they accounted for over half of all investment in Zambia, Burma, and Venezuela, and over 20% in eleven other countries surveyed.[22]

SOEs in the 1970s also handled a large share of their countries' foreign trade: 44% of Mexico's exports and 24% of its imports; 87% of Peru's exports and 27% of its imports; 18% of Brazil's exports and 39% of its imports.[23] More than 95% of international wheat trading in 1973–77 involved SOEs on either the import or export side; in mineral trading, public enterprises handled in the mid-1970s 39% of the copper, 27% of tin and bauxite, and 20% of iron.[24]

In some countries, particularly in Africa, SOEs are a major source of employment. In seven sub-Saharan nations, public enterprises accounted for 40%–74% of all wage employment; in Kenya SOEs provided almost 50% of the public-sector employment.[25] In the early 1980s Ghana's parastatal Cocoa Marketing Board alone accounted for 20% of the formal sector employment.[26] In Argentina in 1975 SOEs employed 8.4% of the labor force. In Turkey in 1983 they employed 9.3% of the nonagricultural workforce.[27]

State-owned enterprises have also served as many nations' principal foreign-exchange earners and tax-revenue generators, such as the oil-exporting nations of Nigeria, Venezuela, and Mexico. This has also been true of other commodity exports: In the late 1970s the Ivory Coast, Madagascar, and Malawi obtained more than one-fourth of their total tax revenues from the surpluses of their agricultural export marketing boards.[28] The 1985 output sales of Argentina's SOEs generated about one-third of the public sector's revenues.[29]

SOEs have also been major conduits of foreign loans. In 1978 new Eurocurrency loans to developing country SOEs passed $12 billion, which constituted almost a third of the total LDC commercial borrowings.[30] During 1970–86, SOEs accounted for over 20% of ninety-nine LDCs' foreign debt and over 50% in such countries as Brazil, Mexico, and Philippines, Portugal, and Zambia.[31] SOE indebtedness was double the private sector's.[32]

Rationale for SOE Creation

It is clear that SOEs are an important economic force in national and international marketplaces. To understand their behavior, we must understand why governments create them. There are many rationales, and several may prevail simultaneously. Ideological predilections toward state control over the economy have undoubtedly influenced some decisions to create SOEs, but SOEs are present across a broad ideological spectrum. For example, the percentage contribution to GDP by SOEs was almost identical in the early 1970s in socialist-oriented India and market-oriented South Korea.[33] The Ivory Coast and Kenya both strongly support and encourage the private sector, but in the former there were about 130 SOEs, and in the latter they were present in almost every sector.[34] Even when a "statist" government is replaced by a "privatist-oriented" government, SOEs often remain economically important. In Argentina, despite such political and ideological shifts, the percentage contribution of SOEs to GNP rose from 6% in 1965 to 8% in 1975.[35]

Among the nonideological rationales for SOEs are economic development needs. Certain types of economic activities essential to the country's development (e.g., infrastructure or social service investments) may either be beyond the private sector's financial capacity or have such low financial returns or high risk that private companies will not undertake them. Consequently, the state fills this entrepreneurial void. Sometimes SOEs are created to counterbalance the economic power of private businesses occupying monopolistic or oligopolistic positions; in these instances the state would be intensifying competitive rivalry.

Some SOEs have resulted from the government's nationalizing private enterprises. This was the origin of many natural-resource SOEs, such as Venezuela's state oil company, which was formed when the government nationalized the multinationals. Similarly, Mexico took over the banking industry when it nationalized local banks in 1983. In East Africa eight of the eleven most populous countries went through major episodes of widespread nationalizations of large private firms.[36] Reasons for nationalization vary in their particulars but generally involve the government's desire to exercise sovereignty over what are seen as critical sectors of the economy. India has used SOEs in the core industries to control the "commanding heights" of the economy.

Other SOEs have come into being when the government has taken over failing private enterprises. These rescue operations are generally aimed at preserving jobs and avoiding the socioeconomic and political costs of increased unemployment or disrupted production.

Another important reason why governments create SOEs is to increase the government's or particular subgroups' political power. An SOE can be a powerful instrument to dole out patronage, increase one's political base, or exercise control so as to erode an opponent's power. SOEs have also been misused as vehicles for misappropriating public funds into private pockets.

Competitive Characteristics

Like every private enterprise, each SOE is unique, so all competitive analyses must ultimately look at the institutional specifics in each industry setting being analyzed. Still, many SOEs share common institutional traits that affect the ways they operate. Understanding these traits will help managers analyze SOE behavior as competitors, buyers, and sellers. SOE characteristics will be examined in five areas: objectives, organization, marketing, finance, and production.

Objectives. The distinctive nature of SOE objectives differentiates the SOE from its private-sector counterpart. Because SOEs are created for various reasons and are subject to pressures from various constituencies, they often have multiple objectives that are internally inconsistent, ambiguous, and not easily measured.[37] For example, in Egypt "from the outset the objectives set forth for state enterprises were in clear conflict with one another. On the one hand performance was to be measured in terms of output, profit and productivity while on the other, government's employment drive meant the gradual deterioration of their financial results."[38] Egypt's SOEs employed about 25% of the nonagricultural labor force in 1985.[39] Sierra Leone's petroleum SOE was supposed to contribute importantly to the government's revenue, but its prices are controlled to keep energy costs low.[40]

To interpret or project SOE behavior, one must recognize the dynamics caused by the nature of its objectives. One should not impute the private sector's objective of profit maximization; it may be politically, socially, or developmentally driven. One should attempt to identify which groups exercise pressure over the SOE and what their objectives are. One should then try to ascertain to whom the SOE is responding. In effect, understanding SOE competitive behavior involves analyzing its constituency relationships. By identifying the direction and degree of pressures, one is better able to design an effective way to interact with the SOE.

Organization. The early theory of SOEs held that their commercial activities would require relatively greater autonomy than other government agencies had in order to cope with exigencies of the marketplace; the central government would set the basic objectives, and the enterprise's autonomous pursuit of these would automatically lead to the desired contribution to societal welfare.[41] In reality, this theory has not held up. Central governments have often gone beyond mere goal-setting to control the operating decisions of the SOE managers. This scrutiny by the central government may create risk averseness among the enterprise managers. In India, reportedly, "public enterprises do not always exercise the powers delegated to them. To exercise these powers would be to assume too high a responsibility and expose them too much to dangers of visible accountability."[42] At the other extreme, some SOEs have operated highly independently with adverse consequences for the countries. For example, the excessive and often unmonitored foreign borrowings of SOEs in Indonesia, Brazil, and Mexico contributed significantly to their external debt crises.

The SOEs' lack of autonomy carries several competitive implications. They will tend to be less flexible and more bureaucratic than private enterprises. Their response times are often longer. As competitive rivals they may be less agile. As buyers their bureaucratic switching costs may be large, thereby creating barriers to entry for new sellers. Although the lack of autonomy hinders SOEs in many ways, it also gives them a special channel into the government's decision-making and often preferred access to resources controlled by the government. This gives them considerable competitive power.

Another organizational characteristic common to many SOEs is the high turnover of top management. SOE managers are often chosen for their political connections rather than their professional competency. When the parties in power change, executive posts in SOEs often look like objectives in a political game of musical chairs. The previous managers exit, taking with them their experience and institutional knowledge (and even company records!). Political shifts even during a single government's term in office are sometimes such that the SOE executive suite appears to have revolving doors. This high turnover severely impairs management continuity and strategic coherence and dilutes the SOEs' competitive strength. It may also lead to erratic behavior as new managers try to move in directions diverging from those of their predecessors. SOE behavior as a rival becomes less predictable, and relations with them as buyers or sellers less dependable. This turnover, however, may create new opportunities for private firms to work with the SOEs because old barriers to entry in the form of relationships with previous clients may be removed.

Marketing. SOEs are frequently more constrained than private firms as to consumers served, products provided, and prices set. Governments often mandate that SOEs provide designated products or services to certain consumer groups with high political or social priority. Low prices for these goods may also be stipulated, even below cost, i.e., subsidized.

Such moves may preclude private companies from servicing those consumer groups and lead to *de facto* market segmentation, with private companies selling different products to different, often more affluent, segments. Government controls over SOE marketing decisions may make them more vulnerable to private competitors able to introduce a broader array of products and services at varying prices to meet varied and shifting consumer preferences. Some countries have formal or informal market-sharing agreements. For example, in one South American country's steel industry, SOEs handle the flat products and private firms the nonflat.

Where the government regulates prices, the presence of an SOE rival may sometimes be desirable. One Indian private-sector manager stated that his problem was that "there is no SOE in my industry."[43] In those industries where SOEs were present, their relative inefficiency led them to negotiate with the government for high prices, which then served as a price umbrella and profit guarantor for the more efficient private companies in the industry. Sometimes an SOE rival can be converted to an ally in bargaining with the government for favorable policies toward the industry as a whole. When the SOE is on the buying end of the marketing transactions, its flexibility in setting prices and terms is often limited by the legal requirement to purchase through public bids. This may, however, have the effect of increasing the SOE's bargaining power as a buyer by intensifying the rivalry among the sellers.

Finance. Unlike private enterprises, SOEs need not be profitable to survive, for governments can subsidize their losses. SOEs also often have preferential access to scarce credit or foreign exchange. These deep, special financial pockets are a source of competitive power. In the past SOEs have also had ready access to international capital markets, but restrictions emanating from the LDC debt crisis have significantly reduced this access. Some countries are now insisting that their SOEs generate profits and become self-financing. The Pakistani government instituted a performance evaluation system that tied management bonuses to achieving after-tax profit targets. This also required that a more rigorous cost-accounting system be developed for management control and evaluation.[44]

The special links into public coffers also carry some disadvantages. Funding of SOEs is often tied into the government's general budgetary process, which introduces political uncertainty and expanded bureaucratic procedures. Financial agility is hindered; this reduces their competitive power. The public controls of SOE finances may impose burdens on suppliers. Cumbersome procedures and slow disbursements from the central government to state enterprises often make SOE settlement of their accounts payable very slow. In Venezuela, for example, the government's agricultural marketing SOE fell two years behind in its payments to farmers for crops it had purchased. Private buyers were able to compete for the farmers' produce much more advantageously by offering immediate payment.[45]

Production. Factory location is a critical determinant of production economics. This decision tends to be more complicated for SOEs than for private companies, because the government often seeks to achieve additional benefits from the plant location such as the development of a remote region, job generation in an area of high unemployment, links to other development projects, or favoring a political ally. The result is that the factory may be operating with a permanent economic handicap. For example, in India one fertilizer SOE was required to locate in an economically disadvantaged area, causing higher investment and operating costs and making the company's cost structure noncompetitive with other SOEs and private producers.[46]

The government sometimes sees SOEs as technology generators, yet their bureaucratic structures are generally not conducive to innovation. More often they are buyers of technology. Licensing of technology is a common mode of interaction between SOEs and MNCs, and sometimes the interaction has taken the form of joint ventures.

Such strategic alliances can be quite advantageous. Unilever has a 55%–45% joint venture with the Kenyan government and dominates the profitable edible-oils market.[47] Piper Aircraft's joint venture with the Brazilian aircraft SOE enabled it to knock its international competitor Cessna out of the Brazilian market.[48] In Tunisia in 1986 several SOEs had international collaborative arrangements with French institutions. Air France had a small equity position and governmental cooperative arrangements with Air Tunisia; Crédit Lyonnais owned 23% of the government's financial institution Union Internationale des Banques; Elf Aquitaine had a 50–50 venture with the government's petroleum research and exploration company; and Meridiens Hotels Group had a franchise with a tourism SOE. In the People's Republic of China, all of the international joint ventures are with SOEs. Although having the government as your partner has significant advantages, it might also lead to demands to pursue activities that make public sense but might not be particularly profitable. Chapter 10 discusses the use of joint ventures as a competitive strategy.

Inventory management is another problematic area for SOEs. This may reflect the risk aversion of SOE managers and their response to incentive systems that punish them more for shortages and production stoppages than for the added costs of excessive or even outdated inventories.

Privatization

In recent years considerable attention has been given to the alternative of "privatizing" SOEs, that is, selling them to private owners or at least shifting their operation to private-sector managers. Interest in this option has various causes. SOE performance often has not lived up to expectations. Instead of being entities that delivered priority goods efficiently to key groups, many have been inefficient, given poor service, and caused a net drain on government funds. In the Dominican Republic, for example, SOEs' financial losses in 1987 amounted to 3.6% of GDP.[49] Almost two-thirds of the SOEs in twelve West African countries showed losses, and 36% had negative net worths. In the early 1980s SOE losses amounted to 4% of GDP for both Niger and Togo. Even in socialist-oriented Tanzania the commissioner for public investment lamented in 1984 that the "public enterprise sector in Tanzania has been in existence for almost 19 years, but the performance has been disappointing."[50] The macroeconomic environment for most LDCs deteriorated during the 1980s: international recession, falling commodity prices, mounting foreign-debt-servicing burdens, deteriorating balance of payments, and rising fiscal deficits. Governments faced reduced economic capacity to absorb SOE losses and to feed their capital needs. Political changes in many countries brought in governments ideologically predisposed toward private enterprise. International agencies such as the IMF and the World Bank also pushed governments toward privatization, as has the U.S. government through its international aid programs.

SOEs have been privatized in several countries. The sale of SOEs presents interesting opportunities for private enterprises to expand or enter new markets previously precluded through the government's ownership, or to acquire assets at an attractive price. Nonetheless, the actual number and value of privatized SOEs have been small in comparison with the totals. One survey of twenty-eight countries revealed that during the 1979–86 period about 10% of 4,100 SOEs had been sold, and 80% of these were in two countries (Chile and Bangladesh).[51] Another survey of fifty-six developing countries revealed that 338 SOEs had been sold: 67% through private sale, 17% through public offering, 13% through sale of assets, and 2% through employee buyout.[52]

There are many barriers to privatization.[53] Political considerations will preclude the disposal of many SOEs on the grounds of national security, sovereignty, social necessity, or political control. But even where policymakers desire privatization, potential private buyers should approach these acquisition opportunities with caution. The SOEs the government most wants to get rid of may be the least viable and thus the least attractive. There is a strong tendency to hold on to money-makers and to shed losers. However, some profitable SOEs, such as Malaysia's shipping line, container corporation, and telecommunication enterprise, have been put up for sale on the premise that private owners would improve services and profits, thereby benefiting consumers and generating higher tax revenues for the government.[54] The subsequent profitability of an SOE being sold may depend on the government's changing some of its basic macropolicies, such as price controls, and the likelihood of that occurring must be carefully assessed. The manager should carry out the type of public-policy analysis described in the previous chapter.

The large size of many SOEs may make their price tag beyond the resources of a private investor and sometimes foreign buyers are excluded. LDC capital markets are thin and often unable to absorb large offerings (see Chapter 7). In 1986, however, the Jamaican government, using an extensive public information campaign, successfully sold off 51% of its equity in the largest bank through a public offering on the local stock exchange.[55] The buyer might be able to negotiate with the government for special loans, installment payments, purchasing out of profits generated after the takeover, or buying only a part of the SOE's operation. For example, in Brazil the sale of one major SOE was accompanied by the offer of the government's development bank to finance 80% of the purchase price with a twelve-year, 12% loan.[56] A further constraint is difficulty in valuing the enterprise and selecting the buyer; these are technically and politically difficult decisions. A buyer should be prepared for accusations of benefiting from political favoritism. To reduce this risk, the government of Togo used three independent audits to determine the fairness of the sales price of two bankrupt textile mills sold to a group of U.S. and Korean investors who then successfully rehabilitated the mills for export operations.[57] In Costa Rica valuation problems initially impeded the sale of a state-owned aluminum mill, ALUNSA.[58] The country's Controller General valued the mill at its replacement value (i.e., original cost adjusted for inflation). The resulting $52 million price tag for a money-losing company far exceeded its perceived market value.

The Controller General, as protector of the national patrimony, refused to change the valuation. Ultimately, the company was sold to a group of Costa Rican investors and a Venezuelan aluminum company for about $7 million. The difference was covered by a local currency credit from the U.S. Agency for International Development; this credit was used to offset the SOE's debt with the Central Bank. ALUNSA was thus purchased free of debts. The Venezuelan company was assisting in supplying the aluminum, an experienced manager was hired, and a $2.2 million investment in productivity-enhancing equipment was being made.

There are forms of privatization other than the outright sale of an SOE to private buyers. These include leasing the assets and engaging in management contracts; governments and private companies in several countries have successfully followed both avenues. One survey of sixteen countries documented eighteen instances of leasing and thirty-seven management contracts.[59] The previously cited survey of fifty-six LDCs revealed forty-five leasing arrangements and fifty-three management contracts. For example, Togo leased a steel mill to foreign and local investors and the Gambia gave a ten-year lease with a buy option for a state hotel to a British hotel company.[60]

Many governments in Latin America, Asia, and Africa are increasing their efforts to sell SOEs. By 1988 fifty-one developing countries had under way or planned 755 privatizations in some form.[61] Nigeria announced in mid-1988 that it would privatize sixty-seven firms, including hotel chains, agricultural and food companies, breweries, and insurance companies. It was also planning to sell majority shares in many of its other SOEs, including banks, the airlines and shipping line, and oil companies.[62] Malaysia has been privatizing its national airlines, shipping company, port facilities, and telecommunications system. The Philippines and Thailand also have significant privatization efforts under way.[63] The Mexican government had divested its minority holdings in 339 firms[64] and agreed in late 1988 to sell Aeromexico to private investors for $350 million and also planned to dispose of its 51% interest in Mexicana Airlines and to sell off dozens of other SOEs, including its truck factory and a large copper mining company.[65] The Philippines had planned or under way 134 privatizations and Brazil had 67.[66] It is certain that privatization efforts will continue and that this will alter industry structure and competitive dynamics. It is equally certain that SOEs will remain significant actors in the LDC competitive environment. Understanding their distinctive nature is essential to effective competitive analysis.

BUSINESS GROUPS

Business groups have different names around the world, such as *chaebol* in Korea, *grupos económicos* in Latin America, or "business houses" in India, but they share many characteristics, particularly the ownership of vast resources and the exercise of tremendous economic power. As an institutional form of economic concentration, these groups often dominate the competitive environment in developing countries. This section[67] will define and describe the business groups and discuss their competitive characteristics.

Definition and Description

A business group is defined as a large, multicompany association that operates in different markets under common financial and management control and maintains a relationship of long-lasting trust and cooperation among group members. Thus, they are large, diverse, and fiduciary.

The magnitude of business groups can be appreciated with a few examples. In 1984 Korea's five biggest business groups were listed among *Fortune* magazine's Top 100 non-U.S. firms, their value-added equaled 12.1% of the nation's total, and their annual growth rate for two decades averaged 30%.[68] Korea's Samsung group would rank in the top fifteen companies in the United States, alongside such firms as Chrysler and K-Mart.[69] In Nicaragua of the early 1970s, four groups held 35% of the financial sector's loans and investments.[70] In Pakistan in 1968 ten groups controlled 33% of all assets of private, Pakistani-controlled firms in the modern manufacturing sector.[71] Of the top 259 firms in the Philippines, overseas Chinese business groups controlled 43% of the commercial and 34% of the manufacturing firms, even though Chinese represent less than 2% of the population.[72] This phenomenon of business concentration is common in many other countries in Asia, Latin America, and Africa.

Business groups' operating diversity is a second distinctive feature. Whereas SOEs and MNCs tend to concentrate their investments in specific industries, business groups' investment strategy involves growth and portfolio balance through diversification into different industries in local markets. In one sense, business groups tend to be mirror opposites of MNCs: They are diversified in their activity but geographically concentrated, whereas MNCs are generally diversified geographically but concentrated in their activity. In Korea one business group maintains prominent positions in twenty-nine different industries.[73] In India thirty-seven of the largest domestic business groups had an average of five activities.[74]

Although the variety of business group activities is wide, a common characteristic is that financial institutions such as banks or insurance companies tend to be at the core of the business groups' operations. These financial intermediaries provide necessary funds for the groups' expansion and become a means of controlling the groups' diverse activities by funds allocation. Business groups with export activities often include a trading company.

The third characteristic of a business group is that relationships among group members and their intragroup behavior are based on loyalty and mutual trust, which is termed a "fiduciary atmosphere."[75] These informal and intricate ties among group members contrast with arm's-length dealings with nongroup members and are substantially stronger than those found in cartels and conglomerates. The loyalty and trust permeating business groups are like those normally associated with family or clan members. This fiduciary atmosphere seems to work as an important binding force that effectively coordinates and controls the diverse activities of member companies and, hence, maintains the group structure with a concentrated economic power.

The fiduciary atmosphere usually originates from family ownership and control, especially in a business group's formation and consolidation stages. Owner families actively participate in management, especially in decisions about resource allocation and appointments to key managerial positions. In many cases, as groups mature and grow, management participation of owner-families diminishes and nonfamily professionals take over management. Ties within overseas Chinese business groups are both familial and cultural, and their management system is distinctive. The family owners specialize in entrepreneurial functions, professional nonfamily members are hired to handle administrative functions, and extended family members carry out custodial functions that serve to control the nonfamily administrators.[76]

A distinction must be made between a business group and a conglomerate. In conglomerates a common parent owns the subsidiaries, generally few operational and personal ties exist among them, and relationships are legal. They tend not to transfer managerial resources among themselves; they are disparate entities with legal bonds. In business groups the ties are personal, and transfers of managerial and financial resources among firms are common.

Competitive Characteristics

Business groups are an organizational response to the distinctive characteristics of LDC environments. They are mainly an effort to overcome or capitalize on imperfections in the marketplace. Small, inefficient input markets characterized by imperfect information and high transaction costs raise uncertainties about supply dependability, quality, and prices. Needed inputs such as management and capital are scarce. Thin markets and underdeveloped institutional mechanisms increase capital costs. Concentrations of power in distribution channels and asymmetrical information availability among consumers impede access to markets. Barriers to entry abound. Government regulatory actions create additional transaction costs and barriers.

Business groups gain competitive advantage by overcoming or exploiting these market imperfections. The business group's social cohesion, large structure, and diversified activities enable it to achieve economies of scale and scope in mobilizing and utilizing various resources (particularly information, capital, and managerial skills), and in marketing outputs and bargaining with government and other industry actors.[77]

Information Collection and Use. A business group's size and diversity increase the volume and flow of information within it. Its participation in many different activities makes its structure a wide-ranging information system. The incremental cost of collecting new information is minimal, because a piece of information generated from one group activity may be used for several other actual or potential activities in the group. Thus, besides economies of information collection, substantial gains can accrue from using the information internally rather than marketing it. The information can be used to accelerate the learning curve of different entities within the group and, in effect, erect a barrier to entry for potential rivals. The group's fiduciary atmosphere facilitates information flow. This wide and efficient information network becomes an important group infrastructure that contributes to the overall efficiency of group activities and creates competitive advantage.

Capital Mobilization and Allocation. The business group, especially in its early stages, usually draws its capital from sources that transcend a single wealthy family, although family capital provides the key equity base. As the group's structure becomes larger and more diversified, it forms an internal financial pool, often in the form of banks or other financial institutions such as insurance companies. This allows it to mobilize external capital and guarantee more reliable and possibly cheaper financial services for group members. Economies of scale in financing are obtained first by reducing transaction costs because (1) the borrowers are known and cash-flow shortages and surpluses among the group's entities can be coordinated, and (2) the group's overall credit standing reduces the risk to outside lenders and thus also the price they charge to the group's individual borrowing entities. The group's superior scanning and financing capability enables it to identify investment opportunities and allocate capital more efficiently than nonbusiness groups.

Where capital is especially scarce and financial institutions are weak, a business group's financial capability gives it extra competitive strength. Either through their own funds or through their superior access to other financial institutions, business groups are often able to enter new businesses as formidable competitors. For example, Pepsico's Mexican snack food subsidiary had its position of industry leader severely challenged when a Mexican business group decided to diversify into snacks from its leading position in the baked-goods field. Its resources allowed it to launch a promotional campaign with advertising expenditures double those of the Pepsico subsidiary.[78]

Despite their economic strength, business groups are vulnerable to financial collapse if their strategic decisions are not congruent with their business environment. The Alfa Group in Mexico expanded dramatically in the 1970s and 1980s by borrowing extensively in the international markets. It failed to analyze adequately the macroeconomic risks inherent and detectable in the government's national strategy.[79] When the Mexican peso collapsed, Alfa's dollar exposure and overextended financial position were unsustainable. One of the country's largest business groups crumbled.

Use of Management Resources. Managerial and entrepreneurial resources are scarce in developing countries. Many managers/entrepreneurs in business groups are members of owner families. This family base is very important, especially in early stages, because it provides such unmarketed qualities as loyalty, mutual trust, and high motivation, thereby substantially reducing monitoring costs. The fiduciary atmosphere permits the formation of larger top management teams with trust and understanding than would otherwise be possible. This facilitates effective coordination of large, diverse group activities through better communication and delegation of authority.

The group structure also increases managerial mobility and their optimal utilization; managers can be shifted among the group's entities, depending on company needs and managerial capabilities. Greater paying power, promotion opportunities, and prestige from association with the group often give business groups a competitive advantage in recruiting managers. On the negative side, family dynamics (such as pressure to appoint unqualified members to key positions, conflicts over personal matters, or family pride dominating business rationality) can be disruptive and demotivate nonfamily members of management. This might be the "Achilles' heel" of business-group competitiveness.

Output Marketing. The business group's power in product markets offers economies of scale and scope in marketing member firms' products. Common distribution channels, equipment, or brands can reduce the incremental costs of marketing new and existing products. Vertical integration can reduce transaction costs and increase flexibility through transfer pricing. Channel control can create barriers to entry. Diversification increases the group's staying power and may intensify rivalry as profitable activities are used to support those experiencing greater competitive pressure. In some countries ethnic-based business groups have concentrated their strategies on channel control (see Chapter 9).

Bargaining Power. Business groups' economic power and importance to the economy strengthen their bargaining power with external actors, be they the government, suppliers, or buyers. Business groups usually have access to top-level government officials, often cultivate political connections, and are thus in an advantageous position to elicit preferential treatment from government. Furthermore, their information system and administrative capabilities enable them to achieve economies of scale in the transaction costs of dealing with government bureaucracy. Groups can designate individuals to specialize in obtaining import permits, foreign-exchange licenses, and so on, for all their business entities. Superior capability in managing the bureaucracy creates competitive advantage. In India, for example, the business groups frequently have a "liaison officer" to handle and accelerate the processing of the multitude of government applications and authorizations. In the Cummins Engines joint venture in India, the local partner was an important business house. Its knowledge of the bureaucratic processes and its established contacts with government decision-makers gave the undertaking a capability that Cummins alone would not have had or obtained easily. As a result, the company was able, for example, to renegotiate successfully the domestic-content schedule, thereby gaining valuable time to develop local suppliers.

Some governments, such as South Korea's, have explicitly used business groups as primary instruments to implement their development strategies. This gave the *chaebols* preferential access to scarce resources and significant influence with government policy-makers. One drawback of the groups' concentrated economic power and high visibility is that they become political targets and may be subject to intensified controls. By the mid-1980s some political backlash was occurring in the form of restrictions on *chaebols* and special credits for small and medium-size businesses. Regime changes can severely affect business groups. For example, when a new government came to power in Nicaragua in 1979, it dismantled the major business groups through expropriation because of their perceived excessive concentration of economic power and ties to the previous regime.

Group Evolution

The structure and behavior of business groups tend to evolve as they and their environments change. The groups' own growth forces internal changes, and the countries' development processes reduce some of the original market imperfections, which enables the groups to shift their activities. Family dominance and direct involvement in the groups' operations diminish. Initially there are generational changes within the family, with the younger leadership having more professional training. As a result, increasing professionalism and meritocracy replace nepotism. The group's growth exceeds the supply of family managers. The overseas Chinese business groups have dealt with this problem by appointing professional managers to administrative positions while retaining entrepreneurial and custodial functions for family members.

Ownership tends to be broadened. Inherited shares may be sold off to outsiders. Joint ventures are established, often with foreign firms but sometimes with new and growing local firms. International ventures are undertaken. There is a clear trend for business groups to become multinational through direct foreign investments in other LDCs and in some developed countries. By 1980 LDC firms had invested between $5 billion and $10 billion abroad and set up more than a thousand subsidiaries.[80]

These Third World multinationals are often extremely effective competitors, especially in other developing countries. For example, in Indonesia, Thailand, and Singapore about one-third of all nonoil or nonmining FDI had come from other LDCs.[81] Hong Kong has been the largest direct investor, putting in about $1.8 billion; its investments account for about 10% of all FDI in Indonesia, Malaysia, and Taiwan.[82] In Taiwan, Hong Kong's FDI exceeded 50% of all FDI in leather, pulp and paper, construction, and transportation. The Third World multinationals' knowledge of LDC environments has enabled them to tailor technologies and operations to that business environment's distinctive demands. The San Miguel business group of the Philippines displaced a major U.S. brewer to become the dominant brewery in Hong Kong; the family-owned Turkish construction company Enka was a leading international contractor in the Gulf States.[83] Third World multinationals have significantly lower overheads because of lower salaries and sparser facilities than developed country MNCs, thereby gaining a cost advantage.[84] Singapore's soft drink manufacturer used its lower cost structure to compete successfully in Indonesia against Coca-Cola and Fanta, and a Singaporean battery company overcame Union Carbide's heavy advertising by pricing 26% lower.[85]

The Third World multinationals also compete against each other. The Korean *chaebol* took away 20% of the Taiwanese Tatung business group's electronics export sales to the United States.[86] The Korean government promoted the establishment in 1975 of general trading companies to increase the country's competitiveness internationally. The *chaebols* were the only business organizations with the resources to carry out these trading operations, and by 1981 they were handling 44% of the country's exports.[87]

The long-term evolution of business groups may be toward a type of MNC–conglomerate hybrid with the institutional history and culture of a business group that may give it a distinctive coherence and diversity. Such an evolutionary path is far from certain. What is certain is that wherever LDC business groups lie on the evolutionary spectrum, they represent a significant force in the domestic environment.

LOCAL FIRMS AND COOPERATIVES

Most indigenous firms do not belong to business groups. These entities range tremendously in size. Most are family-based firms, but some are publicly held corporations, particularly in those LDCs with more highly developed capital and stock markets. A second type of local enterprise found in most LDCs is cooperatives. These operate in many sectors and generally have strong links to the government. We shall examine the competitive characteristics of the local firms first and the cooperatives second.

Competitive Characteristics

Local non-business-group firms tend to operate in only one or a few business activities. They do not have the degree of diversification or economic size of business groups but can be competitively important in their particular industry or market niche. The family-based firms have the same advantages and disadvantages of kinship dynamics as in business groups. However, they may be very dependent on one or a few key individuals and therefore lack the management depth needed for expansion. Those firms that are professionally managed are often aggressive and innovative, relying on their business skills to offset some of the competitive disadvantages they face vis-à-vis economically stronger business groups. Sometimes the non-business-group company will seek out multinationals for a joint venture. This alliance often gives the local firm the greater economic muscle it needs to compete with business groups. For the multinational such a joint venture might be a preferred route into an established market niche.

Cooperatives are, of course, not unique to developing countries, but they have emerged as an organizational form particularly suited to many of the characteristics of the LDC business environment. Most cooperatives are guided by the following set of principles: voluntary association, democratic management, self-help, nonprofit motivation, political and religious neutrality, nondiscrimination, and open membership. Cooperatives are vehicles for gaining economic and political strength through association. They are particularly appealing to small businesspeople, farmers, or even households as a way to gain bargaining power with buyers, suppliers, or the government, and to achieve economies of scale in purchasing, processing, and distribution. Governments often promote cooperatives because they provide an organizational conduit through which public assistance efforts can be more effectively and efficiently provided to these groups. By increasing the leverage and capacity of "atomized" sectors of the economy, cooperatives create a mechanism for improving the distribution of income and political power in a country. In some instances, however, governments use the cooperatives as political instruments.

Cooperatives tend to specialize by activity: savings and loan, agricultural marketing and processing, housing, consumer goods, transportation, and so on. Their presence in a particular sector can be quite important. In Costa Rica, for example, where about 30% of the economically active population in 1985 belonged to cooperatives, agricultural cooperatives produced 45% of the coffee (the principal export), 37% of the beef, and 88% of the ornamental plants (the fastest-growing export), and transportation cooperatives provided 85% of the taxi service.[88] In India the development of the cooperative sector has been an important element in its development strategy since independence. By the mid-1960s there were more than 670,000 industrial, agricultural, credit, and consumer cooperatives with total membership exceeding 41 million.[89] Cooperatives sometimes dominate sectors. Cooperatives are especially important in agribusiness: On a worldwide basis they supply about 20% of the farm inputs and market about 30% of farm production.[90] In Maharashtra, India's largest sugar-producing state, cooperatives produce and process almost 90% of the white sugar.[91]

The cooperatives have competitive strength from their numbers. Sometimes they hold dominant control of a particular resource or service, thus enhancing their bargaining power or competitive strength. For example, the sugar cooperatives in Maharashtra have dominated the private sugar processors. The cooperatives grow sugar cane and have their own sugar mills; this integrated structure makes them both buyers and sellers. The private processors buy from independent sugar cane growers. The cooperative members' returns come from higher sugar cane prices, whereas the private investors get their returns from dividends on the profits from their mill. Thus, the cooperative mill has an organizational structure and objective to pay the farmers high cane prices and the private mills have the opposite incentive. As a result, the farmers prefer to sell to the cooperative and the private mills are being left without sufficient cane to operate their mills economically. Some of the private mills are even converting to cooperatives. The managers of these mills are elected by the farmer members, and support is often given to those managers able to run the mills most efficiently so as to pass on higher prices to the members.[92] Cooperatives' extensive membership gives them political power. Government programs often give cooperatives access to credit at preferential rates and to other forms of economic assistance and protection that can create competitive advantages.

On the weakness side, cooperatives often lack professional managers; for example, only 28% of Costa Rica's cooperatives were managed by professionals. Furthermore, the organizational form sometimes impedes rapid response to changing business conditions. Decisions often have to be delayed while the membership is consulted. Cooperatives have fewer options for raising capital. They are not able to issue equity and must rely on member contributions. Lastly, cooperatives can sometimes be manipulated by governments for political ends.

INFORMAL SECTOR BUSINESSES

Developing country economies, particularly in large cities, abound with enormous numbers of small enterprises that are operated by individuals or families and are not legally constituted. They are not legal in that they do not have formal papers of incorporation or the necessary licenses or permits to operate; they produce socially acceptable goods and services but through an informal system. We are not referring to businesses engaged in producing illegal goods or services such as narcotics or auto thefts, but rather small businesses such as street vendors, tailors, shoemakers, repairmen, carpenters, transporters, light manufacturers, and so forth. These businesses are a significant part of the industry environment. We shall first examine their economic significance and then their competitive characteristics.

Economic Significance

The informal sector has emerged out of economic necessity. The rapid population growth and urbanization prevalent throughout the Third World created massive labor pools that exceeded employment opportunities in the modern, formal sector. To survive, the unemployed created their own jobs, producing goods or services with their own labor and meager economic resources.

Although there is a tendency to discount these activities as economically insignificant to a country and to industry structure, the informal sector is an integral and important part of LDC economies. It employs about half the urban workforce and accounts for about a third of urban income.[93] The informal sector is significant both in the aggregate and within specific sectors. For example, Peru's informal sector accounts for 27% of GNP and 46% of retail output, 45% of transportation, 42% of construction, 20% of personal services, and 16% of manufacturing.[94]

Competitive Characteristics

The behavior and role of the informal sector can be understood by examining its access to resources, production mode, and relations to formal-sector enterprises.

Resource Access. The informal sector is characterized by its low access to resources. Because these entities do not generally exist as legally constituted businesses, they have little access to legal protection or government services for business. In part they may remain illegal to avoid taxes or other government regulations such as wage and benefit levels or license fees. But even if they wish to legalize, there are often bureaucratic and economic barriers. In Peru, for example, researchers documented that to formalize an industrial company properly, one must obtain ten separate documents, which take up to 290 days to process and cost $1,530. Formalizing a commercial firm requires forty-three days and $110.[95] In both instances, considerable personal time and skill are required to deal with the bureaucracy; these economic, time, and skill requirements constitute significant barriers to formalization given the extremely limited resources of most informal sector producers. One of the consequences of their illegal status is that informal-sector firms often have to bribe public officials to avoid being shut down or fined; another consequence is that they have to hide their operations. These aspects increase their operating and transaction costs and impede their access to consumers.

Informal businesses have low access to formal sources of capital. Formal lending institutions generally will not lend to them, so they use their own savings and profits or borrow from family, friends, or informal-sector lenders. The interest rates charged in these very imperfect capital markets are extremely high compared to formal-sector rates. Informal businesses are also at a disadvantage in obtaining imported goods or scarce raw materials. Formal-sector firms are able to obtain government import permits more readily or to bid away scarce supplies; informal firms must often resort to the black market for their sourcing. Informal firms do have high access to cheap labor supplies and to low-income consumer groups.

Production Mode. Informal businesses' production operations are highly labor-intensive, with relatively low capital usage. Studies in India, Kenya, and Ghana, for example, showed that capital invested per job in the informal sector was less than 20% of that in the formal sector.[96] In these low-tech production systems, labor is also lower-skilled and has less formal training. Standardized, high-precision, or high-complexity production methods are difficult for informal enterprises. To increase their access to raw materials and decrease their costs, informal enterprises often recycle materials used by others. This is economically feasible for the informal sector, because the collection and reworking activities are labor-intensive and the wages lower.

Formal Sector Links. Although the existence of a modern, formal sector and a traditional, informal sector suggests a dichotomous structure, in reality the two are linked as suppliers, buyers, or competitors. The formal sector often uses the informal sector as subcontractors.[97] Their lower costs and ability to handle labor-intensive operations make them attractive suppliers. Their nonlegal status, their large number (given the low barriers to entry), and their need for markets reduce the informal sector's bargaining power with the formal sector. The informal sector, in turn, also buys inputs from the formal sector, which again tends to hold a dominant bargaining position over informal enterprises.[98]

Besides their links as buyers and sellers, the two sectors are also sometimes competitors. Informal enterprises tend to concentrate on business catering to individual needs, such as repairs, tailoring, and home services. They often also serve lower-income groups (other members of the informal sector). While in many of these areas the two sectors are involved in distinct product and consumer segments, in other instances they compete directly, such as in shoes, clothing, furniture, food service, and transportation. The main basis of competition in these areas is price.

The informal businesses can be quite competitive because of their low overhead and labor costs as well as their tax avoidance. One international corporation in Thailand decided not to set up an operation to supply its own printing needs and sell to outsiders after a feasibility study revealed that it could not compete in costs with the existing supplier in the informal sector, who ran his company out of his house and used family labor.[99] In Venezuela many small-scale furniture builders sprang up in the 1970s to supply the growing demand of the increasing numbers of apartment dwellers for modular, space-saving furniture.[100] These informal-sector companies were set up in rudimentary facilities in the squatter settlements surrounding Caracas. Their prices were much lower than those charged by retail furniture outlets, and some of these small companies advertised in the newspaper to obtain direct orders. They grew rapidly and became a significant competitive force in the furniture industry.

The Informal Sector's Future

One might expect the informal sector to disappear as the countries develop. However, the demographic structure and process in the developing countries is such that the underlying pressure of burgeoning urban populations will continue to exceed the formal sector's capacity to generate jobs. People will continue to flow into the informal sector. Furthermore, governments are increasingly recognizing the informal sector's economic, social, and political importance and have begun to promulgate policies to reduce some of the barriers facing informal enterprises. The informal sector is an exceptional source of entrepreneurial energy and innovation. Fostering it will be likely to accelerate a country's socioeconomic development. It is highly probable that the future will see an expanding and invigorated informal sector and a blurring of the lines between the informal and formal sectors.

MULTINATIONAL CORPORATIONS

MNCs are strong competitors in most developing countries. Their foreign origin and international links create a distinctive competitive position for them. The nature of this position also depends on the degree to which MNCs deploy global strategies.

Competitive Characteristics

Compared to indigenous firms, MNCs generally have superior access to foreign capital, technology, information, markets, and brands. All of these factors are scarce within LDCs, so the MNCs' ability to tap external sources gives them potential competitive advantage. The MNCs' home governments may also be sources of economic or political support. For example, Great Britain extended large, subsidized credits to Mexico to enable a British MNC to win the construction contract for a billion-dollar steel mill project.[101] Mitsubishi Corporation persuaded the Japanese government to provide economic development assistance to the Kenyan government to enable it to finance Mitsubishi's construction of the international airport at Mombasa. Mitsubishi also secured loans from the Japanese government and the African Development Bank for the government of Malawi for another airport construction project. Japanese trading companies are the initiators of many of Japan's economic assistance projects in developing countries.[102]

On the liability side, the MNCs' foreignness can hinder their competitiveness. Their presence is politically sensitive, and political groups or the government may single them out for restrictive actions. All enterprises are not held equal before the law. The foreign corporation will not, at least initially, know the local environment as well as its domestic competitors do. Furthermore, the MNC usually will not have the contacts and access to government that local firms have. Finally, the MNCs' home governments may impose restrictions on their actions; for example, the U.S. Foreign Corrupt Practices Act makes payments to government officials illegal regardless of the practices of indigenous competitors (see Chapter 6). An even more extreme restriction has been the U.S. government's requiring U.S. MNCs to cease operations in politically unfavored countries, such as Libya and Angola.

MNCs can create competitive advantage through global strategies.[103] As was pointed out in Chapter 2, global industries are one of the vehicles that link the LDCs' national environment with the international environment. Such strategies are based on the premise that the company's operations around the world are interdependent, that its competitive position in one country can significantly influence or be influenced by its own or others' competitive positions in another country. The strategy tries to integrate the MNC's global activities to enhance its competitive power. This involves centralizing some activities in certain countries and coordinating the flow of resources and activities among the MNC's entire network of companies and countries.

Various changes in the international economy are conducive to the globalization of industries. Technological advances in communications and transportation have shrunk time and distance and facilitated physical flows among countries. Capital markets have expanded and have financially linked almost all countries. The spread of MNCs has created global buyers and sellers. Homogenization of product needs is growing. New processes for product development and production offer economies of scale.

The key decisions in formulating a global strategy are where to put each activity and how to coordinate them. The goal is to do this so as to generate a competitive edge through lower costs, higher consumer appeal, greater barriers to entry, or stronger bargaining positions. These decisions and possibilities are shaped in part by the nature of the industry. For example, an industry like aircraft manufacturing that requires very heavy R&D and product-development investment would want to centralize these activities to achieve economies of scales, yet the end markets would be global and would benefit from close coordination. Some parts of the final good might also be economically produced elsewhere and assembled in still another country. Thus, location can also be determined by the comparative advantages that different countries offer.

A global strategy can give an MNC a competitive edge over domestic firms (or rival MNCs not using global strategies), because it increases the MNC's options in suppliers, buyers, and product design and cost. The MNC's bargaining power vis-à-vis its local suppliers and buyers can also be increased by having external alternatives. This can also strengthen the company's position with the government, for the MNC could export into captive markets (other subsidiaries of the MNC) not otherwise available to the country. Similarly, the MNC's dispersion of producing sites might lessen its vulnerability to adverse actions by the government of one country. An MNC's actions or interactions with other MNCs in one country might sometimes appear irrational unless they are interpreted as part of the competitive dynamics of the global industry in which it is operating.

The feasibility and desirability of an MNC's global strategy are shaped, on the one hand, by the nature of the industry and the firm's individual situation and, on the other, by the characteristics of countries' environments. Developing countries often have features that give them an international comparative advantage for certain types of industries and companies. For example, low-cost labor has traditionally attracted labor-intensive industries such as textiles and shoes. Global sourcing dominates the strategies of the sports footwear industry, with companies setting up production facilities or contracts in various developing countries. Much of the electronics industry's move toward offshore production facilities mentioned in Chapter 1 has been driven by global strategies. The existence of natural raw materials such as minerals or forests can also make LDCs part of a global industry. The location of a developing country might give production from there a transportation advantage for regional markets. Some MNCs have centralized research in an LDC for certain types of products common in Third World markets.

Government actions, as a "mega-force" shaping the competitive environment, become a critical factor determining an LDC's attractiveness as part of a global strategy. These actions can significantly impede or facilitate global strategies. On the impediment side, governments can require MNCs to form joint ventures, which might complicate coordination of transfer pricing, investments, and technology flows within the MNC's network. IBM has refused to enter into joint ventures for such reasons. Trade restrictions, technology-transfer controls, and foreign-exchange limits can greatly reduce MNCs' ability to achieve global synergism through international resource flows. Government requirements for domestic content can also limit global sourcing options. The more severe such impediments are, the more an MNC must adapt a country-focused strategy. Other factors such as cultural heterogeneity or infrastructural deficiencies may also make country strategies preferable to global strategies. But it is important to recognize that even within such constrained environments, opportunities to globalize certain subactivities may still exist.

On the facilitating side, governments can provide special fiscal incentives to attract FDI, production licenses to get higher technology into the country, import licenses for export goods, export subsidies, and so forth. A global strategy may give an MNC more options and flexibility in negotiating with the government to obtain some of these positive policies. For example, the MNC might have more ready access to export markets and thus be able to generate foreign exchange to offset its import requirements. For a government, the MNCs might be vehicles for establishing the country as a more viable competitor in a global industry. The Mexican government viewed IBM this way for microcomputers.[104]

THE DEVELOPMENT PROCESS AND COMPETITIVE DYNAMICS

The Third World's distinctive competitive environment arises from its different process and level of development. The five competitor groups (SOEs, business groups, informal sector, local firms and cooperatives, and MNCs) with their particular competitive strengths, weaknesses, and behaviour patterns are institutional responses to that peculiar business environment.

Competitive dynamics are fundamentally affected by two basic characteristics of that environment: concentration and uncertainty. The scarcity of financial and managerial resources, inadequate physical and social infrastructure, deficient information, low factor mobility, and institutional weaknesses impede the functioning of economic and political markets and lead to concentration of private and public power. Economic and political barriers to entry abound and modulate and distort market and competitive forces. A relatively small number of competitors exercise a disproportionately large degree of power. This often leads to implicit or explicit market-sharing arrangements and/or to ruthless squashing of opponents. This economic concentration lies in the modern sectors; the informal sector is the mirror opposite: highly fragmented and intensely competitive.

The development levels and processes also produce greater political and economic uncertainty. On the political side, government policies and actions often suffer discontinuities and are erratic. The rules of the competitive game are frequently unclear and unstable. This is a reflection of the underlying instability of the political actors and weaknesses of political and bureaucratic institutions. Given the mega-force of government, competitive advantage is often dictated more by political actions than business decisions. Consequently, competitive dynamics often focus on attaining political preference as the vehicle to competitive advantage. However, such advantages can be ephemeral, because what has been given can be taken away. The sustainability of politically based competitive advantage can be fragile. This heightens the importance of managing business–government relations as part of the competitive strategy equation (see Chapter 6). Being able to foresee, perhaps influence, and adjust to major changes in government strategy or policies becomes critical to preserving competitive viability. For example, a shift from an ISI to an EPI development strategy (which many LDCs are undertaking) can profoundly change the cost structures, market prospects, and sources of competitive strength of firms. Such policy effects on the business environment increase the economic uncertainty. Additionally, LDCs are generally more exposed to external economic shocks. Shifts in international prices of key exports or imports or access to primary export markets can dramatically affect the general macroeconomic and specific industry situation, and hence competitive dynamics. Contingency planning and operating flexibility become important elements in managing this economic uncertainty.

The foregoing characterizes the general nature of competitive dynamics in the LDC environment. A related key issue is how this might change as countries move forward in the economic development process. Although there is no evolutionary certainty, some tendencies are strong enough to point toward a path. As countries develop, many of the institutional, infrastructural, and informational imperfections in the marketplace are reduced. Markets become more efficient resource allocators. Barriers to entry decline, thereby increasing the numbers and intensity of competition. Government's role in the economy shifts increasingly from direct to indirect mechanisms for the allocation of resources and control of private businesses. As the complexity of the economy grows, the capacity of the state to control it directly lessens. As the economy strengthens, it will become more integrated with the international economy and more open to international competitive pressures on the import and export sides. Evaporating protectionism will fundamentally change the competitive environments in LDCs.

Some aspects of the evolution of the five types of LDC competitors are discernible. SOEs will decrease in number and in their breadth of industry involvement, with the private sector absorbing many of them through privatization. However, many of the larger SOEs will remain as significant businesses in the domestic and international markets. Past inefficiencies and losses will be less tolerated by fiscally strapped governments. It is likely that the surviving SOEs will be more efficient and competitively stronger. Third World business groups will continue to be major competitive forces. Increasingly their management will become more professional and their operations more international. Their presence as global competitors will be significantly felt. MNCs' presence in LDCs will continue to increase as part of the growing development of international networks dictated by global strategies. The MNCs and the LDC business groups will face the key choice of whether to confront each other competitively or to create strategic alliances. Other local LDC firms will expand as the total size of the economy grows; concentration is likely to fall along with entry barriers. Cooperatives will continue to serve as vehicles for individuals to gain economic strength through association, but their evolution is likely to be significantly affected by government attitudes and policies toward them. The informal sector will remain large and will become increasingly integrated with the formal sector.

Although there is no clear map, managers should be aware of the linkages between the development process and competitive dynamics in their country. The nature of the competitive environment will change as the country develops; effective competitive analysis requires this dynamic perspective.

CONCLUSION

This third component of the EAF has facilitated our examination of the structure and dynamics of the LDC business environment at the industry level. The EAF modified Porter's "Five Forces" model for competitive analysis to capture the distinctiveness of the LDC environment. The first modification was to introduce government's actions as a "mega-force" that can dramatically affect the other forces of rivalry, barriers to entry, substitution pressures, and supplier and buyer bargaining power. The second modification was to recognize that LDC environmental factors give rise to special types of industry actors. To understand the competitive environment, a manager must understand how industry participants are likely to act. The EAF therefore takes an institutional focus.

Through institutional analysis we were able to understand the distinctive characteristics of the five main categories of competitors in the LDC business arena: SOEs, business groups, local non-business-group firms and cooperatives, informal-sector producers, and MNCs. We identified each type's competitive strengths and weaknesses and how they might behave as rivals, allies, buyers, and sellers.

This chapter completes the elaboration of our Environmental Analysis Framework. The first component of the EAF is the categorization of environmental phenomena into economic, political, cultural, and demographic factors. These four interrelated groups and their subcategories allow managers to scan and analyze their business environment more systematically and with a sharper focus. These factors shape that environment at each of our four analytical levels: international, national, industry, and firm. The second component of the EAF enables the manager to analyze a government's national strategy and to understand its effect on the business environment. Through the EAF's Public-Policy Impact Chain, the manager can trace and assess potential or actual effects of government strategies, policies, and policy instruments on a firm's overall strategy and functional areas. The third component of the EAF, analyzed in this chapter, uses an institutional perspective to identify the distinctive nature of the key actors in the competitive environment at the industry level.

By applying the EAF, managers can systematically examine environmental characteristics, country strategies, and industry structure and dynamics so as to formulate more effective company strategies. Thus, Part I of the book has provided a conceptual framework and analytical tools for addressing the two core questions of business environment analysis: What should a manager analyze in the environment? and How can a manager assess its relevance to the firm? In elaborating and illustrating the analytical framework, Part I has also striven to identify and deepen the reader's understanding of the distinctive nature of the developing county business environment.

We now move on to Part II of the book, which examines selected key issues in each of the functional areas of management. These five chapters focus more specifically on the main decision areas at the firm level. We shall probe in greater detail certain critical problem areas that tend to emerge from the distinctive nature of the LDC business environment. The purpose is both to increase the manager's understanding of these problems and to provide guidance on how to analyze and deal with them.

Managing the Functional Areas

6

Business–Government Relations

Managing the Mega-Force

In developing countries a company's interactions with government constitute, in many if not most instances, its key external relationship. Managing that relationship effectively is of strategic importance to the success of the firm and should be considered as vital a skill for the general manager as the traditional functions of finance, production, marketing, organization, and control, because government actions affect operations in each of these areas as well as overall corporate strategy. Government relations are critical to both local and foreign investors, but a survey of 233 West German firms found that the most serious constraint to their LDC investments was difficulties in dealing with government officials.[1]

The central issue is *how* to manage the business–government relationship. We can envision this interaction as occurring in a special type of marketplace, the political marketplace. The "products" the company seeks are political goods, mainly in the form of government actions. To operate effectively in this marketplace as in other ones, a company should have a conscious strategy. A good manager does not leave the firm's financial, production, or marketing operations to chance; the same should be true for business–government relations. In formulating the business–government strategy, the manager must answer three questions:

1. *What do I need from whom in the government?*
   This, in effect, specifies the firm's demand for particular political

147

goods and identifies the government suppliers of those goods. (How can the government help my business?)

2. *What does the government entity need that I have and how much does it need it?*

   This assesses how the company can "pay" for the political goods and what the perceived value of the company's "currency" is. (How can my business help the government?)

3. *How should I interact with the government?*

   Having assessed the needs and power of the government and the company, the manager can then elaborate and implement a strategy for dealing with the government.

In the following sections, we shall explore how each of these questions[2] can be answered by (1) understanding political actors' needs and power, (2) assessing the company's fulfillment of those needs, and (3) formulating strategic approaches and operating actions for managing the interactions with government.

UNDERSTANDING GOVERNMENT NEEDS AND POWER: POLITICAL MAPPING

The first requisite for effective business–government relations is understanding the political actors with whom the firm must interact. To accomplish this, a manager can create a political "map" that assembles key information about political actors. The first concept behind this map is specificity. Businesses do not deal with "The Government"; rather, they interact with specific institutions and individuals in national, regional, and local governments. Nongovernmental entities that influence government are also relevant political actors, albeit not the direct dispensers of political goods. Businesses interact with government actors at all levels, depending on the nature of the issue or operation. For example, a major investment approval might involve discussions with a country's president or cabinet ministers, and an import authorization might be handled by a low-level bureaucrat in the customs department. The essential departure point in establishing and maintaining effective business–government relations is recognition of the government's institutional and individual heterogeneity. Careful mapping of the firm's external actors in the government will avoid the false assumption of its monolithic structure. In effect, the company is managing a portfolio of relationships.

Thus, the first step in constructing the political map is to specify *who* are the political actors relevant to the firm.[3] As was described in Chapter 4, the EAF uses the Public-Policy Impact Chain to trace how national strategies and policies and their implementation affect industries and firms; political mapping, in effect, attaches institutional actors to the corresponding decision-making points in that chain, thereby revealing the institutional dimension of the policy process. Managers should approach the elaboration of the map from two perspectives. The first is the top-down or macro-micro view. The manager takes the policy chain and designates the potential relevant actor categories for each type of policy and at each level in the chain. At the national policy level for fiscal policy, for example, the main decision-making institutions might be the Ministry of Finance and the Central Bank, within which are certain key groups and individuals such as the ministers, advisers, or department heads. Implementation of fiscal policy would involve other entities, such as the Bureau of Taxation or some unit handling fiscal expenditures (e.g., subsidies), for which the key decision-makers or administrators could be specified. In this manner, one can identify the government decision-makers involved with each category of policy actions and government operations. One might also note which nongovernment political actors are most influential or involved with each of the government actors, for this knowledge may be important in formulating strategy for dealing with specific government decision-makers. This top-down perspective creates a general map of the potential political actors with whom the company will probably have to deal when important issues arise in various policy areas. It provides a forward-looking view of the political terrain.

The second perspective essential to structuring the map is from the bottom up. This is done by asking the managers of the firm's functional areas to specify with which government functionaries they and their staff interact and why. This allows the map to be precise about the actual past points of interaction between the firm and the government. This view provides a historical view of the political terrain. It ensures relevancy, signals to line management the importance of government relations, and involves them from the beginning in the government relations strategy process.

The following examples illustrate various types of political actors likely to figure in the political map.

National-Level Officials. Within the governmental structure, the chief of state and ministerial heads are key. The relative significance of these positions varies across countries, with individuals, and over time. Some may never be relevant actors in the firm's external environment and therefore may not figure into the relationship network. Others will enter or exit the scene depending on the nature of particular issues. For example, a foreign investment decision may formally be handled through a centralized foreign-investment board,[4] or a major domestic investment might be screened by a government development bank. However, other ministers might be greatly interested in seeing the investments realized or blocked. One has to identify the government's broader decision-making process and actors for the issue at hand. Seeing beyond a government's monolithic façade might enable the firm to rally support from interested entities or counteract resistance from opposing entities. Sometimes those holding national positions will be from the military. Even with a civilian government in power, the military is usually quite influential and should therefore be analyzed.

Bureaucrats. The aforementioned high-level government officials are key because they set the policy agenda and wield significant decision-making power. But their tenure in government, or at least in their current position, is usually transitory. A more permanent fixture is often the civil servant or technician who remains operating the governmental apparatus from one administration to another. Of course, even here there may be very high turnover from one government to another if patronage dominates the hiring process. Yet it is with these bureaucrats that the firm interacts at the operations level. They are the actual governmental gatekeepers. Thus, they become key to maintaining the relationship, because they represent continuity in the long run and operating access in the short run. As one MNC manager put it, "It's better to be well known and have influence with people at the Permanent Secretary level— the real people behind the scenes who do the work. I feel just going door-to-door to Ministers is not the right way."[5]

Although central government officials tend to be principal actors, provincial or city functionaries often significantly affect a firm's operations through building permits, operating regulations, taxes, and services. For example, one U.S. investor in a joint venture in China was having a multitude of startup problems. The local mayor, who was keenly interested in seeing the new joint venture company in his city succeed, was instrumental in removing many of the bottlenecks impeding the firm's progress.[6] These local government actors should also be carefully considered in the political map and the relationship portfolio.

Party Officials. Another set of political actors comprises the officials in political parties. They can hold elected posts at the national or local levels or simply be important figures within the various political parties. Although an apolitical strategy would preclude partisan support of these people, it may be important to develop a direct or indirect relationship with both those in power and those out.

Labor Leaders. A semipolitical group that falls within the government-relations network is the labor union movement. In most LDCs unions are extensions of political parties or movements. This means that labor relations are political relations. One cannot understand union behavior fully unless it is placed in a political context.

State-Owned Enterprises. A final institutional patch in the government quilt is the state-owned enterprise. As described in Chapter 5, SOEs are policy instruments that can significantly affect a company's operations as buyer, supplier, competitor, or partner. Thus, they too should be considered a part of the relationship portfolio.

Pressure Groups. Besides these primary political actors, various pressure groups emerge around specific issues that affect their particular interests, e.g., consumer groups protesting price rises, farmer groups lobbying for higher support prices, or industry associations or business groups pressuring for import protection. Although they are not government entities, they are part of the business–government relationship web. Companies may have to deal with these groups directly or at least understand their effects on the political decision-making process.

===

The second step in political mapping is to designate the *interests* of each actor identified on the map. What is managerially relevant is to understand the government's ideological perspective, political preferences, and economic strategy. A critical managerial skill is the capacity to empathize. Managers must avoid being blinded by their own ideological biases; political ethnocentricity produces managerial myopia. If one cannot understand the government actor's point of view, one cannot accurately predict or interpret its behavior. Conversations with government officials from many different LDCs consistently reveal that they hold in higher esteem those private managers who are able to understand the government's perspective and the reasons for their decisions. In this regard, it is important to reiterate that the government is not monolithic; managers should identify its multiple perspectives and interests.

In assessing actors' interests, a manager should distinguish between (1) formal, explicit organizational goals and informal, unwritten objectives; (2) institutional interests and personal interests; (3) short-term imperatives and longer-term interests; and (4) issue-specific concerns and general concerns. The manager tries to understand what is important to the relevant government actor. These needs and concerns will vary across actors and over time. Identifying the specific nature of interests, especially informal and individual ones, is particularly difficult. Nonetheless, it may be erroneous to assume that an actor will behave in a rational, utility-maximizing manner according to some presumed goals; actual interests must be ascertained. The information-gathering process needed to determine such interests often requires significant interaction with government functionaries to get to know them, or consultation with other businesses that interact with those government entities.

The final step is to assess the actors' *power*. One should examine both its degree and its sources—power being defined as the ability to control or influence the behavior or performance of the business (i.e., supply political goods). The manager can use the EAF, particularly the Public-Policy Impact Chain, to identify the government's specific points of impact on the firm. The government actor's power may come, for example, from being able to give or withhold economic resources (e.g., loans, subsidies, taxes, raw material access, government purchases, or market access or protection), operations authorizations (e.g., import licenses or building permits), or decision-making freedom (e.g., price or wage controls). By assessing the significance of the government action or resource to the firm, the manager has a measure of the government's power and hence the firm-specific political risk. The government also has power from what Lindenberg and Crosby call "soft resources," such as social status.[7] The government can "dispense" prestige to a company or damage the company's image by its pronouncements. For example, in annual recognition ceremonies by the Korean government, a citation as a leading exporter was highly valued by companies and eagerly sought after. The degree of power will depend on the significance of the government actor's decisions to a company at a particular time. Thus, it is relative and dynamic.

Having constructed a political map identifying key political actors, their interests, and their power, a manager can next assess how well the company's resources are able to contribute to the government actors' needs.

MEETING GOVERNMENT'S NEEDS: THE SEARCH FOR CONGRUENCY

The business–government relation is a power relationship. Each party has political, economic, social, or administrative resources that the other desires. At the heart of the relationship is the question: *Who needs what from whom, how much, and when?* Especially with multinationals, it is not that governments necessarily *want* them but rather that they *need* them. The government's needs flow mainly out of its developmental and political strategies, and political mapping identifies the interests of specific actors. In general, the greater the need and the better one company is able to meet that need relative to other companies, the greater will be the firm's bargaining power. Congruency is a source of bargaining power. Government actors will favor those firms able to help them meet their needs. In this section we shall first examine the nature of company resources as a source of power. Second, we shall introduce Economic Cost-Benefit Analysis methodology, which is one approach to quantifying public and private congruency. We conclude the section with a discussion of the nature of bargaining power.

Company Resources: Power Through Congruency

The source of a company's bargaining power is the resources it holds that the government actor desires. The power value of those resources is shaped by the supply-and-demand forces surrounding them. If many companies are offering to meet government's needs, then its power is enhanced. But when there are few companies interested but strong demand by government, the companies' power is increased. Relative position within an industry affects power, with dominant firms carrying more leverage than small ones.

Examples of the types of resources companies can use to meet government needs follow:

1. *Equity capital,* especially as foreign exchange, brought a firm more bargaining power in 1989, when international bank lending was shrinking, than it would have a decade earlier, when petrodollars were flowing through banks to the Third World. There are growing indications that developing countries are competing more aggressively to attract foreign investors.[8]

2. *Technology* is an important determinant of bargaining power; low technology or generic products reduce the company's leverage, whereas

proprietary or patented technology increases it. Technology is increasingly seen by governments as the key to accelerating economic growth. The Executive Director of one Chinese city's development corporation stated that his "most important objective was to attract foreign technology that would enable exports so as to earn foreign exchange."[9] In 1984 the Malaysian government adjusted its foreign investment restrictions so that firms producing higher-technology products using national resources or utilizing new technological processes could own up to 70% rather than 30% of the operation.[10]

3. *Employment* opportunities are often highly valued, given chronic and often growing unemployment in many developing countries. Jobs are valued even more if accompanied by training to improve skills significantly. Job creation is the primary benefit sought by governments when they set up free trade zones. Zimbabwe's Marxist Prime Minister, Robert Mugabe, faced with a 23% unemployment rate, welcomed Heinz Company's investment.[11]

4. *Management or industry expertise,* particularly a proven capacity to operate within constraints imposed by the LDC environment, can be a source of power relative to less experienced firms. Ford Motor Company, for example, has provided technical assistance to Latin American governments to help formulate national policies for their automotive industries.[12]

5. *Infrastructure development,* particularly in less developed regions in a country, may contribute significantly to government needs. In Ghana the largest private producer of aluminum in Africa, VALCO, guaranteed to purchase electric power from the government; this guarantee enabled the government to obtain financing needed to construct a large hydroelectric dam, which in turn was essential to the country's entire industrialization strategy.[13]

6. *Market access* is also relevant; with access to external markets the company has greater power than if it is selling only domestically. One of the primary motivations of both Korea's and Taiwan's seeking out foreign investors was to benefit from their marketing abilities and networks in export markets. One MNC manager in an African country asserted: "We have a strong bargaining position in any fight, because we sit on the marketing system in Europe."[14] A Swedish company was able to get the Indian government to authorize significantly higher licensing fees and royalty payments after the company agreed to purchase specified quantities of exports from India over a five-year period.[15]

7. *Tax* or other budgetary contributions may be particularly valued in countries burdened by large fiscal deficits.

The more a company's actual or proposed operations and resources contribute to the government's goals, the stronger is its bargaining position. This contribution can be determined by constructing a Congruency Assessment Matrix that sets forth on the horizontal axis the resources contributed through the business and on the vertical axis the government's goals or needs. The manager can then assess for each resource whether it makes a positive, neutral, or negative contribution to each of the government goals. Table 6.1 illustrates the matrix using the resources listed above and some common government goals at the national level.

Table 6.1 Congruency Assessment Matrix

Government Needs	Business Resources							
	Cap.	For. Ex.	Tec.	Jobs & Trg.	Mgt.	Infra.	Mkts.	Taxes
Economic								
Employment	o	+[a]	o	+	+	o	o	o
Training	o	o	+	+	+	o	o	o
Bal. of payments	+[b]	+/−[c]	o	o	o	o	o	o
Growth	+	+/−	+	+	+	+	+	+
Productivity	+	o	+	+	+	+	o	o
Infrastructure	+	o	o	o	o	+	o	o
Fiscal revenues	o	o	o	o	o	o	o	+
Political								
Economic power*	o	+/−	o	o	o	o	o	+
Credibility*	+	o	+	+	o	+	o	o
Social								
Education	o	o	+	+	+	o	o	+[d]
Health	o	o	o	o	o	+[e]	o	+
Housing	o	o	o	o	o	+	o	+
Income equity	o	o	o	+[f]	o	o	o	+

[a] If labor is substituting for or reducing imported equipment or materials.

[b] If the capital would otherwise leave the country.

[c] The effect will depend on the net balance of foreign exchange generation and use by the business.

[d] Taxes paid by the business are assumed to contribute to public expenditures in social fields.

[e] A business might provide health services or worker housing directly.

[f] If jobs and training are obtained by relatively more disadvantaged workers, these would have a positive distributive effect.

* Economic power derived from economic resources at the disposal of political decision-makers; credibility derived from visible resources such as factories that politicians can point to as having been generated through their policies toward business.

In practice one would use the political map and company particulars to make the needs and resources more specific to increase the precision of the congruency assessment. One might also add "intangible" resources that the government might value. For example, the cooperation of a major business group might lend credibility to the government's policies, or investment by a prestigious multinational might enhance the country's image and attract more foreign investment. Or a foreign firm might be able to assist the host government in seeking aid from the company's home government, a common practice of Japanese MNCs. The manager should also estimate the government's relative priorities for the needs delineated in the matrix. The matrix identifies possible points of congruency and conflict, foci around which the bargaining process can be mounted. This approach of developing a congruency matrix can be used to analyze and plan the company's interaction with government officials at any level. Even for the individual manager, the thought process embodied in the approach can help in planning an interaction with a specific government functionary. A congruency matrix can be quite elaborate or just sketched on the back of an envelope; investment in developing the matrix should be a function of the importance and complexity of each governmental relationship involved in the issue at hand.

Economic Cost-Benefit Analysis: Quantifying Congruency

The congruency matrix is a qualitative approach to assessing the fit of a company's resources with the government's needs. Many LDC governments evaluate new projects, especially foreign investments, using Economic Cost-Benefit Analysis (ECBA) to quantify the investment's desirability for the country and the degree of congruency or disjuncture between the financial return to the company and the economic return to the country.[16] All projects financed by the World Bank (about $10 billion annually) are required to be evaluated using ECBA. It is important for managers to understand ECBA methodology, because it can lead governments to reject projects profitable to the private investor but deemed unattractive from the public perspective or to pressure companies to make investments that are privately unprofitable but calculated to be publicly desirable. What is good for the company is not always good for the country, and vice versa. One review of 183 projects in thirty-seven countries revealed that about one-third had negative economic effects on the countries' GNP even though profitable for private investors.[17] By understanding why these discrepancies might arise, a manager will be better able to negotiate with the government to find ways to achieve congruency.

A fundamental concept in ECBA is that market prices (i.e., those private businesses use in their transactions and financial calculations), do not always accurately reflect the value of those resources to society. This discrepancy arises because conditions of "perfect competition," which would lead to optimally efficient allocation of resources by the ...g countries. We have seen that ...and price controls, tariffs, subsi- ...along with oligopolistic industry ...what they would be under free- ...no longer reflect the true opportu-

...certain a project's true contribu- ...of its effect on GNP. Private ...act on the individual firm. One ...difference is to view the process ...used in the private company's ...their value to society, with that ...i if used in an alternative way, ...s are termed "shadow prices." ...calculations are made in ECBA.

...services a company produces, ...ts" to society of a project. GNP ...oods and services, and ECBA ...economic benefit of consumption ...ie market prices they are willing ...3A. However, when the project's ...fits should be what the country ...rt the goods. This value would ...cally (which would be distorted ...). The Kirloskar-Cummins joint ...s produced in India at $6,700, ...1 be imported at about $3,500. ...ndia would be valued at $3,500 ...rather than the $6,700 KCL would receive. The adjustment reveals that the project's economic benefits to the country appear much lower than the private financial revenue would indicate. Analogously, if the goods produced are or could be exported, their economic value is the price that could be earned in the export market.

Another adjustment to the revenue/benefits figure may be required when the project's output affects the country's foreign-exchange resources, either by replacing the need to import or by generating export earnings. Government controls on foreign exchange often distort the real value of currency. Rather than use the official exchange rate, a "shadow exchange rate" is estimated. This is usually less than the black market rate but more than the official rate. In India the official exchange rate was Rs.4.76: US$1.00 at the time of the Cummins KCL investment in 1962. Government controls were extensive and the black market rate was much higher; in fact, the rupee was devalued in 1966 by about 50%. If we estimate the shadow exchange rate in 1962 to have been 50% higher, then the value of the KCL production would have to be increased accordingly to reflect the real value of the foreign exchange saved by not importing. That is, the value of the imports would be increased by the additional real cost of the foreign exchange that would have to be used up to acquire them. Thus, the "economic benefit" to the country of the KCL engines would equal the price of imports, $3,500, increased by 50% to reflect the shadow exchange rate premium, increasing the value to $5,250 and hence the attractiveness to the country.

Adjusting Costs. The company's investment and operating costs constitute the resources used up in this project rather than applied to alternative uses in the economy. Thus, they are real costs to the society.

1. *Investment costs.* Capital equipment, buildings, or other fixed assets are entered as costs in ECBA when they are assigned to the project, because at that point their use in other projects is precluded. When they are paid for is disregarded. If any portion of these assets was imported, its import price must be adjusted by the shadow exchange rate. Thus, if 60% of KCL's $5,439,000 plant and equipment investment was imported, then that share of the investment costs would be increased by the shadow exchange rate premium over the official rate, which we estimated above as 50%, or 1.5 times the official rate. The calculation would be:

local currency share   + (foreign exchange share × 1.5)
40% × $5,439,000 +   (60% × $5,439,000 × 1.5)
$2,175,600   + $4,895,100   = $7,070,700

Thus, the total investment costs under ECBA would be valued at $7,070,000 rather than the $5,439,000 actually expended by the private investors.

2. *Labor costs*. The economic opportunity cost of labor to society is not the firm's actual wage bill but what that labor could earn (i.e., contribute to GNP) in its next best alternative use. If there is much unemployment or underemployment, the value or "shadow wage rate" that ECBA would attach would be lower than the nominal wage. If one-fourth of the KCL workforce was drawn from the unskilled labor force, in the ECBA the wage costs would be valued at the shadow wage rate of, say, 40% of the wage being paid by KCL. This adjustment lowers project costs, thereby contributing to a societal return on investment higher than would occur under the private financial return analysis. The skilled workers KCL hired and had other equally remunerative job opportunities in the Poona industrial area, so the market price of their labor was probably a good estimate of their true opportunity costs. Therefore, no wage adjustment would be needed.

3. *Materials and service inputs*. Any imported inputs or local inputs for which there exists the alternative opportunity for importing or exporting would be valued at the international price adjusted by the shadow exchange rate. Nontradable goods, e.g., internal railway transport or nonexportable electric power, would be valued at their local cost.[18] For KCL 70% of its costs was for parts and materials that could have been imported if the government allowed. Even though KCL was obliged to increase its domestic content to almost 85%, the opportunity costs to India would be the import prices of these inputs increased by the shadow exchange rate premium. Whereas the local cost for KCL to acquire these inputs was $4,228 per engine, the import price was estimated at $2,621, which when increased by the shadow exchange rate premium of 1.5 gave an economic cost of $3,931.

4. *Taxes, tariffs, subsidies*. The economic cost of producing a good, unlike private costing, should exclude all direct and indirect taxes, subsidies, and tariffs or duties. These transactions are merely transfers between the private producer and the government and do not produce or use up any real resources. Thus the income, excise, property, and sales taxes and the import duties KCL paid the Indian government and recorded as costs in the private financial analysis are excluded from the ECBA. Similarly excluded are the tax credits and export subsidies KCL received from the government. Although these transfer payments are relevant to the government's fiscal concerns, they do not affect GNP and are therefore excluded from ECBA.

Discounting. As in financial analysis, ECBA calculates a return on investment by discounting the project's life stream of benefits and costs to their present value. The discount rate is the opportunity cost of capital and can be estimated as the weighted average of the real rates of interest of the various alternative sources of capital. The government agency carrying out the ECBA will have estimated this "shadow interest rate." Local economists or those from international development agencies can also provide estimates.

Unlike financial analysis, in ECBA domestic loan amortizations and interest payments are excluded from the cash flow because they are simply financial transfers that do not use up real resources. The loan and equity funds will already have entered the analysis as investment costs; to include them again would be double-counting. However, when the capital has come from abroad, and dividends and debt-servicing payments will flow out of the country, these are real costs to the country because foreign exchange is being lost.[19] These flows would be adjusted by the shadow exchange rate. The net flows are discounted, and if the present value is positive, the project would make a positive contribution to the country's GNP. Alternatively, as with financial analysis, one could calculate an internal rate of return based on the pro-forma flows and then see if this rate is greater than the opportunity cost of capital, i.e., the shadow interest rate. This is analogous to a private firm's hurdle investment rate.

Using ECBA as a Management Tool. Knowing the ECBA methodology ensures, at a minimum, that a manager will understand this "technical language" when it is used by government officials. More ambitiously and importantly, the manager can use ECBA as a management tool in negotiating with governments. It can contribute to the search for congruency between government needs and company operations by identifying and quantifying the divergencies between private-return analyses and ECBA.

Figure 6.1 can help us understand the implications of congruence and noncongruence between the public rate of return on an investment calculated with ECBA (y-axis) and the private rate of return calculated via financial analysis (x-axis). The figure is divided into subfigures (a–d), each one illustrating an additional aspect of the public–private comparison.[20] We shall discuss each subfigure.

Subfigure (a) shows that when the public ECBA and private financial rates of return are equal, say a 20% return, they fall on the congruency line. This means that both the country and the company are benefiting equally from the resources invested in the project. Any deviation from the congruency line means that the project is yielding higher returns for one side than the other. If the rates fall to the left of the congruency line, the resultant noncongruency favors the government; such a point is shown in subfigure (a) as the intersection of a 20% ECBA rate and a 5% private rate. Conversely, if the rates fall to the right of the line, the noncongruency favors the company, as is illustrated by the intersection point of a private rate of 20% and an ECBA rate of 5%.

Congruency of rates of return does not automatically make a project desirable to either a government or a company. What is critical is the absolute levels of the returns. As subfigure (b) shows, governments and companies have "hurdle rates of return" below which any project is unacceptable. These public and private hurdle rates are not necessarily equal, and empirically the private hurdle rates tend to be higher than the public hurdle rate (which is the opportunity cost of capital). In subfigure (b) we have assumed a public hurdle rate of 10% and a private hurdle rate of 20%. Any investment that yields a private internal rate of return less than 20% and a public ECBA rate of less than 10% would be unacceptable to government and company, falling into subfigure (b)'s shaded region of joint unacceptability. Neither party would want to proceed with the project on economic grounds. However, any investment with a private return less than 20% but with a public return of 10% or above would be unacceptable to the company but acceptable to the government; conversely, any investment with a public rate below 10% and a private rate of at least 20% would be rejected by the government but accepted by the company. These disjunctures in return levels place the government and the company in conflict; one party would like to proceed with the investment while the other would not. This situation signals the need to redesign the investment so as to achieve mutually acceptable returns.

If the absolute levels of returns are equal to or above the public and private hurdle rates (10% and 20% in our example), the project can be mutually acceptable, even without congruency. In subfigure (c), we see that if an investment had a private rate of 20% and a public rate of 10%, there is an area of acceptable noncongruency favoring the company. If the public return were 25% instead of 10%, and the private return was still 20%, the acceptable noncongruency would favor the government.

Subfigure (d) depicts the challenge of project design and redesign. First, if the investment can be configured to increase both the public and private returns simultaneously, there are joint gains regardless of noncongruency, i.e., the intersection point of the returns moves outward on the graph. The second challenge is to reduce the noncongruence without reducing the absolute level of return of either part. In subfigure

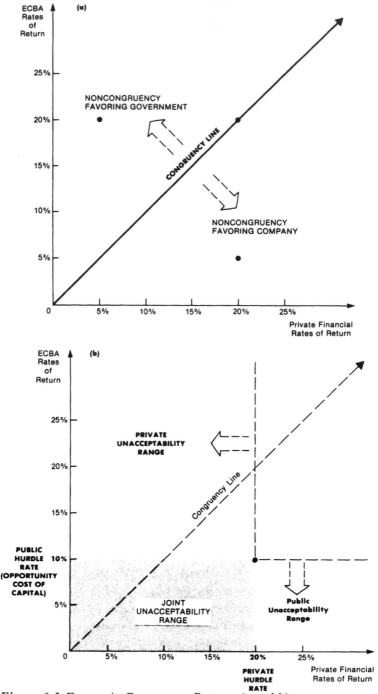

Figure 6.1 Economic Congruency Patterns (a and b)

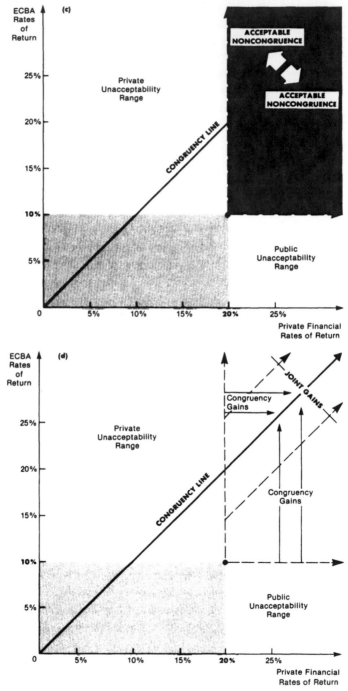

Figure 6.1 Economic Congruency Patterns (c and d)

(d) the intersection point moves closer to the congruency line. These congruency gains lessen the underlying and possibly dysfunctional tension that noncongruence can produce.

Understanding these different aspects of congruency and noncongruency provides a basis for designing ways to reconfigure projects to achieve a positive sum game by increasing the returns from the country's vantage point without necessarily reducing, and perhaps even increasing, the company's returns. Such project adjustments might lead the government to value in its ECBA the company's revenues higher and its costs lower. For example, if the company could profitably add export operations to the project, the value of those export revenues would be increased in the government's ECBA because of the shadow exchange rate premium. KCI succeeded in generating exports, thereby enhancing its attractiveness to the government while strengthening Cummins's global marketing network. Both the public and private rates of return were shifted outward toward the joint gains indicated in subfigure 6.1(d). On the cost side, a company might, for example, adjust its production technology to use more labor-intensive methods and employ more unskilled labor. This might reduce the company's capital investment and lower overall production costs even if the wage bill rose. In the ECBA calculation, labor costs would be reduced as a result of the lower shadow wage rate, thereby increasing the public rate of return. This could produce congruency gains, i.e., the improved public return moves it closer to the private return, which remains unchanged or perhaps increases. Appendix D provides a more detailed example of the ECBA methodology and how it can guide the redesign of investment projects so as to enhance their attractiveness to a country and a company.

Even where governments do not formally use ECBA as an investment screening tool, companies can make these analyses and use them in their presentations to government officials to assure them (and the company itself) that the proposed investment will make a positive economic contribution to the country. Not all economic benefits or costs can be easily quantified, but they should be included qualitatively in the assessment. For example, a positive "externality" would be the construction of an access road from a highway to the factory that also enables neighboring farmers to move their produce to market more efficiently. A negative "externality" might be pollution of a river due to a factory's waste discharges.

The government's goals, of course, are not exclusively economic and cannot be fully captured through ECBA methodology (although technical refinements attaching weights to sociopolitical goals such as income

distribution effects have been developed). However, it and the qualitative approach used in the congruency assessment matrix enable the company to plan its interaction with government better. Before we turn to the strategic approaches to these interactions, some additional comments are in order about the nature of bargaining power.

The Nature of Bargaining Power

Business–government relations inherently involve bargaining.[21] Bargaining power tends to erode over time. The source of bargaining obsolescence is changes in the supply and demand forces for company and government resources. On the demand side, a government's needs change continually as the country develops. The development process makes government needs a moving target; political shifts tend to make the target even more mobile. A company's bargaining power stemming from the contribution of a needed resource erodes as that need evolves into an old or met need. When the source of power is the transfer of assets, leverage begins to evaporate as soon as the transfer has occurred; asset immobility due to the nature of the investment (e.g., a mining project or a paper mill) creates barriers to exit and therefore reduces the company's bargaining power.[22] On the supply side, the emergence of other foreign or local companies willing to supply new resources (such as improved technologies) or changes in industry position (the emergence of a business group's company or an SOE) can reduce the company's bargaining power. The obsolescence phenomenon is seen as relatively inevitable in natural-resource industries.[23] In manufacturing, however, the shift of power to the government does not necessarily occur, particularly for firms that are more technology-intensive and globally integrated.[24] Thus, the bargaining relationship is dynamic, requiring continual monitoring and renewed strategic responses.

Before we move on to the formulation of strategies for interacting with the government, it is important to remember that reactions by the political apparatus are company-specific. Political forces and events carry different implications for different companies, so one must scrutinize the company's specific characteristics to forecast the probable impact. Nonetheless, a set of five general company characteristics might serve as predictive parameters to indicate at least the intensity of the government's scrutiny of and concern about a company:

- *Ownership.* The more the ownership is foreign (including national ethnic minorities), the more politically sensitive is the company's presence.

- *Product.* The more socially basic, economically critical, or politically symbolic a product is, the higher its sociopolitical importance will be and the greater will be the government's concern.
- *Buyers.* The more organized the company's customers are, the greater their lobbying power and ability to elicit government actions.
- *Technology.* The more capital-intensive the technology, given LDCs' generally small market size and scarce capital resources, the greater the likelihood of a concentrated and oligopolistic industry structure, making the firm more subject to government supervision.
- *Size.* The bigger the enterprise, the greater its visibility and political salience.

Close government scrutiny resulting from these company characteristics does not necessarily result in negative political actions. The consequences of the risk are modulated by the company's bargaining strategy and process.

MANAGING GOVERNMENT RELATIONS: STRATEGIC APPROACHES

To manage the diverse portfolio of government relationships effectively, business people must use multiple strategies tailored to the actors and issues at hand. Despite this imperative for diversity, managers can group their strategic approaches into four categories: alter, avoid, accede, and ally.

- *Alter.* The company can bargain to get the government to alter the policy, the instrument, or the action of concern.
- *Avoid.* The company can make strategic moves that bypass the risk or impact of the government's action.
- *Accede.* The company can adjust its operations to comply with a government requirement.
- *Ally.* Sometimes the company can insulate itself from risks by creating strategic alliances.

A key step in choosing among these strategic approaches is establishing clear objectives. This requires assessing both the strategic importance of the issue at hand to the company and its power position. The company's action will engender a reaction by the government entity involved in the process. This possible counter-strategy should be projected; it will be a function of the importance of the issue to the government and its power position. The previous sections provided tools to make these assessments of relative importance and power: political mapping, the congruency matrix, and ECBA reveal the government's needs and how well the company's resources will meet them. Using the Public-Policy Impact Chain, the manager can judge the criticalness to the firm of the impact of specific government actions.

These measures of relative power and importance provide general guidance for selecting among the four approaches. Figure 6.2 presents a choice matrix. If the issue is highly important to the firm relative to the government and the company is in a relatively high power position, then the strategy of choice would be to *alter* the government's action. When the opposite occurs (that is, when the issue is of relatively low importance and the company's power is relatively low), the firm should *accede* to the government's wishes. If the issue is of low importance to the firm but high importance to the government, the company might choose to *avoid* confronting the government even though the firm has relatively high power. Lastly, when the issue is highly important but the firm is in a weak power position, it should strive to *ally* with others to ameliorate the effects of the government action. The "Ally" strategy, besides being used just to insulate the firm from the government's actions, might be chosen to increase the firm's bargaining power so that it can then carry out an "Alter" strategy. In some circumstances other permutations might be called for. For example, if alliances are not feasible but

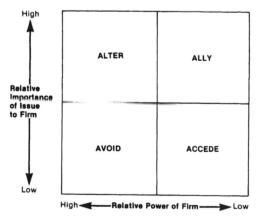

Figure 6.2 Strategic Approaches to Government Relations

avoiding the impact through changes in the company's operation is, then the "Avoid" approach might replace the "Ally" strategy. We shall now elaborate on each of the "Four A" approaches to dealing with the government.

Alter

In attempting to alter the government's policy or action, the manager should remember that the bargaining process is generally a give-and-take phenomenon. As Lax and Sebenius point out, cooperation and competition are both operative in negotiations as the parties try to create value through cooperation and then compete to claim the value created.[25] Value-creation opportunities may exist because of differences in the government's and the firm's evaluation criteria, capabilities, risk aversion, time preferences, forecasts, or outcome valuation.[26] The congruency matrix and ECBA can reveal opportunities for joint gains. What is also needed is creative conflict management. Flexibility and innovativeness are desirable traits in achieving a positive-sum game result. If both business and government come out ahead from the negotiating process, the company may then have the additional bonus of creating goodwill with the government actors involved, and this may enhance future negotiations. Zero-sum games in which the company wins but the government loses, or vice versa, are usually not sustainable as an ongoing bargaining strategy for managing business–government relations.

The types of analysis discussed here enable the manager to be more specific and systematic about which elements of the government's actions should be points for negotiations (an "Alter" strategy) and which should be dealt with through one of the other approaches. For example, KCL faced the technical impossibility of complying in the short run with the government's required level of domestic content. Rather than try to change the basic policy of increasing local production (which was highly important to the government's import-substitution industrialization policy), KCL sought an adjustment in the way the policy was administered, namely, an extension of the deadline for achieving the domestic content levels. The timing was critical to KCL but of less importance to the government, which was interested mainly in having local production increase and obtaining the higher technology Cummins Engine offered. By getting more time, KCL was able to pursue a supplier development program that enabled it to overcome problems caused by the government's policy. In effect, it used an "Alter" strategy that facilitated the later implementation of an "Accede" strategy.

Cummins also used an "Alter" strategy to maintain its 50% position in KCL, even though government legislation in 1973 restricted foreign equity participation to 40%. Cummins was able to use its access to foreign markets as a key resource in meeting the government's need for foreign exchange. KCL began exporting certain engines to Cummins dealers in other countries in the region. These foreign-exchange earnings were very important to the government and led it to authorize the needed import licenses and even award KCL a medal of distinction for its export performance.[27] Additionally, Cummins continued to provide infusions of new technology that contributed to the government's industrial development goal. The government continued to approve industrial licenses for KCL to expand capacity. Both the government and KCL experienced joint gains: The government's development goals were being assisted and KCL's profits were growing. Between 1973 and 1982 the company's net profits increased at a compound annual rate of 39%, reaching $8.2 million in 1982 on revenues of $89.5 million; annual dividends and technical fees to Cummins Engine had almost reached the $2 million level.[28]

IBM failed to get the Indian government to alter its policy requiring minority foreign ownership. The issue was of equally high importance to both IBM and India; neither would give way, so the sovereign power of the host government prevailed and IBM chose to pull out of India. In Mexico, however, IBM succeeded in getting the government to alter its "Mexicanization" requirement so as to allow IBM to retain a wholly owned subsidiary in exchange for increased equity investment, intensified development of local suppliers, and access to IBM's global marketing network. Robeli Libero, president of IBM Latin America, commented: "You have to tune the company's objectives to the country's objectives."[29] Capital, technology, and markets were the key resources creating its bargaining power. Mexican policy-makers saw the presence of "Big Blue" as pulling the country's entire computer industry up to an internationally competitive level in this critical global industry.[30]

Avoid

Avoiding or bypassing the effect of government actions may be possible through adjustments in the company's strategy or its operating procedures. For example, when a Latin American government's price controls on milk made its production unprofitable, several dairies shifted their product line to yogurt and cheese, which were not price-controlled. A tractor manufacturer in another Latin American country overcame the problems

of excess capacity (caused by the government's licensing too many producers for the size of the market) by shifting production to farm implements
and replacement parts. KCL solved the problem of a collapse in demand
for diesel engines (due to the government's tightening of funds for original
equipment manufacturers) by using its facilities to produce on a subcontract basis small-horsepower engines for Kirloskar, manufacturing parts,
taking up job orders for specially designed engines, and seeking out
new users in marine engineering.[31] In countries where restrictions on
foreign investment are particularly onerous, some companies have shifted
from a direct-investment strategy to providing management contracts or
licensing (see Chapter 10).[32]

Accede

The company might choose to adjust its operations to comply with
government requirements for several different reasons. Sometimes there
may be no other choice: The company may simply not have the power
to bargain for a change, or there may be no feasible way to adjust
operations to avoid the impact nor any available alliance. PepsiCo set
a high priority on penetrating the large Indian market, so it complied
with the government's foreign exchange requirements by promising to
earn five times more foreign exchange than it spent on importing Pepsi
ingredients. To accomplish this it will export tomato paste and fruit
juices and carry out research to develop export crops. Robert Beeby,
president of Pepsi-Cola International, explained: "We're selling something that's nonessential, so we have to give them more than we're
getting."[33]

Even when the company might have strong bargaining power, the
issue may not be sufficiently important to justify expending the firm's
scarce "political capital" to negotiate a change in it. One should select
one's battles carefully. For example, a company exporting flower seeds
was required by the government to obtain an agricultural export license
for each shipment. This licensing requirement had been instituted because
in a previous year large exports of grain had left the country short and
had forced food imports. The company could have petitioned for a change
in the policy that would have exempted flower seeds because they were
a nonfood crop. Compliance, however, entailed tolerable (albeit bother-
some) administrative effort. Delays in processing the license requests
were managed by submitting the requests in advance of production.
Thus, the low importance of the issue and the feasibility of compliance
made an "Accede" strategy preferable to an "Alter" strategy. Attempting

to get the government to grant an exemption might have required significant management time, irritated government officials by disrupting existing procedures, and brought unwelcome governmental scrutiny of or interference with other aspects of the company's operations.

Even when other approaches are feasible, acceding might be advantageous. If competitors will be affected more adversely, then compliance creates competitive advantage. Often business groups are able to absorb the impact of government actions more readily than individual firms. For example, the group's diversified businesses allow unaffected operations to carry the adversely affected business, or the group's larger administrative staff and network of contacts might enable it to handle increased bureaucratic burdens imposed by the government. Acceding to a new regulation might actually open up new opportunities. For example, in acceding to the Indian government's requirement by diluting its majority ownership in its Indian subsidiary down to the 40% level, Ciba-Geigy was able to benefit from the privileges bestowed only on Indian companies, which included expanding capacity and producing higher-margin pharmaceutical products.[34] Compliance also might be a way of generating goodwill with the government, which could be of value in subsequent negotiations.

Ally

Developing strategic alliances may be necessary when the company alone does not have sufficient bargaining power to get the government to alter its action or to avoid being exposed to its adverse effects. The "Ally" strategy can be an intermediate strategy to enable a company to implement an "Alter" strategy, or it can be an independent strategy aimed at insulating the company from adverse effects of the government's actions. For example, a joint venture between an MNC and a local company may give both some protection from government actions that they would otherwise not have had. Piper's joint venture with EMBRAER, the Brazilian aircraft manufacturing SOE, insulated it from the import restrictions imposed on other foreign aircraft exporters. Burroughs set up a computer joint venture with India's second largest business group, Tata, which enabled it to expand and fill the void left by IBM's exit. An alliance between a company and a local or state government might offset actions by the federal government. An alliance with the company's workers, suppliers, or customers might preempt actions that would seriously reduce a company's level of operations. Some companies have brought politically influential individuals onto their boards of directors to help insulate their operations from rash or adverse governmental actions. Broadening the network of groups with vested interest in the continuing success of the company is an antidote for obsolescing bargaining power.

Other Options

Another way of dealing with certain kinds of governmental risk is to take out insurance. Multinationals can generally obtain from their home governments political risk insurance that protects their assets from extreme political actions and noncommercial risks such as expropriation, wars and revolution, and inconvertibility exposure. Some insurance also covers losses due to natural disasters. In the United States such insurance can be purchased through the government's Overseas Private Investment Corporation (OPIC). OPIC insurance coverage is limited to 90% of the investment but is also available for retained earnings.[35] Table 6.2 lists insurance availability in seventeen countries. Some large private insurance companies also offer specially designed policies, although they tend to carry rather heavy premiums and vary by the type and location of the investment. Government programs charge annual premiums in the 0.5%– 1.5% range, while private insurers quote rates in the 0.75%–7.0% range. About 20% of the FDI in developing countries between 1977 and 1981 was insured under national programs.[36] In April 1988 ten developed and twenty-five developing countries with the assistance of the World Bank established the Multilateral Investment Guarantee Agency (MIGA), which will also offer insurance against noncommercial risks. The agency has subscribed capital of $1 billion and aims to supplement the existing national programs and serve to improve the investment climate in LDCs.[37]

There are other international mechanisms that companies and governments can utilize to help resolve disputes through mediation or arbitration. These would include the International Centre for Settlement of Investment Disputes (ICSID) and the International Chamber of Commerce (ICC) Court of Arbitration.

A related topic to be discussed is the company's political posture. Companies, particularly larger ones, are inescapably actors in the political arena, because their economic actions have political ramifications. The strategic issue for managers is how to exercise their economic power and therefore their political influence. There are two principal options for a company's political strategy.

The first is a partisan approach, which entails supporting one particular political group rather than others. It can also involve exercising influence

Table 6.2 Foreign Direct Investment Risk Insurance Programs

Country	Insuring Institution	Type of Investments	Annual Premium[a]	Period Covered[b]
Australia	Export Financing Insurance Corp. (EFIC)	Equity Loans Licenses Royalties	1% + 0.5% in-scription fee	1–15 yrs.
Austria	Oesterreicher Kontelbank (OKB)	Equity Loans Licenses Royalties	0.5%	1–20 yrs.
Belgium	Office National du Ducroire (OND)	Equity Loans Profits	0.75%–0.8%	1–15 yrs.
Canada	Export Development Corpo-ration (EDC)	Equity Loans Licenses Royalties Leases Service Contracts	1%	1–15 yrs.
Denmark	Danish International Devel-opment Agency (DA-NIDA)	Equity Loans Licenses Royalties	0.5%	1– 5 yrs.

Table 6.2 Foreign Direct Investment Risk Insurance Programs (*Continued*)

Country	Insuring Institition	Type of Investements	Annual Premium[a]	Period Coverage[b]
Finland	Vientitakuuclitos (VTL)	Equity Loans Licenses Royalties Profits	0.5%–0.7%	1–20 yrs.
France	Banque Francaise du Commerce Exterior (BFCE) & Compagnie Francaise d'Assurance pour le Commerce (COFACE)	Equity Long-term loans Profits	0.4%–0.7%	1–20 yrs.
Germany	Treuarbeit	Equity Loans Licenses Royalties	0.1–0.5% inscription fee	1–20 yrs.
Italy	Special Section for Export Credit Insurance (SACE)	Equity Licenses	0.8%	1–15 yrs.
Japan	Overseas Investment Insurance Scheme	Equity Loans	0.55%–1.3%	1–15 yrs.
Netherlands	Netherlands Credit Insurance Company (NCM)	Equity Loans	0.8%	1–15 yrs.

New Zealand	Export Guarantee Office (EXGO)	Equity	Vary by project	5–15 yrs.
Norway	Export Credit Guarantee Institution (GIEK)	Equity Loans Profits	0.7%	1–20 yrs.
Sweden	Swedish Export Credits Guarantee Board (EKN)	Equity Loans	0.7%	1–20 yrs.
Switzerland	Office for Guarantee of Export risks (GERO)	Equity Loans Profits	1.25% + 4% of profits	1–20 yrs.
United Kingdom	Export Credit Guarantee Department (ECGD)	Equity Loans Licenses Profits	1%	1–15 yrs.
United States	Overseas Private Investment Corporation (OPIC)	Equity Loans Licenses Royalties Leases	1.15%	1–20 yrs.

[a] As % of total investment.
[b] Years represent minimum and maximum periods.

SOURCE: *Investing in Developing Countries* (Paris: Organizations for Economic Co-Operation and Development, 5th Edition, 1983) pp. 39–108).

over a wide range of economic and noneconomic policies and even over the selection of political candidates and government officials. There are many examples of the exercise of this role of political power broker by local business groups and multinationals. This option tends to exist where the degree of development of political institutions is low. Businesses, being more organized, move into this political vacuum to exercise influence. As countries develop and political institutions mature, private businesses tend to be crowded out of the political arena as direct actors, but they still have the option of influence through partisan support. This approach can garner favorable treatment from the government in power as long as it remains in office. When it leaves, either democratically or via a coup d'état, the company's partisan political assets may quickly become liabilities. Companies generally outlast governments, so partisan politics can jeopardize the firm's long-run viability.

The other option is an apolitical stance in which the firm seeks political neutrality and restricts its exercise of power to bargaining about the economic issues surrounding its operation. Some managers mistakenly interpret an apolitical policy to mean noninvolvement in politics. In LDCs' highly politicized environments, involvement is inescapable. In fact, much political skill is needed to implement an apolitical strategy. For example, many MNCs and local companies continued to operate successfully in Nicaragua after the 1979 revolution. They consistently employed an apolitical strategy before and after the revolution, demonstrating considerable political acumen. In contrast, many of the companies that had closely aligned themselves with the previous regime had their businesses expropriated.[38]

MANAGING GOVERNMENT RELATIONS: OPERATING ISSUES

The preceding section emphasized the general strategic approaches to dealing and bargaining with the government. This final section will address three more specific aspects of implementing business–government relations strategies. The first concerns the critical role of communicating with government, the second deals with how companies should organize themselves to handle their government relations, and the third addresses the perplexing problem and risk of corruption, which is often present in interactions with government officials.

Communicating with Government

The business–government relationship can become an asset only through the investment of management time and attention. We have discussed the substance of the investment in the preceding sections. The mechanism through which the investment is made and maintained is mainly a *communications process.*

This should be handled not in an *ad hoc* manner but rather strategically. It should have explicit objectives, a plan for developing specific channels of communication, designated responsibilities for doing the communicating, guidelines for its substance and mode, and systematic processing of the resultant information. Handling the communication process should be an important function of the company's management information and control system.

There should be multiple channels of communication corresponding to the multiplicity of government actors. These channels should be both formal and informal and should involve individuals both outside and inside government. As one MNC manager explained,

> In what is after all a very parochial environment, I feel that this is important. I would say that we haven't cultivated this side enough, and we're taking steps to do so. Informal contacts with people in government are extremely important—far more important than we realize. Because when you do run into trouble as we have . . . you feel that you want friends in court.[39]

Nongovernment political actors identified by political mapping may be key communication conduits and information sources. Breadth of sources provides variety of perspectives and can serve as a cross-check on the validity of gathered data. It also adds flexibility to the communications strategy, because some channels may be more appropriate than others for certain types of communication.

The communications process should be a two-way flow. Gathering data by scanning the political environment can provide an early-warning system and essential inputs to managerial decision-making, but information must also be communicated to the sources. This is necessary both to achieve the company's strategic goals and to create a reciprocal relationship in information flows. The company will often have information useful to government officials but not otherwise available to them. In some situations, however, minimizing interaction with government may be appropriate. For relatively smaller firms, paperwork relationships may be all that is needed; low visibility may increase operating flexibility. But even this approach requires high awareness of political structure and processes.

One purpose of the communications process is to educate government officials about the nature and problems of the business. This can help eliminate misperceptions and place discussions on a more rational, problem-solving basis.[40] This mutual understanding of perspectives and problems is essential to building trust. A closed communications strategy (to give only information that is demanded) breeds suspicion and an inclination for greater control of the company by the government. One large company in a South American country provided the government with cost and output data and technical advice. This openness was viewed as a means of generating the government's trust, helping it to understand the industry, and enabling it to control the misinformation and illegal behavior of the company's competitors.

Organizing for Business–Government Relations

The task of managing multiple relationships with government should not be delegated to a specialized department of government affairs. In developing countries, the impact of government policies and actions on company operations is so pervasive that company personnel in all functional areas and on all levels generally have some degree of interaction with government actors. Organizationally, government relations should be integrated into the entire organization: Responsibility for effective business–government relations must reside with all managers for their respective operating areas. Each should understand and manage his or her piece of the political map. This does not mean, however, that business–government relations should be fragmented and unrelated. Coherence and coordination comes through the overall corporate strategy discussed above, which provides guidance to the line implementers.

Even though responsibility lies mainly with line managers, a staff department for government relations and political analysis can play an important supportive role. Data collection, analysis of specific issues or events, assistance in strategy formulation, and even direct involvement in negotiations are functions that can be of considerable use to top and line managers. As in other areas, some aspects of political analysis can benefit from the expertise of specialists. Political scientists or individuals with extensive experience in government can often provide insights and advice not otherwise available.

Political analysis departments or specialists use a variety of techniques.

The Delphi technique, for example, involves requesting a panel of experts to state their individual opinions on a given political situation. These opinions are then consolidated into a group distributional opinion, which is returned to each individual for modification. This process is repeated several times. Another technique many MNCs use is the "old hands" method. This involves hiring specialists (including former foreign service officers or local political specialists) with in-depth knowledge of a special region or country. Reliance is placed mainly on their intuition and judgment rather than on a systematic analysis. From either of these methods one can develop political scenarios. Other approaches have involved more formal models that attempt to quantify various forms of political risks.[41] Much of the focus to date in the political analysis field has been on political risk *assessment*, and the locus has been the home-country headquarters.

Our approach focuses on political risk *management* by operating managers in the field. It is essential that managers throughout the organization develop the skills of managing their multiple relations with government entities. This requires a clear message from top management regarding the importance of this part of their responsibilities. Mahini and Wells identified four approaches used by MNCs to organize business–government relations in their international network of subsidiaries.[42] In the "Policy Approach," headquarters sets corporate-wide policies on key issues and does not allow deviation by subsidiaries. IBM's nonnegotiable position on joint ventures epitomizes this approach; its high bargaining power due to its technological and marketing strength has enabled it to implement this global policy with high success. (In terms of our strategy framework for business–government relations, IBM has employed an "Alter" strategy to gain exceptions to governments' joint venture requirements.) At the other end of the organizational spectrum is the "Diffuse Approach," in which the subsidiary managers handle business–government relations with little guidance from headquarters. This approach takes full advantage of local managers' knowledge of the country situation and matches responsibility with authority. Companies whose international operations were only a small part of total operations or whose strategy was very country-centered rather than globally integrated used this approach.

In between these extremes was a "Centralized Approach," in which headquarters played a major direct role in business–government relations (often using a special government relations department); however, the bargaining position was negotiable rather than universal. International oil companies used this approach; their operations were so integrated that centralized negotiating positions were essential, and the economic and political importance of the oil sector to the governments required high-level management involvement. Unlike IBM, their bargaining power was not necessarily large relative to the governments' or OPEC's. In many instances an "accede" strategy was inescapable, but the companies' integrated structure meant that consistent actions across countries was essential. Under a "Coordinated Approach" primary responsibility for business–government relations was left with country managers, but headquarters promoted a process of joint consultations and information-sharing across countries to coordinate bargaining positions. The firms using this approach tended to be in global industries that were less integrated internationally than oil, for example, pharmaceuticals or automobiles.

The international organizational approaches to managing business–government relations, like our "4-A" business–government strategies, should be seen as a portfolio of options. Different ones can be selected depending on the specific issue and governmental relation being considered. A monolithic approach to the inherent heterogeneity of government relations is nonsensical. Furthermore, country managers still must manage the direct government relationships regardless of headquarters' organizational approach.

The Corruption Problem

Mordida, matabiche, dash, bribe—every language and country, developed and developing, has its name for it. It is a universal phenomenon that confronts the business manager: the payment by private individuals and organizations to public officials to elicit desired treatment. It is an aspect of business–government relationships that presents the manager with difficult legal and ethical problems.

Bribes take many forms and occur at many levels. At lower bureaucratic levels they are sometimes called "facilitating payments" aimed at accelerating the performance of some public service, such as getting a replacement part out of customs or authorizing a travel visa. Telephone operators in India took payoffs for placing international calls on a priority basis.[43] Government controls create gatekeepers who are always tempted to extract a toll from those wishing to pass through.

Some argue that such payments are desirable: They make bureaucrats more responsive and increase productivity; they compensate for the low wages paid to public servants; and they even constitute a form of income redistribution. Bribes are often seen as minor "fee for service" payments, part of the daily operating cost of doing business. At higher levels of government, payments tend to be larger and are used to influence major decisions. The initiative for payment may come from either the payer or the recipient. In either case, the transaction is generally illegal and unethical, regardless of "common business practices" prevailing in the country. Political payments to influence public decision-makers represent an abuse of power and a distortion of public purpose.

Most developing countries have legal sanctions against bribes, but these often are not consistently enforced. The presumed enforcers may even be beneficiaries of payoffs. It takes considerable political will to confront and overcome corrupt practices, especially when they have become widespread. Corruption is an insidious phenomenon in that the more prevalent it becomes, the more resigned a society becomes to it, so that even honest officials, instead of being praised, may be seen as naïve for not having exploited their positions. However, though bribery may be common, that does not mean it is widely condoned. Taking the higher road may require more patience, but it can produce superior results. A manager in one African country recounted his experience:

> Getting the initial approval for our project was the hard part. Everybody wanted to stick their finger in the pie. We resisted that because we didn't want to get into a favor-giving situation. So we just kept pressing for approval by stressing the benefits of the project for the government and the country: employment, foreign-exchange earnings, and rural development. It took nine months, but we finally got the okay without buying anybody.[44]

For U.S. multinationals, the Foreign Corrupt Practices Act of 1977 creates significant legal penalties if they or their subsidiaries are convicted of making payments directly or indirectly to foreign officials, political parties, or candidates for the purpose of securing the recipient's assistance in obtaining business for the company. The act also carries record-keeping and internal control provisions, thereby placing a special responsibility on companies' management control systems.[45] It applies to all companies registered with the Securities Exchange Commission and is enforced by the SEC and the Department of Justice. Violation of the law can result in fines of up to $10,000 and imprisonment up to five years for convicted executives, and penalties up to $1 million for the offending corporation. Since its passage, various companies have been found guilty, some through internal investigations and self-disclosure, and have paid fines. During the 1970s and early 1980s, thirty U.S. multinationals were reported in the press as having been involved in questionable payments in fifteen Middle Eastern countries.[46] Although somewhat imprecise in its language, the act does not consider facilitating payments to minor government officials who perform clerical or administrative duties to be illegal.

Many MNCs asserted that the act would put them at a competitive disadvantage relative to corporations from other industrialized nations and local companies. Some studies indicate that certain companies lost sales by being precluded from making illegal payments. In two surveys of large multinationals, about 30% reported lost sales.[47] One analyst noted in regard to Saudi Arabia: "While many American firms suffered from the enactment of the Foreign Corrupt Practices Act . . . Korean firms maneuvered their way into the tough market by relying on these risky practices."[48] However, other studies reveal that most companies were able to comply with the act without significantly adverse competitive effects.[49] The act prompted many companies to formulate codes of conduct for their personnel to ensure that illegal payments were precluded as a mechanism for managing their government relationships. Many also require compliance with the code in their contracts with foreign sales agents. While such codes may constitute a constraint, they also remove a former business cost. These freed resources are available to the company to deploy creatively and legally in its marketing and business–government relations to develop offsetting competitive advantages.

Regardless of the legal aspects of corruption, managers must still deal with the ethical aspect. Business ethics is a body of moral principles or values that guide the professional conduct of managers. An individual's ethics shapes behavior, but corporations can also be viewed as having a conscience.[50] Consequently, ethics is the concern of the individual manager and the company. Goodpaster cites three approaches to ethical thinking.[51] The first views ethics as a means to self-interest: We will be fully truthful in our sales promotions because it will retain our customers' patronage. The second sees ethical behavior as imposed by external forces: We shall not bribe government officials because of the dictates of the Foreign Corrupt Practices Act. The third thinks of ethics as an end: To fulfill the responsibility embedded in our authority, we must contribute to the well-being of others. This third perspective is revealed in the Borg-Warner Corporation's statement of beliefs:

Any business is a member of a social system, entitled to the rights and bound by the responsibilities of that membership. Its freedom to pursue economic goals is constrained by law and channeled by the forces of a free market. But these demands are minimal, requiring only that a business provide wanted goods and services, compete fairly, and cause no obvious harm. For some companies that is enough. It is not enough for Borg-Warner. We impose upon ourselves an obligation to reach beyond the minimal. We do so convinced that by making a larger contribution to the society that sustains us, we best assure not only its future vitality, but our own.[52]

When formulating ethical stances, managers should recognize that environments shape ethical perceptions. What is seen as a perfectly ethical practice in one culture might be deemed abhorrent in another. To some extent the Foreign Corrupt Practices Act negates this cultural and ethical relativism and posits a universal professional code of conduct for U.S. companies.[53] For the multinational corporation there is considerable merit in creating a consistent ethical code throughout its global organization. This corporate conscience can serve as a unifying force, create a shared vision, and lead to behavioral coherence. Such a stance can be an asset in recruiting management talent and motivating personnel. A global approach to professional ethics in no way need imply cultural insensitivity; it simply recognizes that in certain spheres of business practice, the company may deviate from a local norm. Among multinationals and local LDC companies, there appears to be a growing concern about and formulation of ethical codes of conduct.

To be effectively implemented, corporate codes of conduct of MNCs or local firms should be accompanied by mechanisms for monitoring compliance. Dow Corning Corporation published its first corporate code of conduct in 1977.[54] To monitor compliance and communicate with employees about the code, the company conducted annual audits. In preparation, local managers filled out a seven-page worksheet of questions about company practices and interactions with government officials, company distributors, customers, and competitors. Managers kept an ongoing file of reports (using a standard form) to record the details of possible code-related incidents. The company's Business Conduct Committee carried out the audits, reviewing actual practices with area management and clarifying interpretations of the code. The company conducted about twenty audits a year. Surveys of employees revealed that their attitudes toward the company's ethics improved every year after it instituted the code.

Clearly, ethical conduct transcends business–government relations. Nonetheless, experience suggests that managing this interface requires special attention to ethics. To ignore corruption is to condone it. And condoning it places the business–government relationship in a precarious position.

CONCLUSION

How well a company manages its government relations will often be a key determinant of its success in a developing country. To manage the relationship strategically, a manager must first identify the key government actors, their needs, and their power. Political mapping and the Public-Policy Impact Chain are tools for doing this.

Next the manager must assess to what extent the company can meet the government's needs with the resources at its disposal. The fit between resources and needs can be examined through the Congruency Assessment matrix. The closer the fit, the greater the company's bargaining power. The company's economic contribution to the country's economy can be quantified through Economic Cost-Benefit Analysis. This methodology can determine the degree of congruence between the public and private returns on an investment and help identify ways in which a company's investment might be reconfigured to increase its contribution to the economy. These contributions determine companies' bargaining power, but bargaining power tends to obsolesce over time unless a company can provide new resources needed by the country.

Business–government relations should be approached strategically. Four main approaches stand out: alter, avoid, accede, and ally. Which strategy to follow will be determined by the company's relative bargaining power and the relative importance of the issue. Various permutations of the "4-A" strategies might be called for, and different approaches will be required for different issues and different government actors. The company's position regarding involvement in the political process is another important strategic issue.

In addition to the overall strategy in approaching government actors, the firm should pay special attention to three operating aspects of managing business–government relations: designing and implementing the communications process, organizing responsibilities and functions for interacting with the government, and dealing with practical and ethical aspects of corruption.

The capacity to manage a firm's relationships with key government actors can be a source of competitive advantage. It requires a significant investment of management time, but that can pay handsome dividends. To neglect it is to place your firm in peril.

7

Finance

Coping with Inflation, Foreign-Exchange Exposure, and Capital Scarcity

Inflation and devaluation are two problem areas in the financial environment of LDCs that are especially strategic because their effects can be potentially devastating to a company. These two phenomena also occur in more developed nations, but not with the same frequency or intensity as in the Third World. A critical third problem is capital scarcity. It, however, is a chronic condition, whereas inflation and devaluation tend to be episodic events that can greatly disrupt a firm's operations and strategy. We shall first examine the nature, consequences, and ways of handling inflation and devaluation. Although we will focus on inflation and devaluation as specific problems, it is important to realize that their emergence may signal broader instability in a country's entire business environment. The challenge for the financial officer is to avoid the myopia of defining inflation or devaluation as narrow technical problems and to recognize the larger implications for adjustments in a company's overall strategic plan. The final section of the chapter will examine financial management problems that arise from capital scarcity, including pressures stemming from the international debt crisis.

INFLATION[1]

Impact on Companies

Many firms have gone bankrupt or suffered severe financial damage because of their inability to deal with the effects of a quick inflationary surge. Managers who have faced the problems of high inflation would undoubtedly find their sentiments echoed in the lament of a Mexican manager grappling with newly accelerating inflation: "It's as if all the rules have been changed; we have to learn how to do business in a totally different environment."[2] It is not simply the high levels of inflation that complicate the financial management task, but also the roller-coaster of price surges and declines. Figure 7.1 reveals how price changes have varied among different LDC regions. Latin America has witnessed by far the greatest inflation. Levels of inflation have risen in the 1970s

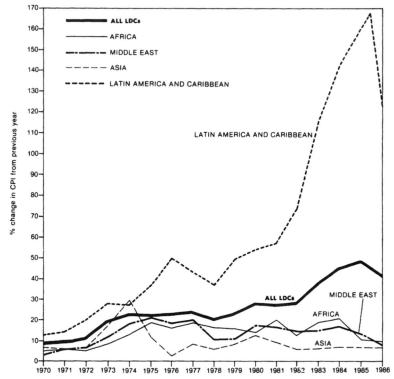

Figure 7.1 Inflation in Developing Countries

SOURCE: Derived from *International Financial Statistics Yearbook, 1986* (Washington, D.C.: IMF, 1986).

and 1980s in part as a result of oil price shocks. For example, the inflation rate in the Philippines between 1957 and 1969 averaged 4% per year, whereas between 1970 and 1984 it rose significantly and fluctuated more widely, ranging between 6% and 43%. This change led one Filipino finance specialist to conclude that "Philippine business firms have to face the fact that inflation will remain a primary unsolved problem in our economy."[3] Between 1983 and 1987 twenty-seven countries had annual inflation rates above 20%, seventeen above 30%, and seven above 100%.[4] Several Latin American countries, including Bolivia, Argentina, Brazil, and Nicaragua, experienced four-digit hyperinflation in the 1980s, leading to the issuance of entirely new currencies in their efforts to restore price stability. An Argentine manager commented on the cost of managing under such conditions: "It's very high in terms of people and overhead just to deal with the price controls, with the everyday analysis of the financial markets, and with the different changes we are suffering in the daily business life."[5] We shall examine five of the problem areas that inflation and government actions to deal with it create: illusory profits and decapitalization, a creeping tax burden, rising finance costs, liquidity complications, and company relationships.

Illusory Profits and Decapitalization. A company's revenues will rise as its products' prices ride the general inflationary spiral upward. This sales rise might actually cloak a decline in physical volume. Nominal profits will be greater than the previous year's, which might even create stockholder pressure to increase dividends, but in fact the real purchasing power of these profits may be even less than those of the previous year. The result is that the company may find itself with shrinking capital in real terms rather than a surplus, as the following simplified example of a trading company illustrates:

	Revenues	Costs	Profits	Cash Balance
Period 1				
Initial cash balance				$1,000
Purchase of merchandise for resale		$1,000		0
Resale of merchandise (50% markup)	$1,500			$1,500
Profit before taxes			$500	
Taxes (at 50% rate)		$250		$1,250
Profits after taxes			$250	
Cash surplus				$1,250

Period 2

Purchase of merchandise for resale		
(100% inflation)	$2,000[a]	
Cash deficit		−$750[b]

[a] Outlay for purchase of merchandise in period 2:

$$\begin{array}{ccc}
\text{cost of merchandise} & \times & 1 + \text{inflation rate} \\
\text{in period 1} & & \\
\$1,000 & \times & 1 + 1.00 \quad = \$2,000
\end{array}$$

[b] Cash deficit is:

$$\begin{array}{ccc}
\text{cash surplus} & - & \text{cost of merchandise} \\
\text{in period 1} & & \text{in period 2} \\
\$1,250 & - & \$2,000 \quad = -\$750
\end{array}$$

The company had a profit of $500 and a total cash inflow of $1,250, but its margin of 50% was insufficient to cover the increase in cost of the replacement inventory, which was rising at the 100% inflation rate. The historical cost of goods sold and sales margin became irrelevant accounting statistics in setting margins adequate to preserve puchasing power. To purchase replacement inventory, the company would have to come up with an additional total of $750 in working capital.

Profitability measures such as return on equity (ROE) or on assets (ROA) lose their meaning when the capital or assets are in historical values and the returns are in current values. From the above example, assume that the original equity put in at the beginning of the year was $1,000. The year-end profit after tax of $250 would give an apparent return on the original equity of 25%. However, if the equity were revalued to take into account the 100% inflation occuring during the year, it would amount to $2,000, and the return in year-end current dollars would be only 12.5%. Inflation can render traditional accounting and financial information misleading. Budgets, standard costing, and variance analysis are crippled.

Creeping Tax Burden. Inflation leads to adverse tax effects. As nominal profits rise the company may be pushed into higher tax brackets if the country uses a progressive corporate tax structure. In addition to this bracket creep, taxes will tend to rise because the tax shield from depreciation decreases. This assumes that under tax regulations the values of depreciable assets remain at their original levels while nominal profits increase, thus lowering the amount of profits shielded from taxes by the fixed depreciation amounts.

Rising Finance Costs. During inflation financing costs can soar: Interest rates rise and working capital requirements expand because of rising prices, thereby yielding higher financing rates on a larger borrowing requirement. The traditional focus on profit before interest and taxes (PBIT) can lead to overlooking the significantly increased impact that interest costs can have on profitability. It is not unusual for interest expense to double or triple as a percentage of sales. Inflation breeds inflationary expectations, which in turn increase people's propensity to spend their current income quickly before its purchasing power is eroded. Interest rates to savers must be increased substantially to entice them to save rather than spend. In Peru in late 1988, for example, inflation was running at an annual rate of 1,400% but the highest bank savings rate was 270%, which made it nonsensical to save.[6] When banks do increase their rates for depositors, the interest rates at which banks will lend also is pushed up.

In some instances, however, inflation might lead to a reduction in finance costs in real terms. For example, in 1987 interest rates for commercial loans in Venezuela were about 13% while the annual inflation rate was 40%. Government regulations prevented banks from charging higher interest rates or attaching an inflation readjustment clause to the loan principal. A company paid back its loan at the end of the year in bolivars worth only 60% of the purchasing power of the original capital. Thus, the firm enjoyed a negative real interest rate of 27% (13% − 40%). Similarly, in Turkey in the late 1970s real interest rates fell to a negative 50%.[7]

Liquidity Complications. Under inflationary conditions, cash and other liquid instruments are wasting assets, in that their real value diminishes daily. There is thus a great incentive to minimize this type of asset; yet inflation simultaneously increases the volume of cash needed for transactions. Volumes expand and speed of handling accelerates. This complexity is magnified by constantly changing values and the proliferation of financial charge arrangements. The larger cash needs, higher interest expenses, and lower credit availibility can combine to create serious liquidity problems for firms.

Company Relationships. Dealing with inflation usually changes the behavior of a company's suppliers, customers, bankers, competitors, employees, and government, therefore causing adjustments in its traditional ways of doing business and interacting with them. This adds to the stress and complexity of devising and implementing solutions. For example, Unilever's Brazilian subsidiary encountered several problems when inflation started accelerating in 1982. Many large wholesalers bought several months worth of Unilever products to hedge against expected price increases. Consumers had also begun to hoard. This surge in demand disrupted production schedules and distribution operations. The stockpiling also dampened demand after the company increased its prices. Furthermore, many consumers switched to lower-priced and lower-quality competing products. The company was burdened by mounting inventories and further production disruptions. The government began imposing price controls to hold down inflation, thereby further constraining the company's operation.[8]

Managing Under Inflation

Managers cannot stop inflation; it comes from macroeconomic and political forces beyond their direct control. They must live with it. Profitabilty is possible, and learning to manage its effects can even create competitive advantage. Thus, even though Brazil in 1988 was moving into four-digit inflation, Britain's Imperial Chemical Industries opened a $65 million polyester film factory. The president of the Brazilian operation, John Matthews, explained: "I am able to persuade my superiors abroad that Brazil has an enormous potential, and we can do business even in a very difficult environment."[9]

Under inflation the financial management dimensions of the business increase in complexity, yet inflation's effects permeate the entire business, not just the realm of the Chief Financial Officer. Thus, a prerequisite to managing effectively is to educate managers to think and operate with an inflationary mindset. Standard operating procedures no longer apply. Managers can take actions in five areas: forecasting inflation, thinking in replacement terms, preserving real margins, shortening credit and stretching payables, and adjusting personnel performance indicators.

Forecast Inflation Rates and Government Actions. In a relatively noninflationary environment, little attention is paid to movements in general price levels. In inflationary environments, predicting price rises becomes central to the management information system. Many groups, including government agencies, industry associations, economic consultants, and company departments (sales, planning, purchasing), may be making inflation forecasts. Managers can better judge the reasonableness of different forecasts (or at least spot ones definitely based on faulty reasoning) if they understand the basic economic and political forces underlying inflation.

Inflation emerges from various causes. Two types are often cited. In "demand-pull" inflation monetary demand for goods exceeds physical supply, thereby pulling prices up. This surge in demand is often associated with deficit spending by the government and expansion of the money supply to cover deficits, i.e., more money chasing fewer goods. Political campaigns are seldom won on austerity platforms. Promising more rather than less is a more appealing political posture. It was not surprising that in Argentina's 1988–89 presidential campaign the leading opposition party candidate (and eventual winner) proposed huge increases in salaries and government spending despite the country's 440% inflation rate.[10]

The second type, "cost-push" inflation, occurs when suppliers of production inputs such as labor or raw materials bid up their prices, which are then passed on to consumers. Sometimes these wage increases are in response to price increases caused by demand-pull forces, thereby creating an interlocking spiral of inflationary pressures. Inflation can also be "imported," as when international prices of a key economic resource have increased. The inflationary impact of oil price increases is the most salient recent example; this triggered cost-push price increases in the oil-importing nations. When a country devalues its currency, imports become more expensive in the local currency. If these imports are essential and their volume remains unchanged, their higher prices will be another source of cost-push pressures.

For exporting LDCs, price increases in international commodity markets (e.g., oil, coffee, tin, copper) have also been a source of "imported" inflationary pressures, but on the revenue rather than on the cost side, as the sudden surge in income creates demand-pull pressures. Governments can offset this imported price pressure from commodity price booms by "sterlizing" the inflow. For example, skyrocketing coffee prices in 1976 caused Costa Rica's coffee export revenues to double. To keep these revenues from flooding the economy with excess liquidity and triggering demand-pull inflation, the government first issued three-year Coffee Savings Bonds. These carried a 12% interest rate with the guarantee that if coffee prices fell below $1 per pound, the holder could sell the bond to the Central Bank without any early conversion penalty. Second, the government increased the interest rate on time deposits. Third, the government banks increased the interest rates on coffee production loans so as to encourage the farmers to use their increased revenues to finance their production. As a result of these actions, almost 80% of the incremental coffee revenues was absorbed, significantly moderating the inflationary pressure.[11]

A third source of inflationary pressure, consumer expectations, grows out of the pre-existing inflation. In an inflationary environment people begin to expect that prices will continue to rise, and they adjust their behavior accordingly. They may tend to hoard or accelerate purchases to take advantage of today's prices. The previously cited example of the Brazilian consumers of Unilever's products exemplifies this psychological mindset and behavior.

Managers need to understand which are the fundamental forces causing the inflation and monitor those. Application of the Environmental Analysis Framework and the Public-Policy Impact Chain, described in Chapter 4, helps the manager understand the role of the government's strategy and policies as both inflation causes and inflation remedies. Clearly government fiscal and monetary policies become focal points of scrutiny, because they help identify inflationary pressures and because specific actions can affect the company's operations. For example, to reduce inflation the government might (1) cut back its expenditures, which might directly or indirectly hurt company sales; (2) tighten credit, thereby affecting the firm's investment projects; or (3) control prices, thus squeezing margins. The Indian government's anti-inflationary reductions in expenditures and credit, for example, caused demand for KCL's engines to plummet.

Government actions on inflation are dictated by both political and economic forces, so both should be examined. How powerful are labor unions in seeking further wage increases? Are the expenditures of the SOEs controllable? Will the government agree to austerity measures demanded by the International Monetary Fund? Analyzing these political and economic forces will help the manager assess the likely direction of public policies and actions, and therefore inflation trends. However, even if measures are taken to reduce inflationary pressures, people's expectations of rising prices create an independent source of upward pressure. Breaking this inflation psychology is also necessary if the policies are to be effective. Sometimes governments attempt to do this by having the country "start fresh" by withdrawing the old currency and creating a new one, instituting price and wage controls, and tightening bank credit. Bolivia's annual inflation rate reached 21,000% in 1984 and resulted in a change in governments; the new administration created a new currency and launched a drastic austerity program that brought inflation down to zero within a few months.[12] In August 1988 the Argentine government declared a bank holiday before announcing a series of measures aimed at braking the 30% per month inflation rate. Governments have to take highly visible steps to signal their resolve and get consumers to begin to alter their inflationary expectations.

Governments publish price indices such as the consumer price index (CPI) or wholesale price index (WPI), which measure past inflation rates. They sometimes also forecast these rates. When inflation becomes chronic, governments may institute indexation systems as part of wage and price controls, whereby input and output prices are adjusted periodically in tandem with changes in the indices. Government indices are important elements in forecasting, but they can be manipulated for political purposes. To keep prices down, governments have been known to alter the mix of goods in the "consumer basket" on which the CPI is calculated. It is not unreasonable to assume that the real rates of inflation exceed those reported or forecast by governments. Choosing the appropriate reference rate is critical to corporate financial forecasting and planning. Indices like the CPI or WPI can vary significantly. For some companies, however, these general indices may not be the most relevant. The relevant inflation rates for a company are those of the prices of its particular mix of inputs and outputs. Different industries and different companies within the same industry can face quite distinct inflation profiles.

Consequently, the manager should forecast these prices by understanding the forces affecting them, studying trends in the company's cost records, and talking to suppliers and buyers. On the other hand, the CPI might be quite useful in formulating an interest-rate forecast. One international banker operating in Turkey indicated that many of the bank's clients use its inflation forecasts to do their own budgeting.[13]

Regardless of the forecasts' source, inflation rates have to be incorporated into operating budgets. The difficulty in predicting inflation rates precisely means that operating budgets should be adjusted periodically, perhaps monthly, using updated inflation-rate estimates. This updating means extra effort, but it is simplified by using financial software that can quickly generate the new pro-formas with revised inflation assumptions. In one Central American country experiencing rapid inflation, no adjustments were made in the original budgets of the government's state-owned enterprises. This failure rendered useless actual-to-budget comparisons and made the financial planning system managerially nonsensical.

Think Replacement. Managers are used to thinking of costs in historical terms. In inflationary environments managers need to think about the cost of replacing goods just sold; their previous purchase price will not be their new purchase price. Although most relevant for pricing decisions, replacement costing is also important for profit calculations. In accounting terms, the last-in-first-out (LIFO) method locates the actual cost of goods closer to the ever rising prices of inflation than first-in-first-out (FIFO). A replacement mentality, however, would use what we call a "next-in-first-out" (NIFO) method.

In the United States such approaches do not conform to standard accounting principles, because relatively little attention has been paid to the managerial realities of inflationary environments.[14] However, in some developing countries with chronic inflation, the accounting profession has developed extensive standards and methods for dealing with inflation in financial reporting. For example, the Argentine National Accounting Association has set forth procedures for expressing all financial statements in constant currency.[15] The basic approach is to restate the value of the assets, liabilities, and equity at the beginning of the period in terms of the value of the currency at the end of the period, using the monthly WPI to derive the constant closing currency values. Income statements are adjusted accordingly to incorporate the results from inflation exposure.

Preserve Real Margins. Inflation often squeezes margins, because costs accelerate faster than sales prices. Action is required on both fronts. Prices should be viewed as moving, not fixed. Pricing based on replacement values will help preserve margins. Margins may have to increase in nominal terms to preserve their purchasing power value in real terms. Price lists or quotes should be continually updated; the longer a price remains fixed, the bigger the effective discount to the buyer. If a delivery date is significantly later than the order date, the price might then be tied to an agreed-upon price index to cover the inflation occurring during the overdue period. These escalator clauses can become a critical issue in the bargaining relationship between buyer and seller. One might even have the buyer provide some of the production inputs to remove the inflation risk on this portion of the product.

Continually raising its prices may cause a business to lose market share if competitors choose to hold prices back. It is a strategic decision. The leading company in one food industry in a Latin American country chose to maintain margins by aggressively increasing prices. Its competitor did not follow and gained market share. The industry leader, however, remained quite profitable despite the volume drop; the competitor was selling more but making less. To avoid the loss in economies of scale from reduced volume, the leader acted on the cost side to reduce fixed costs, tighten cost controls, and increase productivity. This financial and production rationalization put the company in an even stronger position to recapture market share without sacrificing profit margins. The competitor's shrinking margins severely reduced its cash flow, which led to cutbacks in its advertising budget, thus loosening its hold on the newly won market share.

Where governments have imposed price controls, margin preservation becomes part of the business–government negotiating process discussed in the previous chapter. As one Brazilian manager put it: "The negotiations are very time-consuming. Sometimes the government increases keep pace with inflation, but usually they generate a gap between your price and your real costs. You have to have a very accurate control of this so that you can show the government."[16] A bicycle manufacturer in Burkina Faso had to wait eighteen months for a price increase.[17] (Chapter 9 on marketing discusses price controls further.)

Shorten Credit and Stretch Payables. Non-interest-bearing accounts receivable (and cash balances) are to be avoided if competitively possible. The higher the inflation and the longer the grace period for payment, the bigger the effective discount given. Consider the following example contrasting the costs of extending a thirty-day non-interest-bearing credit in a noninflationary environment with an inflationary one:

	0% Inflation	*60% Inflation*
Amount of credit	$10,000	$10,000
Monthly interest rate	1%	6%
Receivable carrying cost	$100	$600[a]
Purchasing power loss	0	$500[b]
Net real revenues	$9,900	$8,900[c]

[a] Receivable carrying cost per month is:

Amount of credit × Monthly interest rate = Receivable
                                            carrying cost
$10,000   ×   0.06   = $600

[b] Purchasing power loss per month is:

Amount of credit × Annual inflation rate/12 = Purchasing
                                              power loss
$10,000   ×   .60 / 12   = $500

[c] Net real revenues per month are:

Amount of − Receivable carrying − Purchasing = Net real
credit sale   cost   power loss   revenue
$10,000   − $600   − $500   = $8,900

We can see that a thirty-day average credit where the annual inflation rate is 60% can reduce real revenues by 10%, thus seriously eroding profits. Interest should be charged for all credit, to cover both working-capital interest costs and inflation erosion (i.e., the interest should be positive in real terms). If the company's bargaining power with the buyer is particularly strong, it might even seek prepayment. To extend credit wisely in an inflationary economy, the manager must recognize that the company is unavoidably and importantly in the financing business. Customer credit should not be considered a peripheral activity. Obviously, credit terms are a competitive tool and should not be set independently of the actions of competitors. However, in inflationary environments free or easy credit can become a deceptively expensive tool. The manager should ask who in the specific situation is best able to provide financing, and how the company might gain or lose competitive advantage through its credit operations. Extra effort also will probably have to be made in collecting receivables.

For a company's payables the converse of the foregoing strategy holds: squeeze as much free or cheap credit out of suppliers as possible. There may indeed be advantageous credit or prices, because there tends to be greater diversity during inflationary periods. It pays to shop around. Inflation distorts market forces and makes price formation less transparent. Each company sets prices based on expectations and forecasts rather than current actuals. Furthermore, different companies may be affected differently by inflation or may opt to use credit competitively in distinct ways. The careful buyer may even be able to find opportunities for credit at negative interest rates, i.e., where the interest rate is less than the inflation rate.

As was mentioned previously, working-capital needs expand and financing costs increase during inflation. Part of a shopping strategy is comparing the terms of supplier credits with bank loans. The company's bargaining power may be greater with one source than with another. For MNC subsidiaries, having access to foreign credit lines or additional equity capital inflows might increase their flexibility and bargaining power. However, such foreign financing increases the parent's capital exposure and devaluation risk, as will be discussed below.

If a company is able to operate on a cash basis on its sales side yet receive credit on its payables side, inflation may prove very profitable. You may end up making more money on this financial arrangement than from the operating aspects of the business. In fact, gains from *de facto* supplier discounts may allow a more aggressive price discounting strategy and a gain in market share. Inflationary environments require new managerial perspectives. Traditional norms for financial liquidity ratios become less appropriate. For example, it may even by desirable in some instances for the acid test ratio (current assets − inventories to current liabilities) to be negative, i.e., minimize cash balances and receivables, increase inventories (which appreciate with inflation), and stretch payables.

Adjust Personnel Performance Indicators. Inflation can distort traditional performance incentive or evaluation systems. Commissions based on a percentage of sales become bloated as a consequence of rising prices that are increased to cover higher replacement and finance costs. A preferable system for measuring and motivating real sales would be one with unit quotas. Budget adherence may not accurately measure managerial competence because of imperfections in the original forecasts of price and cost increases. One should separate out changes in productivity from price change effects. For salaried and wage employees, upward adjustments must be made to avoid decreases in their real incomes, which can cause demotivation and desertion.

=

There is little doubt that inflation complicates the managerial task and poses very serious problems. Inflation, however, is a manageable problem, and companies that learn how to manage it more effectively will create a competitive advantage. Inflation also contributes to exchange rate instability, to which we now turn.[18]

FOREIGN-EXCHANGE EXPOSURE

One of the nightmares of managers with operations in developing countries is to be hit with an unexpected or unreasonable devaluation of the country's currency. The consequent financial reverberations due to the company's foreign-exchange exposure can be severe. The words of a regional manager for Cummins Engine in Venezuela capture the shock:

Almost everybody in America, young and old, remembers where they were when President Kennedy was assassinated. Well, everybody in Venezuela remembers where they were on February 18, 1983, Black Friday. Ever since Black Friday, when the bolivar was devalued, Cummins has had a real set of problems in Venezuela. We're holding

$1.4 million in accounts receivable that's never going to be worth what it was a couple of months ago.[19]

Although devaluations can have devastating effects, they might also enhance a firm's position, for example, by making exports more competitive or by lowering the foreign-exchange value of local liabilities. In both negative and positive cases, handling the foreign-exchange risk is a critical task for financial management in LDCs.

Exchange-Rate Instability

Managing exposure to changes in nominal and real exchange rates is a task faced by businesses worldwide. Even firms operating in only one country must deal with foreign-exchange exposure if they or their competitors import inputs or finished goods into the home market. Although the problem is universal, foreign-exchange exposure in developing countries is intensified by inflation, capital-flow instability, and government regulation.

The Theory of Purchasing Power Parity links inflation to changes in foreign-exchange rates. It holds that if inflation[20] is higher in country A than in country B, the *nominal* exchange rate between the two currencies must adjust to reflect the lower value of A's currency relative to B's if the *real* rate of exchange is to be maintained in equilibrium. In theory, this adjustment will occur automatically if goods are allowed to trade freely and foreign-exchange rates are allowed to fluctuate in response to supply and demand (conditions that seldom exist in developing countries). Since inflation in LDCs is often significantly higher than in more developed countries (as noted in the first part of this chapter), one would expect LDC currencies to depreciate in *nominal* terms in relation to currencies from developed nations.

Relative rates of inflation are by no means the only factors affecting the exchange rate between two currencies. Since the exchange rate is the price of one currency relative to another, it is subject to other supply-and-demand pressures. If people are confident about a currency's strength or if they need it to purchase goods or other assets from that country, there will be a strong demand for it. In contrast, a country's political or economic instability will discourage domestic and foreign actors from holding liquid assets and conducting business in the local currency rather than a foreign currency. Eroding confidence of key economic actors in a country and its currency can lead to capital flight and both *nominal* and *real* relative depreciation of the local currency as demand for it plummets.

LDC governments tend to regulate foreign-exchange transactions closely. Exchange rates are influenced indirectly through import licensing, which serves to reduce artificially the demand for foreign goods and services and in turn the demand for foreign currencies. A more direct way of achieving the same result is to use foreign exchange/capital controls: allocating foreign exchange domestically and restricting the amount of currency that can be taken out of the country creates pressures to counteract the relative depreciation of the local currency that would occur due to capital flight triggered by political instability or economic shocks.

Although import and capital controls can have a significant indirect impact on foreign-exchange rates, direct regulation of those rates represents the most powerful way for the government to influence a firm's foreign-exchange exposure. In the most extreme case, a government may leave nominal exchange rates fixed for months or even years, even with rapid inflation, with the aim of creating a more stable environment for foreign trade, to keep the cost of imported goods down, or out of a belief that the demand for or the supply of the country's exports are relatively inelastic and therefore would not respond to the price effects of a devaluation. Devaluation is often impeded by pressure from groups with a vested interest in maintaining the prevailing rate (e.g., importers) or by a perception that devaluation would be a signal of political weakness (especially if the IMF or a foreign government is pressing for such action). To prop up the nominal exchange rate in this manner, however, the government may affect the supply-and-demand forces on foreign exchange through direct transactions. It may draw down its existing foreign-exchange reserves, borrow foreign exchange from abroad, and ration foreign exchange domestically.

If the currency becomes increasingly overvalued in real terms, pressure to correct the disequilibrium will mount from various sectors: (1) businesses that require imported inputs but no longer have access to import licences and foreign exchange; (2) exporters who find that demand for their products has declined as the real price of their products to foreign buyers has increased; (3) foreign lenders who find interest and principal payments on their loans delayed because of rationing of scarce foreign exchange; and (4) the government finance ministry itself, which finds that a burgeoning black market for foreign exchange and foreign goods is reducing government revenues through smuggling and other unofficial, untaxed transactions. For example, Ghana's currency became increasingly overvalued during the 1976–83 period, and so the revenues from cocoa, the country's principal export, eroded significantly, thereby reducing the price paid to farmers. They decreased their plantings and smuggled much of their remaining production to neighboring countries, where prices were 300% higher. This export diversion further exacerbated the country's foreign-exchange position.[21]

Ultimately, the government is forced to devalue the currency either partially or completely back to equilibrium. These devaluations usually occur with little or no prior warning and hence leave firms operating in the environment extremely vulnerable to the effects of foreign-exchange exposure. When the Ghanaian government finally devalued the cedi in April 1983 from 2.85 to the dollar to 23.38, the working capital needs of firms dependent on the instantly more costly imported inputs skyrocketed. Many firms were catapulted into liquidity crises.[22] Some governments have more visible and predictable devaluation processes, sometimes in the form of monthly "mini-devaluations" or even daily adjustments. By 1986 Ghana was using weekly foreign-exchange auctions to allow market forces to set the exchange rate. The longer a country waits to adjust the exchange rate, the more out of balance it may become and the more drastic the adjustment will have to be.

Coping with Foreign-Exchange Exposure

To manage foreign-exchange risks[23] we offer suggestions in four areas. The first deals with predicting exchange-rate variations; the other three concern specific types of foreign exchange exposure: transaction, translation, and operational.

Predicting Exchange Rates. The financial exposure inherent in foreign-exchange management is due mainly to the risk of exchange-rate variations and the policies governments adopt to address underlying macroeconomic problems. Accordingly, the financial management information system should focus on data that will help forecast changes in the exchange rate. This information must be both economic and political. Because exchange rates are shaped in part by supply-and-demand pressures for the currency, the underlying economic forces must be examined. At the same time, however, LDC governments generally set the exchange rate rather than let free market forces determine it exclusively. Thus, like other policy decisions, the exchange rate is subject to noneconomic political considerations. Forecasts are best able to predict the direction of exchange rate changes; estimating precisely their magnitude and timing is more elusive.

On the economic side, we can refer to the Environmental Analysis Framework to examine macroeconomic phenomena. A company's infor-

Table 7.2 Inflation Rates: United States vs. Mexico

	1983	1984	1985	1986	1987	1988
United States	3.2	4.3	3.5	2.0	3.6	3.8
Mexico	101.6	65.6	57.8	86.2	131.8	114.2
Difference	98.4	61.3	54.3	84.2	128.2	110.4

SOURCE: *International Financial Statistics*, 42, no. 6, (IMF, 1989): 372, 546.

mation system should monitor the relative inflation rates of countries whose exchange rates are being examined. If these inflation rates diverge significantly, an exchange-rate adjustment is likely to follow. Table 7.2 shows how inflation rates in Mexico began to accelerate faster than in the United States, its chief trading partner. The Mexican government kept the exchange rate fixed, but the underlying pressures of this divergence resulted in major devaluations, with the peso-to-dollar rate changing from 23:1 in 1980 to 335:1 by 1985 and 2,000:1 in 1987. In addition to inflation rates, the information system can also examine interest-rate differentials and the rates on forward contracts for the currencies under consideration.

Devaluation pressures are often revealed in the country's balance of payments, which is the other main information source to be monitored. A country's balance-of-payments accounts record international transactions and flows of goods, services, and capital; they thus reveal a country's sources and uses of foreign exchange. Analyzing the trends and factors influencing these different sources and uses can help identify pressures on the exchange rate. Table 7.3 sets forth the major sources and uses of foreign exchange in developing countries that generally warrant monitoring. Although each of these items should be monitored, some key relationships stand out as summary indicators.

Table 7.3 Major Sources and Uses of Foreign Exchange in LDCs

Sources	*Uses*
S-1. exports	U-1. imports
S-2. gifts from foreigners & worker remittances	U-2. interest, dividends, royalties paid to foreigners
S-3. suppliers' credits	U-3. loan and credit repayments
S-4. foreign loans	U-4. investments and deposits abroad
S-5. foreign direct investment	U-5. increase in foreign currency holdings or gold stocks
S-6. decrease in foreign currency or gold stocks	

Trade Balance. This is the difference between the exports and imports of goods and services (S-1 minus U-1). Exports are generally the main foreign-exchange generator, and imports the main user. Understanding the structure of exports is essential to interpreting the meaning of trends. Often one or a few products will dominate exports. Changes in their international prices or their access to major markets can have dramatic effects on foreign-exchange earnings. Similarly, if the foreign-exchange earner is a service such as tourism, domestic unrest or natural disasters might lead to significant shortfalls. Thus, monitoring these dimensions is central to forecasting. Similarly, the composition of imports will often reveal a heavy concentration among certain items. It may also indicate how elastic imports are, i.e., how easily they could be reduced to adjust to export shortfalls. The more economically critical (oil) or socially necessary (basic grains) the imports are, the fewer the degrees of freedom will be to cut back on imports and the greater the probability of trade deficits if exports falter.

Debt Servicing. The tremendous rise in LDC foreign debts has made scrutiny of loan amortization and interest payments (U-2 and U-3) particularly important. Much debt carries variable interest rates; consequently, a small change in international interest rates can greatly increase the amount of foreign exchange flowing out to service the debt. Although private lending to developing countries declined between 1982 and 1985, there was a surge in floating-rate bond lending: 46% of the outstanding LDC debt in 1985 carried floating rates, but three-fourths of this was concentrated in four debtors.[24] Thus, debt levels and international interest rates become items for careful scrutiny by managers concerned with predicting exchange rates. The ratio of debt service to exports can be monitored as an indicator of a country's foreign-exchange generating capacity relative to its debt obligations.

Foreign Aid and Remittances. For some countries, grants (S-2) or loans (S-4) from other governments may be critical to covering their foreign exchange gap. As we noted in Chapter 1, in the mid-1980s official assistance once again became the largest source of foreign capital for developing countries. Managers should identify the relative significance of this item in the country of concern and monitor the political variables, particularly foreign policy, affecting these flows. Where the flow comes not from another government (bilateral aid accounted for two-thirds of the 1986 official flows)[25] but from the International Monetary Fund, one might in some instances witness accompanying policy changes oriented toward austerity measures, tight credit, import reductions, and devaluation. Remittances from workers abroad have been significant sources of foreign exchange for countries like Pakistan, Korea, Turkey, Portugal, and the Philippines. Shifts in foreign demand for these worker services (e.g., a decline in the Middle East due to falling oil revenues, or restrictions on worker immigration) can affect the foreign-exchange situation. Changes in the relative levels of domestic and international real interest rates also influence remittance flows.

Private Foreign Capital. In addition to monitoring public and private loans from abroad, one should also follow the foreign direct investment (S-5) and supplier credits (S-3). The former constitutes long-term capital commitments; its decrease might indicate reduced confidence in the business environment, economic instability, and devaluation probability. Supplier credit is a short-term source. What should be monitored is whether the country is, in effect, using this or other short-term credit to make long-term investments because alternative long-term capital sources are not available. If that is the case, it could portend a liquidity crunch (and an exchange rate crisis) when the returns from long-term investments are not forthcoming to meet the short-term repayment of supplier credits. Although both FDI and export credits to LDCs fell significantly in the first half of the 1980s, both shifted upward in the second half.[26]

Capital Flight. Another devaluation warning flag is private capital outflows, which appear partially in balance-of-payments accounts as increases in claims on foreign entities (e.g., bank deposits abroad, foreign securities, and foreign real estate). Governmental capital controls often try to reduce such flight, but capital still finds ways to flow out. In balance-of-payments statements, the plug item "Errors & Omissions" often includes this illegal capital flight. Official statistics on capital flight are often difficult to obtain and of dubious accuracy. Understandably, some governments tend not to report or to underreport capital flight to minimize the risk of raising further concern and prompting additional flight. Much capital flight is illegal and thus difficult to document, even if the government were inclined to report it. Informal communication channels in the business community may provide indications of the seriousness of the capital flight risk.

World Bank economists estimated that at the end of 1984 private nonbank residents of the eight highest-indebted LDCs had demand and time deposits abroad totaling nearly $47 billion.[27] A study of twenty-three LDCs showed that between 1978 and 1983 these countries added

$381.5 billion to their debt, but no less than $103.1 billion flowed back out as capital flight.[28] For the decade 1975–85, capital flight from developing countries due to fear of loss from hyperinflation, devaluation, or expropriation was estimated at $15 billion a year.[29] Venezuela's capital flight during this period exceeded by 20% its inflows of foreign direct investment and foreign borrowing.[30] Capital flight as a percent of gross external debt for the 1974–82 period was 38% for Mexico and 35% for Argentina but only 4% for Brazil and Peru.[31] Flows tend to surge in response to or anticipation of major economic or political changes. For example, in the mid-1980s Mexico was hit by drops in oil prices and soaring inflation, and the banks were nationalized; $4 billion fled Mexico in 1984, and in the summer of 1985 capital was flowing across the Rio Grande into Texas Commerce Bank at the rate of $3 million to $4 million daily.[32]

Reserve Changes. Another indicator is the net change in the country's foreign-exchange holdings and gold reserves (S-6 and U-5). However, this is a residual account, so it is important to examine the previously discussed sources and uses to explain reserve changes (for example, whether an increase in reserves was due to export earnings or borrowed capital).

Managers should also monitor black market exchange rates. Although these markets are often thin and imperfect, they do signal supply-and-demand pressures from a subsegment of the economy. The larger the market and the greater the divergence from the official exchange rate, the stronger the likelihood of an exchange-rate adjustment. Where there is a local market for gold, changes in its price is another indicator of currency misalignment.

Even if the economic indicators listed here all point toward devaluation, political considerations often impede the decision. One should try to identify and assess such factors. In many countries devaluation is equated with an admission of economic mismanagement and is therefore viewed as political anathema. When the devaluation recommendation comes from the IMF as a condition of its assistance, nationalism often evokes political resistance. Other political economy concerns may influence the decision. For example, for a country whose main exports face a largely inelastic demand or whose prices are denominated in dollars (e.g., oil), the devaluation will not necessarily boost foreign-exchange earnings. Groups adversely affected by a devaluation (such as importers facing higher prices for their imports) will probably exercise political pressure against the devaluation.

Although political factors are important determinants of the timing of devaluations, underlying economic forces cannot go unheeded. Given uncertainties in predicting the magnitude and timing of devaluations, managers could benefit from considering several different politico-economic scenarios with their corresponding government actions. Corporate contingency plans can be formulated for the different scenarios and activated as unfolding events and information point toward one scenario or another. This exercise should include careful assessments of the shape the company would be in if it acted now believing a devaluation would occur and it then did not happen.

Devaluations cannot be forecast with precision, but understanding the pressures can improve the basis for managing the foreign-exchange risk. We now move from examining the large macroeconomic phenomena to analyzing the firm level and the three types of foreign-exchange exposure (transaction, translation, and operational). Each has distinct dimensions and can be handled in different ways.

Transaction Exposure: Critical Issues. Transaction or contractual exposure occurs when a firm agrees to purchase or receive payment for a good at a fixed price in a foreign currency at some future date. Interest and principal payments from borrowing or lending are relevant here as well. If the government holds nominal exchange rates fixed for long intervals of time relative to the contract period, the firm can expect to trade its reference currency for the foreign currency (and vice versa) at the same rate of exchange when the contract is fulfilled as when it was signed; the only transaction exposure the firm faces is the risk of a sudden devaluation. This risk should not be regarded as insignificant, however. Even infrequent currency devaluations often change the whole business environment dramatically; a firm may end up losing much if not most of the contract's value if devaluation occurs before the transaction is completed.

If the government allows its exchange rate to float, the firm will almost surely be exposed to a changing exchange rate. Some LDC governments employ a form of "managed float" in which exchange rates are fixed for only very short periods and are adjusted frequently through mini-devaluations or foreign-exchange auctions aimed at keeping real exchange rates constant. In this discussion, the "managed float" will be considered equivalent to a true float. Although a product's price will probably be set based on anticipated inflation over the period, this will not necessarily protect the firm against possible foreign-exchange losses. The most obvious danger is that the actual rate of inflation will differ from the projected rate. This problem is exacerbated by potential differences between the inflation rate relevant to the exchange rate and the inflation rate applicable to the specific product being sold. In addition, it is common for foreign-exchange markets to lag behind or anticipate inflation differentials, given the weak information infrastructure and correspondingly inadequate price data in many LDCs. Finally, a firm may experience an unanticipated loss or gain on the transaction as a result of political instability or economic shocks that cause the future exchange rate to differ from its original projection.

Transaction Exposure: Managerial Responses. The manager of a firm subject to transaction exposure wants to avoid the possibility that the *nominal* exchange rate applicable to the contract when payment is due may differ from the rate projected when the transaction was agreed upon. In fact, a number of strategic responses are available to the manager, including alternate invoicing, hedging, and transaction balancing.

Alternate invoicing. A firm may be able to avoid foreign-exchange exposure altogether on a transaction by devising a means for purchasing/ receiving payment for the good in its own reference currency. The other firm in the transaction may be amenable to this arrangement for a small fee or without charge if the requesting firm is a high-volume or otherwise powerful buyer or seller. If such an arrangement cannot be struck with current vendors or buyers, the firm may be able to diversify its sources and markets, finding other firms more willing to enter into such an arrangement. Another approach is to lease rather than own assets. This reduces the company's asset exposure.

Hedging. Forward or futures markets allow a firm to agree to buy or sell a particular currency at a specific price on a specific future date. In effect a firm can "lock in" a guaranteed price for the foreign exchange on the day the contract is signed, regardless of how the exchange rate changes. If the predicted change in the exchange rate would produce a loss greater than the cost of the hedge, then hedging would be justified. Certain features of the futures markets, however, tend to limit the flexibility of this strategy in practice. First, futures contracts are bought and sold in multipules of specific units of currency, making it difficult to hedge the exact value of the transaction under consideration. Second, contracts may be available for only a limited number of fixed dates (e.g., the last day of every third month) and thus may not coincide even closely with the planned transaction date. An even greater constraint is imposed if the contracts are for a fixed period. Furthermore, even if a transaction has been hedged through a forward contract, the customer might pay late, causing exposure from having to settle the forward transaction at the existing spot rate and the late payment at a future spot rate. In LDCs late payment is often caused by delivery delays due to transportation deficiencies or foreign-exchange processing delays. Interest rate penalties tied to the exchange rate can help cover this foreign exchange exposure.[33]

Third, and most significant, futures contracts are unavailable for most LDC currencies;[34] as of October 1987 the only developing countries whose currency regulations made forward contracts in their currency possible were Greece, Indonesia, Kuwait, Korea, Malaysia, Mexico, Philippines, Qatar, Singapore, Taiwan, Thailand, and Turkey.[35] Even where allowed, the hedging operations may be slowed down by the government's or company's processing procedures and because many companies may be trying to hedge at the same time, thereby putting excessive demands on the hedging system. The controller of an MNC in Mexico commented on the problems he encountered:

> People may ask: "Why didn't we hedge more of the debt?" Well, let me tell you that it was not that simple. First, the cost of hedging was enormous. . . . Second, once we decided to make the hedge, it wasn't so easy to implement. The whole country had the same idea at the same time. We made the first $6 million hedge. We had all the papers ready for an additional $7.0 million hedge and were in the midst of getting corporate approval when the November devaluation occurred.[36]

Another form of hedging a payable involves converting enough reference currency into foreign currency on the day the transaction is signed to generate the precise amount of funds needed by the required date to pay off the transaction. (The foreign currency is invested in an interest-bearing account in the interim period.) This strategy applies to firms committed to purchasing a good with foreign currency. If the firm were instead to receive payment for a good in foreign currency, it would need to borrow foreign currency at the time of signing, immediately convert it into the reference currency, and then pay the loan back with the foreign currency it received on the date of consummation. The interest rate available for the currency will generally include the inflation anticipated for the period and hence cover the price increase for the good implicitly built into the final purchase price. This strategy may be weakened, however, if government controls keep interest rates below anticipated levels of inflation and hence force the firm to convert more currency up front to execute the hedge. Alternatively, a firm needing to borrow a foreign currency may find the strategy impossible because of credit controls, or too expensive because of high interest rates (induced by capital scarcity in the LDC). To operate effectively in multiple currency markets, the financial management information system has to be designed to obtain the relevant data quickly.

Another approach is to discount a company's receivables with a bank or another company. This removes that asset from the company's devaluation exposure, and the liquidity allows the manager to redeploy the asset into a less exposed position. Given their continuing need for local currencies, multinationals often arrange large exchanges of receivables and currency between themselves or their branches; these paper block or currency swaps serve as a hedging mechanism. Two MNCs might exchange two currencies and then reexchange them after a set period using the original exchange rate, or they might make parallel loans to each other's subsidiaries in different countries. Some international banks have devised services whereby a customer can hedge cross-currency using paper within the bank. It is not a futures market: There is no trade, just a bank customer transaction.

Transaction balancing. A firm that anticipates an inflow (outflow) of foreign exchange on a particular date may be able to arrange for an offsetting transaction to take place at the same time in which other goods are bought (sold) with the same currency, thereby avoiding foreign exchange exposure over the transaction period. Executing this strategy of export–import balancing may be difficult. The only purchases (sales) available at the time may be of a different amount of currency than the transaction one is attempting to balance, or they may occur at a very different time. Nevertheless a firm may be able to minimize its exposure by carefully planning the currency aspects of sourcing and sales in advance, with the aim of balancing the aggregate inflows and outflows of each type of foreign currency used.

Translation Exposure: Critical Issues. Whereas any firm conducting a business transaction in a foreign currency is subject to transaction exposure, only firms with operations in foreign countries are subject to translation or accounting exposure. This exposure results from the need for those foreign operations to be consolidated with the parent company's into a single set of financial statements for the entire firm at regular intervals. Since most line items in a subsidiary's financial statements are listed in the local currency, the value of the firm's assets, equity base, and profits in the parent company's currency will depend on the *nominal* exchange rate used to translate the statements from one currency to the other. MNCs with LDC subsidiaries are particularly concerned about translation exposure, since LDC currencies tend to depreciate relative to currencies in more developed countries.

The translation loss can sometimes transform a star performer into a dog. The Mexican subsidiary of American Telecommunications had tripled its profits in three years, reaching $2.1 million in 1976. However, the devaluation of the peso from 12.50 to the dollar to 19.95 caused a translation loss of $1 million and a transaction loss of $2.3 million, thereby converting the subsidiary from a profitable to a losing operation.[37]

The extent of the parent company's exposure will depend on the translation method required by accounting rules in force in the parent's home country. Although many variations are possible, the three main methods are:

- *Current rate method.* All assets and liabilities[38] are translated at the *current* exchange rate. Income statement items are translated at their *average* rate for the period covered.

- *Monetary/nonmonetary method.* All monetary assets and liabilities are translated at the *current* exchange rate, while all nonmonetary items are translated at their *historic* exchange rate (for each item, the rate in effect on the day the asset was purchased or the liability was incurred). Income statement items related to nonmonetary assets (e.g., cost of goods sold and depreciation) are translated at their *historic* rate, while all other items are translated at their *average* rate for the period.

- *Current/noncurrent method.* All current assets and liabilities are translated at the *current* exchange rate, while all noncurrent items are translated at their *historic* rate. Income statement items related to noncurrent assets and liabilities (e.g., depreciation and interest payments) are translated at their *historic* rate, while all other items are translated at their *average* rate.

Another key component of the relevant accounting system is the treatment of foreign-exchange losses or gains that result from the translation of the subsidiary's balance sheet. In general, the current rate and current/noncurrent methods allow these gains and losses to be accumulated year after year in a separate equity account; only at liquidation will the net gain or loss be recognized. In contrast, the monetary/nonmonetary method usually requires that foreign exchange gains and losses flow through the income statement and be recognized immediately. This requirement may cause earnings to fluctuate dramatically from year to year in the parent's currency, even if they are fairly stable in the local currency.

Translation Exposure: Managerial Responses. Because a firm's translation exposure can be measured in so many different ways, the manager's response to such exposure will depend on (1) the specific accounting rules applicable to the firm and (2) the extent to which management is concerned about the appearance of the operations in accounting terms as different from the underlying state of the company in economic terms. For example, a manager subject to a system that requires foreign-exchange losses or gains to flow through the income statement may be under more pressure to minimize translation exposure than a manager who can report losses or gains under a separate equity account. An additional consideration is the extent to which the exchange rate is likely to change in nominal terms: If the LDC government tends to keep the exchange rate fixed for long periods of time, the manager may be less concerned in the short term about translation exposure. The long-term threat of devaluation, however, should not be ignored.

One fairly straightforward strategy for reducing translation exposure of the balance sheet is the use of a *balance sheet hedge.* Since a firm's net exposure is equal to its exposed assets minus its exposed liabilities,[39] the smaller the difference between these amounts, the lower the exposure. Under the monetary/nonmonetary method, the firm can try to eliminate exposure by equalizing the levels of its exposed assets (such as cash and accounts receivable) and its exposed liabilities (short-term and long-term debt, accrued current liabilities). If the firm believes it need worry only about exposure to relative depreciation of the currency in nominal terms (as is often the case in the LDCs), it might try instead to minimize exposed assets, maximize exposed liabilities, and thereby possibly even achieve foreign-exchange gains. The problem with both strategies is that what makes sense for accounting reasons may not do so for business reasons. For example, reducing accounts receivable by severely restricting sales on credit may also cause the firm to lose a significant proportion of its potential sales.

Under the current/noncurrent method, the firm could also pursue a balance sheet hedge. In this case, it works to equalize exposed current assets and current liabilities. Balance sheet hedges are not really possible under the current rate method, because exposed assets will always exceed exposed liabilities. An exception occurs when the firm has such a high level of assets denominated in the parent company's currency (e.g., in cash or investments) that their value is greater than or equal to the sum of the equity accounts.

As for the exposure of profits to changes in the nominal exchange rate, a firm in the LDC anticipating a depreciation of the local currency may not be able to do much to affect the level of reported (accounting) earnings. However, it may be able to maximize the value of its cash flow by converting as much of it as possible as quickly as possible into the parent company currency. This strategy presupposes that (1) the company does not want or need to retain much of the subsidiary's cash flow in the local country for operating purposes, and (2) the LDC government does not have currency controls that restrict the repatriation of profits—an unlikely scenario in most developing countries.

Operating Exposure: Critical Issues. Unlike transaction and translation exposure, operating exposure relates to changes in *real*, not *nominal*, exchange rates. Operating exposure affects the underlying economics of any firm dealing with foreign buyers, suppliers, or competitors through its impact on input costs, sales prices, and sales volume. A key consideration is the nature of the competitive environment. Operating exposure plus transaction exposure constitutes the company's economic exposure.

When foreign-exchange rates simply adjust to compensate for inflation differentials between currencies, changes in the nominal prices of foreign goods are compensated for. Hence, real prices remain identical from the buyer's or seller's point of view. If exchange rates are fixed artificially, however, or if political instability or economic shocks bring factors other than inflation into the determination of the exchange rate, then real exchange rates will almost certainly change. In LDCs rates are often held fixed in the face of high relative inflation, causing the local currency to become *overvalued* relative to foreign currencies and causing foreign goods to become cheaper relative to local output. On the other hand, if business confidence is shaken by political or economic events while exchange rates are allowed to depreciate, then the local currency may become relatively *undervalued* and local goods correspondingly cheaper.

Operating exposure can affect a firm in many different ways. For example, an MNC's LDC subsidiary using local production inputs while its competitors use imported inputs will face a cost disadvantage when the local currency becomes overvalued. If the company exports, it will also face a competitive disadvantage on the revenue side, assuming that it must cut its local currency prices to compete with other international producers in the target market currency. If the local price is not reduced, the firm will lose sales unless demand for the product is totally inelastic. If a firm is operating in a global industry rather than in separate country markets (i.e., using a global rather than a multidomestic strategy), exchange-rate changes in various countries can have significant differential effects on companies as a consequence of differences in the geographical configurations of their operations and their resultant currency exposures.[40]

The severity of a firm's operating exposure is also heavily influenced by the level of tariffs and the nature of nontariff barriers set by the LDC government and by subsidies and taxes on imports and exports. For example, the potential cost advantage enjoyed by firms importing raw material inputs into an LDC with an overvalued currency may be counterbalanced by high tariffs or made moot by restrictive quotas that bar the goods altogether.

Operating Exposure: Managerial Responses. It is important for a manager to be able to recognize and respond to the often wide-ranging strategic problems and opportunities that characterize operating exposure. Since disequilibria in real exchange rates may last for several months or even years, the firm should strive to maximize its flexibility in sourcing, marketing, and financing.

Sourcing. As a firm's local currency moves out of equilibrium, the company should be in a position to shift its purchases to those suppliers who by virtue of their location can provide inputs at the lowest cost in the local currency. Firms with established relationships with vendors in a variety of countries (or merely indirect connections to such vendors as subsidiaries of the same MNC) can implement such a strategy most easily. If the economics are favorable, the firm may even go so far as to help set a supplier up where one does not yet exist. For example, if the local currency is chronically undervalued, it is to the firm's advantage to shift most of its sourcing to local vendors or to finance a captive supplier if none exists. In any case, the firm may still want to source a limited amount of its inputs from less favorable suppliers in other countries if it feels that maintaining an ongoing relationship may help in the future when strategies need to be reversed. If a company has a global production system in which some of its plants supply others of its plants, then the company may be able to shift production among supplying plants to take advantage of more favorable exchange rates.[41] The feasibility and desirability of shifting among sources will also be affected by the existence of excess capacity and the costs of layoffs.

When a company is sourcing via imports, the resultant price increases might be reduced through negotiations with the government regarding the exchange rate. Sometimes in a devaluation, the government establishes multiple exchange rates that reflect import priorities. In Venezuela's 1983 devaluation, basic foodstuffs were initially allowed to be imported at a Bs.4.3:$1 rate while other goods had to use a Bs.7.50:$1 or a Bs.14:$1 rate, depending on their assigned import priority. Multiple rates create a bargaining opportunity with the government in which the skills in managing business–government relations, discussed in Chapter 6, come to the fore. Favorable treatment, albeit temporary, might be negotiated.

Marketing. The applicable marketing strategies mirror those discussed for sourcing. In general, the firm should be ready to sell to export markets when the local currency is undervalued and ready to boost domestic sales when the currency is overvalued. These strategies require the establishment of relationships with a variety of distributors and/or end buyers and may even involve developing new distribution channels and markets. The firm may also lobby the government to promote trade policies most favorable to its current position. Firms operating with global production and marketing strategies may be in an advantageous position to respond to marketing opportunities created by devaluations. For example, Becton Dickinson developed such a strategy for disposable syringes. When the Mexican peso was devalued, the company was able to shift its production to the Mexican plant, thereby gaining a price advantage over its competitor's U.S. plant.[42]

Financing. Since capital costs may also be regarded as a key factor in the profitability of operations, the firm should also be aware that exchange-rate disequilibria may affect the relative cost of borrowing in one currency rather than another (because of differentials in inflation, interest, and exchange rates discussed previously). The firm that has established its presence in a variety of capital markets will be more able to shift to lower-cost borrowing opportunities than a firm that finances all its capital requirements in a single currency.

CAPITAL SCARCITY

The third finance issue we shall now explore is capital scarcity. First we shall analyze the underlying causes of this scarcity and its consequences for companies. Then we shall examine how firms can deal with the scarcity problem.

Causes and Consequences

Economic conditions, institutional weaknesses, and international debt stand out as primary causes of capital scarcity in general and in the form of foreign exchange.

Economic Conditions. Lower incomes in developing countries are the fundamental constraint on savings. Most individuals and the country as a whole have to spend most of their income on basic necessities, thereby reducing savings capacity. Scarcity increases the cost of capital and decreases its accessibility to many potential borrowers. As was mentioned in the first section of this chapter, inflation also creates a disincentive for saving, because monetary assets tend to lose purchasing power. Savers will tend to invest in real assets such as land rather than monetary instruments until real interest rates become sufficiently positive. For example, since Thailand brought its inflation rate down, the financial depth (measured by currency, demand, time, and savings deposits in commercial banks as a percentage of GNP) rose from 34% in 1980 to 60% in 1987, while inflation-plagued Argentina had a financial depth of 18%.[43] Savings that do accumulate can be reduced even further by capital flight triggered by economic mismanagement, political instability, and fear of devaluation. For example, in Nicaragua in 1978 the intensification of the armed revolution stimulated a capital outflow of $275 million, which wiped out a trade surplus of $92 million, eroding the country's foreign reserves and reducing local liquidity by 7.2%.[44] Additional factors contributing to capital flight are corruption and the shielding of illegal payments, and the aggressive pursuit by international banks of deposits from foreigners. The magnitude of capital flight varies in response to these changing economic and political conditions and events. For all capital-importing countries annual capital flight averaged $7 billion in 1975–78, $22 billion in 1979–82, and $9 billion in 1983–85.[45]

Institutional Weaknesses. LDC financial institutions and markets are often weaker and narrower than in the developed countries. This problem is especially acute for equity capital. In 1985 deposit and central banks held 68% of the financial system's assets in developing countries and 39% in the developed countries, whereas long-term debt securities and equities markets and contractual savings institutions accounted for 47% of the assets in the developed countries and 21% in the LDCs.[46] Although stock markets in LDCs have existed for a long time (Egypt's was founded in 1889), most developing countries do not have stock exchanges. LDC stock markets' size and importance as a source of equity capital vary considerably, as revealed by the partial data in Table 7.4 on LDC stock exchanges. In 1988 the aggregate market capitalization of the stock markets in twenty-five developing countries was about $602 billion. Some of the more economically advanced and larger developing countries, such as Singapore, Korea, Taiwan, Hong Kong, Mexico, and India,

Table 7.4 Developing Country Stock Markets 1987–89[a]

	Number of Companies			Market Capitalization (millions of US$)		
	1987	1988	Percent Change	1987	1988	Percent Change
Latin America/Caribbean						
Argentina	206	186	− 9.7%	$ 1,519	$ 2,025	33.3%
Brazil[b]	590	589	− 0.2%	$ 16,900	$ 32,149	90.2%
Chile	209	205	− 1.9%	$ 5,341	$ 6,849	28.2%
Colombia	96	86	−10.4%	$ 1,255	$ 1,145	− 8.3%
Mexico	233	255	9.4%	$ 12,674	$ 23,630	86.4%
Venezuela	110	66	−40.0%	$ 2,278	$ 1,816	− 20.3%
Asia						
Hong Kong	253	282	11.5%	$ 54,088	$ 74,377	37.5%
India[b]	5460	2238	−59.0%	$ 14,480	$ 23,845	64.7%
Korea	389	502	29.1%	$ 32,905	$ 94,238	186.4%
Malaysia	232	238	2.6%	$ 18,531	$ 23,318	25.8%
Pakistan	379	404	6.6%	$ 1,960	$ 2,460	25.5%
Philippines	138	141	2.2%	$ 2,948	$ 4,280	45.2%
Singapore	317	132	58.4%	$ 17,931	$ 24,049	34.1%
Taiwan	141	163	14.2%	$ 48,634	$120,017	146.8%
Thailand	125	141	12.8%	$ 5,485	$ 8,811	60.6%
Africa						
Kenya	55	55	0.0%	$ —	$ 24	—
Nigeria	100	102	2.0%	$ 974	$ 960	− 1.4%
South Africa	565	754	33.5%	$128,663	$126,094	− 2.0%
Zimbabwe	53	53	0.0%	$ 718	$ 774	7.8%
Others						
Greece	116	119	2.6%	$ —	$ 4,285	—
Israel	269	265	− 1.5%	$ 12,001	$ 5,458	− 54.5%
Jordan	101	106	5.0%	$ 2,643	$ 2,233	− 15.5%
Kuwait	65	65	0.0%	$ 14,196	$ 11,838	− 16.6%
Portugal	143	171	19.6%	$ 8,857	$ 7,172	− 19.0%
Turkey	50	50	0.0%	$ 3,221	$ 1,135	− 64.8%

[a] Other LDCs with stock exchanges but for which data were lacking include Costa Rica, Guatemala, Panama, Trinidad and Tobago, Uruguay, Ivory Coast, Namibia, and Tunisia.
[b] São Paulo and Bombay only.

SOURCES: International Finance Corporation, *Quarterly Review of Emerging Stock Markets*, First Quarter 1988 (Washington, D.C.), p. 8; International Finance Corporation, *Emerging Stock Markets Factbook 1989* (Washington, D.C., 1989), pp. 6, 8–9, 31.

have large-volume stock exchanges, while those in other countries trade relatively few stocks. For example, in 1988 Taiwan's stock exchange had 163 firms listed and a market capitalization of $120 billion, and Korea's exchange had 502 stocks worth $94 billion, whereas only fifty-five stocks were being traded on the Nairobi stock exchange in 1988. India had four exchanges trading several thousand companies' stocks. Guatemala's stock market, founded in 1987, reportedly "opens twice a week for ten minutes and usually closes without any trading."[47] At the end of 1987 the stock markets in Brazil, Mexico, India, and Malaysia were larger than the markets in Australia and Norway, but for most LDCs the stock markets are thin or nonexistent.[48] The thinness has often led to speculative boom-and-bust cycles. Table 7.4 reveals considerable variation in market values and numbers of stocks listed.

Venture-capital firms are neither numerous nor heavily capitalized. Equity investments tend to be private placements. The paucity of equity capital often causes firms to be relatively highly leveraged. However, markets for bonds and other debt instruments are also thin and institutionally underdeveloped. Lastly, the capital that does exist is often highly concentrated and preferentially channeled to business groups rather than being widely accessible.

Public regulation often contributes to institutional weaknesses. In some instances legislation regarding financial institutions and markets is highly restrictive, limiting the flexibility required by equity-oriented financial institutions. In other cases there is too little regulation, leading to fraud or abuse that makes potential capital providers even more risk averse. For example, one study described the financial machinations of two brothers in one Latin American country in the late 1960s. They floated a $20-million stock issue aimed ultimately at gaining control of a company in which they had a minority position. To attract small investors the stock was offered as loan certificates with a guaranteed interest of 3% per month and redeemable at par, which was a "flagrant violation of accepted . . . financial practice, but strangely the Central Bank . . . , the national regulatory agency, failed to take notice."[49] The brothers then had the newly capitalized company guarantee a $2.6-million personal loan to them as directors. With this money they purchased another company, which they in turn resold to the main company for $9 million worth of stock, thereby giving them majority control. Thereafter, they suspended without notice the monthly interest payments and the redemption clause for the original stock issue. Despite clamoring from damaged stockholders, the Central Bank "blandly insisted that the move was outside its proper authority and continued to take no action."[50]

A further impediment to generating investor confidence and capital mobility is insufficient information about companies. This is due to regulatory weaknesses, the closely held nature of companies, limited development of accounting standards,[51] and general information imperfections in developing countries. Furthermore, companies may be reluctant to disclose information because it might be advantageous to competitors or it might lead to tax investigations by governmental authorities.

The lack of reliable information on businesses and markets increases the risk averseness of bankers and pushes them toward demanding greater collateralization. Often businesses are forced to turn to informal money markets, where interest rates are usually exceptionally high. This and high leveraging tend to pressure managers toward a short-run, quick-payback mentality. For example, "most of Taiwan's private firms . . . remain chronically undercapitalized, overindebted, and underaudited, driven into high-interest informal money markets [which supply 30% of business loans] to finance long-term development through short-term loans. They have relied on quick profits from proven technologies, and they have neglected basic research and development."[52] In addition to moneylenders, families, and friends, leasing is a nonbank credit source providing, for example, 8% in Korea and 14% in Malaysia in 1985.[53] Cooperative savings groups of varying degrees of formality are another source. In Togo loans through credit unions grew 33% annually during 1977–86.[54]

Government banking regulations frequently limit interest rates on loans and deposits. As indicated previously, during inflationary times this can even create negative real interest rates, which are a disincentive for banks to lend; they will tend to seek other more remunerative financial-service activities such as foreign-exchange transactions or special unregulated financing. Long-term lending particularly tends to dry up, thereby constraining companies' fixed asset investment programs. Depositors, like the banks, will try to escape these uneconomic government restrictions on capital. In Egypt, for example, negative regulated interest rates led depositors to shift their savings to Islamic banks, which are not strictly deposit-takers, interest-payers, or lenders, and therefore not subject to the banking regulations on interest; they were, therefore, able to pay positive, real "returns" to their "investing savers."[55]

Even when savings and lending rates are positive, banks are not always effective mobilizers of savings. The lack of administrative capacity, marketing skills, and customer orientation is a deterrent to attracting savers. Legislation in some countries requires banks to give lending preference to domestic companies over multinationals; MNCs are often expected to be capital providers rather than users.

Banks are often very slow in processing loans. Given the scarcity of capital, the concentrated structure of most LDC banking industries, and the resultant low level of competition, banks tend to hold the power in the borrower-lender relationship. In those instances where the banks are nationalized, these conditions are further exacerbated. In many developing countries the banking systems are almost entirely state-owned (e.g., Mexico and Costa Rica), and in almost all LDCs state-owned banks exist and often dominate the financial system (e.g., accounting for 40% of the deposits in Argentina and 50% of the bank assets in Greece.)[56] There is also an urban bias in lending, with banking institutions operating mainly in the large metropolitan centers. In India post office savings banks are used in rural areas to collect savings, but they do not make loans.[57]

The aforementioned characteristics reveal some of the chronic institutional weaknesses. However, many LDC financial organizations have been ravaged by inflation, recession, and adverse government regulations during the 1980s and are entering the 1990s in very precarious economic positions. Work by the World Bank indicates that "the number of banks and other financial institutions that are currently insolvent is without precedent in the last 50 years."[58] This suggests even greater institutional fragility and capital scarcity. Some governments, for example Turkey, are permitting the banks to have extra-high margins to offset bad debt losses and equity capital erosions. Preference may be given to existing borrowers in financial distress as the banks attempt to prevent loan defaults. Stronger companies may be crowded out by such distress borrowing or may face higher-cost capital if they do get loans. The same effects would occur if the government is borrowing from the banks directly or through reserve requirements in order to cover fiscal deficits.

International Debt. The mounting burden of servicing international debts has exacerbated capital scarcity in general and foreign-exchange availability in particular. In 1985 LDCs expended $132.6 billion to service $991 billion of debt. The largest debtors and the greatest debt-servicing burdens are in the Western Hemisphere, where in 1986 debt servicing demanded 45% of the countries' export earnings.[59] However, imports of critical goods may be even more important to a country and less postponable than debt-servicing; it is the current account deficit, not just the capital outflows, that causes foreign-exchange scarcity. The World Bank estimated in 1988 that the seventeen top debtors would require about $16 billion annually to cover their projected current account deficits over the next several years (net of any rescheduling or repayments); FDI could provide about $4 billion and multilateral agencies about $4 billion, leaving about $8 billion to be supplied by private banks, which would be double their recent lending rate.[60]

Instead of increasing their financing, banks have been writing off and reducing their LDC loans. In 1988, for example, Security Pacific Corp., the seventh largest bank in the United States, added $350 million to its reserves to cover LDC loan losses; American Express set aside a similar amount and wrote off all its Latin American private-sector corporate loans, having already in 1987 cut its LDC lending by 37%; and in late 1989 Manufacturers Hanover Corp., the sixth-largest U.S. bank, raised its Third World loan loss reserves by almost $1 billion by selling one of its subsidiaries to Japan's Dai-Ichi Kangyo Bank, the world's largest bank group.[61] These developments suggest continuing tightness in the LDCs' supply of capital from external sources. There are, however, some signs of progress. Latin America reduced its interest expense to export ratio from 41% in 1982 to 30% in 1988; annual GNP growth moved from a negative 2% in 1982–83 to a positive 3.4% in 1984–87.[62] Furthermore, not all developing countries find themselves strapped for foreign exchange: In 1987 Taiwan was wallowing in foreign-exchange reserves approaching the level of Japan's, and by 1989 it was giving economic aid to other developing countries. Nonetheless, for almost 40% of the developing countries capital repayments exceed new capital inflows, thereby causing a net reduction in the supply of capital and making foreign exchange particularly scarce.

Dealing with Scarcity

We shall examine three approaches to the problem of capital scarcity: mobilizing private sources, tapping governmental sources, and using the private/public vehicle of debt-equity swaps.

Private Sources. When a resource is scarce the first approach is to economize. For example, when selecting production technologies, one should consider investment savings possible from using more labor-intensive methods rather than capital-intensive ones (see Chapter 8). Working capital financing is generally more available than long-term financing. To overcome the shortage of foreign exchange, every significant use of foreign exchange should be examined for substitution possibilities. For example, one can substitute local supplies for imported inputs, although this may require investments in one's own facilities and/or training of local suppliers to produce to the required specifications. A survey of fifty-two companies in four Latin American countries found that firms in all countries increased their local sourcing to cope with foreign-exchange shortages during 1981–83.[63]

A second approach is to earn your own. Self-financing through retained earnings is often less expensive and more certain. The aforementioned survey also found increased use of self-financing by the companies. Business groups, as was mentioned in Chapter 5, often develop a financial institution as part of their conglomerate to ensure themselves a source of financing as well as to engage in a usually profitable activity. To address the foreign-exchange shortage, some firms expand into export operations even though that was not their original strategy.

Despite the institutional weaknesses and thinness of equity markets, capital can be raised locally. There is often pent-up demand to invest but a lack of opportunities with acceptable risks and rewards. Reputable companies, particularly MNCs, are often perceived as attractive investments. For example, in capitalizing KCL in 1962, Cummins Engine and Kirloskar offered the public 25% of the stock in their joint venture through the Bombay Stock Exchange; it was oversubscribed eightyfold, and the Exchange had to make a pro-rata allocation of five shares per subscriber.[64] Ciba-Geigy sold 25% of its Indian joint venture at 40% over book value.[65] The Kenyan government's offering of 20% of its Kenya Commercial Bank in July 1988, which was the largest single public share issue in the history of the Nairobi Stock Exchange, was oversubscribed three and a quarter times.[66] Private placements and joint ventures are more common than public offerings as mechanisms for raising capital in most LDCs. (Chapter 10 analyzes the pros and cons of joint ventures.)

Banks, finance corporations, and informal money-market lenders are other sources of capital. Bank loans can often be financially attractive in inflationary environments where government limitations on interest charges create negative real interest rates. Finance corporations tend to be more costly but sometimes have greater flexibility in structuring special financing arrangements. Informal money markets are almost always the most expensive source of funds; they service those borrowers unable to tap formal market sources. Supplier credits can sometimes be an important source of working capital, but one must carefully assess the cost. Larger firms can generally get preferential treatment from banks because of their lower risk. Banking relationships are often personalized; social connections may facilitate access. MNCs generally have greater access to international banks abroad and in-country, thanks to ongoing relationships of the parent corporations. This and their access to equity funds from their parents can be a source of competitive advantage in capital-scarce environments. When foreign funding is used, managers must carefully manage the concommitant foreign-exchange exposure, as discussed in the previous section.

Scarcity and institutional weaknesses in developing country financial markets constitute opportunities for financial institutions. International banks with a greater capital base to draw on may be in a competitively stronger position than the many local banks that are on the brink of insolvency. With economic development the needs and sophistication of the financial markets will grow. Firms able to meet those needs will reap attractive rewards.

Public Sources. As part of their development strategies, governments often have special lines of credit, such as for exports or agricultural development, offered through their state-owned banks, or even through private banks. Tapping these sources becomes part of the business–government relations agenda discussed in the previous chapter.

For multinationals, their home governments may also be sources of capital. Where equipment exports are involved, home governments often have financing facilities such as the U.S. Export-Import Bank. Bilateral aid to LDCs is often tied to purchases of equipment or materials from home country suppliers. In setting up its KCL joint venture, Cummins Engine was able to obtain low-cost rupee loans from the U.S. Agency for International Development's local currency funds, thereby reducing the company's foreign-exchange usage and exposure. Japanese firms have frequently used their government's aid program as a financing vehicle for international operations in developing countries. The Japanese government's Overseas Economic Co-operation Fund ties part of its aid to large ventures that are beyond the means of its private investors; it will often take a 30%–40% share in a Japanese investment consortium.[67] In 1987 the Japanese government announced a $2-billion aid package for Southeast Asia, consisting mainly of a loan fund to promote private sector joint ventures between Japanese and ASEAN companies.[68]

Multilateral agencies also can be a capital source. The World Bank provided $12 billion in loans to LDC financial institutions between 1981–87 for disbursement to small and medium scale enterprises; $15 billion more has gone to agricultural and agroindustrial development.[69] About half of the World Bank's $18 billion in loans in 1987 went for infrastructure (transportation, telecommunications, power, water), much of which was acquired in international markets. Similarly, the regional development banks (the Inter-american Development Bank, the Asian Development Bank, and the African Development Bank) may be indirect sources of financing through their loans to governments. Additionally, the World Bank (and to a lesser extent the regional banks) began in 1983 cofinancing operations with commercial lenders. This has been through direct participation in longer-maturity portions of commercial loans, guarantees of later maturities, and contingent obligations to increase financing if interest rate variations increase repayment flows.[70] The OPEC nations, primarily the Arab countries, provided $74 billion in aid during 1974–84, which constituted 22% of aid given by all donors.[71]

The International Finance Corporation (IFC), the equity arm of the World Bank, specializes in coinvestments with private companies in developing countries. The IFC is the largest international source of direct project financing for private investments in the Third World. As of 1988 the IFC had provided financing to about one thousand companies in more than ninety developing countries. Its portfolio was valued at roughly $3 billion, and its annual investment rate was around $1 billion.[72] The IFC invests in a project only if sufficient capital cannot be raised from other sources on reasonable terms. As a coinvestor it will usually provide no more than 25% of the share capital, but will play an active role in mobilizing other investors. During the 1976–86 decade it raised $2 billion from two hundred financial institutions in its syndicated financings. The IFC financial packages range from $1 million to $250 million, but usually the minimum size of a project is $4 million.

As a development finance institution, the IFC will invest only in projects that are privately profitable and developmentally beneficial to the host country. In terms of the congruency analysis in Chapter 6, the IFC projects must fall into the joint acceptability range, with public ECBA and private financial rates of return above the respective hurdle rates. IFC equity investments are considered as national capital in complying with governments' foreign ownership limitations. IFC loans are generally seven to twelve years at commercial variable and fixed rates and may include an initial amortization grace period. The IFC has special loan facilities to serve the particular needs of sub-Saharan Africa and the Caribbean and to assist in debt restructurings.[73] About 14% of IFC's portfolio is in sub-Saharan Africa, with projects ranging from a $0.6-million loan to a Somali packaging company to a $55-million investment in rehabilitating Ghana's largest gold mine. Since 1985 the IFC has also been involved in forty-eight corporate debt restructurings, more than half of them in Latin America and the Caribbean.

In addition to financing, IFC offers technical assistance to investors through its Washington, D.C., headquarters or its twelve country offices. It assists in finding local partners and dealing with host governments and views itself as a catalyst for projects. For example, its long involvement in the Brazilian petrochemical industry enabled it to create a profitable and developmentally important joint venture among a Brazilian SOE, two local Brazilian private firms, a U.S. technical partner, and the IFC.[74]

Debt-Equity Swaps. A final approach to the problem of capital and foreign-exchange scarcity is financial swaps. These new forms of financial transactions emerged as one means of partially extricating governments, private borrowers, and international banks from the debt crisis. The principal form is debt-equity swaps. The specific mechanisms vary, but they generally involve the elements in the following illustrative transaction (also depicted in Figure 7.2):

- A bank holding debt from an LDC wishes to remove this debt from its portfolio because of the perceived repayment risk, so the

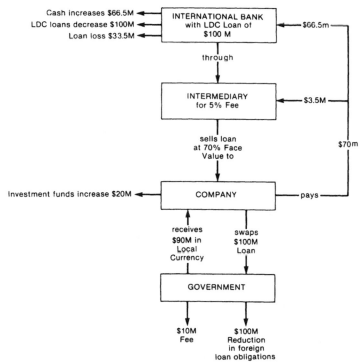

Figure 7.2 Debt-Equity Swap

bank offers to sell $100 million of it at a discount from face value, say 30%.

- An investment banker or other intermediary finds a buyer for the debt paper, which might be a company in need of the debtor country's currency; the intermediary receives, for example, a 5% fee for this service.

- The buyer, assisted by the intermediary, arranges to sell this $100 million debt to the debtor country's central bank at, say, 90% of the face value in local currency equivalent; in effect, they are "swapping" the dollar debt for local currency, with the government charging a 10% fee.

- The company then uses the $90 million worth of local currency to make a local equity investment, e.g., to increase the capacity of its subsidiary's plant.

The advantages of the swap are that the bank cleans up its portfolio by eliminating a bad debt risk and increases its liquidity, although it does incur a loss equal to the discount at which it sold the loan. The purchasing company acquires needed investment capital cheaply: $90 million worth of local currency for a $70 million outlay. The debtor country reduces its foreign debt-servicing burden by $100 million, and the capital is redeployed in productive investments. The financial intermediary earns a $3.5-million service fee. The selling bank may also have various portfolio-management objectives motivating the transaction, such as altering its country mix (concentrating or diversifying), shortening the maturities, or adjusting tax exposures. In some cases two banks might directly swap loans to rebalance their portfolios.

Although the first debt-equity swap reportedly occurred in Turkey in 1980, this secondary market did not significantly increase until the mid-1980s. The transaction volume in 1987 was around $5 billion to $6 billion.[75] It is a thin market but increasingly formalized with quotes on the discount rates at which various countries' debts are being sold. The discount rates differ significantly across countries. For example, in July 1985 Mexican debt was selling at 81 cents on the dollar while Peru was selling at 47 cents. Table 7.5 illustrates how the rates can dramatically shift over time, as a result of changing economic or political conditions. Mexico's rates dropped during a one-year period from 81 cents to 57 cents because of oil price decreases in 1986 and plummeted even further in 1987; Peru's rates fell from 47 cents to 20 cents after the government announced that its debt servicing was going to be linked to export earnings.

Table 7.5 Discounted Levels of Debt of Selected Countries
(*cents per dollar of debt*)

	Mexico	Venezuela	Peru
July 1985	81	82	47
July 1986	57	77	20

SOURCE: Derived from Leroy O. Laney, "The Secondary Market in Developing Country Debt: Some Observations and Policy Implications," *Economic Review* (Federal Reserve Bank of Dallas), July 1987, p. 2.

And Brazil's rate dropped 11 cents after it announced it would cease to pay interest on its loans. The discounts for the heavily indebted countries have ranged from 20% to 90% and have averaged about 55%.[76]

The thinness of the market and the magnitude of the discounts create negotiation opportunities concerning these rates. A critical part of the analysis is risk assessment. One Federal Reserve official observed that "any error in accurately incorporating risk is more likely to come from an inability to read political or sociostructural aspects of a country correctly than from any inaccuracy in measuring economic risk or debt-servicing ability."[77] The deployment of our Environmental Analysis Framework will help in systematically evaluating the possible risks and in capitalizing on others' misassessments and excessive discounts.

European banks have been very active sellers of their debt because they were less constrained than U.S. banks by regulations that would cause discounts to impair their balance sheets. Furthermore, since most international debt is dollar-denominated, the decline of the dollar significantly reduced the value of these loans to Europeans. As a result, the cost of removing these loans from their portfolios was reduced. Regional U.S. banks have also been moving their loans to eliminate these relatively small but troublesome parts of their portfolios. The major international banks were beginning in 1987 to turn on a larger scale into swapping their LDC debt. Shortly after Citibank added $3 billion to its bad-debt reserve in early 1987, it announced that it would be moving heavily into debt-equity swapping. It projected a $5-billion reduction in its LDC loans over the 1987–90 period.[78] But even before Citibank's widely publicized announcement, Bankers Trust had already indicated it would pursue a strategy to convert much of its loan portfolio into equity investments.[79] Japanese banks shifted LDC loans to a collectively owned Cayman Islands factoring company to facilitate their debt-equity swapping operations.[80]

The market-makers of debt-equity swaps were initially major investment bankers. Small entrepreneurial intermediaries have also played major roles in the early stages. For example, the European InterAmerican Finance Corporation handled about one-sixth of all Latin American swaps through 1986.[81] The intermediaries' commissions have ranged from 0.25% to 15%. The government of the Philippines charges a handling fee of 5%–10% for swaps in its country. Large commercial banks have increasingly performed the intermediary function, often finding buyers among their MNC clients.

By mid-1987 three countries had led the way with official debt-equity swap programs: Chile, the Philippines, and Mexico. A description of some of their actions illustrates the experience.

Chile. The Chilean government instituted its program in mid-1985, and over the first twenty months made twenty-five deals converting $1.4 billion of Chile's $21-billion debt. The average discount rate was 35%.[82] Chile's first swap was with the National Bank of Saudi Arabia, which set up a local holding company with $10 million of converted debt that it then invested in local companies. By 1987 the conversion total had risen to $25 million, and the investments were in such operations as fish processing, electric utilities, and gas transmission.[83] Bankers Trust converted its own loans to raise $43 million in local currency, with which it purchased controlling interest in a large insurance company and the country's largest pension-fund manager. The latter had been an SOE that was privatized.[84] The largest transaction to date was by a New Zealand paper products company that purchased $161 million of public sector debt for $115 million, which it then swapped for a 50% holding in a large Chilean natural resource company. Of the total swapped investments, 31% were in the automotive sector, 16% in tourism, 13% in capital goods, and 8% in export assembly operations.[85]

Philippines. Japanese companies have engaged in several swaps to assist their subsidiaries in the Philippines. Japan Airlines bought $1 million for $700,000 plus $100,000 in fees to Citicorp and the Philippine government to refurbish the Manila Garden Hotel owned by a JAL subsidiary. Kawasaki purchased $1.2 million at a 30% discount, which it tendered to the government at 95%, using the pesos to invest in its local subsidiary. Kao Corporation, a soap maker, swapped $17 million to increase the capacity of its coconut oil plant.[86] Several foreign banks have swapped their own debt to acquire positions in local financial institutions: American Express Bank converted $15 million of its debt paper to acquire a 40% interest in the International Corporation Bank; First

National Bank of Boston swapped a portion of its $32 million for a 40% interest in the Commercial Bank of Manila; and First Pacific Ltd., a Hong Kong banking corporation, swapped for shares in the Associated Bank in Manila.[87]

Mexico. Several foreign auto manufacturers swapped debt and used the proceeds to invest in their local facilities. Chrysler purchased $100 million at a 40% discount from European banks and redeemed it at 92 cents from the government, which then released the pesos at three intervals to reduce the inflationary pressure of the emission. One of the main reasons for Chrysler's decision to swap was its need to meet the government's regulation stipulating that it had to earn sufficient foreign exchange to offset its imports. The swap's proceeds not only allowed it to expand capacity to export its sports coupe model to the United States at the price-reducing exchange rate, it also helped to retire $20 million of expensive short-term debt.[88] Volkswagen swapped $140 million, Ford $50 million, Nissan $54 million, and Renault $17 million.[89] Many other companies, ranging from Gillette to Christian Dior to Club Mediterranean, have also arranged swaps. But the biggest deal, formulated in 1987 by Morgan Guaranty Trust, was around $1 billion for the acquisition of a 45% interest in the country's largest business group, Alfa. American Express Bank has established a wholly owned subsidiary to convert its LDC debt and had plans to swap about $150 million of public-sector debt into equity positions in local companies.

=

The other large Latin American debtor, Brazil, had a debt-equity swap program in 1983 and converted $1.8 million but then abandoned it. Critics of swaps in Brazil and other countries raise several objections: The money would have come in anyway; foreigners gain control of local enterprises; government funds should go to higher-priority uses than debt retirement; it is a mechanism to bypass repatriation restrictions, and it is inflationary. Governments generally impose restrictions on the dividend and capital outflow of equity investments. In Chile, for example, profits earned during the first four years may begin to be remitted in the fifth year at a 25% rate and capital may be repatriated after ten years. Others also assert that local currency payments may be inflationary. If swaps are financed through the banking system, the money supply will expand; if they are financed with government bonds to the private sector, interest rates may be pushed up and private borrowers crowded out.[90]

In spite of these objections swaps are increasing, even in Brazil. In mid-1987 Norwest Bank Minneapolis and the Bank of Scotland converted loan paper worth $26 million into a 28.7% equity stake in a major Brazilian paper producer with prospects of at least an annual 4% dividend and the right to repatriate the appreciated capital investment after twelve years.[91] Swaps allow countries to redeploy debt capital in ways that may be more productive than the first time around. One study of ninety-nine debt-equity swaps in Argentina, Brazil, Chile, and Mexico, found that in 61% of the transactions, the investors would not have made the deal without the swap mechanism.[92] Clearly, swaps will not greatly reduce the total LDC debt. Nonetheless, the magnitude will be economically significant at the national level and will create many important financing opportunities for individual companies. Some estimated that the market would be above $50 billion by 1997.[93]

It is likely that innovative forms of swaps will emerge. For example, an IRS ruling allows U.S. companies to convert their dollar debts to local currency, donate the proceeds to U.S. charitable organizations working in the LDC, deduct the donation from its taxes, and take a loss equivalent to the difference between the original value of the loan and the swapped value.[94] Companies will have to use many different financial instruments to execute successfully the major debt restructurings needed to allow them to move forward on a sounder financial footing. For example, Valores Industriales, S.A., one of Mexico's largest private industrial groups, completed in 1989 the restructuring of its $1.7-billion debt through the use of debt-to-equity conversions, debt-to-debt swaps, discounted debt buybacks, debt rescheduling, sale of assets, and new public and private stock offerings. This mix was required to meet the different needs of its sixty-seven creditors and allowed the company to reduce its debt 75%.[95]

CONCLUSION

The task of financial management in LDCs is particularly demanding. Our attention has focused on three critical problem areas: inflation, foreign-exchange exposure, and capital scarcity. Mismanagement in these areas can devastate a company's profits, capital structure, and economic viability.

Inflation can erode capital and profits, increase tax burdens, push up financing costs, complicate liquidity management, and alter relations with suppliers, customers, bankers, competitors, and government. To manage under inflationary conditions, firms should set up their management information systems to monitor and forecast price changes. Accounting methods have to be adjusted to recognize the continual rise in costs; a focus on the future rather than the past is required. Setting prices must be geared toward preserving real margins. Close management of receivables and payables is imperative; one should generally try to shorten credit and lengthen payables. Lastly, personnel performance indicators may require adjustment to avoid distortions due to inflation.

Foreign-exchange exposure arises from shifts in a country's exchange rate. As with inflation, monitoring and predicting changes in the exchange rate become an important part of financial information flows. Transaction exposure occurs when a company agrees to purchase or sell a good or service (including loans) at a fixed price in a foreign currency at a future date. The risk that the values will change because of a shift in exchange rates can be managed through alternate invoicing, various forms of hedging, or transaction balancing. Translation exposure occurs when the financial results of a company's overseas operations are consolidated with the parent's financial statements. The exposure and how to manage it depend in part on the accounting method used to make the translation and how foreign-exchange losses or gains are handled. One should take care that a method (such as balance-sheet hedging) for reducing this accounting risk does not in turn create business problems. Operating exposure arises from the impact on costs and prices of changes in the real exchange rate. Devaluations, for example, can increase the costs of imported inputs or competing goods and decrease the prices of exported goods. Companies can influence their operating exposure by the configuration of their sourcing, markets, and financing.

Capital scarcity is a chronic condition in developing countries, caused by low levels of incomes and savings and weaknesses of financial institutions and markets. The international debt burden is a drain on the capital supply and heightens the scarcity of foreign exchange. To cope with this scarcity, firms must constantly economize on capital uses, perhaps through technology choices. Despite the thinness of capital markets, equity funds can be raised through public offerings if the firms are viewed as reputable. Private placements and joint ventures are the other common routes to equity financing. Multinationals are sometimes discriminated against in local credit allocations; they often also have preferential access to international banks. Institutional weaknesses in capital markets create opportunities for creative and efficient financial institutions. Lastly, debt-to-equity and other forms of financial swaps have emerged as financially attractive capital sources both for companies looking to expand existing operations and for firms designing entry strategies.

Although the problems of inflation, foreign exchange, and capital scarcity are complex and involve many factors in the external environment that are beyond the manager's control, their effects are manageable. Not all firms or managers will be equally disposed or able to respond to these challenges. Those who establish competency will be better poised to convert these critical problems into competitive advantages.

8

Production

Managing Technology

O ur analysis of production issues focuses on the strategically critical area of technology management. To a large extent production technologies in developing countries have been transferred from more technically advanced nations, yet those technologies face very different environments in LDCs. The issue is how to achieve an appropriate technological fit, so we shall concentrate our analysis on technology choice and adaptation. In this chapter's final section we shift our attention to a related aspect of technology management: local procurement. LDC suppliers often are not equipped technologically or managerially to meet the demands of manufacturers and processors, which causes a multitude of quality and cost problems. Handling those supplier problems often involves technology transfer and management issues.

Dealing with the problems of production technology has been a central challenge especially for local and multinational firms engaged in LDC manufacturing for export, because serving the international market intensifies the technological demands. As indicated in Chapter 1, developing countries have become important as manufacturing bases for export, with a more than tenfold increase in manufactured exports since the mid-1970s. By 1986 LDCs were earning more foreign exchange from manufactured exports than from agricultural or mineral exports.[1] In EAF terms, the international environment affects LDC production operations in two key ways: as a technology source and as a market outlet. To highlight the increasingly important role of LDC manufacturing in global production strategies, we shall begin the chapter with a brief description of the growing importance of the "offshore production" phenomenon.

OFFSHORE PRODUCTION

The move toward global production strategies is broad and accelerating. As one manager from National Semiconductor put it, "In today's high tech environment . . . the choice has become not one of 'whether' but of 'where' and 'when'." By the early 1980s National had twenty plants in eight countries, mostly developing nations.[2] The Asia-Pacific countries have been preferred as offshore locations. Between 1966 and 1977 exports of U.S. foreign manufacturing affiliates to the United States rose from 10% to 27% of total sales, with the share for electrical machinery reaching 70%.[3] The upward trend has continued into the 1990s. IBM also relies on LDC suppliers: It is estimated that 73% of the manufacturing cost of its PC consists of components made by Asian producers.[4] Several leading U.S. manufacturers of electromechanical relays have more than half their sales from offshore operations.[5] A similar trend toward overseas production exists among producers of video display terminals.[6] Auto manufacturers, too, are turning to LDCs and are, for example, sourcing from Mexico, whose proximity to the United States reduces transport costs and helps offset lower wage rates in many Asian countries. Wiring harnesses can be produced in Mexico for 25% less than in Detroit and more cheaply than in Taiwan or Korea, thanks to lower freight costs for this relatively bulky product.[7] Latin America's exports of auto products to the United States increased from $0.8 billion in 1981 to $4.2 billion in 1986.[8]

More than a thousand companies from the United States, Japan, Korea, and other countries have established manufacturing facilities in Mexico, over half of them set up during the 1980s. A particular attraction has been the government's *maquiladora* program, which allows a firm to set up assembly or other labor-intensive operations, mainly in special duty free border zones and with certain exemptions from foreign investment restrictions such as on majority ownership.[9] LDC governments try to attract offshore production to meet their pressing need to generate employment for their expanding labor force. In effect, there is a congruence of governments' national development strategies with the MNCs' strategies of developing global production networks. Both wage and skill differences were important factors in AT&T's decision to shift its production of cord telephones to Thailand, thereby freeing up its Singapore plant for manufacturing the more sophisticated cordless phones.[10] Many agribusiness firms, such as seed companies, internationalize for lower labor and land costs and to avail themselves of climatic conditions that permit year-round production from the different sites. Global production strategies entail a country portfolio approach based on complementarity and coordination.

U.S. firms obtain tariff exemptions through their offshore assembly operations. They ship semifinished products abroad and then obtain finished or nearly finished goods back, paying duties only on the value-added abroad. These include products shipped out ready for assembly without further fabrication (item 807 on the U.S. Tariff Schedule), articles sent out for repair or alteration (item 806.20), and nonprecious metals exported for processing (item 806.30). Products exported but not made more valuable, e.g., repackaging (item 800), enter duty-free, as do products with less than 35% value-added from LDCs designated as beneficiaries under the Generalized System of Preferences. Such offshore procurement from LDCs increased forty-one times between 1966 and 1987.[11] By the mid-1980s these imports had reached $9 billion, with Mexico supplying 42%, Malaysia 14%, Singapore 11%, the Philippines 8%, Korea 6%, Taiwan 6%, and Hong Kong 5%.[12] Almost a third of those imports were semiconductors and parts; 20% were televisions, radio apparatus, and office machines; 7% textile products; 4% electrical circuit and conductor equipment; and 4% motors and engines.[13] Most of those imports came from U.S. MNC affiliates assembling abroad, except for textiles and apparel, which tended to be procured from independently owned subcontractors.

It is not just U.S. multinationals that have moved offshore; Japanese firms have also set up international operations. NEC, for example, has extensive overseas facilities, and Hitachi is making color TV sets and other products in Taiwan. Like their U.S. counterparts, Japanese firms are attracted to the lower cost structures in developing countries. In Taiwan, for example, wages for assembly workers in 1983 were $1 per hour, engineers and programmers earned only about $500 monthly, and plant space was 22 cents per square foot, as against $1.40 in Silicon Valley.[14] The Japanese producer of miniature bearings, Minebea, experienced significantly lower production costs in its Thai and Singapore plants because of lower wage and energy costs and through avoidance of Japan's cost escalation due to the yen's rising value. This led the company's vice president to remark, "We're having 'thank-you-high-yen' bargain sales. . . . The competition is sure matching our prices, but the same price which brings us profits is [making] the competition bleed."[15] European firms, more than their Japanese or American counterparts, tend to invest in LDCs to serve local markets rather than to create offshore production sites for exporting to home markets.[16]

In the early 1970s the principal exporters were MNC subsidiaries with manufacturing facilities mainly in the NICs, but indigenous firms have become increasingly significant exporters. By 1980 "50 percent of the television sets exported from Korea, 78 percent of the radios from Taiwan and 80 percent of the phonographs and cassette recorders from Hong Kong" were produced by local firms.[17] Some of these Third World MNCs from Taiwan and Korea, including Tatung, Goldstar, and Samsung, even set up production facilities in the United States and England to overcome emerging trade barriers against their exports. International sourcing is increasingly being seen by experts as critical to ensuring global competitiveness, and the more advanced developing countries, the NIC's, are seen as sources of production and process innovations. Cost advantages are not the only strategic reason to integrate developing countries into the global production strategy.[18]

Offshore production in developing countries offers many attractive advantages, but its benefits are not automatic or guaranteed. Both Tandon and Seagate set up production operations in Singapore and India to obtain competitive advantages in the disk-drive market through lower labor costs. They both experienced rapid growth but later encountered serious problems of product quality and financial losses.[19] Furthermore, labor costs increase over time, eroding the cost advantage. Successful operations in the NICs require careful management of special technological and organizational problems. Those problems are even more acute in LDCs that have lower levels of industrialization yet are edging into the international sourcing equation. They will be at the center of the global production system in the near future. For example, the People's Republic of China has a goal of becoming a major exporter of manufactured goods, and it is very likely that it will achieve that goal. However, the difficulties in setting up manufacturing operations there and in other LDCs are very large. At the heart of managing these production challenges are the tasks of choosing and adapting technologies as well as dealing with local procurement problems.

TECHNOLOGY TRANSFER

An integral part of technology management is the selection of the vehicle for transferring the technology to the developing country. None of the multiple mechanisms for technology transfer is inherently superior to the others. Their appropriateness depends on the characteristics and goals of the supplier and the receiver of the technology, its nature, the industry's competitive situation, the governments' policies and actions, and each country's particular environmental characteristics. In effect, the choice of transfer mechanism will be situation-specific. Furthermore, the same transfer process often uses multiple vehicles. It is appropriate here, however, to delineate briefly the principal vehicles used to transfer technology.

Direct Technology Transfer Mechanisms

Foreign Direct Investment. With FDI the technology transferor is also an investor/owner of the recipient. The transfer is an intrafirm process between parent and subsidiary. For U.S. MNCs the share of technology payments coming through intrafirm transactions rose during the 1970s.[20] The intrafirm technology transfer increases control over the process, although this can become more complicated when the subsidiary is a joint venture (see Chapter 10). In one study of the transfer of 221 innovations to Asian developing countries between 1945 and 1978, 65% were via FDI, including 30% as joint ventures.[21]

Licensing. Licenses often accompany FDI but also serve as separate major transfer mechanisms (Chapter 10 provides a comparative analysis of FDI and licensing). Of the innovation transfers to Asia mentioned above, 35% were through licensing.[22] Korea's Hyundai Motor Company, for example, began as an assembler under licenses and technical agreements with Ford. It later licensed more than thirty technologies from Japan, the United States, and England, as well as set up its own R&D department as part of its strategy to become a successful exporter.[23]

Licenses often contain stipulations regarding quality, prices, volumes, sources of material and equipment inputs, and limitations on exporting, patent transfers, and local R&D. Such restrictions in technology contracts have increasingly come under scrutiny by LDC governments. Many governments require the registration and approval of all technology contracts. Mexico, for example, rejected 35% of the 4,600 agreements reviewed during the 1970s because of high costs or restrictive clauses such as the excessive duration of agreements, prohibition of the use of nonpatented technology or of production after the agreement period, grant-back clauses on innovations by the licensee, submission of agreements to foreign laws, and export restrictions.[24]

Equipment Imports. Machines embody technology, and equipment suppliers are often key information transmitters on their use. Imported equipment can also be copied. When Japan was still a developing country, its main strategy for technology acquisition was captured by the slogan: "The first machine by import, the second by domestic production."[25]

Technical Services and Training. Technology suppliers often provide direct services to the recipients. At one extreme, these services could be constructing a plant on a turnkey basis and training its personnel. Or they might involve training for a specific technology or skill. At another extreme, the transfer might be slower if the foreign company has a management contract giving it responsibility for the actual administration of the operations, within which training would be one aspect. Management contracts are sometimes used to ensure that other technology being transferred will be appropriately utilized.[26]

Public Information. This source includes technical journals, books, and international conferences. Whereas the other transfer vehicles involve active technology providers, these sources are passive and depend on the technology seekers' efforts to obtain the information.

Education. Another transfer vehicle is formal and informal training through degree programs, short courses, or working for the technology-using companies. National educational policies are crucial in this area.

As technology transfer takes place, LDCs' technological capability increases. This capacity can be viewed as an ability to handle increasingly complex technical and organizational tasks of transforming inputs into outputs. Figure 8.1 presents a simplified view of this technology transformation process. There are four rungs on this "Technological Capability Ladder": adoption, adaptation, enhancement, and creation.[27] As one moves up the capability ladder, the technological complexity increases and the level of human skill required rises. At the first level, adoption, the task involves identifying, assessing, and acquiring the technology through one of the transfer mechanisms discussed above. The second level, adaptation, involves making whatever engineering or operational adjustments in the technology are needed to set up and run the production system in the LDC environment. The third level, enhancement, produces improvements in the technology and requires innovative capability. At the top level, a country or firm reaches the technology creation frontier and becomes a generator of new knowledge. At this point the developing country becomes a technology supplier rather than just a buyer. Developing countries vary in their technological capabilities, both in general and in specific industries. It is important for managers to assess these

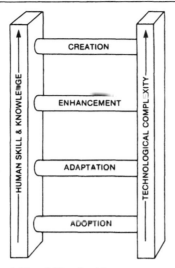

Figure 8.1 Technological Capability Ladder

technological capabilities, because they influence the types of technologies that should be chosen and how they should be transferred, adapted, developed, and managed.

TECHNOLOGY CHOICE AND ADAPTATION

Technology choice is a strategic issue. Different choices can spearhead very distinct types of competitive strategies. For example, one type of technology will achieve a low-cost, high-volume, standardized product strategy, while a different technology is needed for a strategy of high-quality product differentiation. Different technological choices will create distinct capital or technical barriers to entry. The competitive advantage gained from the technology choice is greatly determined by how well the technology fits the particular business environment.

Much discussion about technology choice in LDCs has been reduced to a dichotomous argument between labor-intensity and capital-intensity. This tendency is understandable. The large supply of relatively low-cost labor in most developing countries suggests that they hold a comparative advantage here. Furthermore, social and political pressures caused by growing unemployment make labor-intensive technologies attractive to many LDC governments. These considerations notwithstanding, positing the technology issue as a labor-versus-capital choice is a simplistic reduction of a more complex decision. Some companies mistakenly view technology acquisition as only a decision to purchase machinery rather than as part of a long-term technological strategy. Our approach to technology choice and adaptation aims to capture this broader set of considerations.

Five variables should be weighed in choosing the technology: factor costs, market requirements, technical constraints, input scarcities, and competitive dynamics. The company's strategy interacts with each of these. Furthermore, the issue is not simply selecting one type of technology over another, but also identifying opportunities to adapt the selected type for a better fit, by changing either the technology to fit the environment or the environment to fit the technology.

Factor Costs

Where labor and capital are substitutable in a production technology, their relative costs should be weighed.[28] The first task is to assess the costs correctly, and the second is to consider their importance among the criteria in the choice of technology.

Relatively low nominal wage rates stand out, but they are only the starting point in the cost calculation. As we know from our discussion of the Public-Policy Impact Chain, government actions affect cost structures. Legislated social benefits need to be added. In Mexico, for example, these include 6–14 paid vacation days, five paid national holidays, a Christmas bonus of fifteen days' pay, 15% social security contribution, and a 5% housing fund contribution.[29] Additional benefits, for example, in Colombia were a 4% family subsidy, a 2% education subsidy, and a transportation allowance.[30] Often labor legislation also includes significant severance benefits (e.g., one month's salary for every year employed), which have to be included in the calculation. Turnover rates and concommitant recruiting and training costs should also be considered. One should examine trends rather than just current rates. Rising wage rates in Korea, for example, led Fujitsu in 1983 to end its ten-year-old joint venture in consumer electronics; Singapore's rapidly increasing wages caused similar disincentives for labor-intensive industries.

The hourly or monthly wage and benefits rate is still not the relevant cost. Rather, one is interested in the labor cost per unit of output, because it incorporates labor productivity into the analysis. The potential benefits of cheap labor can be erased by low productivity. For example, wage rates in Haiti were one-fifteenth of those in Mississippi, but unit labor costs were about equal because of productivity differences.[31] In the clothing industry, hourly wage rates in Hong Kong, Taiwan, and South Korea average about 22% of U.S. rates and more than offset their lower productivity levels (averaging about 65% of U.S. levels), giving a unit labor cost less than half that of U.S. producers.[32] Because labor's productivity is affected by interaction with capital equipment configurations, it may change with different mixes and new technologies. For example, some observers foresee for the textile industry that introducing computer-aided design and manufacturing (CAD/CAM) installations in grading, marking, cutting, and sewing will increase productivity sufficiently in industrialized nations' textile mills to overcome lower LDC wage rates. Another consideration in costing is that different firms face different wage rates: MNCs and unionized firms tend to pay higher wages, and informal-sector firms often do not pay legislated fringe benefits or even the minimum wage.

The cost of capital can vary widely depending on the source; different firms have varying access to these sources. (The EAF and the Public-Policy Impact Chain can reveal how government policies will affect different groups' cost of capital.) Government programs often offer subsidized interest rates to stimulate investment in certain regions or particular sectors such as agriculture or new industries. Such government subsidies lower the price of capital and create incentives to opt for more capital-intensive technologies. Furthermore, if those interest rates or principal repayments are not adjusted to compensate for inflation, the interest rates and cost of capital may even be negative, as discussed in Chapter 7. The inward-oriented ISI strategies discussed in Chapter 4 often lead to overvalued exchange rates that make capital equipment imports cheaper. Other government tax policies (depreciation allowances, equipment investment credits, or import duty exemptions) can create a similar bias toward using machines rather than people. Studies have shown that the combined effects of these various policy-induced "market distortions" can significantly reduce capital costs, for example, by 76% in Pakistan and 36% in Tunisia.[33] Ironically, these same governments often have stated goals and other policies aimed at increasing employment.

As was pointed out in the previous chapter, in LDCs capital is generally scarce and financial markets are underdeveloped. Small firms in particular have relatively low access to formal financial institutions. The cost of capital from informal-sector lenders will be much higher and less available. This pushes firms toward more labor-intensive methods.[34] One study of shoe manufacturers and brick factories in Malaysia found that firms without access to bank credit opted for labor-intensive methods, while almost all of those with such credit chose more capital-intensive techniques.[35] In large Indonesian textile mills automatic looms rapidly displaced hand looms, largely because government interest regulations kept annual nominal bank loan rates at 10%; small textile mills had low access to bank credit and faced 80% interest rates in the informal money market. It was financially rational for the large mills to choose the more capital-intensive technology and for the small mills to remain with the labor-intensive. Under an ECBA analysis using a shadow interest rate, the fully automatic looms were found to be uneconomical for the country (although the semi-automatic had an acceptable public rate of return).[36] Another study in Indonesia found that "shortage of funds" was a frequently cited reason for avoiding capital-intensive investment technologies.[37] As mentioned earlier, foreign firms are sometimes restricted in borrowing locally, which forces them into international capital markets. The cost of capital raised abroad should carry an imputed cost for the foreign-exchange devaluation risk.

Different firms in the same industry can end up with different technological choices because they face different costs of capital or labor. Also, firms can opt for different strategies that might lead to weighing factor costs differently. A company following a low-price strategy might be very sensitive to cost differentials possible from different labor–capital configurations; a firm with a strategy of high price and product differentiation would be less concerned with cost differentials and more concerned with the technologies' effect on product characteristics. For example, Lecraw's study of four hundred firms in Thailand found that those exporting into price-competitive markets chose more labor-intensive technologies than similar firms selling in the protected Thai market.[38]

The overall significance of factor-cost differentials to a technology choice decision will be greatly determined by how large a share of the company's costs is composed of labor or capital. For example, one study found that pharmaceutical companies whose labor and depreciation costs amounted to less than 5% of selling price were relatively indifferent to factor-cost differentials when choosing production technology, whereas an elevator manufacturer with labor and depreciation costs of 30% was very attuned to capturing savings through adjustments in the production technology. The latter company's chief industrial engineer stated: "To perform exactly the same function we may use completely automatic equipment in the United States, semiautomatic equipment in Europe, and conventional hand-operated equipment in other areas. The criterion which is used is the relationship of capital cost to the local wage rates modified by the productive efficiency of local labor."[39]

The importance of capital and labor costs relative to price can even be a starting point in analyzing technology choice. If factor costs are relatively unimportant, attention should focus on other criteria. Similarly, when such cost configurations prevail, government policy-makers should not expect to influence companies' technology choice with policies aimed at changing those factor prices. However, the production manager in one large company operating in a smaller LDC said even though labor costs were relatively unimportant (less than 10%) in its operation, the company "feels a sense of social responsibility not to go too high-tech and displace workers."[40]

The market prices of labor and capital might carry very different "shadow prices" in an Economic Cost-Benefit Analysis, such as the case with capital costs in the previously cited example of the Indonesian textile looms. In one study of textile factories and pulp and paper mills in four LDCs, "there was a large disparity between the chosen technologies and the social optimum in terms of capital use and employment," with the selected technologies using one-third more capital and providing half the jobs that the socially optimum technology choices would have.[41]

Market Requirements

Production technologies must be able to respond to the demands of the marketplace in both quantity and quality. Capacity planning is a strategic decision closely tied to technology choice. The relatively small size of many LDC markets reduces the possibilities of economies of scale usually required by capital-intensive technologies. In Brazil, researchers found that for managers of MNC subsidiaries "size of market or scale was, by all odds, the most important determinant of their choice of production technique."[42] In General Motors' Korean joint venture with Daewoo the original production system followed the American mass production model, but the small market allowed only short production runs. The system had to be adjusted to permit the production of smaller quantities of more diversified cars.[43] Studies of companies in Nigeria, Kenya, and India further corroborate the importance of small market size in leading companies' decisions to choose more labor-intensive technologies.[44] A common adaptation in manufacturing firms is to use multipurpose rather than numerous special-purpose machines. Cummins Engine used this approach in its Indian plant. Multipurpose machines can be more fully used on shorter production runs than specialized machines, which would often be idle. A refrigerator producer in a small LDC market used multipurpose machines that could handle various models as well as other appliances; a Filipino carpet maker used 16-inch looms whereas U.S. companies used 200-inch looms.[45] Downscaling equipment and increasing labor-intensity helps deal with small market constraints.

When a market is expanding rapidly, however, a more capital-intensive method might be economically justified, even though it could remain underused during the early years. In some very populous countries, domestic markets for some products permit long production runs and more capital-intensive technologies. For example, Brazil's soft-drink market is the fourth largest in the world, and the country also produces more than a million vehicles annually.

When demand is highly uncertain, perhaps because of the possibility of changes in government policy or political or economic turmoil, it would appear advisable to avoid capital-intensive investments that require a steady volume over which to spread fixed costs. The underlying assumption is that the labor supply is more flexible, but this is not always the case. In one Central American country, when a shirt company tried to meet a surge in demand by having workers work overtime, employees refused because after 6:00 P.M. there was no public transportation to take them back to town. Additionally, sometimes labor legislation makes layoffs very costly, thus almost converting labor from a variable to a fixed cost. In such circumstances, machinery whose output level can be quickly raised or lowered may become the more market-responsive technology.

Not only must managers reconcile the technology to the volume characteristics of the market, they must also ensure that the technology will meet the market's quality requirements. The company's strategy for quality will often dictate the choice of technology. Technology is determined in the first instance by product choice. A firm might choose to produce synthetic rather than all-cotton shirts, but each product category has multiple quality options. Similarly, export markets often require higher quality, yet even they may have different quality segments with varying technological demands. Both the Philippines and Taiwan export canned pineapples to high-income countries, but Philippine exporters sell a very high quality product to the upper end of the market and use capital-intensive technology, while Taiwanese companies use more labor-intensive technologies to produce a lower-quality product that sells very successfully in lower-income segments.[46] Keddie found in Indonesia that firms opting for a high-quality strategy tended to use more capital-intensive techniques. In such industries as cigarettes and flashlight batteries, where market segmentation occurred along price and quality lines, different firms chose distinctly different technologies.[47]

Clearly, one key to technology selection is careful market research to identify the quality requirements of the target consumer segment (see Chapter 9 on marketing). Costlier technologies for products whose quality exceeds that demanded will not be able to capture a price premium to justify the technology investment. Research can also lead to a choice of technology that will differentiate the product by higher quality. Sometimes the buyer's power is great enough to force technology choices on the seller. For example, the Kenyan subsidiary of one multinational manufactured cans for another MNC's subsidiary. The customer demanded that a more mechanized technique be used to create a stronger side seam, and the seller felt obliged to comply because this was a large customer not only in Kenya but for the parent company's subsidiaries in other countries.[48]

Quality is not determined exclusively or ensured by technology choice. Workers' direct inputs and the way they use the technology can significantly affect quality. Insufficient quality-consciousness among production managers and workers remains a problem in many developing countries. To meet the market's quality requirements, management must view training of the workforce as an essential companion to whatever technology is chosen. Production managers in several Latin American countries reported significant improvements in recent years, with increasing use of quality control circles and quality control training. In Latin America Volkswagen's Brazilian subsidiary pioneered the use of quality control circles (QCC), having formed by 1985 a thousand circles involving 10,000 employees. A company manager observed, "We began by copying the Japanese literally and that didn't function very well. We adapted it and now it works well."[49] The MNC Johnson & Johnson and the SOE Embraer were also innovators with QCCs in Brazil. By 1985, six hundred companies in Brazil had QCCs, more than six hundred in Argentina, thirty-one in Colombia, and twelve in Chile; in Mexico and Venezuela there were significant initiatives.[50] Rising quality-consciousness has been stimulated in part by the growing export orientation of countries and companies during the 1980s. Where tariffs or quotas protect local producers from external competition, pressures for quality-enhancing technologies are reduced.

Technical Constraints

Since market characteristics and marketing strategies dictate scale and quality requirements, the issue then becomes whether there are sufficient technical alternatives to meet those requirements. Compliance with market requirements clearly narrows the range of technology choice, and "technical rigidities" do exist. For example, equipment may be essential to carry out certain chemical processes, achieve some levels of physical accuracy, handle indivisible heavy materials, or deal with hazardous materials or processes.[51] Yet experience in LDCs has revealed that even for a given quality and volume there are many opportunities for factor substitution.[52] Managers must avoid the myopic mindset of technological determinism. A systematic examination of the production process often reveals possibilities for substituting labor for machines to achieve lower production costs without sacrificing quality or volume. For example, Pickett and Robson identified seven efficient technological alternatives for producing the same quality and quantity of cotton cloth, and these alternatives had capital–labor ratios ranging from \$9,700 to \$29,500 per worker.[53] The elasticity of substitution, to use an economist's term, is often positive and financially significant. A survey of twenty MNC subsidiaries operating in Kenya found that on the average their technologies were three to four times more labor-intensive than their parents' technologies.[54]

The key to assessing the true extent of technical constraints and the full possibilities of factor substitution is to divide the production process into its stages and subprocesses. In more developed countries the tendency is often toward integrated production technologies with labor-saving linkages. To identify the optimum production configuration in developing countries, one should unbundle the technology and the process. One useful distinction is between stages that transform raw materials and those that handle inputs or outputs. These latter, "peripheral" stages usually offer greater possibilities for factor substitution. It is often the transformation process that produces the required product quality characteristics. Pulp and paper mills, for example, generally use automatic controls, because human error can greatly damage product quality and process efficiency.[55] In contrast, handling operations may have little influence on quality and are thereby relatively free of technical constraints. Of course, for fragile or easily contaminated products, handling can greatly affect quality and therefore technically constrain the process.

Textile production illustrates the range of technology choices. The first stage of opening and cleaning cotton bales has six machines and staffing alternatives and costs, ranging from \$250,000 in machines with four workers to \$430,000 and two workers.[56] The analytical approach is to move through each production stage, costing out technical alternatives, and then find the least-cost combination for the entire process.[57] Other inputs besides labor and capital costs must be included in the calculation, for technologies can have differential effects on other items such as raw materials, energy, and space requirements. Technology adaptations can also greatly enhance labor productivity. For example, the manager of a Kenyan fruit-processing plant quadrupled the productivity of his packing worker by a simple technical change: Instead of packing the cans one by one, the manager added a sheet of metal with twelve holes for empty cans that the worker could then fill simultaneously by shoving the fruit across the sheet and letting it drop into the cans.[58]

Many opportunities for technical substitution are not realized because of lack of information about technological alternatives. Companies from more developed countries often do not systematically assess possibilities for factor substitution. In one study of 282 pairs of foreign-owned and private Brazilian firms matched by size and industry, the foreign companies were found to use more capital-intensive technologies than local firms.[59] There is a tendency for managers to rely on their engineers or equipment suppliers, whose technological orientation is shaped by the industrialized economies and their capital-intensive production systems. Their experience and knowledge do not usually include LDC production systems. Third World MNCs, on the other hand, have been found to employ more labor-intensive technologies than multinationals from industrialized nations. This in part reflects their greater experience and information base with regard to LDC environments. The most appropriate equipment suppliers may, in fact, be located in developing countries. For example, two of the three most labor-intensive weaving technologies could be obtained only from LDC suppliers.[60] Korea's Daewoo, a major producer of textile equipment and fabrics, provided equipment and technical assistance to the fledgling garment industry in Bangladesh; this technology transfer proved to be a key catalyst in spurring export production, which grew from nearly nothing in 1979 to almost $450 million in 1988.[61]

Sometimes secondhand machinery in developed nations can be acquired very inexpensively; it is often amenable to more labor-intensive methods. A Colombian textile manufacturer bought a large equipment complex from a U.S. textile mill that was shifting to a more capital-intensive, labor-saving technology. Given Colombia's lower labor costs, the equipment was highly economical: Savings on the capital equipment more than paid for disassembly, shipment, reassembly, and worker training.[62] One Central American paper mill has successfully used secondhand equipment to economize capital without sacrificing quality. Various MNCs have opted for used equipment, generally from their home-country factories. Although LDC governments are often sensitive about receiving "outdated" technology, it may well be more appropriate to the country's factor endowment. It may also save both the entrepreneur and the country scarce foreign exchange by lowering the cost of capital equipment without any sacrifice in product quality.

One should be cautious in generalizing about the desirability of used equipment, because there can be drawbacks such as lower productivity, difficulties in maintenance, scarcity of spare parts, damage during disassembly and transport, and obsolesence. One Costa Rican manager commented, "We imported used trucks, but maintenance costs were so high we had to throw them out after two years.[63] Although the risks are clearly higher than for new machinery, used-machinery dealers or brokers can help reduce some of the risks with their superior technical knowledge of the equipment, its history, scrap value, and procedures for disassembly, transport, and installation. Yet if technological innovation is very rapid, the risk of obsolesence is greater for used equipment.[64] One Brazilian manager of an aluminum factory observed that importing used equipment was very important in the company's early stages, but it now used state-of-the-art technology.

Managers' backgrounds may also influence the process. Those with production or engineering backgrounds are reportedly more able to see substitution possibilities and seek out relevant information than managers with marketing or finance backgrounds.[65] On the other hand, some contend that engineers tend to choose more sophisticated, capital-intensive technologies and disdain less modern, but more economical, labor-intensive methods.[66] Having both an exposure to labor-intensive technologies and an appreciation of financial implications may be a prerequisite for a broader technological perspective.

The information market about production technologies for LDCs is imperfect. Communication channels within and across countries are not well developed; LDC managers often cite insufficient information as a problem in technology acquisition.[67] For example, a large MNC producing cans ended up using a relatively more expensive technology mainly because its engineers were unaware of more efficient techniques used in other Asian Countries.[68] The costs of obtaining information, although not insignificant, are usually small relative to the possible economic gains from more optimum production design. Equipment suppliers from developed and developing countries are one important source. One should request that their proposals indicate how they would modify their standard technologies to fit factor costs and availabilities in the particular country and site. Visits to the LDC's factories that produce the product or use similar production processes but for different products are invaluable. Local engineers who have consulted with and helped construct, service, or manage factories in the same industry can be excellent information sources in the technological search process. The multinational Philips

Gloeilampenfabrieken built a pilot plant in the Netherlands that simulates conditions prevailing in Africa. They use it to obtain knowledge about how to adapt their technologies to LDC environments to assist manufacturing operations in twenty countries.[69]

A final type of technical constraint is the safety risk. Different types of products and technologies carry varying risk levels in terms of the probability of accidents and the magnitude of the consequences for workers, customers, or the public. Where the risks are high, managers need to choose the technology that will minimize the risks and maximize the safety. In some instances using equipment rather than people can reduce the chance of human error. However, special care must be taken to ensure adequate maintenance of the equipment and safety systems, including the training of personnel. Contingency plans and emergency procedures for handling an industrial accident have to be delineated. In developing countries environmental regulations and industrial safety standards are not always well elaborated or strictly enforced because of administrative weaknesses in the government apparatus. Deficiencies in infrastructure, worker skills, and safety orientation further accentuate the problem. LDCs are higher-risk environments for industrial safety. Consequently, companies have a special need and responsibility to exercise great caution in choosing technologies and to use rigorous safety control systems for high-risk technologies.

The Bhopal, India methyl-isocyanate gas leak, the largest single industrial disaster in history, revealed the horrendous consequences of safety system failures. More than two thousand people were killed and 250,000 injured. Even though Union Carbide had installed five fail-safe systems to prevent this type of accident, "on the night of the accident, every one of those systems was shut down for maintenance or failed to operate effectively."[70] One analyst concluded that "the accident was not caused by the unforeseen failure of some highly sophisticated piece of machinery. It was instead a combination of small errors, postponed maintenance, and poorly trained personnel," and because the government had not "heeded the complaints of unions representing the Bhopal workers."[71] Urban migration and housing shortage in Bhopal led to the rise of a densely populated shantytown adjacent to the industrial plant, raising the exposure risk. Thus, a combination of technological, organizational, sociological, political, and human factors contributed to and amplified the crisis.[72] The disaster caused Union Carbide's stock market value to fall $900 million, resulted in legal and damage liabilities of around $400 million, forced the company into major divestitures in order to block a takeover attempt, and led to an exodus of top management.[73] Clearly, the safety dimension of technology choices and management for LDCs is of strategic and ethical importance.

Input Scarcities

Developing countries are scarcity environments. Production operations often face shortages of skilled workers, materials, energy, and equipment. A production technology can sometimes be selected or adapted to accommodate these input scarcities.

Skilled Workers. One entrepreneur in Kenya chose a highly automated loom technology for his textile plant, in part to overcome the shortage of skilled workers.[74] However, a study of other countries revealed that "five of the seven process steps in textiles contained capital-intensive technologies that used absolutely greater amounts of skilled and supervisory labor than did more labor-intensive technologies."[75] Some observers believe that new electronics technologies will "deskill" many tasks that now require electrical and mechanical skills, thereby reducing bottlenecks caused by shortages of such personnel.[76] For example, numerically controlled machine tools greatly reduce the skill content in that machinists are replaced by more easily trained machine setters and programmers. The growing use of this technology in Argentina is in part due to industrialists' difficulties in recruiting skilled machinists.[77]

It is important to analyze skill categories to ascertain which is scarcer: skilled workers, supervisors, or maintenance technicians. Different technologies will economize on some skills and increase demand for others. In Brazil some managers were reluctant to use transfer equipment because of the need for highly skilled electricians and machine makers, who were scarce and costly relative to machine operators. When transfer equipment was used, it was often modified to economize on skilled labor inputs. "One firm managed to cut its tooling costs substantially by halving the number of stations on its transfer line and increasing the amount of metal cut per station. It did this by tripling the amount of time the work piece stayed at each station. Output per hour fell, but there was a substitution of unskilled for skilled labor."[78]

In contrast, a manager of an automobile plant in Venezuela said he had enough skilled maintenance people and therefore tried to minimize the amount of labor interference in processes using transfer lines. The availability of skilled workers can vary geographically within countries:

In Northeast Brazil skilled labor is scarce and unskilled abundant; in the Southeast the opposite is the case.

Skilled maintenance workers are often in short supply. In one survey technical experts agreed that the most important reason for maladaptation of equipment in LDCs was repair and maintenance difficulties, citing examples of factories with idle equipment because no one knew how to fix it.[79] A principal reason given by managers in Kenya for not using more sophisticated equipment was that it required "greater maintenance and operational knowledge on the part of workers from what is available."[80] Somtimes the problem is not skills, but attitudes. Production supervisors and workers may disdain or deem unimportant the rather mundane "hands-on" imperative of routine maintenance. The lack of a "maintenance ethic" is not uncommon.

The maintenance problem can be approached in several ways: select technologies with proven low-maintenance requirements, purchase equipment from suppliers with strong and locally available service capacity, develop in-house capacity through training and preventive maintenance programs, stock up on spare parts, or invest in backup equipment. One U.S. multinational uses more or less standardized plants in all its subsidiaries to speed up problem diagnosis and simplify repairs.[81] Technological compatibility may be a source of economies within a company's global production system and strategy.

Training is an alternative to technology adaptation and a way to overcome skill scarcity. In general, managers should consider training an integral part of their production investment strategies, for it can help to realize the technology's full productivity potential. The choice of a technology is only the start; how it is used (or misused) will determine its final utility. Modest investments in training can yield dramatic productivity returns: Reportedly, "South Korean high school graduates from rural areas can, after 3-months' training, match Japanese levels of productivity in welding ships, at one-third of the wages."[82] A manager of a German MNC commented on the effectiveness of skill adaptation: "In Singapore graceful Chinese girls achieve results working on heavy presses that men would be hard put to match in Germany."[83]

Adaptation to the demands of the modern production environment can be sociologically difficult for some new factory workers. For example, young Malay women working the night shifts in Malaysia's electronic factories often suffered attacks of uncontrollable shaking and crying.[84] Their Chinese and Indian co-workers were not afflicted. The Malay women attributed the hysteria to evil spirits inhabiting the factories, while industrial sociologists have indicated that it is a reaction to their inability to deal with the tension inherent in the mass production line. The hysteria incidents decline as the workers gain experience, but companies have used local medicine men to exorcise the spirits and Moslem priests to bless new factories. Managers and co-workers have learned to deal with the attacks as a part of the work environment. The afflicted women are excused from work to recuperate. Technology must also achieve an appropriate sociological fit.

MNCs tend to undertake significant efforts in training, a contribution often valued highly by governments. In Nigeria the multinationals and local companies spent about the same amount on training (about 0.14% of sales), but the multinationals expended more than six times as much per employee, partly because of training sessions held abroad.[85] Some multinationals have regional training centers (e.g., Nestlé in Mexico and Siemens in Argentina), where managers from various countries attend courses. Unskilled workers tend to receive on-the-job training or short classroom simulations; some companies (e.g., Philips and GE in Brazil) have literacy programs. Skilled worker training is often the major budget item, with various types of apprenticeships commonly used. Esso Singapore estimated that 10% of its technician days and 3% of its management's time were spent in training. Caterpillar used a full-time training staff at each of its overseas operations. Between 1962 and 1978, Philips International Telecommunications Centre in the Netherlands provided 16,030 weeks of training for 1,155 employees in LDCs.[86] Japanese companies, both at home and abroad, place great emphasis on employee training, especially in achieving quality control norms.[87] GM Venezuela formally trains its workers in a six- to eight-week program that contains a specific section on quality. One seed-exporting company in Africa uses intensively supervised on-the-job training: After a brief classroom orientation, the training moves to the greenhouses, and local supervisors (who themselves had been trained by foreign specialists) work one-on-one with the new worker for three days followed by close monitoring.

The amount of training required to transfer the technology effectively is often underestimated. Cummins Engine concluded that a major reason for the startup production difficulties encountered in the Indian joint venture was that it had not provided sufficient on-site technical training. Similarly, a Swedish tool manufacturer found that shortly after its expatriate engineer ended his technical assistance, the quality of its joint venture's production deteriorated drastically.[88] Where the training is being carried out by foreigners, language and cultural differences may impede the accuracy and the speed of the knowledge transfer.

Training appears most effective when it is carried out as an integral part of the production strategy, is continually updated to ensure relevancy, involves professional training personnel and line production people, and is seen as an ongoing activity that employees will engage in throughout their careers.

Labor turnover is another problem area. The Nigerian subsidiary of one European car manufacturer reported an annual turnover rate of 33%.[89] Additional skills gained through training generally increase labor mobility, so unless the company's economic and social benefits are competitive with outside opportunities, workers may well leave. Private companies often attract skilled workers from public sector agencies, which generally pay less than major companies. Training should be integrated into the company's larger human resource management strategy. For some managers, automation is an escape from the headaches of labor relations. Machines might cost more, but they don't talk back. One LDC manager who was automating to replace some young workers who attached labels by hand did not know if the machine was cheaper than the hand operation but did state that the workers "were a lot of trouble."[90]

Management's attitude toward the workforce and its union is a critical variable in technology choice and adaptation. If workers are viewed as integral to the technology and productivity equation and critical to the firm's success, investing in their development through training and other measures is likely to occur and to produce synergistic results. If workers are seen as expensive and expendable, the introduction of new technologies may meet with worker resistance and conflict.

Materials. Material inputs to the production process are sometimes very scarce. Imported production inputs are often scarce because of import restrictions caused by foreign-exchange shortages. Scarcities may also be due to the underdeveloped stage of input suppliers or the transportation system. Whatever the reason, it is sometimes economically wise and technically feasible to choose technologies that economize on material inputs, especially when material costs are the main cost. For electronics, material costs are often several times larger than the wage bill. An example of technical options is in manufacturing nuts and bolts, where the same quality can be produced by three distinct techniques but each requires different amounts of raw materials: cold forming 1.11 tons, hot forging 1.22 tons, and machining 2.71 tons.[91]

A Swedish company designed equipment to produce paper packaging that allowed sterilized milk to be kept unrefrigerated for up to three months, thereby overcoming the lack of refrigeration in developing countries. The packages were shaped to create a very low surface area to volume ratio, thereby saving on material. To economize on material even more, the Pakistani licensor of the technology developed a locally produced paper that replaced the imported laminated aluminum foil. This reduced shelf life but achieved great savings on material.[92] A Brazilian steel producer developed technology to substitute charcoal for the special metal-grade coking coal that was unavailable locally. A Ghanaian company replaced imported glue with a substance fabricated from locally produced cassava starch and plantain peels.[93] Various techniques for recycling inputs are also used to save materials. A Nigerian firm found a way to convert into tin plate the waste from a large metal-processing company, thereby reducing its raw material costs by 15%.[94]

Packaging technology can become a significant impediment to successful exporting. Export logistics require special handling and packaging that is often not available locally because the product has not been exported before. One manager of a Brazilian wire manufacturer observed, "When we began exporting to the U.S. in 1981, 70% of the complaints about our products were really complaints about packaging. Packaging technology is one of the main differences between advanced industrial countries and lesser-developed countries. We had to improvise on packaging."[95] Guinea-Bissau experienced frequent shortages of beverages due to the lack of bottle caps. In Nicaragua a shortage of bottles led to the use of plastic bags for soft drinks.

An irregular supply of raw materials can create havoc with production scheduling. This may necessitate modifying a normally continuous production process to a semi-batch process. Maintaining larger inventories of raw materials, inputs, or work-in-process inventories is another way to cope with erratic supplies. The manager of one company in Kenya said, "I keep six to twelve months' worth of inventory for certain production inputs because local producers are often unable to produce them due to shortages of key imported inputs."[96] Inventory management in LDC production systems is critical in dealing with the risks of uncertain supplies. "Just-In-Time" systems are crowded out by the need for "Better-Now-Than-Never" approaches.

Government policies can also affect the prices of raw materials and thus the economics of the technology choice. In India, labor-intensive methods were shown to be viable in a price-controlled market but unlikely to be so if free market prices were to reign.[97] In a Latin American country, the government based raw-material import licenses for vegetable oil processors on how much raw material the processors purchased from local farmers. The fact that imports were much cheaper than local raw materials made import licenses highly desirable. One processor invested heavily in biotechnology research to develop higher-yielding seeds. It planned to distribute those seeds to its farmers to increase the quantity of raw materials it would obtain.[98]

Energy. Energy supplies are often erratic and sometimes rationed. A large Tanzanian textile mill was reportedly able to operate at only a quarter of its capacity because of long shutdowns caused by power problems.[99] Consequently, backup generators are often necessary. Some firms in Manila converted mechanized equipment to semimanual equipment to deal with unreliable power supplies.[100] Alternative energy sources can also be sought. For example, one soap manufacturer in Zaire began burning previously discarded palm kernels from which oil for the soap had been extracted.[101] Many sugar mills use cane fiber as fuel after extracting the sugar. A study of Korean textile mills suggested that labor-intensive operations proved to be also energy-intensive as a consequence of energy inefficiencies of the older technologies being used; capital-intensive methods were more energy-efficient because of economies of scale.[102] In one East African country, a flower-exporting company made a large investment in generators to ensure its energy supply. This enabled it to use tissue-culture technology to produce a higher-value product. This justified the capital investment in the energy equipment, which in turn enabled the company to use a more advanced and competitively superior technology.

Equipment and Technologies. A final scarcity is local equipment and technologies. Capital-equipment industries are not well developed in most LDCs, and resources for scientific and technological development are generally severely constrained. Given the lack of a ready supply, companies are forced to carry out local R&D, import technologies, or both. Sometimes the lack of foreign exchange or the existence of import restrictions will make using or developing local equipment imperative. One Latin American manager described one of these constraints: "The most modern machines have a lot of electronic parts. We have to prove to the government that we need this replacement part and that takes two months to a year. Therefore, you must think twice before buying sophisticated equipment."[103]

Constraints on local R&D can be severe. Although developing countries account for 77% of the world's population, they have only 12.6% of the world's R&D scientists and engineers.[104] Whereas Japan has about 60 scientists per 10,000 workers, South Korea has only 20. Many LDC scientists either move abroad or stay in the country of training upon completing advanced programs, which creates a serious "brain drain" on the LDC's scarce technical pool. A manager of an electronics firm lamented, "Our problem with innovating abroad is finding the engineers or even the skilled labor abroad who have the experience with even the simplest circuitry that our people in the U.S. take for granted: it is a real problem."[105] Government policies sometimes inhibit local innovation. A Pakistani manufacturer of pumps, after two years of research, developed the capacity to produce sophisticated engine-block castings suitable for a local tractor manufacturer. The manager explained the problem: "This will save the foreign exchange for the country and make money for ourselves. Our government, however, seems to restrict us to using our foundry to only make castings for pumps that we manufacture. We have been trying for months to get this permission from the Investment Promotion Bureau."[106]

Local R&D tends to increase as the industry matures and as firms gain experience with the environment. In the global electronics industry, initial production operations, for example in Singapore, had almost no local development work by MNCs. Local companies did engage in secondary design and development by applying known technologies. Multinationals trained local engineering staffs, who handled most production adaptation problems. Design engineering began to occur in some of the MNCs' offshore subsidiaries.[107] In the global semiconductor industry, skill-intensive final testing operations and the more specialized assembly of high-value semiconductors were being set up in Hong Kong, Singapore, Taiwan, and South Korea. But large-volume, standardized production of lower-grade semiconductors, involving almost no local development, was increasingly transferred to such lower-wage countries as Indonesia, Malaysia, Thailand, and the Philippines.[108] One study of multinationals' foreign R&D investments indicated that in LDCs they are generally set up as technology-transfer units assisting subsidiaries and usually only in those LDCs with large market potential.[109] In India there is considerable local R&D: Unilever began a research center aimed at vegetable oil processing technologies and products that serves the company as an R&D arm for its Third World operations; Philips developed a simplified radio for villages; Punjab Tractors Ltd. designed and successfully marketed small-horsepower tractors. In some instances, companies have been able to produce equipment locally by copying imports. For example, some Thai firms made copies of packing and end-making machines at about half the cost of imported machines.[110] China copied a catalytic cracker and platform refinery originally exported to Cuba.[111] In many instances these copies are made in violation of other firms' patents. The U.S. International Trade Commission estimated that such infringements cost U.S. firms as much as $61 billion in lost revenues and royalties.[112]

One often encounters examples of ingenuity and invention in production techniques that emerged in response to some obstacle in the LDC business environment. Scarcity fosters innovation. Witness the following description by a manager of an auto manufacturer in Brazil:

> We had a roof panel that you couldn't do only in one stamp because the local supplier of steel, a state-owned company, could not provide that size of blank and importation was prohibited. So, we designed in our plant a way of welding two blanks and we could stamp the two welded blanks into one piece. These adversities sometimes create innovation.[113]

The Mexican firm Hylsa wanted to replace the imported scrap steel it had been using to produce beer bottle caps. The scrap had impurities, and its prices and supplies were too variable. The minimum scale required for producing steel from virgin iron using existing blast, open hearth, or oxygen furnaces exceeded Hylsa's needs. After ten years' research, the company developed and patented a direct-reduction process that fitted the smaller-scale requirement. Hylsa subsequently licensed this technology to firms in Brazil, Venezuela, Indonesia, Iraq, Iran, and Zambia.[114] The small scale constraint led another company to develop pollution control systems for small plants, and Dupont's Mexican subsidiary did the same thing for herbicide production technology. Both technologies were exported to other countries. These firms had moved up to the creation level of the technological capability ladder.

The engineers and production managers of a Venezuela packaging company created a new design for their European-made machinery that was better suited to their workers' habits, the nature of the raw materials, and the pattern of demand. The original manufacturer produced a prototype for them and also added this model to its regular product line.[115] In response to the Brazilian government's decision to produce "gasahol" from sugar cane to reduce oil imports, the automotive industry redesigned engines to run on this new fuel source.

Much innovation occurs through "shop-floor learning" rather than formal research departments, and it often involves redesign and reverse engineering.[116] This was mainly how small machinery manufacturers in Korea acquired their original technology.[117] The manager of a seed-exporting farm in one African country had the following perspective:

I like technology but only in its place. In the U.S. we use fully automated drip irrigation systems. Here we eliminated the flow regulator, the most expensive part, and gave a sample of the tubing to a local company, who produced it at half the cost. We operate this modified drip system manually. A strawberry producer has been trying for two years to get his automated drip system to work. With a simpler system he would have been banking money instead of spending it.[118]

Local producers and end users of technology possess knowledge of the environmental constraints. This enables them to make innovative adaptations of technologies. A Vietnamese artisan and farmer who had been trained as a mechanic for French dredging equipment used the dredging impeller principle to create a low-lift pump for rice irrigation; it was cheaper and more portable than available diesel pumps.[119] The Sudanese Energy Research Council had designed a more efficient charcoal stove, but it was too complicated and costly to manufacture. The Council held a design adaptation contest among local stove makers that resulted in superior designs and marketing of these by the producers even before the contest awards had been given.[120] The scientists at the International Potato Centre in Peru had developed improved varieties to increase storability. Only upon consulting with farmers later did they learn that the farmers' concern was not with duration of storage but sprouting during storage that then required time-consuming pruning. The scientists refocused their research and developed with the farmers new types of storage environments.[121] The interaction of technology producers and users is a vital link in the innovation process.

One impediment to local R&D is the lack of coherent, long-term government strategies for developing certain industries or technologies. This uncertainty reduces the private sector's willingness to invest in research. Nonetheless, several developing countries have begun to export technologies, as Mexico did with its iron-reduction process. Although many technology exports were derived from imported technologies, a significant amount has emerged from original R&D that has allowed them to reach the ''enhancement'' and even the ''creation'' levels of technological capability.[122]

LDC research has not been restricted to low-technology products. South Korea's Samsung Semiconductor and Telecommunications developed 256K DRAM chips in 1984 without a foreign license, thereby moving the country toward becoming a world-class informatics producer. Another sign of Korea's growing technological competence is that by 1980 its exports of customized machinery and steel structures reached

7% of total exports.[123] Propelling Korea's ascent up the technological capability ladder has been the country's investment in its human resources. Between 1977 and 1982 Korea's expenditures on R&D rose from 0.6% of GNP to nearly 1%, and the number of R&D personnel increased from 13,000 to more than 28,000. Korea has increasingly been able to attract back its Western-trained graduates, reversing the "brain drain." Most of this research is carried out by private firms, encouraged by various tax incentives. Universities also do significant research, and public research institutes assist small and large firms. Korea's public educational system has played an important role in the development of the electronics industry. Training in electronics starts in technical high schools, whose graduates constitute most of the industry's skilled workers. Technical junior colleges and engineering departments in colleges provide additional training.[124] Korea's percentage of college-level students in engineering is at least double that in Mexico, Brazil, Argentina, and India.[125]

Korea's national technology strategy and the close cooperation between business and government have been the key to its accelerated technological development. The government created several fiscal incentives for private industry: advance writeoff of funds used for technological development, deduction for R&D personnel development, deduction for commercializing new technologies, and depreciation allowances for R&D equipment.[126] The government also provided special loans for technology development through the Korean Development Bank and the National Investment Fund. Private industry made even larger investments from its own capital. Of particular importance has been the role of the Korean business groups or *chaebol*, whose large financial resources and diversified product lines facilitate their role as technology developers. For example, Samsung, Hyundai, and Lucky-Goldstar invested several billion dollars in semiconductor facilities and research. The government also funds joint industry–government research in microelectronics and other areas, with one such effort aimed at developing 4-megabyte memory technology as well as nonmemory and "upstream technologies."[127]

Korea's increasing technological capability has not proceeded equally across all industries. Although Korea had great success in exporting construction services, its competitive edge rested more on its lower labor costs and higher productivity. By 1981 Korea had overseas construction contracts in the Middle East of about $14 billion (second only to the United States).[128] Other LDCs with lower labor costs entered this market and seriously eroded Korea's competitive advantage. Its attempt to shift to more technology-intensive areas of construction services has been less successful because of the superior technical competency of the more developed nations. Korea has moved up the technological capability level in construction but has not equaled its progress in electronics. Government's research support and subsidized financing have also helped Korea begin production of numerically controlled machine tools, mainly lathes. Taiwan, similarly, has also begun to produce and export these lathes. Both countries, however, continue to rely heavily on Japanese technology for the computerized numerical control units.

The efforts of Korea, and to a lesser extent Taiwan and Singapore, to develop self-sustaining local R&D capacity have reduced their dependency on MNCs as suppliers of technology and distinguish them from other East Asian LDCs. Malaysia in the mid-1980s, for example, was the largest offshore supplier of semiconductors, engaged mainly in the labor-intensive assembly of subcomponents. Its lack of higher-level technological capacity left it with few options when several MNCs pulled out.[129]

Brazil has also made technological development central to its national strategy. Its experience in developing the national computer industry reveals the importance of government actions and public and private alliances.[130] Brazilian computer demand was one of the world's fastest growing and largest markets in the 1970s and 1980s, reaching $5 billion in 1985. Until the mid-1970s the demand was supplied by international computer companies, with IBM holding half the market. In 1976 the government promulgated a national computer policy aimed at developing local capacity. It financed an SOE to spearhead local development and production, thereby assuming the first-mover risks, which were too high for private firms. Groups of decision-makers in various governmental, academic, and private institutions promoted a strategy of technological autonomy. The head of the Brazilian Association of Computer and Peripherals Manufacturers explained the rationale:

We don't care if we aren't state-of-the-art right now. What counts is that Brazilian engineers are learning how to design Brazilian computers. If we don't figure out how to do it ourselves we will lose control of our destiny and be condemned forever as IBM salesmen.[131]

To implement this strategy the government instituted preferential purchasing of national equipment, and increasing restrictions on foreign imports attracted local entrepreneurs and hampered the multinationals. By 1983 one hundred local companies were operating, and their share of sales had passed 60%, while imports fell to 7%. The MNCs lobbied hard against these moves, but by the mid-1980s most had established various commercial and development agreements with local companies.

The Brazilian companies invested heavily to develop their indigenous technological capacity. Their R&D expenditures amounted to 14.4% of sales, as against 6% for American companies. Thus, although it encountered severe difficulties, in a relatively short time Brazil was able to upgrade significantly its indigenous technological capacity in informatics. Some observers, however, asserted that the restrictions on MNCs have seriously slowed Brazil's pace of advancement in the informatics industry. The U.S. government also exercised pressures to get Brazil to reduce its computer import restrictions.

In the capital goods area Brazil has also achieved considerable technological competence with exports of customized machinery and complete plants worth $1.3 billion during 1976–81.[132] Many of these exports were made by business groups whose economic strength and diversity increased their capacity to carry out research and to export. More than half of the locally owned firms received government financial support for their R&D. Brazil is Latin America's leading technology exporter, followed by Argentina and Mexico.[133]

Although much poorer on a per capita basis than Korea and Brazil, India has also placed great emphasis on technological development. Between 1960 and 1980 its pool of scientists and engineers increased almost tenfold to 1.78 million,[134] and R&D expenditures as a percentage of GNP nearly tripled.[135] Annually 150,000 scientists and technicians are added to the country's technology ranks. Exceptional advances have been made in atomic energy, space, agriculture, and some manufacturing sectors. Computers have been an area of emphasis; like Brazil, India initially used an SOE to serve as a "national champion" to lead it toward technological autonomy in this area.[136] India has been a Third World leader in the export of industrial technology, with more than two hundred contracts during the 1980s worth about $2.5 billion. It has had particular success in the design, supply, and construction of technologically complex power stations, but it has also been a leader in the export of consulting services (especially computer programming).[137] Nonetheless, advances are hindered by the lack of effective linkages between government, private industry, and academia. Around 12% of graduating scientific and technical personnel are unable to find professional employment within three years of their graduation.[138]

The capacity for local R&D varies greatly across developing countries, but the trend is clearly upward. As part of a technology management strategy, companies may find that developing this capacity can create competitive advantage by enabling the firm to design technologies that deal more effectively with the many input scarcities, technical constraints, market requirements, and factor cost patterns facing them in the Third World.

Competitive Dynamics

A final factor influencing technology choice is the competitive situation facing a company. In protected markets, insulated by government tariffs or quotas from import competition, competitive pressures on costs and prices are reduced and firms (local or foreign) may become less concerned about seeking least-cost production technologies. SOEs also appear less cost-conscious in their technology choices, perhaps because of the lack of profit motivation or their monopolistic market positions.[139] Other factors related to bureaucratic or political processes might also influence the SOE's choices, such as speed of implementation or favoritism toward politically important technology suppliers. Unfortunately, bribes or kickbacks have also been used in the technology acquisition process.

For private firms operating in protected, low-competition environments, it is logical that the previously mentioned engineer's proclivity to choose more sophisticated technologies, regardless of their cost, will flourish.[140] This apparently irrational "engineering-man" mentality might, in some instances, be competitively advantageous; the higher technologies and product quality might create barriers to entry that protect the company against new competitors, even if the government's import protection walls were removed.

Where companies face strong price competition, managers aggressively seek out low-cost production technologies. One Nigerian company purchased used equipment to set up a factory to manufacture fuel filters. This made the firm's investment 60% less than that of a West German company considering entering with new equipment. The cost differential could not be offset by productivity differences, thus shutting the German firm out of the market.[141] Firms exporting to international markets often face stronger price competition. One study in Taiwan found that foreign firms selling mainly to the protected domestic market used double the fixed assets per worker than other foreign firms in that industry selling in the export market. Intensified competitive pressures led to a cost-reducing, labor-intensive technology choice.[142] For MNCs with global production strategies, technology choice is shaped by the market's demands for specific product characteristics. Nonetheless, managers should also consider how the technology can be adjusted to take advantage of varying factor endowments of different producing sites so as to achieve lower costs systemwide or to fit special needs of customers in LDCs.

Third World MNCs have used their knowledge of these environments to export "appropriate" technology. For example, Taiwan's machinery exports are mainly by small firms to other small firms.[143] Korean paper manufacturing machinery is favored by LDC purchasers because "they are cheaper and embody technology that is both simpler and more labour-intensive than that available elsewhere."[144]

MNCs and LDC business groups have the resources to develop their technological competency as a source of competitive advantage. Korea's *chaebols* have followed this strategy. Hyundai's and Samsung's size and breadth enabled them to carry their heavy machinery divisions during years of excess capacity and losses and "even to take a longer view and to plough money from other divisions into learning, human capital development, and R&D."[145] Samsung's chairman, K. H. Lee, assessed the technology and competition situation this way. "Nowadays Japanese and American companies—particularly in the high-tech fields—avoid technology transfers to preserve their monopolistic hold." Accordingly, Samsung upped its R&D expenditures 30% in 1988 and joined Hyundai, Goldstar, and the Korean government in the joint development of a 4-megabyte chip.[146]

LOCAL PROCUREMENT

The foregoing sections examined the key factors in choosing and adapting technologies, but the viability of a production operation also depends upon the adequacy of its supply of raw materials and other inputs. The supply system must be able to provide acceptable quality in adequate quantities at a reasonable cost at the appropriate time. Given the constraints in the LDC environment, suppliers often fail to meet these quality, quantity, cost, and time requirements. The largest problems with electronic component suppliers, according to manufacturers in Southeast Asian countries, were: (1) insufficient quality (33%); (2) high cost (17%); (3) different product control standards (17%); (4) inaccuracy in meeting design standards (15%); and (5) delivery delays (10%).[147] These problems exist even in some NICs. For example, in Singapore local suppliers to the electronics industry were reported in 1978 to have rejection rates as high as 75%, in contrast with 0.0% for local Japanese subsidiaries serving suppliers. The Singapore suppliers' prices were 40% higher than those in South Korea, Taiwan, and Hong Kong.[148] Singapore's supplier capabilities have improved significantly during the 1980s.

The alternative of importing supplies as a means of bypassing the deficiencies of local suppliers is often precluded by government restrictions on imports and by local-content requirements. National strategies aimed at import substitution have commonly used these policies as a stimulus to develop the nation's industrial capabilities. In the absence of such governmental stipulations, managers will generally prefer to import. For example, pharmaceutical companies in one African country used imported sugar because they considered the local sugar insufficiently white. In India, however, the same companies used the comparable "low-quality" sugar because of government requirements. A similar situation existed for local and imported glass for light bulbs.[149] Substitution does occur when required, but it takes time. In 1960 20% of the demand for automobiles in developing countries was produced locally; by 1980 the figure had risen to 60%, with the percentage of local content in the three largest LDC producers being 98% in Brazil, 95% in Argentina, and 60% in Venezuela. In Asia, India had achieved 100% local content for autos, South Korea 90%, the Philippines 70%, and Taiwan 60%, whereas in Nigeria domestic content was only 30%.[150] In Korea imports used in making exports were 52% of exports in 1971 but had dropped to 29% by 1975.[151] Cummins Engine's joint venture in India achieved 80% domestic content by 1972.[152]

Production imports are allowed in free trade zones. About forty-seven developing countries by 1986 had established 176 free trade zones or export processing zones in which imported production inputs are brought in duty-free to be assembled or manufactured for re-export. Governments' main goal is to generate employment.[153] For example, the zones accounted for 33% of total manufacturing employment in Singapore, 20% in Malaysia, 7% in Sri Lanka, and 3% in the Philippines. The zones have created new opportunities for "young, unmarrried female workers who had not been gainfully employed before."[154] The zones are of varying national importance, accounting for 40% of Malaysia's 1980 manufactured exports and 4% of Korea's.[155] Apparel and electronics have been the main industries locating in these export zones. Although the number of zones doubled during 1975–85, doing business in developing countries generally necessitates facing up to local procurement problems. Even companies in the zones are likely to experience government pressure for more linkages to local suppliers, as suggested by Mexican President Carlos Salinas de Gortari: "The *maquiladora* [export processing zone] generates employment but does not transfer technology. I am more interested in promoting Mexican enterprises that sell to the *maquiladora*."[156]

Supplier deficiencies exist for several reasons. First, suppliers are derived-demand businesses: They do not come into existence or grow until after the industries they are supplying emerge and expand. Consequently, their development generally lags behind the larger industrial development. And because they have less experience and knowledge, they encounter quality and productivity problems. Suppliers initially are often relatively small firms because of the small markets of the emerging industries. Low volumes limit economies of scale and increase costs. Their smallness may also mean capital constraints that impede expansion or investment in more efficient technologies. One advantage, however, of being new is that a firm is not locked into outdated technologies or inefficient worker patterns. If the technology can be appropriately transferred or developed, the new supplier might be able to achieve a superior competitive position relative to older suppliers in other countries.

There are two basic strategies for a company to deal with supplier problems: Do-It-Yourself via backward vertical integration (BVI) or Help-Them-Do-It via subcontractor assistance programs. The particular situation of each company, industry, and country will determine which strategy to follow, because there are intrinsic advantages and disadvantages in both.

The BVI Alternative

Four criteria are particularly relevant: control, capital requirements, flexibility, and costs.

Control. BVI increases the company's control over the quality, quantity, costs, and timing of its inputs. Centralizing the decision-making simplifies communication and facilitates coordination. Where suppliers' quality capabilities are very poor or the demand on their services greatly exceeds their productive capacity, BVI would be favored. This is particularly true when quality requirements for supplies are very high. In the early stages of an industry or in countries with lower levels of industrial development, the absorptive capacity for new technological demands is generally low. One cannot simply open the telephone directory's Yellow Pages and choose from a long list of suppliers. Companies are almost forced in the short run to be their own suppliers because of the shortage of outside suppliers. Even where acceptable firms might exist, the proprietary nature of the company's technologies or products might make the higher control attainable through BVI desirable. Lastly, where only one or a few qualified suppliers exist, their scarcity gives them monopolistic power over the buyer. BVI is a way of avoiding or reducing this disadvantageous bargaining position. Cummins used some BVI to overcome the quality problems it encountered in India. Whereas in its U.S. plants Cummins manufactured 40% of its parts, in India it produced 60% itself.[157]

Capital Requirements. To attain control through BVI, a company must invest in the additional plant, equipment, and personnel development required to produce the production inputs. This increases a company's capital exposure. It might also be uneconomical if the production scale is too low relative to the investment. It may also dilute a firm's distinctive competencies by drawing scarce management resources into a new business activity in which it has little experience or in-house expertise. A multinational may wish to purchase from local suppliers to gain them as allies, rather than displace them and engender their economic and political animosity. On the other side, the integrated system may help the company competitively by increasing capital and organizational barriers to entry.

Flexibility. The capital investments of BVI tend to lock the company into a set supply structure. If the context changes and nonintegrated supply arrangements become advantageous, the integrated firm has less flexibility to respond. For example, if demand is highly erratic or uncertain, in market downturns the integrated firm remains saddled with the fixed costs of supply facilities. For nonintegrated firms, supply costs are variable. The nonintegrated firm is also able to play multiple suppliers off against each other to achieve lower costs and diversify the risks of a single source. Where a firm faces an industry structure with only one or a few suppliers but many buyers, then suppliers have more bargaining power. BVI might be a strategy for reducing this power, even if the company's in-house supply operation provided only a portion of the input needs.

Cost. An integrated system makes for potential efficiencies and economies of scale if production volume is sufficient relative to the investment. Transaction costs may be reduced.[158] Lower variable costs are possible, but higher fixed costs are incurred. Sometimes government policies can significantly influence the economics of integration. For example, price controls in one country were aimed at providing high prices to farmers to stimulate production but to keep food prices low to consumers. Processors' margins were being severely squeezed, so one firm vertically integrated backward to capture the farm-to-factory margin and thereby restored profitability. In another country, a government policy required banks to allocate a certain percentage of their capital to agriculture at interest rates less than half those for industry. One processor integrated into farming as a way of significantly lowering its overall cost of capital.[159]

The Supplier Alternative

If a firm decides not to integrate and is unable to import, it must carefully assess supplier capacity. Failure to do so can be disastrous.

In one Southeast Asian nation a modern, multimillion-dollar beef-processing plant was constructed. The project analysis included national statistics that revealed a large and growing cattle population. Six months after opening, however, the factory was operating at only 8 percent of capacity because it lacked raw material. Contrary to the project analysts' expectations, the statistical cattle did not materialize as beef: the cattle owners were small farmers with transport problems who, because they were unaware of the plant's needs, did not, or could not, alter their custom of selling their cattle to the local abattoir or to middlemen who in turn sold to the abattoirs.[160]

A supplier assistance program must begin with a field-based diagnosis of both the specific problems facing potential suppliers and their causes. The assistance strategy aims at providing resources and incentives to overcome deficiencies. Suppliers' weaknesses can usually be traced to limitations in three areas: knowledge, physical capital, and financial resources. These can be addressed by providing technical assistance, materials and equipment, and financing.

Technical assistance can take many forms depending on suppliers' needs. Skills can be developed through training, visits to other plants, and close supervision and feedback. One large European MNC producing consumer goods has a team of experts whose sole task is to teach suppliers how to meet the company's standards.[161] Where personnel with the requisite minimal background for training in a particular skill do not exist, the company can perform the function itself. For example, some firms do product and process design work themselves and then just teach suppliers how to produce the input.

Where skills exist, the requisite technical assistance might be in the form of blueprints or procedural manuals. The KCL joint venture in India made a concerted effort to work with and train its suppliers' workers to meet the high quality requisites of Cummins Engines' international standards. Where some Indian suppliers were affiliated with other multinationals, Cummins sought assistance for these suppliers from their head offices. Training was also a central part of Cummins's technology transfer to personnel in the KCL facilities. Many early production problems in the plant occurred because it "had not sent in enough technicians initially to set up the operation properly."[162] It later increased its technical assistance efforts, not simply in engineering but also in developing management systems. Otis Elevator was hindered in its technology transfer to local suppliers to its China joint venture by its lack of direct production knowledge and blueprints for many parts that in the United States it purchased from suppliers. It was forced to license the technology from its U.S. suppliers and to engage in reverse engineering.[163]

It may be that the constraints are not on the people side, but rather lack of appropriate machinery, facilities, or material. Sometimes the company can provide these inputs by leasing equipment and providing material of known quality. This increases its control over suppliers and removes some of the causes of quality problems. If the bottleneck is in infrastructure (such as poor transportation or storage), the firm might find it necessary and even desirable to provide these linking services directly to increase control and coordination. Sometimes it is advantageous to locate in an industrial park, where infrastructure is better and also available to suppliers. Plant location decisions, of course, must consider additional factors. For example, after one Central American company moved to an industrial park, tardiness and absenteeism increased substantially. The workers did not own cars, the public transportation routes to the new location were unfamiliar to the workers, and their schedules were inconvenient. The manager adjusted the starting and finishing times by one-half hour to fit the bus schedules and drew up transportation maps for the employees showing them how to get from their residences by bus to the factory.[164]

If suppliers are relatively small yet quite competent, many problems might be solved by providing financing. This, like BVI, does increase capital exposure, but it also gives the company additional leverage with the supplier. In Morocco, European clothing buyers provided the local subcontractors with the cloth; this reduced the producers' working capital requirements while increasing the buyers' quality control over inputs.[165]

Some suppliers' problems may be due to their inability to obtain import permits or other types of bureaucratic approvals. The small size of the suppliers may mean that they do not have the government connections or personnel to deal effectively with the bureaucracy. Assistance in these areas is often quite easy and inexpensive for larger companies; it can be a low-cost, high-leverage form of help to suppliers.

The expedients discussed so far are enabling inputs. The company must also address motivation. Supplier incentive systems need positive and negative rewards. Variable pricing can be used to reward superior performance on any key criteria or to punish deficiencies. Inspection is a critical component in any incentive system. Some Japanese producers have inspectors in the suppliers' plants who have the power to reject goods and even stop production. In part, one tries to create an attitudinal environment in which quality and other delivery requirements are perceived as a common priority. The approach to this task must be tailored to fit the cultural context of the country.

One example of highly effective supplier development is the Singer Company's effort in Taiwan.[166] Singer established its first wholly owned subsidiary in Taiwan in 1963. The Taiwanese sewing machine industry consisted of about 250 assemblers and parts suppliers. Parts were not produced from blueprints, not standardized among producers, and of poor quality. The government approved Singer's investment (over the objection of local producers) but stipulated that Singer must procure more than 80% of its parts from local suppliers and provide them with technical assistance.

Singer provided the suppliers free of charge with blueprints and measuring gauges, foundry patterns, the use of its tool room to make tools and fixtures, guidance for redesigning presses and dies and setting up heat-treatment equipment, and advice in solving problems in casting, plating, and work methods. Training classes were given in inspection methods, use of measurement instruments, heat treatment, and factory management. The company also worked with a vocational high school to train annually 150 bench workers and lathe turners. As for quality control, the company helped suppliers institute their own strict inspection procedures. Singer also had its own inspectors check the quality of purchased parts; it employed five times more inspectors in the Taiwan operation than in its bigger Japanese subsidiary.

Singer's training efforts by the parent's staff were first for the personnel in its own plant; those personnel (with occasional visits from foreign technical professionals) then trained suppliers. Later, the technical staffs of new subsidiaries in India and Indonesia were also trained in the Taiwan plant. Initially the company also sold (at less than the price of imports) some parts manufactured in its plant (partial BVI) to suppliers, who later also began to make these parts. As an additional financial incentive, Singer offered premium prices to suppliers and paid them promptly.

After five years Singer was using all locally produced parts, except for needles in one model. Its exports grew at 12% a year, and by 1975 it was exporting 86% of its output. Singer's efforts helped standardize and upgrade the entire industry's technology and quality. Benefits spread to other sewing machine manufacturers, and industrywide production rose from 91,000 units in 1964 to 2.4 million units in 1978, with 83% exported. Singer's sales account for about 20% of the value of these exports, and its machines sold at a premium price. Thus, Singer used a broad, multifaceted supplier assistance program to transfer production technology effectively. By investing in technical assistance, it generated significant returns in the form of enhanced quality and reduced prices, which enabled it to establish an important and profitable link in its global production network while also helping Taiwan establish an internationally competitive industry.

Fundamentally, supplier assistance aims to create a strategic alliance. Like most relationships, the alliance is shaped by cultural expectations. These may imply certain behavioral patterns of loyalty, like sustaining a supplier even in down periods. Establishing personal friendships and trust relationships may be a prerequisite to forming a supplier–buyer alliance. Such alliances can create competitive advantage and capture many of the benefits of BVI. The combination of close relationships, financing, technical assistance, and relatively simple technology enabled Haiti to become the dominant supplier of baseballs to the United States, with a 95% share of the market.[167] In Hong Kong much of the export system is characterized by a network of merchandisers linked to small independent production units with supporting layers of suppliers. This system is tied together by kinship and personal relationships rather than contracts. Similar exporter-producer-supplier networks exist in Taiwan, where 40,000 small firms account for 80% of the country's exports.[168] Such alliances are also becoming more prevalent in the global auto industry. Mitsubishi Corporation and Mitsubishi Motors (24% owned by Chrysler), which engineered the drive trains and engines and supplies the automatic transmission for Korea's very successful Hyundai Excel, acquired 15% of Hyundai Motor in 1986. In 1987 Hyundai supplied 30,000 Excels for sale in the United States under Mitsubishi's name.[169]

CONCLUSION

Developing countries have become an integral part of global production strategies and systems, and technology management is critical for successful production in developing countries. A key issue is how to transfer technology so that it achieves an appropriate fit with the distinctive LDC environment. Vehicles for transferring technology include foreign direct investment, licensing, imported equipment, technical services and training, public information sources, and education. In addition to choosing the vehicle, managers face the task of choosing among existing technology options or adapting those technologies. Both the transfer and the adaptation decisions should consider the technological capability in the country, industry, and company. The prevailing capability levels (acquisition, adaptation, enhancement, and creation) present different constraints and opportunities for technology management.

In acquiring and adapting technologies, managers should analyze five aspects: factor costs, which consider the relative economic importance of labor and capital; market requirements, which stipulate the demands of the marketplace in quality and quantity; technical constraints, which impose limits on the range of technology options; input scarcities, which include skilled workers, materials, energy, and equipment; and competitive dynamics, which intensify or supress pressures for technological innovation. Technology choice and adaptation require a manager to weigh the relative importance and interrelationships of these factors. The technology decisions are of strategic importance and require a deep understanding of the distinctive demands of the LDC environment.

The foregoing technology considerations are also relevant when dealing with problems that emerge with local suppliers. As was indicated in Chapter 4, governments frequently follow import-substitution strategies that require procurement from local suppliers. But suppliers are often unable to provide acceptable quality in adequate quantities at a reasonable cost at the appropriate time. To deal with these deficiencies, manufacturers or processors can either integrate vertically backward to produce their own inputs, or technically or financially assist suppliers in overcoming their weaknesses. The choice of these alternatives should weigh considerations of control, capital requirements, flexibility, and costs.

It is clear that the distinctive environments of LDCs create special challenges for production operations and technology management. Two trends make meeting these challenges increasingly important and urgent for managers in developing countries: the growing emphasis of LDC governments on national strategies aimed at export promotion, and the emergence of global industries and manufacturing strategies as sources of competitive advantage. The most successful production managers may be those who can reconcile the demands of the international system with the realities of LDC environments.

9

Marketing

Adjusting the Marketing Mix

Developing country environments pose several key challenges to marketing managers. We shall examine the implications for managing of the following elements of the marketing mix: product policy, pricing, promotion, distribution, and market research.[1] The ramifications of LDC environments for global marketing strategies are also addressed. We shall end the chapter by discussing the special role "social marketing" can play in developing countries.

PRODUCT POLICY

At the heart of marketing strategies is product policy, which guides a firm's product choice to achieve an optimal fit with its environment. We shall illustrate how the LDCs' distinctive economic, political, cultural, and demographic characteristics can shape product policy. In effect, we are using the EAF to help formulate product policy. For LDCs, new product development often entails introducing or adjusting products marketed elsewhere but new to the country. We begin with, and give extra attention to, demographics, because LDC demographics, as was pointed out in Chapter 3, are fundamentally different than the more developed nations'.

Demographic Factors

Managers who do not understand the underlying demographics of a country do not fully know their marketplace. Product policy must be rooted in careful market analysis. The demographic dynamics of LDC markets are characterized by expansion, youth, and urbanization, and so managers are dealing with the market parameters of growth, age, and geography.

The significance of population growth to marketing depends on the nature of the product. Demographic expansion drives the demand for such mass-market items as basic goods or services. Population growth trends or changes are central to sales forecasting. The higher LDC birthrates mean that the average family size will be larger (around six rather than the four common in industrialized nations). Furthermore, several generations will often live together, increasing the household size, changing its consumption patterns, and creating decision-making units different from those in small nuclear families. Food items often need to be packaged into larger serving sizes.

In addition to population growth and size data, marketing managers must also focus on age structure. A relevant demographic indicator is the Total Fertility Rate. This is the average number of children that would be born alive to a woman during her lifetime if, during her childbearing years, she were to bear children in accordance with prevailing age-specific fertility rates. Replacement Level Fertility is the demographic term for the fertility level at which each woman gives birth to only enough daughters to replace herself; this rate would be slightly higher than one, because some mothers and daughters will die before their childbearing years are over.[2] Changes in these fertility rates affect a country's age structure. Although the LDC age structure will change, the youth-dominated profile will remain for several decades.

The revelance of this for the marketer will again depend on the nature of the product. Where demand is age-driven the impact will obviously be greatest. More specifically, the developing countries constitute growth markets for baby- and child-oriented products. As birthrates in the industrialized nations have tailed off, Third World demographics have attracted the producers of baby foods, baby-care products, and other children's goods. Developing countries in 1983 constituted about half the $4 billion global market for infant formula products.[3] Furthermore, the market for educational goods and services will expand, because both absolute numbers and enrollment rates are rising. The number of young families is larger, so goods related to starting up households will find broader markets. The youth factor might also be relevant in shaping companies' promotional presentations.

Age structure also affects household composition and economics by shaping the proportion of the population that is of working age. The standard demographic indicator for this relationship is the Dependency

Ratio, defined as the ratio of the population under fifteen and over sixty-four to the population aged 15–64 (which is presumed to be the working age group). The indicator attempts to reveal what share of the population is being supported by the working age group. The higher the ratio, the more dependents have to be supported. The large portion of youngsters in LDCs creates a high dependency ratio. The ninety-nine low- and lower-middle-income countries had an average dependency ratio in 1990 of about 70%; the upper-middle-income countries had a ratio of 65% and the industrialized market economies 48%.[4] Higher ratios suggest greater pressure on household incomes to sustain dependents; at lower income levels more of the income (60%–85%) must go to food and other necessities. Differences exist among low-income countries: In 1990 Sri Lanka's dependency ratio was 61%, but Pakistan's was 92%. Trends also differ: Indonesia's ratio was projected to fall from 82% in 1980 to 60% in 2000, and Liberia's was estimated to rise from 81% to 102%.[5] Marketing managers should scrutinize these differences in levels and trends because of the implications for product policy of their different effects on consumer expenditure patterns.

A refinement in the demographer's traditional definition of the dependency ratio could increase its relevance to marketing managers: The age limits of the working group might be extended, particularly at the younger end. Children, especially in rural areas, are often working productively before age fifteen. Adjustments at the upper end are not as necessary because average life expectancy in the LDCs is only sixty, although it is rising. However, the elderly often engage in child care, which frees other household members for outside work. Widening the age limits would increase the number of working family members and reduce the number of dependents, thereby lowering the dependency ratio. In contrast, one should reduce the number in the workforce by removing those of working age who are unemployed. The dependency ratio would then rise, because the unemployed would be considered economic dependents, not contributors. The denominator should be those economically active within or outside the household.

The final demographic factor affecting product policy is the clear trend in LDCs for the population to concentrate in the country's largest city and for those cities to reach enormous size. This reflects the political centralization and economic concentration that draw people to capital cities or major industrial centers. Table 9.1 lists the share of national populations living in the LDCs' twenty-five largest cities. The rate of net immigration to the principal city appears to decline when a country's per capita income approaches $4,000 (in 1980 dollars); migra-

Table 9.1 National Populations in Major Cities, 1985

Country/City	Urban Population	% of Total Population
Mexico City	17,300,000	21.9%
Brazil		
São Paulo	15,900,000	11.7
Rio de Janeiro	10,400,000	7.7
China		
Shanghai	12,000,000	1.2
Beijing	9,300,000	0.9
Tianjin	7,900,000	0.8
India		
Calcutta	11,000,000	1.4
Bombay	10,100,000	1.3
Delhi	7,400,000	1.0
Madras	5,200,000	0.7
Argentina		
Buenos Aires	10,900,000	35.7
Korea		
Seoul	10,300,000	25.1
Pusan	4,100,000	10.0
Indonesia		
Jakarta	7,900,000	4.9
Egypt		
Cairo	7,700,000	15.9
Iran		
Teheran	7,500,000	16.8
Philippines		
Manila	7,000,000	12.8
Pakistan		
Karachi	6,700,000	7.0
Thailand		
Bangkok	6,100,000	11.8
Peru		
Lima	5,700,000	30.7
Hong Kong	5,100,000	94.4
Bangladesh		
Dacca	4,900,000	4.9
Colombia		
Bogotá	4,500,000	15.9
Iraq		
Baghdad	4,400,000	27.7
Chile		
Santiago	4,200,000	34.7

SOURCE: *Statistical Abstract of the United States: Comparative International Statistics*, 108th ed. (Washington, D.C.: U.S. Department of Commerce, 1988).

tion to smaller urban areas continues, as does the general urbanization process.[6]

Although urban populations are growing throughout the developing world, Table 9.1 clearly reveals significant differences in urbanization levels, with Latin America the most urbanized. The urban-rural population patterns have several important marketing implications. First, for the next few decades the rural population and market in most LDCs will still be sizable. Income levels in the rural areas are lower than in the urban centers; reaching rural consumers is more difficult because of infrastructure deficiencies. Nonetheless, for agriculture-related products and for many consumer products, rural areas are a market that needs to be served and can be economically rewarding. Second, urban centers will be dynamic markets, as their absolute size expands in numbers of consumers and physical spread. Surrounding rural and semirural areas will be incorporated into the expanding metropolis. This clearly has significant implications for the location of distribution outlets and the design of logistics systems. New urban consumers have greater exposure to products and media and are more influenced by the demonstration effects of other consumers. Consumer tastes and habits will change. Rural migrants will shift work patterns and consumption habits. In this demographic transition lie many marketing opportunities.

The flood of migrants, on top of urban births, often expands the population and workforce faster than employment opportunities. Consequently, large low-income population groups grow, accentuating disparities in income distribution and market segments in urban areas. One should not assume, however, that poorer neighborhoods are economically insignificant. There is often considerable economic vitality, as their informal-sector activities generate sustenance and surplus. Their participation in the consumer durable market is not insignificant, as the many TV antennas protruding from roofs in poor neighborhoods reveal. An international marketing manager of a major Japanese electronics firm observed: "What is interesting about electronic products is the hierarchy. I have seen it in India and other countries: Houses don't have a refrigerator or washing machine, but they have a television."[7]

Lastly, urbanization will take these markets along many paths already traveled in industrialized nations and the more advanced developing countries. Goods and services that served those urban consumers will also be demanded by new and growing urban centers. Differences in income level, infrastructure, and purchasing patterns will require special adjustments, but much that already exists will be transferrable.

Economic Factors

Population size and composition do not, of course, fully reveal a market's economic profile, which is a function of income level and distribution, i.e., effective demand. Large but poor populations may not constitute mass markets for higher-priced products that are oriented toward more affluent consumers. Yet in all large-population countries, even those classed as low-income, the market segment of affluent consumers will be significant as a result of the uneven distribution of income. For example, although India is among the poorest countries in per capita income, 20% of its population earns about 52% of its total income.[8] That makes this segment's average income about five times greater than the national average and comparable to averages in middle-income countries. Furthermore, because of India's huge population, this more affluent segment is a significant market in absolute purchasing power: around $80 billion. Even the top 5% of the economic pyramid probably represent a market of $10 billion to $20 billion. Clearly, the LDCs' economic stratification calls for marketing segmentation.

Although lower-income segments have very limited individual income, their aggregate numbers also constitute economically sizable market segments for products in their consumer basket. Food expenditures generally dominate their budgets; as incomes rise, absolute expenditures on food increase, although the types change and the share of total expenditures decreases. If a country has a relatively small population, this may lead companies to broaden their product line or to focus on export markets. Taiwan's Tatung Company did both. Its chairman, T. S. Lin, explained: "With a small domestic market, it is very easy to reach the saturation point. Whenever that happened, we found a new product to develop."[9]

Political Factors

Government regulations can bear directly on product policy. Trade restrictions can eliminate imported products from a company's line. Requirements to earn foreign exchange can force companies to export a wide range of new types of products (see subsequent discussion on countertrade). Some products are banned for health reasons: e.g., cyclamates almost everywhere and saccharine and copper gluconate in Venezuela.[10] Some industries might be restricted to government production, e.g., military goods or natural resource extraction. Some product categories might be reserved for indigenous firms, e.g., microcomputers in Brazil. Price controls can affect the desirability of different products (see pricing discussion below). Some LDC governments (e.g., Kenya, Singapore, Malaysia, and Ecuador)[11] stipulate standard sizes for some types of consumer package goods.

Cultural Factors

A society's values and attitudes influence product preferences. Personal care products often encounter strong social norms or taboos that require significant adjustments in how they are marketed. Food products may confront problems due to religious restrictions. For example, Pillsbury uses vegetable shortening in its cake mixes sold in the Middle East to conform to Islamic restrictions on the use of animal fats.[12] The sale of some products may simply be forbidden on religious grounds, for example, liquor in Pakistan.

=

The foregoing demographic, economic, political, and cultural factors affect not only a firm's overall product policy but also other key marketing areas, such as pricing.

PRICING

A survey of MNC marketing managers found that 45% considered pricing the single most important factor in marketing strategy.[13] Yet in developing countries this critical marketing tool is often partially taken out of managers' hands by government's imposition of price controls. Coping with price controls is therefore the first pricing issue we shall discuss. The second concerns complications in pricing exports.

Price Controls

Governments intervene to set prices for social or political reasons; for example, to keep the prices of basic staples low to benefit urban consumers or to keep prices to farmers high to protect their incomes and stimulate production. They also impose broad price controls as part of their economic strategy to reduce inflation (see Chapter 7). Within our Environmental Analysis Framework, price controls are a clear example of how national strategies are translated into policies and policy instruments which, in turn, directly affect the firm (Chapter 4). Although the extent of price controls can vary considerably (in the Sudan they cover almost all commodities sold, while in Botswana they are almost nonexistent), they are present in most LDCs.

The economic consequences of price controls can be devastating. Gerber Products, for example, had been in Venezuela since 1960, but unprofitable operations forced it to sell out in 1979. It blamed price controls as a principal factor for its losses, which reached $500,000 in the first half of 1979. In that final year, some of Gerber's products were still being sold at 1968 prices because the government had refused repeated requests for price increases.[14] The pharmaceutical company Glaxo cancelled its expansion plans in Pakistan because of price ceilings, and Cadbury-Schweppes sold its Kenya plant in 1982 because of price controls.[15] Also in Kenya in the early 1970s, the government raised the price corn millers had to pay farmers, but the millers were not allowed to increase their prices to pass along this rise in their raw material costs and were thus forced to operate at a loss.[16] Agroindustries frequently find themselves caught in this type of margin squeeze due to governments' setting high support prices for farmers and low retail prices to help consumers.[17]

To deal with price controls, managers might consider two approaches: protecting margins and diversifying the product line.

Protecting Margins. The first way is to negotiate better terms with the government. Price controls are administrative mechanisms and are often open to negotiation. Because governmental decision-makers displace market forces as the shapers of prices, energies previously used to obtain optimum prices in the marketplace must be rechanneled into managing relations with government price-setters.

Negotiations first require a clear understanding of the motives behind price controls. Our methodology of political mapping (Chapter 6) pointed out the need to identify the interests and influence of various groups affecting or being affected by a policy action. In one Asian country a timber-processing company's request to the governmental Price Commission for price increases was repeatedly rejected, even though such adjustments were clearly warranted by increases in the company's costs due to general inflation. Informal consultation revealed two key pieces of information. First, a few congressmen were pressuring the Price Commission to hold prices down because many of their constituents were carpenters who would be hurt by price increases for lumber. Second, a manufacturer of mahogany furniture was also lobbying directly with his personal friend the president against the price rise. With this information, the company revised its price increase request to exclude mahogany and to provide special discounts to small craftsmen. Neither of those product categories was a significant source of revenue in the company's overall line. The Price Commission approved the revised request, and positive margins and profitability were restored.

In some circumstances price controls can be beneficial to private firms, as the following remark by one Latin American manager indicates: "If you are in a business where there are many competitors, it becomes easier to convince the government to raise prices than to deal with twenty or thirty companies. I know some companies under price controls that are more profitable than those without controls."[18]

Price approval is almost always slow, bureaucratically cumbersome, and time-consuming. The same manager remarked: "Fifty percent of management's time is spent developing good business–government relations." As was indicated in Chapter 6, companies should organize expressly to handle this, establishing communication channels and ongoing relationships with the bureaucrats and politicians involved. One company achieved relatively expedient processing of its price-increase requests by having independent auditors document the cost increases and by providing government officials ample access to these figures and other accounting records. The transparency of the process fostered a trust relationship between the government and the company. In this disclosure process both sides must take care to ensure that competitively sensitive cost data or product ingredient compositions are handled with the utmost confidentiality. Thus, when price controls can be negotiated, superior skills in managing business–government relations can create competitive advantage.

Frequently the company is not negotiating a price increase but a subsidy level. In one Latin American country the government established the price vegetable oil processors had to pay farmers for oilseeds and the price to their wholesalers of the processed oil. The government recognized that the resultant margin did not cover processing costs and profit and was willing to pay processors a subsidy to cover the difference. This approach, however, can create considerable friction and suspicion, because there has to be agreement on the cost data and on what is an acceptable profit margin. These negotiations were industrywide. Since an SOE also operated in the industry, private companies persuaded it to join them in presenting a unified request for the subsidy. This increased the private companies' credibility with the government. Since the SOE was less efficient than the private firms, the subsidy, adequate for the SOE, was quite attractive for most of the private firms.

In some instances companies have withdrawn their products or reduced operations when price controls had rendered their business unprofitable.

Coke and Pepsi, for example, pulled their products from the Mexican market in 1983 until they received a price increase that restored positive margins.[19] In Brazil in 1988 Coca-Cola bottlers delayed making $150 million in investments because of margin squeezes from price controls: The government had granted a 14% increase, but a 50% rise was needed to keep up with inflation.[20]

Another approach to protecting margins is to lower the cost floor through rationalizations, cost containment, and productivity-enhancing measures. This is not mutually exclusive with negotiating with government to increase prices. However, where price controls are rigid, superior abilities in cost-reduction can give a firm competitive advantage.

One complication of competing in price-controlled settings is the emergence of black markets for the goods. If the real demand for the goods would call forth a higher price, then some of the goods will be diverted into these channels. Those participating in the black market will have added revenues and competitive advantage. Unfortunately, this behavior penalizes the firm adhering to controls, because it creates an uneven playing field. To overcome this, one company policed its competitors' actions and reported violations to the government. This greatly increased the company's credibility with the government, because it revealed that it was honoring price controls and helping the government overcome its limited administrative capacity to police violators. Where price controls are severely out of line with supply-and-demand realities, creating negative margins, producers will inevitably stop producing, stockpile, or sell into the black market. Thus, the emergence of this type of behavior should be a signal to policy-makers to review their pricing policies to avoid the resultant distortion in resource allocation. In Brazil, failure to adjust prices frozen at unrealistic levels led to hoarding and black markets, which caused the government's initially successful anti-inflation Plan Cruzado to collapse in 1986.

Diversifying. Another way to deal with price-control problems is to diversify away from them. Here, pricing-policy constraints are driving product policy. Obviously many other considerations should also be integrated into a diversification decision. Often products that are very closely related to the price-controlled product, such as by-products, may not be controlled. In one Asian country the price of flour was controlled, but the by-product from wheat milling (usable as animal feed) was not. The flour miller expanded into animal feed processing and later into meat production, which were quite profitable because demand was strong and the products were not price-controlled. An MNC equipment manufacturer in a Latin American country faced price controls for its main product, but none existed for replacement parts or ancillary implements, so it expanded its production of those lines. A large bakery shifted some of its production from price-controlled bread to nonprice-controlled sweet rolls. Similarly, in another country a dairy shifted from price-controlled milk to cheese and yogurt, and a vegetable oil processor added mayonnaise to its product line, because the government considered all these to be nonessential products not requiring price controls. A final form of diversification is market destination. Shifting to export markets is sometimes a feasible and attractive escape from price controls.

Export Pricing

Export products are not usually subject to price controls, except when marketed through a government trading company. However, other complications enter the pricing equation. The first is the possible effects of the country's exchange rate. If it is overvalued, then the effective price is increased to the foreign buyer, or vice versa if the currency is devalued. International revenues are subject to the foreign-exchange risks discussed in Chapter 7. In the international markets, LDC exporters are usually price-takers rather than price-setters. Ghana's cocoa exports in the 1970s generated about 70% of the country's foreign-exchange earnings. The government's Cocoa Marketing Board purchased the cocoa from the farmers at official prices and exported it. As the cedi became increasingly overvalued, the Marketing Board was less able to pay cedi prices to farmers high enough to keep ahead of inflation. Consequently, the official prices to farmers fell in real terms from 10,073 cedis per ton in 1974 to 3,389 cedis in 1983. The farmers smuggled the cocoa to neighboring countries where prices were triple the controlled prices.[21]

Government subsidies and credits can also influence price competitiveness. The Indian government's export subsidies enhanced Cummins's ability to export diesel engines. In contrast, exporters of unfinished leather were hurt by the government's export tax, which aimed to stimulate export of higher-value finished leather products rather than raw material. Foreign tariffs also affect price levels.

Intracompany exports raise special pricing problems. MNC subsidiaries in LDCs often have significant sales to other corporate divisions. Pricing these intracorporate transactions can be a critical part of the company's global strategy. As Arpan indicates: ''Intracorporate sales can so significantly alter the financial results of global operations that they comprise the most important ongoing area of decision making for large multinational corporations."[22]

Transfer prices are financially important because by varying them a corporation can potentially reduce taxes globally or reduce the constraints of foreign-exchange controls. In a high-tax country, for example, raising the transfer price of goods sold to that subsidiary or reducing transfer prices of goods it sells would reduce taxable profits there and increase them in the company's operations in lower-tax countries. Price adjustments may also affect the level of duties levied against company's exports. Where restrictions on profit or capital repatriation exist, higher transfer prices for goods shipped to that country become a vehicle for sending funds out.

While these adjustments might enhance a corporation's global maximization of profits, they occur at the expense of the government's fiscal and foreign exchange coffers. What is good for the company is not necessarily good for the government. Not surprisingly, governments frown upon such manipulations of intracorporate pricing. Because MNCs are often suspected of making advantageous price adjustments, one can expect government scrutiny in this area. Governments tend to require transfer prices to be based on market prices of other companies (or of the subject company in other markets) rather than cost-based prices, because the latter are less verifiable and are thought to be more amenable to manipulation. Such verification, however, is not always possible, because the exported components might be unique to the company.

Transfer prices can be viewed as financial rather than marketing decisions. From either perspective, they become another area for negotiation in which there may be room for accommodation on other grounds. For example, an MNC in an industry with high R&D expenses might be able to convince the government that it would be fair to use cost-based transfer prices since they allow the firm to recover the costs of risky innovation. The market prices of "imitated" products would not represent a reasonable transfer price since the imitators are not innovators. Lall supports this approach:

[I]t is impossible to define a transfer price which is correct in an objective sense. Reference to prices charged by the Transnational Corporation in other markets, or by other firms which do not innovate, are not solutions: the correct transfer price must represent society's view of how to finance risky innovation. . . . What is proposed is that in such cases, the issue of transfer pricing be taken out of the restrictive and misleading context of tax realization and placed in the broader, more complex, but more relevant context of paying for innovation in the framework of TNC dominated international oligopoly. The emphasis should then be on negotiation and detailed evulation rather than on detecting tax evasion.[23]

Because some companies have abused it, transfer pricing stands out as a potentially sensitive aspect of business–government relations.

PROMOTION

Three aspects of promotion merit special attention: media choice, message formulation, and customer relations.

Media Choice

The pattern of media usage for promotion in developing countries differs significantly from that of the more industrialized countries because of three environmental characteristics: (1) Communication infrastructure is relatively less developed; (2) low incomes reduce TV ownership and therefore audience coverage; and (3) low literacy impedes the coverage of print media. Figure 9.1 shows the much lower per capita levels of various media in developing as against developed countries. Figure 9.2 shows that as incomes rise, advertising expenditures rise from around 1% of GNP to about 3%. Advertising levels increase proportionally less than per capita income levels.[24] It is worth noting that advertising has become a more prevalent form of communication in the current LDCs than was the case in the industrialized nations when they were at similar income levels in their development process. This is another indication of how the LDCs' access to modern communications and management technologies has changed their options and development process relative to their predecessors.

Newspapers and Magazines. The low average rate of adult literacy in LDCs (52% as against near total literacy in the developed countries) impedes the coverage of print media. Literacy rates among adult groups also differ. Older adults will have lower literacy than younger ones, reflecting increases in primary school enrollments in recent decades. Since older adults may be key decision-makers in the consumer purchasing unit, newspaper advertising for such households might be relatively less effective. Women tend to have lower literacy rates than men. In the

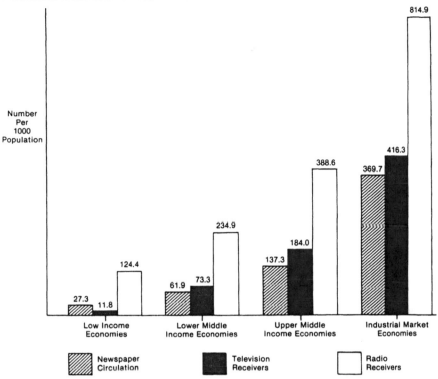

Figure 9.1 Media Usage by Type and Country Levels, 1985

SOURCES: *Statistical Abstract of the U.S.: Comparative International Statistics* (Washington, D.C.: U.S. Department of Commerce, Bureau of Census, 1988); *UN Statistical Yearbook for Asia and the Pacific 1986–87* (Bangkok: UN Economic and Social Commission for Asia and the Pacific, 1988); *Statistical Abstract of Latin America 1987* (Los Angeles: UCLA Latin American Center, 1987).

Ivory Coast, for example, one of two men would be reached by newspapers but only one of four women.[25] (For more country rates, see Chapter 3, Table 3.10). The marketer should identify and analyze the "decision-making unit" in the purchasing process. Gender roles are often relevant here. One marketing expert observed that in one Asian country "the wage-earning male population has an overwhelming decision-making power on almost all purchases, including products for women."[26] The advertising message might have to be directed to the "influencer" rather than the ultimate consumer.

In many countries newspapers are disseminated mainly in urban areas, because distributional weaknesses and lower literacy rates in rural areas hinder distribution. Parkinson provides an example:

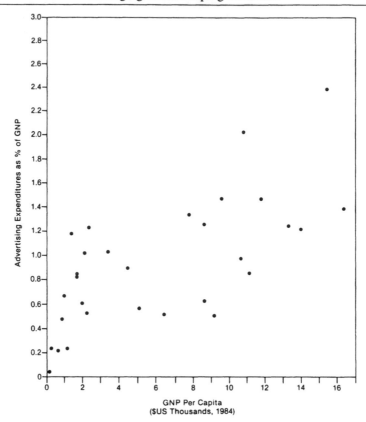

Figure 9.2 Advertising Expenditures in Relation to GNP
SOURCE: Derived from *World Advertising Expenditures in 1985*, 20th ed. (Mamaroneck, N.Y.: Starch Inra Hooper, 1986), p. 10.

[T]he Malawi Book Service has stores in all major towns. Its Mzuzu store, which is in the far north of the country, will display for sale the [one] national newspaper. The most recent copy it is likely to have will be that of the previous day, while it may be complemented by issues of up to a week old, and the customers are delighted to see them there.[27]

The number of newspapers published per 100,000 people averages 0.12 in low- and lower-middle-income countries, 0.98 in upper-middle-income countries, and 2.7 in industrialized nations.[28] About 34% of advertising expenditures goes to print media in low- and lower-middle-income countries: 44% is allocated in upper-middle-income countries; and 50% in industrialized nations.[29] Magazine coverage is considerably more limited than newspapers. Readership is often concentrated in a specific socioeconomic group, so magazine advertising might be effective for products targeted to that market segment. Such targeting, however, is often hampered by lack of audited circulation figures and socioeconomic readership profiles. As literacy levels improve, these print media become more relevant.

Television. Per capita ownership of TVs is still relatively low in developing countries, but it rises quickly with income improvement. In 1986 in India there were 3 TVs per 1,000 people, in Peru 43, in South Korea 238, in the United States 356. The correlation between TVs per capita and GNP per capita has a coefficient (R-squared) of .69.[30] TV ownership is concentrated in urban middle and upper classes and is therefore a very effective medium for reaching those segments. It is wrong, however, to assume that low-income groups cannot also be reached via television. In urban areas, TVs are very high on the purchase priority list of many low-income families, with savings often targeted toward the acquisition of a television. A TV in one household in densely populated low-income neighborhoods is often watched by many families. The number of sets per capita may be low, but the number of watchers to a set is high, hence effective coverage is increased. Television advertising has been shown to have a strong influence across a broad range of socioeconomic strata in urban centers.[31]

Lower-middle-income countries spend the largest share (57%) of their advertising dollars on TV. This figure is 39% in upper-middle-income countries and 21% in industrial market economies. The latter two groups allocate more of their budgets to print media and also engage in direct advertising, such as point-of-sale or mailings, which are used very little in lower-income nations.

Radio. Radio ownership is relatively widespread in LDCs. The emergence of low-cost transistor radios precipitated the rapid dispersion of radios in rural and urban areas and among lower-income groups. Radio ownership in developing countries is more than double TV ownership. Relative to other media, radio has greater coverage in rural areas. In some countries, however, access to radio (and TV) broadcasts for commercial advertisements is restricted by governmental controls. In Saudia Arabia, for example, the government prohibited any commercial radio advertising.[32] Governments often own some or all of the radio or TV stations and restrict lengths and timing of commercials. In lower-income countries advertisers allocate about 15% of their budgets to radio, about

double the share in upper-middle-income countries and developed countries.

Cinema. Motion pictures are relatively important in developing countries. Cinema attendance is a very popular form of recreation, even for
low-income consumers. Commercial advertising is commonly shown
along with the movie. The contrasting importance of cinemas as an
advertising medium is revealed by the fact that 12.6% of Kenya's advertising expenditures were in cinemas but only 0.7% in the United Kingdom.
Because different theaters tend to cater to distinct socioeconomic groups,
one can target an audience through outlet selection.

Billboards and Posters. Although it is very difficult to assess the
effectiveness of these media, they are relatively inexpensive and commonly used in developing countries.

Direct Mail and Telemarketing. Deficiencies in the postal and telephone systems in most developing countries seriously hinder their use
as marketing tools. Mailing lists are not readily available, telephone
lines are scarce, and service is defective. The relatively uncommon use
of these media, however, suggests that opportunities can be tapped when
the infrastructure improves and as creative approaches to overcoming
limitations are devised.

Other Media. Perhaps because of these infrastructural deficiencies,
informal communication channels using social networks are often quite
strong. One Côte d'Ivoire company effectively used a "word of mouth"
approach. A series of meetings with community leaders throughout the
country announced and explained the forthcoming opening of a national
chain of stores.[33] Sound trucks are another way to reach the public
without reliance on formal systems; they can be targeted to specific
geographic areas and groups. In some countries, public buses provide
this message dissemination service. A final promotional approach is the
use of small gifts or special prize drawings.

Message Formulation

One initial difficulty facing advertising in many developing countries
is multilingualism. Ethnic diversity within countries is often quite high.
The sub-Saharan countries have more than two thousand distinct dialects;
two hundred exist in Nigeria alone. India and some other Asian countries

have similar linguistic diversity. Latin America, however, is linguistically more homogeneous, with Spanish dominant (Portuguese in Brazil) but still a second language for some indigenous groups. Sri Lankan advertisers face Tamil-speaking Hindus, Sinhalese-speaking Buddhists, and Muslim and Christian groups.

In an effort to create greater national unity, governments have often promoted one dialect as a unifying official language. Indonesia adopted Bahasa and Kenya chose Swahili, both originally trading languages. Advertising messages have to be translated into multiple dialects to reach different linguistic groups, which are often geographically concentrated. In Nigeria, for example, Ibo is used in the East, Hausa in the North, Yoruba in the West, parts of Kwara State, and Lagos, while English is also used in Lagos and three Eastern states.[34]

For international marketers, language choice and translations have sometimes been the source of advertising blunders, as the following examples reveal:

- One American airline company promoted in Brazil its plush "rendez-vous" lounges on its new planes, only to discover that in Portuguese "rendezvous" was the term used for a room hired for love-making.[35]
- Advertising for General Motors' Nova model in Latin America encountered a snag because in Spanish "no va" means "does not go."[36]
- Residents of a Middle-Eastern country saw an ad about a new auto-suspension system that, in translation, said the car was suspended from the ceiling. Since there are about thirty dialects in the eighteen Arab countries, great care in translation is needed.[37]

The foregoing examples are problems due to semantic errors in translation. Other advertising problems are caused by lack of understanding of cultural norms in the developing country:

- One body powder producer encountered resistance from the Indian public when it placed newspaper ads showing an apparently nude woman dusting herself with the company's talcum powder. Many readers found the ad distasteful and contrary to their standards of decency, certainly not the reaction hoped for by the company.[38]
- A French perfume maker chose to use ads in Saudi Arabia that had been very successful in France for their TV and print campaign. The ads showed a very attractive woman walking down the street with the copy asserting that a thousand eyes would turn her way. This directly conflicted with the Saudis' religious and social custom in which women are veiled and to be seen only by their husbands.[39]

- The American manufacturer of the Monza car advertised in Greece using a model attired in Greece's blue and white colors with her hands outstretched. However, the gesture of holding the hand, palm outward, toward another person is known as the *mounza* and is very insulting. The company was introducing the Monza by giving the audience the *mounza*.[40]

- Color symbolism also differs across countries and ethnic groups. One soft drink company lost sales in Southeast Asia when it changed the color of its vending machines to light ice blue, a color associated there with death and mourning.[41] In Thailand the launching of a toothpaste required changing its color from red to green to be acceptable to the consumers. In another country a company encountered difficulty because its international emblem on its packages was green, and for many in that culture green was symbolic of the jungle with its diseases and dangers.[42]

Cultural sensitivity in designing promotional strategy is critical for all international marketing.[43] Heightened ethnic, linguistic, and social diversity in developing countries makes this variable even more central.

Customer Relations

The foregoing discussions of media have emphasized consumer products. For industrial marketing, personal selling is the main promotional vehicle. Industrial products, particularly more complex equipment, require more detailed and technical information dissemination. The size of the purchase is also often much larger than for consumer items. Consequently, the purchasing process tends to be more complex and lengthy, and requires greater information transmittal and more direct contact with the customer. The importance of this customer relationship is increased in LDCs, because information is less available, the industrial product often involves foreign technology, and customers are often less familiar with the product. These factors tend to make the customer more dependent on the seller, which puts a premium on achieving a trust relationship.

Grow reported an illustrative case of Japanese, American, and Soviet companies' attempts to sell machinery to a Chinese steel-fabricating company, China #1. The Japanese company, Takemitsu Kaisha, made nine visits to the Chinese company between 1973 and 1982, learning about its problems and establishing working relationships with its managers and engineers. When the Chinese sought bids in 1984, Takemitsu put forth a relatively brief $9-million proposal, delineating the equipment needed, the training to be provided, and the importance of the existing relationship. The American company, General Technologies, made one visit to the company and five weeks later submitted an $11-million proposal for a state-of-the-art system. The Soviets offered to supply used equipment that would mesh with existing Russian machinery in use at the Chinese plant. The equipment would be bartered for Chinese grain worth $5 million. Although the Soviet machinery cost less and was more familiar, and the American machinery was more advanced and productive, the Chinese chose the Japanese.

> Time and again, the Chinese manager, engineers and foremen found themselves talking about the Takemitsu proposal in terms of the personal relationships that had developed between the individuals at China #1 and members of the Japanese team. When questions arose in the Chinese discussions about product reliability, maintenance, delivery schedules and unforeseen events, the discussion usually returned to the Chinese confidence in the relationships they had formed with the Japanese. . . . There was a sense that the Japanese firm was a known quantity, that the Takemitsu team members had a greater personal stake in the success of the marketing relationships than other foreigners they had dealt with, and that Takemitsu would be more readily available to handle unexpected problems.[44]

Cummins Engine also used direct and close contact with customers to overcome its marketing crisis when demand from original equipment manufacturers evaporated in the face of the Indian government's credit restrictions and investment cutbacks. It sought potential new users of diesel engines and worked with them to design special engines to meet their specific problems and needs. Direct and close interaction with customers enabled KCL to open new market opportunities. Industrial marketing in LDCs generally involves technology transfer, and this is almost always a hands-on process. Marketers will be more effective if they are able to help the customer sort through the critical factors involved in technology choice and adaptation decisions (as delineated in the previous chapter). Furthermore, customer relations are culturally imbued; marketers must be attuned to customers' cultural norms and expectations.

DISTRIBUTION

Managing LDC distribution systems encounters special problems due to infrastructure deficiencies and domination of channels by particular ethnic groups.

Infrastructure Deficiencies

Weaknesses in transport infrastructure and services, telecommunications, and storage tend to make distribution channels longer than in developed countries. There are more intermediaries between producers and consumers. Geographical isolation, smallness of markets, and lack of national networks create more fragmented and longer channels. It is not unusual for a product to change hands four to eight times before reaching the final consumer. Surplus labor also contributes to the problem as people become petty traders or service laborers, making distribution a labor-intensive undertaking.[45] Channel length and structure tend to increase costs and dilute the producer's channel control. Sometimes importers become powerful in the wholesale channels because of the country's dependence on imports; as the dependence decreases, so does the importers' channel power.

Poor quality of roads often causes greater wear and tear on vehicles. The high price of imported replacement parts and original equipment often make transport costs relatively high. Deficiencies in transport and storage often cause sizable product losses. In agricultural marketing, post-harvest losses due to these deficiencies were estimated to be at least 10%–20% of the crop.[46] Companies may have to utilize different preservatives or packaging to hold up under slower and rougher handling conditions. Foremost Dairy Corporation's joint venture in Thailand overcame the lack of distributors' refrigeration by providing freezers to the multitude of small corner stores and restaurants on a conditional sales contract. Upon fulfillment of the contracted product sales, Foremost "sold" the freezers to the distributors for one dollar.[47]

In addition to these logistical problems, communication deficiencies impede the flow of information and contribute to market imperfections. Prices, supply and demand data, and product flow information are not readily available. Often prices are flexible, with bargaining the norm and fixed prices the exception. The lack of information gives a competitive edge to those entities able to mount management-information systems to gather such data and competitively handicaps those that cannot. Thus, the marketing management information system becomes vitally important.

A strategic decision for a producer is whether to mount one's own distribution system (i.e., vertically integrate forward) or to use existing channels. From one angle, this decision requires the normal analyses, weighing the costs of increased investment and organizational complexity against the benefits of system efficiencies and increased channel control. This is comparable to our analysis in Chapter 8 of the production strategy of backward vertical integration to overcome supplier deficiencies. Forward vertical integration may require engaging in a business activity quite different from the company's traditional areas of experience and competency. For example, in developing countries where capital and commercial credit are scarce, wholesalers must often engage in credit extension activities. As countries and their financial systems develop, this financing function tends to shift from wholesalers to credit institutions. But initially a company wanting to integrate vertically may have to get into the credit business.

From another angle, the integration decision might involve a larger issue: the transferability of modern merchandising systems versus the use of traditional channels. There is a dual tendency for LDC channels to shorten and for more "modern" distribution systems to emerge.[48] The early success of Sears Roebuck in Latin America was largely due to its creation of new distribution channels.[49] Modern systems often arise parallel to traditional outlets to serve more affluent segments. The urban retail level has dual structures: self-service stores, supermarkets, and department stores along with traditional open markets, corner stores, and street vendors.

This duality exists because traditional channels are not easily displaced. Their particular forms have emerged in response to unique social and economic conditions in the environment. Migros, the successful Swiss chain-store operation, was unsuccessful in Turkey reportedly because it "tried to operate its self-service stores, supermarkets, and mobile-selling trucks in the same manner as it operated them in Switzerland, without considering the different needs and characteristics of Turkish food consumers and prevailing environmental conditions."[50] Local distribution structures clearly have strengths. Rather than think about bringing in modern distribution systems to displace traditional ones, one should seek out synergistic combinations. In Mexico, for example, Pepsico's snack food subsidiary, Sabritas, took Pepsi and Frito-Lay's U.S. concept of a direct store delivery system and adapted it to the local channel structure. In the United States, the major outlets are supermarkets; in Mexico the retail structure is dominated by thousands of very small family run outlets. These exist because most consumers are not very mobile, buy in small quantities, shop frequently, and require credit because of constraints of income (low and irregular cash flow) and storage (refrigeration). To accommodate these market characteristics, Sabritas created its own truck fleet with driver-salesmen and then delivered directly to the corner stores, thereby gaining broad access to the mass market through the existing retail structure.[51]

In Ghana, a U.S. company developed a large, modern corn farming operation. It packaged its seed in standard weight containers, an innovation well-received by buyers because a common deficiency in LDC markets is the lack of standard measures and weights; the buyers were local market women, whose existing network enabled rapid and wide coverage.[52] Some new forms take hold because they are similar to existing activities but with distinct attributes. For example, the rise of fast-food franchise outlets in major cities throughout the developing world is a variant of the traditional street-corner vendor or quick lunch stop. In contrast to their customer pattern in the United States, however, these outlets have relatively few drive-through and car customers; they serve mainly pedestrian traffic in high-movement commercial areas.

Ethnic Domination

Another distinctive feature of distribution channels in many LDCs is their domination by certain ethnic groups, for example, Asians in many African countries and overseas Chinese in many Asian countries.[53] The extent of channel control exercised by the overseas Chinese, for example, is very high. In Malaysia 74% of the retail outlets and 72% of the trucks were estimated to be owned by Chinese; in the Philippines, Chinese were 1.4% of the population and owned 33% of the retail outlets, which accounted for two-thirds of the business; in Indonesia and Thailand the economic salience of the Chinese was similar.[54] One survey of 15,000 small businesses in Malaysia found 83% to be Chinese-owned, whereas the Chinese share in the total population was 30%.[55] In some African countries certain tribal groups dominate particular segments of the economy. Sometimes immigrants carve out areas of economic dominance. In the Côte d'Ivoire, Lebanese immigrants dominate urban commerce and Ivorians dominate agriculture and the government bureaucracy.[56]

When ethnic groups control the channels, formulating a distribution strategy requires special analysis to understand how to interact with those ethnic groups. The way these groups operate is distinct and derives from their culture. Cultural analysis becomes essential to distribution analysis. As an illustration, we can draw on the insightful analyses of Limlingan and others of the overseas Chinese.

In commercial channels the Chinese derive significant competitive advantage from their social network and customs. This network serves as an efficient system for information collection and dissemination, giving Chinese firms an important edge over others. In effect, the social system helps overcome informational imperfections in the marketplace. Trust relationships also create financing advantages in environments where access to capital is scarce. Barton's account illustrates these points:

> The major advantage that Chinese merchants had over Vietnamese traders in developing reputations for credit worthiness derived from the nature of Chinese social organisation. The Chinese community functioned as a well-organised system of information, as an arena in which businessmen carried out transactions exposed to the scrutiny of others. By participating in the various associations and gatherings which were constantly being organised in the Chinese community, a businessman had available to him the information, speculation and gossip which formed the subject matter of everyone's conversations. Much of the conversation at Chinese social gatherings centered on the financial affairs of persons not present, with everyone fully realising that his own activities would be freely discussed on occasions where he himself was absent. The task of every businessman, then, was to so conduct himself in his financial affairs as to build and preserve a reputation for trustworthy, reliable and astute behaviour.[57]

Barton's research revealed that Chinese merchants are able to obtain credit at interest rates about half those paid by non-Chinese. The custom for Chinese businessmen is to pay off all debts annually during Chinese New Year, which creates a social control mechanism for credit payment. Furthermore, fulfilling such obligations is important so as to avoid causing loss of face for the kinship clan. This sense of social obligation and family loyalty (with roots in a Confucian value system) also enables much business to be conducted through trust relationships, rather than elaborate and costly administrative control systems. This means that Chinese firms often have leaner and more agile organizational structures, another competitive advantage.

Limlingan observed that Chinese traders are very price-competitive because they tend to use low margin/high turnover strategies. They also vertically integrate forward into transportation and storage. They seldom integrate backward into commodity production, but they do diversify their product lines. This diversification sometimes is intended to obtain credit rather than to profit from that product line. This can create competitive disruption, as the following example reveals. In the Philippines, MNC tire manufacturers used their access to relatively low-cost capital to extend liberal credit terms to attract business. Chinese dealers would purchase large quantities of tires on credit and then sell them at below the purchase price to generate cash for use in their other more profitable trading activities. The loss on the tire sales was considered an interest expense. This "dumping" created considerable discontent among the tire manufacturers' other customers.[58]

In deciding whether to compete against or collaborate with a Chinese or other ethnic distributor, one should realize that one is dealing with a larger sociopolitical system rather than just a single company. Understanding that larger network and its leverage is essential to thorough analysis of the relative power relationships among buyers, suppliers, and competitors. Some dimensions of this network in the Philippines are as follows:

> Perhaps the most important single group to a Chinese business man is the local Chinese Chamber of Commerce. Each Chamber of Commerce provides a forum for discussion, collects and disseminates information about trade conditions, investigates and guarantees the credentials of Chinese business men, settles disputes, conducts research, provides machinery for group action, and acts as a lobby and pressure group to promote the interests of the Chinese in their dealings with the Philippine government officials. Money is collected through the local Chamber for charity work, hospitals, cemeteries, social clubs, and especially the financing of Chinese schools. Chinese businessmen also seek protection through such trade organizations as the Philippine Chinese Hardware Association, Chinese Groceries Association, and the Philippine Manila Chinese Sari Sari Store Association. At present the larger trade associations and the 120 Chambers of Commerce are united in the Federation of Chinese Chambers of Commerce to present a single cohesive front and facilitate business contacts in all the provinces.[59]

Ethnic groups in the channels are potentially strong allies or strong competitors. Understanding their cultural modalities is a prerequisite to interacting with them effectively. There is also an important political dimension. The ethnic groups dominating distribution channels are often minorities. Their relatively better economic position has often bred resentment among majority groups and led to political retaliation. In some instances, they have been excluded from certain economic activities. Many African nations after independence sought to Africanize their distribution systems because they were predominantly controlled by non-Africans. Uganda expelled 50,000 Asians upon ninety days' notice. The Ivory Coast, where less than 15% of the retail outlets were run by Ivorians, chose a gradual approach of creating a government network of stores and a retailer training program for its own people.[60] But civil strife in Lebanon has led to a tenfold increase since 1975 in the Lebanese immigrant community in the Ivory Coast, which is now estimated to be in control of two-thirds of the domestic trade and half the real estate in the capital city.[61]

In ethno-dominated channels and others, personal relationships with distributors are often of vital importance. As one Latin American manager put it: "They prefer to buy from someone they know, that they have good relations with, even if it's not as good a business proposition.[62]

MARKET RESEARCH

The last element in the marketing mix that poses special challenges to the manager is market research. One of the salient characteristics of LDC markets is scarce and imperfect information. We have seen that overcoming information gaps can be strategically important. The market researcher faces problems of data collection and data reliability.

Data Collection

Infrastructural deficiencies impede data collection. Mail and telephone surveys are relatively much more difficult to implement. Telephone ownership is much lower. Often only a third of the urban households have phones, and telephone directories are often outdated. Phone service in Zaïre is so bad that it has sparked the widespread use of walkie-talkies, which are hardly amenable to telesurveys.[63] Mail delivery is often unreliable and slow in many countries.

Nonresponse is another problem for both telephone and mail surveys. In some countries cultural norms inhibit giving information over the phone. Nonetheless, there have been enough positive results with telephone surveys to indicate that they can still be useful. Singer Sewing Machine in Kenya had a 70% cooperation rate in a survey testing consumer awareness of the location of one of its stores. Experiments with mail surveys in Bogotá, Colombia, reportedly increased response rates from 12% to 48% when a small gift was used.[64]

For international marketers adapting survey questionnaires used in other countries, great care is required to ensure language accuracy and linguistic and cultural suitability. The "back translation" approach can be helpful: The translated questionnaire can be translated back into the original language by a third party in an effort to pinpoint misinterpretations.[65]

The limitations of telephone and mail surveys make personal interviews the method of choice, but it, too, has problems. The first difficulty is the lack of trained interviewers; training will be required. A second issue is gender. Women tend to be the main interviewers in developed-nation market research, but they are reportedly more difficult to recruit in LDCs. Perhaps the reason is social norms about appropriate gender roles or the need to make evening calls in urban areas that might not be considered entirely safe.[66] In Moslem countries, in particular, it would be inappropriate for women to be interviewed by strange men. Consequently, female interviewers are imperative.[67] One international research firm has successfully used discussion panels in the Middle East with groups of local women and run by a female researcher.[68]

Even if one is successful in realizing an interview, some data may simply not be available. Cultural norms might make some topics taboo, such as sex, personal hygiene, and family relationships. The extended nature of many family structures may make it very difficult to identify or have access to all the key individuals in the consumer decision-making unit. Interviewees may also be quite reluctant to provide information on family income for fear it might be used by tax authorities. Thus, it is very important to stress the confidentiality of the interviews. Some field evidence suggests that interviewers that are, or look like, college students obtain relatively high rates of cooperation.[69]

In drawing a sample and gathering interview data, one should recognize the potential diversity among regions within a country and attempt to understand the sociopsychological aspects of consumer interests. Cundiff and Higler describe an illustrative experience in Brazil.[70] Campbell Soup undertook a consumer survey in the southern city of Curitiba. It revealed that families consumed soups daily rather than occasionally, as in the United States. This indicated a major market, so the company invested $6 million in a joint venture and $2 million in a national promotion to launch their line of canned soups. There was high recognition and initial sales, but then sales plummeted, leaving the factory operating much below capacity. Investigation revealed that southern consumers, being in a temperate climate, consumed soup more than households in the tropical north. Thus, the sample was nonrepresentative of the national market. It was also discovered that homemakers felt unfulfilled psychologically by the canned soup because it left them with nothing to do. The competition (Lipton and Knorr) had dehydrated soups that allowed homemakers to mix in their own ingredients. The initial high sales apparently reflected curiosity and a desire to store these ready-to-serve soups for an emergency rather than as a regular consumption item.

Data Reliability

One must also be concerned about the reliability of the primary data collected. Some respondent bias is culturally caused. For example, in Asia and the Middle East a "courtesy" bias has been noted: Respondents try to provide information they feel the interviewers will want to hear rather than divulge their true feelings or opinions.[71] Exaggeration is another bias type. The respondent's answer may be shaped to cast a favorable image. In a study of tea consumption in India, over 70% of the respondents from middle-income families claimed to use one of several national brands of tea. These findings were questionable when cross-checked against the fact that over 60% of the tea sold in India was unbranded.[72] Questions should be carefully worded to anticipate, catch, and reduce such respondent biases.

Careful review of respondent answers and interviewer observations can lead to improvements in questionnaires. A consumer research expert in the Philippines recounted such an experience in adjusting an annual survey of low-income urban consumers:

In the earlier surveys, my interviewers reported that when they were talking to some of the downscale housewives about such expenditure items like, for example, "eating out" or "vitamins," several of them seemed reluctant or even looked embarrassed to choose from among the list of the six coping responses the one that "best describes" what they did to the expenditure item concerned. The interpretation that my interviewers gave to this show of reluctance or embarrassment is either the real response was not in the list we were showing them to choose from and it was a response that reflected a situation they were embarrassed about, or else that they simply did not remember what they did.[73]

By adjusting the questionnaire to allow for "cannot recall" and "did not buy or use" responses, the researcher was able to increase the survey's accuracy. The resultant survey findings illustrate the utility of market research among low-income LDC urban dwellers. They revealed six categories of behavior low-income homemakers used to cope with hard economic times: purchase reduction, elimination, usage-economizing, substitution, maintenance, and extenders. The survey data enabled an estimate, for example, that snack food consumption in this consumer segment would fall by 36% through the combination of these coping strategies, but rice consumption would remain steady. The data also revealed that as a usage-economizing and substitution-coping strategy, people used laundry soaps for both personal bathing and clothes. Thus, laundry soap would face added demand while facial soaps and shampoo sales would suffer unless more economical product lines were offered. In pharmaceuticals, consumers became very price sensitive, thus signaling an opportunity to market low-priced lines aggressively. Other opportunities were identified for less expensive products that could substitute for or extend meat dishes.[74]

Another bias problem is sampling error. Often very few reliable data are available on the universe from which samples would be drawn. Population registers, census data, voter registrations, and telephone directories are outdated or incomplete. Population growth rates, migration, and mobility complicate the demographic accuracy of records and maps. This makes selection of blocks for probability sampling difficult. Furthermore, multigenerational families living in the same dwelling complicate the definition of families and households.

These problems sometimes force researchers into the realm of second-best solutions. Instead of random probability samples, they may use quota or convenience samples. Quota sampling is nonprobability sampling in which interviewing quotas are established for various kinds of respondents. Convenient samples are taken in marketplaces and other public gathering locations. For example, in China, which is only beginning to develop a market-oriented economy, manufacturing firms would make product modifications and then place their employees in stores as clerks to ascertain consumers' reactions.[75] These approaches have the obvious weakness of not necessarily being representative of the larger population, so they must be interpreted with caution. The complications of market research design place considerable demand on the skills of researchers. These skills are not in abundant supply in many LDCs, and in some instances less-trained groups have fudged the data. Careful selection of the research group and review of the methodology to be used are recommended. Even in NICs, market research skills may be scarce. In Singapore techniques being used were considered "very basic and rudimentary," although improving rapidly.[76]

Secondary data are also important to market research, but their accuracy is often questionable. For example, in Saudi Arabia an American market survey team verified that even though official government statistics indicated that 10 million frozen chickens had been imported, in actuality 60 million had entered. Similarly, a Japanese company found that 40,000 air conditioners had been imported, even though official figures reported 10,000.[77] The unreliability of official statistics may be due to technical deficiencies, smuggling, or even political manipulation.[78]

GLOBAL MARKETING

A major strategic marketing issue for MNCs is the extent to which global marketing encompassing the LDCs is desirable and feasible. We shall first examine the basic product policy issue of standardization versus adaptation. Then we focus on the globalization issues surrounding advertising. Next, we discuss how government actions and requirements might constrain globalization strategies. Last, we examine the barriers, advantages, and strategies for exporting from LDCs.

Product Policy: Standardization vs. Adaptation

Proponents of standardization point to the tendency of markets to "homogenize" because of the effects of global communications and transportation technology.[79] As higher-income and higher-educated groups become more exposed to international products, they may tend to prefer similar consumer goods, such as TVs, radios, tape recorders, and computers. In these instances, more uniform approaches may be feasible. In the medical products area Becton Dickinson chose to standardize worldwide the design and quality for its syringes and needles. Its quality standards were often more stringent than government requirements. This gave it a competitive edge, and the standardization permitted production economies of scale and competitive pricing.[80]

Despite these forces for standardization, one study of 174 consumer package goods pointed toward adaptation: 90% of the products transferred from developed to developing countries were modified in some way.[81] Some products (often food items or food-preparation equipment like microwave ovens) are more culture-bound and therefore require country-specific tailoring. One large U.S. food producer launched a major campaign to introduce its top-selling U.S. snack food into the Thai market. The local manager described the effort this way:

> What we did was entirely transpose the product straight from the United States and superimpose it in Thailand. Nothing was wrong in the marketing strategy, if you accept the global strategy. Everything was done exactly to the letter. What happened six months later after everything was wiped out was that 95% of the people did not like the product.[82]

It was an expensive failure, because consumers rejected the product's taste; the product formulation was not culturally transferrable. The company later carried out consumer surveys and taste tests that enabled it to reformulate the product and gain acceptance.

Like food, services are often strongly influenced by culture.[83] Because services usually involve personal interaction, social norms regarding interpersonal behavior become relevant to operational design. For example, the degree of attentiveness or formality in customer relations may have to be adapted to the local norms. A culture's attitudes toward basic human nature affect the degree of trust placed in others, and this might influence, for example, the use of self-service approaches. A society's time orientation could affect the speed or timeliness requirements placed on customers and employees. One key to handling these cultural adaptations is to unbundle the service package; many component activities may be amenable to standardization while others will require local tailoring.

Even within the same company different products may require different approaches. For example, Unilever's strategy for its packaged foods leans more toward local adaptation than its approach to detergents, which in turn requires a more nationally differentiated strategy than the company's chemical business.[84]

Advertising

In the promotional area, the globalization focus is on standardization of advertising. The international advertising agency McCann-Erickson claims to have saved $90 million in production costs over two decades by producing worldwide Coca-Cola commercials.[85] Because such global economies of scale can create competitive advantage, the approach merits pursuit. But the previously cited examples of cultural blunders in advertising counsel caution. The uniqueness of local preferences has been the rationale for Nestlé's and Unilever's rejecting the standard global advertising and marketing favored by such other MNC giants as Coca-Cola and Kodak.[86] But even where messages and product names are tailored to the country, the actual production of the advertising materials can sometimes be centralized to obtain production economies of scale. For example, Nestlé produces most of its TV film footage in one location, and Canon produces centrally its camera and other manuals and product literature in multiple languages.[87]

Of all the elements in the marketing mix, advertising deals most intensely with values and is thus the most likely to be affected by local peculiarities. Marketers should therefore involve knowledgeable locals in the cultural testing of global advertising for both linguistic and visual appropriateness. Even Coca-Cola decided to replace its brand name in China because its phonetic pronunciation in Chinese meant "bite the wax tadpole."[88] Varying availability of media channels may also require adaptation of global strategies. Global approaches with some local adjustment may gain the benefits of international economies while still ensuring local effectiveness. The key is to separate the elements of a promotion into those that are country-bound and those that can be centralized. Striking the right balance is not simply a technical issue; it also involves more fundamental consideration of the control relationship between headquarters and local subsidiaries. Organizational tension will be inevitable.[89]

Although the media type and message will require country adaptation, the general strategy regarding advertising's role in the overall marketing strategy may be common across countries. Where the consumer products are relatively new in a market and are competing against traditional products (e.g., laundry detergents, bread, breakfast cereals, and pharmaceuticals), firms have found heavy advertising to be particularly effective in achieving consumer switchovers. MNCs tend to use advertising more heavily than local firms both to penetrate markets and to impede others' entries. The effectiveness of this intensive advertising has also engendered criticism of MNCs for distorting national tastes and hurting local firms.[90]

Market research in LDCs can provide useful information in formulating their global strategies. By gathering data on market evolution in countries at different levels of development, a company may be able to predict and plan more accurately market opportunities that will emerge as a country develops. Even though each country has its own development path, there may be significant similarities in the evolution of market behavior for the same product in different countries.

Government Constraints on Globalization

Government regulations can hinder globalization efforts. Product ingredient laws, packaging specifications, labeling requirements, price controls, and promotional restrictions can necessitate local modifications. For example, the government of Ecuador set new size standards for bottles, forcing the international and local soft drink companies to abandon global package standardization. In Oman the government required tobacco manufacturers to print on their labels "Smoking is a major cause of cancer, lung disease, and diseases of the heart and arteries,"[91] instead of the less explicit wording in the warning labels used in the United States and elsewhere. Other LDC governments restrict the use of foreign brand names, which impedes global branding strategies. Price controls may affect global marketing decisions, because price levels in one country may set precedents for pricing in other countries. One multinational pharmaceutical company, for example, was reluctant to release a new drug because the price suggested by the government price regulators was unacceptably low and the company feared that other governments would require a similar price. However, the company had launched a massive advertising campaign in advance of the product's introduction. To satisfy the clients' built-up demand, the company decided to distribute the drug free until an acceptable price could be negotiated.[92]

Despite these locally mandated constraints and adjustments, regional standardization might still be possible, and some aspects of the marketing mix might still be globalizable. There is another area of government regulation that creates an additional challenge to global marketing strategies: countertrade.

Countertrade can take various forms, but it basically involves a barter-type transaction in which goods from one country are paid for, at least in part, with goods from another country. This can be a direct exchange of one good for another, a counterpurchase agreement to acquire various goods equal in value to the purchased goods, or a buy-back agreement whereby an equipment supplier will take payment in the form of output produced by the supplied equipment.[93] For example, in 1984 Saudi Arabia acquired ten Boeing 747s in exchange for $1 billion worth of oil, and Volkswagen do Brasil announced it would supply $630 million worth of cars to Iraq in exchange for oil, which would then be sold to the Brazilian government's oil company. Colombia paid for Russian and Rumanian buses with coal and coffee. The government later passed a countertrade law stipulating that importers had to export Colombian products of equivalent value, sparking a flurry of new exports by MNCs and local companies that had earlier been serving only the domestic market. General Motors and Chrysler exchanged vehicles for Jamaican bauxite. Malaysia paid for 80% of an electrical equipment contract with Yugoslavia with tin and rubber exports. To generate foreign exchange needed for importing its concentrate, PepsiCo set up a trading subsidiary to market such exports as pineapple and frozen broccoli from Mexico, sesame from Sudan, sisal from Tanzania, and molasses from Nicaragua; Xerox covers its Brazilian imports by exporting steel and venetian blinds.[94]

The volume of countertrade is estimated to be between 5% and 30% of world trade, or $100 to $600 billion.[95] In the mid-1980s, General Electric Trading Company's countertrade commitments exceeded $2.2 billion. Developing countries have become increasingly involved in countertrade for several reasons. The liquidity crises in the 1980s, triggered by falling commodity prices and the burden of servicing international debts, can be partially alleviated by meeting obligations with goods rather than scarce convertible currencies. If the currency is overvalued, countertrade may be a way of overcoming the noncompetitiveness of exports due to the exchange rate distortion. Some countries see long-term countertrade contracts as a way of stabilizing the prices of their commodity exports. Others view countertrade as a means of selling products that would be difficult to market under unrestricted conditions or to stimulate nontraditional exports.

Regardless of the reasons, companies undertaking global marketing are increasingly having to deal with the demands and opportunities of countertrade. Although it can be viewed simply as a financial matter, countertrade is often the deciding factor in whether a sale is made. Furthermore, governments sometimes stipulate which products have to be countertraded, the quantity, and the market destination.[96] Therefore, companies with superior ability to accept and profitably resell counter-traded goods may have a competitive advantage. Global marketing strategies may have to be expanded to include disposal of ancillary countertrade goods as well as the company's main product line.

MAKING IT IN THE EXPORT MARKET

The previous sections have stressed marketing in or into the developing countries. The other side is export marketing from the LDCs. The degree to which this can be globalized also depends on the nature of the constraints and country conditions discussed above. But regardless of the globalizability, export marketing from LDCs offers significant opportunities but also faces serious barriers.

Barriers that have typically impeded exporters include the following:

- *Quality:* Deficient production technologies or different product characteristics or lower quality requirements in domestic markets reduce product acceptability in the international markets.
- *Information:* LDC exporters often do not have adequate knowledge of the requirements and workings of the export markets.
- *Channel Access:* Exporters may face barriers to entry into the distribution channels resulting from concentrated structures, existing supply arrangements, or resistance to trying new suppliers.
- *Logistics:* Transport and storage infrastructure may be inadequate in quality or quantity to meet the logistical demands of the export markets.

- *Competition:* Producers used to low competition in protected domestic markets may find their products and prices unable to compete against more experienced or more efficient producers from other countries.
- Exchange Rates: Government controls may make the currency overvalued, decreasing the exporter's competitiveness.
- Trade Restrictions: Protectionism in various forms on the part of importing countries can reduce the viability of export operations (20% of LDC exports face nontariff barriers, which is double that faced by developed country exports).[97]

On the positive side, LDCs have various potential *sources of comparative advantage* as exporters, including the following:

- *Labor:* Abundant and relatively inexpensive workers, in some countries quite skilled.
- *Natural Resources:* These include minerals, timber, fisheries, land, and energy, giving the countries control over scarce, highly demanded products or lower raw material costs in related industries.
- *Geography:* A country's location can create climatic conditions (e.g., the tropics) that enable the production of special products, or the location might give exporters freight cost advantages to nearby markets.
- Government Actions: Exchange rate, credit, fiscal, and trade policies can create competitive advantage for exporters (as discussed in Chapter 4).

The task for managers seeking to succeed in the export market is to formulate strategies that mold their firms' special competencies so as to reduce the barriers and capitalize on their country's particular sources of comparative advantage. The following five categories of *export strategies* illustrate distinct bases for competing in the international markets:

1. *Cost strategy* is appropriate for products that are price-sensitive and where cost minimization is critical to competitiveness. Labor-intensive goods are especially amenable to this strategy, for example, apparel and electronics assembly. The LDCs where this strategy is most likely to fit are those with large pools of underemployment and unemployment, because of either their big populations (e.g., China, Mexico) or their low levels of development and few alternative economic opportunities (e.g., Haiti, Sri Lanka). The extreme form of this strategy is the use of the export processing zones, where almost the only local input is the labor, with the materials being imported. The viability of the low labor cost/low price strategy erodes as a country develops, because wage

rates rise relative to those in other countries. Sustainability can be preserved by increasing labor productivity and achieving economies of scale to keep unit costs down. Even where labor is not a major cost component, freight savings might make this approach viable, for example, for bulky manufactured components such as auto parts from Mexico for export to the United States.

The export market access barrier is often removed because the producer (especially in the export processing zones) is frequently also the importer as part of an offshore sourcing strategy. Where the exporters are independent they must create links with importers; often this entails producing for private labels. The exporter–importer relationship based on the low price strategy is tenuous. The buyer will usually continue to shop around for better prices from other countries' suppliers. To some extent the exporters can strengthen their position by demonstrating their reliability for on-time deliveries and their responsiveness to buyer needs such as product modifications.

2. *Value strategy* combines cost and quality considerations to create attractive value. This is for products where quality is quite important to the buyers, yet a good price will allow the new exporter to penetrate the market. These products are often more technically sophisticated and producible by the industrially advanced NICs operating higher on the technological capability ladder (Chapter 8, Figure 8.1). The value is created not only by lower factor costs but also by the growing ability to achieve production process innovations and product design enhancements. An example would be the Hyundai car. The company and the country had the human and technical skills to produce a reasonably reliable and comfortable car; production competency and quality control were prerequisites. They then used penetration pricing, sacrificing margin to gain acceptance by distributors and consumers and to generate the volume essential for economies of scale. Aggressive advertising stressed value. The value strategy will increasingly propel LDC export penetration in manufactured goods. LDC business groups will follow this approach in their efforts to internationalize their operations, and the MNCs will use the value opportunities to strengthen their global production and marketing networks. Head-on competition will become more frequent, but so too will opportunities for collaboration (see the next chapter). The MNCs often offer ready-made access to marketing outlets, thereby removing an export barrier to the business groups.

3. *Uniqueness strategy* is for products that cannot be produced in the importing market and can thus be sold on their distinctiveness. Tropical

fruits would be an example. Traditional ones such as bananas and pineapples have well-established distribution channels, largely created through vertically integrated systems developed by MNCs. Newer ones such as mangoes require more intensive education of distributors and consumers; carefully crafted advertising and trade promotion can be quite effective, as revealed by the successful introduction of the Kiwi fruit into the United States. Such artisan products as carpets, furniture, and crafts usually require specialty outlets on the marketing side and significant organization of small producers on the supply side.

4. *Seasonality strategy* is for agricultural products that enter the markets during the off-season for local production, e.g., the winter vegetable and fruit market in the United States. The key to these export operations is high quality control and tight management of the logistical system. Success usually requires close links and coordination between exporters and importers.

5. *Value-added strategy* takes advantage of opportunities for exporters of unprocessed or semiprocessed goods to undertake additional processing prior to export, increasing the value of their exports. Examples would include instant coffee, plywood, cocoa butter, canned meats, frozen and prepackaged vegetables, and fabricated metals, although for some more highly processed products transport costs increase. For some products and major local companies (SOEs or business groups) the path to value-added will be vertical integration into the importing markets by acquiring (or developing) processing and distribution operations. For example, Venezuela's state oil company and private coffee growers in Brazil acquired U.S. companies engaged in downstream processing and marketing operations.

LDCs will become increasingly important actors in the export arena. Successful exporting requires the careful formulation of strategies that fit the company competencies, country context, and export market demands. The effective implementation of these strategies demands managerial expertise in analyzing and dealing with the special problems and conditions examined in the other chapters.

SOCIAL MARKETING

This final section discusses the application of marketing concepts and techniques to critical social problems in developing countries. "Social marketing" strives to change individuals' behavior in socially desirable ways. It is singled out from the commercial marketing discussed so far because it has emerged as a new phenomenon over the past fifteen years, whereas the contribution of marketing in general to economic development has been discussed for several decades. From an economic perspective, Galbraith's and Holton's classic study of Puerto Rico's marketing system in the early 1950s revealed the significant economic savings that could be achieved through improvements in the island's food marketing system.[98] From a management perspective, Drucker's seminal 1958 article pointed to the key role of marketing as an organizing force to dynamize the development process.[99] Much has been written since then. Many concur with Etemad's conclusion that "marketing can be a potent catalyst" in economic development; others would agree with the Dholakias's warning that some marketing institutions and processes can adversely affect development by increasing dependency and concentrating benefits with the wealthier groups.[100] Analyzing this important debate is not within the scope of this book; the purpose of this section is rather to highlight the emerging role of social marketing.[101]

Social marketing in LDCs has been applied mainly to public-health problems where new information and practices have to be disseminated. Among the areas of application have been the following: adoption of family planning methods, in-home use of simple oral rehydration therapy to prevent life-threatening dehydration that often accompanies infant diarrhea, child immunization campaigns, purchase of iodized salt to prevent goiter, AIDS education, and improved hygiene and sanitation practices.

Programs to address these types of problems have generally been the responsibility of government entities or private social organizations. The effectiveness of their efforts has often been reduced because of marketing problems. Common among these have been inadequate information about the target audience's preferences and behavior, poorly designed or delivered communications, and defective distribution systems. The recognition of the applicability to these problems of the techniques of market research, advertising and promotion, distribution systems, pricing policies, and product strategies has led to the emergence of social marketing.

Fox and Kotler cite several successful efforts in the family planning field.[102] The Sri Lankan government's social marketing program comprised the following elements:

- Consumer research revealed wide acceptance of the concept of family planning but low knowledge and use of contraceptive methods.
- Product selection chose condoms, and a brand, Preethi (meaning happiness), was developed.
- Packaging and pricing led to a three-pack design selling for US$0.04, an extremely low price.

- The distribution strategy was for broad coverage through multiple channels, including more than 3,600 pharmacies, teahouses, and grocery and general stores, as well as direct mail and agricultural extension workers.
- Promotion used radio, newspaper, films, booklets, and point-of-purchase displays.

The government cited as measures of the effort's effectiveness Preethi's annual sales of 6 million by 1977 and an estimated total of 60,000 unwanted pregnancies averted.

A similar effort launched in Bangladesh had annual condom sales in 1983 of 50 million pieces and was particularly effective in reaching poor, illiterate, rural fathers.[103] A similar program in Thailand run by a community organization had a cost per recipient half that of the government's program, which did not use social marketing.[104] In rural Kenya, market-research modeling techniques revealed how adjustments in the advertising part of the social marketing effort could identify key ways to increase usage of condoms.[105] One social marketing effort in Kenya involved setting up health and family-planning clinics and activities for workers at various private and parastatal companies.[106] Selected workers were trained as family-planning educators and contraceptive distributors. The program's aim was to increase knowledge about family-planning practices and to improve access to preventive methods. Folk media (local musical or drama groups), posters, direct contact, and word-of-mouth rather than mass media were the vehicles used. Participating companies saw significant benefits from the program. For example, one company with 4,000 employees, 70% of whom were women, provided free housing, subsidized food, day care centers, and health clinics. About 60% of the health-care costs were for the care of women and of children under five. After the family-planning and preventive health-care services were begun, maternity cases fell from thirty-nine deliveries per month to twelve. In another participating company, the number of women on maternity leave dropped from sixty per month to ten.

Such social marketing efforts have increased the effectiveness of family-planning programs in many countries. Some demographic analysts attribute the recent decrease in the LDC fertility rate largely to the introduction of these programs.[107]

As for health and nutrition, an international advertising firm carried out careful market research in Indonesia, involving focus-group interviewing. This research provided the basis for formulating a nutrition education campaign. A series of one-minute messages were designed to promote behavioral changes in nutritional practices and were broadcast extensively over the radio. Follow-up research revealed high effectiveness.[108] In the Philippines a social marketing campaign to introduce oral rehydration therapy (ORT) used focus groups to gain an understanding of mothers' usage of the oral rehydration powder consisting of separate packets of glucose and sodium to be mixed into a liter of water. This consumer research revealed that some mothers dissolved only the sodium and kept the glucose as high-quality sugar for use in guests' coffee. Other mothers found the mixed ORT solution too salty and added sugar to make it more acceptable to their children, thereby imbalancing the treatment. These findings led to further consumer research and adjustments in the product and promotional messages.[109]

A social marketing program in one area of Nigeria aimed to control guinea-worm disease by getting villagers to acquire water filters. The social marketers used a highly participatory approach in which local village health workers were heavily involved in the design and production of the filter, the pricing decisions, the distribution and promotion of the filters, including persuading the local leader to endorse the use of the filters.[110]

In several developing countries governments have launched public education campaigns about AIDS using mass media. In the Philippines, social marketing was also used to increase awareness and change the public's attitudes toward corrupt behavior by government officials.

The foregoing examples show how several elements of the marketing mix can be applied to efforts to alleviate various social problems. Kotler and Roberto set forth five core components in social change campaigns to which the marketing techniques would be applied:

- *Cause.* A social objective that change agents believe will provide a desirable answer to a social problem.
- *Change Agent.* An individual, organization, or alliance that attempts to bring about a social change—that embodies the social change campaign.
- *Target Adopters.* Individuals, groups, or entire populations who are instruments of bringing about change, the target of appeals for change.
- *Channels.* Communication and distribution pathways through which influence and response are exchanged and transmitted back and forth between change agents and target adopters.
- *Change Strategy.* The direction and program adopted by a change agent to affect the change in a target adopter's attitudes and behavior.[111]

Social marketing offers no magic solution to the multitude of social problems facing developing countries. It does, however, hold potential for significantly enhancing programs to address these problems. The marketing management skills that abound in private companies are applicable also outside the normal commercial boundaries of business. This may constitute another area for constructive collaboration between government and business.

Even commercial marketing carries special social responsibility in developing countries. Developed-country products and marketing techniques must be introduced with care and sensitivity, for there is the possibility of crowding out or blemishing local cultural norms. For example, a survey in one Latin American country revealed that one company's heavily advertised symbol was more recognizable to children than their national flag. Accusations of "cultural imperialism" can carry political repercussions.

A company's product and marketing techniques can also lead to consumer injury. The most cited example in recent times has been that of infant formula. A perfectly safe, high-quality, and beneficial product became potentially lethal because of its misfit with the LDC environment. Low-income consumers living in unsanitary environments were often simply unable to use the product in a way that followed the hygienic requisites for safety. Aggressive marketing techniques often enticed poor mothers to switch from cheaper and healthier breast-feeding to bottle-feeding. Faced with severe criticism from consumer advocacy groups and a consumer boycott, the infant formula companies, under the auspices of the World Health Organization, developed a marketing code of conduct that eliminated many of the marketing practices.[112] One Nestlé official reflected on the experience:

> The Nestlé boycott teaches two lessons. The first, which is ignored only at great peril, is that issues that can arise to threaten a company are as likely to be sociopolitical as financial, and that no company, especially a large visible company, is exempt from the possibility of some political crisis arising. Therefore, executives owe it to themselves and their firms to become as competent at managing political issues as they are at managing profit-and-loss issues. In today's world, public policy and profits are equally important to a company's survival.
>
> The second lesson is that if a company commits itself to acquiring sociopolitical competence, and instills that commitment in all ranks, it can become as dynamic and assertive in shaping its political environment as it is in shaping its financial and marketing environment.[113]

A similar example is the marketing in LDCs of potentially dangerous chemical products such as pesticides. Although developing countries account for only 15% of world pesticide use, they suffered more than half of the 750,000 cases of pesticide poisoning and more than three-fourths of the 14,000 deaths.[114] Misuse of the product was a major cause of these poisonings. Illiteracy, inadequate training in handling, repackaging into unsafe containers, and storage near food all contributed to the misuse. The need is clear to adjust marketing and product packaging to reduce the risks of misuse that stem from the LDC environment's characteristics.

Marketing can contribute significantly to the development of the Third World. Managers must be sensitive to the social consequences and contributions of marketing strategies and practices.

CONCLUSION

Marketers in developing countries face a distinctive environment that requires adjustments in the marketing mix. Product policy is particularly affected by LDC demographic structures and dynamics. The high population growth rates affect the market for products whose demand is mainly population-driven. The LDCs' young age composition affects demand profiles, family structures, and purchasing patterns. LDCs' rapid urbanization creates a process of changing consumption patterns for new urban dwellers; however, rural populations remain large markets in most LDCs. Economic factors also shape product policy. In particular, the skewed income distribution patterns create distinct market segments with different product demand patterns. In the political area government regulations can affect the type of products a company can market and the methods for marketing them. Cultural factors shape consumer product preferences and receptivity to marketing approaches.

Pricing policies must often cope with governmental price controls and complications surrounding export pricing. For promotional activities, managers face a very different communications infrastructure and consumer profile, so media choice requires adjustments. Message formulation has to be particularly sensitive to the demands of linguistic diversity and cultural requisites. Customer relations are particularly critical in industrial marketing, given the imperfect information and complications of technology transfer. Distribution strategies are affected by infrastructural deficiencies and the domination of channels by ethnic groups. Market research is hindered by data deficiencies and the lack of skilled researchers.

However, companies able to do research effectively may gain great advantage, because the relative scarcity of information creates a premium value for what is gathered.

A global marketing approach may enable economies of scale for some products, but many will require adaptation to the special demands of LDC environments. Careful scrutiny of the product and consumer characteristics and government regulations is required to identify the feasibility and degree of globalization. Exporting from LDCs offers significant opportunities but also faces several barriers. Successful export strategies blend the company's competencies, the country's comparative advantage, and the export market's requirements. Five distinct bases for competing in the international markets exist: cost, value, uniqueness, seasonality, and value-added.

Deficiencies in LDC marketing infrastructure and processes impede the development of LDCs. Improved marketing management can help accelerate economic growth. Furthermore, social marketing can contribute to the attainment of social goals. Marketers have a special responsibility to ensure that their products and the ways they market them will be compatible with the consumers' circumstances and enhance their well-being.

10

Organization

Assessing Entry, Ownership, and Cultural Effects

In this chapter we shall focus on three key organizational issues. The first regards the strategic choice of the mode of entry into LDCs for foreign companies. The second concerns ownership strategy and the use of joint ventures. The third explores how cultural factors affect organizational structures and processes.

ENTRY MODE

One can conceptualize the choice of a company's involvement in LDCs as a spectrum of modalities in which a firm's asset exposure (financial investment) and the intensity of managerial involvement increase (see Figure 10.1). The least involving form of entry into an LDC is exporting from the home country; this might involve visits and considerable communication but no direct investment in the country nor, necessarily, a continuing relationship after the sale. Licensing (or franchising) would entail closer assessment of the licensee, technical assistance in transferring the technology, and an ongoing relationship for the duration of the licenses, but not necessarily any investment other than the ceding of the proprietary knowledge. Setting up a local sales branch to market the company's exports would require direct investment and management presence. Production subcontracting for export usually entails intensive and continual interaction with the subcontractor and often some form

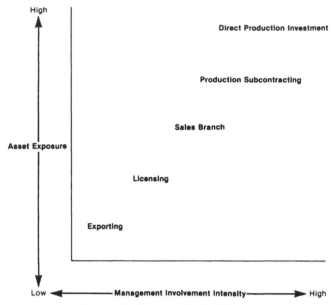

Figure 10.1 Entry Mode Choices

of financing. The most management-intensive and financially exposed form of entry is direct investment in production operations as a wholly owned subsidiary or a joint venture. This depiction of forms of entry is an oversimplification in that firms can combine these modalities. For example, Cummins Engine made a direct investment in its Indian joint venture while simultaneously licensing production technology to the venture. Furthermore, licensees often continue to import parts from the licensor. International production subcontracts sometimes involve licenses or direct investments in the form of equipment and materials. Many organizational permutations are possible.

Choosing the right mode of entry is a complex decision because of the multitude of relevant variables. Our intention is to specify, organize, and analyze these variables. They can be categorized into three groups: country environment, competitive situation, and company characteristics. Although the perspective here is that of the foreign company, the variables are also relevant to deliberations of host country companies as potential licensees or partners. To simplify and highlight the variables, we shall discuss each of the three groups in the context of a choice between licensing and FDI. The analytical approach and the variables used can also be applied to an evaluation of the other entry forms (exporting, sales branch, and production subcontracting).[1] As is implied by our groups, the "right" choice cannot be generalized; it will depend on the specific features of a company, its competitive context, and a country's environment. Our analysis will indicate for each variable how its condition favors FDI or licensing.

Country Environment

Following our Environmental Analysis Framework, we can organize country variables into economic, political (including government policies), and cultural categories:

Economic   Market size and growth
                          Labor: cost
                                 skill
                          Local managerial capacity
                          Infrastructure adequacy
Political   Political risk
                          Government receptiveness to FDI
                          Import controls
                          Foreign-exchange controls
                          Price controls
Cultural   Cultural compatibility

Each of these will be examined as to the condition under which they would favor licensing or direct investment, *holding all other things equal.*

Economic Factors

Market Size. Generally, the larger the market and the higher its rate of growth, the greater the chances for attaining a volume sufficient to justify a direct investment. Managers of technology-intensive firms have expressed preference for direct investment over licensing for large markets, but they did not always follow this preference in practice, perhaps because of more intensive competition in those markets.[2]

Labor Cost. Low labor costs are an attractant for FDI, but as wage levels rise, disinvestment sometimes occurs. For example, low wages were important in drawing foreign investment into Hong Kong, but as costs rose many firms shifted their labor-intensive operations to neighboring countries with lower wages, such as Thailand. A 1984 survey of foreign investors revealed that high labor turnover, labor shortages, and high wages were the three most unfavorable factors in the Hong Kong investment climate.[3]

Labor Skill. The lack of skilled workers raises the risk and costs of FDI. Hong Kong's supply of skilled workers was important in attracting and retaining investors originally and has enabled the country to attract more skill-intensive operations to offset the flight of low-skill operations moving to countries with cheaper labor.

Local Managerial Capacity. The more capable local management is, the greater their ability to absorb outside technology and to mount new operations. This increases the chances of licensing realizing its full income-generating potential. Thus, the management resources available through FDI become less needed.

Infrastructure. If infrastructure is more developed, it will make FDI less risky. For example, Hong Kong's relatively highly developed telecommunications and shipping facilities were key factors in making it attractive as an export base for the eight hundred U.S. companies that had invested more than $5 billion there as of 1984.[4]

Political Factors

Risk. From our discussion of political analysis in Chapters 4 and 6, we know that to be assessed most meaningfully political risk must be considered as industry- and company-specific, rather than as a macro phenomenon. With that in mind, it is clear that the greater the political risk, the more desirable is licensing's lower asset exposure.

Government Receptivity to FDI. Where national strategies have relied heavily on FDI, the investment environment is greatly enhanced. For example, Singapore's export-oriented industrialization was spearheaded by foreign investors. The government placed almost no restrictions on investors and offered them various incentives. Investment grew annually at rates of 40% in 1966–73, 12% in 1973–77, and 24% in 1977–79;[5] foreign firms constituted 13% of the companies but accounted for 50% of the nation's value-added in manufacturing.[6] South Korea also sought FDI and experienced similar FDI growth rates.[7] In contrast, Algeria nationalized most foreign firms in 1966–71 and later discouraged new FDI. Consequently, various forms of licensing and contracting were the involvement modes chosen by foreigners there.[8]

Import Controls. As we know from our discussion in Chapter 4 of the EAF's Public-Policy Impact Chain, it is through specific policy actions that national strategies affect the business environment. If import controls create a protected domestic market, competitive pressures from imports will be lowered, reducing the market risks of FDI. But if import controls create scarcity of previously imported critical inputs, then production problems could arise, thereby increasing operating risks.

Foreign-Exchange Controls. Where governments exercise strong restrictions on foreign-exchange outflows, dividend or capital remissions are often tightly limited. In both Brazil and Korea MNC subsidiaries reportedly used licensing fee payments to their parents as indirect mechanisms for profit remission to circumvent exchange controls.[9] However, some LDC governments closely scrutinize and aggressively tax royalty payments, perhaps to discourage such disguised profit remissions or to encourage equity-capital inflows rather than licensing.

Price Controls. As was discussed in Chapters 7 and 9, price controls can jeopardize profitability, especially during inflation. The MNC food-processing company Gerber moved away from equity investments with their greater asset exposure because in its words "licensing lessens the adverse effects of inflation, price controls and in some cases, the political climate."[10]

Cultural Factors: Compatibility

The greater the differences between the foreign firm's home culture and the LDC's culture, the greater are the operating risks and transaction costs of relating to its subsidiary. Service businesses tend to be culturally more sensitive. Licensing reduces cultural risk by reducing intensity of involvement. It does not, however, eliminate the risk, because interaction with the licensee is still required, but the burden is lightened and shortened.

Competitive Situation

Four variables of industry structure and competitive dynamics appear most relevant to the entry choice: industry concentration, relative competitive strength, local barriers to entry, and risk of market cannibalization.

Industry Concentration. Competitive behavior by multinationals is influenced significantly by industry structure. Where there are relatively few competitors (an oligopolistic industry structure), the competitive dynamics tend to be matching moves.[11] Because direct investments are viewed as strong competitive moves that could capture market share, they tend to be imitated as a defensive measure. Licensing is generally seen as a weaker move and thus less threatening.

Where the industry is more fragmented, licensing tends to become more prevalent. For example, in the petrochemical industry there is a relatively small number of large manufacturers, but engineering contractors also own technology. The engineering firms have a higher proclivity to license than to invest, so this possibility leads manufacturers to license more than they otherwise would.[12]

Relative Competitive Strength. Companies may view the choice of entry mode as dependent on their competitive position within the industry. The companies that tend to license are smaller or weaker ones that may be unable to capture an adequate share of the market to achieve needed economies of scale or volume to justify direct investment. Gerber's previously mentioned strategy of licensing reflects, in part, its position as a relatively smaller player in the industry. Also, latecomers in the industry may use licensing as a way to accelerate the catch-up process.

Local Barriers to Entry. In some instances, local companies are firmly entrenched. Their positions may be protected by government assistance such as production or import licenses or by their control of raw materials or distribution channels. These local competitors may be economically and politically powerful business groups or SOEs. Almost all LDC governments, even those strongly favoring FDI (such as Singapore), exclude foreign investment in certain key industries, for example public utilities, defense manufacturing, and mass media. High local barriers to entry increase the costs and competitive risks of direct investment. Licensing would be favored, although a joint-venture arrangement (see the next section) might overcome some of these barriers and justify FDI.

Market Cannibalization Risk. Licensing carries the risk of creating new competitors. A licensee might eventually export to the licensor's home market or third-country markets in which the licensor is selling. Loss of sales in those primary markets may be far more significant for the licensor than royalty income from licensing. Geographical restrictions in licensing agreements can reduce this risk but are seldom foolproof and sometimes prohibited by local governments. For example, one Swedish tool manufacturer licensed an Indian manufacturer as offshore source for its marginal overseas markets. The Indian licensee did not uphold the Swedish firm's quality standards but continued to export. It became a serious competitive threat in some markets and also jeopardized the Swedish company's international reputation for high quality.[13] The magnitude of such risks will also be influenced by how mature the technology is, as will be discussed in the next section.

Company Characteristics

There are certain characteristics of firms that influence the entry-mode decision:

Product	Maturity
	Brand differentiation
	Line diversity
	Service-intensity
Technology	Maturity
	Stability
	Complexity
	Patentability
Resources	Capital
	Management
	LDC experience
Globalization	International strategy

Although each company may have distinctive product and technology characteristics, most aspects will be common to many firms and would thus apply to the industry as a whole.

Product

Maturity. When a product is far advanced in its life cycle, licensing may offer a way to extend its life in a new market. A local licensee might be able to use existing production resources to exploit the license. The product's shortened longevity and the competitive risk of new substitutes reduce the profit potential of FDI.

Brand Differentiation. When a product is highly differentiated and brand recognition is high, the company has a competitive edge in the marketplace. This reduces the competitive risks of making a direct investment. Licensing puts the brand image at risk in that the licensor has less control over the operations and quality of the licensee than would be the case with FDI.

Line Diversity. Telesio's study of sixty-six multinationals revealed that the more diversified a company's product line, the more likely the use of licenses. The manager of one highly diversified MNC explained the reliance on licenses this way: "We put products into foreign production faster than we can find our own subsidiary managers, capital, and foreign market knowledge."[14] For these companies, breadth and speed of market penetration via licensing are more important than the greater depth and control possible from FDI. Furthermore, the lessened dependence on a single product or a few products may make it less necessary to undertake FDI as a defensive mechanism to protect market share.

Service-Intensity. If the product requires intensive post-purchase servicing by the licensor, it is less amenable to licensing, or at least the transaction costs of supporting the license are increased. The distance between consumers and the foreign-based support service impedes rapid response and effective communication. FDI reduces this distance and increases the certainty of quality performance. When the product itself is a service (rather than service's being part of follow-up support), then FDI becomes more necessary. The obvious exception is franchisable services, such as fast-food businesses. Franchising has expanded rapidly in LDCs: In 1983 there were on average forty-four U.S. franchises per developing country with about twelve outlets per franchise (as against eighty-one franchises and forty-seven outlets in developed nations).[15] Where the services and the attendant management systems can be standardized and readily transferred via training and manuals, this licensing variant becomes feasible.

Technology

Maturity. As with products, when technologies mature, the tendency is for licensing to increase. Access to the technologies grows because imitative inventions circumvent the patent or the proprietary technology is discovered. As ownership spreads, the monopoly profits of the original innovators are eroded, and a race to capture licensing rents ensues.

Stability. Technological longevity varies. The technology of the nine petrochemical products studied by Stobaugh showed a life cycle spanning several decades.[16] Others suffer premature deaths through scientific discovery. Where the technological area is new or undergoing rapid transformation resulting from fundamental breakthroughs, technological advantages are less durable. Technological instability creates competitive uncertainty, and the "first-mover" rewards have to be very high to justify direct investment. Licensing reduces asset exposure to the risk of obsolescence.

Complexity. The more complex the technology, the greater the demands placed on the LDC recipients, and the more likely difficulties in transferring the technology will occur. The wider the gap between the technology's exigencies and the country's absorptive capacity, the more need there is for FDI. The transferor of the technology has to assume a more active role in the process. Low-tech lends itself to licensing but high-tech may not. The high technological demands of Cummins's large diesel engines relative to India's capability in this area called for direct investment and involvement there, whereas the company was able to go the licensing route in subcontracting production to Japan's technologically sophisticated Komatsu corporation.

Patentability. When a technology is patented the company has a more licensable entity. The risk of bypassing or stealing the technology is lessened, because there is a basis for legal recourse in the case of patent infringement. As a protective and preemptive move, MNCs often take out patents in LDCs even though they are not worked there. For example, in Nigeria only 5% of the patents are used.[17] The patent creates a protected licensing opportunity; however, obtaining infringement relief in the courts of the licensee's country will not necessarily be easy, because patent-protection legislation in developing countries is relatively weak.[18] Most developing countries are not signatories to the International Convention for the Protection of Industrial Property or any other international patent agreement. Some developing countries will not honor a foreign patent or will place more severe restrictions on it, such as reducing the protection period. For example, Pfizer's leading antiarthritis drug could not be patented in Argentina because the government wished to promote its domestic pharmaceutical companies; Monsanto will not market its best-selling weedkiller in India because it has no patent protection.[19] A further risk of seeking patent protection is that the required disclosure may enable competitors to discover ways of legally circumventing the patent. Thus, patent protection should be assessed for its breakability. Vulnerability from this perspective would indicate preserving proprietary technology through FDI.

Furthermore, patent protection is not absolute, because "counterfeiters" are hard to identify and control. Some developing countries have increasingly engaged in producing imitation goods. There may be more than $20 billion in fake goods flowing from developing countries. Taiwan reportedly is the main source, followed by South Korea, Thailand, Mexico, and Brazil. In 1983, AT&T revealed a new phone model at a trade show; before it even reached the market a Taiwanese company had replicated, manufactured, and marketed it. The company withdrew the imitation after AT&T lodged a private protest.[20] The Motion Picture Association of America uses five hundred investigators and lawyers in sixty countries to catch bootlegged videotapes.[21] However, by licensing a local company in the key counterfeiting countries, the licensor may be able to create a local ally with a vested interest in policing against imitators. Local companies can use the threat of counterfeiting to obtain licenses. Wells cites the tactics of a local pharmaceutical manufacturer in one Asian country:

> We can copy most drugs quite easily, so the task is to handle the patent problem. Our government requires that patented products be manufactured locally for the patent to hold. Moreover, the government limits royalty payments to 5 percent of sales. Thus, early in the life of a new product, we approach the foreign manufacturer, show him our ability to manufacture the product, and ask for a license. He has little choice. He can try to manufacture locally himself, but he is not very attracted to the small market and realizes that we are likely to produce a substitute product and undercut him so much that his plant will be a failure. Usually we get the license.[22]

The more proprietary and imitable the technology, the greater the need to maintain control and secrecy. This would favor FDI over licensing. The U.S. pharmaceutical MNCs are an example of an industry with high dependence on proprietary technology and a strong preference for FDI over licensing.[23] German chemical and other research-intensive companies also expressed preference for FDI.[24]

Resources

Capital. FDI obviously requires much more capital than licensing. For the capital-constrained firm, licensing offers a mechanism for penetrating a new market without overstretching the company's financing capacity. Consequently, smaller firms tend to favor licensing. For example, the smaller U.S. semiconductor companies tend to subcontract or license independent Asian assemblers rather than undertake FDI.

Management. FDI is much more management-intensive for the investor than licensing. Even if a company has abundant capital, its managers may be fully utilized. The scarcity of managerial resources, especially top management time, should be carefully assessed. Even though new managers can be hired, launching new investments in developing countries generally imposes significant demands on home office management. Start-ups require strategy formulation and strategic deliberations that require top management involvement. This is not to imply that licensing planning and negotiations are not managerially demanding, but the demands are less in duration and scope.

LDC Experience. Just as there are experience curves for technologies which lead to greater efficiencies, so too are there significant gains from greater operating experience in developing countries. As is clear from previous chapters, the LDC environment confronts companies with innumerable, distinctive managerial demands. Those companies with greater LDC experience will be much better positioned to undertake FDI. Much of the experience in one LDC is transferrable to others, because many of the problems are generic. Nonetheless, we have also pointed out in previous chapters that each country is distinct. Consequently, even the LDC-experienced company should approach FDI in a new country with caution. International subcontracting, as an intermediate modality between licensing and FDI, can be used to gain experience and help decide which path to take. In Haiti several multinationals (Sylvania, GTE, Automatic Coil) first contracted with local companies to produce certain components and products; based on positive results of these trials, they proceeded to make direct investments.[25]

Globalization

The more globalized a company's strategy and operations are, the greater will be the need for control and coordination. In general, this would be met better by FDI than by licensing. Larger firms that have shifted component production or assembly offshore as part of a global production and sourcing strategy have tended to opt for FDI rather than licensing. The semiconductor industry illustrates the phenomenon. Fairchild Semiconductor led the industry into Southeast Asia, setting up assembly operations first in Hong Kong and then in neighboring countries. These production sites specialized in labor-intensive, lower-sk   's of production, but they were viewed as an integral part   production system. Product reliability, efficiency, and logisti   tion were essential to preserving the integrity and competi   of an integrated global system. Consequently, the need   and technical control was high. This led Fairchild and producers who followed to set up their own manufacturing subsidiaries rather than license local companies.[26] In lower-technology industries such as garments and footwear, subcontracting rather than full FDI has been used more frequently; these goods are often produced in final form ready for consumer marketing and do not need to be integrated into a global production system as intermediate inputs.

Another example is international banking. As service businesses, banks are less able to license, but, additionally, their FDI is pushed by their global strategies. First, they need to follow their multinational clients. Five major U.S. banks by 1982 had invested more than a quarter of a billion U.S. dollars in fixed asset facilities in Hong Kong. These investments were made to serve the eight hundred U.S. firms there and to coordinate their Asia-Pacific operations. Bank of America made Hong Kong its Far East headquarters and started developing an integrated regional information network.[27]

Many service and manufacturing companies have chosen to invest in Hong Kong to position themselves to market in or source from China as part of their global strategies. One large U.S. multinational made a direct investment in China as a preemptive move because, if "Japanese competitors were to attain leadership in China, they might gain cost reductions which could undercut prices in the U.S. or third country markets."[28]

Although greater globalization tends to favor FDI, global strategies can readily encompass both FDI and licensing along with such other organizational forms as trading and subcontracting. Japanese MNCs in extractive industries, for example, obtain almost half their copper and a third of their iron ore by making production loans to LDC producing companies; for the balance they make direct investments. The loan-and-import approach accommodates those developing countries that wish to retain national ownership of natural resource industries yet need financing and market access. The Japanese get the raw materials they need, earn interest on the loans, reduce their fixed-asset exposure, and exercise control through their marketing operations.[29] A manager can take a portfolio view in which one modality might be more appropriate in one country and a different approach better in another.

Integrating the Variables

Table 10.1 presents a consolidated view of the country, competitive, and company variables and indicates the conditions for each variable that would tend to favor licensing (lic.) or foreign direct investment

Table 10.1 Entry Mode Selection Matrix: Licensing vs. FDI

Types of Variables	Condition of Variables Low ←------→High	
Country Environment		
Economic		
Market size and growth	lic.	FDI
Labor cost	FDI	lic.
Labor skill	lic.	FDI
Local managerial capacity	FDI	lic.
Infrastructure adequacy	lic.	FDI
Political		
Risk	FDI	lic.
Gov't. receptivity to FDI	lic.	FDI
Import controls	lic.	FDI
Capital controls	FDI	lic.
Price controls	FDI	lic.
Cultural		
Compatibility	lic.	FDI
Competitive Situation		
Industry concentration	lic.	FDI
Relative competitive strength	lic.	FDI
Local barriers to entry	FDI	lic.
Cannibalization risk	lic.	FDI
Company Characteristics		
Product		
Maturity	FDI	lic.
Brand differentiation	lic.	FDI
Line diversity	FDI	lic.
Service intensity	lic.	FDI
Technology		
Maturity	FDI	lic.
Stability	lic.	FDI
Complexity	lic.	FDI
Patentability	FDI	lic.
Resources		
Capital	lic.	FDI
Management	lic.	FDI
LDC experience	lic.	FDI
Globalization	lic.	FDI

(FDI), other things being equal. In any particular case some variables would probably suggest FDI while others would point toward licensing, and some of these variables will offset each other. For example, the technology might be highly complex, which would indicate the need for FDI to handle the technology-transfer demands, but the country may also have high levels of managerial competency, which would suggest that local companies might be able to absorb the technology effectively via licensing. Furthermore, a company's actual situation may show a variable to be neither high nor low but medium. The manager's task is to judge the relative importance of the variables, their conditions, and their interaction in terms of their impact on corporate strategy and profitability. The matrix facilitates a systematic analysis of the variables; tradeoffs become clearer. The imperative of managerial judgment remains.

OWNERSHIP STRATEGY

If a company opts for FDI, it then faces a second strategic decision regarding the subsidiary's ownership profile. The initial choice is between a wholly owned subsidiary (WOS) and a joint venture (JV). Similarly, local firms can choose between going it alone or taking on a foreign partner. The trend for multinational companies is to make increasing use of joint ventures in carrying out the FDI. In the early 1900s 10% of the new U.S. subsidiaries in developing and developed countries were JVs; by the 1970s the share was 45%.[30] European[31] and particularly Japanese MNCs show a greater proclivity toward joint ventures than U.S. companies do. For example, in Malaysia 87% of the Japanese subsidiaries were joint ventures, as against 50% for the U.S. MNCs.[32] Japanese MNCs' use of joint ventures is significantly greater in LDCs than in developed nations: In North America 43% of their investments are JVs, whereas in Latin America 78% are, Asia 85%, and Africa 94%.[33]

During 1952–75 the major U.S. multinationals formed most (63%) of their subsidiaries in Latin America, followed by East Asia (13%).[34] The top ten countries in numbers of subsidiaries formed during this period and the percentage share set up as joint ventures are shown in Table 10.2.

During the 1950s the average number of JVs formed annually by the major U.S. multinationals was thirty-two, rising to eighty-three in the

Table 10.2 Countries with Greatest
Numbers of U.S. MNC Subsidiaries,
1952–75

	No. of Subsidiaries	JVs
Mexico	624	39%
Brazil	441	35%
S. Africa	338	26%
Venezuela	322	37%
Panama	224	8%
Argentina	217	34%
Hong Kong	111	15%
Peru	106	31%
Philippines	100	38%
India	93	72%

SOURCE: Harvard Business School, Multinational Enterprise Project Data Base.

1960s and declining to seventy-nine in the 1970s. Joint ventures as a share of total subsidiaries showed important variations over the period. Figure 10.2, derived from the Harvard Business School Multinational Enterprise Project data base, shows the percentage of new subsidiaries that were started as joint ventures in LDCs, in total and by regions. It is evident that the incidence of joint venturing had an upward trend but varied significantly over time and among regions.[35] Joint ventures' share for 1952–75 was 34%; it peaked at 45% in 1965, declined to 27% by 1969, and then moved back to 45% in 1975. As for regional differences, in North Africa/Middle East and South Asia, JVs are relatively more frequent, averaging 51% and 67%, respectively. In East and West Africa and in South Africa, joint ventures' shares are below average: 31% and 25%, respectively. In both East Asia and Latin America, the share of subsidiaries started as JVs in 1969–75 has been about 32%. Within regions, however, significant differences exist. For example, in Mexico 39% of the subsidiaries were JVs, but in Panama only 8% were. Kobrin's analyses reveal that, in general, the past JV patterns have largely continued into the mid-1980s.[36] As of 1985 38% of the LDC subsidiaries were JVs; the share in Latin America was 30%, Asia 44%, Africa 50%, and Northern Africa 81%. Just as the choice of entry mode will vary depending on country, company, and competitive variables, so too will the ownership strategy vary because of these factors.

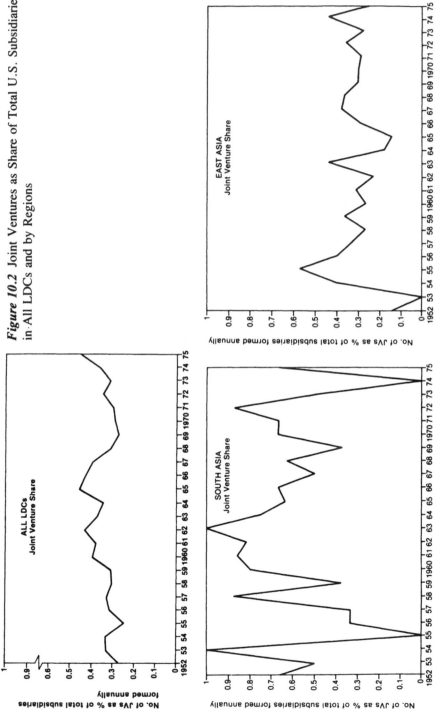

Figure 10.2 Joint Ventures as Share of Total U.S. Subsidiaries in All LDCs and by Regions

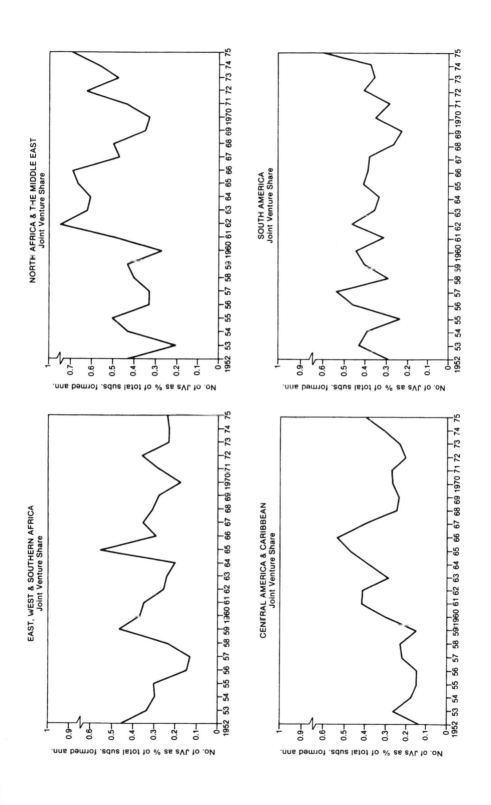

One encounters strikingly different approaches to joint ventures, with IBM saying "never" and Celanese saying "always." Most companies fall in between these two extremes, and even the "purists" have made exceptions. In the following sections we shall examine the strategic roles that JVs can play and the rationale for choosing this cooperative organizational form rather than sole ownership. Then we shall discuss the drawbacks to joint-venturing. Lastly, we present some suggestions for managing JV relationships.

The Strategic Roles of Joint Ventures

The basic concept behind joint ventures is synergy. By joining together, partners are able to accomplish more than they could separately. There is complementarity. Four roles for joint ventures stand out: resource mobilizer, political insurance, cultural guide, and competitive tool.

Resource Mobilizer. By joining forces, partners increase the total capital pool while reducing each one's individual contribution. In effect, capital-sharing can help overcome individual financial constraints while also reducing each partner's asset exposure. Joint ventures often have greater access to local financing than wholly owned foreign subsidiaries, which may be affected by governmental lending restrictions. Thus smaller firms, which are often resource-constrained, find joint ventures attractive.

Management resources are similarly expanded. Local managers have greater knowledge of the operating environment, while the foreign partner may be more able to contribute soft or hard technology. The local firm may have existing facilities and may afford quicker access to local markets and suppliers, while the foreign partner may bring a brand or access to international markets.[37]

H. J. Heinz Company's chairman, Anthony J. F. O'Reilly, pointed to these resources as central to his firm's use of JVs in developing countries:

A joint venture offers the twin advantages of familiarity and facilities . . . . Rather than plant our flag and hope for the best, we believe it far more prudent to seek an experienced and knowledgeable partner in each region we enter. . . . The facilities of an existing enterprise off an important financial advantage in the early stage of an venture. Because so many developing countries find their rrency in short supply, they may have difficulty importing 1 equipment to build a plant. That bottleneck may be avoided factory with equipment and infrastructure in place.[38]

Multibillion-dollar Otis Elevator chose to enter into a joint venture in China rather than license its technology, because only in a JV could it gain access to the potentially huge local market. The Chinese were attracted by the increased access the JV would give to production and management technology and by the prospect of exports into Otis's international markets.[39] A Central American manager emphasized the importance of JVs to technology transfer: "When imported equipment comes from an outside entity, that supplier doesn't really care what happens to it; a joint venture helps you avoid that problem."[40] The technology being sought by local partners can be administrative as well as technical. C. S. Kirloskar, the Managing Director of the KCL joint venture, considered that the most important contribution by Cummins had been its "management technology," a "goal-oriented approach" that facilitated delegation and enhanced control.[41]

Japan has used joint ventures to gain access to raw materials and markets. As of 1980 80% of the manufacturing JVs by the top nine Japanese trading companies have been in developing countries (predominantly in Asia), and in almost 90% of the cases as minority partners.[42] The propensity for joint commercial ventures in contrast to manufacturing ventures is much lower: Only 26% of the trading companies' overseas ventures were in commerce, and only 29% of these were in LDCs; however, joint ventures were still the organizational form of choice (78%). Also, in shifting many of its low-value-added industries (such as textiles, footwear, and toys) to LDCs, small and medium-size Japanese firms have readily entered into JVs to minimize their outlays of capital and management.

Sometimes joint ventures give access to preferential government treatment. As was mentioned in Chapter 6, Ciba-Geigy reduced to 40% its holdings in its Indian JV, thereby gaining classification as an Indian-owned firm, which qualified it for a larger production quota of higher-valued pharmaceuticals than foreign-majority-owned firms received.[43]

Political Insurance. Joint ventures can help manage political risks. Local partners, if chosen carefully, can bring to the venture knowledge of the political system and a set of contacts. Given the critical importance of business–government relations to corporate success, this competency can help the company navigate tumultuous political seas. The partners' political access and knowledge help insure against arbitrary actions by the government or blunders stemming from the foreign partners' political ignorance. Sometimes the state itself is the partner. In Korea, for example, 12% of the foreign investment in 1980 was in JVs with SOEs;[44] in the

People's Republic of China all joint ventures are with government entities. Heinz Company's chairman viewed its joint venture in Zimbabwe this way: "The principal benefit of our government partnership is the ability it gives us to understand the rules and regulations that govern Zimbabwean society."[45] Of course, the local partners' political assets may be perishable; if they are too heavily tied to the government or to one political group and there is a change in the reins of power, the asset may even become a liability.

In many instances, the joint venture is more like "compulsory insurance": It may or may not help you, but the government requires you to have it. Government laws or regulations often require foreign investors to share ownership. A review of government requirements on foreign ownership in forty-seven LDCs revealed that 78% required some degree of local equity participation, at least in some industries.[46] Such regulations are much less frequent in the more developed countries. In countries with restrictions on wholly owned subsidiaries, the share of JVs by the 180 largest U.S. manufacturing MNCs as of the mid-1970s was significantly higher than in the more open developing countries.[47] Franko's analysis in the early 1980s of seventy leading MNCs' subsidiaries in twenty developing countries also revealed that 54% of the 50–50 or minority JVs were concentrated in five countries: Mexico, Brazil, Philippines, Venezuela, and India.[48] These countries aggressively require joint ventures. More than half of the companies in Beamish's 1985 survey indicated that government pressure was the main reason for undertaking the JV in an LDC.[49] Lastly, Kobrin's 1986 survey of 162 of the largest U.S. multinationals showed that in LDCs with requirements for local participation in all foreign investments, 67% of the 563 subsidiaries were joint ventures, while in those LDCs without such strictures, only 29% were JVs.[50] Foreign companies attracted by China's economic opening have generally entered via joint ventures; 96% of the 3,348 foreign investments operating in 1987 were joint ventures,[51] and one observer predicted: "Joint ventures promise to be perhaps the most important form of economic interaction between the U.S. and China."[52]

It is clear that for many companies JVs represent a second-best solution. General Motors, which operates a third of its LDC subsidiaries as equal or minority joint ventures, states that generally this occurs only where required by law.[53] In the pharmaceutical industry JVs are very rare. One Johnson & Johnson executive put it this way:

The type of operations is influenced by host country government policy. In those cases where we have joint ventures, the only reason for having a host country national or nationals as a joint venture partner is because of specific laws precluding a 100% foreign investment.[54]

In most LDCs, the JV requirements are elastic in that their application is handled case by case, opening it to bargaining.[55] In this process, the government may conclude that the benefits of having FDI resources (capital, technology, management, or market access) justify exempting the company from JV requirements. IBM achieved this outcome in Mexico but failed to in India.

Cultural Guide. The local JV partner's knowledge of the social milieu and culturally based business practices can be an important contribution to the undertaking. Of course, a firm could also attain this skill by hiring local managers and personnel in a wholly owned subsidiary, but one needs more than a cultural translator. In many LDCs, business networks are closely entwined with social networks. Social access may be a prerequisite to business access. An equity partner, as contrasted to a simple employee, is more likely to develop a trust relationship with the foreign investor that can lead to effective social and business networking. One survey of sixty-six JVs in LDCs ascertained that the primary partner skill sought by MNCs was knowledge of the local culture, politics, and economy.[56]

Competitive Tool. Joint ventures can create competitive advantage. By establishing a strategic alliance with a local firm, an MNC may be able to create barriers to entry, gain preferential market access, accelerate expansion, or reduce other companies' competitive advantages. The use of JVs in the Indian computer market is illustrative.[57]

The government's strategy for developing the computer industry was to achieve self-sufficiency through development of local private firms and SOEs. It required foreign firms to reduce their holdings to 40% or less. Neither the industry leader, IBM, nor the second firm, Britain's ICL, was successful in bargaining to preserve its wholly owned and majority owned subsidiaries. IBM chose to leave rather than joint venture. ICL decided to use the minority JV route as a strategic move to gain market dominance. In exchange for its compliance, ICL gained a near monopoly in the large system market, with sales tripling between 1979 and 1984 and reaching $22 million.

Burroughs's Indian experience provides another perspective. During the 1960s and early 1970s, it had a distribution agreement in India but had failed to sell a single system. In 1977 it entered into a 50–50 JV with the Tata group, one of India's most powerful and skilled business groups, which was already producing custom software. The JV manufactured software and printers for export to Burroughs and others. Exports reached $42 million by the end of 1984; the average return on equity was over 30%. The partnership had created an inexpensive, high-quality supplier for Burroughs's international system and a base from which Burroughs could penetrate the Indian market. In 1984 the government shifted its goal from self-sufficiency to rapid expansion of computer usage; it opened up the domestic computer market, although the 40% minority ownership requirement remained. Burroughs reduced its share in the JV (as did Tata), set up new manufacturing facilities, and with the strong market knowledge of its joint partner, projected that domestic sales would reach $120 million by 1990 and that export sales would double.

Cessna had been the principal exporter of recreational aircraft to Brazil, which was a major international market for the company. When the government decided to restrict imports, Cessna tried to bargain for continued export access. Piper seized the opportunity and formed a JV with the government's aircraft manufacturing SOE (EMBRAER) to produce the planes locally. This strategic move allowed Piper to capture the Brazilian market from the industry leader; it not only gained preferential access to a protected market, but was also able to generate sizable export sales of its components for the JV's assembly/manufacturing operation.[58]

For the smaller firms in an industry, JVs are a means of overcoming some of their competitors' size advantages. In the auto industry, AMC has used joint venturing as its exclusive entry mode in LDCs. Its willingness to assume minority equity positions has enabled AMC to differentiate itself from the majors with their preference for wholly owned subsidiaries and to gain government approval and support. This strategy successfully enabled AMC to set up operations in China to manufacture the Jeep model for the domestic market.[59] European auto manufacturers, especially Renault, have also been using joint ventures as competitive tools for gaining market access and share.

In the pharmaceutical industry, where 100% ownership is the norm, smaller firms such as Squibb are turning to JVs as a way to catch up to larger firms, especially in markets where governments are demanding local participation and the big companies are resisting.[60] While Coca-Cola pulled out of India rather than disclose its formula and Pepsi tried to overcome opposition from local soda manufacturers to its re-entry into India, the tiny Double-Cola Co. of Chattanooga, Tennessee, joined Indian investors in a JV in 1987, set up bottling plants, and quickly captured a significant market share.[61] Attracted by the 20% annual growth in soft drink consumption, Coca-Cola applied in 1988 for permission from the government to set up a wholly owned factory in an export-processing zone; one-fourth of the concentrate production would be sold locally and the rest exported.[62]

Local independent firms may seek joint ventures with multinationals as a strategy to compete with the larger local business groups. One Argentine manager said, "When foreign companies in our industry want to come into our country, we do all we can to make sure they do a joint venture with us."[63] Third World MNCs often use joint ventures with local firms in foreign countries to overcome their resource constraints and to gain advantage relative to developed country subsidiaries.[64] In Wells's study of 938 manufacturing subsidiaries of Third World MNCs about 90% were JVs;[65] the JV rate for U.S. MNCs was around 40%. Developed country MNCs might be able to increase their competitive advantages by joining Third World MNCs in joint ventures in developing countries. Third World MNCs have lower overhead and personnel costs and are very skilled in certain areas. For example, a JV of an international hotel chain with one of the very good Indian hotel-management firms could lower the chain's costs while capitalizing on the chain's reputation.[66] Indian companies can field a middle-level manager in an LDC for about one-fifth the cost for a U.S. company.[67] A Cleveland construction company combined its technical expertise with the low-cost labor of a Chinese construction enterprise to win a JV bid for a contract in Kuwait that neither alone could have won.[68]

The importance of joint ventures for the global strategies of major corporations is increasing.[69] GM voluntarily undertook a 50–50 venture with Daewoo in Korea and another joint venture with Taiwan Machinery Company (with the government also holding a 20% share) to manufacture heavy-duty trucks. Nissan Motor entered into a JV with a Taiwanese consortium to produce cars. Honda, Toyota, Mitsubishi, Subaru, and Ford have also entered joint ventures in Taiwan.

The Drawbacks of Joint Ventures

The problem areas for joint ventures revolve around conflicting priorities, loss of control, and interaction costs.

Conflicting Priorities. Just as the complementarity of needs and resources is essential to JV synergy, so, too, is the congruency of objectives vital to partner harmony. Yet there are many potential points of conflict.

While partners may agree on profit maximization as the key goal of the undertaking, they may define profits differently. The multinational firm may want to maximize the profitability of its global system, whereas the local partner will see the subsidiary as the relevant unit. The more integrated the subsidiary is into a global network, the greater the likelihood of conflicts. The MNC might wish to supply the subsidiary with inputs on which it can realize profits through attractive transfer pricing, because, for example, the taxes in the exporting country are lower than those in the subsidiary's country. The local partner would be more interested in sourcing from the cheapest supplier or paying a lower transfer price to increase profits in the joint venture. Or the local partner might be a supplier and expect preferential purchasing. The situation would be similar on the sales side. Dow Chemical encountered resistance from its Korean JV partner to buying raw materials from Dow's wholly owned subsidiary rather than from cheaper outside sources. The conflict remained unresolved and ultimately led to Dow's dumping its assets at a $100-million loss.[70] A Korean government proposal in 1980 to merge Hyundai and the GM-Daewoo JV was aborted because Hyundai's goal of producing a "Korean" car for export was incompatible with GM's global production strategy of using Korea to produce one of its "world cars."[71]

Conflicts might also arise on the financial side. The disposition of profits is a common problem area. The partners may have different time preferences for profit returns, leading to disagreement over when and at what levels dividends should be declared. Increases in capitalization can also be touchy because of different degrees of risk aversion to increased asset exposure or differences in financial strength. A U.S. manufacturer of industrial machinery planned to expand its Argentine operations through reinvesting profits, but the local partner sought immediate payout of dividends. The conflict led the U.S. firm to sell out at a loss.[72]

Conflict can increase because the partners' situations change, causing their priorities to shift. Complementarity can evaporate as each partner absorbs the other's contributions and competencies. The national learns the technology and the foreigner learns the environment; the original need for each other diminishes. Unrejuvenated joint ventures are fertile grounds for discontent. An additional problem is that the players change. JV agreements are often embedded in the personal relationships of the original architects. Many of the understandings are unwritten, inscribed only on the bonds of personal trust. So when key players on either side leave the companies or shift into other areas of responsibility, the newcomers may bring different perspectives and priorities. In one joint venture between a Swedish firm and an Indian company, the chairman was a third partner who served as a bridge between the two companies; when death removed him as an interlocuter, disputes and misunderstandings soon emerged, almost killing the joint venture.[73]

Loss of Control. A major disadvantage of joint ventures is loss of control over decision-making. Some companies view their autonomy as more essential to success than others. Firms with global strategies can see JVs as potential impediments to effective and efficient systemwide coordination of their production, marketing, and financing networks. For companies with proprietary technology, JVs have the potential of becoming disastrous leaks in their security systems. The risk of creating a competitor is real. Furthermore, for companies with very high-quality products and strong brand names, loss of control over production and marketing jeopardizes their key success determinants.

Gillette exemplifies many of these characteristics. It maintains high and internationally uniform quality standards for its razor blades; its brand recognition and franchise are one of its most valuable assets; it sources and markets globally to achieve maximum capacity utilization and economies of scale; it has patented and proprietary process and product technology; it is a financially strong industry leader; and it has extensive international experience. The company has a very strong preference for 100% ownership and has no LDC joint ventures in its razor blade business, except for India and China, where it made minority investments as a means of entering two new markets that hold strong long-term prospects.[74]

The control issue may be exacerbated when the ownership is minority rather than majority. When India issued its requirement for 40% foreign ownership, ICL was already in a majority-owned JV. Sharing ownership was not a problem, but the shift from 60% to a minority 40% share gave it great concern because of the control implications. Killing's research indicates that JVs with one clearly dominant partner tended to have fewer difficulties than when the management was shared.[75] The involvement of personnel from both partners in JV management can create tension around issues of authority and allegiance.

Interaction Costs. While a JV generally reduces the amount of management resources each partner has to deploy individually, there is still a significant amount of managerial time required to interact with each other. The difficulties of communication across organizations are generally greater than within them. One may have to reconcile different management styles, administrative systems, cultural norms, and languages. In addition, much of the interaction might be spent on negotiating and bargaining to deal with control issues or conflicting priorities.

Managing the Relationship

Successful joint ventures are made, not born. Like any close and enduring relationship, it must be worked at to realize its full potential. The following are brief suggestions to enhance the prospects for a fruitful partnership.

Carefully assess complementarity.

First, know thyself! Specify clearly your own needs and weaknesses as well as your strengths and what you can bring to the deal. Do the same for the candidate partner. Assess the match. Is there duplication of strengths? Are there unfilled needs? What are the relative bargaining powers? What will joining together enable you to do that you could not have done on your own? If the complementarity and synergy are unclear or too ephemeral, stop before you start; broken engagements are less painful and costly than divorces.

Know your partner.

Before one enters the joint venture, it is critical to penetrate the superficies observable in business meetings. This means going beyond the due-diligence measures of credit references. Talk with the partner's suppliers, customers, competitors, other partners, and its own employees. How does the company interact with others? How dependable is it? What are its business practices? Are its ethical standards congruent with yours? Is its human-relations management philosophy compatible with yours? If possible, set up a trial relationship (such as a buyer, supplier, or distributor) to test your ability to work together. Once in the joint venture, the longer you work together, the better you will know each other. But before entering the JV, the better you know each other, the longer you will end up working together.

Achieve goal and strategy congruency.

The partners must have common goals and share the same vision of the business. A U.S. and a Latin American manufacturer of an industrial product were attracted to setting up a JV because their competencies and limitations appeared very complementary. The effort floundered, however, because they could not agree on whether the operation should sell mainly to the domestic market or export to the United States. Clarify the business concept and plan, for ambiguity can cloak fundamental disagreements. Make sure that the JV's chosen manager is receiving consistent and compatible objectives and directions from both partners.[76] Conflicting signals and demands produce managerial schizophrenia.

Identify conflict points.

Points of conflict are inevitable; goals, priorities, and perspectives never perfectly mesh. Conflicts can be better managed by spotting them ahead of time and figuring out how to handle them. Don't ignore them with the hope that goodwill will solve anything that arises. Plan for them, assess their seriousness, and take preventive measures. For example, the basis for transactions with the partners' parent companies could be spelled out. Conflict cannot be avoided, but it can be managed.

Make clear rules.

Rights and responsibilities should be spelled out clearly in the partnership agreements. The form, quantities, and timing of respective resource contributions should be delineated. Specify the authority of the management and the decisions reserved for the board. Try to give operating authority to one of the parents and clarify the relationships of the parents' personnel in those operating positions.

Good legal counsel can help partners clarify their expectations and reduce the risk of "free riders." Nonetheless, most legal instruments will be only as good as the signatories. Rules may help preserve continuity if the managers who structured the original agreements are replaced. Rule-making has to be culturally compatible; an overlegalistic approach might be counterproductive. (See the subsequent section, "Culture and Organization.")

Make transactions transparent.

Suspicion is the cancer of collaboration. If one partner thinks the other is cloaking its actions or intentions, it may presume that such behavior is trying to create one-sided gain. The suspicion may not be well-founded, but it can quickly lead to reciprocal withholding and zero-sum game behavior. The antidote is to be open in one's dealings with the JV partner. If some information must remain proprietary, this should be explained. Partners need not share all, but transparency reduces misunderstanding.

Communicate clearly and often.

Physical and cultural distances complicate communications. Nothing breeds concern like the unknown. Infrequent and imperfect communication can easily cause misunderstandings and turn insignificant operating problems into organizational crises. Set up a system of regularly scheduled communications to keep the partners informed of progress. Use consultative communications to elicit partner advice on strategic issues. Be particularly sensitive to the cultural dimensions of your communications (see the final section of this chapter). One successful U.S.–Korean 50–50 joint venture used monthly board meetings and a mutually chosen outside director to resolve any disputes on managerial policies.[77]

Control creatively.

Loss of control is not synonymous with loss of ownership. Equity holdings are only one source of control, and not even necessarily the most effective. In a study of fifty-two Indian–U.S. JVs, control did not become an issue of conflict; generally the Indians controlled the management of operations and the Americans controlled the technology. Both were essential to the companies' success; countervailing control created balance.[78] This equation worked for Cummins and Kirloskar in their Indian venture. Gillette gave up majority equity control in one of its subsidiaries but achieved operating control via a management contract. International mining companies with minority positions in the Dominican Republic and Ghana have also used management contracts.[79] Control can be exercised through other key elements such as brands, production inputs, or market access. Bylaws can be written to require approval by both partners of certain strategic decisions, such as dividends, capital increases, and the like, irrespective of their equity shares. Compliance with government requirements to reduce ownership to a minority status has often been achieved without losing control by selling the majority to the public or to other passive investors, who are interested in earning a return but not in operating the company. Japanese trading companies held minority positions in 90% of their overseas manufacturing investments but exercised control through supplying inputs and marketing output.[80]

Share equitably.

Opportunities will arise to take advantage of your partner, to gain at the other's expense. These situations may occur quite legitimately within the terms of the JV through changes in the environment that affect the partners differently or changes in the partners' situations. Some imbalance is inevitable. If it is minimal and occurs in both directions over time, there is no problem. If, however, the pie begins to be sliced so that one side continually receives much larger pieces than originally intended, then divisive feelings of inequity will begin to boil. When one partner feels shorted, it has a great incentive to find ways to correct the imbalance. The means may be cloaked and insidious, thus placing the well-being of the venture in jeopardy. One Latin American manager emphasized mutuality: "To insure the long-term success of the joint venture, compromise must be perceived by all sides as being a mutual thing."[81]

Fairness and the perception of fairness are prerequisites to preserving goodwill. Both gains and losses must be shared equitably, regardless of the formal written obligations. In the KCL joint venture in India, Cummins Engine voluntarily waived its royalty payments on the technology license during the difficult startup years of 1964–67; this gesture created considerable goodwill and trust with the partner, which greatly facilitated the resolution of other conflicts. Similarly, Swedchem agreed to delay collection of its licensing royalty payments from its Indian "partner" to help out during a period of financial austerity. This deepened the trust relationship.[82] Fairness has its dividends. A Mexican manager with a record of fifteen successful joint ventures commented, "So far, we have enjoyed very successful experiences with all our foreign partners. Profits and growth in an environment of trust and mutual respect have been the golden rules of our relationships."[83] Trust accelerates conflict resolution, facilitates delegation and management autonomy, and enhances flexibility.

Be flexible.

Even though it is important to lay out "rules and responsibilities" clearly, it is impossible to foresee all constraints and opportunities. LDC business environments are often intensely unpredictable. Don't be a prisoner of your original business plan and JV agreement. Being legalistic can rigidify relationships and reduce responsiveness to changing business conditions. One should be open to ancillary agreements that allow for wider roles and forms of interaction. A change in tax laws in the home or host country might make the original remuneration mechanisms less than optimal for one or both partners. Flexibility can sometimes be built into the relationship from the beginning through contingency planning. Fundamentally, flexibility is a managerial state of mind. Openness to change and a norm of collaborative problem-solving will help JV partners cope with unforeseen difficulties and capitalize on emerging opportunities.

Review and revise.

Flexibility aims to achieve response capability to sporadic environmental shifts; there remains, however, the need to review periodically and systematically the JV's basic rationale and strategy. Complementarity is an obsolescing phenomenon. As a partner's original contributions meet and satisfy the other's needs, complementarity shrinks. It is very useful to assess at regular intervals the joint venture's costs and benefits. Erosion may be inevitable, but revitalization is also possible. One should try to identify new inputs or activities that enhance the synergy. Sometimes this entails realigning roles and responsibilities. For example, in 1982 GM transferred most operations management functions to its Korean partner Daewoo, whose intimate knowledge of the special conditions of the Korean market and suppliers enabled it to redesign production, inventory management, and quality control systems to fit the Korean environment. This shift contributed significantly to turning the operation into a profitable and expanding business.[84] The investment required to develop the partner relationship is usually sizable, and it often constitutes a nonreplicable asset. Consequently, it holds the potential for generating distinctive competitive advantages. A JV's capacity for self-renewal will be greater the deeper the partners' respect for, trust in, and commitment to each other are.

Know when to exit.

Keeping a joint venture vitalized can be very beneficial, but it is important to know when the venture has outlived its usefulness. Exit, like entry, is a strategic move. When the joint venture no longer fits the company's overall strategy, or when partner conflicts become irreconcilable and the costs of achieving complementarity outweigh the benefits, then the firm should end the relationship. JV obsolescence dictates termination. It may simply be that the original decision to set up a joint venture was a mistake or that changed external conditions invalidated the original rationale for the joint venture.[85] Figure 10.3 shows the degree and nature of JV instability among U.S. MNCs in developing countries during 1952–75. About 25% of the subsidiaries experienced some type of change in ownership status, with changes occuring almost as frequently in JVs as in WOSs. Of the JVs experiencing changes, 47% were disposed

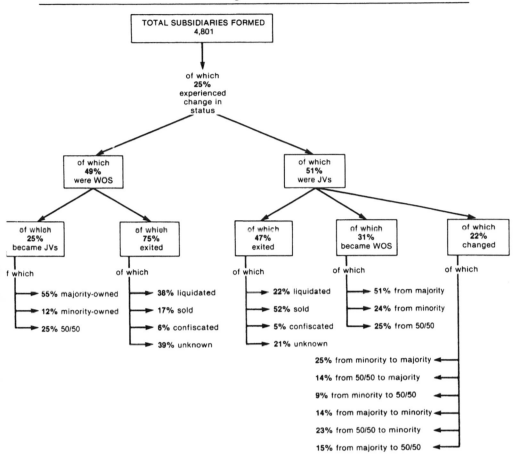

Figure 10.3 Changes in Ownership Status of U.S. MNC Subsidiaries in LDCs, 1952–75
SOURCE: Derived from Harvard Business School Multinational Enterprise Data Base.

of mainly through liquidation or sale and 31% were converted to WOSs, principally from majority-owned JVs. The other 22% remained as JVs but had ownership changes, with almost equal shifts from minority to majority as the reverse. Of the ownership changes in the WOSs, 25% became JVs (mostly majority owned or 50–50); the other 75% were liquidated or sold, with a small share being confiscated. Other smaller surveys found JV instability rates in the 45%–50% range.[86]

How to exit becomes the issue. One can sell out to the partner or buy the partner out. If the business is desirable but the control and other costs of partnership are too high relative to the benefits, then a buyout is in order. Sometimes the exit decision is not driven by deficiencies in the JV partner or operations *per se*, but rather by changes in the company's global situation that create a lack of fit of the industry or the country with the company's global strategy. In these instances, the company would be revisiting its entry-mode deliberations discussed in the first section of this chapter, but in reverse. A shift from FDI to licensing might be in order. Thus, JVs can obsolesce because of changes in the external business environment, internal shifts in either of the partners' operations or strategies, or altered costs and benefits resulting from the joint venture's own successes, failures, or strategy shifts. In fact the JV can be conceived of from its inception as having a finite duration. As a manager of a leading Brazilian construction company explained:

> The company has always sought, as a basic principle, to develop the technology required for the execution of the various types of works in our field with its own resources. However, whenever necessary, it establishes associations with foreign companies that possess high technology in specific areas. Such associations have brought a significant contribution to our technological development. The total or partial absorption of each technology, depending on the project, marks the end of these associations.[87]

JV instability is an adjustment indicator, not a failure indicator. Change is not necessarily negative; like any organizational form, JVs should last only as long as the form fits the function.

Whatever the reasons for termination, exit with grace. Your actions have a tendency to follow you. Bullying out the local partner in a takeover could create an enemy who might reappear as a competitor, with the government on its side. Or a rapid pullout from the country might leave the local company precariously in the lurch, creating resentment and retaliation. One Central American government even sued a hastily departed MNC for breach of contract. A manager of one MNC recounted the precariousness of ending a partnership in an Asian country:

> It was going to be a shock to the local partner for us to pull out, but they were representing us in ways that were clearly not acceptable. Our management in New York thought, "Well, it's not working. We'll make a change. There are plenty of others who want to work with us. We'll file the papers and that will be the end of it." It has been a far more traumatic experience than that would have suggested.

The partner raised many legal, social, and political difficulties for us about getting paid what we were owed, obtaining work permits for our expats, getting licenses approved, and trying to find a new partner. It was a very, very messy divorce. In Southeast Asia your relationships really play a key role in trying to establish yourself strategically.[88]

How a multinational behaves in one country is reviewed by governments and local companies in other countries; an unsavory exit might disturb positive existing relationships or impede new ones. Exit can be facilitated by specifying the mechanism with the partner in the beginning: for example, mutual rights to buy the other out on the same terms. But as long as a company does not exit, then management must deal with the last, and perhaps most pervasive, dimension of organizational strategy: culture.

CULTURE AND ORGANIZATION

We saw in the previous chapters on finance, production, and marketing how it is necessary to make adjustments in financial approaches, production technologies, and marketing processes and products to operate effectively in the distinct LDC business environments. So, too, must managers adjust their organizational design strategies to fit the cultural dictates of the host country. Whereas one can identify clear trends toward global homogenization of financial instruments, technologies, and markets, organizational structures and processes may be the most culture-bound and least susceptible to global standardization. Although technologies and market conditions significantly affect organizational processes independent of cultural differences,[89] several studies, including Hofstede's sixty-seven-country survey of 88,000 employees in one MNC and Laurent's ten-country survey of managers in various companies, clearly reveal very distinct, culturally based attitudes, values, and approaches to work activities.[90]

Achieving cultural congruency is a strategic issue because of its importance and scope. Many business opportunities have been lost or JV operations crippled because of failures in understanding or in managing cultural diversity; getting the economics right may be futile if you've got the culture wrong. One cannot effectively address the cultural dimension by tinkering with some narrow organizational aspect. Culture is communication's companion; all key relationships and interactions are culturally shaped. Thus, cultural understanding and effective cross-cultural communication are critical for the internal relations between expatriates and local employees, between JV partners, and between headquarters and subsidiary, as well as for the external relations with government officials, suppliers, and customers. To illustrate where and how the cultural dimension can affect the organization, we shall examine the following areas: organizational structure and decision-making processes, group dynamics, personnel management, planning and scheduling, and communications. We shall explore these issues in terms of national or societal values, attitudes, and behavior. One should keep in mind that within countries, across groups, and among individuals there may be significant diversity and departures from the national norm.

Organizational Structure and Decision-Making

Societies vary in their values and attitudes toward authority and equality, which in turn influence how they structure relationships in organizations. Those countries that prefer more authoritarian relationships tend toward hierarchical organizational structures; those that prefer more equal distribution of power are less accepting of such structures. Hofstede refers to this value dimension as "power distance"; his studies indicate that LDCs tend to be more accepting of hierarchical orders, whereas the United States and most other Western developed nations have a stronger preference for equality in relationships.

The imposition of an "egalitarian" organizational design on a hierarchical culture, or vice versa, risks causing great dissonance among the employees; cultural expectations and behavior will conflict with the organizational dictates. Canadian expatriates working under a Filipino manager found his close supervision of employees' work and behavior very demotivating, interpreting it as a sign of distrust in his subordinates. The supervisor's actions conflicted with the expatriate's cultural expectation of relationships with one's supervisor. The Filipino manager, however, saw his style as meeting the employees' expectations that their supervisor would show his caring through close involvement.[91] Cultural perceptions about the basic nature of humans (i.e., their inherent trustworthiness) will also affect managers' attitudes about supervision, delegation, and control.

The relationships between superior and subordinate will vary. The hierarchical culture may expect the manager to be paternalistic, assuming responsibility for employee welfare and providing strong guidance while receiving loyalty and obedience in return. One study found that 95% of the surveyed Pakistani employees visualized their relationship with their immediate superiors as mainly that of a son to his father. Intimate dialogues with one's boss often began with, "Sir, you are like a father to me." A comparative survey found that subordinates in the United States saw their bosses in nonfamily terms such as friend or enemy.[92] Employees in a paternalistic culture will expect the manager's obligation to them to extend beyond the workplace and into their family situations. In countries with a Chinese cultural heritage, such as Hong Kong, Singapore, and Taiwan, Confucian roots and family structures manifest themselves in business structures and processes characterized by paternalism, dependency, and respect for order.[93] T. S. Lin, the chairman of Taiwan's fifth largest firm, "continues to run Tatung much like a grand patriarch. His approach to managers is professional and to other employees unabashedly paternalistic."[94]

Personnel interactions can also be affected by societal attitudes toward gender roles and relationships. A manager in one African country commented, "We have problems if a woman has to give instructions to a man."[95] To increase the effectiveness of women placed in managerial positions of authority, one needs to be aware of traditions and attitudes toward gender roles to handle possible dissonance that might be created by shifting roles and relationships.

Cultural attitudes affect decision-making processes. More autocratic decision-making fits better in hierarchical cultures, where participative decision-making would be less congruent. For example, one study found that most Indian managers and subordinates preferred an autocratic style and close supervision. Frequent consultation with subordinates might be perceived as revealing managerial incompetency.[96] Most Italian managers in Laurent's study felt it important that they have ready, precise answers to most of their subordinates' questions to maintain their credibility as experts. (Latin American managers have been found to share similar attitudes.) In contrast, most of the U.S., Swedish, Dutch, and British managers saw this as unimportant, viewing their job as helping subordinates discover solutions rather than suppressing their initiative and creativity with their own answers.[97] U.S., Swedish, and British managers agreed that it might be necessary to bypass their superior to have efficient work relationships; Italian managers felt that adhering to the formal hierarchical structure was essential. Thus, a well-intentioned bypass by a U.S. expatriate could be viewed as insubordination and disrespect by an Italian manager, and an Italian employee's failure to bypass could be seen by an American manager as wasteful and bureaucratic, whereas it was meant to be a respectful and efficient use of formal channels. The grounds for cultural misunderstanding are fertile; frustration and animosity can quickly take root. Paternalistic and hierarchical structures can also suppress subordinates' willingness to assume decision-making responsibilities; the buck gets passed upward and often floods top managers with relatively minor administrative decisions.

Different attitudes toward hierarchy and equality also manifest themselves in varying forms of privilege and status. Managers from a culture where status differences are minimized may create dissonance by rejecting the normal trappings and formalities bestowed on their positions in a more hierarchical culture.

Group Dynamics

The ways in which groups are used in the workplace are significantly influenced by cultural values concerning individualism versus group orientation, or "collectivism" in Hofstede's terms. LDCs (and Japan) tend to be more collectivist; group affiliation and loyalty are of paramount importance there, group welfare is placed above individual welfare, and the group protects and cares for its members. The Anglo and Nordic developed countries tend to value individualism more.

Japan and China reportedly share certain group decision-making practices.[98] This involves consulting the principal members of a group before a full meeting so that consensus can be reached without letting dissent emerge in the final meeting. This is known as *nemawashi* in Japanese (pruning minor roots of tree before planting) and *yunning* in Chinese (fermentation in wine production). A second practice is for individuals at lower levels to present proposals to higher levels; this "bottom-up" process of involving subordinates in the decision process is known as *ringi* in Japan and "consultations with the masses" in China.

In the group-oriented culture, the business unit is one of the social groups in which the norms of mutual obligation and loyalty prevail. Fundamentally, group cohesion is trust-based, so personal relationships are important. Managers from individualistic societies tend to be very task-oriented; in a group-oriented society a prerequisite to performing the task is establishing a trust relationship with the group. This may involve interacting socially rather than just in a business setting. Group norms and actions can serve as organizational control mechanisms.

In group cultures, singling out individuals for either punishment or praise can create tension; this action is more common and accepted in individualistic societies. Causing loss of face is to be avoided; maintaining group harmony is to be sought. Whereas frankness and openness are

admirable managerial traits in individualistic cultures, the
very disturbing in group-oriented ones. The art of indirectnes

Personnel Management

Culture impinges on many aspects of personnel management. Criteria
for selection and promotion can be strongly influenced by culture. In
one survey of Arab executives, two-thirds considered loyalty more important than efficiency in choosing employees.[99] One joint venture between
a Swedish and an Indian company was jeopardized when the local partner
sought to hire mainly relatives because of their loyalty, whereas the
Swedes felt competency should be the only consideration.[100] Japanese
MNCs have encountered difficulties in recruiting high-quality local managers because of their reluctance to promote locals into higher management
ranks. This reluctance stems from the Japanese premium on loyalty derived
from membership in the parent company.[101] Transfers of personnel into
a group-oriented culture may be complicated by the reluctance of insiders
to accept outsiders based simply on their competency. Membership is
not competency-based; it has to be earned. If the society holds age in
high respect, promotion of a younger, more productive employee over
an older one may cause great dissonance. Societies also have different
attitudes toward gender roles, and this constrains employee recruitment,
assignments, and promotions. Cultural ascription may overshadow individual achievement. In the Chinese culture nepotism, which values family
membership over competency, is considered a virtue.[102] In some cultures
employee loyalty is to their organizations; in others it is to specific
people.

Incentive systems can also be culturally complicated. One should not
assume that motivations are weighted equally across cultures. Economic
incentives always count, but employees may be more interested in optimiz-
ing than in maximizing their income. One American company raised
the hourly rate of its Mexican employees to stimulate them to work
more hours. They worked less, saying, "We can now make enough
money to live and enjoy life in less time than previously."[103] Economists
call this a "backward bending supply curve." It stems from cultural
values toward work, pleasure, and materialism. Some societies see work
as an end; others view it more as a means.

Noneconomic incentives like praise or reprimand are also bound up
with culture. As was indicated previously, singling out an individual
for praise in a group-oriented culture may create embarrassment rather

than positive motivation. Dismissal for incompetence may not be culturally acceptable. A small study of firms in Singapore indicated that almost all managers would not fire an employee for poor performance but would shift the individual to a different position. However, dismissal would occur if the employee had broken the trust expectations inherent in the paternalistic relationship.[104] Evaluation systems with standardized rating forms intrude on the personal bonds in paternalistic superior-subordinate relationships. "In fact, the whole notion of 'objective' assessment, embodying as it does negative as well as positive comments, does not slide easily into a society where [there is] such a premium . . . on avoidance of the unpleasant and acute sensitivity to psychic comfort."[105]

When U.S. electronics firms first set up factories in Malaysia, many gave their workers uniforms as a benefit and to create a sense of identification with the company. However, the Western-style short-sleeved and knee-length dresses revealed arms and legs, which was culturally unacceptable. The uniforms were subsequently modified to the customary long-sleeved blouses and ankle-length skirts.[106]

Planning and Scheduling

Attitudes toward time and environment affect planning. Cultures vary in their perceptions of the controllability or mutability of their environments. Where these are low or thought to be determined by divinity, the resultant fatalism erodes the rationale for planning. As an individual from one Asian country put it, "We don't like to think about things far into the future; we equate it with just dreaming. Why bother?"[107] Where a society is more future-oriented than present- or past-oriented, planning is more culturally compatible.

Some cultures, like that of the United States, view time as a finite and scarce resource and therefore put a premium on punctuality and time efficiency. Other cultures view time as infinite and abundant. In Latin America, meetings seldom start on time. Although this grates on the North American, it is neither a social nor an economic offense within the Latin's cultural context. Differing time orientations can lead to very distinct perceptions about the importance of adhering to completion or delivery dates, thereby introducing greater uncertainty into scheduling. In some cultures important decisions are expected to take more time; quick decisiveness could signal that the issue was unimportant rather than critical and urgent.[108]

Societies also differ in their attitudes toward the allocation of time for work and nonwork activities. Religious and political holidays preclude work. One Latin American production manager lamented that in his country fifteen Mondays were holidays. Another said that his company's attempt to schedule work during the holidays was unsuccessful. Its workers agreed to come to work at bonus wage rates, but the firm's suppliers were not working, which crippled the production line.[109] Although a company can sometimes alter cultural norms within its organization, it has little control over outside groups.

Communications

Cultural variances can cause major communication barriers. Cultures can fall at very different points on the attitudinal spectrums of emotionality versus objectivity, aggressiveness versus passivity, formality versus informality, directness versus indirectness, and personalism versus impersonalism. Some forms of expression that are suitable in one culture are inappropriate or easily misunderstood in another. Cross-cultural communication requires a sensitivity to these differences.

Whereas a Latin or an Arab might use emotionality in persuasion or negotiations, the North American might appeal more to logic and facts. The North American would tend to be more frank, straightforward, and argumentative; the Malaysian, less open, more indirect, and not overtly aggressive. The Malaysian might be quite formal; the American, more casual. The Asian or the Latin might view the interaction as a personal relationship; the American, as an impersonal business task requiring little personal involvement.[110] Chinese negotiators place great emphasis on friendship, and this derives from their concept of *guanxi,* a relationship between individuals that allows them to make unlimited demands on each other. Pye cites the comments of an American businessman:

Each time I go back to China it can be embarrassing because someone whom you once negotiated with but have forgotten will greet you as a long lost friend. They'll act as though you had never been away . . . you know you have to go on to other things and you can't get yourself all tied up with the problems of a particular chap. But that is not the way they are. They expect that when you come back again you will remember everything about them and you'll be ready to become even more friendly. It can get a bit thick, but that is just their way of doing business.[111]

The chairman of Heinz & Company also emphasized the importance of relationships: "Because the legal system in China remains less formal than that in the West, a joint venture operation requires the forging of strong and lasting personal bonds. We have made sure to keep in contact with important Chinese officials throughout our involvement with their country.''[112]

Hall cites an example of an American sales executive who failed to close a deal in Mexico because he could focus only on the business aspects rather than the personal dimensions of the transaction. The Mexican Minister explained his rejection of the American's offer:

> I like the American's equipment and it makes sense to deal with North Americans who are near us and whose price is right. But I could never be friends with this man. He is not my kind of human being and we have nothing in common. He is not *simpático*. If I can't be friends and he is not *simpático,* I can't depend on him to treat me right. I tried everything, every conceivable situation, and only once did we seem to understand each other. If we could be friends, he would feel obligated to me and this obligation would give me some control. Without control, how do I know he will deliver what he says he will at the price he quotes?[113]

One needs to tailor culturally how one gives or receives good or bad news, criticizes or praises, defends one's position or challenges another's, and requests assistance or gives orders. For example, Pye points out that "the Chinese frequently appear to be agreeing when they respond by saying that it is 'possible.' The answer, however, is often an ambiguous way of saying 'no'."[114] Fieq observes that to avoid overt verbal clashes, "Thais may hold back rather than come to grips with the question at hand if it would involve difference of opinion. Surface harmony will be preserved, but the problem will be left unresolved."[115] Harrison asserts that "the North American often blunders when negotiating in the Brazilian business world, largely because many of the qualities esteemed by his North American associates—aggressive confrontation of problems, an eager offering of suggestions and solutions, and a desire to 'get straight to the point'—are precisely the qualities a Brazilian finds disquieting and even offensive."[116]

Culture also influences the role of nonverbal factors in communication. In "high-context" countries the physical setting and procedural formalities and rituals are part of business rather than impediments to "getting down to business." They communicate information about the parties and their attitudes. Attitudes toward space also affect communication; cultures view personal proximity differently. For Latins, closeness and physical contact during conversation are common, whereas Anglos tend to remain physically distant. Space can be viewed more as a private or public resource, to be guarded or shared. Americans hold meetings in privacy in closed offices; Middle Easterners tend to have fewer private quarters and frequently more people coming and going during meetings.

Legal systems and their use in business communications also vary across cultures. The costliness of cultural misunderstanding in this area is illustrated in Adler's description of the experience of a Canadian businessman. His Egyptian host offered partnership in a joint venture, and the delighted Canadian suggested they meet the following morning with their lawyers to work out the details. The Egyptians never showed. They saw the request for lawyers as a sign of mistrust, whereas the Canadian had seen it as facilitating the agreement.[117] Other similar business practices that would be deemed "due diligence" in one culture might be offensive in another. For example, in trying to establish a venture in Abu Dhabi, a U.S. architectural firm consulted the potential partner's bank to ascertain his creditworthiness. A bank staff member reported this to the prospective partner, who perceived this as an insult to his integrity and cancelled the negotiations.[118] One U.S. lawyer with a decade of experience in negotiations in the PRC indicated that Western lawyers viewed contracts as legal documents delineating rights and responsibilities and consequences for nonperformance, but the Chinese saw contracts as commercial documents designating the transaction's desired outcome with little attention to the possibility of a breakdown. This latter reluctance is seen as being in part "a cultural aversion to confronting openly the possibility of conflicts between parties."[119] Another experienced manager depicted the cultural reality thus: "There is seldom a legally enforceable position in China. More often there is an equilibrium of mutually perceived interests. The key here is perception. When that changes, so does the basis for the agreement."[120]

Managing the Cultural Variable

The foregoing analyses have indicated how relevant cultural factors are to organizational structure and processes. This section will briefly suggest some actions that managers can take to manage the cultural variable more effectively.

Identify the cultural parameters.

The first step in dealing effectively with cultural factors is to identify them explicitly. Because culture is so pervasive, it is easy to take it for granted and assume that one knows it. By delineating one's own cultural norms and perceptions and those of the foreign culture with which one is interacting, one can become more sensitive to their importance and to cross-cultural differences. The categories used in the EAF for cultural factors are a starting point in the identification process: social structures and dynamics, perceptions of human nature, attitudes toward time and space, religious values, gender roles, and language.

Develop cultural sensitivity.

Managers and employees, expatriates and locals can increase their cultural capabilities through self-education and specialized training. This area of human-resource management is generally neglected in international firms. Cultural preparation is preventive medicine; taking it ahead of time can prevent many serious mistakes later. Japanese companies reportedly give special preparation to managers going abroad.[121] During the year before going abroad, they are trained in the language, culture, and business practices of the country. Upon arriving there, the managers are assigned mentors to help them understand the local situation and resolve any problems. In evaluating a manager's performance, the first year in the country is considered one of learning about the local business environment. Cultural competency is learnable.

Understand managerial implications.

Being culturally cognizant and sensitive is a necessary but insufficient condition for effective cultural management. The key additional ability is understanding the managerial implications of cultural phenomena. Table 10.3 presents a summary of the cultural value and attitude parameters we have analyzed and the managerial areas affected by them. The cultural parameters are presented as a series of dichotomies, but they are really spectrums. The manager should assess where on that spectrum the country in question lies, what type of managerial response that cultural trait would call for, how congruent the company's actual organizational structure and practices are with the cultural dictate, and what the performance consequences are of conforming or deviating from the cultural norm. For example, if the society is characterized by hierarchical organizational structures, paternalistic manager–employee relationships, and autocratic decision-making, but the company is trying to use an egalitarian structure with expectations of employee self-reliance and highly participative decision-making processes, the manager should expect considerable dissonance resulting from the deviation from the cultural norms. Planned

Table 10.3 Management Impact Areas of Cultural Factors

Management Area	Cultural Value and Attitude Parameters
Organizational structures	*Social structures:* Hierarchical ←---------→ Egalitarian Vertical ←-----------→ Horizontal Familial ←---------→ Institutional High-status Low-status differentiation ←--------→ differentiation
Manager–employee relations	*Societal relationships:* Authoritarian ←--------→ Democratic Paternalistic ←---------→ Self-reliant Personal ←----------→ Functional
Decision-making	*Decision processes:* Autocratic ←------- ..... → Participative Unilateral ←---------→ Consultative
Group behavior	*Interpersonal orientation:* Collectivism ←---------→ Individualism Group welfare ←--------→ Self-interest Other-oriented ←--------→ Task-oriented
Communication	*Personal interactions:* Personalized ←---------→ Impersonal Closed ←-----------→ Open Formal ←-----------→ Informal Indirect ←----------→ Direct Passive ←----------→ Aggressive
Incentives and evaluation	*Motivation:* Economic ←----------→ Noneconomic Work ←------------→ Pleasure Loyalty ←-----------→ Competency Role Merit ascription ←---------→ achievement
Control	*Human nature perceptions:* Intrinsic good ←--------→ Intrinsic evil Trust ←------------→ Distrust Cooperative ←--------→ Conflictive Malleable ←----------→ Unchangeable
Time management and planning	*Time perceptions:* Infinite resource ←-------→ Finite resource Present-oriented ←-------→ Future-oriented Imprecise ←---------→ Precise Controllable ←--------→ Uncontrollable
Spatial relationships	*Space perceptions:* Private ←-----------→ Public Nearness ←---------→ Farness Aesthetics ←---------→ Functionality

deviation may produce significant benefits, but unplanned deviation can create organizational disasters.

Some MNCs have explicit strategies to create a uniform "company culture" in all its subsidiaries regardless of the country culture. This serves as an organizational control mechanism for headquarters and as a vehicle for increasing the international interchangeability of its personnel. This approach requires extensive training and higher levels of headquarters–subsidiary personnel interaction. One MNC using this culture–creating approach expended almost twice as much on headquarters–subsidiary travel than another company that opted for a nonacculturation approach. The culture-creating company relied heavily on direct interaction, and the other firm used more written communication.[122]

Avoid ethnocentricism.

It is easy to slip into the perilous pitfall of ethnocentricism; the assumption that your (sub)culture's modality is "best" may be the quickest way to create a problem. We are all prisoners of our own national culture and the narrower subcultures of our closer social groupings. What is "best" in one setting may be managerially ineffective in another. One should resist the immediate instinct to be culturally normative, because this can suffocate understanding and insights.

Seek cultural complementarity.

Cultural differences can be an asset rather than a liability; different perspectives and approaches, if effectively shared and integrated, can lead to superior solutions. Cultural synergies should be sought out. It may be feasible and desirable to adopt an organizational strategy that intentionally goes counter to the cultural norms. But to do this requires great cultural knowledge and sensitivity. One has to understand deeply the multiple attitudinal and behavioral dimensions being changed to assess their elasticity and to predict and manage the new social dynamic that is being engineered. Sometimes a company's operations can be differentiated and competitive advantage gained by achieving behavior that differs from the cultural norm. One study of Thai managers suggests that their training in Western management concepts may lead to adjustments in traditional cultural behavioral patterns somewhere in between Western norms and Thai norms.[123] Cultural congruency and differentiation may both offer important opportunities for organizational effectiveness.

CONCLUSION

We have examined three critical organizational issues. First was the choice of organizational form for entering developing countries (exporting, licensing, sales branch, production subcontracting, and direct production investment). These alternatives can be systematically evaluated using three sets of variables related to the country environment, competitive situation, and company characteristics. The country environment variables emerging from the EAF are economic (market size and growth, labor costs and skills, local managerial capacity, and infrastructure adequacy), political (risk, governmental receptiveness to FDI, and regulatory controls), and cultural (compatibility). The competitive situation variables include industry concentration, relative competitive strength, local barriers to entry, and the risk of market cannibalization. The company characteristics considered concern the product (maturity, brand differentiation, line diversity, and service intensity), technology (maturity, stability, complexity, and patentability), resources (capital, management, and LDC experience), and the degree and nature of a company's globalization. To decide on the entry mode, the manager ascertains which of the entry forms are favored by the prevailing conditions of each of these variables, and then assesses the relative importance and interaction of these variables.

The second critical organizational issue explored was the ownership strategy to be pursued in setting up operations in a developing country. Joint ventures have been used with significant frequency. The basic concept behind them is the complementarity and synergy attainable through the alliance. Joint ventures can provide resources needed by the partners, can serve as a form of political insurance (sometimes mandatory), give cultural guidance, and create competitive advantage. Problems can arise from conflicting priorities, loss of control, and excessive costs of interaction. Changes in ownership status of joint ventures and wholly owned subsidiaries is common in response to these problems and to changing circumstances of the company, industry, or country. Suggestions for enhancing the effectiveness of JV relationships include: carefully assessing the partners' complementarity; knowing the partner well, achieving goal and strategy congruency; identifying conflict points; setting forth clear rules; making transactions transparent; communicating clearly and often; controlling creatively; sharing equitably; being flexible; reviewing and revising; and knowing when to exit. Joint ventures are not easy to manage, but if managed well they can be a powerful organizational form.

The final area analyzed was the role of culture in organizational design and processes. Managers need to identify, understand, and managerially interpret cultural forces. This can be done by relating certain sets of cultural values, attitudes, and behavior to the organizational areas they most affect. These would include social structures' impact on organizational structures, societal relationships on manager–employee relations, decision processes on decision-making, interpersonal orientation on group behavior, personal interaction on communications, motivation on incentives and evaluation, perceptions of human nature on control, perceptions of time on time management and planning, and perceptions of space on spatial relations. To manage the cultural factors more effectively, one should avoid ethnocentricism and seek out potential complementarities and synergies across cultures and subcultures. Successful management in developing countries requires cultural sensitivity along with economic acumen and political dexterity.

11

Toward the Future

We now turn our vision toward the twenty-first century and offer brief final reflections on the evolving business environment and management challenges in developing countries. For this future perspective we shall again peer through the EAF's conceptual lenses to examine economic, political, cultural, and demographic dimensions of the LDC environment. As we delineate possible future outlines of the Third World, it is important to reiterate the first chapter's observation: behind the generalizations lies great diversity, to which managers must be sensitive.

THE EVOLVING BUSINESS ENVIRONMENT

Demographic Dimensions

We begin with population variables because they are among the most predictable components of the equation. Demographic changes occur relatively slowly, and their future effects on LDC business environments are more clearly discernible. Population expansion will be almost entirely a Third World phenomenon. Although current LDC birthrates will continue to fall, health improvements will increase infant survival rates, thereby keeping annual population growth up near 2%. By the year 2000 four of every five consumers and six out of every seven children under fifteen will reside in the Third World (see Chapter 3, Figures 3.3 and 3.4).[1] By about 2050 India will be the world's most populous country with 1.7 billion people, surpassing China, and Nigeria will have moved up to third place with a fivefold increase to 529 million people; 86% of the world's population will be in today's developing countries and Africa's share will have almost doubled to 21%, while Asia's will

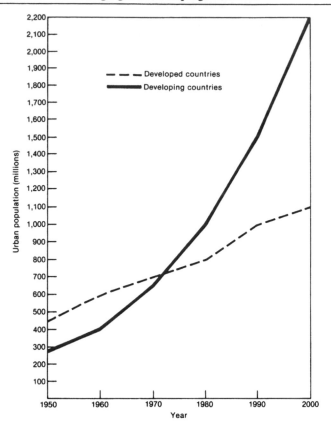

Figure 11.1 Urban Population Growth
SOURCE: James E. Austin, *Confronting Urban Malnutrition* (Baltimore: Johns Hopkins University Press, 1980), p. 4.

remain about 58% and Latin America's and the Caribbean's about 9%.[2]

Urbanization will continue its rapid climb, so that by 2000 city dwellers in LDCs will be double those developed nations (Figure 11.1); twenty of the world's twenty-five largest cities will be in the Third World, with Mexico City topping the list at 31 million people (Table 11.1). Despite rapid urbanization, most of Africa's and low-income Asia's population will remain rural. By 2050 the LDCs' rural population will have increased by 1 billion.[3]

With most of the world's consumers, although less affluent, residing in LDCs, many firms view the Third World as the strategic growth area of the future. Witness Heinz chairman Anthony O'Reilly's observation:

In 1980, we conducted an internal company review of global investment

Table 11.1 World's Largest Cities in 2000 (millions)

Mexico City	31	Madras	13
São Paulo	26	Manila	12
Tokyo/Yokohama	24	Bangkok/Thornburi	12
New York/New Jersey	23	Buenos Aires metrop.	12
Shanghai	23	Delhi	12
Beijing	20	Karachi	12
Rio de Janeiro	19	Bogotá	12
Calcutta	17	Tehran	11
Bombay metrop.	17	Baghdad	11
Jakarta	17	Istanbul	11
Seoul	14	Osaka/Kobe	11
Los Angeles metrop.	14	Paris	11
Cairo/Giza/Imbaba	13		

SOURCE: *World Development Report 1984* (New York: Oxford University Press for the World Bank, 1984), p. 68.

potential. Our first unsettling discovery was that at that time 85% of the world's population had not been exposed to the Heinz brand. We also found—and it remains true today—that in the mature markets of Europe and the North American continent food consumption was not growing by more than one percent. If we wanted significant expansion in volume, we would have to look beyond the industrialized West.[4]

Similarly, with soft drink consumption growing at 20% in markets like India (as against 5% in the United States), the major cola companies are battling to penetrate the Indian market, with one industry analyst projecting: "India won't affect earnings estimates for the next three years, but it could be in the top 10 markets in the next 15 years."[5] The president of the multinational food company CPC International, which doubled its investment in Brazil in 1988, remarked: "A market of 140 million people with a per-capita income of less than $2,000 simply has possibilities too great to ignore."[6] The Brazilian market will be 180 million by 2000 and 279 million by 2050. LDCs will increasingly be the demand locus for demographically driven products.

Concurrent with the growing consumer base, the LDCs' high population growth rates and young age structure create a rapidly expanding labor force. This may provide countries and companies with an abundant supply of relatively low-cost labor that can be a source of competitive advantage. This cost advantage erodes as countries advance economically and wages increase. Thus, comparative labor cost advantages will continue to shift from the advancing to the less-advanced LDCs. The need to generate employment opportunities for the burgeoning workforce will be an increasingly high priority for LDC governments. In 1985 they faced the need to find 29 million jobs for new entrants to the workforce; in the year 2000 there will be 41 million entering the labor pool.[7] In 1980 Colombia had a working age population of 15 million; by 2000 it will be 25 million. Bangladesh's job seekers will grow from 48 million to 84 million.[8] Private sector companies will increasingly be sought to hire and train new workers. Employment generation will be increasingly central to business–government relations. Informal sector activities will continue to be an important labor absorber.

The concentration of the population in the under-fifteen group places increasing demands on the LDCs' educational systems and budgets. For high-fertility countries like Kenya the school age population will continue to expand rapidly, but for countries such as Colombia, China, and Korea where fertility rates are declining, the growth will be slower. The growing demands on scarce government revenues means public spending per student and student–teacher ratios will continue to deteriorate in many countries.[9] The quality of education will erode. Yet as technologies advance, labor skill rather than labor cost will become more critical to international competitiveness. Cheap labor by itself will be a less important source of comparative advantage. This skill gap will widen. Those developing countries and companies that more aggressively and effectively address this gap will gain competitive advantage. For companies the importance of on-the-job training will grow; skill development must become central to firms' human resource management strategies.

Burgeoning population will squeeze other resources as well. In 1971–75 there was 0.35 hectares of cropland per capita in developing countries; by 2000 it will be reduced to 0.19.[10] Land scarcity is one factor motivating migration to the cities. Deforestation and erosion continue to lower the productivity of the land. The rate of deforestation in tropical countries has exceeded reforestation by ten to twenty times, partially because of the 2.5 billion people who gather firewood as their principal source of energy.[11] LDCs' food production capacity will continue to be strained. Improvements in agricultural productivity in general and among subsistence farmers will help food supply adequacy, but income inequalities will continue to restrict poor families' access to food. It is likely that by 2000 there will still be about 400 million people suffering from significant calorie deficits.[12] Agriculture and food adequacy will be of high priority to LDC governments: agribusinesses, big and small, will continue to play important roles in Third World economies.

Economic Dimensions

We cast our economic focus first on LDC growth prospects. The World Bank's projections for 1988–95 show an acceleration in LDC growth rates (see Table 11.2). The higher growth rate scenario assumes that macroeconomic imbalances within and among the developed countries are reduced, particularly in the United States (declining fiscal and trade deficits, lower real interest rates, dollar depreciation). In the developing countries the scenario assumes that governments will also make adjustments to reduce fiscal deficits and inflation, avoid currency overvaluation, achieve institutional reforms in the public sector, and accelerate their exports of manufacture. GDP growth in this scenario will be 4.6% per year, up from the recession-pocked 1980–88 average of 4.0%. If these assumptions do not fully hold, the low growth scenario projects a rate of 3.7%.

Different types of LDCs are expected to experience different growth rates. Oil exporters will be the slow-growth countries (barring major oil price rises); the highly indebted nations (many being oil exporters) and the sub-Saharan countries will also grow below average. The high-debt countries' investment and therefore growth will be severely constrained by the capital outflows for debt servicing. Exporters of manufactures, especially in Asia, will experience the highest growth rates, particularly if the industrialized nations experience stronger growth and lower protectionism. These average annual rates will, of course, have yearly variations, with some countries experiencing major deviations. Economic instability, including inflation and foreign exchange rate volatility, will continue to plague the Third World. The LDCs' large population growth reduces the aggregate economic gains when coverted to a per capita basis, wiping them out entirely in sub-Saharan Africa.

In general LDCs will be economically expanding business environments. Rising incomes will lead to higher and more diversified consumption. Absolute expenditures on food increase, but as a share of the total budget they decrease. Consumers will broaden the range of products they purchase and diversify their diets, often shifting to foods perceived to be of higher quality or status. With still higher incomes, demand for consumer durables increases. Consumer goods businesses will be fueled by these income-driven expenditure shifts and the population expansion mentioned above. The number of people with annual income under $135 will decline by about one-third by 2000, but the share of national income going to the poorest 40% would stay about 15%.[13] Markets will continue

Table 11.2 Growth of Real GDP and GDP per Capita (average annual percentage change)

	Real GDP			Real GDP/Capita		
		1988–95			1988–95	
	1980–88	Adjustment with Growth	Low	1980–88	Adjustment with Growth	Low
Low & middle-income countries	4.0	4.6	3.7	2.0	2.7	1.8
Sub-Saharan Africa	0.5	3.2	3.1	−2.5	0.1	−0.1
Asia	7.3	6.0	4.9	5.5	4.3	3.2
Europe, Mideast, N. Africa	2.9	3.5	2.8	0.7	1.6	0.8
Latin America & Caribbean	1.7	3.1	2.3	−0.6	1.2	0.4
17 highly indebted countries	1.3	3.2	2.3	−1.2	1.0	0.2
High-income OECD countries	2.7	2.6	2.4	2.1	2.1	1.9

SOURCE: World Development Report 1989, p. 21.

to have very distinct economic segments because of this income skewedness. Widespread poverty will remain a stark reality, but there will be growing middle classes.

Industrial goods will also be in strong demand as governments continue to promote industrial development. The nature of the goods will, of course, depend on each country's level of industrialization. On average, manufacturing accounted for 10% of GDP in Africa but 20% in Latin America, with Asia in between.[14] In Africa and Asia manufacturing's share of the economy will continue to expand; in Latin America it will remain relatively stable. The type of businesses and equipment needed can vary significantly, but all markets present important opportunities.

Past paths of industrialization, however, will not necessarily be followed in the future. LDCs will find technological leapfrogging increasingly possible because of greater access to new technologies. LDCs' underdevelopment, paradoxically, may accelerate their development: They are less locked into old technologies financially, physically, and institutionally. The microelectronics revolution and its sister in telecommunications are profoundly transforming the entire business world and carry significant implications for developing countries.[15]

Information-processing technologies present both problems and opportunities. They may help LDCs deal with many problems stemming from "imperfect information" that characterizes LDC environments, but this will require overcoming deficiencies in infrastructure and personnel. In some instances leapfrogging will be possible, e.g., adopting fiber optics in telecommunication infrastructure development. With appropriate training programs some LDCs will increasingly make information services such as data processing and programming an important part of their exports. To the extent that electronic controls and programming reduce the costs of changes in production models and schedules, small-batch, flexible production will become more economically feasible. This may transform small markets or market segments that were previously precluded because of the requisite of large-scale production into attractive opportunities.

Traditional barriers to entry and sources of competitive advantage will be affected by accelerating technological diffusion. The "four dragons" will have company, as several other developing countries rapidly advance economically and technologically. How successfully countries and companies exploit these opportunities will greatly depend on how well they adapt their strategic vision, policies, and socioeconomic organization to the new technologies. As we have seen, the distinctive LDC environments will require adjustments quite different from those in mature industrial countries. Thus, the technological horizon reveals major change, entrepreneurial opportunities, and managerial pitfalls.

Technological transformations will continue into the next century as a driving force in developing countries. In the shorter run, many LDCs are undergoing economic structural adjustment. Global recession in the 1980s and the economic burden of their international debts have required countries to take several measures that significantly affect their future business environments. Serious balance of payments problems, often accompanied by large fiscal deficits and inflation, led many countries (often grudgingly) to seek IMF assistance. By 1987 almost half the developing countries were engaged in stabilization programs with the IMF. Although these programs are tailored to the specifics of each country, they commonly include exchange-rate devaluation, import restrictions, reductions in government expenditure and credit, and tax increases.

These economic adjustment measures create problems for some businesses and opportunities for others. Domestic demand may plummet under austerity measures. So if your business depends on the domestic market, particularly when the IMF comes to town, get prepared for a sales downturn. Cuts in government subsidies for basic goods or services may cause suffering, social unrest, unemployment, and political disturbances; reductions in other government spending and programs may dramatically affect certain industries. For example, Ghana's austerity program slashed maintenance expenditures for roads, ports, and railways; consequently, when international prices rose, mineral and timber exporters were held back by the resultant infrastructure deficiencies.[16] Many LDC financial institutions will have to be restructured or fail because their loan portfolios are so impaired. The economic difficulties of the 1980s left them with an unprecedented impairment of their solvency. Bank liquidations have occurred, for example, in Argentina, Chile, Egypt, Guinea, Kenya, Malaysia, and the Philippines; in eighteen countries 50% of the loans of the industrial development finance institutions were in arrears.[17] Devaluation will make imports more costly but exports more cost competitive. If your business is export-oriented, the economic adjustment policies may facilitate a rapid expansion in sales. Learning to live through these adjustment processes (which will be repeated in many countries) will be a managerial necessity. Managers can use the Public-Policy Impact Chain (Chapter 4) to project and analyze systematically the impact of the adjustment policies on their particular industry and company.

If effective, the adjustment programs produce greater monetary and exchange-rate stability and a more positive investment climate. A good example of this transformation is Ghana, which by 1982 found itself in terrible straits:

- GNP was shrinking 3% per year.
- Per capita incomes had declined by one-third since 1970.
- Savings as a percentage of GNP had fallen 77% to 3.9%.
- Government's fiscal deficit had risen to 7% of GDP and was absorbing most savings.
- Inflation was averaging 35%, triple the rest of sub-Saharan Africa.
- Exports had collapsed from 28% of GDP to 3%.
- Skilled Ghanaians were fleeing the country.[18]

In 1983 Ghana instituted an economic reform program with IMF and World Bank assistance. Over the ensuing three years the government devalued the cedi from 2.3 cedis to 90 cedis to the dollar, cut the fiscal deficit to 1.5% of GDP and government borrowing to 0.6%. It removed most price controls and increased real prices to producers. Real GDP rose to more than 5% per year; inflation fell below 8%; all major exports expanded in volume, and their constant value grew 26% in 1986 causing the trade deficit to fall to 6% of GDP.

The adjustment processes occurring in Ghana and other LDCs, however, are more than short-run economic realignments. They are changes in strategy and structure. There is a growing shift toward outward-oriented development strategies. Import substitution and domestic market protection remain, but they are increasingly being used more selectively as part of governments' efforts to make their industries internationally competitive. This shift is driven by the imperative of generating foreign exchange to service their external debt and by the desire to emulate the economic growth achieved by some countries' export-led growth strategies. Governments have also been reshaping their economic roles to give the private sector and market forces greater influence. The privatization of SOEs is continuing evidence of this.

LDC export growth will reduce the debt burden: Between 1987 and 1995 long-term debt as a percentage of GNP is projected to fall from 37.7% to 23.9% and debt service as a percentage of exports from 20.2% to 15.6% (although it will remain around 37% for the highly indebted countries).[19] To succeed as exporters, LDCs are restructuring their economies and institutions to promote industries where they hold or can develop comparative advantage. Such restructuring requires many years, because it means altering the traditional roles and ingrained behavior of government institutions and private businesses; it also calls for redeploying capital and labor to different industries where they can be used more efficiently. To facilitate such transformations the World Bank has increasingly provided structural and sectoral adjustment loans and technical assistance (about 20% of the Banks' total lending, with fifty-nine countries receiving such long-term loans during 1980–88). These provide the additional resources to carry out the policy and institutional reforms required to achieve sustainable growth over the medium term. Similarly, the IMF created new structural adjustment lending facilities ($11.4 billion in 1990) to provide multiyear funding to low-income countries facing high indebtedness and declining export commodity prices.[20] The reduced flow of private lending gives the World Bank, the IMF, and bilateral public lenders increased leverage in encouraging governments to pursue such restructuring. These adjustment loans and the government reforms will catalyze new flows of private capital.[21]

This growing export orientation, in one sense, is part of the larger phenomenon of globalization. Unrelenting technological advances in transportation, telecommunications, and information-processing will continue to shrink time and space. National markets will grow more interdependent. LDCs will become more significant actors in global industries and be increasingly integrated into global sourcing, production, marketing, and financing strategies. Capital flows to the Third World will be constrained in the short run but eventually will increase, although continued U.S. trade and fiscal deficits will have first call on capital from such surplus countries as Japan. Private lending may not grow much in the aggregate during the 1990s, but it will be selectively significant for the more creditworthy LDCs. By the turn of the century, the current "debt crisis" will have been largely resolved through a combination of writeoffs, conversions, repayments, and restructurings. Bank lending to the Third World will rise slowly from the ashes. In the interim, multilateral and bilateral official loans will play a larger role. FDI will also increase. LDC governments will aggressively seek foreign investors. Strategic alliances between MNCs and LDC companies will become more common and their forms of cooperation more diverse. LDC business groups will increasingly move abroad, and these Third World MNCs will become significant competitive forces in other LDCs and in developed countries.

Because government action can significantly influence international competitiveness, it is likely that business–government relations will become ever more important as companies and countries turn outward. In the international trade area there is a growing number of bilateral and multilateral arrangements. Protectionist pressures and bilateral political interests will impede "free trade" and foster "managed trade." Governments will continue to be important architects of the international business environment.

Political Dimensions

LDC governments will continue to be less stable than in developed countries but more stable than they have been historically. Political institutions and processes will become stronger. The resurgence of democracies and receding of military governments is likely to continue, but many democracies are fragile. Authoritarian regimes will resurface, but with less frequency and duration. Countries with extreme and unimproving socioeconomic inequalities will be prone to violent government overthrows. Governments unable to remedy major macroeconomic problems will be subject to coups.

As mentioned above, there will be some realigning of public and private economic roles. LDC governments, however, will continue to be a "mega-force" in the economy even as they withdraw from some areas and rely more on the private sector. Although governments are increasingly recognizing the economic and administrative limits of the state, they will not necessarily relinquish public authority or responsibility. There will be a groping search for new public–private arrangements; what may emerge are different forms of business–government interaction and collaboration in the economic and social areas.

Internationally, LDC governments will seek political-economic arrangements. As mentioned above, this is part of the shift to outward-oriented strategies. Some agreements will be bilateral among neighboring countries and will focus on the joint development of specific industries or resources to capture economies of scale or gain competitive advantages in international markets. Other attempts will focus on revitalizing regional common markets or trading agreements. In the past these arrangements attempted to expand each country's market beyond its borders while still maintaining high import barriers for the region as a whole. This approach, driven by import-substitution strategies, will have to be rethought to fit the emerging export-oriented strategies. This may lead to very different regional industry configurations that will be capable of competing effectively in international markets. The economic benefits of cooperation may lead nations to put aside or resolve long-standing political differences.

Cultural Dimensions

One of the many paradoxes in developing countries is that so much changes yet so much seems the same. Part of the explanation for this lies in culture's constancy: Cultural values, beliefs, attitudes, practices, and social structures are deeply rooted and evolve slowly. Cultural change does occur, but it is generally less visible than political, economic, and demographic changes; these, in turn, affect culture and create adjustment pressures. Some dimensions of culture seem less changeable: attitudes toward time and space, perceptions about basic human nature, and values related to individualism versus collectivism. But social structure and dynamics seem more amenable to change, albeit incremental and slow. The pressures of urbanization appear to alter somewhat traditional family structures and social behavior. Gender roles also seem to be shifting as female access to education has increased. Businesses have many chances to open nontraditional employment opportunities to women.

CRITICAL MANAGERIAL CAPABILITIES

To be successful in any business environment, one of course needs competency in strategic analysis and functional management. To meet the distinctive demands of the LDC environments, seven additional capabilities stand out as particularly critical. Together they constitute a managerial perspective and mindset attuned to the special challenges of LDCs.

1. *Applying environmental analysis* is fundamental to effective strategic management. Myopia is a most precarious perspective for managers in developing countries. Viewing one's business context narrowly blinds one to external forces that could critically affect the profitability and even survival of the firm. Dealing with such forces and events on an *ad hoc* or reactive basis reduces options and constrains managerial discretion. Analyzing the environment systematically and systemically provides a solid basis for planning strategically and for reacting to unforeseen events analytically rather than haphazardly.

2. *Handling business–government relations* carefully is essential to success in developing countries. Government is a mega-force; its actions permeate the LDC business environment. Managers need to know who the key government and political actors are, their goals and interests, and the basis of their power. Managers must understand the government official's perspective; the capacity to empathize is crucial to comprehension and communication. Understanding public policy is a prerequisite

to formulating effective private strategies. Firms seeing themselves as agents of development with a mission of contributing to the betterment of the country in which they are operating will be better able to build a positive relationship with the government. Rather than start from the premise of an adversarial relationship, managers should continually search for and create congruency between company and country goals.

3. *Managing change* is a critical capability, because the business environment is often in a tumultuous state of flux, both economically and politically. The concentration of economic activities and the fragility of institutions expose the business environment to significant disruptions resulting from economic events, such as a large price drop in the country's major export or an eruption of inflation. On the political side, regimes can change suddenly, and even within an administration policies are often drastically and inexplicably altered. Change is the norm. One needs to expect disruptions, predict them, and find ways to insulate operations or adjust them quickly. Contingency planning, strategic flexibility, and operational agility become important managerial skills.

4. *Capitalizing on constraints* is a major management challenge because market imperfections and resource inadequacies abound. Rather than let these gaps and deficiencies stifle operations, managers must see them as opportunities. Each one that a firm overcomes can be a source of competitive advantage. Innovating is critical to cope with both the frequent changes and the multiple constraints in the business environment. Standard procedures and traditional methods will often be inadequate to the new demands. Solutions are not easy or immediate, but finding ways to do without scarce resources or creating new ways to carry out essential tasks can lead to superior results. Such creativity abounds in developing countries, because it has been cultivated by the continued need to cope with scarcity. This talent has to be encouraged and tapped as part of the corporate culture. Constraint management becomes a critical competitive tool. Patience, perseverance, and innovation are essential ingredients.

5. *Being culturally sensitive* is essential to ensuring that a business's economic strategy is compatible with cultural dictates. This becomes especially critical for cross-cultural interactions and communications. One first needs to be cognizant of one's own culturally based values, attitudes, and behavior and then identify how those vary in the other culture and adjust one's actions accordingly. Managers should also search out opportunities for creating cross-cultural synergy by combining positive attributes of different cultures in complementary ways. Being able to

discern and interpret underlying shifts in a culture may be critical to ensuring cultural compatibility and to discovering new business opportunities.

6. *Being socially concerned* is integral to responsible management. Developing countries are beset with pressing socioeconomic problems and social needs. The intensity and pervasiveness of poverty produce widespread human suffering. Managers must view their businesses as part of this larger community and define their responsibility as helping to meet community needs. Businesses and managers have skills, resources, and institutional influence that can be mobilized very effectively to address social needs. In fact, they are often uniquely positioned to alter socioeconomic and even political conditions. Social responsibility and ethical sensitivity are essential to strategic management.

7. *Thinking globally* is the final imperative, given the growing economic integration of the developed and developing countries. Companies need to determine the roles that their LDC operations will play in their global production, marketing, and financing strategies and networks. Firms operating in only one country still need to have a global perspective for sourcing and for dealing with import competition. Managers should explore opportunities for creating new types of alliances and arrangements in and across developing countries. Changes in international economic relations and the growing globalization of industries call for organizational innovation.

=

Third World nations face enormous problems in their struggle to develop. Managers and businesses play a critical role in the development process. Quality management may be the Third World's scarcest resource; those countries and companies best able to mobilize and strengthen management capability will surge forward. Managers face a multitude of challenges as they operate in this very demanding business environment. They also carry a significant responsibility for contributing to the betterment of the societies they are operating in. It is the author's fervent hope that this book has strengthened their ability and willingness to meet those challenges and carry those responsibilities.

Appendixes

Four Dimensions
of Development
Country Values

(Countries Listed by GNP/Capita)

Country	GNP/Capita for 1987 (U.S.$)	GNP/Capita Growth 1965–87	Industry as a % of GDP 1987	PQLI Index 1985
Ethiopia	130	0.1	18	27
Chad	150	−2.0	18	–
Zaïre	150	−2.4	33	51
Bangladesh	160	0.3	13	31
Malawi	160	1.4	18	27
Nepal	160	0.5	14[a]	30
Mozambique	170	–	12	–
Tanzania	180	−0.4	8	61
Burkina Faso	190	1.6	25	20
Madagascar	210	−1.8	16	–
Mali	210	–	12	27
Burundi	250	1.6	14	35
Zambia	250	−2.1	36	48
Niger	260	−2.2	24	27
Uganda	260	−2.7	5	49
China	290	5.2	49	75
Somalia	290	0.3	9	17
Togo	290	0.0	18	37
India	300	1.8	30	46
Rwanda	300	1.6	23	–
Sierra Leone	300	0.2	19	26
Benin	310	0.2	14	38

Country	GNP/Capita for 1987 (U.S.$)	GNP/Capita Growth 1965–87	Industry as a % of GDP 1987	PQLI Index 1985
C.Afr.Rep.	330	−0.3	13	33
Kenya	330	1.9	19	56
Sudan	330	−0.5	15	39
Pakistan	350	2.5	28	27
Haiti	360	0.5	–	–
Lesotho	370	4.7	28	22
Nigeria	370	1.1	43	49
Ghana	390	−1.6	16	48
Sri Lanka	400	3.0	27	85
Mauritania	440	−0.4	22	30
Indonesia	450	4.5	33	58
Liberia	450	−1.6	28[a]	41
Senegal	520	−0.6	27	30
Bolivia	580	−0.5	24	53
Zimbabwe	580	0.9	43	64
Philippines	590	1.7	33	75
Yemen AR	590	–	17	28
Morocco	610	1.8	31	49
Egypt	680	3.5	25	57
Papua N.G.	700	0.8	26[a]	69
Dominican Rep.	730	2.3	30[a]	70
Ivory Coast	740	1.0	25	40
Honduras	810	0.7	24	63
Nicaragua	830	−2.5	34[a]	71
Thailand	850	3.9	35	79
El Salvador	860	−0.4	22	69
Congo	870	4.2	33	57
Jamaica	940	−1.5	41	91
Guatemala	950	1.2	–	–
Cameroon	970	3.8	31	47
Paraguay	990	3.4	26	80
Ecuador	1,040	3.2	31	73
Botswana	1,050	8.9	57	–
Tunisia	1,180	3.6	32	65
Turkey	1,210	2.6	36	67
Colombia	1,240	2.7	35	77
Chile	1,310	0.2	–	88
Peru	1,470	0.2	33	69
Mauritius	1,490	3.2	32	–
Jordan	1,560	–	28	71

Country	GNP/Capita for 1987 (U.S.$)	GNP/Capita Growth 1965–87	Industry as a % of GDP 1987	PQLI Index 1985
Costa Rica	1,610	1.5	29	91
Syria	1,640	3.3	19	71
Malaysia	1,810	4.1	–	73
Mexico	1,830	2.5	34[a]	80
S. Africa	1,890	0.6	44	–
Brazil	2,020	4.1	38[a]	74
Uruguay	2,190	1.4	32	90
Hungary	2,240	3.8	40	–
Panama	2,240	2.4	18[a]	–
Argentina	2,390	0.1	43	89
Yugoslavia	2,480	3.7	43	87
Algeria	2,680	3.2	42	50
Korea	2,690	6.4	43	86
Gabon	2,700	1.1	41	–
Portugal	2,830	3.2	40	86
Venezuela	3,230	−0.9	38	83
Greece	4,020	3.1	29	91
Trin. & Tob.	4,210	1.3	39	91
Libya	5,460	−2.3	–	–
Oman	5,810	8.0	43[a]	–
Spain	6,010	2.3	37[a]	–
Ireland	6,120	2.0	37[a]	–
S. Arabia	6,200	4.0	50[a]	45
Israel	6,800	2.5	–	–
N. Zealand	7,750	0.9	31[a]	96
Singapore	7,940	7.2	38	89
Hong Kong[b]	8,070	6.2	29[a]	95
Italy	10,350	2.7	34[a]	96
U.K.	10,420	1.7	38[a]	91
Australia	11,100	1.8	33[a]	97
Belgium	11,480	2.6	31	96
Netherlands	11,860	2.1	30	98
Austria	11,980	3.1	37	96
France	12,790	2.7	31[a]	98
Germany	14,400	2.5	38[a]	96
Finland	14,470	3.2	35	98
Kuwait	14,610	−4.0	51[a]	–
Denmark	14,930	1.9	29	98
Canada	15,160	2.7	35[a]	97
Sweden	15,550	1.8	35	99

Country	GNP/Capita for 1987 (U.S.$)	GNP/Capita Growth 1965–87	Industry as a % of GDP 1987	PQLI Index 1985
Japan	15,760	4.2	41	99
U.A.E.	15,830	–	57[a]	–
Norway	17,190	3.5	35	99
U.S.A.	18,530	1.5	30[a]	97
Switzerland	21,330	1.4	–	–

[a] Figures for years other than specified.
[b] GNP data refer to GDP.
NOTE: Some countries are not listed for lack of data.

SOURCES: World Bank, *World Development Report 1989* (New York: Oxford University Press, 1989), pp. 164–69; PQLI Index from John Sewell, *et al.* (eds.), *U.S. Foreign Policy and the Third World: Agenda 1985–86* (New York: TransAction Books, in cooperation with the Overseas Development Council, 1985), pp. 214–18.

Four Dimensions
of Development
Country Rankings
(from Lowest to Highest)

Rank	GNP/Capita for 1987 (U.S.$)	GNP/Capita Growth 1965–87	Industry as % of GDP 1987	PQLI Index 1985
1	Ethiopia	Kuwait	Nepal[a]	Somalia
2	Chad	Uganda	Panama[a]	Burk. Faso
3	Zaïre	Nicaragua	Papua N.G.[a]	Lesotho
4	Bangladesh	Zaïre	Liberia[a]	Sra. Leone
5	Malawi	Niger	Hong Kong[a,b]	Mali
6	Nepal	Zambia	U.S.A.	Ethiopia
7	Tanzania	Chad	Dom. Rep.[a]	Pakistan
8	Burk. Faso	Madagascar	France[a]	Niger
9	Madagascar	Ghana	N. Zealand[a]	Malawi
10	Burundi	Liberia	Australia[a]	Yemen AR
11	Zambia	Jamaica	Italy[a]	Senegal
12	Niger	Venezuela	Mexico[a]	Mauritania
13	Uganda	Senegal	Nicaragua[a]	Nepal
14	China	Bolivia	Canada[a]	Bangladesh
15	Somalia	Sudan	Spain[a]	C.Afr.Rep.
16	Togo	El Salvador	Ireland[a]	Burundi
17	India	Tanzania	Germany	Togo
18	Rwanda	Mauritania	Brazil[a]	Benin
19	Sra. Leone	C.Afr.Rep.	U.K.[a]	Sudan
20	Benin	Togo	Oman[a]	Ivory Coast
21	C.Afr.Rep.	Ethiopia	S. Arabia[a]	Liberia
22	Kenya	Argentina	Kuwait[a]	S. Arabia
23	Sudan	Benin	Uganda	India

Rank	GNP/Capita for 1987 (U.S.$)	GNP/Capita Growth 1965–87	Industry as % of GDP 1987	PQLI Index 1985
24	Pakistan	Peru	Tanzania	Cameroon
25	Lesotho	Sra. Leone	Somalia	Zambia
26	Nigeria	Somalia	C.Afr.Rep.	Ghana
27	Ghana	Bangladesh	Bangladesh	Morocco
28	Sri Lanka	Nepal	Burundi	Uganda
29	Mauritania	S. Africa	Benin	Nigeria
30	Indonesia	Honduras	Sudan	Algeria
31	Liberia	Papua N.G.	Madagascar	Zaïre
32	Senegal	N. Zealand	Ghana	Bolivia
33	Bolivia	Zimbabwe	Ethiopia	Kenya
34	Zimbabwe	Ivory Coast	Togo	Egypt
35	Philippines	Gabon	Malawi	Congo
36	Morocco	Nigeria	Chad	Indonesia
37	Egypt	Trin. & Tob.	Sierra Leone	Tanzania
38	Papua N.G.	Uruguay	Kenya	Honduras
39	Dom. Rep.	Malawi	Syria	Zimbabwe
40	Ivory Coast	U.S.A.	El Salvador	Tunisia
41	Honduras	Costa Rica	Mauritania	Turkey
42	Nicaragua	Burk. Faso	Rwanda	Papua N.G.
43	Thailand	Burundi	Bolivia	Peru
44	El Salvador	Rwanda	Niger	El Salvador
45	Congo	U.K.	Honduras	Dom. Rep.
46	Jamaica	Philippines	Egypt	Jordan
47	Cameroon	Sweden	Ivory Coast	Syria
48	Paraguay	Australia	Burk. Faso	Nicaragua
49	Ecuador	Morocco	Paraguay	Ecuador
50	Botswana	India	Senegal	Malaysia
51	Tunisia	Denmark	Sri Lanka	Brazil
52	Turkey	Kenya	Pakistan	Philippines
53	Colombia	Ireland	Lesotho	China
54	Peru	Netherlands	Costa Rica	Colombia
55	Mauritius	Spain	Greece	Thailand
56	Costa Rica	Dom. Rep.	Denmark	Paraguay
57	Syria	Panama	Netherlands	Mexico
58	Mexico	Pakistan	India	Venezuela
59	S. Africa	Mexico	Ecuador	Sri Lanka
60	Brazil	Germany	Cameroon	Korea
61	Uruguay	Belgium	Belgium	Portugal
62	Hungary	Turkey	Morocco	Yugoslavia
63	Panama	Italy	Tunisia	Chile
64	Argentina	Canada	Uruguay	Singapore

Rank	GNP/Capita for 1987 (U.S.$)	GNP/Capita Growth 1965–87	Industry as % of GDP 1987	PQLI Index 1985
65	Yugoslavia	France	Mauritius	Argentina
66	Algeria	Colombia	Peru	Uruguay
67	Korea	Sri Lanka	Indonesia	Costa Rica
68	Gabon	Greece	Zaïre	Greece
69	Portugal	Austria	Congo	Trin. & Tob.
70	Venezuela	Ecuador	Philippines	Jamaica
71	Greece	Mauritius	Colombia	U.K.
72	Trin. & Tob.	Finland	Thailand	Hong Kong[b]
73	Oman	Portugal	Sweden	Germany
74	Spain	Algeria	Norway	Italy
75	Ireland	Syria	Finland	N. Zealand
76	S. Arabia	Paraguay	Turkey	Austria
77	N. Zealand	Norway	Zambia	Belgium
78	Singapore	Egypt	Austria	Australia
79	Hong Kong[b]	Tunisia	Singapore	U.S.A.
80	Italy	Yugoslavia	Venezuela	Canada
81	U.K.	Cameroon	Trin. & Tob.	Denmark
82	Australia	Hungary	Hungary	France
83	Belgium	Thailand	Portugal	Netherlands
84	Netherlands	S. Arabia	Jamaica	Finland
85	Austria	Brazil	Gabon	Norway
86	France	Congo	Japan	Sweden
87	Germany	Japan	Algeria	Japan
88	Finland	Indonesia	Argentina	
89	Kuwait	Lesotho	Nigeria	
90	Denmark	China	Korea	
91	Canada	Hong Kong[b]	Yugoslavia	
92	Sweden	Korea	Zimbabwe	
93	Japan	Singapore	S. Africa	
94	Norway	Oman	China	
95	U.S.A.	Botswana	Botswana	

[a] Figures for years other than specified.
[b] GNP data refer to GDP.

SOURCES: World Bank, *World Development Report 1989* (New York: Oxford University Press, 1989), pp. 164–69; PQLI Index from John Sewell *et al.*, (eds.), *U.S. Foreign Policy and the Third World: Agenda 1985–86* (New York: TransAction Books, in cooperation with the Overseas Development Council, 1985), pp. 214–18.

C

Income Distribution

(Listed in Improving Order)

	Gini Coefficient	Year of Study
Ecuador	0.63	1970
Zimbabwe	0.62	1969
Gabon	0.61	1968
Honduras	0.61	1968
Kenya	0.60	1970
Mexico	0.57	1969
South Africa	0.56	1965
Iran	0.56	1971
Panama	0.56	1970
Turkey	0.55	1968
Venezuela	0.54	1976
Tanzania	0.52	1968
Colombia	0.52	1974
Malaysia	0.52	1970
Ivory Coast	0.52	1970
Senegal	0.51	1970
Thailand	0.50	1969
Chile	0.50	1968
Brazil	0.50	1970
Philippines	0.49	1971
Costa Rica	0.47	1971
Malawi	0.45	1969
Congo	0.45	1958
India	0.43	1965
France	0.42	1970
Japan	0.41	1971
United States	0.40	1972
Germany (West)	0.40	1973

	Gini Coefficient	Year of Study
Sri Lanka	0.38	1973
Korea (South)	0.35	1970

SOURCES: Nanak Kakwani, *Income Inequality and Poverty* (New York: Oxford University Press for the World Bank, 1980); Jacques Lecaillon, *et al.*, *Income Distribution and Economic Development* (Geneva: International Labour Office, 1984).

Economic
Cost-Benefit Analysis
Project Example

The purpose of this appendix is to present to the reader a simple example of economic cost-benefit analysis (ECBA), as a supplement to the explanation in Chapter 6. The appendix first describes a proposed investment and the corresponding private financial analysis.[*] Then it carries out an economic cost-benefit analysis and explains the differences between the financial and the economic analyses. Lastly, alternative ways in which the project could be modified to change the financial and economic returns are presented.

PROJECT DESCRIPTION

Proto International, a U.S. multinational that manufactured industrial machinery and parts, had submitted a proposal to the Finance Ministry of Zandia to manufacture steel rings, an essential part of most industrial machinery.

Investment

The proposed plant would produce 6 million rings, Zandia's current level of imports. Imported machinery and equipment would cost $12

---

[*] Project data originally from UNICAP, Ltd. (A), Harvard Business School Case (379–070), prepared by Lokhi Banerji under the supervision of James E. Austin.

million and would be installed over a period of three years. Future growth of demand could be accommodated by increasing the plant's size. It was estimated that an increase to 12 million rings capacity could be achieved with an additional investment of $4 million. The factory would be set up on government-owned land that had no alternative use.

Revenues

Zandia imported rings at the average CIF price of $1.50 per ring. Though the official exchange rate was fixed at Lp.7.50 per U.S. dollar, the rings retailed at the average price of Lp.15.75, reflecting supply shortages due to the quantitative import restrictions imposed by the government on these products. Proto's selling price would be Lp.15 each.

Operating Costs

Exhibit 1 (at the end of the appendix) shows the annual operating costs for the project. The salaried personnel will consist of 50% expatriates for the first two years of production. From the third year on this would be reduced to only 25% in accordance with the Zandian government's policy to hire locals.

Of the wage earners, 250 would be skilled workers earning Lp.1120 per month, plus the usual 25% for social security, leave, and other worker benefits. These workers would be hired from the unskilled construction and industrial workforce and given sufficient training. They currently earned Lp.700 per month. The rest of the workers would be 550 unskilled laborers, who would be paid Lp.560 per month plus 25% and would be recruited from the surrounding rural areas. The average income for farm workers, allowing for both subsistence production and idle days, was roughly Lp.210 per month. An alternative technological option existed in which more labor-intensive technology could be used, requiring four times as many workers and reducing the investment in plant and equipment by $1.2 million. Under this alternative, imported materials would be reduced to $1.067 million, for a drastic reduction in the importation of spare parts for machinery would occur. Also, the number of salaried personnel would double to provide adequate support and supervision to the larger workforce.

Transport costs, as shown in Exhibit 1, reflect the average rates charged by Zandian Railways. The actual operating costs of carrying the additional tonnage for this plant would be 50% of the average cost. The import content of rail transport was about 75%.

To ensure a smooth flow of materials, inventories of imported goods would be maintained at the level of three months' usage. Since domestic materials were readily available, no inventory would be necessary for these.

Housing

To house the eight hundred workers, the government's Housing Corporation would build houses, which would be in place when production started. The average cost of a house was Lp.24,000, to be financed by loans from the government's Development Bank at 6% annual interest. Proto would be charged annually 5% of its total wage bill, and the company would recover this amount from the workers.

Finance

Of the $12-million investment, $8 million would be received as a loan from a New York bank. The loan would be repayable in five equal installments from the year the plant was expected to begin production, and the interest is 8% on the outstanding balance. The remaining investment funds would be equity supplied by Proto. Interest payments before production startup in the fourth year would be made from Proto's New York headquarters.

Proto's hurdle rate of return on equity was 10% after taxes. The company would repatriate the net cash flow in U.S. dollars and use it in other projects.

Taxes

The corporate income tax in Zandia was 50%. The income tax payable by expatriate workers on their gross income averaged 25%.

BASIC ANALYSIS OF THE PROJECT

Since the basic purpose of the appendix is to illustate the ECBA technique, we shall assume that all figures provided are reliable (e.g., we shall assume there is a market for 6 million rings, there will be no inflation taken into account, etc.). In actual practice, assumptions should be examined through sensitivity analysis.

To differentiate clearly between a private financial analysis and ECBA, both will be developed. We start by showing the basic calculations leading to the private analysis.

A. Financial Analysis

1. Investment. Twelve million dollars at the current exchange rate of Lp.7.5 per $1 equals a total investment of Lp.90 million. The investment should be spread out in equal disbursements in years 1–3. An additional investment in working capital must be made to provide the raw materials for the first three months of operation. Since the new materials (Exhibit 1, p. 396) have an annual cost of Lp.34.5 million, the three-month supply is one-fourth of that, Lp.8.625 million. This investment in working capital is recovered at the end of the fifth year, once the inventory is used up and the corresponding rings are sold.

2. Revenues. Six million rings at Lp.15 each provide a revenue of Lp.90 million per year in years 4–8.

3. Operating Costs. The operating costs (see Exhibit 1) are Lp.52 million per year.

4. Amortization and Interest. Since the total debt is $8 million (Lp.60 million) over two years, with an interest rate of 8%, then the debt flows are as follows (all figures in millions of Lp.):

		Debt	
Year	Principal	Interest	Balance
1		2.4[a]	30
2		4.8	60
3		4.8	60
4	12[b]	4.8	48[c]
5	12	3.84	36
6	12	2.88	24
7	12	1.92	12
8	12	0.96	0

[a] The interest payments are equal to the balance to date times the interest rate (Lp.30 × 0.08 = Lp.2.4).
[b] The principal payments are one fifth of the total debt contracted (Lp.60/5 = Lp.12).
[c] The balance is the debt at the end of period t minus the principal repaid during that year (Lp.60 − Lp.12 = Lp.48).

As can be seen from the calculations above, during the first two years there are positive flows of Lp.30 million each, corresponding to the disbursement of the loan. In each of the following five years there are principal payments of Lp.12 million each (assumed to occur at the end of the period) and interest payments equal to the balance of the previous year times the interest rate.

5. *Depreciation*. The depreciation is taken into consideration because it provides a fiscal shield by increasing the operating expenses by a fifth of the total investment each year (Lp.90/5 = Lp.18). However, since the depreciation does not imply an actual disbursement of funds, it is added to the cash flow after the taxes to be paid have been calculated.

6. *Taxes*. Since the tax rate for corporations in Zandia is 50%, half of each year's operating profits must be disbursed as payments to the government. The resulting cash flow is shown in Exhibit 2 (p. 397).

7. *Net Present Value*. The net present value results from discounting each year's flow to its present value and then adding all discounted flows. The discount factor used is that which the company has established as its expected return on equity after taxes (10%). In this case the net present value is a positive Lp.7.11 million, indicating that the project has an internal private rate of return of over 10%, the company's hurdle rate of return. From this analysis, company analysts would conclude that the project, as presented, should be developed (all else being equal).

In the next section, the same project is analyzed by applying the ECBA technique. The idea is to show how ECBA would adjust the basic financial analysis presented above.

B. Economic Cost-Benefit Analysis

1. *Investment*. The private investments in years 1–3 are not considered, since they exist only if the project is carried out. They have no opportunity cost in Zandia, for they belong to the company and their use in the project does not preclude the government from investing in any other project.

In year 3 the government must invest Lp.19.2 million to cover the development of the housing project for eight hundred workers. Each house costs Lp.24,000. The assumption is that the housing cost is attributable to this project. Without it the houses would not be built.

2. *Benefits*. The project's socioeconomic benefits differ from the revenues calculated for the financial analysis. The project's rings would replace imports and therefore save foreign exchange. The sale of 6 million rings is therefore valued at the shadow exchange rate (SER), which (we assume) has been determined by the Planning Commission to be Lp.10.5 per $1 rather than the official exchange rate of Lp.7.50. Since

the average CIF price of the rings is $1.50, the project's total benefits are $1.50 × Lp.10.5 × 6 million = Lp.94.5 million. Note that this is the same as selling 6 million rings at Lp. 15.75, the current average retail price of rings.

Housing is a benefit of the project no less than the rings. It is a good produced because of the project. Workers would pay 5% of their wages annually for these houses. Since the total wages to be paid are Lp.8.82 million per year, then the housing benefits are valued at Lp.0.441 million per year (Lp.8.82 × 0.05 = Lp.0.441).

3. Interest. Interest expenses must be considered in the economic analysis, since they represent a loss of foreign exchange for the country that would not occur if the project did not exist. If the loans had been local, interest expenses would not appear in the calculations since they would not use up any real resources. The flows are equal to the interest amounts shown in the financial analysis increased by a premium equal to the relationship between the shadow exchange rate (SER) and the official exchange rate (OER) (SER/OER = Lp.10.5/Lp.7.5 = 1.4). Since in the first three years the interest will be paid by Proto's New York office, they must be excluded from ECBA, for during those years they will have no effect on the country's foreign exchange resources. The interest to be included in the ECBA flows are (all figures in million Lp.):

Year	Interest	SER/OER Factor	Adjusted Interest
1	0.00	1.4	0.00
2	0.00	1.4	0.00
3	0.00	1.4	0.00
4	−4.40	1.4	−6.72
5	−3.84	1.4	−5.38
6	−2.88	1.4	−4.03
7	−1.92	1.4	−2.69
8	−0.96	1.4	−1.34

4. Operating Costs. The operating costs are wages, salaries, materials, transportation, and land.

a. *Wages.* Wages in ECBA are what the workers would have earned in the next best alternative occupation, i.e., their opportunity costs. Accordingly, ECBA values wages at less than the wages the company would actually pay. Skilled workers' wages have to be adjusted to reflect the fact that, were it not for the training provided by the project, they would continue to be unskilled, earning only Lp.700 per month, or a total for the 250 of them of Lp.2.1 million per year (Lp.700 × 250 × 12 = Lp.2.1 million). Unskilled workers would be recruited out of the farming sector, where average wages were only Lp.210 per month. The project would provide jobs to 550 such workers, for a total of Lp.1.386 million per year (Lp.210 × 550 × 12 = Lp.1.386 million).

b. *Salaries*. The salaries, which in the financial analysis were always Lp.2 million, have to be adjusted to reflect that half the workers are expatriates subject to income taxes of 25%, who will repatriate their salaries in foreign exchange. The total salaries are Lp.1.0 million, i.e., the local personnel plus Lp.0.75 million (Lp.1.0 − 25% of Lp.1.0 = Lp.0.75), corresponding to the expatriate personnel after taxes. Since the expatriates repatriate their incomes, their salaries must be adjusted to reflect the social cost of foreign exchange, Lp.10.5 per $1.00; therefore, their actual cost for the government analyst is Lp.1.05 million (Lp.0.75 × [10.5/7.5]. The total cost of salaried personnel is Lp.2.05 million for the first two years. After the third year salaried expatriates are reduced to 25% of salaried personnel, and their total cost is equivalently changed to a total of Lp.2.025 million.

c. *Materials*. There are Lp.30 million of imported materials per year. Since they are imported, their costs have to be adjusted to reflect the real cost of the foreign exchange by multiplying them by the SER/OER factor of 1.4. The costs have already been converted to Lp. at the official exchange rate. The materials costs are Lp.42 million for years 4–8. The 15% duty on materials is excluded from ECBA because it is a transfer payment. It does not use up any real resources.

d. *Transportation*. Transportation costs have to reflect the fact that 75% of them are imported and the real marginal operating cost for this plant would be 50% of the average. The ECBA cost is Lp.0.125 (.25 of the local component times the marginal rate of Lp.0.5) plus Lp.0.525 (.75 of the imported component times the expected rate and adjusted by the SER/OER factor of 1.4).

e. *Land*. Since the land presumably has no alternative use, its rent does not constitute a cost for the project from the ECBA viewpoint.

=

Total operating costs are given in the following tables (all figures are in millions of Lp.):

Year	Wages(1)	Salaries(2)	Materials(3)	Transport(4)
4	3.49	2.05	47.5	0.65
5	3.49	2.05	47.5	0.65
6	3.49	2.025	47.5	0.65
7	3.49	2.025	47.5	0.65
8	3.49	2.025	47.5	0.65

(1) Wages of plant personnel.
(2) Salaries to local and expatriate personnel.
(3) Includes both local and imported materials.
(4) The costs of transportation reflect the fact that the plant will have a lower operating cost.

The total operating cost for each year is:

Year	Operating Cost
4	53.69 million
5	53.69 million
6	53.665 million
7	53.665 million
8	53.665 million

5. *Repatriation of Funds by PROTO.* The firm will repatriate all funds that "rightfully" belong to it. These are given by the depreciation expenses plus the net profits from operation. Since these funds are in Lp., they too have to be adjusted to reflect the real cost of foreign-exchange loss to the country and should therefore be multiplied by the foreign-exchange premium of 1.4. These repatriation flows are (all figures in millions of Lp.):

Depreciation Expenses	Operating Profits	SER/OER	Adjusted Cost of Repatriation
18	7.6	1.4	35.84
18	8.08	1.4	36.512
18	8.56	1.4	37.184
18	9.04	1.4	37.856
18	13.84	1.4	38.528

6. *Net Present Value.* As with the financial flow, the net present value results from discounting all the individual flows to their present value and then adding all the present values together. The difference is that the discount rate applied in ECBA is the shadow price of capital

(social rate of discount), given at 15% by the Planning Commission. The result is a negative NPV of Lp.14.87 million, indicating that the project is not acceptable under ECBA. Thus, although the project would be acceptable to the company, it would be rejected by the government. The complete ECBA flows are shown in Exhibit 3 (p. 398).

PROJECT MODIFICATIONS

As explained in the section dedicated to ECBA in Chapter 6, if a project does not meet the hurdle rate, be it private or public, the manager should explore modifications that might increase its attractiveness to one or another sector. In this case, the project meets the private sector's rate requirements but not the public sector's. The challenge is to see whether the project could be redesigned to generate a positive return for the country under ECBA while still meeting the company's hurdle rate. The following project modifications will be examined:

- Increase the project size to 12 million rings of productive capacity and export the extra production of 6 million rings.
- Use more labor-intensive technology in manufacturing to increase employment as much as possible and to reduce the capital investments required.
- Propose the initial project again, but this time offering 50% of the equity to the local government.

These alternatives are obviously not exhaustive nor mutually exclusive. They are meant only as illustrations of ways in which governments and private sectors can seek increased congruence through project redesign.

Expansion and Export

The first alternative proposed, the expansion of the project to 12 million rings, results in the following modifications to the financial analysis previously carried out.

A. *Financial Analysis*

1. Investment. Total investments would grow to Lp.120 million, resulting from a $4 million increase from the original project. We assume that the additional investment would be covered by the company's equity, for there is no evidence that loans would be available. The investment in working capital to cover three months of imported materials' stock would also double to Lp.17.25 million.

2. Revenues. Income would increase by Lp.67.5 million as a result of the export sale of the 6 million additional rings. This is equivalent to selling 6 million rings at $1.50 each and multiplying the result by the official exchange rate of Lp.7.50. Total revenues increase, therefore, to Lp.157.5 million.

3. Operating Costs. All operating costs, with the exception of rent (a fixed cost), would be doubled if capacity were increased to 12 million rings. The result is total operating costs of Lp.103.82 million.

4. Depreciation. Depreciation would increase to Lp.24 million per year, resulting from the increase in investments to a total of Lp.120 million, previously explained. The resulting private cash flow is shown in Exhibit 4 (p. 399).

B. Economic Cost-Benefit Analysis

The analysis of this alternative using ECBA would require the following modifications to the analysis.

1. Benefits. From the ECBA viewpoint, revenues would double since the country would not only stop importing the rings, it would export 6 million rings to other markets. The additional 6 million rings are valued, like the first 6 million, at Lp.15.75, since they represent foreign-exchange earnings for Zandia. The total benefits from the rings, from an ECBA perspective, are: 12 million rings at $1.50 each multiplied by the shadow exchange rate of Lp.10.5 per $1. This results in benefits of Lp.189 million.

2. Housing. Since the size of the project doubles, benefits from housing also double, passing from Lp.0.44 million to Lp.0.88 million. The investment in housing, previously Lp.19.20 million, now doubles to Lp.38.40 million.

3. Repatriation Flows. Repatriation flows result from Proto's transfer of funds from Zandia to projects in other parts of the world. The repatriation flows are equal to the net financial profits (shown in Exhibit 4) plus the depreciation flows, multiplied by the SER/OER factor of 1.4. The resulting ECBA cash flow is presented in Exhibit 5 (p. 400).

C. Net Present Values: Financial Analysis vs. ECBA

As can be seen from the cash flows in Exhibits 4 and 5, under the alternative of expand and export, the project continues to be attractive for the company and becomes attractive for the Zandian government. The corresponding net present values are: for the private sector Lp.11.01 million and for the public sector Lp.36.72 million. This results from the fact that the additional benefits in housing and foreign-exchange earnings more than offset the increase in costs and investments to be realized by the government. Revenues increase more than investments through economies of production design. Amortization outflows are proportionately less than the increase in foreign-exchange earnings to the country. The increase in NPV from the private perspective results from the attainment of economies of scale in production that more than offset the increase in costs and the fall in the average selling price of the rings.

Labor-Intensive Technology

The second alternative is to use a more labor-intensive technology to increase the benefits to the country via employment and housing. The modifications in the project's analysis from the implementation of this alternative are:

A. Financial Analysis

1. Investment. The investment in plant and equipment would fall to Lp.81 million, at the same time reducing the depreciation costs to Lp.16.2 million. Investments in working capital were drastically reduced because under this alternative three months of imported materials represented only Lp.2.3 million. The rest of the figures remained equal to those of the original project.

2. Operating Costs. The number of workers would increase to 3,200 (1,000 would be skilled and 2,200 unskilled). Twice as many salaried personnel would be needed and materials costs would fall to just Lp.9.2 million ($1.067 million multiplied by Lp.7.5 plus 15% import duty). The resulting operating costs would be Lp.55.16 million for the first two years and Lp.55.14 for the last three years of the project. The resulting cash flow is presented in Exhibit 6 (p. 401).

B. Economic Cost-Benefit Analysis

The analysis of this alternative under ECBA requires the following modifications to the original ECBA cash flow.

1. Housing. Housing benefits would quadruple: Four times as many workers would benefit from the program. The original figure of Lp.0.44 million is, therefore, multiplied by four, yielding housing benefits of

Lp.1.76 million. Likewise, the government's investment in the housing program has to quadruple relative to the initial project, increasing from Lp.19.2 million to Lp.76.8 million.

2. *Operating Costs.* Operating costs would change substantially to reflect the labor-intensive technology. Wages for 1,000 skilled workers would be (1,000 × Lp.700 × 12 months) Lp.8.4 million, and wages for unskilled labor would be (2,200 × Lp.210 × 12 months) Lp.5.04 million. The salaries would be exactly double those of the original project, under ECBA. The costs of imported materials would be greatly reduced to reflect the decrease in purchases of spare parts for imported equipment. The costs of imported materials of Lp.8 million would have to be adjusted to reflect the relationship between the official exchange rate and the shadow exchange rate by multiplying their value by the SER/OER factor of 1.4 (Lp.8 million × 1.4 = Lp.11.2 million). The other costs (transportation and rent) would remain equal to those of the ECBA for the original project. The resulting operating costs are Lp.34.84 million for the first two years and Lp.34.81 million for the last three years.

3. *Repatriation Flows.* The new repatriation flows would be modified to reflect the profits and depreciation flows existent under this alternative. The resulting cash flow is shown in Exhibit 7. The treatment given them is similar to that given to the profits and depreciation, under ECBA, of the original project.

C. Net Present Values: Financial Analysis vs. ECBA

The net present values of the project, Lp.8.76 million under private financial analysis and Lp.1.52 million under ECBA, are better than those of the original project. The reason there is such a marked improvement in the ECBA result is that under this alternative the repatriation flows decrease considerably because of lower depreciation flows, plus there are marginal benefits thanks to increased housing and employment. The improvement in the private results is due to the decrease in the investment of funds in plant and equipment and in working capital.

Joint Venture with the Government

A similar procedure would be followed to analyze the impact of involving the government as a 50% equity partner in the project. The results from the implementation of this alternative are: The private rate of return remains equal to that of the original project, the absolute amount being reduced by 50%. For the government, however, the results are quite different, since the government would not have to disburse funds to the project. These funds now enter the ECBA cash flow as investments because they have an alternative use and opportunity cost. The rest of the analysis would be basically equal to that shown in Exhibit 3. The NPV under ECBA for this alternative is a negative Lp.14 million.

CONCLUSION

Two things should result from reading and studying of this appendix. The reader should now understand the basic technique behind ECBA and the fact that private and public desirability are not necessarily equal. From the analyses realized, it is clear that, all else being equal, the expansion and export alternative is the most desirable for both the private company and the government. We have shown how a project that initially fell in an area of unacceptable noncongruence becomes attractive to both sectors through creative modification and continued analysis. The project, in the technical language of Chapter 6, moved up the congruency line and achieved gains for both the private and public sector until it fell into the area of acceptable noncongruence. It surpassed the hurdle rates established by Proto and the government of Zandia.

Many other alternatives could be tested, but these should suffice for illustration. It is important to mention once more that a complete analysis would include questions and factors to account for uncertainty in supply, marketing, sociopolitical context, and many other variables that should be considered in evaluating investments in LDCs. Many of the factors that should be addressed in the different areas are discussed in depth in the main text of this book.

Exhibit 1 Annual Operating Costs for the Project (Lp. millions)

Wages	
Skilled	4.20
Unskilled	4.62
Salaries	2.00
Imported materials	30.00
(duty at 15%)	4.50
Local materials	5.50
Transportation	1.00
Rent for the land	0.18
Total annual cost	52.00

Exhibit 2 Cash Flow for the Original Project (Lp. Millions)

Year	1	2	3	4	5	6	7	8
1. Revenues				90.00	90.00	90.00	90.00	90.00
2. Operating costs				(52.00)	(52.00)	(52.00)	(52.00)	(52.00)
3. Depreciation				(18.00)	(18.00)	(18.00)	(18.00)	(18.00)
4. Interest expenses	(2.40)	(4.80)	(4.80)	(4.80)	(3.84)	(2.88)	(1.92)	(0.96)
5. Operating profits	(2.40)	(4.80)	(4.80)	15.20	16.16	17.12	18.08	19.04
6. Taxes	0.00	0.00	0.00	7.60	8.08	8.56	9.04	9.52
7. Profits after tax[a]	(2.40)	(4.80)	(4.80)	7.60	8.08	8.56	9.04	9.52
8. Investments:								
Plant, equipment	(30.00)	(30.00)	(30.00)					
Working capital			(8.63)					8.63
9. Depreciation flow				18.00	18.00	18.00	18.00	18.00
10. Debt flows:								
Disbursements	30.00	30.00						
Princ. repayment			(43.43)	(12.00)	(12.00)	(12.00)	(12.00)	(12.00)
11. Net cash flows	(2.40)	(4.80)	(43.43)	13.60	14.08	14.56	15.04	24.15
12. NPV factor @ 10%	1.00	0.91	0.83	0.75	0.68	0.62	0.56	0.51
13. Discounted flows	(2.40)	(4.36)	(35.87)	10.21	9.62	9.04	8.48	12.39
NPV:	7.11							

[a] No tax loss carry forward.

Exhibit 3 ECBA Cash Flow for the Original Project (Lp. Millions)

Year	1	2	3	4	5	6	7	8
1. Benefits				94.50	94.50	94.50	94.50	94.50
2. Housing benefits				0.44	0.44	0.44	0.44	0.44
3. Net benefits				94.94	94.94	94.94	94.94	94.94
4. Housing investment			(19.20)					
5. Operating costs				(53.69)	(53.69)	(53.67)	(53.67)	(53.67)
6. Interest expenses				(6.72)	(5.38)	(4.03)	(2.69)	(1.34)
7. Net flows	0.00	0.00	(19.20)	34.53	35.87	37.24	38.59	39.93
8. Repatriation flows				(35.84)	(36.51)	(37.18)	(37.86)	(38.53)
9. Net economic flows	0.00	0.00	(19.20)	(1.31)	(0.64)	0.06	0.73	1.40
10. NPV factor @ 15%	1.00	0.87	0.76	0.66	0.57	0.50	0.43	0.38
11. Discounted flows	0.00	0.00	(14.52)	(0.86)	(0.37)	0.03	0.32	0.53
NPV:	(14.87)							

Exhibit 4 Private Cash Flow for the Expansion and Export Alternative (Lp. Millions)

Year	1	2	3	4	5	6	7	8
1. Revenues				157.50	157.50	157.50	157.50	157.50
2. Operating costs				(103.82)	(103.82)	(103.82)	(103.82)	(103.82)
3. Depreciation				(24.00)	(24.00)	(24.00)	(24.00)	(24.00)
4. Interest expenses	(2.40)	(4.80)	(4.80)	(4.80)	(3.84)	(2.88)	(1.92)	(0.96)
5. Operating profits	(2.40)	(4.80)	(4.80)	24.88	25.84	26.80	27.76	28.72
6. Taxes	0.00	0.00	0.00	12.44	12.92	13.40	13.88	14.36
7. Profits after tax	(2.40)	(4.80)	(4.80)	12.44	12.92	13.40	13.88	14.36
8. Investments:								
Plant, equipment	(40.00)	(40.00)	(40.00)					
Working capital			(17.25)					17.25
9. Depreciation flow				24.00	24.00	24.00	24.00	24.00
10. Debt flows:								
Disbursements	30.00	30.00						
Princ. repayment				(12.00)	(12.00)	(12.00)	(12.00)	(12.00)
11. Net cash flows	(12.40)	(14.80)	(62.05)	24.44	24.92	25.40	25.88	43.61
12. NPV factor @ 10%	1.00	0.91	0.83	0.75	0.68	0.62	0.56	0.51
13. Discounted flows	(12.40)	(13.45)	(51.25)	18.35	17.02	15.77	14.60	22.37
NPV:	11.01							

Exhibit 5 ECBA Cash Flow for the Expansion and Export Alternative (Lp. Millions)

Year	1	2	3	4	5	6	7	8
1. Benefits				189.00	189.00	189.00	189.00	189.00
2. Housing benefits				0.88	0.88	0.88	0.88	0.88
3. Net benefits				189.88	189.88	189.88	189.88	189.88
4. Housing investment			(38.40)					
5. Operating costs				(107.38)	(107.38)	(107.35)	(107.35)	(107.35)
6. Interest expenses				(6.72)	(5.38)	(4.03)	(2.69)	(1.34)
7. Net flows	0.00	0.00	(38.40)	75.78	77.12	78.50	79.84	81.19
8. Repatriation flows				(51.01)	(51.68)	(52.36)	(53.03)	(53.70)
9. Net economic flows	0.00	0.00	(38.40)	24.77	25.44	26.14	26.81	27.49
10. NPV factor @ 15%	1.00	0.87	0.76	0.66	0.57	0.50	0.43	0.38
11. Discounted flows	0.00	0.00	(29.03)	16.30	14.55	12.99	11.58	10.33
NPV:	36.72							

Exhibit 6 Private Cash Flow for the Labor-Intensive Alternative (Lp. Millions)

Year	1	2	3	4	5	6	7	8
1. Revenues				90.00	90.00	90.00	90.00	90.00
2. Operating costs				(55.16)	(55.16)	(55.16)	(55.16)	(55.16)
3. Depreciation				(16.20)	(16.20)	(16.20)	(16.20)	(16.20)
4. Interest expenses	(2.40)	(4.80)	(4.80)	(4.80)	(3.84)	(2.88)	(1.92)	(0.96)
5. Operating profits	(2.40)	(4.80)	(4.80)	13.84	14.80	15.76	16.72	17.68
6. Taxes	0.00	0.00	0.00	6.92	7.40	7.88	8.36	8.84
7. Profits after tax	(2.40)	(4.80)	(4.80)	6.92	7.40	7.88	8.36	8.84
8. Investments:								
Plant, equipment	(30.00)	(30.00)	(21.00)					
Working capital			(2.30)					2.30
9. Depreciation flow				16.20	16.20	16.20	16.20	16.20
10. Debt flows:								
Disbursements	30.00	30.00						
Princ. repayment			(28.10)	(12.00)	(12.00)	(12.00)	(12.00)	(12.00)
11. Net cash flows	(2.40)	(4.80)	(28.10)	11.12	11.60	12.08	12.56	15.34
12. NPV factor @ 10%	1.00	0.91	0.83	0.75	0.68	0.62	0.56	0.51
13. Discounted flows	(2.40)	(4.36)	(23.21)	8.35	7.92	7.50	7.08	7.87
NPV:	8.76							

Exhibit 7 ECBA Cash Flow for the Labor-Intensive Alternative (Lp. Millions)

Year	1	2	3	4	5	6	7	8
1. Benefits				94.50	94.50	94.50	94.50	94.50
2. Housing benefits				1.76	1.76	1.76	1.76	1.76
3. Net benefits				97.26	96.26	96.26	96.26	96.26
4. Housing investment			(76.80)					
5. Operating costs				(34.84)	(34.84)	(34.81)	(34.81)	(34.81)
6. Interest expenses				(6.72)	(5.38)	(4.03)	(2.69)	(1.34)
7. Net flows	0.00	0.00	(76.80)	54.70	56.04	57.42	58.76	60.11
8. Repatriation flows				(32.36)	(33.04)	(33.71)	(34.38)	(35.05)
9. Net economic flows	0.00	0.00	(76.80)	22.34	23.00	23.71	24.38	25.06
10. NPV factor @ 15%	1.00	0.87	0.76	0.66	0.57	0.50	0.43	0.38
11. Discounted flows	0.00	0.00	(58.07)	14.70	13.16	11.78	10.53	9.42
NPV:	1.52							

Notes

CHAPTER 1

The Management Challenge

1. James E. Austin, "Cummins Engine in India," Harvard Business School case 9–379–072, 1978, rev. 1985; Jack Baranson, *Manufacturing Problems in India: The Cummins Diesel Experience* (Syracuse: Syracuse University Press, 1967).

2. Carlos Sequeira, "Electrohogar, S.A.," IPADE case, 1985.

3. Kenneth Hoadley and James E. Austin, "Sabritas S.A. de C.V.," Harvard Business School case 381–096, 1981, rev. 1986.

4. Alan Cowell, "Egypt Faces an Economic Squeeze," *New York Times,* June 26, 1989, D9. Herein the American definition of "billion" is used, that is, 1 billion equals one thousand million.

5. For purposes of consistency we will consider as developing countries those so designated by the World Bank in the annual *World Development Report.* These include ninety-nine countries classified as developing economies (including Taiwan and newly independent Namibia), four high-income oil exporters, thirty-two countries with less than 1 million population, and seven nonreporting members of the World Bank from the Eastern block.

6. My T. Vu, Edward Bos, and Rodolfo A. Bulatao, "Asia Region Population Projections: 1988–89 Edition," World Bank, Population and Human Resources Department, Policy Planning and Research Working Paper, 1988, pp. 32, 33.

7. *World Development Report 1986* (New York: Oxford University Press for the World Bank), Table A.4, p. 155 (excludes nonmarket economies)

8. *IMF International Financial Statistics: Supplement on Trade,* Supplemental Series, no. 15 (Washington, D.C.: IMF, 1988), p. 99.

9. Dieter Schumacher, "Determinants of the Major Industrialized Countries' Exports to Developing Countries," *World Development,* 16, no. 11 (1988): 1317.

10. Derived from United Nations, *Statistical Yearbook 1982* (New York: U.N., 1985), pp. 52, 53.

11. Christopher A. Bartlett and Gary Gerttula, "Note on the Paper Machinery Industry," Harvard Business School case, 9–383–185, 1983.

12. U. Srinivasa Rangan and Christopher A. Bartlett, "Caterpillar Tractor Company," Harvard Business School case, 9–385–276, 1985, rev. 1988.

13. *IMF International Financial Statistics: Supplement on Trade,* Supplemental Series, no. 15 (Washington, D.C.: IMF, 1988), p. 99.

14. Derived from U.S. Department of Commerce data, *Foreign Trade Highlights* (Washington, D.C.: Office of Trade and Investment Analysis, 1987), pp. A-063, A-119.

15. David Goldsborough and Iqbal Zaidi, "Transmission of Economic Influences from Industrial to Developing Countries," *Staff Studies for the World Economic Outlook* (Washington, D.C.: IMF, July 1986), p. 192.

16. Alan V. Deardorff, "The Directions of Developing-Country Trade: Examples of Pure Theory," in Oli Havrylyshyn (ed.), *Exports of Developing Countries: How Direction Affects Performance* (Washington, D.C.: World Bank, 1987), pp. 2–21.

17. James E. Austin, Frank J. Aguilar, and Jiang-sheng Jin, "Nike in China," Harvard Business School case, 9–386–065, rev. 1988.

18. "A.T.&T. to Build Plant in Thailand," *New York Times,* June 24, 1988, p. D4.

19. Constantinos C. Markides and Norman Berg, "Manufacturing Offshore Is Bad Business," *HBR,* 88, no. 5 (September–October 1988): p. 115.

20. David J. Collis and Michael E. Porter, "Tatung Company (B)," Harvard Business School case 9–385–174, rev. February 1986, pp. 1–2.

21. Jimichi Goto, Paula Holmes, and Paul Mes, *The Caribbean: Export Preferences and Performance* (Washington, D.C.: World Bank, 1988), p. x.

22. Otto Kreye, Jürgen Heinrichs, and Folker Frobel, "Export Processing Zones in Developing Countries: Results of a New Survey;" International Labour Office Multinational Enterprises Programme, Working Paper no. 43, 1987, p. 1.

23. *World Development Report 1988* (New York: Oxford University Press for the World Bank), pp. 250–51.

24. Kreye, Heinrichs, and Frobel, "Export Processing Zones," p. 4.

25. *The International Corporate 1000: A Directory of Those Who Manage the World's Leading 1000 Corporations* (New York: Monitor), 1989.

26. "Business in the Developing World," *The Economist,* December 26, 1987, p. 86.

27. Jon Sigurdson and Pradeep Bhargava, "The Challenge of the Electronic Industry in China and India," in Staffan Jacobsson and Jon Sigurdson (eds.), *Technological Trends and Challenges in Electronics: Dominance of the Industrialized World and Responses in the Third World* (Lund, Sweden: Research Policy Institute, University of Lund, 1983), p. 250.

28. Andrew Tanzer, "Samsung: South Korea Marches to Its Own Drummer," *Forbes,* May 16, 1988, p. 86.

29. Alice H. Amsden and Linsu Kim, "The Role of Transnational Corporations in the Production and Exports of the Korean Automobile Industry," Harvard Business School Working Paper 9–785–063, June 1985, p. 17.

30. David Goldsborough and Iqbal Zaidi, "Transmission of Economic Influences" (note 15 above), p. 176.

31. For an analysis of government export financing, see Philip A. Wellons, *Passing the Buck: Banks, Governments, and Third World Debt* (Boston: Harvard Business School Press, 1987).

32. *World Development Report 1989,* p. 23.

33. Goldsborough and Zaidi, "Transmission of Economic Influences," pp. 151, 155, 176.

34. K. Burke Dillon, Luis Duran-Downing, with Miranda Xafa, "Officially Supported Export Credits: Developments and Prospects," *IMF World Economic and Financial Surveys,* February 1988.

35. *World Debt Tables 1988–89* (Washington, D.C.: World Bank, 1989), vol. I, p. 2, and vol. II, pp. 42, 262.

36. Derived from *World Debt Tables 1987–88,* vol. 2 (Country Debt Tables) (Washington, D.C.: IMF, 1988).

37. Louis T. Wells, Jr. (ed.), *The Product Life Cycle and International Trade* (Boston: Harvard Business School, 1972); J. M. Finger, "A New View of the Product Cycle Theory," *Weltwirtschaftliches Archiv,* 111 (1975): 79–99; Seev Hirsch, "The Product Cycle Model of International Trade: A Multi-Country Cross-Section Analysis," *Oxford Bulletin of Economics and Statistics,* 37 (1975): 305–17; Raymond Vernon, "The Product Cycle Hypothesis in a New International Environment," *Oxford Bulletin of Economics and Statistics,* 41 (1979): 255–67.

38. Guy Pfefferman and Dale R. Weigel, "The Private Sector and the Policy Environment," *Finance & Development,* December 1988, pp. 26–27.

39. Derived from *World Development Report 1985* (New York: Oxford University Press for the World Bank, 1985), p. 126.

40. David J. Goldsborough, "Investment Trends and Prospects: The Link with Bank Lending," in Theodore H. Moran (ed.), *Investing in Development: New Roles for Private Capital* (New Brunswick, N.J.: TransAction Books, 1986).

41. Kiyoshi Kojima and Terutomo Ozawa, *Japan's General Trading Companies: Merchants of Economic Development* (Paris: OECD, 1984), p. 43; the top nine trading companies accounted for half of the overseas investments of Japan's top fifty multinationals, p. 16.

42. Derived from *Balance of Payments Statistics Yearbook* (Washington, D.C.: IMF, 1984), pp. 643–55.

43. Derived from *International Investment and Multinational Enterprises: Recent Trends in International Direct Investment* (Paris: OECD, 1987), pp. 186–210.

44. Bohn-young Koo, "New Forms of Foreign Investment in Korea," in Charles Oman (ed.), *New Forms of International Investment in Developing Countries: The National Perspective* (Paris: OECD, 1984), p. 106.

45. The foreign assets are assumed to be in the same sector as the companies' principal line of business.

46. Tomás Otto Kohn, "International Entrepreneurship: Foreign Direct Investment by Small U.S.-Based Manufacturing Firms," doctoral dissertation, Harvard University Graduate School of Business Administration, 1988, p. 10.

47. Joseph C. Wheeler, *Development Cooperation: 1987 Report* (Paris: OECD, 1987), p. 51.

48. *World Development Report 1989* (New York: Oxford University Press for the World Bank).

49. *Ibid.*, p. 223.

50. "Average Japanese Income Reported Higher than U.S.," *Miami Herald,* October 14, 1988, p. 5A.

51. *World Development Report 1989*, pp. 168–69.

52. *Ibid.*

53. James G. Brown, "Improving Agroindustries in Developing Countries," *Finance & Development*, June 1986, p. 42.

54. John Sewell *et al.* (eds.), *U.S. Foreign Policy and the Third World: Agenda 1985–86* (New Brunswick, N.J.: TransAction Books, 1985), pp. 214–18. The PQLI operates on a 0-to-100 scale, starting with the worst literacy, infant mortality, and life expectancy rates ever recorded and rising to the best rates expected anywhere by the year 2000.

55. See Appendix C for sources.

56. *World Development Report 1989*, pp. 164–65.

CHAPTER 2

Environmental Analysis Framework

1. Stephen D. Younger, "Ghana: Economic Recovery Program—A Case Study of Stabilization and Structural Adjustment in Sub-Saharan Africa," *Successful Development in Africa*, EDI Development Policy Case Series, no. 1 (Washington, D.C.: World Bank, 1989), p. 138.

CHAPTER 3
The Environmental Factors

1. Dale D. Murphy provided key assistance in the preparation of the initial drafts of this chapter.

2. For a general primer, see Gerald M. Meier (ed.), *Leading Issues in Economic Development*, 5th ed. (New York: Oxford University Press, 1989).

3. Catherine B. Hill and D. Nelson Mokgethi, "Botswana: Macroeconomic Management of Commodity Booms, 1975–86," *Successful Development in Africa*, EDI Development Policy Case Series, no. 1 (Washington, D.C.: World Bank), 1989, pp. 174–75.

4. *Statistical Yearbook of Indonesia 1984* (Jakarta: Biro Pusat Statistik, 1985), p. 84; *Country Report: Indonesia* (London: The Economist Intelligence Unit, 1988), nos. 1, 2, 3, p. 2 and centerfold; *Statistical Abstract of Latin America 1987* (Los Angeles: UCLA Press, 1988), pp. 432–33, 447, 449; *Revista del Banco de la República* (Bogotá: Banco de la República), 49, no. 585: 953; 50, no. 591: 145; 55, no. 651: 139.

5. Stephen D. Younger, "Ghana: Economic Recovery Program—A Case Study of Stabilization and Structural Adjustment in Sub-Saharan Africa," *Successful Development in Africa*, EDI Development Case Series, no. 1 (Washington, D.C.: World Bank, 1989), p. 142.

6. N. T. Wang, "United States and China: Business Beyond Trade—An Overview," *Columbia Journal of World Business*, Spring 1986, p. 4.

7. Omotunde E. G. Johnson, "Labor Markets, External Development, and Unemployment in Developing Countries," *Staff Studies for the World Economic Outlook* (Washington, D.C.: IMF, July 1986), p. 58.

8. These are China, Brazil, India, Mexico, South Korea, Saudi Arabia, Indonesia, Poland, Taiwan, Argentina, Yugoslavia, Algeria, South Africa, and Turkey.

9. *World Development Report 1989* (New York: Oxford University Press for the World Bank, 1989), pp. 164–65.

10. *World Development Report 1989*, pp. 180–81.

11. *World Development Report 1988*, pp. 272–73, based on data from twenty-eight LDCs and eighteen developed countries for various years; between 1967 and 1977 income distribution in LDCs worsened. Meier, *Leading Issues in Economic Development*, p. 128.

12. Simon Kuznets speculated in 1954 that traditional peasant societies were initially relatively equitable, then rapid economic growth benefited a small upper class, creating inequities, before the benefits trickled down to the masses. Simon Kuznets, "Economic Growth and Income Inequality," *American Economic Review*, 45 (1954): 1–28. See also Jacques Lecaillon *et al.*, *Income Distribution and Economic Development: An Analytical Survey* (Geneva: International Labour Office, 1984).

13. Edilberto Segura, "Industrial, Trade and Financial Sector Policies to Foster Private Enterprises in Developing Countries," *Columbia Journal of World Business*, Spring 1988, p. 23.

14. *World Development Report 1988*, pp. 270–71.

15. *Statistical Abstract of Latin America 1987* (Los Angeles: UCLA Latin American Center, UCLA Press, 1988), p. 787.

16. *World Development Report 1989*, calculated from Tables 1 and 8, pp. 164–65 and 198–99.

17. A special issue of *World Development*, vol. 15, no. 5 (1987), analyzes various aspects of world commodity economy; for an overview, see Alfred Maizels, "Commodities in Crisis: An Overview of the Main Issues," pp. 537–49.

18. See Robert J. Saunders *et al.*, *Telecommuications and Economic Development* (Baltimore: Johns Hopkins University Press for the World Bank, 1983), pp. 50–54, 61–69.

19. See Figure 3.2 sources.

20. Michael Hiltzik, "Zaïre: Private Enterprise Fills the Void," *Boston Globe*, December 4, 1988, p. A116.

21. U. Srinivasa Rangan and Christopher Bartlett, "Caterpillar Tractor Co.," Harvard Business School case, 9–385–276, April 1988, p. 21.

22. David Lamb, *The Africans* (New York: Random House, 1982), pp. 351–52.

23. Humberto Vásquez M., José de Mesa, and Teresa Gisbert, *Manual de Historia de Bolivia* (La Paz: Gisbert y Cía., S.A., 1984).

24. A clear articulation of this theory is Samuel P. Huntington's *Political Order in Changing Societies* (New Haven: Yale University Press, 1968). Empirical efforts to prove or disprove the theory have been inconclusive. See Ekkart Zimmermann, *Political Violence, Crises, and Revolutions: Theories and Research* (Boston: G. K. Hall, 1983).

25. Thomas L. Brewer, "Interactive Reaction Function Models in Country Risk Analysis: Measuring and Forecasting Stability and Instability," paper presented at the Annual Meeting of the Academy of International Business, Chicago, 1987.

26. Huntington, *Political Order*, p. 165.

27. George C. Lodge and Ezra F. Vogel (eds.), *Ideology and National Competitiveness: An Analysis of Nine Countries* (Boston: Harvard Business School Press, 1987), p. 2. Also see George C. Lodge, *The New American Ideology* (New York: Knopf, 1975); Martin Seliger, *Ideology and Politics* (London: George Allen & Unwin, 1976); and John B. Thompson, *Studies in the Theory of Ideology* (Berkeley: University of California Press), 1984.

28. Lodge and Vogel, *Ideology and National Competitiveness*, Chapter 11.

29. For example, Robert O. Keohane and Joseph S. Nye, *Power and Interdependence: World Politics in Transition* (Boston: Little, Brown, 1977).

30. See Robert Gilpin, *War and Change in World Politics* (Cambridge: Cambridge University Press, 1981), pp. 231–44; Hayward Alker, "The Decline of the Superstates: Rise of New World Order?" paper presented to the International Political Science Association, Paris, 1985; and Robert O. Keohane, *After Hegemony: Cooperation and Discord in the World Political Economy* (Princeton, N.J.: Princeton University Press, 1984). Kenneth Waltz argues that balance-of-power politics will maintain the bipolar system in *Theory of International Politics* (Reading, Mass.: Addison-Wesley, 1979).

31. See Fernando Cardoso and Enzo Faletto, *Dependency and Development in Latin America,* trans. Marjory Mattingly Urquidi (Berkeley: University of California Press, 1979); Immanuel Wallerstein, *The Capitalist World Economy: Essays* (New York: Cambridge University Press, 1979); Theda Skocpol, "Wallerstein's World Capitalist System: A Theoretical and Historical Critique," *American Journal of Sociology,* 82 (March 1977): 1075–90; and Anthony Brewer, *Marxist Theories of Imperialism: A Critical Survey* (London: Routledge & Kegan Paul, 1980).

32. Tagi Sagafi-Nejad, "Egypt," *World Development,* 12, nos. 5/6 (1984): 567–73.

33. Geert Hofstede, *Culture's Consequences: International Differences in Work Related Values* (Beverly Hills: Sage Publications, 1980); Geert Hofstede, "Motivation, Leadership, and Organizations: Do American Theories Apply Abroad?" *Organizational Dynamics,* Summer 1980, pp. 42–63; Geert Hofstede, "Cultural Dimensions in Management and Planning," *Asia Pacific Journal of Management,* 1 (January 1984): 81–99.

34. For a managerially oriented treatment of this and other cultural variables, see Henry W. Lane and Joseph J. Distefano, *International Management Behavior: From Policy to Practice* (Scarborough, Ontario: Nelson Canada, 1988).

35. For a methodology for carrying out such gender analysis, see Catherine Overholt *et al.* (eds.), *Gender Roles in Development Projects: A Case Book* (West Hartford, Conn.: Kumarian Press, 1985).

36. United Nations Centre for Transnational Corporations and International Labour Office, *Women Workers in Multinational Corporations in Developing Countries* (Geneva: International Labour Office, 1985), p. 7.

37. Arthur S. Banks and Robert B. Textor, *A Cross-Polity Survey* (Cambridge: MIT Press, 1963).

38. Vern Tepstra and Kenneth David, *The Cultural Environment of International Business,* 2nd ed. (Cincinnati: South-Western Publishing Co., 1985), pp. 20, 28.

39. Lamb, *The Africans* (note 22 above), p. 14.

40. High-income oil exporters and China are excluded from the population and mortality statistics. Population growth rates for China averaged 1.5% in the decade 1975–85 (low for its income level) while life expectancy was unusually high at sixty-nine years. For high income oil exporters, in contrast, the population growth rate was 5.1%, while life expectancy was low: only sixty-three years.

41. The primary source for population statistics in this section is: the World Bank's *Population Change and Economic Development* (New York: Oxford University Press, 1985).

42. My T. Vu, Edward Bos, and Rodolfo A. Bulatao, "Asia Region Population Projections: 1988–89 Edition," World Bank, Population and Human Resources Department, Policy, Planning, and Research Working Paper, 1988, pp. 28, 50, 70.

43. *Ibid.*, pp. 52, 54, 84.

44. *World Development Report 1989*, pp. 224–25.

45. *World Development Report 1984*, pp. 68, 69.

46. International Labour Office, *World Labour Report*, 1 (1985): 101.

47. Huntington, *Political Order in Changing Societies* (note 24 above), pp. 299–306.

48. *World Development Report 1988*, pp. 286–87.

49. UNICEF, *The State of the World's Children 1988* (New York and London: Oxford University Press, 1988), pp. 64, 68–69.

CHAPTER 4

Interpreting National Strategies

1. Vincent S. R. Brandt, "Korea," in George C. Lodge and Ezra F. Vogel (eds.), *Ideology and National Competitiveness: An Analysis of Nine Countries* (Boston: Harvard Business School Press, 1987), pp. 207–39.

2. *World Development Report 1988* (New York: Oxford University Press for the World Bank, 1988), pp. 274–75.

3. S. Ghosal and Christopher A. Bartlett, "Matsushita Electric Industrial (MEI) in 1987," Harvard Business School case, 388–144, 1988, p. 6.

4. William R. Cline, "Can the East Asian Model of Development Be Generalized?" *World Development*, 10, no. 2 (1982): 81–90; Gustav Ranis, "Can the East Asian Model of Development Be Generalized? A Comment," *World Development*, 13, no. 4 (1985): 543–45; William R. Cline, "Reply," *World Development*, 13, no. 4 (1985): 547–48.

5. Anne O. Krueger, "Import Substitution Versus Export Promotion," *Finance & Development*, 22, no. 2 (June 1985): 21.

6. Brian Levy, "Korean and Taiwanese Firms as International Competitors: The Challenges Ahead," *Columbia Journal of World Business*, Spring 1988, pp. 43–51.

7. Stephan Haggard, "The Newly Industrializing Countries in the International System," *World Politics*, 38, no. 2 (January 1986): 343–70.

8. Krueger, "Import Substitution," p. 21.

9. Elvio Baldinelli, quoted in Norman Gall, "The Four Horsemen Ride Again," *Forbes*, July 28, 1986, p. 98.

10. Bela Balassa, *Change and Challenge in the World Economy* (New York: St. Martin's Press, 1985).

11. Chalmers Johnson, "The Industrial Policy Debate Re-examined," *California Management Review*, 27, no. 1 (1984): 75.

12. Michael Roemer, "Resource-Based Industrialization," in Gerald M. Meier and William F. Steel (eds.), *Industrial Adjustment in Sub-Saharan Africa* (New York: Oxford University Press, 1989), pp. 38–45.

13. James E. Austin and Gustavo Esteva (eds.), *Food Policy in Mexico: The Search for Self-Sufficiency* (Ithaca, N.Y.: Cornell University Press, 1987).

14. James Brooke, "Ivory Coast: African Success Story Built on Rich Farms and Stable Politics," *New York Times International*, April 26, 1988, p. 8.

15. Morton Owen Schapiro and Stephen Wainaina, "Kenya: A Case Study of the Production and Export of Horticultural Commodities," *Successful Development in Africa*, EDI Development Policy Case Series, no. 1 (Washington, D.C.: World Bank, 1989), pp. 79–94.

16. Renato Baumann and Helson C. Braga, "Export Financing in LDCs: The Role of Subsidies for Export Performance in Brazil," *World Development*, 16, no. 7 (1988): 821–33.

17. Noel Ramírez, *El Empresario y Su Entorno Económico* (San José, Costa Rica: EDUCA, 1987), p. 169.

18. *Ibid.*

19. C. D. Jebuni, J. Love, and D. J. C. Forsyth, "Market Structure and LDCs' Manufactured Export Performance," *World Development*, 16, no. 12 (1988): 1520; Peter A. Petri, "Korea's Export Niche: Origins and Prospects," *World Development*, 16, no. 1 (1988): 48.

20. Rundheersing Bheenick and Morton Owen Schapiro, "Mauritius: A Case Study of the Export Processing Zone," *Successful Development*, pp. 97–126.

21. *World Development Report 1989*, p. 56.

22. Alice H. Amsden, "Private Enterprise: The Issue of Business-Government Control," *Columbia Journal of World Business*, Spring 1988, pp. 37–42.

23. Stephen E. Guisinger and Associates, *Investment Incentives and Performance Requirements* (New York: Praeger Publishers, 1985), pp. 37–55; Stephen Guisinger, "Host-Country Policies to Attract and Control Foreign Investment," in Theodore H. Moran (ed.), *Investing in Development: New Roles for Private Capital?* (New Brunswick: TransAction Books, 1986), pp. 157–172.

24. This section is based on information from two Harvard Business School case studies—Lokhi Banerji, John Ince, and James E. Austin, "Industrialization Strategy in India," 378–130, 1977, and James E. Austin, "Cummins Engine in India," 379–072, 1978—and from Jack Baranson, *Manufacturing Problems in India: The Cummins Diesel Experience* (Syracuse, N.Y.: Syracuse University Press, 1967).

CHAPTER 5

Understanding Industry Structure and Competitive Dynamics

1. Michael E. Porter, *Competitive Strategy* (New York: Free Press, 1980), and *Competitive Advantage* (New York: Free Press, 1985).

2. *World Development Report 1989* (New York: Oxford University Press for the World Bank, 1989), pp. 55, 57.

3. Edward Felton, Jr., and Ralph Z. Sorenson, "Republic Flour Mills," Asian Institute of Management case, ICH 12M30, 1970.

4. Gordon R. Bond and Ray A. Goldberg, "John Deere de Mexico, S.A. de C.V.," Harvard Business School case, 9–313–239, 1968.

5. Melissa H. Birch, "Industrial Policy and the Brazilian Information-Processing Industry," Colgate Darden Graduate School of Business Administration, University of Virginia, UVA-G-283, 1985.

6. James E. Austin and John C. Ickis, "Managing After the Revolutionaries Have Won," *Harvard Business Review,* May–June 1986, p. 104.

7. James E. Austin, "State-Owned Enterprises: The Other Visible Hand," in Ray A. Goldberg (ed.), *Global Agribusiness Now and in the Year 2000* (Boston: Harvard Business School Press, forthcoming); John Waterbury, "The Political Context of Public Sector Reform and Privatization in Egypt, India, Mexico and Turkey," paper presented at the Institutional Perspectives on Third World Development Seminar Series, MIT Center for International Studies, November 30, 1988, mimeo, p. 28.

8. Malcolm Gillis, "The Role of State Enterprises in Economic Development," *Social Research,* 47 (Summer 1980): 253.

9. Ravi Ramamurti, *State-Owned Enterprises in High Technology Industries* (New York: Praeger, 1987), pp. 17–19.

10. For Brazil and India, Leroy P. Jones and Edward S. Mason, "Role of Economic Factors in Determining the Size and Structure of the Public-Enterprise Sector in Less-Developed Countries with Mixed Economies," in Leroy P. Jones (ed.), *Public Enterprise in Less-Developed Countries* (Cambridge: Cambridge University Press, 1982), p. 41; for Mexico, Gustavo Esteva, "La Economía Política de la Empresa Pública en México," mimeo, n.d., p. 1.

11. "World Business Directory: 1987 Rankings," *Fortune,* Special Issue, 1988.

12. Lucian Rapp, "Public Multinational Enterprises and Strategic Decision-Making," Multinational Enterprise Programme, ILO, Working Paper no. 34, 1986, p. 7.

13. Derived from records provided by the company.

14. Anthony Vanclyk, "Ethiopian Airlines Looks Closer to Home to Strengthen African Leadership Role," *Airline Executive,* April 1982, p. 13.

15. Jones and Mason, "Role of Economic Factors," p. 23; Elliot Berg, "Privatization: Developing a Pragmatic Approach," *Economic Impact,* 57, no. 1 (1987): 6–11.

16. Ramamurti, *State-Owned Enterprises,* p. 5.

17. Jones and Mason, "Role of Economic Factors," p. 22, 1972 data.

18. Brian Levy, "State Owned Enterprises in Developing Countries," *World Development,* 16, no. 10 (October 1988): 1202.

19. Jones and Mason, "Role of Economic Factors," p. 22.

20. John Nellis, "Performance of African Public Enterprises," in Gerald M. Meier and William F. Steel (eds.), *Industrial Adjustment in Sub-Saharan Africa* (New York: Oxford University Press, 1989), p. 219.

21. Austin, "State-Owned Enterprises" (note 7 above).

22. *World Development Report 1988* (see note 2 above), p. 168.

23. Alfred H. Saulniers, "State Trading Organizations: A Bias Decision Model and Application," Institute of Latin American Studies, Technical Papers Series, no. 28, University of Texas at Austin, 1980, p. 2.

24. For wheat, Alex F. McCalla and Andrew Schmitz, "State Trading in Grain," p. 55, and for minerals, Walter C. Labys, "The Role of State Trading in Mineral Commodity Markets," pp. 83, 89, 93, 98, both in M. M. Kostecki (ed.), *State Trading in International Markets: Theory and Practice of Industrialized and Developing Countries* (New York: St. Martin's Press, 1982).

25. *Accelerated Development in Sub-Saharan Africa: An Agenda for Action* (Washington, D.C.: World Bank, 1981), p. 40; Republic of Kenya Ministry of Economic Planning and Development, *Economic Survey, 1979* (Nairobi: Government Printer, 1979), p. 50; Horacio Boneo, "Political Regimes

and Public Enterprises,'' Second Boston Area Public Enterprise Group (BAPEG) Conference, April 1980, mimeo, p. 16.

26. Tony Killick and Simon Commander, "State Divestiture as a Policy Instrument in Developing Countries," *World Development*, 16, no. 12 (1988): 1466.

27. Waterbury, "The Political Context" (note 7 above), p. 7.

28. *Accelerated Development*, p. 40.

29. *World Development Report 1988*, p. 173.

30. "State in the Market," *Economist*, December 30, 1978, p. 41; Gillis, "The Role of State Enterprises" (note 8 above), p. 257 footnotes 13, 14.

31. *World Development Report 1988*, p. 170.

32. *World Development Report 1989*, p. 57.

33. Jones and Mason, "Role of Economic Factors" (note 10 above), p. 21.

34. Nicola Swainson, *The Development of Corporate Capitalism in Kenya, 1918–77* (London: Heinemann, 1980); Jacqueline Dutheil de la Rochere, *L'etat et le Developpement Economique de la Côte d'Ivoire* (Paris: Editions Pedone, 1977).

35. Boneo, "Political Regimes and Public Enterprises," p. 5.

36. Donald B. Keesing, "Manufacturing in East Africa," in Meier and Steel, *Industrial Adjustment* (note 20 above), p. 84.

37. Raymond Vernon, "Linking Managers with Ministers: Dilemmas of the State-Owned Enterprise," *Journal of Policy Analysis and Management*, 4, no. 1 (1984): 39–55.

38. Heba Ahmad Handoussa, "The Impact of Economic Liberalization on the Performance of Egypt's Public Sector Industry," Second BAPEG Conference, April 1980, mimeo, p. 3.

39. Waterbury, "The Political Context" (note 7 above), p. 7.

40. World Bank Staff, "Problems of Public Enterprises in Sierra Leone," in Meier and Steel, *Industrial Adjustment*, p. 225.

41. Herbert Morrison, *Socialisation and Transport* (London: Constable, 1933).

42. P. K. Basu, "Linkage Between Policy and Performance: Empirical and Theoretical Considerations on Public Enterprises in Mixed Economy LDCs," Second BAPEG Conference, April 1980, mimeo, p. 8.

43. Personal interview.

44. *World Development Report 1988*, p. 177.

45. James E. Austin and Michael Buckley, "Food Marketing Public Enterprises: Mexico Versus Venezuela," in K. L. K. Rao (ed.), *Marketing Perspectives of Public Enterprises in Developing Countries* (Ljubljana, Yugoslavia: International Center for Public Enterprises, 1986), pp. 166–93.

46. Austin, "State-Owned Enterprises" (note 7 above).

47. *The Economist*, December 26, 1987, p. 85.

48. Ravi Ramamurti and James E. Austin, "Empresa Brasileira de Aeronautica, S.A. (EMBRAER)," Harvard Business School case, 9–383–090, 1982.

49. Data provided by Fundación Economía y Desarrollo based on an analysis of the financial statements of the country's major SOEs.

50. Nellis, "Performance of African Public Enterprises" (note 20 above), pp. 219–20.

51. Elliot Berg and Mary M. Shirley, "Divestiture in Developing Countries," World Bank Discussion Papers, June 1987, pp. 21–22.

52. Charles Vuylsteke, "Techniques of Privatization of State-Owned Enterprises: Methods and Implementation," World Bank Technical Paper, no. 88, 1988; statistics in text derived from Table I, pp. 164–72.

53. James E. Austin, Lawrence H. Wortzel, and John F. Coburn, "Privatizing State-Owned Enterprises: Hopes and Realities," *Columbia Journal of World Business*, 21, no. 3 (Fall 1986): 51–60.

54. Berg and Shirley, "Divestiture," p. 6.

55. *World Development Report 1988*, p. 179.

56. Vuylsteke, "Techniques of Privatization," p. 146.

57. *World Development Report 1988*, p. 180.

58. Alexander C. Tomlinson and Ismael Benavides, "Evaluation of the Divestiture Program of Corporación Costarricense de Desarrollo, S.A. Costa Rica 1984–1988," Center for Privatization, Washington, D.C., Project no. 71, May 1988.

59. Berg and Shirley, "Divestiture," p. 23.

60. Vuylsteke, "Techniques of Privatization," pp. 38, 169–72.

61. Rebecca Candoy-Sekse with Anne Ruiz Palmer, "Techniques of Privatization of State-Owned Enterprises," vol. III, World Bank Technical Paper no. 90, May 1989.

62. "Nigeria to Sell 67 Firms," *Daily Nation* (Nairobi), July 16, 1988.

63. L. Gray Cowan, "A Global Overview of Privatization," in Steve H. Hanke (ed.), *Privatization and Development* (San Francisco: ICS Press, 1987), pp. 11, 12.

64. Waterbury, "The Political Context" (note 7 above), p. 28.

65. Matt Moffett, "Mexico Plans Aeromexico Sale for $350 Million," *Wall Street Journal*, October 26, 1988, p. A18.

66. Vuylsteke, "Techniques of Privatization," pp. 169–72.

67. This section draws on the technical note "Business Groups in Developing Countries," prepared by Richardo S. de León and Seok Ki Kim under the supervision of Professor James E. Austin, Harvard Business School, 386–111, 1986.

68. *Fortune*, August 19, 1985, pp. 183–85; Tamio Hattori, "The Relationship Between Zaibatsu and Family Structure: The Korean Case," in Akio Okochi and Shigeaki Yasuoka (eds.), *Family Business in the Era of Industrial Growth: Its Ownership and Management* (Tokyo: University of Tokyo Press, 1984), p. 121.

69. Andrew Tanzer, "Samsung: South Korea Marches to Its Own Drummer," *Forbes*, May 16, 1988, p. 84.

70. Harry W. Strachan, *Family and Other Business Groups in Economic Development: The Case of Nicaragua* (New York: Praeger, 1976), pp. 47–51.

71. Lawrence J. White, *Industrial Concentration and Economic Power in Pakistan* (Princeton, N.J.: Princeton University Press, 1974), p. 65.

72. G. L. Hicks and S. G. Redding, "Culture and Corporate Performance in the Philippines: The Chinese Puzzle," in *Essays in Development Economics in Honor of Harry T. Oshima* (Manila: Philippine Institute for Development Studies, 1982), p. 205.

73. At the two-digit SIC level; Seok Ki Kim, "Chaebol in Korean Environment: Samsung Group, Its Entrepreneurial History, Sources of Expansion, and Evolution of Structure and Scope," unpublished mimeo, 1984, p. 43.

74. Nathaniel H. Leff, "Industrial Organization and Entrepreneurship in the Developing Countries: The Economic Groups," *Economic Development and Cultural Change*, July 1978, p. 665.

75. Strachan, *Family and Other Business Groups*, p. 3.

76. Victor S. Limlingan, "The Overseas Chinese in ASEAN: Business Strategies and Management Practices," unpublished dissertation, Harvard University Graduate School of Business Administration, Boston, 1986, pp. 273–75, subsequently published in 1986 by Vita Development Corporation, Paisig, Metro Manila, Philippines.

77. Although the business-group phenomenon can be partially explained by the arguments posited in agency theory—John W. Pratt and Richard J. Zeckhauser (eds.), *Principals and Agents: The Structure of Business* (Harvard Business School Press, 1985)—and those in the transaction-cost approach—Oliver E. Williamson, "The Economics of Organization: The Transaction Cost Approach," *American Journal of Sociology*, 87, no. 3 (1981): 548–77—business groups appear to reflect also social factors that ensure stability of relationships over time and permit inter- and intra-organizational links not entirely captured in the mentioned theoretical constructs.

78. Kenneth Hoadley and James E. Austin, "Sabritas," Harvard Business School case, 381–096, 1981.

79. Richard Vietor, "Mexico: Crisis of Confidence," Harvard Business School case, 9–383–148, 1983, rev. 1986.

80. Louis T. Wells, Jr., *Third World Multinationals: The Rise of Foreign Investment from Developing Countries* (Cambridge: MIT Press, 1983), pp. 2, 10; Khushi M. Khan, "Multinationals from the South," in Khan (ed.), *Multinationals of the South* (New York: St. Martin's Press, 1986), pp. 1–14; Krishna Kumar and Maxwell G. McLeod (eds.), *Multinationals from Developing Countries* (Lexington, Mass.: Lexington Books, 1981).

81. Wells, *Third World Multinationals*, p. 5.

82. Edward K. Y. Chen, "Hong Kong," *World Development*, 12, no. 5/6 (1984): 482–83.

83. *The Economist*, December 26, 1987, p. 85.

84. Wells, *Third World Multinationals*, pp. 33–34.

85. *Ibid.*, pp. 51, 63.

86. Jules Arbose and Don Shapiro, "Tatung Rides Out Recession with Confucian Calm," *International Management*, January 1983, pp. 22–27.

87. Dong Sung Cho, "Anatomy of Korea's General Trading Company," Harvard Business School Working Paper, 784–055, January 1984.

88. *Datos Básicos del Sector Cooperativo Costarricense* (San José, Costa Rica: Instituto Nacional de Fomento Cooperativo, 1986).

89. S. Uddin and M. Rahman, *The Cooperative Sector of India after Independence* (New Delhi: S. Chand & Co., 1978).

90. Chip Hance and Ray A. Goldberg, "American Rice: A Farmers Cooperative Goes Public," Harvard Business School case, 589–044, 1988, p. 2.

91. D. M. Attwood and B. S. Baviskar, "Why Do Some Co-operatives Work but Not Others?" *Economic and Political Weekly*, 22, no. 26 (June 27, 1987): pp. A-40.

92. Donald Atwood, "Does Competition Help Cooperation?" paper presented at the International Perspectives on Third World Development Seminar Series, MIT Center for International Studies, November 2, 1988, mimeo.

93. S. V. Sethuraman (ed.), *The Urban Informal Sector in Developing Countries: Employment, Poverty, and Environment* (Geneva: International Labour Office, 1981), p. 8; Omotunde E. G. Johnson, "Labor Markets, External Developments, and Unemployment in Developing Countries," *Staff Studies for the World Economic Outlook*, Washington, D.C.: IMF, July 1986, p. 52.

94. Data from the Instituto Nacional de Estadísticas, Lima, Peru, cited in the Harvard Business School case study "The Informal Sector in Peru," prepared by Tomás Urreiztieta and James Garrett under the supervision of James E. Austin, Harvard Business School case, 386–022, 1985; Hernando de Soto, *El Otro Sendero: La Revolución Informal* (Bogotá, Colombia: Editorial Oveja Negra, 1987), published in English as *The Other Path* (New York: Harper & Row, 1989).

95. For an extensive analysis of Peru's informal sector, see de Soto, *El Otro Sendero*.

96. A. N. Bose, *Calcutta and Rural Bengal: Small Sector Symbiosis* (Calcutta: International Labour Organization, 1978), p. 96; William J. House, "Nairobi's Informal Sector: A Reservoir of Dynamic Enterpreneurs or a Residual Pool of Surplus Labour?" Working Paper No. 347, Institute of Development Studies (Nairobi, Kenya: University of Nairobi, 1979), pp. 7–8; William F. Steel, *Small-Scale Employment and Production in Developing Countries: Evidence from Ghana* (New York: Praeger, 1977), Chapter 4.

97. Victor E. Tokman, "An Exploration into the Nature of Informal-Formal Sector Relationships," *World Development*, 6 (September–October 1978): 1065–75.

98. Chris Gerry, "Petty Production and Capitalistic Production in Dakar: The Crisis of the Self-Employed," *World Development*, 6 (September–October 1978): 1147–60; Ray Bromley, "The Urban Informal Sector: Critical Perspectives," *World Development*, 6, (September–October 1978): 1033–40.

99. Direct interview.

100. Robert N. Gwynne, *Industrialization and Urbanization in Latin America* (Baltimore: Johns Hopkins University Press, 1986), pp. 160–161.

101. Philip A. Wellons, *Passing the Buck: Banks, Governments, and Third World Debt* (Boston: Harvard Business School Press, 1987), Chapter 1.

102. Kiyoshi Kojima and Terutomo Ozawa, *Japan's General Trading Companies: Merchants of Economic Development* (Paris: OECD, 1984).

103. Michael E. Porter (ed.), *Competition in Global Industries* (Boston: Harvard Business School Press, 1986).

104. Allen Sangines-Krause, James E. Austin, and Dennis J. Encarnation, "Mexico and the Microcomputers" (A), (B), (C), Harvard Business School cases, 2–386–182–84, 1986.

CHAPTER 6

Business–Government Relations: Managing the Mega-Force

1. Keith Marsden and Therese Belot, "Impact of Regulations and Taxation on Private Industry," in Gerald M. Meier and William F. Steel (eds.), *Industrial Adjustment in Sub-Saharan Africa* (New York: Oxford University Press, 1989), pp. 163–68; Jurgen Riedel, "Attitudes in the Federal Republic of Germany to the Policies of Developing Countries Regarding Foreign Investors," *Industry and Development*, 13 (1984): 1–38.

2. In the study of applied political economy, political scientists have elaborated various sets of analytical questions; of particular utility are Harold Lasswell,

Politics: Who Gets What, When, and How (New York: Meridian Books, 1958); Warren Ilchman and Norman Thomas Uphoff, *The Political Economy of Change* (Berkeley: University of California Press, 1969); and Marc Lindenberg and Benjamin Crosby, *Managing Development: The Political Dimension* (West Hartford, Conn.: Kumarian Press, 1981).

3. Lindenberg and Crosby, *Managing Development,* carefully elaborate and illustrate mapping methodology with particular emphasis on the perspectives of public-sector and nonbusiness actors; my application of mapping techniques to private business managers has benefited from these authors' approach and from Marc Lindenberg's insightful suggestions.

4. Encarnation and Wells indicate a trend toward more centralized handling of foreign investment decisions by governments. Dennis J. Encarnation and Louis T. Wells, Jr., "Sovereignty en Garde: Negotiating with Foreign Investors," *International Organization,* 39, no. 1 (Winter 1985): 47–78; idem, "Competitive Strategies in Global Industries: A View from Host Governments," in Michael E. Porter (ed.), *Competition in Global Industries* (Boston: Harvard Business School Press, 1986), pp. 267–90.

5. Steven W. Langdon, "Export-Oriented Industrialization Through the Multinational Corporation: Evidence from Kenya," in Ahamed Idris-Soven, Elizabeth Idris-Soven, and Mary K. Vaughan (eds.), *The World as a Company Town: Multinational Corporations and Social Change* (The Hague: Moulton Publishers, 1978), p. 304.

6. William H. Davidson, "Creating and Managing Joint Ventures in China," *California Management Review,* 24, no. 4 (1987): 79.

7. Lindenberg and Crosby, *Managing Development,* p. 47.

8. Encarnation and Wells, "Sovereignty en Garde," p. 47.

9. Personal interview.

10. Thomas L. Brewer, Kenneth David, and Linda Y. C. Lim, with Robert S. Corredera, *Investing in Developing Countries: A Guide for Executives* (Lexington, Mass.: Lexington Books, 1986), p. 97.

11. Louis Kraar, "How to Sell to Cashless Buyers," *Fortune,* November 7, 1988, p. 154.

12. Amir Mahini and Louis T. Wells, Jr., "Government Relations in the Global Firm," in Michael E. Porter (ed.), *Competition in Global Industries* (Boston: Harvard Business School Press, 1986), p. 306.

13. George Botchie, "Employment and Multinational Enterprises in Export Processing Zones: The Cases of Liberia and Ghana," International Labour Office Working Paper no. 30, 1984, p. 24.

14. Langdon, "Export-Oriented Industrialization," p. 306.

15. Carl G. Thunman, *Technology Licensing to Distant Markets: Interaction Between Swedish and Indian Firms* (Stockholm: Almqvist & Wiksell International, 1988), p. 97.

16. This section is derived mainly from Lokhi Banerji and James Austin, "Economic Cost-Benefit Analysis," *Harvard Business School* technical note, 9–379–073, 1978. Space limitations force us to simplify and abbreviate our treatment of this methodology. For a more detailed elaboration of the underlying methodology, see Michael Roemer and Joseph J. Stern, *The Appraisal of Development Projects: A Practical Guide to Project Analysis with Case Studies and Solutions* (New York: Praeger, 1975); I. M. D. Little and James A. Mirrlees, *Project Appraisal and Planning for Developing Countries* (New York: Basic Books, 1974), and Louis T. Wells, Jr., "Social Cost/Benefit Analysis for MNCs," *Harvard Business Review*, March–April 1975, reprint no. 75211.

17. Dennis J. Encarnation and Louis T. Wells, Jr., "Evaluating Foreign Investment," in Theodore H. Moran (ed.), *Investing in Development: New Roles for Private Capital?* (New Brunswick, N.J.: TransAction Books, 1985), pp. 61–86.

18. The economic cost of these nontradables should be the marginal cost of providing the increment required by the project. These would exclude overhead costs that would have been incurred regardless of the project, even though the private market price includes an overhead charge.

19. If foreign capital would not otherwise be available were the particular project under consideration not implemented, these resources have no opportunity cost for the country, and therefore the investment generated by these funds would not be entered as investment costs in plant and equipment. Profit and debt repayments, however, would still enter as costs.

20. Dennis Encarnation provided useful suggestions in the initial conceptualization of these figures.

21. For an analysis of bargaining from a managerial perspective, see David A. Lax and James K. Sebenius, *The Manager As Negotiator: Bargaining for Cooperation and Competitive Gain* (New York: Free Press, 1986). For analyses of business–government bargaining issues involving multinationals see the following: Raymond A. Vernon, *Storm over the Multinationals: The Real Issues* (Cambridge: Harvard University Press, 1977); *idem,* "Sovereignty at Bay: Ten Years After," *International Organization,* 35, no. 3 (Summer 1981): 517–29; David N. Smith and Louis T. Wells, Jr., *Negotiating Third-World Mineral Agreements: Promises as Prologue* (Cambridge: Ballinger Publishing Company, 1975); Nathan Fagre and Louis T. Wells, Jr., "Bargaining Power of Multinationals and Host Governments," *Journal of International Business Studies,* Fall 1982, pp. 9–23; Donald J. Lecraw, "Bargaining Power, Ownership, and Profitability of Transnational Corporations in Developing Countries," *Journal of International Business Studies,* Spring/Summer 1984, pp. 27–43; Thomas N. Gladwin and Ingo Walter, *Multinationals Under Fire: Lessons in the Management of Conflict* (New York: John Wiley & Sons, 1980); Yves L. Doz and C. K. Prahalad,

"How MNCs Cope with Host Government Intervention," *Harvard Business Review*, March–April 1980, pp. 149–57; Louis T. Wells, Jr., "Negotiating with Third World Governments," *Harvard Business Review*, January–February 1977, pp. 72–80.

22. Vernon, "Sovereignty at Bay"; Vernon, *Storm over Multinationals; Ray-mond A. Vernon, "The Obsolescing Bargain: A Key Factor in Political Risk," in Mark B. Winchester (ed.), *The International Essays for Business Decision Makers*, vol. 5 (Houston: Center for International Business, 1980).

23. C. Fred Bergsten, Thomas Horst, and Theodore H. Moran, *American Multi-nationals and American Interests* (Washington, D.C.: Brookings Institution, 1978).

24. These conclusions are based on Stephen Kobrin's analysis of 563 manufactur-ing subsidiaries operating in forty-nine developing countries: "Testing the Bargaining Hypothesis in the Manufacturing Sector in Developing Coun-tries," *International Organization*, 41, no. 4 (Autumn, 1987): 609–38.

25. Lax and Sebenius, *Manager as Negotiator*.

26. *Ibid.*

27. G. R. Kulkarni, "Kirloskar Cummins Limited," Indian Institute of Manage-ment, Ahmedabad, 1973.

28. Dennis J. Encarnation and Sushil Vachani, "Foreign Ownership: When Hosts Change the Rules," *Harvard Business Review*, September–October, 1985, p. 158.

29. Louis Kraar, "How to Sell to Cashless Buyers," *Fortune*, Nov. 7, 1988, p. 147.

30. Alan Sangines-Krause, James E. Austin, and Dennis J. Encarnation, "Micro-computers in Mexico (A), (B), (C)," Harvard Business School cases, 386-182–84, 1986.

31. Kulkarni, "Kirloskar Cummins Limited."

32. For a multicountry study on such alternative forms, see Charles Oman (ed.), *New Forms of International Investment in Developing Countries* (Paris: OECD, 1984).

33. Kraar, "How to Sell," p. 147.

34. Encarnation and Vachani, "Foreign Ownership," pp. 153–54.

35. Brewer *et al.*, *Investing in Developing Countries* (note 10 above), p. 226.

36. Ibrahim F. I. Shihata, "Increasing Private Capital Flows to LDCs," *Finance & Development*, December 1984, p. 8.

37. Ibrahim F. I. Shihata, "Encouraging International Corporate Investment: The Role of the Multilateral Investment Guarantee Agency," *Columbia Journal of World Business*, Spring 1988, pp. 11–18.

38. James E. Austin and John C. Ickis, "Managing After the Revolutionaries Have Won," *Harvard Business Review*, May–June 1986, pp. 103–9.

39. Langdon, "Export Oriented Industrialization" (note 5 above), p. 305.

40. José de la Torre, "Foreign Investment and Economic Development: Conflict and Negotiation," *Journal of International Business Studies*, Fall 1981, pp. 9–32.

41. For reviews of various political analysis methodologies, see Stephen J. Kobrin, "Political Assessment by International Firms: Models or Methodologies?" *Journal of Policy Modeling*, 3 (1981): 251–70; Jerry Rogers (ed.), *Global Risk Assessments: Issues, Concepts and Applications*, Books 1 and 2 (Riverside, Calif.: Global Risk Assessments, Inc., 1986); also vol. 3, 1988; Thomas L. Brewer (ed.), *Political Risks In International Business* (New York: Praeger, 1985); Thomas L. Brewer, "Country Creditworthiness and Country Instability in International Banking," Georgetown University School of Business Administration, Working Paper no. 88–66, 1988.

42. Amir Mahini and Louis T. Wells, Jr., "Government Relations in the Global Firm," in Porter (ed.), *Competition in Global Industries* (note 12 above), pp. 291–312.

43. Salim Rashid, "Public Utilities in Egalitarian LDC's: The Role of Bribery in Achieving Pareto Efficiency," *Kyklos*, 34, Fasc 3 (1981): 448–60. See also N. Vijay Jagannathan, "Corruption, Delivery Systems, and Property Rights," *World Development*, 14, no. 1 (1986): 127–32.

44. Personal interview.

45. Hurd Baruch, "The Foreign Corrupt Practices Act," *Harvard Business Review*, January–February 1979, reprint no. 79101.

46. Kate Gillespie, "Middle East Response to the U.S. Foreign Corrupt Practices Act," *California Management Review*, 29, no. 4 (Summer 1987): 11.

47. Suk H. Kim, "On Repealing the Foreign Corrupt Practices Act: Survey and Assessment," *Columbia Journal of World Business*, 16, no. 3 (Fall 1981): 17; U.S. General Accounting Office, *Impact of Foreign Corrupt Practices Act on U.S. Business*, March 4, 1981, p. 14.

48. Chung In Moon, "Korean Contractors in Saudi Arabia: Their Rise and Fall," *Middle East Journal*, 40, no. 4 (Autumn 1986): 621.

49. John L. Graham, "Foreign Corrupt Practices: A Manager's Guide," *Columbia Journal of World Business*, 18, no. 3 (Fall 1983): 89–94; Barry Richman, "Can We Prevent Questionable Foreign Payments?" *Business Horizons*, June 1979, pp. 14–19; Manuel A. Tipgos, "Compliance with the Foreign Corrupt Practices Act," *Financial Executive*, 49, no. 8 (August 1981): 38–48.

50. John B. Matthews and Kenneth E. Goodpaster, "Can a Corporation Have a Conscience?" *Harvard Business Review*, January–February 1982, pp. 132–141.

51. Kenneth E. Goodpaster, "The Challenge of Sustaining Corporate Conscience," *The Notre Dame Journal of Law, Ethics & Public Policy*, 2 (1987): 825–48.

52. From a company document titled "The Beliefs of Borg-Warner: To Reach Beyond the Minimal," reprinted in John B. Matthews, Kenneth E. Goodpaster, and Laura L. Nash, *Policies and Persons: A Casebook in Business Ethics* (New York: McGraw-Hill, 1985), p. 150.

53. For an elaboration of various concepts or ethical relativism, see John B. Matthews and Kenneth E. Goodpaster, "Relativism in Ethics," Harvard Business School technical note, 381-097, 1981.

54. David E. Whiteside and Kenneth E. Goodpaster, "Dow Corning Corporation: Business Conduct and Global Values," Harvard Business School, 385-018, 1984.

CHAPTER 7

Finance: Coping with Inflation, Foreign-Exchange Exposure, and Capital Scarcity

1. Francisco Roman provided important research assistance on this section.

2. Carlos Sequeira, "Electrohogar," IPADE case, 1985.

3. Cesar G. Saldaña, *Financial Management in the Philippine Setting* (Quezon City: AFA Publications, 1985), p. 17.

4. *World Development Report 1989* (New York: Oxford University Press for the World Bank, 1989), p. 63.

5. Personal interview.

6. James F. Smith, "Hyper-inflation Wreaks Havoc," *Boston Globe*, November 20, 1988, p. A10.

7. Alan Roe and Paul A. Popiel, "Managing Financial Adjustment in Middle-Income Countries," Economic Development Institute of the World Bank, Policy Seminar Report, no. 11, 1988, p. 15.

8. John H. Young, "Industrias Gessy-Lever Limitada," Harvard Business School case, 9–385–295, 1985.

9. Julia Michaels and Roger Cohen, "Foreigners Boost Investments in Brazil Despite Its Daunting Economic Problems," *Wall Street Journal*, October 26, 1988, p. A18.

10. Daniel Drosdoff, "Silent Killer Threatens Democracies," *Boston Globe*, October 2, 1988, p. A8.

11. Noel Ramírez, *El Empresario y Su Entorno Económico* (San José, Costa Rica: EDUCA, 1987), pp. 83–84.

12. Drosdoff, "Silent Killer," p. A9.

13. Personal interview.

14. One study documented that, in accordance with Financial Accounting Standard no. 33, about 1,500 large companies presented as supplementary information selected constant and current cost data in the back of their annual

reports, where it was often ignored. Alan H. Seed III, "Inflation Accounting: How It Aids the Financial Executive," *Financial Executive*, December 1982, p. 15. The complexities of financial accounting under inflationary conditions have sparked considerable controversy within the accounting profession. See David I. Fisher (ed.), *Managing in Inflation* (New York: Conference Board, 1978); Geoffrey Whittington, *Inflation Accounting: An Introduction to the Debate* (Cambridge: Cambridge University Press, 1983); Elwood L. Miller, "What's Wrong with Price-Level Accounting," *Harvard Business Review*, November–December 1978, pp. 113–15.

15. Appreciation is expressed to Deloitte, Haskins & Sells—Argentina for providing the relevant technical documentation on inflation accounting.

16. Personal interview.

17. Keith Marsden and Therese Belot, "Impact of Regulations and Taxation on Private Industry," in Gerald M. Meier and William F. Steel (eds.), *Industrial Development in Sub-Saharan Africa* (New York: Oxford University Press, 1989), p. 167.

18. Willis Emmons provided valuable assistance in the initial research and drafting of the following sections on foreign-exchange management.

19. John C. Whitney, "Cummins Engine Company, Inc.: Black Friday," Harvard Business School case, 9–586–122, 1986.

20. In this context, the relevant measure of inflation is the weighted-average inflation rate of goods and services *traded externally*, as opposed to increases in the country's consumer price index, GNP deflator, etc.

21. Stephen D. Younger, "Ghana: Economic Recovery Program—A Case Study of Stabilization and Structural Adjustment in Sub-Saharan Africa," EDI Development Policy Case Series, no. 1 (Washington, D.C.: World Bank, 1989), pp. 131–32.

22. *Ibid.*, pp. 140, 145–46.

23. For a detailed examination of foreign-exchange management, see Chapters 5–7 of David K. Eiteman and Arthur I. Stonehill, *Multinational Business Finance*, 4th ed. (Reading, Mass.: Addison-Wesley, 1986).

24. *Financing and External Debt of Developing Countries: 1985 Survey* (Paris: OECD, 1986), p. 54.

25. Joseph C. Wheeler, *Development Cooperation* (Paris: OECD, 1987), p. 46.

26. *Financing and External Debt of Developing Countries: 1987 Survey* (Paris: OECD, 1987), pp. 22–23.

27. Mohsin S. Khan and Nadeem Ul Haque, "Capital Flight from Developing Countries," *Finance & Development*, March 1987, p. 4.

28. Lenny Glynn and Peter Koenig, "The Capital Flight Crisis," *Institutional Investor*, 18, no. 11 (November 1984): 304.

29. Michael Deppler and Martin Williamson, "Capital Flight: Concepts, Measurements, and Issues," *Staff Studies for the World Economic Outlook* (Washington, D.C.: IMF, August 1987), pp. 39–58.

30. Michele Fratianni, "Encouraging Capital Flows to Developing Countries," *Business Horizons*, 30, no. 4 (July–August 1987): 48.

31. Khan and Ul Haque, "Capital Flight from Developing Countries," p. 4.

32. Gary Hector, "Nervous Money Keeps on Fleeing," *Fortune*, 112, no. 14 (December 23, 1985): 104.

33. David M. Meerschwam, "Optimal Trade Contracts Under Exchange Rate Flexibility," Harvard Business School Working Paper, 9–786–015, 1985.

34. Currency options are another hedging technique. The option contract gives the holder the right (but not the obligation unless under forward contracts) to buy or sell a set amount of a certain currency at a specific exchange rate before the maturity date. However, such options are also largely unavailable for most LDC currencies.

35. Information supplied by Citibank.

36. Tomás Kohn and Christopher Bartlett, "Compañía Telefónica Mexicana (CTM) ATI in Mexico," Harvard Business School case, 9–387–115, rev. July 87, 1987, p. 13.

37. *Ibid.*, p. 7.

38. In this section, the term "liabilities" refers to all items on the right-hand side of the balance sheet except for equity accounts.

39. Note that any assets or liabilities denominated in the parent company's currency are not considered to be exposed. An example of this would be loans from the parent company or from banks located in the parent country.

40. Donald R. Lessard, "Finance and Global Competition: Exploiting Financial Scope and Coping with Volatile Exchange Rates," in Michael E. Porter (ed.), *Competition in Global Industries* (Boston: Harvard Business School Press, 1986), pp. 147–84.

41. M. Therese Flaherty, "Coordinating International Manufacturing and Technology," in Porter, *Competition in Global Industries*, pp. 83–109.

42. Marquise R. Cvar, "Case Studies in Global Competition: Patterns of Success and Failure," in Porter, *Competition in Global Industries*, p. 489.

43. *World Development Report 1989* (note 4 above), p. 64.

44. Ramírez, *El Empresario y Su Entorno Económico* (note 11 above), p. 66.

45. For an extensive treatment of the relationships between the capital flight and international debt problems see Donald R. Lessard and John Williamson (eds.), *Capital Flight and Third World Debt* (Washington, D.C.: Institute for International Economics, 1987); John Williamson and Donald R. Lessard, *Capital Flight: The Problem and Policy Responses* (Washington, D.C.:

Institute for International Economics, November 1987), p. 16; Michael Deppler and Martin Williamson, "Capital Flight: Concepts, Measurement, and Issues," *Staff Studies for the World Economic Outlook*, IMF, August 1987, pp. 39–58.

46. *World Development Report 1989*, p. 39.

47. Personal communication.

48. David Gill and Peter Tropper, "Emerging Stock Markets in Developing Countries," *Finance & Development*, December 1988, p. 29.

49. Deltec Research Project, "New Strategies for Multinational Enterprise in the Third World: Deltec in Brazil and Argentina," in Ahamed Idris-Soven, Elizabeth Idris-Soven, and Mary K. Vaughan (eds.), *The World as a Company Town: Multinational Corporations and Social Change* (The Hague: Moulton, 1978), p. 234.

50. *Ibid.*, p. 235.

51. Roger Y. W. Tang and Esther Tse, "Accounting Technology Transfer to Less Developed Countries and the Singapore Experience," *Columbia Journal of World Business*, Summer 1986, pp. 85–95.

52. Edwin A. Winckler, "Statism and Familism on Taiwan," in George C. Lodge and Ezra F. Vogel (eds.), *Ideology and National Competitiveness* (Boston: Harvard Business School Press, 1987), p. 198.

53. *World Development Report 1989*, p. 106.

54. *Ibid.*, p. 118.

55. Alan Roe and Paul A. Popiel, "Managing Financial Adjustment in Middle-Income Countries," Economic Development Institute of the World Bank, Policy Seminar Report, no. 11, 1988, pp. 15–26.

56. Morris I. Blejer and Silvia B. Sagari, "Sequencing the Liberalization of Financial Markets," *Finance & Development*, March 1988, p. 20.

57. Anand G. Chandavarkar, "The Financial Pull of Urban Areas in LDCs," *Finance & Development*, June 1985, pp. 24–27.

58. Roe and Popiel, "Managing Financial Adjustment," p. 21.

59. *Financing and External Debt* (note 24 above), pp. 52, 62–63.

60. David R. Bock, "The Bank's Role in Resolving the Debt Crisis," *Finance & Development*, 25, no. 2 (June 1988): 7.

61. "Another Bank Boosts Reserves to Cover Loans," *Globe and Mail* (Toronto), January 13, 1988; "Japanese Buy Stake in N.Y. Bank," *Boston Globe*, September 19, 1989, p. 41.

62. William R. Cline, "International Debt: Progress and Strategy," *Finance & Development*, 29, no. 2 (June 1988): 10.

63. Jerry Haar and William Renforth, "Reaction to Economic Crisis: Trade and Finance of U.S. Firms Operating in Latin America," *Columbia Journal of World Business*, Fall 1986, pp. 11–18.

64. G. R. Kulkarni, "Kirkoskar Cummins Limited," Indian Institute of Management case, Ahmedabad, 1973.

65. Dennis J. Encarnation and Sushil Vachani, "Foreign Ownership: When Hosts Change the Rules," *Harvard Business Review*, September–October 1985, pp. 153–54.

66. "Demand for KCB Shares Exceeds Offer Three-fold," *Daily Nation* (Nairobi), July 27, 1988.

67. Kiyoshi Kojima and Terutomo Ozawa, *Japan's General Trading Companies: Merchants of Economic Development* (Paris: OECD, 1984), pp. 49–50.

68. "Japan Unveils $2 Billion Asean Aid Package," *Financial Times*, December 16, 1987, p. 1.

69. Mary Shirley, "Promoting the Private Sector," *Finance & Development*, March 1988, p. 41

70. Klaus P. Regling, "New Financing Approaches in the Debt Strategy," *Finance & Development*, March 1988, pp. 7–8.

71. Ibrahim F. I. Shihata and Naiem A. Sherbiny, "A Review of OPEC Aid Efforts," *Finance & Development*, March 1986, p. 19.

72. "How to Work with IFC," IFC, undated.

73. Guy C. Antoine, "IFC's Initiatives in Sub-Saharan Africa," *Finance & Development*, December 1988, p. 37; Peter C. Jones, "Corporate Debt Restructuring in LDCs," *Finance & Development*, December 1988, p. 36.

74. "IFC: A Guide to Investing in the Developing World," IFC, undated.

75. Joseph Ganitsky and Gerardo Lema, "Foreign Investment through Debt-Equity Swaps," *Sloan Management Review*, 29, no. 2 (Winter 1988): 22.

76. Regling, "New Financing Approaches," p. 8.

77. Leroy O. Laney, "The Secondary Market in Developing Country Debt: Some Observations and Policy Implications," *Economic Review* (Federal Reserve Bank of Dallas), July 1987, p. 9.

78. Edwin A. Finn, Jr., "There Goes the Neighborhood," *Forbes*, June 29, 1987, p. 36; John Liscio, "Truth in Lending or What Has Citicorp Wrought?" *Barron's*, May 25, 1987, p. 11.

79. Rosemary Werrett, "Guide to Debt-Equity Swapping in Key Latin American Countries," a special report published by Latin American Information Services, Inc., 1987, p. 20.

80. Finn, "There Goes the Neighborhood," p. 37.

81. *Ibid.*, p. 35.

82. Andrew Marton, "The Debate over Debt-for-Equity Swaps," *Institutional Investor*, 21, no. 2 (February 1987): 178.

83. Brian Hannon and Scott Gould, "Debt/Equity Swaps Help Latin America out of Its Debt Dilemma," *Business America*, January 19, 1987, p. 5.

84. Marton, "Debate," p. 180.

85. Werrett, "Guide to Debt-Equity Swapping," p. 31.

86. Lyal Houghton, "Getting to Grips with Debt-Equity Swaps," *Euromoney,* March 1987, p. 152.

87. *Debt-Equity Swaps* (New York: Business International Corporation, 1987), p. 91.

88. Werrett, "Guide to Debt-Equity Swapping," pp. 36–44.

89. Marton, "Debate," p. 180; Finn, "There Goes the Neighborhood," p. 37.

90. Michael Blackwell and Simon Nocera, "The Impact of Debt to Equity Conversion," *Finance & Development,* June 1988, pp. 15–17.

91. Werrett, "Guide to Debt-Equity Swaps," p. 54.

92. Joel Bergsman and Wayne Edisis, "Debt-Equity Swaps and Foreign Direct Investment in Latin America," International Finance Corporation Discussion Paper no. 2, 1988, pp. 7–8.

93. Marton, "Debate," p. 180.

94. "Banks Are Offered Way to Write Off Third World Loans," *Wall Street Journal,* November 19, 1987, p. 44.

95. *World Development Report 1989* (note 4 above), p. 83.

CHAPTER 8

Production: Managing Technology

1. Christian Moran, "A Structural Model for Developing Countries' Manufactured Exports," *The World Bank Economic Review,* 2, no. 3 (September 1988): 322.

2. Roger Holmberg, "For National Semiconductor, Offshore Is on Target," *Chilton's Distribution,* October 1982, p. 55.

3. Joseph Grunwald and Kenneth Flamm, *The Global Factory: Foreign Assembly in International Trade* (Washington, D.C.: Brookings Institution, 1985), p. 4.

4. Michael Hergert and Robin Hergert, "NEC Corporation's Entry into European Microcomputers," *Journal of Management Case Studies,* 3, no. 2 (1987): 125.

5. Bob Vinton, "U.S. Firms Increasing Offshore Production," *Electronic News,* May 2, 1983, Supplement, "Relays," p. 12.

6. John M. Granger, "VDTs: Doing More for Less," *Computerworld,* January 19, 1987, p. S1.

7. Daniel T. Jones and James P. Womack, "Developing Countries and the Future of the Automobile Industry," *World Development,* 13, no. 3 (1985): 405.

8. Douglas A. Fraser and B. J. Widick, "The Challenges of Competitiveness: A Labor View," in Martin K. Star (ed.), *Global Competitiveness* (New York: W. W. Norton, 1988), p. 181.

9. Coopers & Lybrand, "Manufacturing Help South of the Border," *Executive Briefing*, May 1988, pp. 6–10.

10. "A.T.&T. to Build Plant in Thailand," *New York Times*, June 24, 1988, p. D4.

11. Constantinos C. Markides and Norman Berg, "Manufacturing Offshore Is Bad Business," *Harvard Business Review*, 88, no. 5 (September–October 1988): 115.

12. Grunwald and Flamm, *Global Factory*, p. 13.

13. *Ibid.*, derived from Table 2–3, p. 17.

14. Robert Batt, "Analyst Urges U.S. Firms to Produce Offshore," *Computerworld*, August 22, 1983, p. 74.

15. Minoru Inaba, "Offshore Manufacturing Pays Off for Minebea," *American Metal Market*, November 17, 1986, p. 30.

16. Grunwald and Flamm, *Global Factory*, p. 5.

17. Lawrence H. Wortzel and Heidi Vernon Wortzel, "Export Marketing Strategies for NIC and LDC-Based Firms," *Columbia Journal of World Business*, 16, no. 1 (Spring 1981): 51.

18. M. Therese Flaherty, "International Sourcing: Beyond Catalog Shopping and Franchising," in K. Ferdows (ed.), *Managing International Manufacturing* (Amsterdam: North Holland–Elsevier Science Publishers B.V., 1989), pp. 95–124.

19. Joel Kotkin, "The Case for Manufacturing in America," *Inc.*, March 1985, p. 60.

20. Frances Stewart, "International Technology Transfer: Issues and Policy Options," Staff Working Paper no. 344, World Bank, 1979.

21. William H. Davidson, "Trends in the International Transfer of U.S. Technology to Pacific Basin Nations," *Proceedings of the Academy of International Business: Asia-Pacific Dimensions of International Business*, December 18–20, 1979, p. 92.

22. *Ibid.*

23. Alice H. Amsden and Linsu Kim, "The Role of Transnational Corporations in the Production and Exports of the Korean Automobile Industry," Harvard Business School Working Paper, 9–785–063, June 1985, p. 7.

24. Stewart, "International Technology Transfer," p. 59.

25. *Ibid.*, p. 9.

26. Sven Olaf Hegstad and Ian Newport, "Management Contracts; Main Features and Design Issues," World Bank Technical Paper, no. 65, 1987.

27. This depiction draws upon the work of Carl S. Dahlman and Mariluz Cortés, "Mexico," *World Development*, 12, no. 5/6 (1984): 601–24.

28. For a conceptual discussion of labor and capital intensity, see A. S. Bhalla, "The Concept and Measurement of Labour Intensity," in A. S. Bhalla (ed.), *Technology and Employment in Industry: A Case Study Approach*, 3rd ed. (Geneva: ILO, 1985), pp. 17–39.

29. Coopers & Lybrand, "Manufacturing Help" (note 9 above), p. 10.

30. Thomas L. Brewer, Kenneth David, and Linda Y. C. Lim, with Robert S. Corredera, *Investing in Developing Countries: A Guide for Executives* (Lexington, Mass.: Lexington Books, 1986), p. 177.

31. Jean-Robert Estime, "International Subcontracting: The Case of Haiti," in Dimitri Germidis (ed.), *International Subcontracting: A New Form of Investment* (Paris: OECD, 1980), p. 104.

32. Kurt Hoffman, "Clothing, Chips and Competitive Advantage: The Impact of Microelectronics on Trade and Production in the Garment Industry," *World Development*, 13, no. 3 (March 1985): 373.

33. Bela Balassa, "The Interaction of Factor and Product Market Distortions in Developing Countries," *World Development*, 16, no. 4 (April 1988): 449–63; Anne O. Krueger, *Trade and Employment in Developing Countries 3: Synthesis and Conclusions* (Chicago: University of Chicago Press, 1983).

34. Nicolas Jequier, *Technology Choice and Employment Generation by Multinational Enterprises in Developing Countries* (Geneva: International Labour Office, 1984), p. 23.

35. Chee Peng Lim, "Manufacture of Leather Shoes and Bricks in Malaysia," in Bhalla, *Technology and Employment*, pp. 251–92.

36. Hal Hill, "Choice of Technique in the Indonesian Weaving Industry," *Economic Development and Cultural Change*, 31, no. 2 (January 1983): 339–53.

37. James Keddie, "More on Production Techniques in Indonesia," in Robert Stobaugh and Louis T. Wells, Jr. (eds.), *Technology Crossing Borders: The Choice, Transfer, and Management of International Technology Flows* (Boston: Harvard Business School Press, 1984), p. 74.

38. Donald J. Lecraw, "Choice of Technology in Thailand," in Stobaugh and Wells, *Technology Crossing Borders*, Chapter 5.

39. Wayne A. Yeoman, "Selection of Production Processes by U.S.-Based Multinational Enterprises," in Stobaugh and Wells, *Technology Crossing Borders*, p. 30.

40. Personal interview.

41. Michel Amsalem, "Technology Choice for Textiles and Paper Manufacture," in Stobaugh and Wells, *Technology Crossing Borders*, pp. 118, 120.

42. Samuel A. Morley and Gordon W. Smith, "Adaptation by Foreign Firms to Labor Abundance in Brazil," in James H. Street and Dilmus D. James (eds.) *Technological Progress in Latin America: The Prospects for Overcoming Dependency* (Boulder, Colo.: Westview Press, 1979), p. 201.

43. Amsden and Kim, "Role of Transnational Corporations" (note 23 above), p. 12.

44. Jequier, *Technology Choice,* Chapter 2.

45. Louis T. Wells, Jr., *Third World Multinationals* (Cambridge: MIT Press, 1983), p. 22.

46. Frances Stewart, "Overview and Conclusions," in Frances Stewart (ed.), *Macro-Policies for Appropriate Technology in Developing Countries* (Boulder, Colo.: Westview Press, 1987), p. 291.

47. James Keddie, "More on Production Techniques in Indonesia," in Stobaugh and Wells, *Technology Crossing Borders,* Chapter 4.

48. C. Cooper, R. Kaplinsky, R. Bell, and W. Satyarakwit, "Choice of Techniques for Can Making in Kenya, Tanzania, and Thailand," in Bhalla, *Technology and Employment* (note 28 above), pp. 100–101.

49. Enrique Ogliastri, *Gerencia Japonesa y Círculos de Participación* (Bogotá: Editorial Norma, 1988), p. 36.

50. *Ibid.,* pp. 36–37.

51. David J. C. Forsyth, Norman S. McBain, and Robert F. Solomon, "Technical Rigidity and Appropriate Technology in Less Developed Countries," *World Development,* 8, no. 5–6 (May–June 1980): 371–98.

52. Lawrence J. White, "Appropriate Factor Proportions for Manufacturing in Less Developed Countries: A Survey of the Evidence," in Austin Robinson (ed.), *Appropriate Technologies for Third World Development* (London: Macmillan, 1979), pp. 300–341; Gustav Ranis, "Appropriate Technologies in the Dual Economy: Reflections on Philippine and Taiwanese Experience," in Robinson, *Appropriate Technologies,* pp. 140–59; Gerald K. Boon, *Technology and Employment in Footwear Manufacturing* (Rockville, Md.: Sitjhoff & Noordhoff, 1980); idem, *Technology Transfer in Fibres, Textile and Apparel* (Rockville, Md.: Sitjhoff & Noordhoff, 1981); James Keddie and William Cleghorn, *Brewing in Developing Countries* (Edinburgh: Scottish Academic Press, 1979); idem, *Brick Manufacture in Developing Countries* (Edinburgh: Scottish Academic Press, 1980); M. M. Huq and C. C. Prendergast, *The Machine Tool Industry in Developing Countries* (Edinburgh: Scottish Academic Press, 1983).

53. James Pickett and Robert Robson, *Manual on the Choice of Industrial Technique in Developing Countries* (Paris: OECD, 1986), p. 32.

54. Irving Gershenberg, "Multinational Enterprises, "Transfer of Managerial Know-how, Technology Choice and Employment Effects: A Case Study

of Kenya," Working Paper 28, International Labour Office, 1983, p. 14.

55. Amsalem, "Technology Choice" (note 41 above), p. 123.

56. Pickett and Robson, *Manual*, p. 40.

57. Pickett and Robson provide detailed examples of this procedure; *ibid*.

58. Howard Pack, "The Substitution of Labour for Capital in Kenyan Manufacturing," *The Economic Journal*, 86 (1976): 56.

59. Larry N. Willmore, "The Comparative Performance of Foreign and Domestic Firms in Brazil," *World Development*, 14, no. 4 (1986): 489–502.

60. Amsalem, "Technology Choice," pp. 121–22.

61. Personal interview, World Bank, Industrial Development Division.

62. James E. Austin, *Agroindustrial Project Analysis* (Baltimore: Johns Hopkins University Press, 1981), p. 125.

63. Personal interview.

64. For a case example, see C. Cooper and R. Kaplinsky with R. Turner, "Second-Hand Equipment in Developing Countries: Jute Processing Machinery in Kenya," in Bhalla, *Technology and Employment* (note 28 above), pp. 129–57.

65. Pack, "Substitution of Labour," p. 53.

66. Louis T. Wells, Jr., "Economic Man and Engineering Man," in Stobaugh and Wells, *Technology Crossing Borders* (note 37 above), pp. 47–68.

67. Allen D. Jedlicka and Albert H. Rubenstein, "Acquiring and Using Technological Information: Barriers Perceived by Colombian Industrialists," in Street and James, *Technological Progress in Latin America* (note 42 above), p. 111–19.

68. Cooper *et al.*, "Choice of Techniques" (note 48 above), p. 113.

69. *Multinationals' Training Practices and Development* (Geneva: ILO, 1981), pp. 3, 22.

70. Richard D. Conway and Molly Conway, "For Risk Managers, Bhopal Provides Lessons," *National Underwriter*, November 22, 1985, p. 32.

71. S. Prakash Sethi, "Inhuman Errors and Industrial Crises," *Columbia Journal of World Business*, Spring 1987, p. 103.

72. Paul Shrivastava, *Bhopal: Anatomy of a Crisis* (Cambridge: Ballinger, 1987).

73. Richard I. Kirkland, Jr., "Union Carbide: Coping with Catastrophe," *Fortune*, January 7, 1985; James R. Norman, "A New Union Carbide Slowly Starting to Gel," *Business Week*, April 18, 1988, pp. 68–69.

74. Jequier, *Technology Choice* (note 34 above), p. 23.

75. Amsalem, "Technology Choice" (note 41 above), p. 114.

76. Luc Soete, "International Diffusion of Technology, Industrial Development and Technological Leapfrogging," *World Development,* 13, no. 3 (1985): 417.

77. Daniel Chudnovsky, "The Duffusion and Production of Numerically Controlled Machine Tools with Special Reference to Argentina," *World Development,* 16, no. 6 (1988): 723–32.

78. Morley and Smith, "Adaptation by Foreign Firms" (note 42 above), p. 215.

79. Simon Teitel, "On the Concept of Appropriate Technology for Less Industrialized Countries," *Technological Forecasting and Social Change,* 11 (1978): 364.

80. Gershenberg, "Multinational Enterprises" (note 54 above), p. 14.

81. Cooper *et al.,* "Choice of Techniques" (note 48 above), pp. 118–19.

82. Pickett and Robson, *Manual* (note 53 above), p. 52.

83. Otto Kreye, Jurgen Heinrichs, and Folker Frobel, "Export Processing Zones in Developing Countries," International Labour Office, Working Paper no. 43, 1987, p. 18.

84. Brewer *et al., Investing in Developing Countries* (note 30 above), pp. 167–71.

85. *Multinationals' Training Practices* (note 69 above), p. 2.

86. *Ibid.,* pp. 2, 21.

87. David Garvin, "Japanese Quality Management," *Columbia Journal of World Business,* vol. 19, no. 3 (1984); Kaoru Ishikawa, *What Is Total Quality Control? The Japanese Way* (Englewood Cliffs, N.J.: Prentice-Hall, 1985).

88. Carl G. Thunman, *Technology Licensing to Distant Markets: Interaction Between Swedish and Indian Firms* (Stockholm: Almqvist & Wiksell International, 1988), p. 141.

89. Jequier, *Technology Choice* (note 34 above), p. 30.

90. Wells, "Economic Man and Engineering Man" (note 66 above), p. 52.

91. Pickett and Robson, *Manual,* p. 50.

92. Louis T. Wells, Jr., "Milkpak (A)," Lahore Graduate School of Business Administration case, 08–0666–87–1, 1986.

93. Wells, *Third World Multinationals* (note 45 above), p. 38.

94. C. N. S. Nambudiri, "Third World Multinationals: Technology Choice and Employment Generation in Nigeria," International Labour Office, Working Paper no. 25, 1983, p. 13.

95. Personal interview.

96. Personal interview.

97. C. G. Baron, "Sugar Processing Techniques in India," in Bhalla, *Technology and Employment* (note 28 above), pp. 181–211.

98. Personal research.

99. "Power Cuts Cripple Mill," *The Standard*, July 28, 1988, p. 9.

100. Susumu Watanabe, "Multinational Enterprises, Employment and Technology Adaptations," in Pradip K. Ghosh (ed.), *Multi-National Corporations and Third World Development* (Westport, Conn.: Greenwood Press, 1984), pp. 176–77.

101. Patti Waldmeir, "Where Management Is More a Matter of Improvisation," *Financial Times*, November 4, 1985, p. 14.

102. Haider Ali Khan, "Technology Choice in the Energy and Textile Sectors in the Republic of Korea," in Bhalla, *Technology and Employment*, pp. 361–87.

103. Personal interview.

104. Aaron Segal *et al.*, *Learning by Doing: Science and Technology in the Developing World* (Boulder, Colo.: Westview Press, 1987), p. 2.

105. Frank C. Schuller, "Foreign Innovation by U.S. Multinationals," doctoral dissertation, Harvard University, Graduate School of Business Administration, 1982, p. IV-6.

106. Louis T. Wells, Jr., and Eshan-ul-Haque, "KSB (Pakistan)," Lahore Graduate School of Business Administration case, 16–003–87–3, 1986.

107. Linda Lim, "Multinational Firms and Manufacturing for Export in Less-Developed Countries: The Case of the Electronics Industry in Malaysia and Singapore," doctoral dissertation, University of Michigan, Ann Arbor, 1978, pp. 425–27.

108. J. W. Henderson, "The New International Division of Labour and American Semiconductor Production in Southeast Asia," in C. J. Dixon, D. Drakakis-Smith, and H. D. Watts (eds.), *Multinational Corporations and the Third World* (London: Croom Helm, 1986), pp. 91–117.

109. Robert C. Ronstadt, "R&D Abroad by U.S. Multinationals," in Stobaugh and Wells, *Technology Crossing Borders* (note 37 above), Chapter 11.

110. Cooper *et al.*, "Choice of Techniques" (note 48 above), p. 114.

111. Stewart, "International Technology Transfer" (note 20 above), p. 9.

112. Clemens P. Work, Don L. Boroughs, Mike Tharp, and Nanci Magoun, "Whose Property Is This Anyway?" *U.S. News & World Report*, November 14, 1988, p. 50.

113. Personal interview.

114. Dahlman and Cortés, "Mexico" (note 27 above), p. 611.

115. George T. Kastner, "La Gerencia de Manufactura en Venezuela: Producir a Como de Lugar," mimeo, March 1988.

116. Segal *et al.*, *Learning by Doing* (note 104 above), pp. 43–44.

117. Alice H. Amsden and Linsu Kim, "A Technological Perspective on the General Machinery Industry in the Republic of Korea," Harvard Business School Working Paper, 9–784–075, May 1984, p. 19.

118. Personal interview.

119. Matthew S. Gamser, "Innovation, Technical Assistance, and Development: The Importance of Technology Users," *World Development*, 16, no. 6 (1988): 711–21.

120. *Ibid.*

121. *Ibid.*

122. *Technology Exports from Developing Countries: Argentina and Portugal*, Development and Transfer of Technology Series, no. 17 (New York: United Nations Industrial Development Organization, 1983).

123. Amsden and Kim, "Technological Perspective," p. 10.

124. Joseph S. Chung, "Korea," in Francis W. Rushing and Carole Ganz Brown (eds.), *National Policies for Developing High Technology Industries: International Comparisons* (Boulder, Colo.: Westview Press, 1986), pp. 143–72.

125. Based on research by Carl F. Dahlman, cited in Amsden and Kim, "Technological Perspective," p. 32.

126. Thomas R. Howell, William A. Noellert, Janet H. MacLaughlin, and Alan W. Wolff, *The Microelectronics Race: The Impact of Government Policy on International Competition* (Boulder, Colo.: Westview Press, 1988), pp. 148–64.

127. *Ibid.*, p. 160.

128. Sooyong Kim, "The Korean Construction Industry as an Exporter of Services," *World Bank Economic Review*, 2, no. 2 (May 1988): 225–38.

129. Wenlee Ting, "East Asia: Pathways to Success," in Segal *et al.*, *Learning by Doing* (note 104 above), pp. 134–35.

130. The following description is based on Emanuel Adler's article "Ideological 'Guerrillas' and the Quest for Technological Autonomy: Brazil's Domestic Computer Industry," *International Organization*, 40, no. 3 (1986): 673–705.

131. *Wall Street Journal*, May 13, 1985, p. 27.

132. Francisco Colman Sercovich, "Brazil," *World Development*, 12, no. 5/6 (1984): 578.

133. Simon Teitel and Francisco Colman Sercovich, "Latin America," *World Development*, 12, no. 5/6 (1984): 645–60.

134. W. W. Rostow, *Rich Countries and Poor Countries: Reflections on the Past, Lessons for the Future* (Boulder, Colo.: Westview Press, 1987), p. 143.

135. Ward Morehouse and Brijen Gupta, "India: Success and Failure," in Segal *et al.*, *Learning by Doing*, p. 199.

136. Joseph M. Grieco, *Between Dependency and Autonomy: India's Experience with the International Computer Industry* (Berkeley: University of California Press, 1984).

137. Sanjaya Lall, "India's Economic Relations with the South," in Oli Havrylyshyn (ed.), *Works of Developing Countries: How Direction Affects Performance* (Washington, D.C.: World Bank, 1987), p. 110.

138. Morehouse and Gupta, "India: Success and Failure," p. 205.

139. Amsalem, "Technology Choice" (note 41 above), p. 125.

140. Wells, "Economic Man and Engineering Man" (note 66 above), p. 48.

141. C. N. S. Nambudiri, "Third World Multinationals: Technology Choice and Employment Generation in Nigeria," International Labour Office Working Paper 25, 1983, pp. 12–13.

142. Gustav Ranis and Chi Schive, "Direct Foreign Investment in Taiwan's Development," in Walter Galenson (ed.), *Foreign Trade and Investment: Economic Development in the Newly Industrializing Asian Countries* (Madison: University of Wisconsin Press, 1985), pp. 106, 115.

143. Alice H. Amsden, "Taiwan," *World Development*, 12, no. 5/6 (1984): 496.

144. Larry E. Westphal, Yung W. Rhee, Linsu Kim, and Alice H. Amsden, "Republic of Korea," *World Development*, 12, no. 5/6 (1984): 524.

145. Amsden and Kim, "Technological Perspective" (note 117 above), p. 17.

146. Andrew Tanzer, "Samsung: South Korea Marches to Its Own Drummer," *Forbes*, May 16, 1988, p. 88.

147. Kikai Shiko Kyokai, "Research on International Competitiveness of Component Industry," 1980, mimeo.

148. Lim, "Multinational Firms" (note 107 above), p. 453.

149. Gershenberg, "Multinational Enterprises" (note 54 above), pp. 13–14.

150. Data from the sixteen LDCs with annual production in 1980 of more than 25,000 cars. Jones and Womack, "Developing Countries and Future of Automobile Industry" (note 7 above), pp. 396–97.

151. Susumu Wantanabe, "International Subcontracting and Regional Economic Integration of the ASEAN Countries: The Role of Multinationals," in Germidis, *International Subcontracting* (note 31 above), p. 222.

152. G. Kulkarni, "Kirloskar Cummins Limited," Indian Institute of Management, 1973, p. 10.

153. Kreye, Heinrichs, and Frobel, "Export Processing Zones" (note 83 above), p. 6.

154. Rudy Maex, "Employment and Multinationals in Asian Export Processing Zones," International Labour Office Working Paper 26, 1983, p. 65.

155. *Ibid.*, p. 63.

156. "A Talk with Salinas," *Business Week*, July 4, 1988, p. 47.

157. James C. Austin, "Cummins Engine in India," Harvard Business School case, 379–072, 1978.

158. Benjamin Klein, Robert G. Crawford, and Armen A. Alchian, "Vertical Integration, Appropriable Rents, and the Competitive Contracting Process," *Journal of Law & Economics*, 21 (1978): 297–326; Oliver E. Williamson, "Transaction-Cost Economics: The Governance of Contractual Relations," *Journal of Law & Economics*, 22 (1979): 233–61.

159. Personal research.

160. Austin, *Agroindustrial Project Analysis* (note 62 above), p. 106.

161. Lim, "Multinational Firms" (note 107 above), p. 455.

162. Jack Baranson, *Manufacturing Problems in India: The Cummins Diesel Experience* (Syracuse: Syracuse University Press, 1967), p. 103.

163. Steven R. Hendryx, "Implementation of a Technology Transfer Joint Venture in the People's Republic of China: A Management Perspective," *Columbia Journal of World Business*, Spring 1986, p. 61.

164. Field research.

165. See Claude Berthomieu and Anne Hanaut, "International Subcontracting: The Case of Morocco," in Germidis, *International Subcontracting* (note 31 above), pp. 108–36.

166. This example is drawn from Chi Schive, "Technology Transfer Through Direct Foreign Investment: A Case Study of Taiwan Singer," *Proceedings of the Academy of International Business: Asia-Pacific Dimensions of International Business*, December 18–20, 1979, Honolulu, Hawaii, pp. 113–22.

167. Estime, "Case of Haiti" (note 31 above), p. 99.

168. Ting, "East Asia" (note 129 above), p. 145.

169. Marc Bauchamp, "Foot in the Door," *Forbes*, December 29, 1986, p. 34.

CHAPTER 9

Marketing: Adjusting the Marketing Mix

1. Alvin Wint provided valuable research assistance in the preparation of this chapter.

2. This would be equivalent to a Net Reproduction Rate of 1.0, which considers both the age-specific fertility and age-specific mortality rates.

3. James E. Post, "Assessing the Nestlé Boycott: Corporate Accountability and Human Rights," *California Management Review*, 27, no. 2 (Winter 1985): 121.

4. My T. Vu, Eduard Bos, and Rodolfo A. Bulatao, "Asia Region Population Projections: 1988–89 Edition," World Bank, Policy, Planning, and Research Working Paper 115, 1988, pp. 82, 84, 86, 90.

5. *Population Change and Economic Development* (New York: Oxford University Press for the World Bank, 1984), averages calculated from data in Table 2, p. 154.

6. Daniel R. Vining, Jr., "The Growth of Core Urban Regions in Developing Countries," *Population and Development Review*, 11, no. 3 (1985): 499.

7. Personal interview.

8. Montek S. Ahluwalia, "Income Inequality: Some Dimensions of the Problem," in Hollis Chenery *et al.*, *Redistribution with Growth* (London: Oxford University Press, 1974), pp. 8–9.

9. Jules Arbose and Don Shapiro, "Tatung Rides Out Recession with Confucian Calm," *International Management*, January 1983, p. 23.

10. John S. Hill and Richard R. Still, "Adapting Products to LDC Tastes," *Harvard Business Review*, March–April 1984, p. 98.

11. *Ibid.*, p. 95.

12. *Ibid.*, p. 98.

13. James C. Baker and John K. Ryans, Jr., "Some Aspects of International Pricing: A Neglected Area of Management Policy," in *idem* (eds.), *Multinational Marketing: Dimensions in Strategy* (Columbus, Ohio: Grid, Inc., 1975), p. 145.

14. Subhash C. Jain, *International Marketing Management*, 2d ed. (Boston: Kent Publishing, 1987), p. 469.

15. Victor H. Frank, Jr., "Living with Price Controls Abroad," *Harvard Business Review*, March–April 1984, pp. 139, 140.

16. J. M. Parkinson, "Marketing in Lesser Developed Countries," *Quarterly Review of Marketing* (UK), 11, no. 1 (Autumn 1985): 14.

17. James E. Austin, *Agroindustrial Project Analysis* (Baltimore: Johns Hopkins University Press, 1981), p. 48.

18. Personal communication.

19. Frank, "Living with Price Controls Abroad," p. 139.

20. Julia Michaels and Roger Cohen, "Foreigners Boost Investments in Brazil Despite Its Daunting Economic Problems," *Wall Street Journal*, October 28, 1988, p. A18.

21. Stephen D. Younger, "Ghana: Economic Recovery Program—A Case Study of Stabilization and Structural Adjustment in Sub-Saharan Africa,"

EDI Development Policy Case Series, no. 1 (Washington, D.C.: World Bank, 1989), pp. 132–33.

22. Jeffrey S. Arpan, "Multinational Firm Pricing in International Markets," in Subhash C. Jain and Lewis R. Tucker, Jr. (eds.), *International Marketing: Managerial Perspectives* (Boston: CBI Publishing, 1979), p. 380.

23. Sanjaya Lall, "Transfer Pricing and Developing Countries," in Gerald M. Meier (ed.), *Pricing Policy for Development Management* (Baltimore: Johns Hopkins University Press, 1983), pp. 146–48.

24. James and Lister computed an R-squared of 0.31 when regressing per capita national income on advertising as a percentage of GNP. Jeffrey James and Stephen Lister, "Galbraith Revisited: Advertising in Non-affluent Societies," *World Development, 8,* no. 1 (January 1980): 89. Leff and Farley, using a refined analysis relating advertising to the manufacturing sector (where advertising would be more relevant than for the primary sector) and employing per capita income levels based on purchasing power, document the less than proportionate rise. Nathaniel H. Leff and John U. Farley, "Advertising Expenditures in the Developing World," *Journal of International Business Studies,* 11, no. 2 (1980): 68–69.

25. Françoise Simon-Miller, "African Marketing: The Next Frontier," in G. S. Kindra (ed.), *Marketing in Developing Countries* (New York: St. Martin's Press, 1984), p. 125.

26. Personal communication.

27. Parkinson, "Marketing in Lesser Developed Countries" (note 16 above), p. 13.

28. Source for newspaper circulation and for other media coverage cited in subsequent sections is *World Advertising Expenditures in 1985,* 20th ed. (Mamaroneck, N.Y.: Starch Inra Hooper, 1986), pp. 22–23.

29. *Ibid.,* pp. 20–21.

30. From an analysis of thirty countries; standard error of coefficient: 0.00319.

31. William H. Cunningham, Russell M. Moore, and Isabella C. M. Cunningham, "Urban Markets in Industrializing Countries: The São Paulo Experience," *Journal of Marketing,* 38, no. 2 (April 1974): 2–12.

32. Erdener Kaynak, *Marketing in the Third World* (New York: Praeger, 1982), p. 209.

33. Simon-Miller, "African Marketing," p. 125.

34. *Ibid.*

35. David Ricks, Marilyn Y. C. Fu, and Jeffrey S. Arpan, *International Business Blunders* (Columbus, Ohio: Grid, Inc., 1974), p. 11.

36. "Speaking to Your Market," *Mass High Tech,* July 20–August 2, 1987, p. 15.

37. Jain, *International Marketing Management* (note 14 above), p. 530.

38. David A. Ricks, Jeffrey S. Arpan, Marilyn Y. C. Fu, "Pitfalls in Advertising Overseas," *Journal of Advertising Research,* 14, no. 6 (December 1974): 50.

39. "Speaking to Your Market," p. 16; Essam Mahmoud and Gillian Rice point out another religious dimension to be considered: Under the tenets of Islam great deference is to be paid to parents, especially fathers; therefore in advertising to the teenage market the message might be wise to stress parental advice and approval. See Essam Mahmoud and Gillian Rice, "Marketing Problems in LDCs: The Case of Egypt," in Kindra, *Marketing in Developing Countries* (note 25 above), p. 87.

40. "Speaking to Your Market," p. 15.

41. Michael R. Czinkota and Ilkka A. Ronkainen, *International Marketing* (Chicago: Dryden Press, 1988), p. 226.

42. "Speaking to Your Market," pp. 14–15.

43. James M. Carmen and Robert M. March, "How Important for Marketing Are Cultural Differences Between Similar Nations?" *Australian Marketing Researcher,* 3, no. 1 (Summer 1979): 5–6.

44. Roy F. Grow, "Japanese and American Firms in China: Lessons of a New Market," *Columbia Journal of World Business,* 21, no. 1 (Spring 1986): 52–53.

45. Many consider Japan's distribution channels to be relatively inefficient and lengthy because as Japan moved from a developing to a developed country much of the labor displacement was absorbed into distribution activities.

46. E. R. Pariser, "Post-Harvest Food Losses in Developing Countries," in J. Price Gittinger, Joanne Leslie, and Caroline Hoisington, *Food Policy: Integrating Supply, Distribution, and Consumption* (Baltimore: Johns Hopkins University Press, 1987), pp. 309–25.

47. Vern Terpstra, *International Marketing,* 2d ed. (New York: Holt, Rinehart & Winston, 1978), pp. 117–88.

48. Philip R. Cateora, *International Marketing,* 6th ed. (Homewood, Ill.: R. D. Irwin, 1987), Chapter 19.

49. Peter F. Drucker, "Marketing and Economic Development," *Journal of Marketing,* 22, no. 3 (January 1958): 257.

50. Kaynak, *Marketing in the Third World* (note 32 above), p. 246.

51. Kenneth Hoadley and James Austin, "Sabritas," Harvard Business School case, 381–096, 1981.

52. Thomas Wenstrand and Ray A. Goldberg, "Ejura Farms Ghana Ltd.," Harvard Business School case, 373-322, 1973.

53. Douglas S. G. Norvell and Robert Morey, "Ethnodomination in the Channels of Distribution of Third World Nations," *Journal of the Academy of Marketing Science,* 11, no. 3 (1983): 204–15.

54. Victor Limlingan, "The Overseas Chinese in ASEAN: Business Strategies and Management Practices," doctoral dissertation, Harvard Business School, 1986, pp. 8, 13. Published in 1986 by Vita Development Corporation, Paisig, Metro Manila, Philippines.

55. Gregory Thong Tin Sin, "The Management of Chinese Small-Business Enterprises in Malaysia," *Asia Pacific Journal of Management*, May 1987, p. 179.

56. James Brooke, "Ivory Coast: African Success Story Built on Rich Farms and Stable Politics," *New York Times International*, April 26, 1988, p. 48.

57. Clifton A. Barton, "Trust and Credit: Some Observations Regarding Business Strategies of Overseas Chinese Traders in South Vietnam," in Linda Y. C. Lim and L. A. Peter Gosling (eds.), *The Chinese in Southeast Asia. Volume 1: Ethnicity and Economic Activity* (Singapore: Maruzen Asia, 1983), p. 59; see also Limlingan, "Overseas Chinese," Chapter 4.

58. Limlingan, "Overseas Chinese," Chapter 4.

59. D. Stanley Eitzen, "Two Minorities: The Jews of Poland and the Chinese of the Philippines," *Jewish Journal of Sociology*, 10, no. 2 (December 1968): 230.

60. Guy Haik and Frank Meissner, "Africanization of Marketing in the Ivory Coast," in Dov Izraeli, Dafna N. Izraeli, and Frank Meissner (eds.), *Marketing Systems for Developing Countries* (New York: John Wiley & Sons, 1976), vol. 1, pp. 148–59.

61. Brooke, "Ivory Coast: African Success Story," p. A8.

62. Personal interview.

63. Michael Roddy, "Zaïre's Phones Create a Walkie-Talkie Market," *Boston Globe*, November 24, 1988.

64. John Z. Kracmar, *Marketing Research in the Developing Countries: A Handbook* (New York: Praeger, 1971), pp. 201–3.

65. Cateora, *International Marketing* (note 48 above), p. 271.

66. Erdener Kaynak, "Marketing Research Techniques and Approaches for LDCs," in Kindra, *Marketing in Developing Countries* (note 25 above), pp. 238–52.

67. Edward Cundiff and Marye Tharp Hilger, *Marketing in the International Environment*, 2d ed. (Englewood Cliffs, N.J.: Prentice-Hall, 1988), p. 247.

68. Personal Communication, Prof. H. E. Beaton.

69. Harper W. Boyd, R. E. Frank, W. F. Massey, and M. Zoheir, "On the Use of Marketing Research in the Emerging Economies," *Journal of Marketing Research*, 1, no. 4 (November 1964): 23.

70. Cundiff and Hilger, *Marketing in International Environment*, pp. 267–69.

71. Kaynak, "Marketing-Research Techniques," p. 247.

72. Jain, *International Marketing Management* (note 14 above), p. 330.

73. Eduardo L. Roberto, "Consumer Coping Behavior in Difficult Times: Year III," Asian Institute of Management Occasional Papers no. 14, June 1986.

74. Eduardo L. Roberto, "Coping with Difficult Times: The Case of the Metro Manila Downscale Consumers," Asian Institute of Management Occasional Papers, October 1984.

75. Richard H. Hotton, "Marketing and the Modernization of China," *California Management Review*, 27, no. 4 (1985): 39.

76. James P. Neelankavil, "A Coming of Age: Marketing Research in Developing Countries—The Case of Singapore," *Proceedings of the Academy of International Business: Asia-Pacific Dimensions of International Business,* December 18–20, 1979, p. 616.

77. John F. Maloney, "In Saudi Arabia, Sands, Statistics Can Be Shifty," *Marketing News,* July 2, 1976, p. 76.

78. Gerald D. Sentell, "Recognizing and Overcoming Environmentally-Induced Obstacles to Marketing Research in Less-Developed Countries of the Asia-Pacific Region," *Proceedings of the Academy of International Business, Asia-Pacific Dimensions of International Business,* December 18–20, 1979, pp. 632–33.

79. Theodore Levitt, "The Globalization of Markets," *Harvard Business Review,* 83, no. 3 (May–June 1983): 92–102; Kenichi Ohmae, *Triad Power: The Coming Shape of Global Competition* (New York: Free Press, 1985).

80. Marquise R. Cvar, "Case Studies in Global Competition: Patterns of Success and Failure," in Michael E. Porter (ed.), *Competition in Global Industries* (Boston: Harvard Business School Press, 1986), pp. 488–92.

81. Hill and Still, "Adapting Products to LDC Tastes" (note 10 above), p. 94.

82. Personal interview.

83. Dorothy I. Riddle, *Service-Led Growth: The Role of the Service Sector in World Development* (New York: Praeger, 1986), pp. 151–70.

84. Christopher A. Bartlett and Sumantra Ghosal, "Managing Across Borders: New Organizational Responses," *Sloan Management Review,* 29, no. 1 (1987): 45–46.

85. John A. Quelch and Edward J. Hoff, "Customizing Global Marketing," *Harvard Business Review,* 86, no. 3 (May–June 1986): 62.

86. Philippe d'Antin, "The Nestlé Product Manager as Demigod," in Baker and Ryans, *Multinational Marketing* (note 13 above), p. 126.

87. Hirotaka Takeuchi and Michael E. Porter, "Three Roles of International Marketing in Global Strategy," in Porter, *Competition in Global Industries,* p. 122.

88. Hill and Still, "Adapting Products to LDC Tastes," p. 100.

89. Tom Lester, "The Issue Globalists Don't Talk About," *International Management*, September 1987, pp. 37–38.

90. Rhys Jenkins, "Transnational Corporations and Third World Consumption: Implications of Competitive Strategies," *World Development*, 16, no. 11 (1988): 1363–1770.

91. Hill and Still, "Adapting Products to LDC Tastes," p. 95.

92. Amir Mahini and Louis T. Wells, Jr., "Government Relations in Global Firms," in Porter, *Competition in Global Industries*, p. 292.

93. OECD, *Countertrade: Developing Country Practices* (Paris: OECD, 1985), pp. 31–36.

94. Louis Kraar, "How to Sell to Cashless Buyers," *Fortune*, November 7, 1988, p. 150.

95. OECD, *Countertrade*, p. 12; Stephen S. Cohen and John Zysman, "Countertrade, Offsets, Barter, and Buybacks," *California Management Review*, 28, no. 2 (1986): 42.

96. Donald J. Lecraw, "Countertrade: A Form of Cooperative International Business Arrangement," in Farok J. Contractor and Peter Lorange (eds.), *Cooperative Strategies in International Business* (Lexington, Mass.: Lexington Books, 1988), pp. 423–42.

97. *World Development Report 1989* (New York: Oxford University Press for the World Bank, 1989), p. 15.

98. John Kenneth Galbraith and Richard H. Holton, *Marketing Efficiency in Puerto Rico* (Cambridge: Harvard University Press, 1955).

99. Drucker, "Marketing and Economic Development" (note 49 above).

100. Hamid Etemad, "Is Marketing the Catalyst in the Economic Development Process?" pp. 29–56, and Nikhilesh Dholakia and Ruby Roy Dholakia, "Missing Links: Marketing and the Newer Theories of Development," pp. 57–75, both in Kindra, *Marketing in Developing Countries* (note 25 above).

101. For a broader discussion of marketing's role in society, including ethical responsibilities and consumerism, see William Lazer and Eugene J. Kelley, *Social Marketing: Perspectives and Viewpoints* (Homewood, Ill.: Richard D. Irwin, 1973).

102. Karen F. A. Fox and Philip Kotler, "The Marketing of Social Causes: The First 10 Years," *Journal of Marketing*, 44, no. 4 (Fall 1980): 24–33; Kotler was one of the early theorists in the field of social marketing.

103. William P. Schellstede and Robert L. Ciszewski, "Social Marketing of Contraceptives in Bangladesh," *Studies in Family Planning*, 15, no. 1 (January–February 1984): 30–39; V. Kasturi Rangan, "Population Services International: Social Marketing Project in Bangladesh," Harvard Business School case, 9–586–013, rev. November 1986, p. 1.

104. Fox and Kotler, "Marketing of Social Causes," p. 28.

105. T. R. L. Black and John U. Farley, "The Application of Market Research in Contraceptive Social Marketing in a Rural Area of Kenya," *Journal of the Market Research Society,* 21, no. 1 (January 1979): 30–43.

106. Personal interview, John Snow, Inc., Family Planning Private Sector Project.

107. Donald J. Bogue and Amy Ong Tsui, "Zero World Population Growth?" *Public Interest,* no. 55 (Spring 1979): 99–113; *Population Change and Economic Development* (note 5 above), p. 77.

108. Richard K. Manoff, "When the 'Client' Is Human Life Itself," *Advertising Age,* August 22, 1983, pp. 4–5; *idem,* Social Marketing: New Imperative for Public Health (New York: Praeger Publishers, 1985).

109. Philip Kotler and Eduardo L: Roberto, *Social Marketing: Strategies for Changing Public Behavior* (New York: Free Press, 1989), pp. 69–70.

110. *Ibid.,* pp. 243–45.

111. *Ibid.,* pp. 17–18.

112. Kathryn Sikkink, "Codes of Conduct for Transnational Corporations: The Case of the WHO/UNICEF Code," *International Organization,* 40, no. 4 (1986): 815–40; S. Prakash Sethi, Hamid Etemad, and K. A. N. Luther, "New Sociopolitical Forces: The Globalization of Conflict," *Journal of Business Strategy,* 6, no. 4 (Spring 1986): 24–31.

113. Rafael D. Pagan, Jr., "The Nestlé Boycott: Implications for Strategic Business Planning," *Journal of Business Strategy,* 6, no. 4 (Spring 1986): 13.

114. David E. Whiteside and Kenneth E. Goodpaster, "Velsicol Chemical Corporation (A)," Harvard Business School case, 385-021, 1984.

CHAPTER 10

Organization: Assessing Entry, Ownership, and Cultural Effects

1. For a discussion of export marketing, see Franklin R. Root, *Entry Strategies for International Markets* (Lexington, Mass.: Lexington Books, 1987), Chapter 3.

2. Robert Stobaugh, *Innovation and Competition: The Global Management of Petrochemical Products* (Boston: Harvard Business School Press, 1988), p. 90–91.

3. Tien-tung Hsueh and Tun-oy Woo, "U.S. Direct Investment in Hong Kong: The Present Situation and Prospects," *Columbia Journal of World Business,* 21, no. 1 (Spring 1986): 80.

4. *Ibid.,* p. 76.

5. Charles Oman, *New Forms of International Investment in Developing Countries* (Paris: OECD, 1984), p. 58.

6. Pang Eng Fong, "Foreign Indirect Investment in Singapore," in Charles Oman (ed.), *New Forms of International Investment in Developing Countries: The National Perspective* (Paris: OECD, 1984), p. 171.

7. Oman, *New Forms*, p. 54.

8. *Ibid.*, pp. 48–49.

9. *Ibid.*, p. 57.

10. Lawrence G. Franko, "New Forms of Investment in Developing Countries by U.S. Companies: A Five Industry Comparison," *Columbia Journal of World Business*, 22, no. 2 (Summer 1987): 47.

11. Frederick T. Knickerbocker, *Oligopolistic Reaction and Multinational Enterprise* (Boston: Division of Research, Harvard University Graduate School of Business Administration, Boston, 1973).

12. Robert Stobaugh, "Channels for Technology Transfer: The Petrochemical Industry," in Robert Stobaugh and Louis T. Wells, Jr. (eds.), *Technology Crossing Borders* (Boston: Harvard Business School Press, 1984), p. 165.

13. G. Paulsson, "Licensing Industrial Technology to Developing Countries: The Operations of Swedish Firms in India," *Aussenwertschaft*, 41 Jahrgang, Heft IV, Ruegger, pp. 533–49.

14. Piero Telesio, *Technology Licensing and Multinational Enterprise* (New York: Praeger, 1979), p. 18.

15. Dorothy I. Riddle, *Service-Led Growth: The Role of the Service Sector in World Development* (New York: Praeger, 1986), p. 186; see also Michael R. Czinkota and Ilkka A. Ronkainen, *International Marketing* (Chicago: Dryden Press, 1988), Chapter 13.

16. Stobaugh, "Channels for Technology Transfer," p. 173.

17. Owen T. Adikibi, "The Multinational Corporation and Monopoly of Patents in Nigeria," *World Development*, 16, no. 4 (1988): 517.

18. Raymond Vernon, *Exploring the Global Economy: Emerging Issues in Trade and Investment* (Lanham, Md.: University Press of America, 1985), p. 77.

19. Clemens P. Work, Don L. Boroughs, Mike Tharp, and Nanci Magoun, "Whose Property Is This Anyway?" *U.S. News & World Report*, November 14, 1988, pp. 51–52.

20. "The Counterfeit Trade," *Business Week*, December 16, 1985, pp. 64–72.

21. Work *et al.*, "Whose Property," p. 51.

22. Louis T. Wells, Jr., *Third World Multinationals: The Rise of Foreign Investment from Developing Countries* (Cambridge: MIT Press, 1983), p. 64.

23. Franko, "New Forms" (note 10 above), pp. 48–49.

24. Christian Pollak, "Non-Equity Forms of German Industrial Co-operation," in Oman, *New Forms* (note 6 above), p. 238.

25. Jean-Robert Estime, "International Subcontracting: The Case of Haiti," in Dimitri Germidis (ed.), *International Subcontracting: A New Form of Investment* (Paris: OECD, 1980), p. 103.

26. J. W. Henderson, "The New International Division of Labour and American Semiconductor Production in Southeast Asia," in C. J. Dixon, D. Drakakis-Smith, and H. D. Watts (eds.), *Multinational Corporations and the Third World* (London: Croom Helm, 1986), Chapter 5; Warren E. Davis and Daryl G. Hatano, "The American Semiconductor Industry and the Ascendancy of East Asia," *California Management Review*, 27, no. 4 (Summer 1985): 128–43.

27. Hseuh and Woo, "U.S. Direct Investment" (note 3 above), p. 81.

28. John D. Daniels, Jeffrey Krug, and Douglas Nigh, "U.S. Joint Ventures in China: Motivation and Management of Political Risk," *California Management Review*, 27, no. 4 (Summer 1985): 49.

29. Terutomo Ozawa, "Japan's 'Revealed Preference' for the 'New Forms' of Investment: A Stock-Taking Assessment," in Oman, *New Forms*, p. 203.

30. Derived from Harvard Business School's Multinational Enterprise Project data base.

31. Lawrence G. Franko, *The European Multinationals: A Renewed Challenge to American and British Big Business* (London: Harper & Row Ltd., 1976).

32. Tan Siew Ee and M. Kulasingam, "The Malaysian Experience with New Forms of International Investment," in Oman, *New Forms*, p. 115.

33. Ozawa, "Japan's 'Revealed Preference'," p. 201.

34. Derived from Harvard Business School Multinational Enterprise data base; covers firms listed in *Fortune's* 500 with at least six international subsidiaries.

35. Gomes-Casseres's analyses for both developed and developing countries revealed several peaks and valleys within this generally upward trend. Benjamin Gomes-Casseres, "Joint Venture Cycles: The Evolution of Ownership Strategies of U.S. MNEs, 1945–75," in Farok J. Contractor and Peter Lorange (eds.), *Cooperative Strategies in International Business* (Lexington, Mass.: Lexington Books, 1988), pp. 111–28.

36. Stephen J. Kobrin, "Trends in Ownership of U.S. Manufacturing Subsidiaries in Developing Countries: An Interindustry Analysis," in Contractor and Lorange, *Cooperative Strategies*, pp. 129–42.

37. John M. Stopford and Louis T. Wells, Jr., *Managing the Multinational Enterprise: Organization of the Firm and Ownership of the Subsidiaries* (New York: Basic Books, 1972), Chapter 9.

38. Anthony J. F. O'Reilly, "Establishing Successful Joint Ventures in Developing Nations: A CEO's Perspective," *Columbia Journal of World Business*, 23, no. 1 (Spring 1988): 66.

39. Steven R. Hendryx, "Implementation of a Technology Transfer Joint Venture in the People's Republic of China: A Management Perspective," *Columbia Journal of World Business,* 21, no. 1 (Spring 1986): 57–66.

40. Personal interview.

41. G. R. Kulkarni, "Kirloskar Cummins Limited," Indian Institute of Management, Ahmedabad, 1973.

42. See Kiyoshi Kojima and Terutomo Ozawa, *Japan's General Trading Companies: Merchants of Economic Development* (Paris: OECD, 1984), pp. 97, 98, 100.

43. Dennis J. Encarnation and Sushil Vachani, "Foreign Ownership: When Hosts Change the Rules," *Harvard Business Review,* 85, no. 5 (September–October 1985): 154.

44. Bohn-Young Koo, "New Forms of Foreign Investment in Korea," in Oman, *New Forms* (note 6 above), p. 13.

45. O'Reilly, "Establishing Successful Joint Ventures," p. 66.

46. Based on data from *Business International*—"Changing Investment Rules and Regulations at a Glance," June 29, 1987, pp. 204–6; "Round-up of Global Investment Rules," June 29, 1987, p. 201; "Licensing Regulations in 18 Nations," March 7, 1988, pp. 68, 69; and "Investment Regulations in 18 Nations: Wrap-up of Worldwide Conditions," October 26, 1984, p. 341—as well as from "Summary of Measures Affecting Members' Exchange and Trade Systems, 1986," in *Annual Report on Exchange Arrangements and Exchange Restrictions* (Washington, D.C.: IMF, 1986) pp. 44–61.

47. For additional analyses see Benjamin Gomes-Casseres, "Multinational Ownership Strategies," doctoral dissertation, Harvard University Graduate School of Business Administration, 1985, and *idem,* "Joint Venture Cycles" (note 35 above).

48. Franko, "New Forms" (note 31 above), p. 54.

49. Paul W. Beamish, "The Characteristics of Joint Ventures in Developed and Developing Countries," *Columbia Journal of World Business,* 20, no. 3 (Fall 1985): 14.

50. Stephen J. Kobrin, "Trends" (note 36 above), pp. 138–39.

51. Phillip D. Grub, "A Yen for Yuan: Trading and Investing in the China Market," *Business Horizons,* 30, no. 4 (July–August 1987): 18

52. William H. Davidson, "Creating and Managing Joint Ventures in China," *California Management Review,* 29, no. 4 (Summer 1987): 77.

53. Franko, "New Forms," p. 42.

54. *Ibid.,* pp. 47–48.

55. N. Fagre and Louis T. Wells, Jr., "Bargaining Power of Multinationals and Host Governments," *Journal of International Business Studies,* Fall 1982, pp. 9–23.

56. Beamish, "Characteristic of Joint Ventures," p. 13.

57. Joseph M. Grieco, "Between Dependence and Autonomy: India's Experiences with the International Computer Industry," doctoral dissertation, Cornell University, 1982.

58. Ravi Ramamurti and James E. Austin, "Empresa Brasileira de Aeronautica S.A. EMBRAER," Harvard Business School case, 383–090, 1982.

59. Franko, "New Forms," p. 43.

60. *Ibid.*, p. 48.

61. Sheila Tefft, Cheryl Debes, and Dean Foust, "The Mouse That Roared at Pepsi," *Business Week*, September 7, 1987, p. 42.

62. James R. Schiffman, "Coca-Cola Seeking Approval to Build a Plant in India," *Wall Street Journal*, November 17, 1988, p. B6.

63. Personal interview.

64. Seamus G. Connolly, "Joint Ventures with Third World Multinationals: A New Form of Entry to International Markets," *Columbia Journal of World Business*, 19, no. 2 (Summer 1984): 18–22.

65. Wells, *Third World Multinationals* (note 22 above), pp. 2–3.

66. *Ibid.*

67. Connolly, "Joint Ventures," p. 19.

68. *Ibid.*, p. 21.

69. Kathryn Rudie Harrigan, "Joint Ventures and Global Strategies," *Columbia Journal of World Business*, 19, no. 2 (Summer 1984); 7–16.

70. William A. Dymsza, "Successes and Failures of Joint Ventures in Developing Countries: Lessons from Experience," in Contractor and Lorange, *Cooperative Strategies* (note 35 above), p. 421.

71. Alice H. Amsden and Linsu Kim, "The Role of Transnational Corporations in the Production and Exports of the Korean Automobile Industry," Harvard Business School Working Paper, 9–785–063, rev. 6/85, p. 5.

72. Dymsza, "Successes and Failures," p. 417.

73. Syed Akmal Hyder, "A Case of Joint Venture Between an Indian and a Swedish Partner," Working Paper, Department of Business Administration, University of Uppsala, Sweden, 1986.

74. Gomes-Casseres, "Multinational Ownership Strategies" (note 47 above), pp. 565–67.

75. J. Peter Killing, *Strategies for Joint Venture Success* (New York: Praeger, 1983).

76. Jean-Louis Schaan and Paul W. Beamish, "Joint Venture General Managers in LDCs," in Contractor and Lorange, *Cooperative Strategies*, pp. 279–300.

77. Dyszma, "Success and Failures," p. 415.

78. John I. Reynolds, "The 'Pinched Shoe' Effect of International Joint Ventures," *Columbia Journal of World Business*, 19, no. 2 (Summer 1984): 23–29.

79. Sven Olaf Hegsted and Ian Newport, "Management Contracts: Main Features and Design Issues," World Bank Technical Paper no. 65, July 1987, p. 12.

80. Kojima and Ozawa, *Japan's General Trading Companies* (note 42 above), pp. 43, 98.

81. Schaan and Beamish, "Joint Venture General Managers," p. 284.

82. Carl G. Thunman, *Technology Licensing to Distant Markets: Interactions Between Swedish and Indian Firms* (Stockholm: Almqvist & Wiksell International, 1988), p. 103.

83. Killing, *Strategies*, p. 82.

84. Amsden and Kim, "Role of Transnational Corporations" (note 71 above) p. 12.

85. Benjamin Gomes-Casseres, "Joint Venture Instability: Is It a Problem?" *Columbia Journal of World Business*, 22, no. 2 (Summer 1987): 97–102.

86. Beamish, "Characteristics of Joint Ventures" (note 49 above), p. 14.

87. Francisco Colman Sercovich, "Brazil," *World Development*, 2, no. 5/6 (1984): 594.

88. Personal interview.

89. Anant R. Neghandi, "Cross-Cultural Management Research: Trend and Future Directions," *Journal of International Business Studies*, Fall 1983, pp. 17–28.

90. Geert Hofstede, *Culture's Consequences: International Differences in Work-Related Values* (Beverly Hills, Calif.: Sage Publications, 1980); *idem*, "Motivation, Leadership, and Organizations: Do American Theories Apply Abroad?" *Organizational Dynamics*, Summer 1980, pp. 42–63; *idem*, "The Cultural Relativity of Organizational Practices and Theory," *Journal of International Business Studies*, Fall 1983, pp. 75–89; *idem*, "Cultural Dimensions in Management and Planning," *Asia Pacific Journal of Management*, 1, no. 2 (January 1984): 81–99; André Laurent, "The Cultural Diversity of Western Conceptions of Management," *International Studies of Management & Organization*, 13, no. 1–2 (Spring–Summer 1983); 75–96.

91. Nancy J. Adler, *International Dimensions of Organizational Behavior* (Boston: Kent Publishing Company, 1986), p. 31.

92. Syed Mumtaz Saeed, *Managerial Challenge in the Third World* (New York: Praeger, 1986), p. 26.

93. S. G. Redding, "The Study of Managerial Ideology Among Overseas Chinese Owner-Managers," *Asia Pacific Journal of Management*, 4, no.

3 (May 1987): 167–77; Lucian W. Pye, *Asian Power and Politics: The Cultural Dimensions of Authority* (Cambridge: Harvard University Press, 1985).

94. Jules Arbose and Don Shapiro, "Tatung Rides Out Recession with Confucian Calm," *International Management*, January 1983, p. 22.

95. Personal interview.

96. Sudhir Kakar, "Authority Patterns and Subordinate Behavior in Indian Organizations," *Administrative Science Quarterly*, 16, no. 3 (September 1971); 298–307.

97. Laurent, "Cultural Diversity," p. 86.

98. Xu Lian Cang, "A Cross-cultural Study on the Leadership Behavior of Chinese and Japanese Executives," *Asia Pacific Journal of Management*, 4, no. 3 (May 1987): 203–9.

99. Adler, *International Dimensions*, p. 36.

100. Hyder, "Case of Joint Venture" (note 73 above).

101. Michael Yoshino and Thomas B. Lifson, *The Invisible Link: Japan's Sogo Sosha and the Organization of Trade* (Cambridge: MIT Press, 1986), p. 175.

102. Gregory Thong Tin Sin, "The Management of Chinese Small-Business Enterprises in Malaysia," *Asia Pacific Journal of Management*, 4, no. 3 (May 1987): 182.

103. Adler, *International Dimensions*, p. 132.

104. Chong Li Choy, "History and Managerial Culture in Singapore: 'Pragmatism,' 'Openness' and 'Paternalism'," *Asia Pacific Journal of Management*, 4, no. 3 (May 1987): 139.

105. John Paul Fieq, *Thais and North Americans* (Chicago: Intercultural Press, 1980), p. 66.

106. Thomas L. Brewer, Kenneth David, and Linda Y. C. Lim, with Robert S. Corredera, *Investing in Developing Countries: A Guide for Executives* (Lexington, Mass.: Lexington Books, 1986), pp. 167–71.

107. Fieq, *Thais and North Americans*, p. 72.

108. Edward T. Hall, "The Silent Language in Overseas Business," *Harvard Business Review*, 38, no. 3 (May–June 1960): 87–96.

109. Personal interview.

110. E. S. Glenn, D. Witmeyer, and K. A. Stevenson, "Cultural Styles of Persuasion," *International Journal of Intercultural Relations*, 1, no. 3 (Fall 1984): 52–66; Pierre Casse, *Training for the Multicultural Manager: A Practical and Cross-Cultural Approach to the Management of People* (Washington, D.C.: Sietar International, 1982).

111. Lucian Pye, *Chinese Commercial Negotiating Style* (Cambridge, Mass.: Oelgeschlager, Gunn & Hain, 1982), pp. 88–89.

112. O'Reilly, "Establishing Successful Joint Ventures" (note 38 above), p. 69.

113. Hall, "Silent Language," p. 95.

114. Pye, *Chinese Commercial Negotiating Style*, p. 80.

115. Fieq, *Thais and North Americans*, p. 70.

116. Phyllis A. Harrison, *Behaving Brazilian: A Comparison of Brazilian and North American Social Behavior* (Rowley, Mass.: Newbury House Publishers, 1983), p. 72.

117. Adler, *International Dimensions* (note 91 above), p. 92.

118. Personal communication.

119. Stanley B. Lubman, "Negotiations in China: Observations of a Lawyer," in Robert A. Kapp (ed.), *Communicating with China* (Chicago: Intercultural Press, 1983), pp. 64–65.

120. Howard Myers, "The China Business Puzzle," *Business Horizons*, 30, no. 4 (July–August 1987): 27.

121. F. T. Murray and Alice Haller Murray, "Global Managers for Global Businesses," in Henry W. Lane and Joseph J. Distefano (eds.), *International Management Behavior* (Scarborough, Ontario: Nelson Canada, 1988), p. 83, reprinted from *Sloan Management Review*, 27, no. 2 (Winter 1986): 75–80.

122. Alfred M. Jaeger, "The Transfer of Organizational Culture Overseas: An Approach to Control in the Multinational Corporation," *Journal of International Business Studies*, Fall 1983, pp. 91–114.

123. Somkao Runglertkrengkrai and Suda Engkaninan, "The Pattern of Managerial Behaviour in Thai Culture," *Asia Pacific Journal of Management*, 5, no. 1 (September 1987): 8–15.

CHAPTER 11
Toward the Future

1. Pradip Ghosh (ed.), *Population, Environment, and Resources in the Third World in Development* (Meriden, Conn.: Greenwood Press, 1984), p. 120.

2. My T. Vu, Eduard Bos, and Rodolfo A. Bulatao, "Europe, Middle East, and North Africa Region Population Projections: 1988–89 Edition," World Bank, Policy, Planning, and Research Working Paper 117, 1988, p. 32.

3. *Ibid.*

4. Anthony J. F. O'Reilly, "Establishing Successful Joint Ventures in Developing Nations: A CEO's Perspective," *Columbia Journal of World Business*, 23, no. 1 (Spring 1988): 65.

5. James R. Schiffman, "Coca-Cola, After an 11-Year Absence, Seeks to Re-Enter Huge Market in India," *Wall Street Journal*, November 17, 1988, p. B6.

6. Julia Michaels and Roger Cohen, "Foreigners Boost Investments in Brazil Despite Its Daunting Economic Problems," *Wall Street Journal*, October 26, 1988, p. A18.

7. *Labour Force: 1950–2000—World Summary*, vol. 5 (Geneva: International Labour Office, 1979), p. 49.

8. *Population Change and Economic Development* (New York: Oxford University Press for the World Bank, 1984), p. 26.

9. *Ibid.*, pp. 44–46.

10. *World Resources 1986* (New York: Basic Books for World Resources Institute and International Institute for Environment and Development, 1986), p. 47.

11. *Ibid.*, p. 68.

12. World Bank calculations estimated that in 1990 there would be 341–511 millions with daily deficits of more than 250 calories. Shlomo Reutlinger and Marcelo Selowsky, *Malnutrition and Poverty: Magnitude and Policy Options* (Baltimore: Johns Hopkins University Press, 1976), p. 31.

13. *Population Change and Economic Development*, p. 43.

14. Derived from *World Development Report 1988* (New York: Oxford University Press for the World Bank, 1988), pp. 226–27.

15. Carlota Perez, "Microelectronics, Long Waves and World Structural Change: New Perspectives for Developing Countries," *World Development*, 13, no. 3 (1985): 441–63.

16. Stephen D. Younger, "Ghana: Economic Recovery Program—A Case Study of Stabilization and Structural Adjustment in Sub-Saharan Africa," EDI Development Policy Case Series, no. 1 (Washington, D.C.: World Bank, 1989), pp. 141–42.

17. *World Development Report 1989*, pp. 60, 71.

18. Younger, "Ghana: Economic Recovery," pp. 130, 143–45.

19. *World Development Report 1988*, p. 38.

20. Constantine Michalopoulos, "World Bank Lending for Structural Adjustment," *Finance & Development*, June 1987, pp. 25–28.

21. Michael W. Bell and Robert L. Sheehy, "Helping Structural Adjustment in Low-Income Countries," *Finance & Development*, December 1987, pp. 13–16.

Index

Printed in the United States
66298LVS00003B/51

9 780743 236294